MW01029012

THE BECOMING BEAUTY TRILOGY

BEFORE BEAUTY, BLINDING BEAUTY, & BEAUTY BEHELD

BRITTANY FICHTER

THE CLASSICAL KINGDOMS COLLECTION BOOKS 1-3

The Becoming Beauty Trilogy / Brittany Fichter. -- 1st ed.

Edited by Katherine Stephen, Mark Swift, and Meredith Tennant

Cover Art and Design by Sanja Gombar at BookCoverForYou.com

ISBN: 978-1548324971

❀ Created with Vellum

BEFORE BEAUTY: A RETELLING OF BEAUTY AND THE BEAST

THE BECOMING BEAUTY TRILOGY, BOOK 1

~

The Classical Kingdoms Collection Book One

To my husband, Stephen. You'll always be my knight in shining armor, my Prince Charming, and my best friend. Thank you for always believing in me and supporting my dreams, even when it means the laundry doesn't get done.

1

EYES OF THE GIRL

"*E*verard! I know you are here, son. I can feel you."

Ever slipped, grabbing a low branch at the last second and saving himself from a painful fall. What was his father doing here?

"Coming, Father." Curiosity and a little fear mingled in Ever's stomach as he extricated himself from the tree. If his father had come to fetch him personally, rather than sending a servant, whatever he wanted to speak of must be important.

"Yes, Father?" He dropped from the lowest branch just before his father.

"Ah. Garin said you would be here. I want you to return to your chambers and prepare for the procession."

Ever knew better than to question his father, but he was confused. The procession was still two hours away.

As though Ever had spoken his thoughts, his father answered them. "This year you will be riding in the procession with me." Ever turned and looked up at his father in wonder. He'd never been allowed to hold a place in any of the capitol processions.

"Thirteen years is far old enough," his father continued as they began walking back to the Fortress, "to be seen as a leader. When you take the throne one day, I want them to be confident in your strength and ability to protect them. If we begin showing them now that you are indeed serious about your duty, they will accept you readily, even hungrily when I am gone."

"Yes, Father."

"And as this is your first official public appearance as crowned prince, I have new expectations for you, duties which if you neglect today or any other time, could be disastrous to your future rule. Do you understand?" Rodrigue turned his fiery gray eyes to glare down at Ever. Ever nodded ruefully. He had a feeling he wouldn't like these rules.

"First, you must remember that you are to be present with the people, but that you are above them. That includes the servants. You are not to speak with them publicly unless giving an order." The king shook his head. "While I wish you would adopt these habits in court, the way I've been telling you to for years, you cannot forget them in public. Our strength makes us responsible for these people. We must protect them from our enemies at all costs. But in order to be vigilant, we must be removed. You cannot be scanning the horizon for spies, so to speak, when you are giving your attention to one or two peasants in particular. Distraction makes us vulnerable."

"Will we be looking for spies during the procession, Father?"

"We are always looking for spies. You are no longer a child, Everard, and today is the day I expect you to begin acting like a man. Now go to your chambers, and the tailor should have your clothes ready. You will meet your mother on the front lawn when you're finished. I will be there soon after."

Ever did as he was told. When he arrived on the Fortress steps, his mother was already on her horse. He bowed to her, and she gave him a small smile and nod before turning to instruct one of her ladies-in-waiting about the smelling salts she needed to forget the stench of her mount.

Ever had only ever seen the procession from the Fortress balconies, but the procession was grander in person than he had ever imagined. His horse was positioned behind his parents' horses. All around them, tall flags with the royal wolf seal were raised up high on blue velvet squares edged with gold braided trim. The procession always began at the Fortress, moving down the mountainside and into Soudain. Once in the city, it snaked through prominent streets before returning back up the mountain in a giant loop.

Since the monarchs were at the end of the procession, the first performers were returning to the Fortress by the time the royals even left. His father's best soldiers were scattered in groups of six throughout the performers, and more were stationed along the procession path. They wore no bright colors. Gaudy men had never been of any use in battle, his father always said. They were too easy for the enemy to see. So instead of wearing the Fortress colors of blue, green, and white, his father's men simply had the image of the wolf impressed upon their chest plates in black silver, burned into the metal by the finest artisan blacksmiths in all of Destin.

Ever had to remind himself to look regal instead of gawking. He'd never been allowed much time in the capital city. Soudain was too full of distractions to be good for a young prince, his father had always said. But now, Ever had his laurel crown, the one he would wear until he became king. And with his crown came a new sort of freedom, under the watchful eye of his father. And freedom was beautiful, Ever decided.

The streets glowed with the brilliant orange of the setting sun over the mountain, and flames lit the tops of the lampposts that stood on every corner.

Families crowded one another on the edges of the streets to wave to their rulers. They bowed low before his father and mother, but Ever couldn't help noticing that their smiles nearly disappeared whenever the king turned to glance in their directions. Fear, Ever decided, was the overarching emotion they wore. To Ever they remained bowed, but he noticed many dared a peek at their prince. A number of them, particularly the girls, gambled a smile. He would nod and turn back to the street, hoping his actions were as his father expected.

As his horse rounded a corner, a movement in the crowd caught his eye. A few boys were pushing to get to a better spot in line. One of them shoved too hard, and a girl who was standing at the edge of the crowd was knocked right into the street. Without thinking, Ever hopped off his horse and bent down to help her up. She was lanky, with auburn hair and large midnight blue eyes. Her family most likely belonged to the skilled worker class, as the dress she wore was simple, but neat and tidy.

As soon as his hand touched hers, his face reddened with shame, and he could feel his father's icy glare upon his back. So much for staying removed from the crowd. Helping the girl stand, he nodded quickly at her and turned to get back on his horse. His father would have some choice words for him later. For now, he didn't dare look at the king. The procession had come to a halt, and though the people watched the actions of their young prince with looks of sudden pride, none of their opinions mattered. He had failed his father.

Eager to be on his way and ready to forget the whole ordeal, Ever was nearly on his horse when he felt a tug on his sleeve and a gasp from the crowd. Turning, he saw that the girl had lost her bewildered expression of shock, and had followed him to his horse, even daring to do what his servants did not.

"Thank you, Your Highness." She looked up at him with eager eyes.

Anger pulsed through him. Why couldn't she just let him alone? Impatient to be rid of her, he roughly pushed her hand off his arm. As he often did, however, Ever forgot the amount of power that coursed through him. What he'd meant as a simple brush of the arm shot blue fire down his arm and into hers. She fell backward, right in front of a cart horse. The horse startled and reared, and with two sickening cracks, landed on the girl's wrist and ankle. Ever watched in horror as she screamed, and the villagers rushed to her side.

"Everard!" His father's voice was sharper than he'd ever heard it. Slowly, he tore his gaze away from the mess he'd made to look at the king. "On your horse!" The fury in Rodrigue's words was unmistakable, and Ever miserably nodded and climbed back on his horse to finish the procession. But as he rode, he could hold his head high no longer, and every time he closed his eyes, the look of pain on the child's face was there before him.

Ever's father was not kind that evening after the celebration was over. "Not only did you deliberately disobey me, but you made the situation worse with that wretched temper of yours! Now we have one more cripple to live on the streets and beg, one more unproductive citizen to waste precious resources on!"

Ever doubted she would live on the streets, judging by the clothes she was wearing, not that his father would ever notice that kind of thing. But his father was right. He'd added one more helpless, unproductive citizen to his kingdom, one more thread of weakness for the enemy to target.

His mother said little about the incident, except to complain that the pause in the procession had been bad for her hair. Garin and Gigi were the only ones who seemed to understand how he felt.

"And is the young prince wanting some hot cider tonight?" Garin slipped in that evening, as he often did when his duties were done. Despite the enormous load of work that King Rodrigue placed on the steward, Garin always seemed to have time for Ever. This night, however, not even Garin could cheer him up. Ever shook his head as he stared sullenly into the fire.

"Come now, Your Highness." Gigi, the Fortress's head kitchen matron, slipped in from behind Garin. Despite Ever's protests, she set a cup of steaming cider down beside his bed, and proceeded to adjust the pillows around him. "Tomorrow will be a better day." She gave him a gentle smile from beneath her mop of silver curls, and patted his cheek affectionately with a soft hand before wishing him goodnight, leaving him alone with Garin.

Garin walked around the room straightening chairs as Ever sipped his drink. The only sounds were the crackle of the fire and the scrape of furniture against the floor.

"I did something bad today," Ever finally spoke, his voice cracking twice.

Instead of denying it, as all of the other courtiers had done, however, Garin spoke with his usual honesty. "I heard about that. How badly do you think she was injured?"

"It looked pretty bad," Ever admitted.

Garin just nodded. He waited a few moments before speaking, and Ever found himself strangely anxious to hear what the older man would say. Disappointing his father had been bad enough. He didn't know if he could bear to have the steward disappointed in him as well.

"We all make mistakes, Sire." Garin finally folded his arms and leaned against the side of Ever's bed. "Some, unfortunately, cannot be mended as easily as others. I have found, in my humble experience, that when we hold positions of power, our mistakes often hurt more than just ourselves. They hurt others. It is something we must live with." He was quiet for a moment before adding, "But the important thing is that we learn from our mistakes. What you did today was indeed unkind. But you will be no better off if you simply regret it. You must learn from it so that you never hurt another like that again. Everyone makes mistakes, Ever, but a true leader takes the knowledge he gains with him, and he applies it towards his future.

"Now," he gave Ever a smile, his eyes crinkling kindly in an expression very different from the one Ever's father had worn when they'd parted, "it is time for you to sleep. As Gigi always says, tomorrow will be a new day."

Ever hoped their kind words would make sleep easier, but the moment he shut his eyes, he saw the look of hurt and betrayal in the girl's dark eyes once again.

2

OPPORTUNITY

*T*he incident with the girl took longer to forget than Ever had first hoped, but eventually, with the help of his father, he learned to shut the guilt out, along with other distracting thoughts. For that was his duty, his father said.

"Other kings live in soulless buildings, cold and austere castles that provide little motivation for defense other than their own personal comforts. But this place, our Fortress," Rodrigue ran his hand lovingly over the marble walls as they walked, "this Fortress is the source of our strength. It is what sets us apart from others of our rank. It must be protected at all costs, and its kingdom as well. There is no other like it, and never will there be again. And it knows," he turned a sharp eye to Ever, "when we lose our focus. Keep your eyes on the horizon, Everard. You never know who might be coming to steal that focus and this Fortress from you."

Ever's father, always able to focus on the horizon, was like a statue with eyes that never wavered, or even blinked for that matter. Ever didn't have that kind of vision, the ability to naturally block out all but the goal. Instead, he was inclined to notice the slight changes in seasons, or when a servant was acting unusually.

From a young age, he had loved exploring the Fortress grounds. He found peace, a quiet communion of the soul with the colossal citadel when he was deep in its sheltering greenery or underneath its stone arches. As he grew older, it took great effort for him to throw off the childhood desire to pause sometimes and simply exist in the secret places of his beloved home. It was also somewhat painful to treat the servants like people other than his friends, particularly those who had been just that during his solitary childhood years. And yet, his father said, it was what he must do in order to protect it all from the destructive forces of those who would destroy such a paradise.

Little by little, however, under Rodrigue's guidance, Ever gained the ability to focus as his father did. His strength, which had been unusual even when he was a small child, was honed, and by the time he was twenty-six years of age, he had been wrought into the warrior prince not even his father could have dreamed of, or so Rodrigue would exclaim. The girl's face had faded into little more than a bad memory. She only resurfaced when he was tempted to feel guilt, which, thanks to his father, wasn't often. She reappeared, however, the night his mother died.

Ever was out riding his horse, training with some of the archers, when a distant figure waved him down. As he approached, Ever could see Garin's thin frame, and something in his stomach flopped uneasily. While he'd obeyed his father and cut sociable ties with most of the servants, he'd not been able to tear himself from Garin. Out of respect for his father, they didn't flaunt their conversations, but if the steward was coming out to find him personally, something had to be wrong.

"Your Highness," Garin bowed in his saddle as he rode up to the men, "you might wish to cut today's practice short. I have… a message for you."

Dismissing his men, Ever guided his horse over to Garin's. The steward's graying black hair was messy, as though he'd pulled it back in a hurry, and his clothes, for once, were rumpled. "Your Highness… Ever." He finally looked Ever in the eye. "I'm afraid I am not quite obeying your father's order, but I thought you should know before he called you."

Ever gawked at the steward. While Garin often stretched boundaries and rules, he had never disobeyed King Rodrigue outright.

"Your mother has died," Garin continued in a quiet voice. "The fever was just too much. Today she slipped away from us while she slept. Your father wanted me to wait until he could tell everyone, but I thought you should at least have time…" His voice faded, but Ever nodded unhappily. As much as Ever had become his father's protégé, he still was unable to completely block feelings like Rodrigue wished him to. Garin had known he would need time to think before he was called before the entire court to hear the news.

Garin claimed he had an obligation to attend to after that, leaving Ever alone before the courtiers were gathered for the official announcement. Ever struggled to pin down the emotions that flooded him. That there were emotions was undeniable, and none of his father's training could banish them. Strangely, however, what bothered him most, he finally decided, was that he was not sad.

Ever had spent years watching his servants interact with their families, and as a young child, had even joined them when his father wasn't looking. The parents would call, and the children would respond with shrieks of delight, running to their parents for hugs and kisses. It had never been so with his family. His father had shown him affection in his own way throughout the years by preparing him to be the best king he knew how. Queen Louise, though, had never seemed to feel the maternal affection Ever saw in the servants and even the mothers of noble blood. He and the queen were amiable enough, and had greeted one another always with respect and kindness, but there was never anything more. Guilt, Ever realized, was the emotion that ran through him. He felt guilty because he recognized very quickly that her death did not bring him pain. He would have felt more pain if Gigi had died.

On the night of his mother's death, the girl's face visited him in his sleep for the first time in years. The pain in her eyes and her look of utter heartbreak broke his heart. He might have been able to ignore her in his wakeful hours, but at night, he was hers.

He wasn't yet completely recovered from the queen's death when his father announced that it was time for Ever to choose a bride. All of the eligible women and girls of proper status and bloodlines from the surrounding kingdoms were invited, and within a week, they had arrived at the steps of the Fortress, each aspiring to be the next princess of the most powerful kingdom in the land. Ever watched them descend from their great coaches, each girl glittering more brightly than the one before her, decked with jewels and pearls and silks.

"You look as though someone has just handed you a prison sentence," Garin teased him while they prepared.

"Is there any chance my father will rely on the Fortress tradition to choose one?" Ever asked glumly.

Garin's smile vanished, and he shook his head. "I doubt it. As much as your father loves the Fortress, there hasn't been a queen chosen the old way in three generations. Your father will be evaluating the political strengths of each union, rather than the girl herself."

Ever could only nod. He'd suspected as much.

Queen Louise had been a duchess from a neighboring country, and her marriage to his father had joined their armies as allies. It had been a wise political match, to be sure. Still, Ever was decidedly against having the same relationship with his wife as King Rodrigue had fostered with his mother, one of polite greetings and farewells in passing. And yet, it seemed an unavoidable fate. Within an hour, he was presented to the court and was obligated to begin dancing.

The weather was fair, and the moon shined brightly upon the balcony on which dozens of couples twirled in time alongside him. Fortunately for Ever, though there were many, many girls, he was a good dancer, and making conversation was easy for him. Beautiful faces and lovely smiles were everywhere, and sweet greetings and giggles filled his ears. He had no idea as to how he would choose one, but as always, he was sure he would choose to honor his father's wishes. His reluctance aside, the evening was faring tolerably until he suddenly found himself face-to-face with a woman he more than recognized.

Princess Nevina was indeed a beauty, but not in the typical sense. Nothing about her was delicate. Her dress, made of black, silky feathers sewn together tightly with gold threads, was cut low to reveal her generous proportions. Her arms were also bare, and boasted sturdy muscles, not large, but rock solid. Her hair was dark like her dress, and her eyes were a surprising green against her bronze skin. Every move she made was lithe, and her eyes glowed brightly as she looked Ever up and down shrewdly before accepting the hand he'd unconsciously extended.

"Everard," her low voice was smooth, "it has been a long while since we've met on such amiable terms. I think in our separation you might have outgrown your father."

"Perhaps so." Ever's voice sounded strange in his own ears, tight. He had not expected the Tumenian princess to be among the invited guests that night. As they began the dance, he dared an accusatory glance at Garin, who shook his head ever so slightly. That meant his father had invited her. Had Rodrigue lost his mind?

Nevina was right. The princess of Tumen and the prince of Destin had not last parted on pleasant terms. Actually, they were rarely on amiable terms. Introduced as young children, as most of the royals were at this ball or that tournament, they had gotten to know one another well enough. Nevina was unlike the other children, however, in that the moment Ever had laid eyes upon her, he'd realized she had a deep strength almost akin to his own.

But where Ever's strength was one of light and life, the young princess's power had been heavy, nearly sickening. She'd immediately seemed to be aware of her effect on him, too, on that first night they met, for she'd smiled when Ever had to asked Garin to accompany him back to his chambers early, away from the tournament festivities.

He had been seven then. As they got older, not only did he train himself to resist her powers, but even to mute them as well. The two young royals had met again when they were eleven, and much to Nevina's outrage, not only did Ever stop her attempts at tormenting him, he'd stopped her attempts at tormenting anyone else at the gathering as well.

Their encounters had been sporadic after that. They didn't see each other often, as Tumen's continuous push for influence among the surrounding nations strained its relationship with Destin. The year Ever had turned twenty-one, diplomats had begun to report that Tumen was giving up its ambitious goals, and desired nothing more than peace. But Ever had been skeptical. Even if her father was seeking to give up his ancestors' dark power in order to obtain peaceful relations, Ever never doubted for a moment that the princess had every intention of keeping and using those powers to boost Tumen's strength, with or without her father's blessing. Recently, however, it seemed that her schemes had been interrupted by an unexpected arrival.

"Come now, Prince." Nevina gave a little laugh, jolting him out of memories and back to the present. "Let bygones be bygones. Our kingdoms have grown beyond their conflicts, have they not?"

"I certainly hope so," Ever responded curtly. He doubted it, however, as he watched the gold fire dance around her green eyes.

"Then dance with me as you would a woman who might actually deserve you." She drew herself closer to him.

Ever's heart beat even faster as he tried to keep a chivalrous distance between them, looking desperately for his father over her shoulder as they turned.

"I hear things have changed in Tumen." He tried conversing again, desperate to keep her from continually pressing her body against his. It was distracting, and he could see people beginning to notice. Court gossip was inevitable, but this was one tryst he did *not* want gossiped about.

"If you are referring to the birth of my brother, then yes." Her eyes tightened just enough for him to see the gold fire within them roar in spite of her apparent calm.

"I'm sure there are many men desirous of your hand." Ever's voice was polite, but he made sure Nevina didn't miss his words' significance. "You have much to offer."

"Pray tell then," the princess purred, "why exactly am I here?"

"Sire!" A small voice interrupted their spin.

Sending up a prayer of thanks, Ever stopped dancing and released the princess so he could turn and talk to the boy who suddenly stood beside them. It was inappropriate behavior for a servant, but the boy was young, and Ever was grateful for the break in the conversation. Before he could appropriately reprimand the boy, however, Nevina had reached down and slapped the child across the cheek. Ever couldn't keep the indignation from his face as he turned to gape at her.

"You dare touch my servant?" His voice carried loudly, and for once, he didn't care. The music stopped as everyone watched.

"Prince Everard!" She glared back. "His impertinence was an insult to me and my kingdom. If anyone should be apologizing, it should be you. In my country, our servants know their place!"

"I do not care how you abuse your useless Chiens! My people are in the service of the Fortress, and you will not touch them!"

"So this is the strength you boast of, you who are revered far and wide." Her voice suddenly grew cool and quiet, and somehow, even more unnerving. "And yet, you do not have enough control over your own to allow you a single dance with me."

"Get to the point, Nevina."

"Your Fortress is weakening, Everard Perrin Auguste Fortier." Her mouth curved up in a strange smile, and her eyes were nearly closed as she spoke.

She had been waiting for this. Like a vicious cat of prey, she had been waiting for the opportunity to test and push him. Her brother had taken her throne, and now she wanted Everard's kingdom. Now she was searching for any chance to challenge him for it. This revelation infuriated him even more.

"Get out of my home. Leave my kingdom, and do not return!" Ever thundered.

"Oh, we will be leaving." Nevina's captain of the guard was suddenly at her side, glaring at him. Nevina's golden flames blazed even more brightly as her captain spoke. "We cannot, however, allow this insult to our sovereign to go unchallenged."

"Soon," Nevina's voice became a purr once again, "as you watch your men fall, Everard, remember who it was that caused the bloodshed. Know that it was your own weakness and cowardice that was your undoing."

Ever gritted his teeth as she waved her hand at him dismissively.

"Let us take our leave of this place, Captain. We will be back soon enough." With that they turned, Nevina's skinny Chien girl hobbling along behind them as quickly as she could.

Somehow, Ever's betrothal ball had become a declaration of war.

3

PIECES

"My prince." A young man knelt at the entrance of Ever's tent. Ever gave him a quick glance and nod before returning to the map that was spread out before him and his favorite general.

"Acelet, I understand what you're saying, but the plan won't work if we move out a moment before dawn. I won't give them the upper hand of the night. The whole reason we planned this for the morning was so they wouldn't be able to use the hawks. We will have more than enough time to send scouts ahead and split our men here."

General Acelet's sharp eyes followed every move Ever's hands made on the map. Impatience was in the general's face when he finally jerked his chin at the disheveled figure still waiting in the corner of the tent.

"You're one of the king's men, aren't you? What are you doing here?"

"Prince Everard, your father bade me to deliver this!"

For the first time, Ever looked directly at the young man, who thrust a sealed, water-stained parchment at him. His hands trembled and his clothes were tattered. Something must have gone very wrong. Rodrigue had been adamant that their regiments not communicate between campaigns.

"Where is Corbin? Why did the king send you instead?"

The young man could have been no older than seventeen. His thin shoulders shook as he spoke, though whether from fear or being soaked by his rainy trek, Ever couldn't tell.

"Corbin is dead, Sire. I barely made it out before they took the camp completely."

"Dead?" General Acelet stared at him in disbelief. "That man has been the king's favorite messenger for twenty years." He frowned at the skinny boy. "I find it hard to believe that the enemy could get close enough to kill one of the king's favorites."

The young man paled and glanced at Ever. Seeing that he was expected to speak, he went on, his voice trembling. "The king's campaign was unsuccessful. We took too long to reach the valley, and it was nightfall when we arrived. Princess Nevina was upon us before we could set the defenses. Her men burned our supply wagons on the first night, and the hawks and her guards have kept us trapped in our own tents ever since. Not that they needed the monsters." His eyes clouded. "The darkness the princess sends over us is... It's too much." He finally looked straight at Ever. "Your father says he cannot master it."

Fury rippled through Ever. All thoughts of the map aside, he strode over to the young man and grabbed him by the shirt. "I don't know what game you think you're playing," he snarled, "but no matter who has bought your allegiance, you will regret blaspheming my father's name with such insults of weakness."

"Sire!" The young man desperately pointed to the letter still in the prince's other hand. "I beg you, read the letter! I cannot read, but the king spoke the words aloud as he wrote them. I heard as I waited in his tent!"

Ever glared at him for a moment longer before dropping him at Acelet's feet. When he finally held the seal up to the light, he could see that the wax was still unbroken, so the young man could not possibly have read it. A wolf with jewel shaped eyes stood over the corpse of a serpent, baring its teeth and crouching for another pounce. An uncomfortable voice in Ever's head wondered if the messenger might be telling the truth, but he dismissed the thought before it was complete. Breaking the seal, he read what his father had written in a hasty hand.

Everard,

Our campaign has failed. Nevina's hawks have multiplied greatly since our last encounter. Whether through informant or traitor, they knew the location of our first encampment, and were upon us before the first night had passed. We lost many men to the hawks and even more to the arrows they rained upon us in the dark. The siege would have been manageable if their arrows had not burned our supplies, also.

Her worst weapon, however, has been the dreams. More men have gone mad with each passing night from the visions of confusion and blackness that the abominable princess sends. And those who avoid sleep begin to lose their minds to exhaustion. I am finding my own thoughts difficult to follow as I fight the darkness. It is with shame that I admit I cannot match her power. We cannot wait until tomorrow. You must come now.

For the first time since he had become a man, Ever felt a cold shiver run down his back, despite the misty heat of the spring rain. His father had never been as powerful as Ever was, but he'd never been rendered helpless in battle. Was he completely unable to protect anyone but himself? Numbly, the prince read the letter again. He could feel Acelet's eyes on his face, keenly measuring his reaction.

"What does the king say, Your Grace?"

Ever straightened his shoulders and cleared his face of all emotion. "Nevina has apparently gathered numbers greater than we had anticipated," he answered carefully.

"Will we be moving out earlier then?"

Ever took a deep breath before shaking his head. "No. I will not give her the advantage of the night the way my father did. I can protect us here, but not in the mountain passes. We will move in the morning as we had planned."

Acelet bowed his head in acknowledgment and excused himself to finish making arrangements, taking the unfortunate messenger with him. Ever returned to the bench and looked at the map again. As he traced the paths his men would take the next morning, his mind drifted back to the days of planning he'd spent with his father. He couldn't understand what had gone wrong. They had been so careful.

Within an hour of Nevina's challenge, the guests had been dismissed from Ever's ball, none of them announced as his bride. For that, Ever had been grateful, but he'd had little time to revel. Immediately, he was called to his father's study to choose spies and run through battle scenarios. There they had chosen where to break the army into two camps, one on the mountain and one in the valley.

"I don't want Nevina close to the Fortress. She knows too much," King Rodrigue had said. "I want to cut her off in the desert valley just north of the border. If my men wait in the valley before she arrives, you can bring your men through the mountains to close in on her from the east side."

"How do we know when she plans to attack?" Ever had asked.

"Acelet has sent spies, but he believes it will be within two weeks. If we leave soon, we should be ready by the time she reaches the valley. Even if she guesses that we'll cut her off, she will expect to see your forces coming from the south, directly from the Fortress. You will wait here." His father had pointed to a crevice on the backside of one of the desert mountains north of the Fortress. "Instead of coming from the south, you'll be poised to pour down from the east."

Ever had nodded. He knew the place well. There were large caves there that would shield the men from view, should Nevina send her trained hawks in for a closer look. The large caverns would allow him not only to hide two hundred men from Nevina's spying eyes, but they were close enough in proximity for him to shield his men's minds from her visions as well.

"I'll send a runner to the valley to let you know when we've arrived," Ever had begun, but his father was already shaking his head.

"No messengers. No communications of any sort. You may be able to shield your men in the caves, but you cannot be expected to do it for runners as well. I will be too busy to look for messengers. Without our protection, the men could easily be discovered. Nevina would have the information out of them in minutes. We will simply have to be precise."

They'd continued to strategize until Rodrigue was satisfied with every detail. But when they were through, as Ever had turned to go to his chambers, he'd stopped and asked his father the question that had bothered him all evening.

"Father, there is one thing I don't understand. Why was she even invited? Was I supposed to ask for her hand in marriage?"

His father had sighed. "It was a foolish hope on my part. Our relations have been better these past few years. I believed we could forge a union between our powers that would prevent future wars of this sort."

"But their power is not like ours." Ever had frowned. "It is one of deception and darkness. The Fortress would never abide that sort of queen."

"Everard." His father had fixed his gaze on him in a strange way. "I will be honest with you. Where I once felt the strength of the Fortress run through my heart and mind, there is emptiness now. I do not feel its direction anymore. Only its raw power. It is up to us now more than ever to protect our home in these strange times."

Rodrigue had been so confident in their plans. And he'd had every reason to be. King Rodrigue had never lost a battle. Small skirmishes happened often with some of the border lords, but few kings were foolhardy enough to challenge Rodrigue directly. With the strength of the Fortress and the harsh determination of its monarchs, Destin's borders had not been breached in over two hundred years. Most of the king's great battles had been fought coming to the aid of their allies in neighboring lands. Rodriguez had followed in the footsteps of his fathers, and it had served him well. He had known nothing but the study of warfare since boyhood, under the watchful eye of his own father. So when Ever and Rodrigue had drawn up plans against Nevina, there had been no bravado in the king's schemes, nor had there been a false confidence. The preparation had been as straightforward and focused as the king's plans always were.

And yet, as they'd strategized in the king's study, Ever hadn't been able to ignore the waning light in his father's eyes. The glowing rings of blue fire that encircled his pupils had been growing dimmer for years, but Ever had lacked both the courage and the heart to bring it to his father's attention. It would have drawn both shame and outrage to question the strength of the Fortress's power that resided within him. Besides, the Fortress wouldn't allow his father to falter in the midst of his greatest battle. Ever had been sure of it.

But now, here on the mountain as that battle raged, Ever felt the fear stir within him as he reread the lines his father had written. The Fortress had indeed allowed his father's power to weaken, enough for him to call for help in a way he never had before, enough for his men to die horrible deaths of fear and fire as the king cowered in his bed, hoping his son would save him. Every weakness Rodrigue had ever despised, he had assumed in sending that letter.

In his weakness, Ever decided, his father must have succumbed to the shadowy deceptions of his enemy. Nevina's suggestions of hopelessness and confusion must have galled him into sending the messenger. And Ever knew that when his father was once again in his right mind, he would look back on Ever's decisions now and judge them as harshly as he ever had. Ever had been right in telling Acelet to stick to the plan. Besides, it didn't matter if the situation was as dire as his father had described. His men would not survive the night outside the caves. They would have to wait until dawn.

The next morning, the sun rose bright and hot, and as soon as its rays touched the mountain paths, Ever's men fanned out. They crouched along the rocky paths, awaiting Ever's signal to move. Ever lay down on a ledge that jutted out over the valley, and he crawled towards its edge to get a better view.

It seemed that the situation had gone from bad to worse since the messenger had been sent. Throughout his father's camp, Tumen's yellow banner fluttered brazenly over the tents. Those of his father's men that he could see were sitting cross-legged on the ground, chained to one another and watched by guards. Not only had Nevina attacked his father, she had beaten him soundly. It was alarming how quickly her strange band of ragtag vagabonds had grown into an army of hundreds.

Still, from the arrangement of her regiments, it was clear that Nevina expected Ever's reinforcements to come from the south. Ever breathed a sigh of relief as he realized he still had the upper hand. The dark princess might have many men, but her powers were limited. As terrifying as they were, most of Nevina's monstrous hawks could not stand to fly by day, and her men's arrows did not shoot as straight without the dark of night to guide them. Without the winged scouts to circle the skies, the enemy wouldn't see Ever's men until it was too late. Satisfied, Ever gave Acelet the nod. The general, in turn, motioned to his archers to begin the assault.

Their arrows filled the morning sky, sending the enemy scrambling as Ever's footmen began to descend upon the camp. Ever poured his strength into his men as they moved. He could feel Nevina attempting to fill their minds with visions, but she could not penetrate the shield he had created around them. Her rogue forces were caught off guard as Ever's men surrounded the camp. In just minutes, his father's men were freed, and the valley once again belonged to Destin.

Most of the enemy had fled in fear by the time Ever followed his men down into the valley. He surveyed the carnage, and was somewhat surprised at how little blood had been shed. None of his own men had been lost, although he had no idea what kind of damage had been inflicted upon his father's men before he'd arrived.

The same couldn't be said for Nevina. Although it seemed that the princess herself had escaped unscathed, her numbers were devastated. Acelet had the captives that remained rounded up and executed on the spot.

And yet, in spite of the enormous victory, Ever's stomach churned as he entered the king's tent. King Rodrigue tossed and turned in his makeshift bed, moaning. Beads of sweat ran down his white temples. His appearance was so shockingly altered that even the healer hesitated before walking to his side. The arms that had been hard as rock when the king had left the Fortress were now thin and shaking. The king's face was haggard, and his features emaciated. When he turned to look into Ever's eyes, he didn't look like the most feared king in the realm, but a frightened old man.

Ever immediately ordered everyone out. The healer grumbled, but Ever still sent him away. How had his father lost all of his strength to Nevina's power so quickly? But as he moved in closer, Ever could see that the blue fire in his father's eyes was nearly extinguished. This was something only the power of the Fortress could heal, and the only two persons with that strength were staring at one another from across the room.

Ever needed to work fast. Pulling his gloves off, he knelt by his father's side. He took his father's hand and clutched it tightly in both of his. Closing his eyes, he focused on the dim light his father was still clinging to.

As he focused on his father's mind, the enemy's power bit back at him with a surprising force, nearly knocking Ever over. Ever gasped and dug in harder. He hadn't known his father could suffer the power of evil like this. The princess's darkness had indeed grown in their years apart. The desire to tremble filled him greatly, but he could not give in. He tried with all his might to reignite the fire in his father's eyes, but every time he pushed, it flickered dangerously.

"Son," Rodrigue rasped.

Ever opened his eyes to see his father staring at the wineskin of water on his small bedside table.

"Father, I need to draw her power out. You must help me." Ever felt as though he were talking to a child. His father shook his head, however, looking again at the water. Frowning, Ever let go of his hand and gave him the water instead.

After the king drank, he whispered, "Why didn't you come?"

The look that passed through Rodrigue's eyes pierced Ever to the heart. Was his father actually blaming him?

"You know I couldn't have protected my men in the pass at night. If we had tried, my men would have been in the same position as yours." His words were as close to a rebuke as he had ever dared to give his father, but the frustration that welled up within him was nearly more than Ever could bear.

After thinking for a moment, the king nodded heavily and laid his head back down. Ever picked up his hand again, but the king withdrew it.

"Everard, my mistake was not arriving too late, as you might think. My mistakes have been years in the making." He gave Ever a tired smile. "My eyes are dimming. I know you've noticed." He closed his eyes. "I've left my people unprotected. I could see it in the Chiens' eyes when Nevina took the camp." He grabbed Ever's shirt and pulled himself up, suddenly glaring at his son through leaden eyes. "The Fortress has chosen a new king, one that will be a better king than I. But it will reject you, too, if you ignore the cry of our people. You must protect them!"

Rodrigue fell back into the bed. Ever tried once again to take his hand, but the king whispered, "Just let me go, Son. The spirit of the Fortress will carry me to my fathers, and I will rest with them. It's your turn now."

And with those words, the king was gone. In a dirty tent with one candle to light the room, the great warrior king had admitted defeat and left his son to pick up the pieces.

"Your Highness." Acelet knelt at the doorway of the tent. "The grief of the kingdom is with you."

Ever swallowed hard and finally stood, still staring at his father's body. "How are the survivors?"

"Not well, Sire. I'm afraid I must ask you to go to them. Many have gone mad from the dreams. There's nothing else I can do."

With a nod, Ever turned sharply and left his father's body. He had work to do, and he was suddenly grateful for the princess's poison. The work of healing would occupy his mind for now. Deep down, however, he knew he would have to mourn sooner or later. And for all the monsters he could slay, for all the darkness he could pierce with his light, for all the unearthly strength that he possessed, he did not know how to mourn. And it terrified him.

～

The king was properly lamented by his subjects, but Ever got the uneasy feeling that it was more out of respect than true affection. Although the Fortress courtiers and servants wore black, and offered him all the right words in the wake of his father's death, he often heard them speaking excitedly of his upcoming coronation when they thought he couldn't hear. This irritated him more and more as the week drew to a close.

"Shall I tell them you wish to be left alone until the midday meal?" Garin calmly gestured to the manservants present that they could leave. Before answering, Ever put his head in his hands and took a deep breath.

Although his annoyance at one of his lords still lingered, he sought to control himself. His father had taught him not to share too much with his servants, but Ever had never quite been able to sever the connection he had with the Fortress steward. During the early years when he was still too young to be of much use to his father, Garin had been there. And Ever needed him now more than ever before.

"I am supposed to meet with the Duke of Sud Colline in an hour." The duke was prudish, and had been since they were boys. If Ever was too blunt, his distant cousin was just as likely to speak for an hour without actually getting to his point. Tolerating his cousin's pontificating was the last thing Ever was in the mood for.

Garin put his hand on Ever's shoulder and spoke softly. "I don't think it would be too much to ask that your subjects give you time to mourn. It's only been six days, and the funeral is tonight." Ever groaned, and Garin walked to the door. "I will speak to your cousin. If he is not satisfied with my words, then he shall simply have to remain unsatisfied."

At this, Ever couldn't help giving Garin a small smile. Garin smiled back and bowed before leaving the prince alone.

Unfortunately, while the solitude allowed him to elude his courtiers, it made it even harder for him to avoid his own thoughts. The sensation of helplessness settled upon him quickly as he wandered over to the balcony that overlooked the mountain. Ever hated feeling helpless.

He had heard others wonder at this particular balcony's purpose, as it showed nothing of the kingdom or its boundaries, but it was one of his favorite spots in the Fortress. It faced the peak of the mountain, just higher than the slope the Fortress was built upon, rather than the valley and its city that spread out below. It gave the illusion of solitude more than any of the other windows in the citadel. The lush green tree line abruptly ended below the bare summit, which was losing its winter cap. During the warm months the summit was covered in nothing but dirt, but in the winter it was covered in crisp, clean snow.

He closed his eyes and imagined how the snow would feel now. He had hiked there once as a child. Though it was still considered part of the Fortress grounds, none of the groundkeepers ventured that high. Ever had been young when he'd hiked it, only nine, too young to venture out on his own, but old enough to know better. Still, he recalled how the snow had felt as he'd buried his bare hands in it, how quickly they'd numbed. If only he could feel that numbness now. If only he could shove his heart in the snow and leave it there. His desires did not make a difference, however, as the guilt was going nowhere fast. No matter how much he prayed, there was no numbing of the heart. Neither the Fortress nor the Maker seemed to care about what he wanted these days.

Rodrigue had always lectured Ever that guilt was pointless. "It forces you to look inward," he'd growled once when he had caught Ever apologizing to a servant. "It leaves you open, susceptible to attack by others. When you are focused inward, you're distracted. A distracted king is a king begging for enemies to try their strength on your borders."

And Ever had tried. He'd learned over the years how to ignore the feelings that grew within him. It was hard for a child born with such strong affections as he had been. But he had trained himself to push those feelings away, to lock them up by focusing on what needed to be done. And yet, this was a guilt he couldn't push away.

It's not fair, he thought to himself as he turned back to prepare for the funeral. He'd gone over every detail, every scenario in his head. He'd searched for any way he possibly could have saved his father. But each scenario he imagined still ended the same way. He had obeyed his father's instructions down to the letter, and in the end, Ever knew he had made the right decision to wait.

And yet, that did not erase the guilt that now coursed through his veins and made his face run hot and his eyes moisten at the corners.

The funeral was perfect down to the last detail, thanks to Garin. The tapestries had been drawn, shutting out the light of the fainting sun. Candles lit the huge hall only enough to see the casket at the head of the room. The black coffin had been polished so well that Ever could see his dim reflection in its sides as he approached it. His father lay inside in his military robes, a gold braid draped across his chest. In his hands he held a scepter carved out of chestnut wood with a small blue crystal at its tip. The royal holy man uttered words of tribute to King Rodrigue, describing to the kneeling mourners the king's great feats and his daring victories, but all Ever could focus on was his father's face. It was stern now, just as it had always been. Except for the night of his death. Then, it had been full of fright.

Just like the girl's had been.

Ever nearly took a step backward when her face flashed before his eyes. He had tried his best to push her away, but her midnight blue eyes, wide with terror, had followed him in his dreams every night since his father's death.

It was all her fault.

Ever had never had a reason to feel great guilt before she'd stumbled, literally, into his path. His anger flared suddenly as he struggled to keep up with the holy man's words. He was sure the guilt over his father's death would have been easier to push aside if it hadn't also been for the lingering guilt brought by the nameless peasant who haunted the dreams of her prince.

4

STRONGER THAN WINE

"Find Solomon for me," Garin called to one of the servant girls as she ran past him.

As far as any guest was concerned, the coronation ceremony was going splendidly. The aromas of the seven course feast were wafting out of the kitchens, filling the halls with the smells of wild boar, aged cheeses, and spiced stews. Candles lit every corner of the Fortress, brightening it like the day. Wine flowed freely, making the guests even merrier as they awaited the coronation of their beloved prince. Unfortunately, Garin had the feeling that the guests weren't the only ones enjoying drinks tonight.

He wound his way through the guests as he quietly searched for Ever. It shouldn't be so hard to locate the man who was an hour away from being crowned king. Thankfully, none of the guests seemed to suspect anything. Even before they had begun to partake of the drinks, their faces had been alight with the hopes and dreams that rested on young Ever's shoulders.

King Rodrigue had been a good king by most standards, and Garin had sworn his loyalty to him without question, just as he had done with Rodrigue's father, and his father before him, and their fathers before them. But Everard was different. Even those who knew little of the incredible power that flowed through the prince knew he was special.

Though Rodrigue had missed the prince's birth, as he'd been off on a campaign against one of the border lords, Garin had been there. The queen's labor had been difficult and long. Garin had done his best to keep the Fortress servants productive, though that was difficult with Louise's screams echoing down the stone halls.

In one moment, everything had been normal, but the moment the queen's wails had stopped, a strange sensation had filled the air. The Fortress hadn't felt like such on the day of Rodrigue's birth, Garin had recalled. In fact, Garin had not felt anything like that in a long, long time.

"What are you up to?" he'd muttered to the Fortress as he made his way to the queen's chambers, squeezing between the serving girls as they ran to and fro with clean blankets and whatever else the midwife ordered. There had been no words from the Fortress in response, only an even stronger tugging at his heart, one that bid him to walk more quickly.

As soon as he stood outside the queen's door, a chambermaid scurried out, nearly running right into him. "Begging your pardon, Master Garin," she'd curtsied, "but I was just sent to find you. They think you should see this."

Garin followed her into the room, the privacy curtains closing the queen's bed off from his view. The midwife had already expertly cleaned the child, and was swaddling him as Garin approached. But no words needed to be said. Garin had nearly gasped aloud as he'd drawn closer.

Inside each of the child's eyes was a bright ring of blue fire against the gray irises, encircling the pupil. No monarch that Garin had seen had ever been born with the strength of the Fortress so evident. Not like this.

What made it even more surprising was the weak fire Ever's father, grandfather, and great-grandfather had all held. And the queen had no fire at all. Garin had known immediately that this child had a purpose, one that the Fortress hadn't given to a king in generations. He had also known it was his job to help the boy find that purpose, for Rodrigue, as passionate as he was, would be too blinded by his own agenda to value what truly set the child apart.

In the week that followed Rodrigue's death, Garin's fears had been rekindled, his concern that the king's myopic focus would have disastrous consequences in one as powerful and sensitive to the world as Ever. With each day that the prince came closer to being crowned king, he had seemed closer to losing himself. Each day, he had trained harder and eaten less than the one before, and each night he had nightmares that made him cry out. Each night, he had called out about the girl.

Garin wasn't the only one concerned for the prince. The other servants, though less familiar with the ways of the Fortress than he, had become increasingly unnerved by the prince's erratic behavior as well. And now, when the prince could not be found an hour before his coronation, Garin had a sick feeling that it was going to all come crashing down that night.

"You sent for me, sir?" Solomon hastened to the steward's side.

"Yes, I did. Do you know where the prince is?"

The man grimaced a bit. "Forgive me, sir, but I am not supposed to tell you."

Ah, so Ever was going to play that game, was he? Garin huffed impatiently. "Well then, why don't you tell me where he *isn't*?"

Solomon relaxed a bit. Glancing up at the king's study, he said quietly, "The prince is not in his chambers or with his guests." He paused before adding, "He is also *not* drinking *wine*."

Garin sighed and nodded as he headed up one of the spiraling staircases, away from the bustle of the grand entrance, where guests were still being received.

"Your Highness." He cracked the ornate wooden door open. "You've never had more than a few glasses of wine. Are you sure this is a good evening to begin something stronger?" Opening the door further, he saw Ever out on the small balcony that overlooked the back lawn. He was slumped against the door frame, his powerful shoulders hunched.

"The crowds made it too hard to think." Ever's words were slightly slurred.

"Yes, they often do that," Garin said cautiously as he joined the prince on the balcony.

Ever's face was twisted into an emotion that tugged at the steward's heart. Despite the savior Prince Everard had become to many, defeating the dark forces of the north, Ever, the young prince, was still there underneath, and he was grieving.

"But the quiet is even worse. Still," Ever finally stood and walked back to his father's desk, "I have finally understood. I know now why Nevina led her men to attack, why my father died. And it wasn't my fault!" He slammed his hand down on the desk with a bang.

"You are right. It wasn't your fault."

"It was their fault!"

"Their fault?" The uneasy feeling wiggled in Garin's heart.

"Call my advisers, Garin," Ever ordered, taking another swig from the flask in his left hand. "I am going to stop these threats once and for all!"

"Sire, it is the night of your coronation. Surely this can wait until tomorrow," Garin suggested hopefully.

"It cannot. My father always said our enemies would be waiting, and he was right. We must cut them off now!"

With a sigh, the steward did as Ever bid. It didn't take long for all of the prince's advisers to gather in the king's study.

"You all know my father believed the strength of the Fortress was our great secret in defending our land," Ever began, his words still slightly blended. His advisers exchanged wary looks, but he went on. "He taught me to look for weaknesses in our lines, and to search for the chinks in the armor of our great army. After much thought, I have realized that the lack of strength in our men wasn't what allowed the enemy to inflict such vicious casualties."

"Your Highness," General Acelet stepped forward cautiously, "the darkness in our enemy's power was one we hadn't anticipated."

But Ever waved him off. "Just hear what I have to say. Our chink wasn't in the strength of our men, but in the weaknesses of our people. We have too long coddled the unproductive citizens, the weak that inhabit the streets of our cities and live off the hard work of others."

"Sire," Garin gently reminded him, "they haven't lived off of the grain of the Fortress in years. Your father cut off assistance to the churches long ago."

"It doesn't matter!" Ever turned to his steward and jabbed a finger at him. "If we did not have these beggars, these diseased and lame lying in our streets and in our churches, Nevina never would have dared to attack us. There wouldn't have been a weakness to exploit! And I have decided that it will never happen again!" As Ever uttered his next words, Garin felt sick.

"I command that our land be purged of its weakness. You will all go out and make sure that those who cannot contribute to our strength are no longer a threat to Destin's well-being."

General Acelet's face was white and his voice quivered. "You cannot be suggesting that we kill our sick and crippled!"

"That is exactly what I'm saying, General! You are to begin tonight, after the coronation." Ever strode up to his favorite general unevenly, and leaned his face so close to the man their noses nearly touched. "And if you don't have the manhood to carry out my orders, then I will have to find someone else who will."

"Please, Your Highness," Dagin, the horse master, pleaded, "it is late, and the ceremony is about to begin. Please allow us to wait until the morning to reconsider and discuss this again."

"If one more soul questions my order, then he will find the same fate as the diseased that will be soon cleared from the streets," Ever barked. "Now, it's time for my coronation. Garin?"

Nodding blankly, Garin struggled to quickly help Ever into his ceremonial robes, which had been haphazardly tossed over a chair. The other men each bowed to the prince in turn, their faces pale and full of fear. They hastened away, leaving Garin to his charge.

Garin searched desperately for something, anything that might change the prince's mind, but from the look on Ever's face, there was much drink left in his body, and addressing him would only make him angrier. So Garin kept quiet, but that didn't mean he would sit idly by as Ever stained his hands with innocent blood. If Garin could not prevent all of it from spilling, perhaps he could put off some.

As soon as the prince was dressed, Garin excused himself. Running back to his chambers, he whipped parchment and a quill from his desk. The ink smeared as he wrote in haste, but the words were legible. He hailed the first servant he saw.

"Give this to Edgar. Tell him to take it to Ansel Marchand in Soudain. And tell Edgar that if he values his position here at the Fortress, there must be no delay. That goes for you, too! Now hurry!"

As soon as his message had been dispatched, Garin tried to regain control of himself. In all of his years at the Fortress, he had never felt such a sense of dread. The prince who had always been the Fortress's favored one, more than any other king Garin had seen, was quickly bringing something evil upon them all.

What can I do to stop this? he begged the Fortress silently as he strode back to the throne room where the ceremony was beginning. As he took his place in the back, he noticed many of the other advisers returning as well, from errands similar to his, he was sure.

Ever had somehow managed to get himself down the aisle and before the holy man without rousing much suspicion from the guests. Now, as he stood before them all, laying his hand on the Holy Writ, Garin felt a pang of sorrow. This should have been an eve of joy, not one of murderous bloodshed. The kingdom had waited for its beloved prince, its jewel, to become their sovereign since the day he was born.

Before the prince could utter the ceremonial vows, however, the priest abruptly withdrew the Holy Writ and took a step backward. Uneasy murmurs spread through the crowd as the old man's face pulled into a frown and his eyes became engulfed completely with blue flame.

"Everard Perrin Auguste Fortier, son of Rodrigue, son of Damien the Fourth, the Fortress has declared you unfit to wear this crown." A gasp went up from the assembly. "From the day of your birth," the priest continued, "you were gifted with a strength unknown to other men. Because of your callousness, however, what has never been done before will take place tonight."

The old man raised his head and turned his fire-laden eyes upon the ceiling. "The Fortress will go dark, and you, Prince Everard, will be a prisoner of your own making. Before life can be found in this sacred place once again, a new strength must be found. What has been broken must be remade. The one who was strong must be willing to die. Only then can the Fortress and the kingdom have the protector they deserve."

As the priest finished speaking, a dreadful grinding sound filled the hall. Garin fell to his knees, holding his ears, trying desperately to block the noise as the lights began to go out, one by one. The world around him seemed to rise, and rushing winds burst through the great doors. As they swept through the people, each body began to disappear. Then all was silent, and there was no light.

5

BELLE

"*Y*our eyes are sparkling." Deline smiled at her daughter.

Isa beamed back. "It's perfect." And it was. The dress was simple, but it was everything she could have hoped for. The gauzy white made her feel like she was floating in a cloud. Her arms were covered in lace, and her veil made the world look like a mist filled the room. Best of all, the long gown covered all but the toes of her shoes. If she stood still and buried her left hand in the layers of white material, it was impossible to see the crook of her ankle or how her wrist turned inward.

"No, Baby." Her mother wiped a tear from her eye. "*You* are perfect."

Isa fought the tears that threatened to spill down her own face. She still could not believe that this happiness should be hers. At one time, she'd thought that it never could be.

It was hard to imagine that just months ago, she'd been running for her life. After receiving a midnight letter from a friend at the Fortress, Isa's father had dragged the family out of bed, whispering severely that there were to be no candles or fires lit. Deline had wept as Isa's father and brother had bundled her up and buried her beneath a load of supplies in the horse cart and fled the city in the dark of night. For three days, they had waited up in a deserted mountain cottage before Deline had been able to send word that Isa would be safe again. The Fortress had gone dark, and the royal order had never been carried out.

Still, when they had returned, the neighbors said Ansel should send his daughter with the Caregivers. It had been a close call. While years had passed since the Fortress monarchs had shown true interest in the welfare of its poor, everyone had hoped their new king would bring about a more merciful reign. Instead, Isa had very nearly been killed in her sleep by the first edict of the young prince. No one knew when the Fortress would awaken, the neighbors said, and then what would become of Isa? No, her father had argued, much to Isa's relief. Isa would stay.

It wasn't that Isa disliked the Caregivers. They seemed kind enough. Merchants by trade, they would come with great varieties of foreign wares, many which her father sold in his mercantile. They did not trade only for money, however. Everyone knew the Caregivers by the black metal rings they wore. Those rings, they claimed, were a sign of asylum for anyone who needed sanctuary. Unbeknownst to the king and his elite, those who could not provide for themselves could be smuggled out with the Caregivers to their own country, where they were given fitting jobs, food, and shelter.

This was all fine and good, but it had always bothered Isa that those who left were not allowed to contact their families. It was too dangerous for letters even, Marko said.

Marko was one of the Caregivers who visited Soudain most. An old family friend, Ansel often purchased his goods for the mercantile. Marko was a good-natured man, and ever since she was a small child, he had never come to the mercantile without sweets for Isa and her brother and sister. He was fiercely built for a tradesman, and would have frightened her if she hadn't known him for so long. His long hair was always pulled back into a tight knot at the back of his head, and he smelled of campfire smoke. Marko had visited not long after the Fortress went dark, and he had also strongly advised Ansel and Deline to send Isa with him.

"It is too dangerous to leave her here!" he had argued, gesturing in the direction of the Fortress with one of his large arms.

"I will not send my daughter off by herself to a place I have never been, and will likely never see," Ansel had answered his friend in a steady voice.

"You could come with her! We would happily take you back with us, all of you!"

"It would be too conspicuous." Her father had shaken his head. "I'm on Soudain's city council. They would notice when I left. No, I will care for my daughter. She will be safe with her family."

That had been the end of that discussion, and Isa was grateful. After a few weeks, the Fortress had remained dark, and the urgings of well-meaning family and friends had stopped. Life had begun to return to normal. Well, better than normal for Isa. Raoul had asked her to marry him.

Isa smiled to herself as her mother repinned her tresses one more time. Tonight, everything would change. Tonight, Raoul would return from his journey with his father, and she would become the wife of the future city chancellor. She imagined, as she often had in the last few months, what it would feel like to see him again. They'd exchanged letters, she more than he, several times since he had gone. His father kept him busy with political meetings and social events, so his letters were far and few between, but such was the life of a chancellor. Isa refused to be bothered by his full schedule. It was simply a pleasure to write to him, something most women wouldn't have been able to do. But tonight, she would have no need for quill or paper. This would be the night she would wed the one who had been able to see her in spite of her brokenness.

"Now, we have no time for crying." Deline wiped both her face and her daughter's. "The guests will be here soon, and I can already hear your aunt ordering everyone around. I will be back up when it's time."

Isa watched as her mother left, and felt a familiar pang. She would miss her mother. Most women would have been nearly beside themselves with worry, trying desperately to get their grown daughters married, particularly if they were Isa's age and still unwed. But not Deline.

"You'll always have a home here," Deline had told Isa on the day she had gotten engaged. "No matter how old you are or how many years pass, you can always come home."

With those words in mind, Isa carefully practiced the wedding dance as she waited impatiently. She had decided to forgo her sturdy walking boots in favor of the beautiful white slippers her father had commissioned the tailor to make for her. They would make dancing more difficult, but she was determined not to give anyone a reason to smirk or whisper. She would be as beautiful and graceful as any bride this night.

"Isa." Deline finally opened the door. "He's here. It's time."

Taking a shaky breath, Isa tested her ankle once more before beginning down the stairs. It seemed like the whole city was there, crowded into her parents' home. Friends, neighbors, and family smiled at her as she slowly descended, but they weren't the ones she was looking for.

Her groom stood by the door next to his father. Straight backed, he held his head high. His brown coat was clean, despite having just returned from a long journey, and his black boots shined. Slicked back with oil, his neatly trimmed hair matched his boots. What she was most interested in, however, were his eyes. Dark brown, nearly black they were so dark, they reflected the light of the dying sun as sunset passed through the shuttered room. And they were looking right back at her.

As soon as she saw him, she remembered just how handsome he was, why all of the other girls had been so jealous when he had proposed to her. That a crippled girl should have the son of the chancellor was unthinkable. She, who couldn't walk evenly, didn't deserve the responsibilities of being his wife, they said. And yet, he had chosen her.

Isa walked as carefully as she could, making sure not to teeter in front of the crowd, until she was finally standing before him.

His dark eyes were wide and his face was taut, as though he were afraid. She knew the feeling. Cautiously, she curtsied. "My lord." She murmured the first words of ceremony, just as she'd been practicing. "May my life strength be bound to yours."

"Isabelle," he whispered, "we need to talk. Alone."

Isa stared back at him, momentarily unsure of what to say or do. Not only had he failed to give the ceremonial response, but he'd called her Isabelle. He hadn't called her Isabelle since they were children. Nodding slightly, she began to tremble as she followed him to the back door of the house. Whispers and gasps went up as they walked. In addition to all her other woes, Isa miserably admitted to herself that wearing the silken slippers had been a bad idea as she struggled towards the door. After a few slow steps, Raoul stiffly offered her his arm. Silently, everyone watched them leave.

Isa's mind was spinning. They should have begun the ceremonial dance by now. She felt as if she were stepping out of one of her daydreams and into a nightmare. As they sat on the garden's low stone wall, she realized she didn't want to hear what he had to say.

"Isabelle, we've been apart for some time now," Raoul began slowly, his gentle voice strained.

Isa nodded silently, staring at him with fear knocking her heart about in her chest.

"You know my father took me along so I would learn about how other chancellors and governors lived. He says that living here can sometimes blind us to the traditions that people of our station must carry on. It is too easy to get wrapped up in what we desire for ourselves, and what we truly need in order to best serve the people."

Isa nodded again. She had known this, as he had written about it in one of his first letters.

"We saw many other administrators while we were gone. Eight, actually. Some lived like lords, and others had little more than their people. But they all had had one thing in common." Raoul dropped his eyes the ground.

It took Isa a moment to realize that he was talking about her. "Their wives," she whispered. Raoul nodded. She had to swallow hard before she could speak again. "So, you are saying that I'm unfit to be a chancellor's wife."

"Now wait–" he began to correct her, but she held her hand up.

"I can read and write, which is more than you can say for many men in this wretched city. I can figure the sums of the treasury better than you can! How is that an unsuitable match for a chancellor? What more could you possibly want?"

"I need a woman who could exercise leadership in my stead if something happened!"

"No! No, what you mean is that you want a mindless ninny who can stand by your side without having to lean on you for support! A flawless flirt who can charm visiting politicians with her grace and allure! You want a woman without a crooked hand or a lame foot!"

"Belle–"

"Don't call me that!" She was shouting now. "Just tell me one thing. Was this your idea or your father's?"

He stared at her for a long moment before softly answering. "It was my father's wish for me to see how others lived, but it was my choice to live like them. I want what's best for this city."

"Then take what you want and go." Isa's father was suddenly beside him. "But before you do, I want you to know that neither you nor your father are welcome in my mercantile or my house ever again." Ansel wore a look of deep hatred that Isa had never seen before. "Men without honor have no place in my home."

With a weak nod, Raoul looked silently down at her hand.

Isa realized what he wanted, and angry tears spilled down her face as she yanked the ring off her finger and shoved it at him. No words seemed to come to the young man as he stared down at the silver band, so after a long moment, he simply turned and walked out the back gate. Isa and her father sat in silence for an immeasurable time before she was finally brave enough to speak.

"Is everyone still inside?"

"No, your mother cleared them out after I asked Chancellor Dupont what his son was up to."

Isa nodded, and before she knew it, her father had drawn her close and held her tightly. She could hold back no more, and before long, she realized she was wailing. She'd felt pain before, like the day the prince had shoved her into the way of the rearing horse. She'd felt grief when she'd realized that she could no longer dance. She had felt sorrow when the other children left her alone to find more suitable play spots, places she could not walk to or climb.

But Raoul had always been the one to tell her things would be well, to stay with her when the others had run off. He had been the one to ask her to dance at all the town festivals when no other men dared to. Raoul had been the one to nickname her Belle. He had believed she was worth marrying, despite her handicaps. But he had lied. And none of the pain she had ever known compared to this.

Isa cried into her father's shirt until she could no longer sit up straight. It wasn't until she was tucked into her own bed that she realized she must have dozed off. She was still in her white dress, but she didn't bother getting up to change. Instead, she lay in bed and listened to her parents through her little attic floor.

"Did he say why?" her mother asked.

"Some nonsense about how it was acceptable for his son to befriend a crippled girl, and even ask her to go dancing sometimes." Ansel's voice was low, but Isa could hear the dishes they were collecting clatter and bang much louder than necessary. "But as Raoul's father, it was his responsibility to direct him towards important matters, now that he's a man. He didn't say as much, but I can tell you right now that Isa is the reason Dupont took him on the trip, to show him what a chancellor's wife ought to be." At that moment, a dish shattered and Ansel cursed. Isa's parents were silent for a long time before Deline spoke again.

"I'm worried about her, Ansel. I've never seen her like that."

Isa's father gave a loud sigh, and Isa could imagine him running his hand through his graying hair. "Me, too. But she's a strong girl. She'll get through it. She has to."

Dawn was slow to come the next morning. Isa had drifted in and out of a tearful slumber, and the light brought little relief. Finally, Megane got out of her bed and crawled in with Isa. Isa held her little sister tightly, which released another set of tears. Megane watched her anxiously, but was silent until it was time to get dressed.

"You should fold that nicely," she said as Isa crumpled the wedding dress and threw it in the drawer. "Then it won't be wrinkled for the next time."

"There won't be a next time, Megs."

"Why not?"

"Because men don't want crippled women for their wives." Isa spat out the words before she remembered whom she was talking to. Megane's eyes grew wide and she hurried out of the room. Isa felt badly for speaking to her sister in such a way, but she couldn't cleanse the bitter words from her mouth.

As she collapsed back onto the bed, she felt her anger grow. Not just for Raoul, but for all the girls who had told her cripples don't get husbands, and for those people who stared at her sympathetically every time she walked the city streets. The women who had nudged and winked at her as the wedding day had approached. For her small bed that should have lain empty last night. But most of all, for the prince.

If it hadn't been for him, she never would have been a cripple. She would have continued to dance, to run, and to grow and laugh with the other children. She would have been called beautiful by more than Raoul as she became a woman. The touch of a loving husband would have been hers by now, and maybe even children, as some of her friends had. It didn't matter that no one had seen the prince since the Fortress had gone dark. Isa suddenly hated the man with a vengeance she hadn't known herself capable of until that instant.

The day didn't bring much improvement for the family. After they spent all day cleaning up what should have been a wedding feast, Ansel came home from the city council meeting with grim news.

"The chancellor wants someone to visit the other cities and towns to see if their tradesmen have suffered as we have since the Fortress went dark."

"And let me guess," Deline sighed, "he chose you."

"He's just angry that you stood up to him last night!" Isa's younger brother, Launce, muttered over his stew.

"I believe you're right," Ansel said to his son, "but whether he's angry or not makes no difference. The other council members agreed to it. I leave tomorrow."

"How long will you be gone, Papa?" Megane asked.

"Quite a while, sweetheart." Ansel lifted his youngest daughter out of her chair and into his lap.

"You're not going all the way to the western coast, are you?" Deline frowned. "Surely they wouldn't make you go that far!"

"Unfortunately, yes. I'll probably be gone until the leaves change color. But do not worry." He kissed his wife. "I will do my best to be back before the first snow."

So Ansel left the next morning with all his provisions in saddle bags on one of the family horses. Goodbyes were tearful, all except for the one he exchanged with Isa. Isa felt as if there were no more tears left to shed in the whole world.

The rest of the family watched as he made his way east towards the mountain pass, but Isa turned and went back inside. Looking at the pass meant seeing the Fortress as it rose up out of the mountain's side. And looking at the Fortress meant looking towards Prince Everard.

6

ASYLUM

*A*nsel wrapped his cloak around himself even tighter as he started down the mountain. His journey had taken even longer than he'd thought, and the eve of his return looked as though it might have to be postponed. The black clouds above him were heavy with snow, and a long descent still stretched out ahead of him. Even in good weather, it would have taken him three hours to make it down the mountain to Soudain, but the biting wind whistled eerily, as if to guarantee him that his return would take him much longer than that.

The trip had not been encouraging. The other cities and towns Ansel had visited were also suffering. Trade and travel had slowed to a crawl after the Fortress had gone dark. Without the protection of the Fortress and its kings, fear had driven many of the smaller towns to close their borders, and those that had remained open saw few tradesmen or merchants. Ansel would be forever grateful that the darkening of the Fortress had spared his daughter's life, but he now hoped that he had enough in his own mercantile to feed his family, much less those who came to purchase food throughout the winter.

Another large gust of wind interrupted Ansel's thoughts, and when he looked up, he realized that white flurries were already beginning to descend. Within moments, it was nearly impossible to see the road. He stopped where he was and quickly considered what he should do. There were no cottages this high up the mountain that he could seek shelter in. In fact, the only thing that he could possibly reach before the blizzard fully struck would be the Fortress. And the Fortress was dark.

After the Fortress had closed, the townspeople had whispered to one another of curses and all other sorts of dark magic. Ansel had paid little attention to it at the time, simply thankful that whatever had happened had kept Isa alive. Besides, he was a practical man. He didn't have the time to sit around fretting about gossip born of idle minds. Now that he was suddenly faced with the possibility of visiting the great Fortress, however, Ansel had to admit that he felt a bit of unease. Even if there were nothing to the rumors, his family's last run-in with the prince had turned out to be more than disastrous. Still, no matter how the prince felt about him, Ansel had friends there among the servants. Surely when they saw who was knocking upon their doors, they would be willing to open up and provide him simple respite in their quarters until the storm had passed. The prince need not even know.

By the time Ansel was able to make out the post that marked the way to the servants' entrance, the biting air made it hard to concentrate. He coaxed his tired horse onto the dirt path, which was now nearly invisible for the snow, and not a moment too soon, he reached the stables.

Ansel should have felt relief at making it safely to a shelter, and yet, a wave of anxiety hit him as he pushed open the heavy wooden door. There were a few dim torches lit, but no grooms came to greet him, and his sense of dread increased. Everyone knew that like his father had been, the prince was an avid horseman. He surely would have left at least two groomsmen to watch over his favorite warhorses in such a storm.

"Hello?" Ansel called out. No one answered. His disquiet grew as he guided his horse into an empty stall. The other horses whinnied at him. They looked strangely thin for being the king's animals. Peering closer, Ansel saw that they had feed in their troughs, but not much. The Fortress must be suffering from food shortages as well, he realized. In accordance, he took only enough to give his beast a few mouthfuls. He would pay the steward back when he found him. After brushing his animal and making sure he had clean hay, Ansel bundled back up to make the cold trek to the servants' entrance.

The Fortress's greeting was eerily similar to the one he had received in the stables. When no one responded to his knocks, Ansel let himself in. As soon as the door was shut, however, he found that unlike in the stables, not one candle was lit. And not only was the citadel as dark as night, but it was just as quiet, too. No voices echoed down the stone halls. There were no whispers of children, or even footsteps to break the silence.

Something, a suspicious feeling, kept him from calling out. Instead he felt his way down the corridor to where he knew the servants' kitchen would be. When he found it, there was one lone candle lit on the long wooden table, and a weak fire in the large hearth. As long as Ansel had been visiting the Fortress to do business and speak with friends, such as the steward, there had always been people and food in this place. Women were always chasing giggling children away from the freshly baked bread, and hungry young men Launce's age were always hanging about looking for leftovers.

But now, aside from the small flames, there was no one. After a long, uneventful wait on the threshold, Ansel slowly entered the large room. He found some old bread and aged cheese in one of the cabinets. The food was so dry it was nearly inedible, but Ansel was hungry enough to try and stomach it.

A flicker of light against the wall caught his eye. There was something about the way the shadow danced that unnerved him. It was too much like a human's shadow. Shaking his head, he went back to eating. The exhaustion and cold must be getting to him, he thought. When the shadow moved again, however, more boldly this time, Ansel froze with food still in his mouth. Fear made his limbs feel strange, and he began to shiver harder than he had outside.

After a long moment of staring, he finally gained enough courage to swallow the rest of his bite. Unable to ignore his morbid curiosity any longer, he stood up slowly to face the strange silhouette.

It was really too large to be cast by the poor flames of the hearth or the candle on the table, and that bothered Ansel. After he'd stared at it for a long moment, it moved again, jumping three feet down the wall towards the door. Another long minute later, it moved even farther, and Ansel got the feeling he was supposed to follow.

The game continued out of the kitchen and down the hall towards the servants' chambers. Unable to see the shadow in the dark of the hall, Ansel went back and took the lone candle, for that seemed to be what the shadow wanted him to do. After coming this far, what other choice did he have?

As he followed, he got the feeling that this shadow wasn't the only one. The farther he walked, the more invisible eyes he felt on him. Even stranger than that, however, was the sensation that the eyes were familiar. And though the feeling should have sent him running back into the storm, he instinctively felt he could trust the strange apparitions. Either that, or the ancient food he'd just eaten was meddling with his ability to reason.

Unlike the shadows, however, the Fortress itself was as unfriendly as he'd ever seen it. The darkness was nearly suffocating. Walking in it felt like walking deeper and deeper into a tomb. The air was musty and damp, and it smelled as if neither door nor window had been opened in decades. What had happened to the kingdom's beacon of shining light, the sacred place of protection? What kind of power could overcome it? This thought set him trembling more than anything else he'd encountered yet. Perhaps the gossip was not as farfetched as he'd first believed.

The shadow kept him moving quickly down the corridors, but he paused before the throne room. Through the open doors, there was one light, the brightest of any he'd seen, that shone through the high windows above the throne. All of the other windows were covered, their tapestries drawn closed. It was moonlight, Ansel realized, that was coming through the highest of windows. The storm must have abated.

As his eyes began to adjust to the new light, he realized that the grand room had been decorated and left that way. He could only guess it had been set for the great coronation ceremony, as that had been the night everything had gone dark. He turned to go back into the hallway when a voice spoke from behind him.

"And how is it that a commoner escaped the curse of the Fortress?"

Ansel slowly turned. As he peered more closely, he realized that the throne, though hidden in shadow from the moon's rays, was not empty. A dark figure sat hunched in it. Its voice was soft and terrible, and Ansel trembled so that he dropped the candle, and it sputtered out upon the floor.

"I beg your pardon, my lord?" Ansel called back timidly.

"All of my servants, my soldiers, and even my home itself were cursed into this blackness. No one has come or gone for months. And yet, you come in as if you own the place."

"I beg your forgiveness, Sire." Ansel hurried forward and knelt, bowing his head. "I sought shelter from the storm. If I had stayed outside I would have died. I did not mean to intrude."

Two thin rings of blue fire appeared through the darkness, fixing their depths upon him, and Ansel's fear nearly overwhelmed him.

"What is your name?"

"Ansel Marchand of Soudain, Your Highness."

"And what are you doing out in such a storm?"

"I sit on Soudain's city council, and I was sent to visit other parts of Destin to inquire about their matters of trade."

"So you thought it would be acceptable to trespass on sacred ground for this?"

At this question, Ansel swallowed hard, praying his response would not be considered impertinent.

"I beg your pardon, Sire, but was the Fortress not a place of asylum for the weary in the days of old?"

The prince was silent for a moment. Finally, his shadow leaned back. "It does seem that the Fortress has spared you, though I cannot understand why. But perhaps," the prince spoke slowly, "you can be of use to me."

Ansel's heart skipped a beat. What in the heavens could the prince need with him?

"But first, I need to know why you were willing to enter a place that is cursed. What makes your life so worth living that you would risk meeting with phantoms?"

Ansel's words became lodged in his throat. After narrowly escaping the royal edict meant for Isa, he could not tell the prince about his family. So he remained silent.

"You would defy your prince?" For the first time, the terrible voice rose, which made it only more awful. Still, Ansel would not speak.

"If you are unwilling to answer me, I will have no choice than to find out for myself. I suppose you have heard of my strength?"

Of course Ansel had. Though few knew how the monarchs' power worked, everyone knew that their kings, and sometimes their queens, wielded a special gift. It had been the very reason Destin was the most feared kingdom in the realm. And it was most definitely not the kind of power Ansel wanted involved with Isa.

"It would not be difficult for me," Everard continued, "to find whomever or whatever you're protecting. It also would not be difficult for me to share the sickness of this place with them."

Defenseless against such a threat, Ansel closed his eyes and spoke, his voice barely above a whisper. "I have a family, Your Highness. I promised them I would come home safely."

"Tell me about this family."

"You wouldn't be interested in the family of a common merchant, Sire. We are much like other families of our kind."

The prince paused again for a moment before replying. "No, I don't think you are. You're too careful, too protective of them. Oh come now, don't be so surprised. I've given my life to studying strategy and defense, and you, trades-man, are putting up all your defenses. Now, I truly do wish to hear about your family. As you can guess, I get few visitors at the moment. Entertain me."

Ansel swallowed hard before answering. King Rodrigue had despised weak-ness, and after his son's attempt to weed out Ansel's daughter, it appeared the prince despised it as well. Ansel chose his words carefully. "My wife is a shrewd woman, and runs my store as well as I do. She has also taught all of the children to be of use there. The youngest, Megane, is just a child, but she already shows a talent for weaving. Launce, my boy, is nineteen, and he's training to take over the mercantile one day. My oldest daughter..." Ansel's voice faltered for a moment. What if the prince knew her name? What if he remembered her? "My oldest daughter has a strong heart and a quick mind like no other."

The prince held up his hand, and Ansel stopped.

"A strong heart, you say. What is this daughter's name?"

Ansel faltered again before answering. "Isabelle, Sire."

"And what about her heart makes it so strong?" The prince's voice was cyni-cal, but Ansel detected a keen interest in it. His heart pounded as he struggled to answer the prince's question.

"She... suffered an injury as a child, but she never gave up. She was deter-mined to be strong once again, and she is. Isabelle never gives up hope." Ansel prayed that would be the end of the prince's interest in his daughter, that the assurance of her strength and productivity would be enough, but he had no way of knowing. The prince's expressions were hidden in the dark. Only those fiery blue rings could be seen. It seemed like a very long time that the two men sat there in silence, one kneeling and the other hunching in his throne. Finally, the prince spoke.

"So, Ansel Marchand, I have an assignment for you." His voice was quiet and terrible again.

"Yes, Sire?"

"When the road is clear enough to return, you will go back to your home. Isabelle will gather her things and say goodbye to her family and friends. Then you will bring her back here to me before dusk on the third day. Three days should be more than enough time for her to make her farewells properly."

Ansel felt as though his heart had stopped and his lungs had collapsed. He fought for his voice as he threw himself at his prince's feet.

"Your Highness, please! There must be some mistake! Take me! I will stay here in the stead of your servants! I will do anything you ask of me! But this I cannot do!"

"You can," the prince said testily, "and you will."

"No!" Ansel rose to his feet, rage overcoming his fear. "I will not give my child to you! You may sit here in the darkness of your great Fortress, but outside of it, you are nothing! If you were still in power, the trade routes would no longer be filled with robbers and vagabonds, and Destin would once again thrive! You, Sire, cannot make me do such a thing!"

"Oh, but I can. Have you forgotten my threat? I may not leave the Fortress, but that doesn't mean my power is limited by gates or byways or walls. With just a wave of my hand, I can send this dark sickness upon your whole family as well. I'm sure your daughter who is strong of heart wouldn't want such a thing to befall her brother or sister or mother. No, sir, I do not think you are willing to risk your entire family's well-being for one."

Ansel's knees gave out, and he collapsed onto the cold stone floor, cursing himself for ever setting foot in the wretched citadel. It would have been better if he'd died in the storm.

"Take him away." The prince flicked his hand, and invisible beings grasped Ansel by the arms and dragged him out of the throne room. The unseen hands were gentle but firm as they laid him in a bed that smelled of dust. He struggled to get up, but they held him in place. Eventually, he could fight no longer, and fatigue won. But even in sleep, he could not escape the torment of the guilt that consumed him.

In the middle of the night, he was awakened by an idea that had slipped into his dreams. Cautiously, he sat up. It appeared the shadows had left him alone once he'd stopped struggling. He scurried to put on his boots and winter coverings. They were not entirely dry yet, as the fire the shadows had built in his room was very weak, but he hardly noticed. There was a way to keep Isa safe.

In three days' time, she and the rest of the family would be far away, and the prince would have to end these vile, continuous attempts on her life. Ansel wondered if the prince knew about his attempted escape as he sneaked out to his horse, but since no one stopped him, he pressed on toward the stables. The animal stamped its feet when he arrived, seeming as desperate to leave the place as he was.

Less than an hour later, they were on their way home. Snow had made the mountain road nearly impassable, but the merchant could not have cared less. Isa would be safe, his family would be together, and Heaven help the man that tried to stop him.

7

SOMETHING TERRIBLE

*I*n the months since the almost wedding, Megane had tried her best to stay out of Isa's way. Launce had stopped his teasing and replaced it with muttered threats about what he would do if he ever got his hands on Raoul. Deline had taken over Isa's hardest chores, and had suggested as many ways as she could think of to get Isa out of the house. Picnics were planned, the horses were taken for rides in the country, and Isa's favorite dinner was made more often than ever before. Despite their well-laid plans, however, Isa found joy in none of it. Outings were quiet and awkward, as the other three attempted to draw her into their jokes and stories, and Isa scurried back into the house as soon as she was able.

Isa knew they were trying, but there was simply little she had to say to anyone, and everything that should be said could be spoken at home. Leaving the house was perilous, fraught with reminders that other people were still living their happy lives, continuing to move through time. That Raoul was still living his life in the city without her. To Isa, time would stand still forever.

Despite Isa's objections, however, four months after Ansel had set out on his journey, Deline continued to insist that life would eventually get better. And she insisted that Isa move along with it.

There had been a snow the night before, ridiculously early for the season. Still, the ground looked pretty all covered in white, and Deline seemed to think the new scene might cheer her daughter. So Isa, much to her disdain, was goaded into accompanying her mother to the tailor's shop, where she was forced to answer trivial questions as to how she was faring.

"Deline! Isa!"

Isa and her mother turned to see a plump little woman running toward them, the look on her face promising juicy gossip. Surely enough, before any greetings could be exchanged, Margot was speaking.

"Have you heard?" Her voice nearly squeaked with excitement. "Have you heard about young Master Raoul?"

Though she managed to drop her eyes to the ground, Isa's heart beat unevenly. Out of the corner of her eye, she saw her mother give her an uneasy look.

"Isa, why don't you go inside and prepare some tea? I could use a warm drink, and I believe our guest could use one, also."

But Margot shook her head, her words tumbling out faster than Isa could walk. "No, I believe Miss Isa should hear this, and she'll know just how fortunate she is not to have married that horrible young man."

"Margot, I–" her mother tried to interject, but the older woman just kept talking.

"I was just down to the butcher's shop this morning, when Harriet Bissette skipped into the town square to show off her ring. Can you believe it, Isa? He gave her exactly the same ring that he gave you!"

His grandmother's ring. Isa's thumb instinctively moved to rub the spot that, for two months, had been occupied by the silver band. Not so long ago, he'd placed that ring on her own finger. Suddenly, it was hard to breathe.

"...Less than a year, and he's already proposed to a second girl!"

"Really, Margot!" Deline protested, but their neighbor babbled on.

"Isa, you should count it a blessing that you two were not wed! You have a lovely face, my dear, but with your lame leg and hand and all, you wouldn't have been able to hold him. Better to be alone and keep your dignity than to know your man is off chasing other women because you can't satisfy him!" And with that, she spotted another neighbor, and was gone before Isa or Deline could say another word.

Isa bolted for the door before any other well-intentioned friend or relative could find her, and ran upstairs as quickly as her ankle would allow. Deline was faster, however, and she followed her daughter into the attic before Isa could get the door closed.

"I don't want to talk about it!" Isa threw her things down on the bed and went to stare out the window.

"Isa, you knew it was bound to happen."

"That doesn't mean I want to hear about it. This is why I don't leave the house!"

"You can't stay locked up in this attic forever," Deline said. "We have tried to be kind to you, to be sensitive to things that remind you of him. But you can't live the rest of your life hiding from the world."

"What if I don't want to be part of the world?" Isa finally turned and faced her mother. "Thanks to our hero prince, the world thinks I'm good for nothing anyway! There is a reason all the women my age are expecting babies, and their little sisters are getting married, and I'm not. Is it so much to ask that my nose not be rubbed in my loss? That I get to simply remain where at least I know I'm wanted?"

"But you can't do that!" Deline was shouting, too.

"And why not?"

"Because you were born for more than that!"

Before Isa could reply, however, Launce burst into the room, out of breath. "Mum, Isa, Father's home. Something is wrong."

In a flash, Deline was downstairs. It took Isa longer to make her way down the wooden steps, but when she finally did, she could see that something was indeed wrong. Ansel's face was pale, and no matter how many blankets Megane and Launce piled upon him, he shivered. What frightened Isa the most, however, was the wild feverish look in his eyes. He looked like a dog cornered in an alley.

Ten minutes passed before his teeth stopped chattering enough for him to speak a single sentence. When he did speak, he asked Megane to take care of his horse.

"Let Launce do it," Deline told him as the girl bounded off. "She's been dying to see you, and the horse will take at least half an hour."

"I know." Ansel finally looked up from the tea they'd placed in his hands. "But I have something I must tell you all, and I am afraid it will frighten her."

At this, they all stopped what they were doing and stared. Isa felt a chill touch her heart. For though he spoke to them all, he was looking at her.

"We must pack what little we can with great haste. Take only what you need. I will send a message to Marko. We are leaving tonight after the sun sets."

Dumbfounded, Isa looked at her mother and brother, but they seemed to be as much at a loss as she was.

"We're doing what?" Launce was the first one to find his voice.

"We're leaving with the Caregivers tonight. All of us."

"But... why?" Deline frowned.

"Father," Isa put her hands on her father's arm and knelt beside him, "what happened?" Her touch seemed to calm his breathing some, but when his eyes met hers, they were wild with worry.

"Isa," his voice was hollow and old, "it is all my fault. I have done something terrible, and I cannot undo it. This is the only way I know how to save you. I... I was caught out on the mountain when the storm hit. I was afraid I would freeze, so I took the only familiar path I could find." Ansel swallowed loudly before looking beseechingly at the rest of his family. "I sought the shelter of the Fortress."

The silence was deafening as a familiar feeling stirred in Isa's heart. She suddenly knew what kind of turn her father's journey had taken.

"The place is surely cursed," Ansel spoke again, shaking his head at his tea. "I used to laugh at such superstitions, but there was hardly a light in the entire stronghold."

"The servants?" Deline placed her hand over her heart.

"Shadows… phantoms. I do not know. There are no bodies to serve the prince, but the spirits are certainly not lacking. And they do his bidding as well as any staff." He shivered. "And then there was the prince. I don't know how, but he somehow escaped the enchantment. At least, he still has a body I mean. I couldn't see much for the darkness. He saw me, however, and he demanded to know about my family."

A sob suddenly wrenched itself from Ansel's body. "He said he would send a plague upon you all with his power if I did not obey! Isa, forgive me!" Her father dropped his tea cup on the floor and clutched her hands, his brown eyes desperately searching hers. "I tried so hard to shield you. I told him only of your strengths, and as little as I could. And yet," Ansel's voice became a whisper, "he has demanded that you come to the Fortress to stay with him."

Isa stared back in horror. Even under a curse, would he never stop? Why couldn't he simply let her be? As the fear moved through her, however, it was quickly replaced with an even stronger emotion. How dare he? How dare this man threaten her family, using them as leverage to wage this strange war upon her?

"We can make him leave his hiding hole to come here and face us like a man! We could gather a militia!" Launce was fuming when Isa realized they were still talking.

"No, we do not know the true strength of his power," Ansel said. "It would be best if we simply went with the Caregivers. They are our fastest means of escape. I don't think he'll be able to reach us on the third day if we leave tonight. We'll be nearly out of the kingdom by then."

Isa quietly stood and slipped back up to her attic. No one seemed to notice, as they all continued to plan. Her family meant well, but their attempts would be fruitless. They didn't know the true power the prince wielded. She did.

The accident had taken place fourteen years before, when she was only nine, but the day was etched into her memory like writing on a tombstone. Lean and nimble, she'd woven her way through the crowd to the street to see the handsome young prince as he'd ridden by. She'd seen him from a distance a number of times when visiting the Fortress with her father, but that was the closest she had ever been. Someone had bumped her from behind, however, and it had sent her sprawling right into his horse's path.

How noble he had looked when he had jumped down to help her up. It had taken her a moment before she could shake the giddy fog from her mind, and by then, he had left her side. Instinctively, she'd run and grabbed his sleeve, unaware at the time that it was inappropriate to touch a sovereign.

The pain of the horse's hooves had been excruciating, but what she had never told anyone was that the pain hit before the horse's heavy hooves ever touched her. The moment he shook her off, a searing white heat had shot through her, as if he'd taken a branding iron and made her blood burn. The animal that had trampled her seconds later had left its mark for the rest of the world to see, but Isa could still recall the first pain more clearly than that of her broken ankle and wrist.

If the prince had threatened her family, Isa had no doubt that he had both the ability and the intentions to carry through with his plans, Caregivers or not.

Isa would have to go to the Fortress.

She had nearly started back downstairs to tell her family, when she quickly realized that they would never listen. Her father would die before he let her go, and her headstrong brother would probably get himself killed as well. She would need to leave before they had a chance to try anything foolish, or suspected her of doing the same. So she went back downstairs, but stayed quiet. Her father was instructing them on how to prepare for their journey.

"We must bring as little as possible and go about our business as normal for the rest of the day. I don't want anyone aware that we're all leaving. Only the Caregivers will know."

"And our mercantile?" Everyone turned to see little Megane standing in the doorway, her face white.

"I am sorry, Megs." Ansel sighed and held his arms out to her. "I didn't see you standing there. No, we will have to leave our shop. But it will be alright. We will have one another, and we will set up a new life in the new land where Marko takes us. But we must not tell anyone, you understand? Anyone at all."

Megane nodded seriously, her golden curls and round blue eyes shining brightly in the fire's light.

"That's my girl." Ansel put his hand gently on her head before dismissing them all to do as they were told.

With a tight throat, Isa managed to grab both of her parents in a hug. They hugged her back, but Isa was sure they simply believed her to be afraid. They didn't know that it was probably the last embrace they would ever share.

Wiping her suddenly watery eyes on her sleeve, Isa finally turned and headed back to her room. She had few belongings of any real value. A silver hairbrush from her parents and a change of clothes were all she could find to put in her bag. Megane had left her own bag open on her bed, so Isa slipped her favorite childhood doll inside of it. Her sister had always admired the doll, and though Megane was nearly too old for playthings, she might find it a comforting reminder of Isa after she was gone.

With that settled, Isa realized that she needed an excuse to leave the house, particularly as her father had just returned with such urgent news. Immediately, her thoughts went to her horse. After losing her ability to run and dance, Ansel had taught his daughter to find respite in the freedom of riding. It had become a way of escape for Isa over the years, giving her a chance to feel the wind rush past her as she moved unhindered over the earth. Her parents would think nothing of her taking one last ride through the countryside.

"I'm going out for a ride," Isa announced to her family. It took all of her will to steady her voice as she spoke. "I... I need to think."

They nodded sympathetically, and her mother threw her favorite green cloak around Isa's shoulders.

"Use mine. It's warmer than yours. We will be leaving just after nightfall, so be back soon."

Trying to smile, Isa nodded and headed out to the stable. Using the special step her father had made for her, she was soon on her horse and headed towards the mountain.

~

Isa had never feared the mountain. As a child, she had run up and down its familiar face with her brother and friends like mountain goats. More hill than cliff, its slopes were gentle, and its peak was rounded off at the top. It would take a few hours to get to the Fortress because of the melting snow drifts that still stood from the last night's storm, but the path would be easy enough to find. An ancient tree marked its beginning, towering over all of its neighbors. From there, the path ran right alongside a stream carved every spring by snowmelt.

Beginning up the path again felt strange. Isa hadn't visited the Fortress since the incident with the prince. It was strenuous for her ankle, and her father had thought it best if she wasn't near any of the royals. The last time she'd set foot on this path was when she was young and free, able to run and dance without a care in the world. And now she was headed for the domain of the man who had taken it all from her, strong leg, strong hand, even her wedding.

Isa shuddered as she tried not think about what he could possibly want from her. Did he know who she was, or had he simply chosen to pour out his wrath on the first passerby he could find?

Though the legends of the Fortress monarchs had always painted them with at least decent senses of honor and chivalry, Isa had heard stories of how the rulers of other lands treated their wives and concubines. She wondered if that was what he wanted of her.

Even amidst such dire thoughts, Isa was never left alone with her fear, however, for her anger at what he had done, what he might want her to do, burned deep inside as well. She would go, but she would not go quietly.

As the slope got a bit steeper, Isa had to focus more on guiding her horse along the snowy trail. The higher they climbed, however, Isa began to sense that she wasn't alone. She looked around warily, hoping to spot a harmless animal in the brush or the trees, but she could see nothing. The forest was silent. Not even squirrels chattered. She tried to focus on the road ahead, pushing her horse just a bit faster. But the closer she got to the Fortress, the more she felt the prying eyes.

When she spotted the Fortress entrance, Isa let out a sigh of relief and dismay, thinking she had made it. At that moment, however, something large flew out of the bushes and slammed into her, knocking her off her horse.

"Launce!" she gasped as she stared up into the face of her brother.

He ignored her question. "Isa, what are you thinking? I thought you might get curious, but I didn't think you would actually be stupid enough to go!"

"If you get off of me, I'll tell you!"

Launce sat back enough to allow her to stand up. Isa scolded herself silently. She should have known her brother wouldn't let her leave without a goodbye. Actually, she knew he wouldn't let her leave at all. That was why she'd slipped out of the house when she had thought he was out visiting his sweetheart one last time. Apparently, he'd been able to read her better than she had thought.

"Father might think we can outrun the prince's powers, but he's wrong," she said.

Launce stared back at her with unforgiving eyes. "So I am simply supposed to let you run off to live with the madman prince?"

For the first time, Isa wondered if she would actually be able to follow through with her plan. Launce was strong, and though she was tall for a woman, he was a whole head taller. It would be nothing for him to pick her up and take her home against her will.

"Would you sentence Megane to a slow death of sickness and pain?" she asked quietly. His eyes widened a bit, so she continued. "Because he's strong enough. Launce, I've felt it! When the prince touched me in the street all those years ago, I felt his power! It was more painful than I can describe. I don't know what he wants me for, but I *do* know that I want none of it near Megane. Or Mother or Father. Besides, if I don't do as he says, do you think he'll really spare me? My fate is sealed either way." Isa sighed and leaned against her horse, closing her eyes. "But the rest of you have a chance, particularly Megs." She opened her eyes to plead with him. "Let me do this for her. Please don't take it away from me." She drew in a shaky breath and added, "I don't think either one of us could live with ourselves if something happened to her."

The icy look had melted from Launce's face, leaving the torn, helpless expression of the little boy Isa remembered from long ago. She breathed an inner sigh of relief as she saw her words sink in. Launce had always been protective of her, but they had grown up as a team. Megane, on the other hand, was the baby. Pranks they had played on one another were simply not played on her. The unspoken rule was that she was to be protected above all else. And this was Isa's only hope for convincing her brother to let her go.

She knew she had won when she saw tears welling up his eyes. Without another word, her little brother pulled her into a hug, and Isa clung to him, the fear and anguish of separation suddenly surrounding her.

"You must keep Father from coming for me," she sniffled into Launce's shoulder, her words rushed. "You have to remind him that whether I stay or go, the prince will have me in sickness or captivity. I will be a happier captive if I know you are all safe."

Launce finally pulled out of the embrace, still glaring at her. But he helped her back up on her horse and gave her a stiff nod before turning back down the path.

Feeling even more alone than before, Isa turned her horse off of the main road, and the Fortress came into full view. The great stronghold was nothing new to Isa. She'd visited it many times with Ansel as a child, but never had she seen it so empty.

The lofty battlements looked cold and foreboding without the soldiers at their posts, and the great front gate was closed. It seemed the prince wanted her to ask permission before entering his domain, to remind her of just how small and insignificant she was.

The old resentment flared up again as Isa stared at the distant, lofty gate. Prince Everard might be forcing her to come, but that didn't mean she was going to play by his rules.

Isa turned her horse abruptly away from the front entrance. Skirting the outer wall, she headed around to the back of the Fortress, hoping the hole hadn't been patched up.

The bushes had grown since she'd last visited, but to her relief, the gap hadn't been discovered. When she was small, the servant children had shown her the opening in the outer wall, explaining how they used it to get in and out of the Fortress without their parents' knowledge. It was covered by a dense thicket of foliage, barely big enough for Isa's horse. But once she made it through, she was very glad she had come this way.

Much less intimidating, the servants' entrance was smaller and had fewer grandiose architectures. If she'd gone farther down the road, Isa would have made it to the servant's gate. What had been open for her father, however, must have been visited by some sort of spirit keeper, for the back gate was now closed.

Isa rode through the open fields, noticing for the first time a strange set of great statues that filled half of the meadow behind the Fortress. They seemed innumerable, large effigies neatly lined up in perfect rows and columns. Snow covered most of the figures, but there was something eerily human about them. They most definitely hadn't been there when she was little. Each one had unique features, carved of stone, and yet giving the impression that they could walk away whenever they pleased.

When Isa finally arrived at the royal stables, she took as long as she possibly could to feed and groom her horse. As she worked, she seriously considered spending that night in the stable. Her animal was warm and familiar. He was safe. But, Isa reminded herself, she had not abandoned her family to hide in a stable. She had come with a purpose, and no one would be safe until she fulfilled it.

"Good night, my dear friend." She softly rubbed the horse one last time. "I will come to see you as soon as I can." Then, with a deep breath and a prayer, Isa left the stable and headed for the servants' door of the Fortress.

The moment Isa crossed the threshold, her nerve nearly fled. The sun was almost set behind her, but the darkness before her was thick and terrifying. It was as though a black fog had filled the once pristine, shining marble halls. The air smelled heavily of mildew and dust. After letting the door close behind her, she stood still, hoping her eyes would somehow adjust to the blackness.

In spite of her fear, as she gave pause, something deep down inside of Isa hoped this entrance would annoy the prince. She couldn't bear to give him the satisfaction of making her feel insignificant. Not any more than he already had, at least.

She finally spotted one single candle sitting on a table not far from the door. She nearly lost both the candle and her balance, however, when something cold brushed against her arm. Her hand shook as she held the flame up, trying to see what had touched her. But there was only the empty hall to see.

Isa nearly screamed when two more breezes gave her gentle pushes from behind. Only then did she remember Ansel's warnings about the shadows. Drawing Deline's cloak about her as tightly as she could, Isa decided it would be best to do as they wished. Ansel had seemed to think they meant him no harm.

Isa was pushed down a number of large empty halls and up several flights of stairs before she was allowed to rest. To her relief, a door was finally opened before her by invisible hands, that led not into another hall or passageway, but instead, a rather small room with a dim fire inside of a large hearth.

The fire didn't completely chase away the darkness, but it lit the room enough that Isa could see that it had once been a very grand room. The tapestries and carpets that were now riddled with moth holes and covered in dust must have once been very beautiful, and were most likely made of rare, expensive fabrics. An oversized bed with a tall post at each corner filled much of the room, its head against the wall, next to the fire. A large wooden writing desk was placed across from the bed, near the windows that faced south.

"Thank you," Isa whispered to the shadows, tears coming to her eye as she recognized the lights of Soudain in the distance at the foot of the mountain. There were the sentries, the ones that stood guard at the town entrance at night with their torches. Her father had been right. The shadows at least weren't malicious. If she was to be trapped in this place, at least she could sleep with her beloved city in sight.

That seemed to be the end of the shadows' kindnesses, however. Before she knew it, Isa was shoved over to a large wardrobe in the far corner of the room. She gasped as it opened on its own to reveal a large variety of dresses. Like the once lavish room, these gowns had been incredibly luxurious at one time. But they, too, smelled like wet dust. Isa stared at them stupidly for a moment before she realized why she was there.

"Am I supposed to put one of these on?" She felt silly asking the empty room. In response, however, the shadows nudged her one step closer to the wardrobe. "These are all far too extravagant for me." She shook her head. "I don't need anything like this." Again, she received a push. It seemed she had no choice. So after glaring behind her, hoping the shadows would catch on to her annoyance,

Isa picked the simplest of the gowns. If she was going to be introduced to the man who had tried three times now to steal her life, she would not be made a fool in princess's rags.

The gown she chose was simple, but still luxurious. The main fabric was a dark blue that crisscrossed the white bodice with intricate silver stitching. It was a dress her peers would have given anything to wear in the city. Despite the fine craftsmanship, however, the dress smelled as awful as the rest of the Fortress.

Not even allowed to take her own gown off by herself, Isa was subjected to much pulling and pushing as it was tugged off of her like a farmer might shear a sheep. She could feel pulls and pushes at her sturdy boots as well, but she adamantly refused to let those leave her feet. She wasn't entirely sure that she'd be able to walk through the length of the palace without them.

"You can do anything else to me that you wish," she scowled at the fussing shadows, "but those are not coming off until I am ready for bed."

Eventually, to her relief, they left her boots alone and began to fuss with her hair instead, which, admittedly, was rather messy from her journey up the mountain in the cold wind.

Finally, she was ready. At least, she supposed she was ready once the shadows stopped their constant poking and prodding at her clothes, and began instead to escort her towards the door. Isa was getting used being pushed or pulled from all directions by that time, however, so she went willingly when they prodded her out the door once more. This time, much to her relief, the halls were just a bit brighter. Someone or something had lit torches and placed them along the walls. With light now to walk by, she moved somewhat confidently.

Until she turned a corner and ran smack into the prince.

His shout of surprise was the first real sound Isa had heard since leaving her horse. It mingled in the air with her own startled cry as they both fell back a step. Immediately, Isa half knelt, half fell into a curtsy. As much as she had meant to be brave, a deep fear quickly wriggled into her heart. She would soon find out what awful plans he had for her, and she suddenly didn't know if she could bear it.

"Your Highness!" her voice quivered strangely. "Please forgive me."

It took the prince a moment to recover his own voice, it seemed, but when he spoke, it was surprisingly rich, blunt as his words were.

"Are you Isabelle?"

"Yes, Sire." As if any other sane woman would sneak into the cursed citadel. An awkward silence ensued as she continued to kneel and he stood over her.

"Why didn't you arrive during the daytime hours?" he finally asked.

"I beg your pardon?" Isa had to keep herself from looking up in response to the strange question.

"I told your father that you must come during the day!" His voice was petulant.

Isa had nothing to say to this.

"He didn't tell you, did he?"

Isa shook her head.

"You came on your own?"

For fear of giving away her family's plans, Isa remained quiet. She was here, but if he found out her family had planned to flee, he might kill her father anyway. She wouldn't put such treachery past him.

There was another long pause before the prince cleared his throat, his voice a little less sullen when he spoke again. "Isabelle, you may stand when I speak with you from now on. I dislike speaking to the floor."

As she stood, Isabelle dared to look at her prince for the first time in fourteen years. She nearly gasped aloud. He was nothing like she'd expected. His hands were hidden in the folds of his clothes, but the part of his chin that showed was thin and pale, nearly chalky. Most of his face was covered by the hooded cloak he wore, but even through the thick fabric, she could see his nearly emaciated frame. His back was so bent that he was nearly the same height as she was. In fact, the way he stood and moved was much the way her grandfather had done before he died. But her grandfather had suffered from severe joint pain for years, and the prince should have been only twenty-seven years in age, four years older than herself.

It seemed her father had been wrong. The curse had touched the prince as well. This couldn't possibly be the hero prince the children sang songs about, the one who had slain dozens in battle. And yet, here he was.

"You weren't supposed to be here for two more days," he growled. "How did you get in?"

"Near the servants' entrance, Sire." Isa tried to keep the small smile off her face. At least she had succeeded in doing something her own way. "I thought it only appropriate, as I am to be your servant."

"It is true that–Look up at me." He interrupted himself, suddenly removing his hood. "I want to see you better."

Isa couldn't have looked away if she'd wanted to. His face was gaunt. Dark circles seemed painted below his eyes, and his skin appeared fragile, as though someone had stretched it too thinly over his sharp cheekbones. His golden, unkempt hair reached to his shoulders, making his ashen cheeks look even more sunken.

But what really drew her gaze were his eyes. They were the only parts of his face that stood out more than his thin nose, but not because they were frightening as the rest of him was. The prince's eyes would have been gray if not for the thin rings of blue fire that encircled his pupils. They blazed in a strange, beautiful rhythm that made her want to lean in closer. Unfortunately, she realized, those deep, extraordinary eyes were glaring at her with a very real hatred.

He remembers me.

So he hadn't brought her to the Fortress for revenge. The surprise and loathing on his face was so intense that Isa would have wilted under it, had she not been already battling similar feelings of her own. They stood glowering at one another for a long moment before his expression became more controlled. When he spoke again, his voice was slow and deliberate.

"Yes, you are my servant, but not the kind you think."

"Then, Your Highness," Isa spat out, "what am I here for?"

He watched her, a strange look on his face, for a minute longer before answering. "You are here to help me break the curse."

Isa nearly fell back a step. She had imagined many horrible endings to her time with the prince, but none of them had involved breaking a curse. She was both relieved and horrified.

"I can do that?"

"We will see. Now, I assume you're tired from your journey. You will be served supper in your chambers tonight, but tomorrow, you will dine with me." And with that, the prince turned slowly and began to limp away. Still in shock, Isa stared as he paused one more time. "Oh, and one more thing," he said without turning around. "You are safe on the Fortress grounds by day, but you must never venture out after dark. I cannot protect you then."

8

RIDDLES

*S*hock, anger, and confusion clouded Ever's mind, making it hard to think as he began the long trek up the tower steps. It couldn't be *her*. It just couldn't. And yet, the crippled woman who had stood before him was just the right age, and injured in all of the right places.

Even more telling, though, were her eyes. The eyes that had haunted him for so many years, large and midnight blue, had stared right up at him from within his own home. From the moment he'd recognized her, it had taken all of his combat training to chase the angst from his face.

Of all the girls in the kingdom, why did *she* have to be the one? What kind of vengeful trick had that rat of a merchant played on him? He had promised Ever a woman of strength, and had given him a cripple instead. Ever contented himself with plotting how he would get even with the merchant, until he remembered the desperation in the man's pleas when he'd asked to stay in his daughter's stead. Besides, Ansel had boasted of Isabelle's strength of heart; he'd said nothing of her body.

Ever considered this as he continued the slow climb up the stone steps. Could this Isabelle's heart have the strength the Fortress demanded? If so, it certainly wasn't like his strength. She could barely get off the floor from her kneeling position, let alone fight a battle. And yet, there had been a spark in her dark eyes that had hinted at something fierce beneath the surface. *There is nothing to lose*, the voice of reason suggested to him, *by allowing her to try.*

It wasn't as though he had any better choices. In the months after the curse, he had very nearly gone mad, shuffling around the Fortress in his new prison of a body, raving at the stone walls like a lunatic. Anything was preferable to *that* state of anxiety.

Once he finally reached the top of the tower, Ever walked over to the north side of the round, glass-enclosed room, and glared down at the valley just beyond the mountain's northern foothill.

News of the darkened Fortress had spread fast, it seemed. Nevina had made her camp just a month after the curse had fallen, and even now, showed no sign of leaving. From the number of fires that burned, the rogue Tumenian forces were still hurting from their last defeat. If nothing else, Ever comforted himself, their last battle had produced a bit of fear in their northern enemies, one that should make them think long and hard before attacking hastily again. It would buy him some time. He just hoped it would be enough time to reclaim his home.

The great Fortress, which had been his constant companion and guardian since childhood, had abandoned him. He no longer felt the familiar presence pushing or pulling him in different directions. There was no gentle guiding company, no personal familiarity with all that surrounded him. The sorrow he felt at losing his courtiers and servants was nothing compared to this. Losing his parents was nothing.

For weeks, all he had wanted was death. If the Fortress was so intent on forsaking him, he had cried out, then why couldn't it simply let him die? Without the Fortress, Ever didn't know where he belonged or what his purpose was. Without the Fortress, Ever was nothing.

Only the servants, damned to existence as shadows, had managed to keep him alive. After days and nights of walking and screaming into the eternal night, he would awaken to find himself wearing new clothes and with food in his belly. In time, he had eventually realized that if he focused, he could sense the servants' emotions. That had made it a little less lonely. His real saving grace, however, had been the evening when he first heard Garin speak.

The day had been much like the others, one filled with Ever's rants at the Fortress, when the shadow that acted most like Gigi forced a bowl of thin soup into his hands. Ever had protested, but the shadow would not let him rest until he'd begun to eat.

"How does it taste, Sire?"

Ever had very nearly choked on his food when Garin's calm voice first broke the silence. Once Ever had regained his composure, he demanded to know where the others were, hoping that perhaps the curse was lifting on its own. But it wasn't to be. As always, the unusual steward had either found a way around the rule of silence, or was exempt from it. As disappointed as he was about the others, Ever had been immensely grateful for even this small improvement.

Still, life had seemed bleak and hopeless for a long time after that. The curse was a riddle, and he didn't know how to interpret it. But now he had the girl.

"Garin," Ever called quietly.

"Yes, Sire?" Garin's shadow flitted to stand before him.

Keeping his eyes on the fires below, Ever asked, "What do you think of her?"

The steward paused for a moment before answering. "In truth, Sire, your question isn't an easy one to answer. I have known young Isabelle since she was a child, before the accident even."

Ever couldn't conceal his shock as he whipped his head around to look for the familiar face that wasn't there. "You never told me that!"

"My apologies, Your Highness, but you were young, and struggled greatly with the incident yourself. I didn't want to make you even more anxious about it."

Ever let that sink in for a moment. "She was the one you went to warn on the night of the coronation, wasn't she?" he asked softly. He hadn't missed the sudden disappearance of his steward, as well as many of his other officials after his crazed order had been issued. Ever had been drunk, but the details of all that he'd said and done that night were somehow burned into his memory.

"Yes." Garin's voice was quiet, too. "I knew her father."

The affection in Garin's voice surprised Ever.

"The holy man said that what has been broken must be remade. Obviously, I have been broken. I need to be remade, preferably before Nevina regroups and strikes again. Next, the one who was strong must be willing to die." He paused. How many times had he been willing to die in battle before? "If she heals me, I can prove my willingness to die by facing Nevina on the battlefield."

"And the last requirement?" Garin's voice was skeptical. "Where do you suppose you shall find a new strength?"

"She is strong."

"And assuming she has been gifted with the Fortress's strength, how do you plan to take it for yourself?"

Ever didn't answer immediately. His mind was racing faster than his heart, which was probably for the better. He was still in shock at the revelation of the girl's identity, but even amidst his surprise and horror, his mind had already begun to piece together the answer to his riddle. It would be best not to dwell on the repercussions of the logical solution to his curse, however, for it would make him sick to his stomach. But then again, he would do anything to be free. He would do anything to save his people from Nevina.

"It would not be theft," Ever said slowly, "if we were wed. Our strengths would be united, and we could break the curse together."

"This is all assuming she has the strength you're looking for," Garin said. Ever could imagine his mentor crossing his arms and glaring at him over the bridge of his long, thin nose.

"She is strong. I don't know how, but there is a strength inside of her. She must be the one to bring the new strength, to heal me, to make me ready to face death again and break the curse!"

"I'm not arguing that she has a strength. I've suspected as much since the first time I met her as a small girl," Garin said. "What I'm wondering at is your audacity to assume she would marry you after your not-so-inconsequential meeting as children."

"I will be giving her more than any woman from her station could ever dream of. She will be queen, surrounded by every luxury she could ever imagine, and the Fortress's strength, too. Even," Ever sulked, "if she's not madly in love with me at the time."

"Neither gold nor power can mend a broken heart."

"Tomorrow we will see whether or not she has the new strength the Fortress is searching for. If she does, I will find a way to—"

"Be careful, Everard." Garin's voice had a sudden edge to it. "She is not like the court women you are familiar with. Her past and her present have put her in a very precarious place."

Ever didn't bother asking how Garin knew such things. Just as Garin's origins were unknown, his methods of getting information were mysteries best untouched as well. The steward wasn't finished, however.

"And if the Fortress has brought her here, then it has an interest in her, and nothing good will come of meddling vainly with her heart. I've known this girl for a long time, and believe me when I say that she is one who cannot be easily purchased."

A moment later, Ever heard Garin sigh, and when he spoke again his voice was more resigned. "Her father was here on a business matter not long before the Fortress went dark. He told me that a young man had recently begun to draw her from her sorrows, but from the look in her eyes tonight, that future she envisioned with him is no more, broken curse or no. Reaching her... it will take time and sincerity. Pushing her before she is ready will only hurt you both."

"I don't have the time for sincerity," Ever retorted.

"What will you do then, Sire, if she refuses you? Will you force her into wedlock against her will?"

"Garin, I am asking you for your help so that is never a decision I have to make!" Ever huffed. The conversation had taken a turn he didn't like, and Garin's tone of a loving mentor was grating on his ears. "*If* she is the one to break the curse, I will seek to give her anything her heart desires. And if that cannot sway her, it will be your duty to find something that can."

With that, Ever laid down on his pallet, positioned so that he could look through the tower's window walls down at the north foot of the mountain. Doing so, he felt the dangerous beginnings of hope spark inside of him, despite his attempts to quell them. Nothing could be sure, however, until he saw whether or not the Fortress had truly chosen her for her strength. And that test would have to wait until the next night.

9

LONELY DANCER

*I*sa tossed yet again in a vain attempt to sleep, but the musty smell of the bed and the revelation of the prince's purpose in summoning her kept her awake. What had possessed him to think she could unlock the secrets of the realm's oldest source of power?

Isa had heard the stories growing up, tales of the monarchs' strength, great feats of cunning and bravery that were only possible because of the light of the Fortress, strength that was conceived within the Fortress itself. Those were legends that parents told to their children at bedtime, but no one knew much beyond them. Tradition dictated that only the monarchs truly understood their own power, and if the commoners were wise, they would leave it that way.

But Isa's childhood brush with the prince's power had stirred the curiosity inside of her. She wanted to know, and despite all her desire to return home and be rid of this devilish place, she found a small piece of her heart yearning to unravel its knot of mystery.

Not that such a desire mitigated her fear at all, for she also found herself completely terrified. How was she supposed to address the power that had ruined her limbs? More importantly, how was she to even begin breaking the curse? And what would he do to her if she failed?

Isa rose early while the sky was still gray and listless. It was a morning typical of mid-autumn. Still, she noticed that perhaps for the light of the day, the smell of dust wasn't quite as strong as it had been when she'd laid down the night before. *The morning is meant for deep breaths and new beginnings, Isa*, Deline would always say. And it felt this morning that she was right.

As Isa managed to swallow the dry biscuit and old apple left on her bedside table by invisible hands, she realized her own clothes had been returned to her during the night. After getting dressed, Isa decided that the first thing to do would be to find the Fortress library. She heard tales of such rooms, where books were more numerous than flowers in a garden. She had never seen a library, however, and had only glimpsed at real books a few times in her life. Most collections of books existed in great castles and mansions. In the millennium since the Fortress had come into being, *someone* must have made written records about the great power it wielded.

"Please take me to the Fortress library," Isa addressed the shadows. A slight thrill wriggled down her spine as she waited for the servants to usher her to such a wondrous room. Instead of the familiar pushes and pulls she had grown somewhat accustomed to, however, she felt all of the shadows disappear. Surprised and irritated, Isa shook her head and begrudgingly wandered out of her room on her own.

She wasn't quite brave enough to look for the room all alone just yet. So, heading to the front of the stronghold instead, Isa saw the grand entrance for the first time.

Covered in dust and cobwebs, giant columns soared above her, supporting monstrous arches that were loftier than any church steeple in the city. The ceiling was so high and so dark that Isa couldn't make out any of its details at the very top. In fact, the interior was nearly as dark as it had been the night before, as all the tapestries were closed. She was again glad that she had arrived by the back entrance. For coming in through this grand hall would surely have intimidated her.

As she cautiously approached the towering doors, they opened for her without a sound, revealing the relief of the outdoors. Most of the snow from the storm two days earlier had melted, making Isa's walk to the stable much easier.

Isa spent as long as she could out in the stable, feeding and brushing her animal. It was comforting to breathe in his familiar scent. She talked to him as she worked, telling him what a good horse he was, and how he wouldn't believe the things she had seen the night before. They went for a quick outing around the grounds, but Isa was too nervous to take him very far. As much as she enjoyed it, however, eventually there was no more she could do for her friend, so she put him back in the stables and returned to the winding outdoor paths to explore the front lawn.

The Fortress lawn had at one point been the most spectacular arrangement of gardens and statues one could ever hope to see. But now, beneath the melting snow, the flowers lay brown and brittle, as did the trees. Everything was overgrown or wasting away. Isa wandered through the ivy covered statues of wolves and the dying shrubs that were wrapped around them, without knowing where she was headed. No birds sang and no chipmunks twittered. There weren't even the sounds of bugs as she moved through the gardens. Isa thought back to her childhood visits of the Fortress, trying to remember if the gardens had always been this quiet, or if the curse had made them that way.

After wandering through several of the smaller gardens without finding respite, she had nearly turned back to the stables, when one garden in particular caught her eye. It was a rose garden.

The bushes had been allowed to grow tall, and had been planted in such a way as to provide walls of privacy for those who would walk the paths laid in stone between them. Isa walked about the entire circular garden, and found that there were four paths that wound towards the center, one stretching inward from each direction. Despite the vines being brown and dry without a flower to be seen, Isa found herself drawn to their beauty. She cautiously entered the northern path, towards the garden's center.

The rosebushes that made up the garden stood at least three feet higher than Isa's head on each side. Isa followed the winding path inward to find a small courtyard in the center of the garden. The courtyard was large enough that it could have fit her new bed inside of it. A bench made of multicolored stones sat along the edge of the tall, once pruned bushes, where it would have been hidden from the sun had the sun been shining.

Instead of a floor of cobblestone, as the garden paths had, Isa found herself standing upon the most beautiful stone mosaic she had ever seen. A rose larger than Isa was tall had been carefully laid out with colorful stones. Agate gave the rose its shades of red, while light and dark green jade pieces filled the leaves and stem. The giant rose was encircled by blue angelite and white opal. Isa knelt reverently to touch the piece of art. Every single stone had been polished down to make the surface perfectly flat.

As she knelt there, a small flame of rebellion was suddenly ignited within Isa, and the longer she looked at the mosaic, the more the flame grew. If she couldn't go home, and she couldn't visit the library, then she would dance.

Slowly, she walked to the center of the mosaic. The center was deep enough that Isa felt delightfully hidden by the tall bushes, not that there were many people about to watch. Still, the privacy was delicious. Isa had no idea as to what she could expect of her body. It had been a long time since she had danced. Gingerly, she extended her right arm. Then, as well as she could, she pointed her left foot.

Before she had finished the first twirl, Isa's ankle gave out, and she collapsed into a heap on the cold stone. Angry tears welled up in her eyes as she imagined how her former peers would have laughed at her if they could see her now. Her neighbors would have shaken their heads sympathetically, and even her parents would have urged her to stop before she hurt herself. The shame was still just as strong as it had been the day the healer had told her that she would never dance again.

But they aren't here, a voice inside of her whispered. It didn't matter if the girls she'd once danced with would laugh, and it didn't matter how many times she fell. Isa was all alone now, and there was no one to stop her. Wiping the tears from her eyes, she stood up resolutely and stretched her arms out again.

Her form was stiff, and nothing about her movements looked effortless or graceful. Her left wrist wouldn't lay straight, and her ankle was too weak for the leaps. And yet, in spite of herself, Isa began to smile. Sweat ran down her back and soaked her dress, and her hair fell out of place. With each movement, however, her body began to recall the fluid energy that had once flowed through it. Even if just a moment, nothing in the world could have made her happier.

Isa danced until her ankle nearly gave out. Exhausted, she fell onto the stone bench to rest. Only then did she realize that one of the shadows must have brought her a midday meal. It was simple food, and as it had been that morning, was so dry that she could hardly swallow it, but Isa's hunger drove her to eat it all.

"Thank you," she called out to whatever phantom had thought to bring her food all the way out in the garden. She expected no reply but was pleasantly surprised when a quick breeze gently brushed her cheek.

Once she was done, she knew her ankle would last no longer that day, so Isa stood up and limped back to her room, where she dozed until the shadows awakened her in time for supper.

Isa had been dreading supper with the prince all day, trying not to think of it as she had gone about her other activities. But now, she could ignore it no longer. She steeled herself and donned a mask of composure. Despite his great fall from the man he had been, the prince had somehow maintained an air of supreme superiority during their exchange the day before. Isa's manners were by no means lacking, but court etiquette was something she had never learned. She refused to lose her temper and give him another reason to look down upon her.

As the shadows began to brush her hair, a large bath on the other side of the hearth was drawn. Isa hadn't noticed it there before. A warm bath would be nice, she thought, until she walked over to it and realized the water was just as dirty as the rest of the Fortress was.

She balked. "You cannot mean for me to wash in that. I'll be filthier when I get out than when I get in."

In response, some brave shadow snatched up a rag, dipped it in the water, and began to vigorously scrub one of her arms. Isa let out a yelp as the cold water touched her skin. In response, other shadows began to do the same. Apparently, her unwillingness to get in was not a problem for them. Muttering at the shadows, Isa cringed throughout the entire bath, snatching away the drying cloth when it was finally presented to her. Then, as she had been the night before, Isa was dragged over to the wardrobe of musty dresses.

"Where is the one I wore last night?" She gave a doubtful look at the rest of the fancy gowns that hanged before her. "Just so you know," she grumbled, rifling through the piles of lace and frills, "I am not keen on all this finery. Your prince brought me here as a servant, and a servant's wear is much more what I would prefer to appear in."

The shadows paid no heed to her speech, however. They snatched the gown that Isa had last touched out of her hands, and then pushed her over to the writing desk, which had been quickly transformed into a vanity. Deft, invisible hands pulled her hair up into intricate curls and tucked them neatly into one another, while other sets of hands did their best to brush the smudges off the burgundy and cream dress. Another draped a necklace of dull red agate around her neck.

When the shadows were finally satisfied with her hair and jewelry and gown, Isa looked around for her boots. She had taken them off when she'd fallen asleep earlier that afternoon. Her heart fell into her stomach when she realized that the only shoes she could find were red velvet slippers.

"Where are my boots?" she cried out.

The invisible hands, still adjusting her hair here and there, paused, but then continued as if she hadn't spoken.

Her voice got a bit louder as she asked again. "Where are my boots? You cannot mean for me to wear these!"

When she again received no response, Isa pulled up her skirts to reveal her crooked ankle. "I can hardly walk without those boots! I don't know how you expect me to get to supper if I cannot walk! Now please, give me my boots back!"

But the boots never appeared, and nothing Isa said or threatened to do made them reappear. Finally, she was bullied out of the room without them. Defeated, it took her three times as long to reach the dining hall as it would have if she'd had her boots.

Prince Everard was already seated by the time Isa arrived. She could tell by the gentle windy shoves to her back that she was late, but she didn't care. Perhaps that would teach them to think twice the next time they wanted to give her such foolish shoes.

"Isabelle." Everard stood slowly when she entered the room.

"Your Highness." Isa gave him the best curtsy she could manage before collapsing into the chair after her long trek. When they were both seated, unseen servants placed food on the table before them. The light was a little better in this room because of the multiple fireplaces that were lit, and the candles that were scattered about the table, but that didn't do much to alter the heaviness of the mood that filled the space around them.

Isa supposed it was probably polite for the guest to praise something about the home or the food or the décor to the host, but she could think of nothing to say. Still angry about the boots, and reminded again of how much the prince irritated her, Isa stared sullenly at her plate, sneaking angry looks at her host every so often.

He still wore the long, thick cloak. Isa presumed it was to cover a nearly skeletal body that would have matched his face and neck. His dark golden hair had been cut much shorter than it had been the night before, however, and it now shone weakly in the firelight. The deep hollows under his eyes made it look as if he had constant bruises. It was hard to imagine that this man had ever fought against any foe and lived to tell the tale.

Prince Everard was the one to finally break the silence. His voice was distant, but surprisingly polite, very different in tone than it had been the night before. "Your quarters are comfortable, I presume?"

"Yes, Your Highness."

"And the servants have provided you with everything you've required?"

"I suppose you could say that." Isa glared at the ground, thinking of how much her ankle already ached after walking from the bedroom. Another silence ensued as Isa tried to eat the bland stew that had been set before them, the clinking of their spoons making the lack of conversation even louder. Eventually, Everard took a deep breath before finally asking a question Isa could not give a simple answer to.

"So what do you think of the Fortress so far?"

Isa's face began to burn as all the emotions that had been boiling inside of her rose to the surface. "It would be easier to fulfill my purpose here if I were allowed to visit your library, but your servants this morning refused to assist me when I asked," she snapped.

For a moment, the prince stared at her, surprise making his gray eyes look even larger in his gaunt face than usual. "You think you are to break the spell by reading about it?" His musical voice had a hint of amusement to it that annoyed Isa even more.

"I was raised in the city. And as I only know as much about the Fortress as any other commoner, I don't see any other way to learn about it. I cannot be expected to break a curse that I know nothing about!"

Prince Everard gave a low chuckle before putting his spoon down and leaning toward her over the table. "Miss Isabelle, I am proficient in four languages, including the two dead tongues that existed before the birth of this land. I was trained to read the markings of the ancient symbols that were carved into the tombs of my forefathers. I have had access to the sacred writings all of my life, and I have been living alone in this great crypt for six months. What do you think I have been doing in all of that time?"

To that, Isa had no response.

"Believe me," he continued more seriously, "if the curse could be broken by reading, I would have found it by now." Holding her resentful gaze, he added, "I have ordered my servants to give you full access to the Fortress so that you know my good will. Except to the Tower of Annals. The Tower of Annals is sacred, and even the servants have restricted access to that place. Only a few are allowed to accompany me there."

Isa wondered how he knew which shadows really did accompany him there, but she didn't ask. Instead, she found herself still protesting her lack of books.

"I still know nothing of this place or its true history. I can't even begin to consider how I am to break the curse if I am completely ignorant!"

At this, displeasure seemed to surface on the prince's face for the first time, which up until now, had been a mask of cool reserve. "Ask the servants for any specific books you require, but by no means are you to enter the Tower of Annals. Do you understand?"

Isa nodded. For a moment, the blue fire in his eyes flashed, and in spite of herself, Isa felt a bit frightened. Briefly, she could see the warrior prince. The warrior quickly disappeared, however, when the flashing dimmed and he slowly stood. As he shuffled towards her, Isa was again reminded her of her aged grandfather.

The prince extended Isa a black gloved hand. "Miss Isabelle, would you do me the honor of dancing with me?"

Isa felt her mouth drop open in horror, and panic filled her. All of the confidence she'd fought so hard to keep slipped away in that instant, and before she knew it, she was begging, pleading not to dance. Tears ran down her face as she looked up at him. "Your Highness, I have come here in accordance with your will! I have worn the dresses, eaten your food, and agreed to live in your home! Please do not humiliate me in this way. I beg of you!"

As she wept, surprise showed in his eyes again, but he did not relent. "This is something you must do if you wish to help me break the curse," he said quietly as she sobbed.

Still, she could not rise, so he reached down and took her hand, leading her out of the tall dining hall doors to an outdoor balcony.

The balcony was larger by far than the entire dining hall. Even more strange was its floor. A hundred couples could have danced upon it. And instead of the typical stone, it was covered by a beautiful, clear crystal, as smooth as a pool of water. Unlike anything else Isa had yet seen in the Fortress or its grounds, the crystal floor was completely spotless. As she stared at the way the moonlight reflected from it, she doubted a speck of dust could be found lingering upon it.

As they approached the center, invisible musicians began to play, their beautiful, haunting melody echoing over the mountain. As magnificent as the music was, however, Isa could not enjoy it.

They were an awkward couple, able to do little more than sway back and forth, and not even in time to the music. It seemed as if the prince's knees were as stiff as Isa had suspected from the beginning. Her own ankle throbbed with pain as the little slipper left it completely unsupported. As the dance went on, Isa, to her horror, was forced to lean against her partner more and more. The dancing she had done earlier that day had already used most of her ankle's strength, and without her boots, it was all she could do to cling to the prince's arms and pray not to fall.

Worse than the pain, however, was the acute knowledge that Prince Everard was only the second man who had ever been willing to dance with her. The warmth of his gloved hand on her waist and the closeness of his body to hers was nearly unbearable. It was too much like the last time Raoul had danced with her. They had been at a town festival, and his eyes had gleamed with joy as he'd twirled her in circles over and over again, despite the disapproving looks of his parents. That had been the night he'd proposed.

Tears began once again to run down Isa's face, and she knew the prince was watching her curiously. Yet, he said nothing. By the time the dance was finished, Isa could continue no longer.

"I beg of you, Sire, if you have any pity in your heart at all, please just let me go. I cannot go on tonight." Isa hated appearing so weak in front of the prince. Her goal from the start had been to appear strong, to let him know that she was not a coward, nor was she coming willingly. But the pain of her ankle and the pain in her heart had grown too great to bear.

Nodding, he stepped back and bowed slightly. Isa didn't even attempt to curtsy as she did her best to begin limping back to her room.

10

UNEXPECTED VISITOR

*E*ver left the balcony tired and sore, but pleased nonetheless. Learning that his plan might actually succeed had been well worth the physical aches.

The dance itself had been a disaster. Ever had never danced with a partner so unwilling that she wept, and never had he felt so pathetic or inept himself. And yet, while they had danced, he had seen what the girl's untrained eyes could not, especially as she had spent the entire duration of the dance crying. Beneath her shuffling feet, the crystal floor had given off the barest hint of a blue glow. It certainly wasn't the bright shine that Ever's ancestors had used to find their wives in the stories, so she clearly was not yet ready to be queen.

But she could be.

There was *some* sort of power within her, enough, perhaps, to awaken the power of the Fortress that had all but disappeared since the curse.

Back in the Tower of Annals, Ever stiffly sank into the warm bath his servants had prepared for him. He had long ago ceased caring about the dirty water. The relief that it brought his body was too great to sacrifice for some grime. Two of the shadows removed his gloves and began to gently rub a potent salve into his hands. He closed his eyes and leaned his head back, not wishing to ruin his good spirits by the sight of his claw-like hands, or any part of his body for that matter.

He was no longer used to the physical strain it took to dance, and the pain was enough to make his eyes prick. His pain reminded him all the more of why he must succeed in preparing this strange girl to carry the Fortress's power. At the rate his strength was leaving him, he would not survive the next spring.

After getting redressed, Ever slowly moved to his pallet on the low sofa.

Although his mood had improved with the revelation of Isabelle's potential, the fires at the northern foot of the mountain sobered him once again.

Ever lowered himself to his side where he could watch the fires from the pallet, but could not keep his thoughts on the princess's militia for long, despite his efforts. Instead, his mind kept wandering back to the strange girl across the castle.

He had been right when he'd first guessed that she despised him. The flash of her eyes had not been lost on him whenever she'd responded to his questions. It seemed he was incapable of pleasing her.

Strangely enough, Ever found that this disappointed him. Of course, her willingness to carry the power of the Fortress would speed her strength, and that was enough reason in itself to try to gain her better graces. Still, he had hated her for so many years. Why was he interested at all in what she thought of him now?

The odd desire for her respect had first surfaced earlier that day when he'd seen her dancing in the rose garden. She was by no means a lovely dancer, but there was something about her that had made him watch a few moments longer. He had happened to look out of the tower window just in time to see her fall to the ground, and had nearly sent a servant to check on her when she had gotten up and tried again. Why would she try again?

After spending so many years hating her for haunting his dreams, it felt wrong to see her as anything but a means to his end. And yet, he had to admit that after one day of having her as a guest in his home, he could see what her father had meant when he'd said she had a strong heart. A woman who would willingly turn herself in to live as a servant in an accursed castle with the man who had made her lame as a child, that woman was worthy of respect. Getting up and continuing to dance after falling so hard was worthy of respect. A small voice in his head wondered if perhaps, he had taken even more from the young woman than just her ability to walk. But this wasn't something he was yet ready to consider.

He also wondered at her reaction to dancing on the balcony. She had spent her entire morning dancing. Why would she be so upset at dancing with him? It couldn't be that she was embarrassed. His bent back and stiff joints should make it obvious that he would dance poorly, too. But then, he hadn't missed the way she had shuddered when he had touched her hand, or how her eyes had widened when he'd stepped into the bright moonlight.

This also bothered him more than he wanted to admit: that of all the important pieces of the puzzle, his vanity was meddling with his mind. But he shook his head; there was nothing more he could do than go on with the charade. Whatever he felt about her, he would need to convince her that his desires were true.

"Are they now?"

Ever gritted his teeth at the sound of the familiar voice. He would just ignore her. Unfortunately, that didn't seem to deter Nevina tonight.

"I was wondering how you've been keeping entertained, and now I see. She's a pretty little thing, Everard. You must be enjoying yourself."

"What do you want?" Ever bolted up, frustration making his blood boil. He could no longer see the room around him, only Nevina's face. That was to be expected. What he *hadn't* expected was for her to succeed in breaking into his head so early in the night. Usually she wasn't so bold, waiting until he had fallen into a dreamlike state. But then, he usually had a greater amount of strength to keep her out. He tried not to let her see his alarm.

"Ah, there you are. I knew the righteous Everard wouldn't allow his precious reputation to be questioned. Which is rather humorous, as my sources tell me the girl didn't come of her own accord."

"You did not answer my question." Though she couldn't see it, he flexed his fingers. Just a moment more. He just had to keep her talking as his hand warmed with the growing flame. It just wasn't quite enough. "I will not ask you again. What do you want?"

"I want to know what *you* want with her."

That was an odd request. "You think I would tell you that?"

"You wouldn't have summoned her unless she was special." She leaned forward, her green eyes daring him to argue. Before she could speak again, Ever flicked his wrist, sending the fire in his hand from his fingertips up to his head. The blue burst of flame filled his mind, and in a moment, the dark princess was gone.

He leaned back, taking in deep breaths. At one time, purging Nevina from his mind would have tired him just enough to make him ready for sleep. This purge, however, made it nearly impossible for Ever to open his eyes. He lay there, too drained to even sit up, asking the Fortress again and again why it allowed Nevina to plague him so. As he'd expected, no answer came. There hadn't been an answer since the curse had fallen. Instead, a cool wisp of air moved to his side.

"She was here," Garin's voice was grim, "wasn't she?"

Ever nodded.

"I am sorry, Ever. I do not know how she got in."

"It wasn't your fault." Ever pulled himself into a sitting position on his pallet. "I should have been watching more closely. I suppose I was more distracted than usual." He rubbed his eyes. "She hasn't sought me out since the curse began. I wasn't on my guard."

"Nor was I. But what did she want?"

Ever stared into the fire, the hopes he'd allowed himself just a few hours before now going up like the smoke from the flames.

"She knows about the girl."

11

NEVER AGAIN

*R*aoul's arms felt warm and strong as he twirled her around the bonfire in time to the music. And for once, Isa was able to keep time, too. No longer crooked or weak, her ankle worked just as well as his. A part of her mind flickered, just enough to warn her that this was a dream. It would be prudent for her to wake up. But this was such a warm dream! She would only stay a few more minutes, she promised herself.

Before she could finish the thought, however, the grip Raoul kept her on her arm and waist tightened. Instead of smiling, her betrothed was suddenly glaring at her, his dark eyes gleaming with resentment. He didn't let go. His hands continued to squeeze her until it was nearly painful. Isa tried to pull away from the dance, but he only held on tight. When she looked back up from his hands to his face, though, Isa knew why. Raoul's lovely black locks had lightened to a dull gold, and his face was deathly thin.

Wake up! Isa tried to shake herself. The dream she had hoped to eke out was now one she wrestled to escape. She could feel herself thrashing beneath her covers, sweat rolling down her neck and making her hair sticky. But the harder she shook herself, the more determined her dance partner was to keep her. It was a dance in which she was both unwanted, and yet forced to be a part of. Round and around they went, the Raoul-prince dragging her along as though she were a rag doll without a will.

The bonfire in her dream also began to grow in intensity and light. At first, Isa thought the heat was from the way she wrestled with her covers, struggling to awaken. But with each turn of their steps, the fire grew hotter, until it became hard to breathe. If she didn't break free soon, she was going to suffocate.

The shriek Isa let forth was inaudible. She didn't know to whom she was calling for help. There was no one to hear her except the shadows and the prince. Still, she tried. But no sound came from her lips.

Just as she thought she might die of fright, the iron arms began to loosen their grip. A warm sensation, like that of a playful summer breeze, fluttered along her body. It touched first her head, then her arms and legs. Each place that it caressed was loosed from the nightmare's bindings. She looked up from her dream body to see her hated dance partner back up one step, then two.

Then he was gone. Isa's eyelids fluttered open to see that the sun had already risen high in the autumn sky. She stayed there for a long time, allowing herself to breathe deeply and drink in the freedom of being able to move her limbs as she wished. Still, Isa wasn't completely convinced that the visions were only dreams, not terrible memories.

Only as the haze of the dream began to clear away, and Isa began to more clearly recall the actual details from the night before, did she begin to discern truth from reality. As she did remember, she wasn't sure the truth was really any better than the dreams had been. The silken slippers, the lonely dance, and the hopelessness came back to her piece by piece. And as each miserable moment returned, a new determination began to set in.

Never again would she be a part of that story. Her dreams might taunt her, but when she was awake and conscious, Isa's feelings and intentions would be her own. She was through letting the shadow servants bully her, no matter how many orders Prince Everard gave them. She wasn't going to wear the slippers. It would be her boots, or no dancing at all. And if indeed the prince insisted on dancing again, she would choose to hold her head high, not lower it in shame with tears running down her face.

Maybe her mother had been right. There was a time to mourn what she had lost, but she could see now that self-pity had made her weak and vulnerable. She would never be powerless like that again.

In addition to her new sense of resolve, as she became more fully awake, Isa continued to sense the strange new presence that had liberated her. Oddly, she innately knew that the presence which comforted her didn't belong to any of the servants that were usually hovering nearby. This was a different kind of comfort, more potent than that of any human company she'd ever encountered before. And as much as she was confused by it, the new presence had somehow transformed the Fortress in her eyes overnight. The smells of dust and mildew were noticeably less powerful this morning, and the bed she slept in had felt just as familiar as the pallet in her parents' attic.

The presence didn't fade as she got dressed. Her boots and clothes had been returned to her during the night, and Isa took the new shine of her boots as a sort of apology from the servants.

"I accept your apology," she announced to the shadows as she pulled the boots on. "But do not think that means you can take them again tonight. If the prince wants to dance, I will be wearing the boots or there will be no dance at all, understand?"

The shadows brushed by her in annoyed, sharp breezes, and Isa felt a sense of laughter from the walls around her. What was this strange presence that heard both her dreams and her words? What else did it know or hear?

"Oh," she called out once more to the servants, knowing they would listen even if they didn't want to. "And tell your prince I need books on the early history of this place. That should be a mild enough request to suit him."

The sense of the presence still didn't depart as Isa left her room. Instead, it felt close, wrapping around her the way her mother's cloak did. As she walked through the towering halls and out to the stable, Isa wondered if the presence had been there her whole life. How else would it have known her so well? And if it had been with her, how had she missed it before this? It felt as though her eyes were just being opened.

After tending to her horse, Isa returned to the rose garden. As confirmation of her suspicions that something was different, there was a single rose bud on the hedges when she arrived. It grew near the spot where she had fallen the day before. The flower was small, to be sure, and still tightly closed, but the bright sliver of pink was impossible to miss against the otherwise brown hedge.

"What is this place," Isa murmured to her new companion, "that roses should bloom just before the dawn of winter?" In response, a breeze smelling of lavender caught her dress and twirled it gently against her legs. Isa smiled, remembering her reason for coming to the garden in the first place. It was time for her to dance.

She tested her ankle before beginning. It was now tucked safely in her boots, and to her surprise, bore none of the pain from the night before. Satisfied, Isa began. Again, her movements were neither fluid nor confident the way they had been when she was a child. In fact, the muscles in her arms and legs were sore from the day before, and possibly even less coordinated. Still, as a whole, Isa felt just a little more poised, a little more prepared for the steps this time.

A few hours later, as she headed in for the midday meal, Isa realized with a start that for the first time in years she felt like she had a purpose here. And as much as she hated being held against her will, and even if the prince was a despicable human being, she desperately wanted a purpose, one that went beyond tending her parents' store for the rest of her life. If she was somehow able to miraculously restore the Fortress as Prince Everard wanted her to do, it wouldn't be done for him. It would be done for the kingdom. And wasn't that a cause noble enough to desire?

Before she could reach the Fortress, however, the sharp breezes caught her up and began yanking her along once again. These were not the warm, soft breezes she had felt that morning from the friendly presence, but rather those of the unmistakable shadow servants.

"If you're going to order me about so," Isa huffed as they shoved her up a new set of stairs on the right side of the grand entrance, "you could at least ask nicely first." The little breezes paused, as though considering what she had said, but then took up their pushing once again.

Finally, she was dumped outside a very large door on the third level of the Fortress's south wing. Isa blinked at the ornately carved door with its fine amethyst studded golden handle, and wondered whether she was supposed to knock or wait. Her question was answered when shuffling footsteps rounded a corner nearby.

Prince Everard approached her in his slow, stiff fashion, which annoyed Isa more, considering how hurried her servants had seemed. Still, she couldn't help the curiosity that arose when the prince stopped beside her and pulled a large brass key from his cloak.

"As you will presumably be staying with us for some time," the prince said in his rumbling voice, "I would like for you to feel at home."

Isa couldn't help frowning a bit as he unlocked the door. His words sounded rehearsed. When she had first come to the Fortress, he had made it crystal clear that she was his servant, someone to carry out his whim against her will. Last night's dance had been a reminder of that as well. A man of honor never forced a lady to dance.

As the prince opened the door, however, Isa gasped. Inside was the most luxurious room she had ever seen. It far outweighed any daydream Isa had ever conjured up, and most likely even that of her more well-to-do childhood friends in Soudain. Lavender silk was draped and hung from every surface and window, and the furniture was gilded in gold and silver. A bed nearly the size of Isa's old attic room stood in the corner, surrounded by little tables, chairs, dressers, and vanities, each which was decked with little boxes, some the size of her thumb, and others larger than her face. The boxes were made of all colors and grains of wood, hewn stone, thin, shiny metals, and some even of shells. In a daze, Isa wandered over to the nearest vanity and touched it to make sure she wasn't dreaming once again.

"It was more lavish before the curse was cast," Prince Everard said from behind her, sounding quite bored. "The gold and silver have tarnished some, but I supposed you could find a few baubles to please you."

Understanding hit Isa. He was trying to buy her loyalty. After abducting her and making her privy to the hate within his soul, he was attempting to purchase her affections. Well, Isa wasn't that cheap. It took every bit of self-control for her not to turn around and slam the door in his face.

Still, as angry as she was, she might as well use the chance to learn more about her captor, if nothing else. "It is lovely." She tried to make her voice cool and reserved, pausing to open one of the boxes atop the vanity. The jewel encrusted silver bracelet inside of it nearly took her breath away, and she had to focus to keep her face unaffected. "Whose room was this?"

"My mother's."

This time, Isa was unable to keep the surprise from her face, and a sudden sense of pity warred with her disdain. "I am sorry."

"There is no need for that." The prince walked over to another, larger vanity, and carelessly flipped open more of the boxes. "She was ill. Death comes for all of us." He held out a thin golden necklace with a jewel nearly the size of Isa's thumb. "Would you like this?"

"Surely you cannot mean for me to take any of the queen's belongings!" Isa stuttered, taking a step back. "I am only a commoner!"

"I assure you, nothing in this room will affect me, whether it leaves or remains."

Isa watched him for another moment before her conscience got the better of her. She should at least choose one item. Even if he *was* trying to purchase her good will, it would be rude to ignore such an offering. And though Isa's parents were commoners, they had taught Isa well. She was never rude.

Isa resumed perusing the little items, but their sheer number was overwhelming. Diamonds, emeralds, rubies, sapphires, opals, coral, and amethysts made the room sparkle, even in the dim light that the dusty windows let through. Such jewels were breathtaking, but far too expensive for Isa's taste.

Just when she was about to give up and take something simply to say she had done it, Isa spotted a little round stone in the corner of one of the dustier boxes. When she lifted it, she was delighted to find what looked like a rose. The little ball of stone was rough, and looked as though someone has pressed red sand together until it stuck. Little lips of pink stuck out, layered in a circular pattern so that they looked like petals.

"What is this?" she asked.

"It's called a desert rose stone."

Isa jumped a little at the nearness of his voice. The prince had silently come up to stand behind her as she gazed at the stone scene. He was frowning at the little stone as she held it. "You like that?"

"It's simple," she said, turning it over in her hands. "But beautiful. I've never seen anything like it. Did a wizard make it?"

"We wouldn't keep a wizard's work here." He looked slightly disgusted. "It came into being by natural means in the desert. Something having to do with the wind, I think."

She looked back at him and smiled politely. "Your mother must have treasured this."

"Hardly." The prince snorted. "It was too common for her taste."

"How do you know?" As the words left her lips, Isa wondered at her sudden audacity to speak to the prince as though she were his equal. But he didn't seem to mind.

"She told me as much when I gave it to her."

For a long moment, Isa was trapped in his fiery gaze as she felt her mouth open a bit in horror.

"I was eight," he said more softly as he held a grizzled hand out. She gave him the stone, and he studied it as he spoke. "I was out with my father on a diplomatic journey in a neighboring country. We were passing through a desert, and I found it along the path."

"And she didn't like it?" Isa was still at a loss as to how a mother could reject a gift from her son.

"If I recall correctly, her words were, 'Everard, the sentiment was kind, but such gifts are below my station, and below yours. Next time, ask your father to help you find something.'" He handed the stone back to Isa. "I cannot see why you should want this over the gems, but if you wish for it, it's yours."

"I do wish it." Isa defiantly curled her fingers around the stone protectively. "I shall keep it beside my bed. It will be nice to look at if I have another bad dream."

The prince's fiery eyes softened slightly before they snapped wide open. "Wait. You had a bad dream? Here?"

Isa nodded. She hadn't meant to let that slip. But he was glaring at her again with that frightening intensity. "What was your dream about?" He grabbed her shoulders with his gloved hands and squeezed. "Tell me everything!"

Fear suddenly made Isa nauseous as his eyes burned into hers. "It was only a dream…" she stammered. Seeing, however, that he wasn't convinced, she managed to tell all she could of the dream, though her face grew hot as she revealed the visions that had so played on her insecurities.

Then he was gone, faster than she would have imagined him capable of. Suddenly all alone, Isa looked down at the little stone carving in her hand. She was somehow even more confused than she had been that morning.

12

THREATS AND PROMISES

"Don't do this." Garin's voice echoed behind Ever as he limped up to the tower. "It's exactly what she wants!"

But Ever kept going. Nevina had taken this too far. Isabelle had seemed reluctant to share her dream, but what little he had gotten out of her had told him that Nevina had indeed visited his guest in her dreams. Besides, if he stopped and considered what he was about to do, the risk to his mind and to his body might make him waver. And he didn't have time for that.

"As soon as I realized Nevina was in Isabelle's room, I went to her, but the Fortress was already there, expelling Nevina by the time I arrived. All is well, and we will now be on our guard for Isabelle as well. There is no need to give the princess what she wants."

"And you didn't tell me?"

"I knew you would react–"

"Six years since she's penetrated our defenses!" Ever paused and shouted into the air. "And now she thinks she can come in and play games. No." He shook his head and resumed his march to the tower. "I am taking this to her."

"You know why she's slipping through," Garin said sadly. "And if you spend too much of your fire on this, what good will it do? You will only tire faster, and she will penetrate eventually. If you just ask the Fortress–"

"No." Ever reached the top of the stairs and stormed into the tower. He sat down hard on his pallet. "I am going to end this now. She might think this curse gives her an excuse to meddle in my world, but she is sorely mistaken." And before Garin could say another word, Ever closed his eyes and did what he never had before.

Since he was a small boy, Ever had built up walls within his mind to keep his enemy out, a labyrinth to confuse and expel her attempts at invading his dreams and musings. But never had he tried to find her. He had never felt desperate enough to risk entering the princess's poisonous mind. Until now.

Finding her was more work than Ever had expected. He pictured the way down the mountain to her camp, moved in his mind through the brush and trees, between the filthy, stinking men she employed, and searched each tent when he couldn't find her roaming the camp. By the time he located her mind, he could feel sweat dripping down his temples, and Garin saying something from a distance. But he was too far gone to pull back now.

"Well, look at you." Nevina put down the parchment she had been examining, and leaned back, crossing her legs as though he were merely paying a social call. His mind's eye was fuzzy, and the colors were off, but Ever didn't miss the spark of delight in her eyes. "I was beginning to think you wouldn't come, and I had terrified your poor little girl for nothing."

"You stay away from her!" If Ever's body had been with his mind, he would have thrown something. "She knows nothing of this world. This is between you and me."

"Or you'll what? Punish me?" Nevina laughed and ran a hand through her dark hair. "But I don't see what I've done wrong." She leaned forward. "I want her, Everard. And I have a deal for you, if you're not too thick-headed to at least consider it."

"I want no part in your darkness."

"So let me see if I am correct," Nevina said. "You coerce a girl, whom, if my informants are right, you managed to cripple years ago, to come to the Fortress against her will. And from the looks of her dreams, it seems she is to help you with breaking the curse." A small smile lit her lips. "And you accuse *me* of darkness?"

Ever wanted to spit in the woman's face. He wanted to curse her with every filthy word he knew. Unfortunately, she was right. Guilt began to work its way from his heart out towards his limbs, which warmed them uncomfortably.

"As much as I enjoy it, your guilt is not what I invited you down here for." Nevina stood and put a pair of spectacles on as she picked up her parchment again. "You were right. This girl has promise."

Ever stiffened.

"I want you to give her to me."

"What for?" Ever gritted his teeth.

Nevina shrugged. "I really don't know. But since my father had seen it fit to swear off my family's ways, disregarding thousands of years of power and heritage, I am a bit outnumbered. Besides, I could give her what you won't, or can't. I could heal her."

Anger flamed hot inside of Ever, and he clenched his fists. What he wouldn't give to knock this vixen into her eternal punishment now. "I told you, you will not touch her."

"See, that is what I do not understand!" Nevina gave a short laugh and waved her hand at him. "From the look you gave her last night, at least the one she conjured up in her dreams, you hate her. I don't recall you ever giving even me such a look! So why hide this girl away when you dislike her to begin with? Here is what I propose." She shoved the parchment at Ever. A cursory glance revealed that it was a contract. "Give her to me," Nevina said, "and I will leave Destin. I will even heal her, if it assuages your conscience. But keep her from me, and I will hunt you both until the day you die. Either way, Everard," she leaned so close he could see the blemishes in her skin, "you have placed her in my sights. I want her, and whatever happens to her, now or after your death, is on your head."

She held the contract out a moment longer, but when he said nothing, she crumpled it carelessly and threw it on the ground. "Then so be it. I have business elsewhere, which should make you happy. But I will be back." She leveled a look of hate at Ever before flashing him that familiar that smile he hated so much. "And when I return, I hope to find your sentiments have changed, for her sake."

"I won't let you!" Ever spat out, but holding her in the dream state was weakening him too much for it to sound threatening.

"Oh, you will. I have seen you in her dreams, and I know that whatever has befallen the Fortress is changing you. If anyone keeps me out, it will be your watchdog. But Garin can't be there every moment of every day, can he?"

And with that, she dismissed him. Ever woke up, panting as though he hadn't swallowed water in ages. Garin was there, wiping his brow and face with a cool cloth. Though Ever couldn't see him as he did it, he could sense his steward's calming presence, and it began to draw him back to a place of speech.

"What does she want?" Garin's voice was gentle.

It took Ever a moment to find his voice. Garin had been right. Ever's venture into his enemy's mind had taken much more power from him than he had expected. "She..." Ever stopped and licked his parched lips. "She wants Isabelle."

Garin said something, but Ever couldn't focus enough to hear him. All he could think about was Nevina's talk of his broken honor. It killed him to admit it, but she was right. As much as he disliked the girl, he had placed Isabelle directly in danger's path, an act far from honorable. No longer was the girl there simply to help him unravel the curse. Now she was fodder for his most hated enemy.

"Ever?"

"What?"

"I was asking you what you will do to protect her."

Ever took a deep breath. A thousand options flashed in his mind, but he already knew which he had to choose. And it made him guiltier than ever.

"We stay the course."

13

WHAT KIND OF PRINCE?

*I*sa slammed the book shut and leaned back in frustration. A week she had been at the Fortress, and still she knew almost nothing about her reason for being there, only that there was a curse, and that she was supposed to break it. To make matters worse, the books Prince Everard continued to send her said little about the special power the monarchs wielded. The histories she was given reported uses of the power, but none told her how it worked or where it came from.

"I don't understand," she said to the friendly presence. "What can I do when I know nothing, and have nothing to contribute? Why does he think I could be the one to break the curse?" She stood and went to the window to look down on Soudain. Would he have put such faith in her if he'd known who she was first?

Would he be speaking with her more if she were anyone else?

Never in her life had Isa ever thought she might crave the prince's company. She hated him, after all. But one week alone with the silent shadows had Isa ready to talk with anyone. But it didn't matter what she wanted, for after he had stormed off like a madman from his mother's chambers, Isa hadn't seen any sign that he even existed. She hadn't been pushed or pulled into any stuffy dresses, nor had she been forced to wear the silken slippers. Her meals had even been brought to her room, or wherever she happened to be at the moment.

At first, the solitude had been a welcome relief. But the silence had begun to grow noisy, and Isa grew to realize she would have been more than happy to have an argument with the man she despised so much. Only the friendly presence had kept her going through the motions. Isa had even found herself talking aloud to it. She wondered if the shadows thought her insane, but then again, it really didn't matter to her. At least the presence was there.

"I don't suppose–Ow!" A sharp little breeze began to wrestle the rag from her head that she used to tie her hair back for dancing. But the little breeze didn't stop. To her delight and annoyance, the shadows began to race around her, removing clothes and preparing her for the bath that had somehow been brought up without her noticing. Was she to see him tonight?

Isa gave a little shiver. Despite her resolutions from the week before, and her desire to speak with someone living, she still dreaded the anticipation of his touch, should he want to dance with her again. The nightmare of Prince Everard and Raoul was still fresh in her mind, despite the time that had passed since. But, Isa supposed, this was part of the price to pay for seeing another human. For that, she would put up with the servants' tricks and the prince's ill temper. She just didn't want to be alone again.

This evening she didn't get to choose her gown. A dress of light green velvet and cream silk was shoved at her. She endured all the shadows' pushing and pulling, however, until she was once again handed a set of dreadful, lovely silken slippers.

Isa folded her arms and stood firmly in place. "We've discussed this. I am not wearing those tonight. It's my boots or nothing."

To her amazement, one of the little shadows dove furiously at her feet, nearly knocking her over.

Indignation rose up inside of her. "If you think I am going to supper without my boots, you are sorely mistaken!" Then she stamped her foot down hard on the stone floor to make her point.

The shadows began to swirl about her, and with a bit of fear, Isa wondered if they would continue to behave as people without bodies when they were angry, or true ghosts. Before she had too much time to worry, however, that faithful presence seemed to flood the room, and the shadows went scattering. She could feel their annoyance as they put up her hair after that, but nothing more was done about the boots.

Just moments before she was ready to leave her room for the dining hall, a knock sounded at her door. When she answered it, to her amazement, Prince Everard was waiting. He still wore the thick cloak, but underneath he was wearing what appeared to be a somewhat clean garment of deep brown with silver threads. It was too large for his frail body, but she had to admit that distinguished attire didn't look uncomely. Deep bags lay beneath his eyes, as though he hadn't slept in weeks. He did look as though he'd cut and washed his hair, however, as it was combed and parted neatly, the golden strands glinting in the weak light from her fireplace.

He shocked her even more by giving her a stiff bow and somewhat awkwardly extending his arm. "Good evening, Miss Isabelle. Will you allow me to escort you to supper?"

Not quite sure what she was doing, Isa accepted his hand, as if in a daze. Inwardly, she berated herself for so readily taking it, her willingness to touch the man that she loathed so. And to her annoyance, she found that she also wished desperately to stare into his strange fiery eyes. Though all else about him was too upsetting to look at for very long, she could have gazed into the rings of blue forever.

They walked in silence to the dining hall. Their progress was slow, and their uneven steps made scuffing sounds echo down the great stone corridors. Isa did grudgingly admit to herself that it was nice for once not to be the slow one. The man beside her was every bit as slow as she was. Somewhere in the back of her mind, she wondered what he had looked and walked like before the curse.

After the incident at the parade, Isa had avoided all events at which the prince had made public appearances. Following his later public appearances, Isa's friends had always reported with giggles that they had nearly swooned at the sight of him. *How straight he stood!* they would exclaim. And though he wasn't the tallest man in the court, Isa had heard, he'd carried himself powerfully, and that one swipe of his fist could knock a strong man unconscious.

With a start, Isa realized that the prince had fallen much harder than she had first guessed. He, who had grown up with respect and strength, was reduced to walking at the speed of a lame peasant woman. It was ironic. And yet, her revelation brought her less satisfaction than she would have expected.

Supper had been laid out by the time they arrived. Again, once they were seated, the prince started the conversation, his voice polite and distant.

"Were the books I sent to your liking?"

"They were... satisfactory in regards to history, Your Highness."

"But?"

Isa looked up from her stew to see the prince raising one of his eyebrows. He must have caught the tenor of dissatisfaction in her voice. She sighed. "It would be easier if I were simply allowed to browse the library on my own."

But the prince was already shaking his head. "That is out of the question."

Isa nodded, a bit peeved that he had pried the request out of her when she hadn't meant to make it.

He wasn't done, however. Leaning forward, he cocked his head. "Out of curiosity, why are you so intent on finding the books on your own?"

Isa felt annoyance rise up within her again as she pushed her bits of meat and potatoes around the bowl. "I need to know more about the magic." As if it weren't obvious enough.

"Magic?" He raised that eyebrow again, and Isa scoffed a bit.

"Surely you cannot think that the rest of the world experiences life as... as you do here. In the real world, shadows do not serve supper. Hundreds of life-sized statues, each as different as a man from his neighbor, do not suddenly appear on a lawn and look as though they have been there for decades. Doors do not open on their own, nor do instruments to play without musicians.

"Besides, you cannot pretend that all these strange things have begun only since the casting of the curse. In Soudain, even small children know that the Fortress holds a special power. Whatever happened to this place came from within. I can feel it. *That* is what I need to know more about." Isa sat back and took a breath, finally glad to have gotten the chance to vent.

He didn't answer immediately, but gave her a long, shrewd look, distracting her with those strange storm gray and blue eyes. When he did speak, his answer was slow and deliberate.

"What you call *magic* does indeed exist, but there is no book in the Tower of Annals or any other place that can explain it." His eyes turned dark, and his deep voice became bitter. "It cannot be written about. It does not have that kind of nature. Many have tried, but none has succeeded, and in their frustration, they burned or destroyed what little they attempted. If you have questions, you will have to content yourself with asking me. Do you understand?"

Isa wanted to retort that it is impossible to ask a man who is never around, but instead nodded, a bit taken aback by the sudden storm in his voice. He had gone from being distantly civil to temperamental once again.

They ate in silence until he added, more softly this time, "I know the... strength of this Fortress better than any other creature, living or dead. What I need you to understand is that if I simply told you what you wish to know, you would never be able to break the curse. There are things about this place that you must discover for yourself before the curse can be touched. Knowledge will be revealed to you by the Fortress itself, should you need it."

Isa stared at him, dumbfounded, as he stared sadly out into night sky through the tall windows behind her. She was still trying to understand what he meant, when he spoke in his polite voice once more.

"Are the slippers my servants chose for you not to your liking?"

Isa broke out of her reverie and without thinking, looked down at her feet. "The slippers are fine," she said, "but I prefer boots."

His expression was so quizzical that she sighed and explained. "After the... *accident*, my father had the cobbler make me boots that could support my ankle. Without them, I can hardly walk, much less dance. Your servants stole my boots that last night and forced me to wear the slippers." Isa's voice hitched with sudden emotion on the last words, reminded suddenly of the last time she had tried to wear slippers at home. Gathering her resolve, she said more forcefully, "I told them that if I was to dance tonight, I would do it in my boots. I am not about to go to bed completely lame again."

"Oh." Prince Everard frowned in thought for a moment. "I'm sorry to hear that. I will tell them to stop bothering you about it. And... I am sorry they treated you that way. They can be a bit overzealous to please sometimes."

Isa nearly dropped her spoon as the apology fell from the prince's lips. It was the last thing she had expected from the man. All she could utter was a hesitant, "Thank you."

Before long, the prince stood and held out his hand. It was time for the dreaded dancing again. But this time, Isa was more prepared. The boots made her feel more confident. So did the friendly presence that followed her out onto the balcony. Isa still shuddered a bit when the prince's gloved hand held her waist, and she did not find a single moment of the awkward partnering enjoyable. The despair she had felt during the last dance was gone, though, and this time, she was more prepared to fight the memories of Raoul's dances as they moved in their slow circles. She still had no idea as to why the prince insisted on such a strange ritual, especially when it most likely made him sore as well, but she now knew she was at least capable of meeting the task. And when the dance was over, she departed feeling more like herself, feeling victorious.

As she turned the corner of the dining hall, however, curiosity flared up. There was much that the prince wasn't telling her, much she desperately needed to know if she were ever to break this curse. A reckless idea sprang into her mind, and without pause, she acted upon it.

Instead of returning to her room, she hid behind a large column until Prince Everard had gone up the steps of the southern wing.

"I am sure you want me to break this curse just as much as he does," Isa hissed at the shadows around her, "so if you dare tell him what I am about to do, know that I will stop trying to break the curse, and you will be stuck like this forever!" She felt the shadows' disapproval, but sensed them leaving her, one by one.

When the prince had been gone long enough to get a head start, she followed him up the large winding staircase as quietly as she could. She ascended past level upon level. On each level was a hall to her left and to her right. Down each hall were many doors that were larger than the ones in her wing of the Fortress. Isa guessed that the largest of the doors on the highest level led to Prince Everard's personal chambers. She had little interest in those.

She had fallen behind purposefully so he wouldn't hear her foot when it dragged, and she hoped now that he would be in his chambers, sleeping so she could explore freely. She wasn't sure what exactly she was looking for, only that there must be some part of the Fortress that might tell her what the stories wouldn't. And she had a hunch that the library, or rather, the Tower of Annals, was up the dark flight of steps that led skyward from the highest level on the southern wing.

After a long while of climbing the steps to the tower, Isa wondered if her plan had been a good one. Even in the boots, her ankle was beginning to throb from all the stairs she'd taken, even before she was near the top.

By the time she'd ascended the last step, Isa had concluded that the tower she climbed must be the one that made the Fortress visible for miles. In the sunlight, it was easy to see the reflection of the glass that encircled the entire chamber. As a child, this place had stirred her curiosity and imagination. What kind of room would have only windows for walls? And that curiosity was rekindled inside of her now. Remembering the prince's warning about the Tower of Annals, however, Isa restrained herself from actually entering. Instead, she knelt at the keyhole.

The circular room was larger than she had anticipated, but it was indeed encased by windows all around. Shelves of books filled most of the space, with the exception of the center, where there was built a large stone fireplace. The fireplace was surrounded by various chairs, tables, sofas, and even an oddly placed wardrobe.

Instead of the empty room she had expected to see, however, Prince Everard was sitting on a low sofa with his hands stretched out before him. Shadows gently removed the long gloves he always wore, revealing thin, gnarled fingers beneath. They were so knotted that even when he flexed them they stayed curled. Only a weak fire from a hearth and moonlight from the wall of windows lit the space, but the pain on the prince's face was obvious. She couldn't help but pity him.

"I will improve," the prince said in a tired voice. Isa jumped, afraid he knew that she was there. But just as she turned to flee back down the steps, he spoke again, this time, as though answering a question. "She said nothing of it, but I knew she was curious."

Isa knelt again against the door, straining to hear more. Who was he talking to?

"Please, Garin," the prince moaned, "can we talk of this later? My head feels like a battering ram."

Isa felt her heart jump again, but this time, it was a leap of hope. She hadn't heard the name of her father's old friend since he had written to save her life the night of the purge that should have been. She owed him her life. Was he here as a shadow? If he was, she would feel much better. She had always liked and respected the Fortress steward.

Before she could dwell on this too much, however, Isa saw what she had been looking for for the past week. Her gasp was nearly audible as a blue fire, much like that in his eyes, began to encircle the prince's hands. It filled the room with a blue glow, and Prince Everard put his head back, grimacing even harder, a soft groan escaping him.

The scene lasted only a few seconds before the fire went out. When it was done, the prince's fingers were just a bit straighter. After curling and flexing them a few times, he slowly stood and pulled a sword from his belt, one Isa hadn't noticed beneath the cloak. Laying it down beside him, he faced the windows and slowly stretched out on a thin pallet that had been laid upon one of the low sofas near the window wall. When she realized that he meant to sleep there, she turned and began her trek back down the stairs, not wanting to impose upon his privacy.

She struggled to sleep that night. As much as she hated to admit it, Isa couldn't be as angry with the prince as she felt she deserved to be. He had seemed so proud when he had first greeted her, and the hate in his eyes had been real. And yet, the pain in his face this night had been real, too. Isa knew that kind of pain, what it felt like to go to sleep in discomfort. In her family, however, she had never gone to bed without a cup of tea from her mother, something to ease the pain. And with the tea had always been a warm embrace and sweet words.

But Prince Everard was all alone in his pain without a human hand to bring him comfort. And from what little she had seen of the late King Rodrigue and Queen Monica, Isa doubted they had been the kind to spend time kissing away the hurt that his childhood exploits had brought him. Suddenly, for all his splendor and power, the prince seemed far more impoverished than she had ever suspected.

And then there was the soldier's pallet. What kind of prince went to sleep with his sword, watching over his kingdom even though he could hardly walk?

Over and over again, Isa tried to answer the riddles that her adventure had brought her. But the only answer she found was that perhaps, just perhaps, the prince wasn't the man she had hated for so long.

14

ARROWS THAT BURN

*I*n the weeks that followed, Isa fell into a routine that wasn't altogether unpleasant. No snow had fallen since the early autumn storm her father had gotten caught in, so Isa continued her trips to the rose garden daily. And although her ankle and wrist were broken beyond repair, as the town healer had told her when she was a child, Isa felt her body growing stronger.

The garden grew stronger, too. Each day, not only did she revel in the dance, but also in the new roses that were slowly beginning to find their way back into the garden, despite the growing cold.

Isa also found daily relief in being away from the town gossip and sympathetic looks. Here, she wasn't the town cripple. She had a purpose, confusing as it may be. And though she missed her family dearly, Isa felt for the first time as though she might find a way to make them proud.

Her most earnest prayer of thanks, however, was for having escaped Raoul's wedding. The nuptials would have been impossible to ignore, had Isa still lived in Soudain. The marriage of the chancellor's only son would be at its height by now, the talk of the city. Her neighbors' outrage at his betrayal of her hadn't even lasted a week. By the time the wedding arrived, she would have been completely forgotten, and everyone would be anxious to see the beautiful bride who had so quickly captured Raoul's heart. The wedding would come and go, and Isa was immensely grateful not to even need an excuse for her absence.

If she was honest with herself, the nightly dances still bothered her. They were too close to the moments that had been her most cherished until recently. Raoul's cruel words continued to mock her as well when she let her guard slip. Nevertheless, her heartache wasn't any worse at the Fortress than it had been at home. And at least here, she was free to remain alone for the majority of the time, without family and friends trying to "keep her busy," as they put it. Well, the servants were always nearby, but at least they never nagged her about being social.

In order to escape the lonely thoughts of her once beloved, Isa buried herself in reading the books that the prince sent to her. They weren't very interesting, mostly names of monarchs and dry lists of their accomplishments, but they were a distraction at least. And as Prince Everard promised, his servants never made a move for her boots again.

It wasn't long before a sort of truce had formed between them, the prince learning how better to curb his tongue, and Isa striving to keep her tone at least civil, and sometimes kind. He even surprised her one evening by sending over a salve with his servants when he noticed that her left wrist was sore at dinner.

The invisible, ever-near presence also continued to make Isa's life at the Fortress more enjoyable. She found herself talking to it when she was lonely, telling it how much she missed her family, how the prince confused her, and on hard days, even about Raoul. And though she no longer feared that the prince would do something beastly during their suppers, Isa was still afraid to tell him about her invisible friend, fearing he might order it away. This made asking him questions about the *strength*, as he called it, even more difficult, for she knew there was some tie between the magic and her constant companion. But whenever she tried to ask, the right words simply wouldn't come.

Isa could sense the prince was struggling daily, not only with the physical pain she'd witnessed in the tower, but with an even deeper despair. Not wanting to upset him, the only way she could think to phrase her questions was based on the dry stories of past kings and their feats. Still, she never learned very much that way. He would answer her direct questions, but never supplied any more information than was absolutely necessary. And though she was actually enjoying parts of her new life, if she was honest with herself, Isa wondered how, if ever, she was to break the curse. She still had no idea as to what she was doing.

It was a dark, chilly evening, a time of true winter, however, when things finally changed.

"Isabelle." The prince leaned back from his supper and gave her a mischievous grin Isa had never seen before. It was annoyingly cute. "Yours is a long name, and not terribly easy to say. Where did you get it?"

He was being ridiculous. The prince had the most elegant, sophisticated speech Isa had ever heard. He was goading her. But this was a subject which Isa did not wish to touch.

"My mother named me after the Isabelle flower," she replied somewhat stiffly. Although she had secretly never loved her full name either, speaking of her mother was still difficult.

"Isabelle flower? I've never heard of such a thing."

"It's a common miniature rose that grows in the shade," Isa explained. "I'm sure it has an official name in your Tower of Annals somewhere, but in Soudain, it's simply called the Isabelle."

The prince smiled again with that boyish look, and said, "I don't think I will call you Isabelle anymore. It takes too long to say. I think I shall call you *Belle* instead."

Isa's face flushed a hot red. "I don't–Please don't call me that, Your Highness."

"Why not?" There was no distance in his voice now as he leaned forward towards her, only genuine curiosity, which made it all the worse.

"I..." she stammered, searching for words as panic rose in her chest. After all this time, she had thought she was stronger than this. "I beg your pardon, but I just don't want it!"

Everard sat back again and scoffed. "I am not ordering you as the prince. I'm asking you as a fellow human who might enjoy some *real* conversation sometimes." Isa didn't answer, so he continued. "You've only been here for what, eight weeks? I have lived here for eight months on my own. I can sense that I am not your favorite person in the world, so believe me when I say you were never my first choice in companion either."

For some reason, that stung more than Isa would have expected.

But the prince continued with his cruel tirade. "Still, I have tried to get to know you, to get you to open up just a little! But for some reason, you think you're above common civilities–"

"Civilities?" Isa snapped. Suddenly, she didn't care if she was speaking to the prince. He had crossed a line. "I didn't think it was very *civil* when you forced me here against my will, or when you made me dance with you, or when you compelled me to accept a task I still do not understand! What *civility* was there when you ended my childhood before I was ten? And even less civil was your warrant for my death last spring! You were the reason I was abandoned on my wedding day! You took everything from me! And yet, after all that *civility*, you have the audacity to sit here and demand to know why I hate that name!"

The prince sat in his chair looking astonished, but Isa didn't wait for him to recover. Grabbing her mother's cloak from her chair, she threw it around her shoulders as she stomped down the steps to the nearest ground level door. She heard him yelling for her as she moved, but he wasn't fast enough to catch her.

Throwing open the door, she ran out onto the back lawn. Gusts of snowflakes were just beginning to whip furiously in the air around her, but Isa didn't care. Tears streamed down her face as she plunged headfirst towards the statues. Only after a few minutes of trudging through the accumulating snow with the frigid air penetrating her clothing, though, did she begin to wonder where she was going. All she'd wanted was to get away from the prince. But the snow was falling heavily, and she couldn't walk far in snow, even with her boots.

It didn't take her long to reach the statues, where she hoped to find some shelter from the wind before getting completely turned around. She started to breathe a sigh of relief when she reached the tall stone figures, but before she could rest, an arrow of flame fell from the sky, narrowly missing her.

With a shriek, Isa turned back towards the Fortress, but the rising snow and the stiffness of her ankle made her progress slow. More arrows followed, one of them finally catching her skirts on fire and singeing her leg. It knocked her over, the snow extinguishing the flames, but before she could rise, a monstrous creature appeared in the sky.

It was so large that Isa could see the rings of fire in its eyes, even from a distance, but the fire wasn't blue like Prince Everard's. It was gold, and it flamed brighter and brighter as the bird dove straight at her. Isa cried out as it struck her calf with its large beak, just above the place the arrow had scorched. Pain shot up to her thigh, and with it, the awful realization that like the creatures of the Fortress, this bird was no typical bird of prey. The hawk made a large arc over her in the sky, and had turned to dive at her again when a sword was suddenly thrust between the fowl and its prey.

Isa turned to see Prince Everard's hunched form standing above her. He shook with the effort to keep the sword raised so high, but the hawk stopped before it could finish its plunge.

"Go!" he ordered.

Isa scrambled to stand, crying out at the burning in her leg. Together, they pushed back towards the castle. Their progress was sluggish, however, and though the prince kept his sword raised, the bird regained its confidence and began to strike at them once more. Over and over it struck. But it didn't touch her again.

By the time they were pulled back into the Fortress by shadowed hands, Isa was more exhausted and frightened than she'd ever been in her life. The pain in her leg was agonizing. But her alarm grew even greater when she turned to look at the prince.

His neck, arms, and face were covered in gashes that bled, and his skin was a deathly white. He dropped his sword on the floor when the servants slammed the door shut behind them, but instead of collapsing, he gripped her arm and dragged her to the nearest chair. Wordlessly, Isa let him. Shadows rushed around to feed the nearest fireplace as he fairly tossed her into the seat.

"Pull up your dress," he barked.

Shocked, Isa stared at him.

"If I don't tend to your leg, you will lose it! Would you like that?"

Still unable to speak, Isa shook her head and slowly lifted her blackened gown up to her knee. The flesh on her shin was shiny and dark red, and as soon as she saw it, the pain was nearly unbearable. Above the burn was a large gash from which blood was dripping down. The sight made her suddenly very dizzy, and it took all of her strength not to faint.

To distract herself, she tried to focus on Prince Everard's eyes. He had stiffly dropped to his knees, and was yelling out orders to the servants, calling for specific herbs and bandages. It was only then that she recalled his warning from her first evening there, telling her never to leave the Fortress at night. Guilt settled over her as she continued to stare into her prince's eyes.

His face was simultaneously pale and flushed. Beads of sweat ran down his temples, making lines in the dirt and soot that covered his face. The blue fire in his eyes was blazing more brightly than she had ever seen it, and with a start, she realized the presence that had followed her around for the past weeks was in him as well. She suddenly understood that it was the presence itself from which his strength was derived.

Seeing him there, covered in blood and soot, looking nearly weak enough to pass out himself, and yet tending to her wound, Isa's stomach did a strange flop. By that time, the servants had surrounded them with all sorts of herbs, salves, water, and bandages. His claw-like hands shook as he removed his gloves, but he still somehow moved more quickly than she had seen him do since arriving at the Fortress. Expertly, he mixed the herbs with his fingers and rubbed them on her wound.

"What were you thinking?" His voice was low and dangerous.

"I... I'm sorry," Isa whispered.

"Do you not remember me specifically telling you to stay inside at night?" he exploded.

Isa could only stare at him with sorrowful eyes.

"You were nearly killed out there! You do not seem to understand that your life is no longer your own! You're still under the delusion that what you do only affects you! Let me put this simply. If you die, I do not stand a chance at restoring the Fortress or the kingdom! Think about that next time you're of the mind to do something foolish!"

"I'm sorry," Isa whispered again. And she was. If it hadn't been for her infernal temper, neither of them would be bleeding right now. He might have been cruel, but it was she who had lost self-control and foolishly run out into the storm. She should have been stronger than that.

The prince took a deep breath and stopped working. "I'm sorry, Isabelle. My words aren't meant to hurt you. I am frustrated because I should have been better able to protect you."

In that moment, Isa saw a flash of the warrior he had once been, and the shame he owned now for what he had become.

"You don't know," he said, briefly closing his eyes, "what it's like to be a soldier, to stand guard at the gates of evil, to know without a doubt that you can overcome it. And then to have it all stripped away as your kingdom slowly burns to the ground."

An awkward quiet settled over them for what felt like an eternity. The prince continued to treat her wound, and Isa watched, trying to digest all that he had said. No matter how much she wished to deny it, what he had said made more sense of his many strange moods. She felt as though she were gaining a peek into the prince's calloused soul, and any doubt that the prince had a heart of flesh buried somewhere within him fled her like a thief in the night. Finally, Isa could stand the silence no more.

"You are quite skilled with wounds."

The prince didn't look up as he carefully wrapped her leg in a long, white cloth. "Rarely in battle is there a healer to be found when he is needed. All of my men are required to learn the basic healing skills. If they do not, many soldiers die."

"Who were they, the people that attacked us?" Isa tried to quiet her hammering heart.

He didn't answer until he had finished wrapping her leg and his gloves were back on. Finally, he looked her in the eyes. There was no playfulness there this time, no spite, nothing but an earnest frustration. He measured her for a long moment before saying, "Come with me. There is something you need to see."

Isa wasn't sure she would be able to walk, but as soon as she stood up, she could feel the expertise of the prince's work. There was hardly any pain aside from the usual ache of her ankle as she followed him to the stairs she had snuck up once before.

"What you are about to see has only ever been seen by the Fortress kings and queens and their closest confidantes. It is sacred, the heart of the Fortress. But," he turned to her with that strange contemplative look, "if you can truly break the curse, it will affect more than just this Fortress and its inhabitants. What happens in this room determines the fate of our world and that of our enemies."

When they finally reached the top of the tower, Isa could see sweat still trickling down the prince's neck in the weak torchlight. She was breathing hard herself from the effort of the long climb. When he unlocked the door, however, the view made her forget the exhaustion. She gasped as she stepped into the tower of windows. He led her over to the north side of the circular room. From there, she could see a great encampment at the foot of the mountain. Despite the dark, hundreds of fires lit up the night. They made it easy to see the countless rows of tents that stood beside them.

"You can't see them from your room," he said quietly. "I put you there on purpose so that you couldn't, but that is the enemy."

"Who are they? What are they waiting for?" Her heart began to thump unevenly again.

"In the thousand years that this Fortress has stood, it has never gone dark. Tonight's attack was a warning, a taunt. They are reminding me that they're watching."

"Why do they hate you so much?" Isa turned away from the fires to look at him.

"The Fortress isn't the only source of power and strength in the world." He stared down at the enemy, his eyes troubled. "And yet, Destin is different from all of the other kingdoms. Since our kingdom was conceived, we have been the strongest of all." He paused. "What did you learn of the first king, Cassiel, in the books I sent to you?"

Isa racked her memory, running quickly through the dozens of droll histories she'd been reading.

"Wasn't he once a knight for another kingdom?"

Everard nodded. "He was a low-ranking knight of a nearby land, a man of little consequence. On an errand for the king, he entered the lower country of his liege's land, what is now Soudain, and saw the injustices being inflicted upon the people because of his proud king's negligence.

"The Maker's hand was upon Cassiel as he set out to right the wrongs that evil had brought upon the people of the southern land, the atrocities that the nobles of Cassiel's land ignored. In less than ten years, he had turned a barren wasteland full of impoverished souls into a safe and prosperous haven. As a result, the people there were blessed with rich soil and flowing streams.

"In addition, the Maker gifted him with the Fortress, a home from which he could draw a special strength to do justice and provide mercy. That strength was passed on to his descendants as well. That is why the Fortress is more than just a castle. It has been a place of light and hope for a millennium." The prince placed his hand upon one of the glass walls and ran his fingers down the long pane. "Until now," he added in a quiet voice.

"How is it then that this… strength is disappearing so quickly? If the Fortress was created with such power, how can they attack us so ruthlessly?" Isa couldn't tear her eyes away from the fires below.

"There are other powers that wander this earth." Prince Everard frowned. "They have never been able to match the strength given this place, but that doesn't mean they should ever be underestimated. Our greatest enemy, Tumen, has been a source of dark power for hundreds of years, a thorn in our side." Turning from the window, the prince shook his head and sank into a chair.

"Not long before he died, my father sought an alliance with Tumen. My betrothal ball put an end to that, however, thanks to the true intentions of their Princess Nevina, and some ill-chosen words on my part."

The idea of Everard having a betrothal ball was troublesome to Isa for some reason, but she ignored the irksome feeling it caused in her gut, and asked a more appropriate question instead.

"I still cannot understand where their power comes from. How were they able to hit me so well through the snowstorm? To see me even? And why would they attack only at night? Surely it would be easier by day."

"Greed is a powerful weapon of its own." The prince gave her a strange, hard smile. "Cultivated and nourished enough, it can be twisted into an asset of surprising force. King Cassiel was born in Tumen, and served its king until he left to right the injustices he found here. Tumen has always believed that because Cassiel was one of its own knights, Destin rightfully belongs to the Tumenian king. Their rage at being denied sovereignty of this land has become their weapon. The Tumenian power is nearly as old as that of the Fortress, only it is one shrouded in evil. It thrives in the dark of night."

"As for her desire to my throne, Princess Nevina, until recently, was the declared heir of Tumen's throne. When she was small, her father trained her in the ways of their ancestors. She proved to be strong, and many Tumenians believed she would be the one to restore Destin to them.

"This ambition has long made them unpopular with the other kingdoms, and while the Tumenian king has since claimed to have given up his dark powers in order to seek peace, Nevina never had any such intentions. But just when she was at the cusp of taking the sovereignty she'd been promised since birth, needing only a husband to seal the throne for herself, the birth of her younger brother took the kingdom by surprise, and Nevina lost her claim to the throne."

"So the princess is allowed to run about doing whatever she wishes now? Despite her father's claims at peace?"

"Her people have always loved her, and Nevina is clever. She is using their affection to garner support, and has continued to grow her numbers with her promises of the richness and bounty of our land. And for all his claims of peace, her father has done nothing to stop her." Prince Everard shook his head, his next words taking Isa by surprise.

"I fear, however, that her greed is not the power that has threatened this kingdom most in these last generations. She is merely taking advantage of what my fathers and I have been giving her."

Isa waited for him to go on, but it was a long moment before he spoke again.

"We've been able to hold Tumen off for centuries. With each generation, however, they have grown stronger. My father, his father, and even his father did everything they could to ensure our allies' loyalties and to minimize Destin's weaknesses. But the more we've striven, the harder it has become to contain them. And now they wait."

As she pondered his words and watched his eyes, Isa had a sudden flash of insight. "The curse didn't just affect your body. You are losing your power, too, aren't you?"

His eyes once again flaming a duller fire, Everard smiled wryly. "The strength that has flowed through the blood of my ancestors has been diminishing for generations." He swallowed loudly. "It seems my line is no longer fit to bear the burden of power any longer. At least, not until this curse is broken."

Understanding shook her to the core. Isa finally understood his desperation to break the curse. The prince, like her, hungered to fulfill his purpose. Everyone knew King Rodrigue had raised his son to be a warrior prince to protect Destin. And yet, after all he'd done, everything he had tried to do, it still wasn't enough. He was losing everything that he had ever held dear. And as much as she wanted to blame him, Isa was slowly having to admit that perhaps a stronger force was at work in their lives, one that not even the great prince had control over.

And it was breaking him, as it had broken her. Isa fought the sudden desire to reach out and touch him, to embrace him and tell him everything would be alright. Instead, she kept her hands firmly in her lap and decided to answer his question from earlier that evening.

"It's not your fault that I hate the name Belle," she said softly.

Everard turned from staring at the fires again to look at her, his open expression suddenly making him look very young. Isa tried not to get trapped in his gaze.

"I was engaged." Her voice quivered, the pain resurfacing as she spoke. "His name is Raoul. After the injury, I was very alone. The other children didn't want to wait for the crippled girl to constantly catch up, and he was the only one who still saw me for me. He would come over and play with me when I was healing and couldn't leave the house, and he would bring me things that made me smile, like flowers from a field, or apples from an orchard we used to explore.

"As we got older," Isa smiled at the memory in spite of herself, "he was the only one who ever asked me to dance. He called me Belle because," Isa's voice caught, and she had to whisper so she wouldn't cry. "He said I was the hidden flower, the one that was too beautiful for other people to see." Despite her resolve to stay strong, warm tears coursed silently down her cheeks.

"What happened?"

When Isa looked up at him, the prince's face was full of what looked like sincere concern. Isa's hand went to her crooked wrist without thinking. "He proposed to me just after the Fortress went dark, then left immediately with his father on a long journey. His father is the city chancellor, and has been preparing his son for the position since he was born. Apparently, he wanted Raoul to see what a true leader's wife should look like."

Isa's voice hitched again, and instead of stopping, her tears fell harder. The shame of the memory made her face hot. "He returned on our wedding day. He told me… He made it very clear that I was unfit to be the wife of a chancellor, that my weaknesses made me unable to fulfill the role that being his wife would require. I wasn't enough."

Unable to hold in the sobs, Isa put her head in her hands and wept. The pain of being broken was much fresher than she thought it would be by now. Raoul had managed to break her again, just when she had thought she was about to be healed. It felt as if she would never be whole again. This shame and sorrow of not being enough would follow her forever.

It was a few moments before she was calm enough to look into the eyes of her prince, and suddenly, she felt humiliated. What foolishness had possessed her to think he cared or wanted to know her pathetic love story? He had greater concerns on his mind.

When she was finally brave enough to steal a glance at him, however, Prince Everard's face looked like one of those carved upon the stone statues that stood outside. His jaw was set tightly, and the blue in his eyes blazed brightly once more. She was a bit frightened at first, until she realized he didn't seem angry with her. He said nothing, though, as he walked over to the window again and stared down at the enemy below.

"My family calls me Isa," she finally volunteered.

"And my friends call me Ever," he answered solemnly.

Isa couldn't help but wonder if she was supposed to call him this, too. Was she now considered a friend? As she puzzled over this, he quietly added, "For what it's worth, I still think Belle is more fitting."

In a daze, Isa simply gazed up at him. Silence settled over them again, the fire's crackling making the only sounds as the evening drew late.

"You should go to bed soon," he finally said in a rough voice.

Isa knew he was right, but her eyes wandered back to the campfires below. Fear rushed through her every time she looked at them.

"You don't have to be afraid." The prince was now looking at her with a gentleness she'd never seen before on his face. "They've been here for months, and their princess is gone. They won't attack again tonight."

Isa nodded, but her eyes once again locked upon the fires, her leg beginning to throb where the bird had slashed it.

Without warning, Everard began to sing. Isa knew none of the words. They seemed as ancient as the Fortress which surrounded her, but the rich tones of the prince's voice conveyed the meaning just as easily as if she'd spoken the language.

Gentle one who shivers with fear
Tremble no more in your fright.
One who is stronger watches over you
No harm shall meet thee tonight.

As if under a spell, Isa found herself dozing off against the arm of the chair she sat in. She was vaguely aware of airy hands lifting her, floating her to her chambers on a breeze.

She didn't dream of Raoul that night, or even the flaming arrows. Instead, Ever's rich voice serenaded her to a place of peace and rest, and it was with a smile on her face that Isa fell asleep.

15

WHAT SHE THINKS

*I*sa didn't dance the next day. Ever made sure of that. He ordered his servants to keep her in bed and tend to her leg, no matter what kind of fight she put up.

"You could heal her, Sire," Garin suggested gently.

But Ever shook his head. "I can't spend any strength that is not absolutely necessary. With the proper care, she will soon heal on her own." Deep down, however, he knew he was being selfish. Not only was he hoarding the strength he had recently spent so easily upon himself, but he was also planning on using her required bed rest as an excuse to visit her where she couldn't escape his attention.

"I would like for you to come with me this morning, to learn what she thinks of me," Ever said as his servants helped him to dress.

Garin gave a polite snort. "Your Highness, I can tell you that now. She has absolutely no idea what she thinks about you. But you know I will be there with you, as I always am."

The visit was somewhat awkward. Ever thought about bringing flowers, but as the only live ones on the Fortress grounds were in Isa's beloved rose garden, he decided against it. Instead, he brought more books.

She answered him politely through the door when he knocked, and Ever grinned to himself as the female shadows flitted about angrily when he entered. They didn't think it proper for the prince to visit a woman in her bedchambers, but they settled down somewhat when Garin floated in behind him.

After sharing such deep emotions the night before, neither Isa nor Ever seemed to know quite what to say, but the air between them was most assuredly altered.

It didn't help that Ever found himself continually distracted by the way her wavy auburn hair framed her heart-shaped face. The servants had left it down since she was in bed, and it was a surprising length. Its gentle waves gave her a softer appearance, making her look more vulnerable than she'd looked the night before. Multiple times, he caught himself wondering what it would feel like to touch her face.

By the end of the visit, not much had truly been said between the two humans in the room, but Ever could hear Garin smothering his chuckles, and realized that the female servants were very ready to shoo him out. Apparently, his thoughts hadn't been as well hidden as he had believed them to be.

Within a few weeks, Isa's leg was nearly healed, thanks to Ever's quick binding skills. Ever felt a bit bad about this. He knew that if he really wanted to, he could heal her using his strength. If she suspected his selfishness, however, she gave nothing away. Instead, their relationship seemed to improve.

While they were not exactly what Ever would consider to be friends, he found that she no longer sent him scathing looks over her supper, and she ceased to tremble when he led her to the dance floor each night. While she was far from throwing herself at him, it seemed that at least her hatred of him had subsided. And if Isa's actions didn't confuse him enough, Ever's own emotions finished the job.

"You must guard yourself, son," Rodrigue had told Ever after his first ball. The poor prince had been dumbstruck by the great number of eligible beauties that had paraded themselves in front of the young man that night, hoping to capture his attention before he was old enough to make a decision. "A worthy queen will bear you children, but she can easily become a distraction as well. You must protect this kingdom before all else, and that includes your queen."

King Rodrigue had lived by his word. Queen Louise rarely saw her husband. Rumor had it that the king had all but stopped visiting the queen's chambers once Ever was born. Always training the soldiers, always on a campaign, and forever consulting with his generals, Rodrigue had believed his marital duties fulfilled when his wife produced a son. Just as he abstained from all strong drink and any food that might be considered gluttonous, just as he slept keeping watch from the sacred Tower of Annals, he had denied himself the company of a woman, all in the name of duty.

For years, Ever had tried to follow his father's instructions, but just as the idea of choosing a wife based on politics had made him apprehensive, ignoring the draw he now felt to Isa seemed impossible. Finally, tired of being at war with his logic and his desires one day, he called Garin.

"Have you discovered something that will win her affections?"

"Do you mean something that will win her heart, or something that will hasten your plan?"

Ever rolled his eyes. "I don't see what difference it makes," he snapped. "If the plan is going to work, she might as well be happy about it."

Despite the steward's shadowy appearance, Ever could just imagine Garin's mouth turning down at one corner, and the thin wrinkles around his eyes deepening as they always did when he didn't approve of something. "As for the plan," Garin said, "you can see for yourself that the crystal floor glows brighter each night. As for *earning* her love, she no longer despises you, if that's what you are asking."

Ever gave a short, humorless laugh. "While I would agree that that is a start, I am asking what I should do next. I've never–I don't even know where to start." Ever walked out onto the tower's balcony. A breeze ruffled his left sleeve as Garin came to stand beside him. The air was warmer today than it had been for a long time. An early spring was on its way.

"No man has ever truly mastered the way to a woman's heart." Garin's voice was kinder this time. "And anyone who thinks he has doesn't deserve her."

They were silent for a moment as the sound of a lone jay was carried to them on the wind. It had been a long time since any bird had dared to makes its home on the Fortress grounds. In spite of his misgivings, Ever found a small shred of comfort in the lonely sound.

"You know about the old way of choosing a queen on the crystal balcony," Garin said softly. "There is something your father never told you though, probably because his father never told him."

Ever turned in surprise to the steward's voice, forgetting, as he often did, that he couldn't see Garin.

Garin continued. "It is true that the young ladies would present themselves to the future king. It is also true that they would dance on the crystal floor until one showed a sufficient fire of her own to make it glow, just as you're attempting to do with Isa. But the kings of old didn't stop there. You see, any king could find a woman of worth by looking for an answer from the crystal floor, but a wise king would realize that the Fortress had chosen for him a jewel, a pillar of strength to be his helper, his partner in guarding Destin."

Ever could hear the smile in his mentor's voice as he spoke.

"In the stories you begged me to tell when you were small, the queens weren't treated as delicate flowers to be left in their chambers, produce children, and amuse themselves until they died. They were advisers to their husbands, and their words were regarded more highly than generals', for the wise kings trusted that the Fortress had chosen for them only the best. A number of the great queens even learned to wield the strength just as well as, if not better than, their husbands could."

"What happened?" Ever frowned. He had always prided himself in knowing the history of the Fortress. How had he not known this?

"The kings stopped trusting the Fortress, to put it simply." Garin suddenly sounded tired. "They believed they knew best, and as a result, the queens were chosen for alliances and politics, rather than virtue and strength. With all due respect to your mother, of course, the bright lights that burned by the kings' sides disappeared."

"That's all quite interesting." Ever shook his head to clear it and turned to go back inside. It was nearly time for his daily ride, something he insisted on continuing as long as he was physically able. "But I don't see how that is going to help me with Isa."

"It's really quite simple, Your Highness," Garin said after calling for two shadow servants to prepare Ever's riding things. "If you saw a jewel buried in the dirt, what would you do?"

"I'd pick it up."

"But you wouldn't just pick it up and stick it in your saddlebag, would you? You would lift it gently. You'd take your time so as not to scratch it. And once you had it in your hands, you wouldn't allow it to stay filthy. You would brush the dirt off, polish it. And the more you worked, the brighter it would shine."

"Garin, please, I didn't sleep last night, and my mind is not up to answering your riddles."

"Everard, Isa is the jewel, one that has been drawn to the Fortress just as the queens of old were. And just as a jewel needs someone to help it shine, so does this woman. Heartbreak isn't easy to clean up. Lift her up, make her see her worth, and she might surprise you with her brilliance."

By this time, they were on their way down to the stables. Once they were there, Ever painfully pulled himself up onto his horse. He pushed the animal into a quick canter, but he could hear Garin call out from behind him.

"The Fortress has brought her to you for a reason, Ever! You might want to reconsider trusting it to help both of you break the curse!"

Ever didn't answer as he rode quickly towards the north end of the Fortress grounds. His joints ached with each of the horse's steps, but riding was the only way he could move fast enough to think to his satisfaction. As usual, Garin's answers to his questions had only served to breed more of the unknown.

As he made his way, however, Ever suddenly felt as though he were being watched. Surely enough, when he turned around, a large pair of dark eyes were following him from the grand entrance where Isa stood in the doorway. She looked nervous. Ever's curiosity got the best of him, and he cut his ride short. His father would have been appalled.

"Can I help you, my lady?" he called out, somewhat shocked at his confidence as the words left his mouth.

Isa gave him a half smile. "I would like to go out, but I am not sure if the weather agrees with me."

Ever noticed the catch in her voice, however, and saw right through her brave face. He brought his horse up to the grand doors, still held open by the shadows as Isa lingered on the threshold.

"There's nothing to be afraid of." As he spoke, he realized he sounded like a commander insulting one of his cowardly soldiers. "Remember, the danger is only at night. Their birds and archers can't see well until the sun has set." Why was it so hard to soften his voice?

Isa smiled, but he could still see her trembling hands. Suddenly wondering if he could do as Garin had advised, he stiffly dismounted and held his arm out to her. "Would you like me to accompany you to the garden?"

The young woman studied him for a moment, tilting her head a bit as she stared at him with those dark eyes. Ever wasn't sure what she saw there, but she finally nodded lightly and took his arm.

Together, they shuffled down the stone path to the rose garden. And for the first time since the curse had fallen, Ever didn't mind the slow pace. The warmth of her arm felt nice on his, and the soft way she grasped his wrist made his heart jump unevenly. She kept her head down, staring at the ground as they walked, but Ever longed to lift her chin so she would look him in the eyes.

Though he escorted her to supper every night, this felt different, more intimate outside in the thin sunlight that was almost warm. For all his father's training in self-denial and duty, he felt like an adolescent again. With a bit of disgust, he realized his constantly growing desire to be near her was somewhat akin to that of a puppy.

"Would you mind if we go somewhere else today?" he asked as they approached the rose garden, suddenly desperate to keep her arm and her attention.

Isa turned to him with wide eyes. "Where would you like to go?"

Ever honestly had no idea. The question had been spontaneous, so he said the first thing that came to mind. "If you're going to live here, you might as well know a bit about the grounds. They hold more stories than one would think by looking at them now."

Isa's eyes stayed wide, as if this was the last thing she had expected, but to his relief, she nodded. And so, they began to explore the many gardens that had once adorned the Fortress's front lawns. Ever pointed out places in the foliage and shrubs where he had played in the days of his boyhood. As he told her stories of how he had evaded his tutors and hidden with the servant children, Isa seemed to relax. She even laughed a few times when he mentioned some particularly ornery tricks he had played on Garin.

"You really love this place," Isa said as they stopped to rest on a stone bench in the ancient Garden of the Queens.

"I was born with a love for this place," Ever answered uncomfortably. "As a child, I never felt alone. Even when I escaped to be on my own, I always felt loved and protected. It was as if the Fortress itself had wrapped its arms around me. I felt special."

"But you don't feel that way now?"

Ever sighed. Isa's guesses as to his feelings were getting better, and she was fast approaching a conversation he preferred not even to have with himself.

"I used to know how I felt. I knew what the Fortress was doing. It was a part of me. But ever since this curse, since this sickness has fallen, I have felt alone." He let out a gusty breath. "To be perfectly honest, the Fortress has abandoned me. Garin always told me the Fortress never abandoned anyone it chose, but I can't say I believe that anymore."

"Oh," was all Isa said. Ever watched her out of the corner of his eye. She stared at her left wrist, turning it over again and again in her lap, tracing out the lines in her skin with her other hand. As she did, Ever suddenly found himself staring at her lips. They looked soft, and he resisted the sudden urge to touch them. Before his thoughts could wander further, however, Isa spoke again.

"Garin seems wise. At least, I always thought so."

"You can hear Garin, too?" Ever froze. Was she that strong already?

But Isa shook her head, a small smile on those soft lips. "No, but I knew him as a child. He and my father were friends. He was always kind to me." She leaned towards him just a bit, a sudden curiosity in her eyes. "The last time I saw him was when he was in town a year ago, before the Fortress went dark. He didn't look as if he'd aged a bit since the day I first met him!" Her voice fell to an excited whisper. "What exactly *is* he?"

Ever chuckled. "Honestly? A mystery. He's been the steward here for as long as I've been alive, and I believe as long as my father was alive as well. In fact, there's no one here who can remember a time before Garin. Believe me, I've asked everyone. He's just as much a part of the Fortress as the walls and the tapestries. It's strange though, just as our power has not been written of much, neither has he. And yet, he seems to have been always there."

"If that's true, he must have some of that... What did you call it? Strength. He must have some of that strength, too, right?"

"Yes and no." Ever picked up a stick and began to idly draw with it in the gravel at his feet. "While he doesn't wield the strength of the Fortress the way the monarchs do, he has a strange resistance to the powers of our dark enemies. It is as if the monarchs were placed here to guard the Fortress and the kingdom, and Garin was placed here to guard the monarchs. He guarded me, at least," Ever added solemnly. "If it hadn't been for Garin, I might have grown up devoid of affections completely."

Isa watched him with curious eyes. It felt empowering to have her look at him without anger or fear.

"So you didn't see your parents often?"

Ever snorted, hearing the questions she was really asking. "My father was rarely around, and when he was, he was either training his troops for battle or preparing me for the life of a soldier. My mother loved parties and balls, and rarely had time for anything else. I went through a series of governesses as a child, largely because I wore most of them out before they had time to acclimate to palace life. Garin and the servants were the ones who watched out for me, and it was only because of them that I knew anyone else had a family that was more closely knit than mine."

"I see." Isa paused for a moment before a small smile grew on her face and a slight blush colored her cheeks. "I doubt you were that hard to love as a child."

"And how would you know that?" Ever let out a laugh.

Her smile widened. "When I would accompany my father here to do business, I would sometimes watch you from afar."

Ever felt like his heart might beat out of his chest, but he swallowed and tried to keep his voice even. "And what did you think?"

Isa gave a little laugh and leaned back, closing her eyes as the sun moved out from behind the clouds. Ever didn't even pretend to look away this time, staring as rudely as it was possible. But she had him truly curious. And her smile was lovely.

"I thought you seemed kind, different from your father. Not that he was unkind," she hastened to say. "But you talked to the servants as if they were real people. I think you even spotted me staring once, while you were out riding."

As she spoke this time, however, her face fell. Guilt and shame flooded him as Ever realized the direction of her thoughts. He wanted to fall on the ground, to beg for her forgiveness, but he couldn't get his feet to move. Instead, he closed his eyes.

"I know my words now can never make up for what I did to you. I won't attempt to excuse my actions either. But," he took a deep breath, "I need you to know that I wasn't the monster you must have thought me for so many years, not even the monster I am now. I was a boy who was struggling, trying to be someone he wasn't."

Isa was silent, and he was terrified to look at her, so he continued in a rush. "The memory of your face has haunted me for years, the way you looked at me when you fell. You changed me that day. You showed me what evil I was capable of if I didn't learn to control my strength. But I couldn't accept it. It was too much to bear to realize that I could be a beast. It was easier to hate you instead."

Finally, he drew his eyes up to meet hers. They were guarded, her lips parting slightly.

"Please," he whispered, "know that I wasn't always as I am today. Know that I am sorrier than I can ever express."

Her eyes stayed wary, and her hands shook a bit as they clutched her skirts tightly. But she uttered the most beautiful words he had ever heard.

"I believe you."

They walked back to the Fortress in silence after that, not even speaking a word when they parted. Too tired to resume his ride, Ever went to the stables and simply sat beside his horse. The day had certainly not turned out the way he had expected. But as much as he hated to admit it, Garin had been right, at least about Isa. It had taken a long time for her to look at, much less speak to him with any level of confidence or warmth. He just hoped it wouldn't take too much longer for her to move beyond mere warmth. His strength was still waning quickly, and there wasn't much time left.

16

CLOSE

*A*s spring drew closer, and Ever's strength did indeed dwindle, Isa's grew visibly by the day. It wasn't long before the rose garden was fairly glowing with its brilliant blooms of not only pink, but also red, yellow, peach, white, violet, and even blue. The snow melted and was not replaced. Even the blue jays returned to nest in the crevices of the Fortress's roof.

Ever might have attributed it to the cycles of nature if it hadn't been that Isa's favorite paths were always the ones to return far before the others. And when he went to escort her to supper one evening, Ever noticed the smell of fresh vanilla in the halls of the northern wing near Isa's room. Nostalgia and panic hit him as he recalled that before the curse, Gigi had always placed sprigs of the plant all over the Fortress. It seemed now that she was at it again.

The dark, wet stones in the walls and floors began to slowly regain their white marble swirls, and dust and dirt no longer covered every surface.

The gradual lifting of the curse was undeniable, however, the day Ever heard a shriek from Isa's room. He did his best to race towards her, alarm pushing him so fast he nearly tripped down the stairs of the tower. He arrived, breathless, to find Isa's door open. Rushing in, he stopped short to see Isa and one of the servant women laughing and embracing, happy tears running down their faces. The servant was the first to spot him, and pulling herself from Isa's embrace, bowed low.

"Your Highness!"

Ever looked in shock from one woman to the other.

"Ever!" Isa's smile was brighter than any he'd seen before. She was glowing. "This is Cerise! She and I were good friends when we were children!" Then, after pulling her friend back into another hug, Isa asked him, "But how can it be? What brought her back?"

It took all of Ever's self-control to attempt an even answer. "Your strength must be growing."

"I have strength?" Isa's face changed to one of amazement. "You mean, the kind that you have?"

"It would seem so," was all Ever could say before turning and storming out of the room. He could see the confusion and hurt in Isa's eyes at his hasty and rather rude departure, but as he walked back down the hall, he could hear the two women laughing and talking again.

Ever knew he should be happy. He had been right about her after all. Isa truly was the key to freeing the Fortress from its curse. But this was all wrong. Her power was supposed to include healing *him*.

He had noticed the servants' shadows growing thicker in the recent weeks, and there were other signs like the return of the birds and the green of the gardens. But as the Fortress was loosed from the darkness that had held it captive and alone, Ever had continued to grow weaker.

He tried to understand what had gone wrong. He had heard Isa talking to the Fortress when she thought he couldn't hear her, which meant she had discovered its presence unaided. The very presence that had abandoned him. It was a presence very few people could sense. To his knowledge, not even Rodrigue had ever been able to feel it as she seemed to now. She already had a strength greater than many of the kings, it appeared, and she wasn't even aware of it. She was healing everyone and everything around her without effort. Everything but him.

For the first time in a long time, Ever wondered if his plan would truly work. Even if he did marry her, would she be able to heal him? The Fortress was indeed preparing her for something great, but it seemed to be excluding him completely. Anger gathered in the pit of Ever's stomach.

The Fortress had betrayed him, and worse, had brought in a stranger to replace him. Even more cruel, the woman it had brought was the one woman in the world he had ever found irresistible. This anger made Ever even more determined to carry out his plan. She would soon be ready to become a keeper of the Fortress. He would marry her, she would heal him, and all would be restored. His duty would go on. It just had to.

Preparing for supper was difficult for Ever that night. Resentment for Isa filled his heart as he shuffled down the hall to escort her to the dining hall. And yet, when Isa answered his knock that night, he felt his breath leave him.

She had always been lovely, but tonight, she looked every part a princess. Her blue eyes sparkled with excitement, and her cheeks were faintly flushed with color. The joy in her smile was dazzling. For the first time, she no longer looked like a stranger in her own body, a terrified doe ready to duck at the first sign of danger. Tonight, she stood as erectly as her ankle would allow her, and she smiled with confidence. It was perhaps the confidence that allowed all the rest to shine. And as much as Ever resented her growing power, he couldn't help but gawk at the young woman who stood before him now.

As she took his arm, out of the corner of his eye, Ever noticed a little pink object on the white vanity behind her. It was the rose stone she'd picked out of his mother's room on that first day. He was surprised she still had it, and a bit curious. That she had taken it in the first place, rather than the jewels, had perplexed him enough. What woman chose a child's gift over luxurious jewelry? But then, to his knowledge, Isa wasn't a typical woman.

He wanted to ask, but for once, Isa didn't stop talking that night. She had endless questions about what had happened with Cerise, and Ever soon found himself at a loss for words, something he wasn't accustomed to. He kept getting lost in his own thoughts as he stared at her. Confusion stirred within him, feelings he couldn't put a name to. Years of nothing but war and his father's ever watchful eye had kept his eyes averted from women, and now it was as if he'd never seen one before. His bitterness and admiration for her, and the guilt for how he was using her, all warred within him.

"You haven't heard a word I've said, have you?" Isa wore a bemused smile.

Ever smiled politely in return. "I apologize. I've had much on my mind today."

"Why are you doing that?" She suddenly leaned forward and rested her chin on her right fist.

"Doing what?"

"Treating me differently, like a lady?"

Because he'd made it very clear in the beginning that she was his servant, a captive in this hell of a prison. Ever paused before answering. It was hard for him to find words for the torrents of emotions and desires that suddenly raged inside of him, and he wasn't sure he really wanted to.

"Isa, I know I wasn't the perfect gentleman when you arrived, far from it." He stood stiffly and went to stare into the night sky through the great window behind her. "I used to think I knew what I was doing at all times. Rules and regulations made sense. You do what you're told and the world moves along rightly. But this," he gestured at the dining hall with a sweep of his arm, "I am not accustomed to this kind of living. I don't have rules to follow, and I don't have words to speak." He turned pleading eyes upon her, begging her silently for forgiveness for a sin she didn't know he was committing even now as he spoke. "I'm trying. I want to be a good man, but sometimes I fear there's not enough grace in the world to make me into who I should truly be."

Isa stared at him silently. How he wanted to know what she was thinking behind those eyes. Would she be able to forgive him if she found out how he was trying to use her?

"I think you are a good man." Her voice was nearly inaudible. "I just think..." Then she shook her head and lowered her eyes to the floor. "I am sorry. It's not my place to judge."

"No, I want to hear." Ever returned to the table.

"I think," Isa said slowly, "that you've just lost your way. I think you've forgotten the simple goodness of this place, the goodness you knew as a child.

Not that I know much of war, but it seems like your father's pursuit of it, if I may say so, was more than a simple desire to protect Destin. Sometimes we can get so caught up in protecting ourselves that we forget to see what's truly before us."

A thoughtful look filled her eyes as she stared into the fireplace. "But the longer I'm in this place, the more I'm convinced the Fortress is more than capable of protecting itself. Instead, I feel as if it is more concerned with my heart than my head."

She smiled at him again, and he couldn't help but wonder if she was right. If only she knew what he had been through. But then, perhaps he didn't want her to. He had given her enough loss without grieving her more. Instead, he asked her to dance.

"Of course." She looked up at him with that sweet innocence that sent his heart pounding in his ears.

Slowly, they shuffled out to the dance floor. Though they'd been going through the motions for months, Ever felt something different tonight as he took Isa's crooked hand in one of his own and her waist in the other. Frustration inside him howled as he realized the hand that held hers looked just as thin and frail beneath the glove as the girl's did. Likewise, the hunch in his back put them eye to eye. Her good hand held his left arm, and if it hadn't been for all his clothes, could have nearly encircled it.

The familiar shame filled him as he recalled how far he'd fallen. Just a year ago, his arm had been solid and four times as large as it was now. Isa was tall for a woman, but he should have stood a good three inches above her. A year ago, he would have been able to protect this beautiful creature from anything that threatened to harm her. Now, she was probably just as capable of protecting herself, if not more.

He wondered if there was any possibility that she could ever see him not as a captor or a king, but as a man. Could she ever respect him? Could she look up to him, trust him to keep her safe? Could she desire him?

Even as they danced, the warmth of her skin radiated through his gloves, and suddenly, the correct posture the dance commanded wasn't close enough. Somewhere in the back of his mind, Ever remembered his tutors' instructions about proper distances between a man and a woman, and it took all his willpower to adhere to them.

As the dance came to an end, however, he realized with panic that she was going to leave him, as she did every night. When the music died, instead of immediately turning back to her chambers, however, Isa seemed to suddenly be struggling as he was.

Though the music still played, Ever stopped moving. Suddenly, his hands were too hot within his gloves. His vanity screamed at him to stop, but he took the glove off anyway. The lack of physical contact with others had never bothered him. Even before the curse, Ever had rarely made physical contact with other humans, aside from combat practice. But now, with a will of their own, his thin, gnarled fingers brushed her cheek, then her nose, then her lips. It was like touching a sunbeam. Her breathing hitched, but she stood as though in a trance. Could she truly be entranced by him?

"Why did you choose my mother's stone?" he whispered.

"What?" She blinked a few times.

"When I took you to my mother's room. Why didn't you choose jewels or gold instead?"

"Yours was a gift of love," she said, her eyes sparkling in the light of the moon. "I wanted to hope that there was love within you still..." Her fingers trembled slightly as she placed them over his heart.

Without thinking, he leaned forward.

Her breath was uneven as their faces touched. She lifted her chin just a little, and for a moment, his lips rested on hers.

Then, slowly, Isa pulled away. Her eyes pierced his, full of fear. Bit by bit, her fingers loosed themselves from his own, and before he knew it, she had fallen back a step. Then two. Then, without a word, she was gone.

As Ever walked back to the Tower of Annals, guilt crashed over him, like the never-ending waves on a beach. Here he was, falling in love with her, and yet, as Garin had pointed out, he was pushing her towards a cliff from which there was no return. She clearly wasn't ready for him. But he was dying. He would have to continue with the plan.

Despite his determination to carry out his schemes, Ever was haunted that night by midnight blue eyes. Large and frightened, they watched him as they had for all his life. And in his sleep, Ever couldn't help but weep.

17

IRONCLAD DREAMS

"*Y*ou seem unhappy."

Isa jumped a little as the prince lowered himself onto the stone bench beside her. Usually, she heard his approach by the dragging of his feet, but she had been distracted this morning. She twirled the rose in her hands again, wondering how much the prince would really like to hear what was on her mind.

Not that he had been unkind to her as of late. In fact, in the week following their near kiss, he'd been more chivalrous than ever. He had asked her constantly if she was in need of any new clothing or amusements, and had even changed Cerise's work assignment to Isa's room so that they could be near one another. On one night, he had even had the servants light the rose garden with hundreds of candles so that she could walk the green maze in the night. Everything had been done from a distance. His offers were courteous, but respectful, often sent through Cerise instead of being given face-to-face. Still, she had found herself avoiding him. She could see the hurt in his eyes when she immediately returned to her chambers after the dance every night. But she really was at a loss for what to do.

It wasn't that she hadn't wanted him to kiss her. Every muscle in her body had wanted nothing more than to meet his lips on the balcony that night. That her feelings could change so quickly was frightening, however. Everard Fortier had gone from being the evil prince who had ruined her life thrice, to a sweet companion whose company she found herself craving increasingly. What would her family say?

It was this sentiment that had brought her outside to the rose garden so early. She couldn't bring herself to dance, but being outside made her feel a bit closer to home, now that the days were warmer and the sun shined more often.

If she closed her eyes and focused on the warmth of the sunbeams, she could sometimes pretend she was back in her parents' garden, sitting on the little stone wall behind the house. She could almost hear her mother's tools scraping in the garden dirt, and Megane running around after the chickens. She wished so much that she could ask her mother for advice. Was this right? Were her feelings leading her down a trustworthy path? Isa imagined her mother's responses, sometimes for and sometimes against, but she shied away from imagining what her father or Launce might say.

"Well…" Ever's voice brought her back to the present. He'd dropped his eyes to the ground and had begun to stand again. "I suppose if you–"

"No, I'm sorry." Isa grabbed his arm and tugged him back down. "I don't mean to be rude. I was just thinking about my family." She sighed as he settled in and looked at her expectantly. His eyes were serious, standing out from his haggard face even more than usual in the early spring sunlight that filtered through the clouds. She half expected him to scoff or get angry, but instead, he simply nodded, so she continued.

"I just wish I could tell them that I'm safe. But even more than that," she paused shyly before finishing in a whisper, "that I'm happy."

The prince stared at her for a moment before the apprehension melted from his face, and he was suddenly left beaming. The expression looked a bit strange in the gaunt, ashen face, but it wasn't unpleasant either. Isa decided that she rather liked it.

"I think that can be arranged. Is there a token, something you could send with a letter so that they would know it was from you? I'm afraid your father will trust little that I send."

Isa laughed and nodded. "I'll send this rose." Touching its petals, she added, "It's just about to bloom."

Ever stood up again, still smiling. "I will send Garin since your father knows him. Perhaps he will believe the words of an old friend."

"Is he human again?" Isa suddenly sat on the edge of her seat, thrilled with the idea of seeing another familiar face. More servants had been turning every day, but they were mostly the ones tending to her.

Ever gave her an even bigger grin, suddenly looking a bit boyish. "I woke up this morning to find him hovering over my pallet like a mother pheasant. Although," he paused, "I'm not entirely sure he was ever human to begin with."

The joy in Ever's voice was infectious, and Isa found herself suddenly feeling lighthearted. Perhaps she would dance this morning after all.

Her good mood lasted throughout the remainder of the day and into the evening. Supper was more animated than usual as well, as Ever kept her laughing with stories from when he was a small boy. Even dancing was less awkward. He didn't try to kiss her again, and Isa nearly allowed herself to enjoy the warmth of his arms.

When she lay down in bed that evening, as the servants scurried around to prepare her bedchamber for the chill of the night, Isa imagined how her family would react to Garin's message. Her mother would cry, and Megane would snatch the rose up to dry and save it. Launce would let out a few insolent remarks to the Fortress steward, and Ansel, even more. But even with all the carrying on, Isa knew the rose would mean hope for them where there had been none before.

As the servants finished their tasks, and Isa began to drift off, she heard thunder in the distance. It grew closer as her eyelids grew heavy.

"Pardon me."

Startled, Isa's eyes flew open and she tried to sit up, searching in the darkness. Her fire was out and her room had grown cold, which was strange. The servants never let her fire go out.

"Cerise?" she called out nervously. But Cerise didn't answer.

Instead, the strange woman's voice sounded again in the night. Slowly, a face began to appear before her, then a body. Isa shrank back as the woman's muscles were made visible by the increasing lightning outside her window.

"Isabelle?" Her voice was low and smooth.

Isa leapt from her bed and threw herself against the door, pulling with all of her might at the handle. But it was locked.

The woman held up her hands. "I promise I didn't come here to hurt you. I came to talk."

"Talk?" Isa's voice sounded too high.

"I know who you are, Isabelle."

Isa froze, her back pressed against the door.

"I also know that the prince has wronged you in more way than one." The woman leaned forward, her silhouette lighting up in the night. She was sitting backwards on Isa's vanity chair that had somehow been moved over in front of the fireplace, which, to Isa's surprise, was suddenly glowing with embers. Isa tried to move her leg closer to the edge of the bed again. It felt stuck. Isa gasped as she looked down to see that she was now sitting in a chair as well. Her arms and legs were bound to her seat. Isa yanked, but the rope didn't give an inch.

"I'm sorry for the inconvenience," the woman said, waving her hand at Isa. "I knew you would run before I had the chance to explain myself. The least you can do is listen to me, woman to woman. Then I will be gone, I promise."

As her eyes adjusted, Isa could see that the woman was very handsome, but she immediately sensed that this woman was also very, very dangerous. Her slick black hair was pulled back tightly into a knot, and her dress was slit up both sides so that long legs wrapped in men's trousers could stick out. Her unladylike position on the chair and the muscles that ran up and down her bared arms made Isa feel even more powerless. The woman's green eyes were bright, and would have been beautiful if they hadn't been so threatening. It was only then that Isa realized the light that filled the room was coming more from those eyes than the fire's embers. They were filled with rings of golden flame.

Isa sat, petrified. Who was this terrifying creature, and where had they brought her? For she surely wasn't in her room any longer. She tried to open her mouth to scream for Ever, Garin, the servants, anyone who would hear her, but nothing came out.

"See now? This is why I had to bind you." The woman shook her head. "Since you obviously can't escape, and no one has heard you, you might as well listen to what I have to say."

Isa considered this for a moment before ceasing to struggle against her ropes. The woman had a point. Isa was going nowhere fast. She had no choice but to listen. Maybe after the woman spoke, she would simply leave, and Isa would be returned to the Fortress somehow.

"I have been watching your dreams," the woman began.

Isa wondered how that was even possible.

"You were wise when you first arrived here, back when you hated him, feared him with everything in you." She gave Isa a coy smile and wagged her finger. "But just as all women are with him, you were drawn in. Oh yes," she gave Isa a wry smile, "I know the draw. More than most women, actually."

Despite her current situation, Isa frowned. What did that mean?

But the woman continued. "He is a fine specimen of a man. Or was, at least. The draw was even stronger before he wasted away so. You should have seen him in his prime!" She looked almost… sad, Isa thought. "But no matter what he says or does," the woman continued in a harder voice, "you will always be his captive."

Isa frowned, unsure of why this strange woman was telling her all this. While she couldn't deny that his early days had indeed been terrible, it seemed unfair to allow the man she knew now to be spoken about as such. "He's changing," she squeaked, her voice nervous and her throat dry. "He's a different person than he was then."

"He's stopped insulting you, so now you think it's love?" All traces of her smile were gone from woman's face, and the golden fire of her eyes bored into Isa. "I was hoping you would be wise enough to see through him as you did at first, but obviously you're as foolish as the rest of them."

Taking Isa's chin firmly in her hand, the woman jerked her face up so Isa had to look her in the eyes. "He is using you, Isabelle. A man like that cannot love. For power he sold his soul, and you along with it."

Isa wanted to cover her ears and hide, but the woman continued to speak, and Isa continued to hear.

"The prince wants to use your power for his own ends, to heal his own self." She let go of Isa's chin and sat back in her chair again, her eyes suddenly brilliant. "But the end he's conceived for you does not have to come true!"

"What are you saying?"

"I am offering to let you join me. You will be no one's captive, and your power will be sung of for generations to come! If you allow me, I can help you reach heights of glory you never dreamed of! Together," she leaned forward and laid her hand on Isa's wrist, "we could heal you, erase the scars that he inflicted upon you! There would be no limit to what we could do."

For a moment, her words painted a picture in Isa's mind. Release from the agonizingly slow gait, and being recognized as more than just the cripple. What would it feel like, Isa wondered, to go wherever she wanted? Could she truly make her own destiny? A part of her yearned for that, for the freedom to go where she wanted and to do as she wished. No rules, no restrictions, no one to tell her she was incapable.

It was then that Isa noticed the thin young man standing behind the woman. Ashen and glassy-eyed, he watched Isa numbly. Isa felt her mouth drop in horror at the sight of the familiar face.

"What's your decision?" The woman's voice snapped her attention back to their conversation.

"My decision?"

"Be my ally!" The woman's eyes were bright and fierce. "Together, we can take him down! You can have your revenge after all these years! You and I could rule this land together! Make it what we wish!"

"But I don't want revenge," Isa whispered. And as the words left her lips, Isa realized in her heart, that she had forgiven him. When had that happened?

As Isa was wondering over this sudden revelation, the woman's eyes went flat, and the golden flames roared. "Then you have made your choice." Abruptly, she stood, and she and the sickly young man began to retreat into the darkness.

It felt like only seconds had passed after they left, when the room suddenly began to move from uncomfortably warm to scorching. Sweat dripped down Isa's temples. When she blinked again, she was back in her room, but her return brought little relief, as the room was now ablaze with the golden tongues of fire that had been dancing in the woman's eyes. Tied to a chair once more, Isa screamed until her throat ached.

The flames grew higher, and the smoke made it harder to breathe by the second. Gasping, Isa tried to stand so she could pull herself to the door, but all she succeeded in doing was tipping her chair over so her face was even closer to the blaze. She cried out in anguish as the flames began to lick her body. Spots began to fill her vision. Just as she was about to give in and let the blistering room take her, however, a faint voice called her name.

She was too weak to respond. Agony filled Isa as she realized that she was about to die in the inferno alone. And yet, the voice called again, slightly louder this time. And it didn't stop. Something cool touched her hand. Then her head.

Slowly, Isa began to realize that the voice that called to her was actually singing. It was Ever's voice, and the words he used were in the ancient tongue he had serenaded her with in the Tower of Annals. Little by little, the flames were quenched, and the cool of the night began to touch her burned, charred body.

It seemed like years, but eventually, she was able to open her eyes, and to her surprise, she was still in her room. There was no fire. Not even a single candle burned. Only the moon drenched the room in its blue light. Anxious faces were everywhere. A female servant changed the cool cloth on her forehead.

What surprised her most, though, was Ever. His eyes were closed and his face was strained. His whole body shook as he still continued to sing, blue light encircling their clasped hands.

Isa stared at it in wonder. She tried to find her voice, and only after a full minute of trying could she croak out his name.

"She's awake!" Gigi, the kitchen mistress, cried. The other servants surrounding her seemed to let out their breath all at the same time. Finally, Ever opened his eyes and stopped singing. He continued to grip her hand, however.

"What happened?" she asked faintly.

Ever took a deep, slow breath, as though it was difficult to even speak. "It appears our enemy has noticed your growing strength. Unfortunately, with strength comes a greater sensitivity to the darkness she harnesses."

"I don't know what that means."

"It means you had a night terror. Nevina must have returned from gathering men and taken notice of you."

"She spoke to me." Isa tried to swallow, recalling the woman's cruel words.

"Yes, she sometimes does that."

"Have you had one of these dreams before?"

Ever nodded grimly. "My sensitivity to the presence of the Tumenian power began when I was seven."

Isa tried to imagine young Ever with the type of night terror she had just experienced, but that a child should suffer so was too horrible to dwell on.

Ever finally let go of her hand and leaned back in his chair. "Garin had to stay outside my door every night for a whole year while I learned to manage the dreams."

"Do you still have them?" Isa was nearly too afraid to ask. She never wanted to experience that again.

"I do, but they no longer disorient me so. They remind me instead of what I am protecting my people from." In the moonlight, a strange look crossed the prince's face as he suddenly studied Isa with a critical eye. "What did she tell you?"

The question caught Isa off guard. While the woman who had tried to kill her seemed anything but trustworthy, Isa suddenly wondered about her warning that Ever was using her. Could any of it be true?

"She told me lots of things," she said cautiously. "But it was more *whom* I saw that frightened me." Ever looked at her expectantly, so she continued. "There was a young man standing behind her. He didn't speak, but he held her weapons. His skin was pale, and he looked as though he might be starving.

"I knew him as a child," she sighed. "He was born with a bad lung. His parents fell into poverty as they searched far and wide for healing, but no herbalist or healer could help him. I haven't seen him since–I haven't seen him for years," she quickly amended, realizing she'd nearly told Ever of the Care-givers. While the prince had certainly changed since she'd come to the Fortress, Isa wasn't sure she wanted to tell him about how her young friend's parents had sent him off in hopes of a better life in Tumen. She doubted he would understand the desperation of the sick and their families that had led them to make such a decision.

As if to confirm her concerns, Ever was already shaking his head. "He's a Chien."

"A Chien?"

Ever nodded, a look of disgust on his face. "It's the soldiers' term for Destinian traitors. They are servants in the Tumenian royal court, well-to-do homes, and on the battle lines, although the term slave might be more accurate. Anyhow, they leave Destin, thinking our northern neighbor, Nevina's father, will welcome them into the arms of grace for a long and happy life."

Isa felt her heart falter for a moment. The young man had not looked happy or healthy. "What do they do with them?" she asked unevenly.

"They cut their tongues out to ensure their silence and complete dependence. When they are thoroughly beaten in both body and spirit, they are given away to nobles and royalty, sometimes even influential commoners as free labor." Ever shook his head. "They often accompany their benefactors to royal gatherings." Under his breath he added, "Their just reward for leaving."

At this, Isa's face grew hot, and her resolution to keep quiet about the people's Tumenian salvation dissolved. "Well, thanks to you, I was nearly one of them!"

Ever stared at her, but Isa didn't stop.

"Do you think those people leave because they want to? While your father was cutting off all supply to the churches for the sick and the lame, the Caregivers began telling people they could come with them, that they would hide them in their supply carts and bring them to a place where they would receive food and clothing. It was a new start, they promised, one that would allow the unfortunate to begin new lives, to find work and make a living for themselves."

"What stopped you?" The prince frowned unhappily.

Exhausted from the dream and the outburst, she leaned back into her pillows. "Our neighbors urged my father to send me for years. I might find a husband there, they argued, one who didn't mind a damaged wife. He outright refused though." Isa fixed him with her most dangerous glare. "Until he met you."

A long silence stretched out between them. The servants had slowed their frantic pace by now, but Gigi gently laid another compress on her forehead. "You mustn't push yourself too hard," she murmured, giving Ever a very pointed look at the door.

He missed it or ignored it, however, and spoke instead, a fierce look on his face. "How did you know how to find these Caregivers?"

"They always wear black metal rings."

At this, the fire in the prince's eyes leapt. "Another misstep," he murmured, his voice nearly inaudible.

"What?"

"My family," he said slowly, rubbing his eyes with both hands, "has long valued strength above all else. In earnest, we've sought to protect this kingdom as well as we can. But it seems that in so emphasizing the strong, we've forgotten the weak. And now our enemies are in the heart of the kingdom being welcomed, even sheltered, thanks to our negligence."

The sky was beginning to lighten as he stood up and turned to go. "Perhaps the Fortress is right to strip me of my power."

Though the servants filed out after him, leaving her alone to rest, Isa could not sleep for a long time. The fear that the dreams would return mingled with what Ever had said.

Whether the woman from her dream believed it or not, Ever *was* changing. Anxiety still lingered when Isa thought of the woman's words, but the touch of his hands, the way he had trembled while he'd worked to bring her out of the dream was a comfort. No. The woman could not know everything as she pretended.

As Isa considered these things, Gigi walked back into Isa's room and gently pushed her back into a sleeping position. "You don't need to be afraid, my dear. Ever will guard your dreams until Garin gets back. My guess is that she chose tonight because Garin had to stay in town for the storm. You are safe now, though."

Gigi seemed ready to move into the next room after that, but something in Isa's expression must have changed her mind. Instead, she sat on the edge of the bed and drew Isa into a warm, soft embrace. Isa could have stayed in that hug forever. It was like feeling her mother's arms around her once again.

Isa must have been more tired than she knew, however, for soon Gigi was gently laying her back into the pillows, where she drifted into directionless, unmemorable dreams.

NEEDED

*E*ver couldn't remember a worse night since the curse had fallen. Drawing Isa from the dream had taken more power from him than he'd expected. And he had nearly been too late.

After Garin had left for Soudain with the message for Isa's family, everything had gone on as usual. Supper had been enjoyable, and Isa had even seemed to enjoy dancing with him. When they had parted ways, the air had smelled of rain. Ever had looked forward to the sound of a thunderstorm lulling him to sleep. He'd also hoped Nevina's men would get a good drenching as they continued to wait at the foot of the mountain. The witch might be strong, but she had no power over the weather.

But the feeling of peace hadn't lasted long. He'd felt it before the servants had run to him, the princess's return to the valley jolting him from his sleep. Her heavy, stifling aggression had wafted into his dreams just moments before Cerise, Isa's childhood friend, had come pounding on the tower door.

"Your Highness! Gigi says you must come to Isa's chambers! She says it's a night terror!"

Ever had leapt off his pallet so quickly that he had nearly tripped and fallen on the floor. His sore bones and stiff muscles protested as he moved, but he hardly noticed them. Staggering down the tower steps and through the great halls as quickly as he could, he had begged the Fortress to protect her.

And he was furious with himself for not foreseeing this. She must have returned earlier, but waited until she knew Garin was gone. Soudain was a decently large city, but word spread fast. Any spies Nevina had planted there would have reported quickly that Garin was in town, away from the Fortress.

Garin had always made Nevina nervous, so she would have seen his absence as a golden opportunity. She must have suspected that with only the prince guarding the Fortress's inhabitants, it would be easy to slip past him. Garin would have at least made her intrusion a challenge. But with Ever, the only challenge had been, it seemed, to wait until he slept.

As he had run, Ever had imagined all of the horrible things the princess could be doing to Isa, and a cold, steely fear had gripped his heart. With it, however, a searing hatred bubbled up as well. He had been caught unaware the last time Nevina had attacked. But not this time. This time, he would do whatever it took to chase the dark princess from his home.

Isa had been unresponsive to his initial attempts to draw her from the nightmare. He'd cursed Nevina as he struggled to keep Isa from falling completely into her grasp. Isa's face had been ghostly, and sweat sheened her skin. As her breathing had faltered, Ever had desperately poured even more strength into drawing the poison from her mind. For a moment, it felt as if he was losing his father again. *But no*, a part of his mind had whispered to him. *This would be far worse.*

Hours had passed as he'd gripped her soft, crooked hand in his own bent claws. The servants had watched in panic. Nothing like this had happened in the Fortress since he was a small child, and even then, few had ever been privy to those awful episodes, spare Garin, Gigi, and the few servants who had assisted them. Not even his parents had known about the horrible nights he had passed, screaming as the darkness had tried time and time again to poison his mind. And this time, Nevina had done it to Isa.

Now that it was all over, Ever felt more drained than he'd ever been in his life, and yet, he couldn't sleep. The new knowledge that Nevina was handing out weapons of her power to these strange Caregivers in Soudain disturbed him. How long had the Tumenians been infiltrating the capital and wearing weapons of dark magic?

King Rodrigue had once suggested that he and Ever create similar weapons for their own men, talismans to hold a bit of the monarchs' strength. Ever had pleaded with him not to, however. Such power wasn't meant for just anyone, only those the Fortress had chosen, he had insisted. Ever had been grateful when his father listened to him, but apparently, the idea was not original to Rodrigue. Who knew how many men Nevina now had in Soudain, armed with her twisted rings?

Ever hobbled over to the great wardrobe in the center of the room, just beside the hearth. A weak shine spilled out from the wardrobe as he removed the ring from its case. Sitting, he turned it over again and again in his hands.

If he had removed this ring from its case ten years before, it would have lit the whole tower in its brilliance the moment he'd touched it. Even a year ago, the ring had still shined for him when they had taken it from the Louise's finger and given it to him for safekeeping. Now its shine was little more than a reflection from the sun that was just beginning to rise. As he held the ring, his shame warred with desperation as it never had before.

Ever finally fell into a restless sleep with the ring still clasped in his hand.

When he awakened, it was nearly noon, and he could see Isa venturing out to the rose garden. He had a sudden urge to go to her. Without thinking about what he was doing, he put the ring away and made his way down to the girl.

She was already dancing by the time he arrived. He stood at the edge of the walk so as not to startle her. When she finally stopped, he could see that her cheeks were flushed with the effort, and dark circles hung beneath her eyes. She wore an expression of deep concentration as she danced today. When she heard him approach, however, she stopped and dipped into a quick curtsy.

"Do you mind if I watch?" Ever gestured to the stone bench nearby.

She gave him a wry smile. "My guess is that you *have* been watching, otherwise you wouldn't have known where to find me."

Ever smiled and conceded it was thus. He was impressed as she resumed her movements. Compared to the first time he'd seen her dance, her legs seemed to have grown noticeably stronger, and she was more confident in her lunges and turns. Even beneath her look of intense focus, a tranquil smile lit her lips as she moved. Sometimes, she would close her eyes briefly as she slowed, as if being blind would make a movement just right.

"Where did you learn?" he asked when she was finished.

A bit breathless, Isa sat down beside him. "I started dancing when I was very small. Too young, really. I would go to the smaller square when I was four, and I would watch the Soudain dancers practice. I would mimic them, too. Madame Nicolette saw me once, and decided that I had some talent."

"I remember her," Ever said. "She brought her students to the Fortress to perform at celebrations. I remember hearing that they performed at official city events as well."

Isa nodded. "She took me under her wing, and I became her special pupil as I grew older." Isa's eyes took a far-off look. "I'm not sure if I was really as good as she claimed, or if it was simply all the extra instruction, but by the time I was eight, there was talk that I would—" She stopped suddenly and shook her head at the ground. "It doesn't matter now. That was a long time ago."

The wistfulness in her voice made Ever suddenly uncomfortable. Still, for some morbid reason, he wanted to know. "Please tell me."

After a moment, Isa spoke slowly. "There was talk that I would be her lead dancer by the time I was twelve."

Ever sat quietly as the weight of his foolish boyhood temper threatened to drown him. In addition to all the other things he had taken from her, this future had been stolen as well. As always, there was one more sin, one more piece of her life that he had stolen in his youthful foolishness and never sought to repair.

"I am sorry," was all he could say. He didn't dare to look into her eyes.

"I think that's why I was so angry for so many years." When she spoke, however, Isa's voice wasn't tearful as he'd feared it might be, or testy as she deserved to be, but thoughtful instead. "I felt like I'd been robbed of my purpose, like I had no other reason to survive, other than not to be a burden to my family. I needed to be needed."

An odd wave of boldness struck Ever, and he reached up and gently cupped her face in his hand, turning it so that she had to look into his eyes. "You're needed here." As he touched her, a foreign energy rippled through him. Even more enthralling was that she simply gazed back at him, and to his delight, she didn't pull away.

"Why?" she breathed. "Why do you need me?"

"In truth, I'm not sure why the Fortress chose you," he admitted, still holding her face. "But the Fortress doesn't choose people by accident. What I do know is that we needed a light in the darkness of this curse, a beacon to follow in the night. You have been, and will continue to be that light."

He let go of her chin, but ran his fingers lightly across her jawbone, and to his surprise, she smiled hesitantly. Gingerly, with a great deal of reluctance, he pulled his hand back before it decided to touch her again on its own accord. "Do you feel like you're needed now?" he asked breathlessly.

She studied him for what felt like a long time before answering. "I'm beginning to."

An idea hit him, and with it, a pang of guilt, but he acted upon it anyway. "Come with me. I need to show you something."

19

MAKE IT RIGHT

*B*ack in the Tower of Annals, he went to the wardrobe for the second time that day and opened up the case. "This is the Queen's Ring. Every queen has worn this since the Fortress was created."

"It's lovely," Isa whispered, staring wide-eyed at the silver ring. At its center, a flat, round blue crystal was surrounded by smaller white crystals peeking out from silver vines that weaved in and out of one another. Still holding the ring, Ever led her over to the full-length oval mirror that stood near one of the window walls. Gently, he pressed the ring into her right palm.

"Now," he pointed to the mirror, "look."

Isa gasped as she gazed into the glass. Her eyes flamed bright blue, and the ring threw bright streaks of its own light across the room as soon as she touched it.

"What's happening?" she murmured.

"Your power has been maturing since you arrived. You just weren't ready to see it. Until now." Taking her by the shoulders, he pulled her away from the mirror to face him. "You are stronger than you think, Isabelle."

"But... I don't know what to do with it, or even how it works!" she protested, still looking at the mirror.

"I can teach you!" he insisted, hoping to quell her fears before she thought too long about them. "And the Fortress will give you what you need! Your power is still young, but you cannot deny that you've brought the Fortress back to life!"

Isa frowned a bit. "You're still not healed. And neither are the soldiers."

Ever wished briefly that he hadn't told her about the stone army that still stood on the back lawn. "You will be capable of even more very soon. Trust me." The words tasted sour as he spoke them.

Isa stared at the ring for a long time. As she did, Ever couldn't help noticing the fine lines of her jaw, and the way she quirked one eyebrow up as she thought. How had he not seen her beauty for what it was when she'd arrived on that first day?

"Tell me about Nevina." She turned to Ever. Suspicion suddenly filled her eyes. "Why does she hate you so?"

Ever walked over to the window and pulled his hands up behind his back for lack of something better to do with them. Even now, a soldier's stance was more comfortable than any other standing or sitting position he knew. "Princess Nevina and I are not so different," he whispered, wishing with all of his heart that it weren't the truth. How much more had he grown to be like her since his father had died?

"In what way?"

"We were the only children in our circles that were born with powers. What made us different was the purpose and use of our power. The Fortress's power was always meant to protect and defend, while the Tumenian strength was made to steal. The irony of it is," Ever frowned, "that if it hadn't been for Garin and Gigi, I most likely would have grown up just like her."

"She resents you for your bloodline?"

"Clandestine feuds play a part in it, yes, but her resentment runs deeper. Even as a child, she played games, stealing into my dreams and toying with my mind. Over the years, I outgrew it. Outgrew her. But as different as we were, and whether or not we liked it, we shared our outcast position."

"Outcast?" Isa stared at him as though he'd lost his mind. A smug part of his mind wondered if she looked... jealous? "How could the future king of Destin be an outcast?"

"Power is a guarantor of much, including loneliness." Ever gave her a hard smile. "It's hard to make friends when all of the other children are terrified of you. She flaunted her power, and I tried to hide mine, but in the end, it mattered little. We were always in a world apart from everyone else." He paused, then added quietly, "I suppose she thought we would one day find enough common ground to overlook our differences."

"She wanted to marry you?" Isa stood straighter, and Ever couldn't help the little smile that escaped him.

"She came to my betrothal ball, but only too late did I realize she had chosen to take one of two paths. Either I would marry her and give her the queenship her baby brother had robbed her of, or she would take my kingdom and accept the crown herself." He sighed and rubbed the blue crystal as it sat in his hands. "Unfortunately, this curse gave her the chance to do what she couldn't have even dreamed of attempting two years ago."

"So why hasn't she taken it yet?" Isa straightened her shoulders. "I do not mean to be rude, but she seems to have attacked again and again without accomplishing much, despite the Fortress's compromised state. What is stopping her?"

For most of his life, Ever would have answered that the Fortress was keeping her out, but now he simply couldn't. Instead, he gave her a wry smile. "I am not completely without use as of yet." He spread his arms, and Isa let out a small chuckle. "And then there's Garin. Then there's you." By this time, however, all amusement was gone. Ever limped back to Isa and took her hands, placing the ring against her palm once more. Again, the brilliant blue filled the room.

"Me?"

"You have a power Nevina has coveted all of her life," Ever said, drawing her closer until he could feel her breath. "You are kind and good," he lifted her chin, "and the sweetness of your heart makes you more beautiful than she can ever hope to be."

Though his intentions were muddled enough, Ever meant every word. Isa was everything Nevina was not. Everything he was not.

To his surprise, Isa gently pulled his hand from her face and held it. For a long moment, she stared at the black glove. Then, without a word, she slowly removed it. Ever wanted to stop her. She shouldn't have to see him like this. It was bad enough that his back had hunched and his knees were stiff and sore. His face looked as though he hadn't eaten or seen the sun for weeks. But as her fingers brushed his, he closed his eyes. The last time he'd held a human hand had been the night his father died.

"So many scars," she murmured as she turned his hand over in her own.

"Many battles," was all he could say through gritted teeth.

"But I thought you had the Fortress's strength back when you fought them."

"Just because one wields power does not mean he cannot be hurt." Ever kept his eyes closed as she continued to hold his hand. Her touch, as gentle as it was, filled him with a desire that burned.

"Is that why she attacked me?" Isa's voice was barely above a whisper. "Because she wants to kill me before I am strong?"

"She attacked you because she knows that you are strong now. And the stronger you grow, the more you can hurt her." He opened his eyes to see her large blue ones staring back at him. "You know, with the help of this ring, you could stop her if you chose to."

"I really don't think I could."

"Isabelle," Ever said, "if you believe nothing else, then believe this. You have a strength within you that even past kings of the Fortress could never dream of."

With that, he withdrew his hand and took the ring to put it back in the wardrobe, but it nearly killed him to do so. Isa watched him with that suspicious frown as he turned back to her, but he ignored the look, taking her by the hand and leading her to the door. "I will see you tonight. We still have much to discuss, but you need to rest first. Last night was a long one."

She gave him a funny look.

"What is it?"

She hesitated and her face turned bright red as she stared at the floor. If Ever hadn't been curious before, he was most definitely so now. He took her hands in his, once again basking in her warmth on the hand without the glove. "What is it?" he asked again, softly this time.

"When she was speaking to me in the dream," Isa began hesitantly, "she said that you had captured the hearts of many?"

Understanding made him nearly giddy with relief. This, he could answer honestly. "The title itself has brought countless women who could care less about who I am or what I look like. I promise you though, that none have ever turned my head..." he took a deep breath. "Before now."

At this, she broke into a glorious smile before turning once more and beginning her descent.

As she left, she passed Garin on his way up. "Sire." He gave Ever a long, dissatisfied look up and down. "You should be resting."

"I take it, then, that you've heard."

"The servants can speak of nothing else." Garin frowned as he followed Ever back into the tower and set down the silver tray he'd brought up with him. He poured a glass of something that smelled like nectar tea and handed it to Ever. "I thought Nevina might try something while I was gone, but I didn't think she would be so bold. However," he glanced back toward the door, "I see that the night's events haven't frightened young Isa off completely."

"She is ready, Garin." Ever had taken the ring out again, unable to keep it locked away this morning, it seemed, and was turning the silver band over in his hands once more.

Garin frowned again, even more deeply this time, the thin lines on his forehead wrinkling in disapproval. "If that is so, then why do you look so guilty?" When Ever didn't answer, his expression softened a bit. "You love her, don't you?"

Ever still couldn't answer. His mentor, however, was too familiar with his ways to be fooled.

"You know you could heal her now."

"I would if I could!" Ever threw his hands up in frustration. "But if I used that kind of power now, my flame would be extinguished." He shook his head and walked over to the window wall to stare at the great valley below. "If we wed soon, we can defeat Nevina and move on." Ever sighed, suddenly feeling like all of the air had left his lungs. "I'll pay her back one day. I will make it right. One day, she'll understand..." His voice trailed off. He wasn't even convincing himself, let alone the steward.

"Or," Garin said, "she will be unprepared and vulnerable, and she won't be able to heal you even after you wed. You will die, and she'll be left to challenge a powerful enemy, and to rule a cursed castle without a guide or companion." He shook his head. "What kind of life is that for the woman you love?"

"What choice do I have?" Ever exploded. He dropped into a chair and buried his head in his hands. "Either way I die. Either way, I lose her."

Garin's voice was kinder this time. "Ever, has it crossed your mind that perhaps the Fortress hasn't done all of this simply to spite you? That perhaps, there is a lesson to be learned?"

Ever looked at him miserably, so Garin continued. "If she was truly ready, she wouldn't have trembled so as she ran down those steps just now. Gigi says we nearly lost her last night."

Ever didn't answer.

"Just as you weren't ready to face Nevina when you were seven, I'm telling you, Isa is not ready now. Trust the Fortress! You weren't born with your strength by accident, and she wasn't brought here by chance. There's a purpose in all of this, I promise! The Fortress never forsakes its chosen! The fact that it brought Isa to you should be proof enough for that."

But Ever shook his head. "Unfortunately, as much as I would like to, last night made one thing very clear."

"And what is that?"

"The Fortress no longer cares what befalls us even within its own walls–"

"Everard!"

But Ever just walked away. He would have to do this on his own.

20

THE BEST LAID PLANS

*A*s soon as she returned to her chambers, Gigi fussed at Isa until she agreed to lie down and rest before supper. But it was hard to sleep. The memory of last night's terror still lingered fresh in her mind. Even stronger than the memory of the terror, though, was the foreign excitement and trepidation she felt in her body and soul every time she thought of the prince. Somewhere within her, she still felt unsure about the raw honesty of their conversation about Nevina, but her misgivings couldn't compare with the way she had felt when he'd placed the ring on her finger, or the way he had looked at her when she'd opened her eyes from the dream. Her doubts could not break her hope.

How odd to think that just at the end of last summer, she had been abandoned and directionless. Now, at the dawn of this spring, she had both a purpose and, she hoped, someone who cared as much about her as much as she did him. The way he had looked at her that morning had sent shivers across her shoulders. The fervor of his protection through her terrors, and how he somehow believed in her even when she couldn't believe in herself, were all pieces of a dream she could never have imagined. And in the rose garden, when he had touched her face so softly, a strange desire within her had awakened, one that filled her with a kind of longing she hadn't felt for anyone before, not even Raoul. So for Gigi's sake, she pretended to sleep, but really, all Isa could do was think of Ever.

Her act of sleeping must have looked real enough, because the servants began to speak to one another in the next room over. Not quite ready to get up yet, she lay there quietly, and Isa soon found herself drawn into their conversation.

"Do you think it is true? That the prince will propose tonight?" The younger servant's voice was full of excitement and intrigue.

"Gigi says we must not talk about such things. It's not our place." Cerise's voice was less enthusiastic. She lowered it to add, "I will admit though, that I am worried. I don't think she's ready. I just wish he would give her more time."

"But he doesn't have time!" the younger one argued. "His fire burns duller with each day! At least, that's what Solomon says."

"Then I'm afraid he might be too late." Cerise paused. "Perhaps Prince Everard was never meant to be king. Perhaps he was meant to prepare the way for her. At least…" She paused. "At least, if we must lose him, we would have someone to follow in his place." There was sadness in Cerise's voice. She spoke so softly now that Isa had to strain to hear, the deafening beat of her heart making it nearly impossible to listen in.

"But the curse demands that she heal him, or the rest of its requirements will never be fulfilled!"

Isa's mouth fell open in horror. The curse *demanded*? Ever had never told her the curse had specific demands! She began to panic. How was she supposed to heal him, especially if he was as close to death now as they made it sound?

The younger servant spoke again, this time in a comforting voice. "Perhaps she is ready. Every time she's on the crystal floor it shines more brightly. And she's brought back most of the Fortress! She brought us back!"

"I think that no matter what we say or do or think, he will be proposing soon. That was his plan from the start, so we'd better be ready." Cerise's voice was cross. "I also think we should be done talking of this now."

As their conversation turned in a different direction, Isa lay in a miserable daze, wishing that this was a nightmare Ever or Garin could wake her from. She had known at the beginning of her stay at the Fortress that Ever's designs were self-serving. How could they not be? He had threatened Ansel with the lives of his family to get Isa to the Fortress. Then, when she had arrived, he'd given her such looks of cold disdain and hatred that she had wondered why he'd summoned her in the first place.

But then he had begun to change. Isa was sure he had. The gentle words he spoke to her, the way he looked at her, the confidence he'd shown in her abilities, the trembling in his fingers every time he reached for her hand or her face. He certainly wasn't the same man she had met last autumn.

Or perhaps, the cruel voice of reason whispered, *just perhaps, he is a very good actor.*

The woman's words came back to her from the night before. *For power he sold his soul, and you along with it.*

He'd failed to tell her of the curse's requirement that she heal him, and he had failed to mention his approaching death. And now, he was apparently pushing her towards an end the servants didn't think she was ready for, whatever it was. Where were the lies amongst the truths?

Not long after this revelation, Gigi and her hoard of handmaidens arrived to prepare Isa for supper as they always did. With their humanity, certain manners had returned, it seemed, for they no longer shoved her about as they had before.

And for weeks now, the bathwater had been clean, and the clothes had been fresh. Generally, just for fun, Isa might protest the way her hair was prepared that evening, or the color of her gown. Tonight, though, Isa allowed them to dress her in whatever they wanted, however they wished. For she found that after hearing the servants' discussion, she cared little for the details of the night.

They were unusually meticulous as they readied her this night. Gigi ran around, shaking her head at everything the younger women did, clucking her tongue and demanding they do it again. She, like Cerise, seemed on edge.

This night's gown was more exquisite than any Isa had ever laid eyes on. It was a deep blue velvet. Ribbons were weaved through the bodice, beaded with pearls and diamonds, and the arms were draped with silver lace. The blue parted at the bottom to reveal skirts of cream colored silk beneath them. Without a word Isa allowed them to pull the thick skirts over her head and fuss with them to their hearts' content.

Isa caught Gigi's eye while the servants put the finishing touches on her gown, and as they looked at one another, she nearly began to cry. Gigi laid a soft hand on Isa's cheek and gave her a sad smile.

"You look like a princess, my dear."

Isa wanted to weep. Instead of weeping, however, she stepped into her boots and let the others finish fixing her hair. Finally, she heard the dreaded knock at the door. It was time.

When the door opened, Isa's heart flopped in her chest. He was holding a single blue rose, looking just as nervous as she felt. Instead of his black hood, he wore a deep blue coat and what had once been fitted black trousers. His boots were polished so that they reflected the light of the fire in her hearth.

He trembled a bit as he stood there, and his face looked thinner than ever. His hunch was so deep now that she stood a bit taller than he. And yet, she wanted him so badly it made her heart ache.

The fire in his eyes flamed brighter for a moment when he saw her. Finally, he cleared his throat. "My lady, would you join me?"

Nodding, she accepted his arm. Neither of them spoke as they slowly made their way to the dining hall. Isa was sure he could hear her heart trying to beat out of her chest, and she didn't dare meet his eyes until he had walked them right through the dining hall and directly out onto the balcony. Sitting her down on one of the dozens of stone benches that surrounded the crystalline floor, he lowered himself beside her, taking her hands in his gloved ones.

"I can honestly say I never thought it would be this way," he finally said.

Isa watched him, but said nothing.

"When you arrived," he continued, "I thought I was gaining one more person to help solve the puzzle. But I never expected you to change so many things." He swallowed hard. "For years, the memory of you tormented me, and I hated you even more when you appeared in my home. But there was nothing I could do. You had come, and I was desperate enough to use any means to break the curse.

"But you!" He was suddenly staring into her eyes with that pleading, disarming look of his. "You began to teach me that there is healing in love. I think I began to love you without even being aware of it. The night you ran out…" He shook his head and his jaw clenched a bit at the memory. "I thought I had lost you. I hadn't realized how much I needed you before that." He took a deep breath. "That fool from Soudain didn't deserve you, and I'm glad he ran like a coward. You are too rare a creature to belong to someone like him."

Isa's heart cracked a little more with each word he spoke. She wanted so desperately to believe him, but with each confession of love, he also failed to confess his secrets. He was still lying to her, even now as he moved stiffly from the bench to drop down on one knee.

"I love you, Isabelle Marchand. Will you marry me?"

Isa's heart plunged and soared as he spoke the words. Conflicting desires raged within her as she stared at the crystal ring he pulled from his pocket.

She wanted to desperately to say yes. In a way, her heart already was and would always be his. And yet, angry tears threatened to fall as she knew he still hadn't told her the truth.

Her decision was made, however, when Cerise's words echoed in her mind, while she gazed miserably at his expression of hope. Lies or truth aside, he would die if he wasn't healed soon.

She couldn't let him die.

Without a word, she stretched out her hand. Perhaps she could make herself ready. She had to.

Her hand shook as he slipped the blue crystal ring onto her finger. As he did so, the air around them began to quiver.

A pillar of blue fire shot up into the air toward the heavens, engulfing them. Isa screamed as she saw the true power of the Fortress for the first time. She felt the weight of new burdens settling on her shoulders. Destin's well-being and the faces of its citizens began to flash before her eyes. A familiar heat beat at her back, and she recognized the scorch of the evil fire that had nearly consumed her the night before.

Isa struggled to stay upright as the burdens and enemies were heaped upon her, piling one atop another. She tried to steel herself, to face the evil that challenged the light. People's faces flashed before her, and she tried to memorize them. They needed someone to lead them. For hers was a burden, it suddenly felt, that no one else could bear. If she couldn't heal the prince now, it would all come crashing down onto her.

Isa clenched her jaw and looked at the broken man before her. Reaching out with trembling fingers, she tried to touch him, to heal his broken form. Before she could reach him, however, she felt her strength slipping away. It all began to collapse around her. The evil advanced, and the cry of innocent blood echoed in her ears as she failed to hold it all up.

Yanking the ring off, Isa shoved it at Ever, and the column immediately disappeared. With it went the people and their cries. There were no more enemies. The only sound left was her own haggard choking.

"I'm not strong enough!" she sobbed. She could nearly hear the sound of her heart tearing itself in two. She had wanted so much to be ready. Her soul had longed to find his words of confidence in her fulfilled. Why couldn't his words have been true?

While she mourned, anger began to seep in with the heartache as she gasped, still trying to catch her breath. He had known she wasn't ready. And yet, he had still asked.

Ever placed his hand on her shoulder, but Isa shoved it off. "How could you do that to me?" she choked out as tears ran down her face. "I trusted you!"

The prince hesitated.

"Tell me about the curse!" she shouted. "Tell me what you hid from me!"

After another moment of hesitation, he closed his eyes. "Before life can be found in this sacred place once again, a new strength must be found. What has been broken must be remade. The one who was strong must be willing to die. Only then can the Fortress and the kingdom again have the protector they deserve." After he finished speaking, he reached again for her, but she drew back.

"So I was supposed to heal you? How can the broken heal the broken, Everard?" Her anger was so great that she trembled. "I thought you loved me, but I can see now that all along I was just part of your plan!"

Ever stared at her with a long, sorrowful look. Before he said anything, he suddenly tilted his head and closed his eyes as though he were listening to something invisible, which annoyed Isa more. What else was she missing? It was a moment before he spoke, and when he did, his voice was cold.

"If that is how you feel, then there is no place for you here." Stiffly, he drew himself to his feet. His face lost all of its openness, and suddenly, even in his pallor, he looked like a soldier. "Garin," he called. The steward ran over, his own face full of sorrow. "Put Isabelle in one of the carriages. You are to take her as far from Destin as you can. She is never to return."

Isa felt a wave of horror wash over her. "Wait! What are you doing? I turn down your proposal, and you send me into exile?"

But no matter how many demands she made or how much she begged, he wouldn't consent. He wouldn't even discuss it. As she continued to protest, Garin gently took her by the shoulders and led her from the balcony, leaving Ever alone to stare down at the statues on the back lawn.

Gigi was instructed to get her into proper riding gear. Her chamber was oddly quiet as the servants scurried about it. Her gown was exchanged for a soft leather riding skirt and a simple white shirt under her mother's cloak. Isa tried in vain to ask Gigi and Cerise what was going on, but no one would speak a word to her, other than to order her about.

Before Isa was hurried from her room, however, Gigi drew her into a tight embrace, then handed her the bag she had first brought to the Fortress. By the weight of it, Isa could tell its contents had been added to.

Without time for proper goodbyes, she was whisked away to the stables where a coach, all black, awaited her. Isa tried one more time to beg Garin to allow her to speak with Ever, but he gently shook his head and drew her inside.

Isa left the Fortress more confused and hurt than she had been when she had arrived. "Why?" She turned miserably to Garin, who sat on the padded bench across from her. "Why would he do all of this, push me so hard and then send me away? I want to help! I just don't know how."

"I know you do, my dear," Garin said kindly. "But you are not ready, and that is why you couldn't accept the Queen's Ring. The prince does not want you near when the Tumenian princess attacks."

Isa felt the blood drain from her face. "They're going to attack? But he still has no army! It's not ready! And Ever's so weak..."

Garin nodded gravely. "We don't know when, but Everard senses it will be soon."

"But why do I have to go so far? That means it will take a long time for you to return to him!"

"Princess Nevina will not be satisfied with simply taking the prince's life. She knows who you are now, and she knows that you are valuable to him. If she found you, and she will try, she would commit acts of unfathomable cruelty against you out of spite. So no, I will not be returning."

Isa stared at him in shock. From the prince's birth on, she'd been told, and even while bound to a shadow's existence, Garin had rarely left Ever's side. And now he was leaving his charge forever in order to protect her.

Even more surprising was Ever's last act of chivalry. He had prepared himself for certain death by sending his most trusted confidante away to keep Isa safe. True enough, his behavior towards her had been unfair and assuming, as Nevina had predicted it would be. But she couldn't leave. Not yet. As deeply as he had wounded her, she could not just let him die. Desperately, she tried to think of something, anything that might change the steward's mind, or at least delay her departure.

"Please, just... just let me see my family one more time before I go. I need to let them know that I'm safe."

Garin glared at her, but didn't immediately refuse her request.

"One day." She reached out and took his leathery hand. "I just need one night and one day with them."

Finally, Garin nodded, and Isa could have collapsed with relief, but leaned back against the coach cushion instead. She had bought herself one chance to escape. Now she must plan to make sure it wasn't in vain.

The hour was late by the time the coach reached Isa's family's stable. Launce was the first one to see her. He shouted for the others as he sprinted towards them. Within seconds, everyone was there, hugging, laughing, and crying. It took Isa a while to untangle herself so she could point out Garin's presence. Ansel's greeting wasn't nearly as enthusiastic as it would have been at one time, but he did at least invite the steward inside.

"My Isa!" Deline held her tightly and whispered her name over and over again as if she were a small child. And Isa wished she could stay in her mother's arms forever and never let go. But all too soon, they followed everyone else into the house, and her heart grew heavy as she thought about the heartbreak that was once again about to take place.

"I assume you are home to stay?" Ansel posed it as a question, but with the threatening look he shot at Garin, Isa knew he wasn't giving her a choice. Garin opened his mouth to answer, but Isa spoke quickly, sending him a warning look.

"I wanted to see you," she simply said. She was just putting off the inevitable, she knew, but perhaps they could have one night of joy before she had to hurt them again. Launce, Megane, and Ansel began to pepper her with questions, but much to Isa's relief, Deline saw how tired she was. It wasn't long before she was tucked in her little bed with Megane snuggling at her side.

Isa reflected upon how miserable she had been the last time she'd slept in the cozy attic room. Now, she would give anything just to have more time there with her little sister by her side, and her parents and brother downstairs. Garin had chosen to sleep in the stable with the coachman, so Deline, always the gracious host, had made sure they had more blankets than they could possibly use.

Garin's choice of a bed annoyed Isa, as it meant she couldn't sneak out during the night. Escape would simply have to wait until the morning. As much as she needed to stay awake and plan her flight, though, sleep's call was too strong, and Isa soon succumbed to the night.

21

REVELATIONS

*T*he next morning, Isa woke up later than she had planned. The sun was already high, and judging from the smells wafting up from the kitchen, everyone else had already eaten. Reaching into the bag, Isa searched around for her silver brush. While she searched, her hand bumped something hard and smooth. Her hand shook as she pulled the little stone out of the bag.

Gigi must have sent it with her, or maybe Cerise. Either way, Isa ran her fingers across the sandstone petals, a strange longing sensation stinging the edges of her heart. Before she could begin to cry, she scrambled to find the brush she'd been looking for. Then she thrust the little chunk of stone into her reticule before heading downstairs.

As she ate her biscuits and fruit, Deline told her that Garin had gone into the town to look at some official council reports with Ansel. Isa had nearly darted out to the stables then and there, until her mother informed her that all of the horses had been taken by the men.

Isa should have been ecstatic to pass the quiet morning with her mother and sister. She tried to soak up every detail, every smell and sound of her old home as she waited for the men to return, but no peace came. Instead, she felt only the urge to go.

By the time afternoon rolled around, however, and Garin had still not returned, Isa decided to quietly slip out for a walk. Perhaps, while she was out, she could find a horse to borrow.

"Isa!"

Isa drew a deep breath before taking her hand from the door and turning to her younger sister with a forced smile. She had been so close.

"Where are you going?"

"Out for a walk."

"Oh! I'll come, too! Let me get my coins!"

Isa had to bite her tongue as her sister dashed off to find her coin purse. Still, she realized, it might be beneficial to bring Megane after all. It would lower her parents' suspicion if they realized she had gone out. No one would think she was about to escape if she was out with her little sister.

Isa felt some guilt about taking her sister out, only to know that they wouldn't be returning together, but Megane was long old enough to walk home from the market by herself. In fact, Isa knew that her little sister did so daily on errands for their father. And, Isa thought guiltily, what she was about to do, saving Ever and the Fortress from the Tumenians, would eventually save them all. Including Megane.

If she *could* save them, that was.

The air was cool enough that Isa was able to bring her cloak along and draw the hood without looking out of place. Despite her limp, few people seemed to recognize her in the bustle of the busy day. This was good, as the lack of greetings gave her time to think.

Now that she was out and about, however, it seemed unlikely that she should find anyone willing to give their horse to her, particularly without much money. If this venture didn't work, how could she change Garin's mind? As Ever's most loyal servant and companion, Garin seemed the least likely of all the servants to disobey the prince.

When Isa and Megane reached the market, Isa was surprised by how little was out to sell. Just last spring, every stall had been filled with ripe, brightly colored fruits and vegetables, fresh bread, salted fish, wild game, and even sweets and pastries. She'd assumed the Fortress's food had been sparse and bland because of its isolation. But while she'd been gone, it seemed, the people of Soudain had been making do with even less. The sickness of the Fortress must have seeped out of its borders and into the rest of the kingdom, like burning tar rolling down a hill. Fear made Isa shiver as she realized just how much was at stake under the weight of the curse. It went far beyond healing Ever and his soldiers, or even defeating Nevina and her men at the foot of the mountain. The whole kingdom that had thrived on light was crumbling in the dark. Isa suddenly felt a pang of sympathy for the prince. She was beginning to understand why he was so very desperate.

Isa was pulled out of her musings by a cry of delight from Megane. "Isa! Look! The Caregivers are back! So many of them!"

Dozens of brown coaches began rolling into the marketplace. Isa had to work to keep the horror from her face as Megane ran off in search of Marko, and it took everything in Isa to raise suspicion by calling after her.

"Isabelle? Isa Marchand?" a familiar voice exclaimed, despite the fact that her hood was still drawn. Turning, Isa gritted her teeth as she saw her old neighbor hurrying towards her.

"Hello, Margot." She forced herself to smile.

"You're back!" The plump woman stopped and gaped at her. She didn't gape long enough, however, to let Isa speak. "You are just in time! They'll be leaving tonight!"

Isa frowned. "Who is leaving?"

"Why, the Caregivers! Marko says they're putting an end to the prince's abuse! Tonight, they're going to take us, anyone who wants, right from under his nose!"

Isa shivered. Just the memory of the flaming arrows and diving hawks made her leg tingle. "You are sure it's tonight?" Isa struggled to keep her voice even.

Margot nodded enthusiastically. "Just think, dear! You and your family will finally be free of that wretched monster locked away in the Fortress!"

Whirling around, Isa began to call for Megane, but just as she spotted her sister, another familiar face appeared.

"Isa!" Marko boomed, holding his arms out, no doubt expecting the same friendly embrace she had always given him. If only she had known then what cruelties those arms had wrought.

Terror gripped Isa as she grabbed Megane's hand. Pushing her ankle as fast as it would go, she took off in the other direction. It was impossible to continue moving at such a difficult pace for long, however, so Isa turned down the first alley she could find, away from the crowds and mostly hidden from sight.

"Megane," she whispered breathlessly, "I need you to do something for me of the utmost importance. It will keep you and Launce and Mother and Father safe. But you must do *exactly* as I say. Can you do that?"

"What about you? You just came home!" Megane whimpered.

Leaning down, Isa kissed her face and drew her into a tight hug. "I know, Megs," she said. "But if I don't do this, many people will get hurt. I am relying on you. Now, can you help me?"

Wiping away tears, Megane nodded.

"Alright, I need you to go home and tell Mother and Father that I love them very much. Tell them that I am going away to keep you all safe."

Just before she sent her little sister off, however, a man's large frame loomed at the entrance of the alley. Marko watched them, his face dark.

"I wish you wouldn't have done that," he said as he began to walk towards them. Isa pushed Megane behind her as she stood to face the Caregiver. For the first time, she noticed his black metal ring glowing a dull gold as he tightened his right hand into a fist.

"Run, Megane!" Isa screamed. Megane escaped, but Marko reached out and grabbed Isa roughly.

"I have no desire to do this, believe me," he said as he pinned her against the wall. She tried to scream, but he covered her face with his hand. "But you just had to take his side. And my princess can't forgive that."

Isa struggled, but he was too strong. She began to see spots as he kept his hand clamped over her mouth and nose.

"You don't have to worry about him suffering for too long," he whispered in her ear. "He won't last much longer with or without you."

Fortress! she screamed silently. As the cry left Isa's mind, something sparked inside of her. It was familiar, and yet, she had never felt anything like this before. The feeling bled out from her heart, and flowed through the rest of her body. It was warm as it rolled through her veins and into her hands and feet.

Marko gave a cry of pain and flew backward, smacking his head against the building behind them. Blue liquid flame shot out of Isa's fingertips, nearly blinding her as it flared all around, and the force of it nearly made her lose her own balance. Relief at being safe from Marko was followed immediately by panic as Isa realized she couldn't move. The blue flame had engulfed her completely, and she stood frozen with her arms stretched forward while the flame continued to flow out of her body and into the man on the ground.

"Isabelle!" Garin's voice sounded from a distance.

Isa wanted so much to scream for help, but she couldn't move. Seconds later, cool, rough hands took her own, and the flame began channeling into them. They stood that way for what felt like an eternity. In amazement, Isa watched as Garin took the brunt of the raw power that streamed from her. *Don't let it hurt him*, she begged the Fortress.

But as he held her gaze, the man who had bowed to Ever's every wish no longer looked like a castle steward. Instead, he looked like something completely other, something powerful. His eyes blazed a fierce blue, and his skin became white like snow. The lines of age that edged his eyes and mouth disappeared. His arms were powerful, and just for a second, Isa thought she glimpsed a pair of large silver wings on his back.

Whether vision or truth, however, it only lasted for the blink of an eye. Slowly, the flame began to ebb, and bit by bit, Isa could move again. As it slowed, Garin began to look more like himself.

"What was that?" Isa gasped.

"That was the power of the Fortress."

"No, what you just did! How did you do that?"

Garin gave her a small smile. "You don't think the Maker would forge such a great source of power as the Fortress without giving it a keeper now and then, do you?"

"That was amazing though," Isa whispered. "Garin, what *are* you?"

"Only a simple servant, my dear."

"But–"

"There is no one servant more important than another. My purpose is simply a bit… different than that of the others. But we don't have time for this kind of talk. We need to be off, for the day is growing late."

Before he was finished speaking, however, Isa was already heading back toward the street. Garin caught up with her easily, and in silence, they walked as quickly as they could back to Isa's home.

Instead using the front door, however, Isa went directly to the stables.

"And where do you think you're going?" Garin asked as Isa led her father's horse from his stall.

"I am going back. The princess is attacking tonight."

"And how do you know this?"

Isa gave an impatient huff as she began to saddle the horse. They didn't have time for this. "The Caregivers have arrived in town, more than I've ever seen before. I was told that they are planning to take the kingdom by force. They're clearing the streets first, however, by offering to save those of us who want to escape."

"And you think that I will simply allow you to waltz off into the arms of the enemy?"

Isa stopped and looked straight at him.

"We can help Ever."

"Absolutely not!" Garin crossed his arms. "You are coming with me. We are leaving this place, just as Everard instructed! If something happened to you, your blood would be on my head! Do you remember a word I said about what they will do to you?"

"It doesn't matter." Isa shook her head and climbed up onto the horse. "He needs me." As she spoke, thin blue flames licked the reins, making the horse whinny loudly. "I am going back, Garin, and you are welcome to come with me if you so desire."

"And what makes you so sure you can help him after what happened last night?"

"Last night, I didn't understand. I couldn't see that because the Fortress has chosen me, it will give me the strength that I need to bear the burden." Despite her words, she hoped Garin wouldn't see the trembling of her hands.

Garin stood with his arms folded, watching her with an unreadable expression. Finally, a slow smile spread across his face. "Very well." He bowed his head in concession, before pulling something small from his pocket and handing it to her.

"You mean you won't stop me?" She looked at him in confusion.

"I mean you're ready."

22

WILLING

"Please!" Ever's shout echoed both up and down the tower as he slammed his fist on the stone wall of the tower passage. "Come back to me! I am doing all I know how!"

Instead of answering, however, the Fortress stayed silent, and Ever felt his heart beat once, twice out of rhythm, just enough to bring him to his knees. As he knelt to try and catch his breath on the winding steps, he thought about the night before for the thousandth time. What had gone wrong?

If Garin had been there, he would have said that Ever needed to just trust the Fortress. But really, Ever wondered, what could possess him to trust the very force that had stolen the life from his body and leave him alone and cursed?

He had hoped that Isa could be made ready by a speedy marriage. It had been the perfect plan, the answer to the riddle. The ring would focus her strength, he had assured himself countless times before. It would make up for whatever control she was still lacking. But when the time had come, the ring had done no such thing, and at the moment when he could have tried to pick up the pieces, his straying senses had picked up the sound of damnation instead. Nevina's battle horn had sounded.

It had taken all of Ever's willpower to harden his face as he exiled the girl he loved. Not that it would help in the end. His enemy was brutal and cruel, and he knew it was only a matter of time before she turned her rage on Isa when he was dead and gone. Nevina would hunt her down. Sending Garin with her was the only hope he could think of to give her.

As they had prepared her to leave, the girl sobbing the entire time, a small voice in his head had whispered that he could heal her as a parting gift. But no, he'd thought. That would have taken all of his remaining strength, and without his strength, he would die.

You're going to die anyway, his conscience had prodded.

If I die, he'd snapped at the annoying voice in his head, *who will be here to guard the kingdom one last time?* And so he had sent her away to her doom.

The look on her face had been heartbreaking, the same expression she'd worn as a small child when he had broken her the first time. Only this time, breaking her had felt like crushing a piece of himself. She hadn't seen it, but tears had run down his face as he'd watched her coach race off into the evening light. And now, there was nothing left for him to do but beg and plead with the Fortress.

"I don't understand!" He shouted up at the tower's peak. "Isa had a new strength!"

But she didn't stay, the voice whispered in his head.

"She brought healing!" he argued

But she didn't heal everything.

"What about me?" he pleaded desperately. "I was strong, and I have been willing to die. My whole life I have been willing to die! How many times have I gone into battle and risked my life?"

You don't seem ready to die now.

No matter how much he begged, the Fortress itself remained cold. There was no comforting presence, no gentle peace that he had once taken for granted. Beaten, he pulled himself painfully to his feet, and slowly climbed back up the steps and into the tower. Leaning hard on the stone balcony, he leaned over to see Nevina's army's progress below.

They would be at the gates within minutes. The halls were silent beneath him, as he'd given the servants instructions to hide as best as they could. Deep down, he knew that the hope he had given them was vain. He hadn't told his loyal friends how their enemies would silence them forever, how the Tumenians would break their bodies and their spirits. Instead, it was easier to force a smile and tell Gigi that she and the others might make it if they stayed quiet for long enough. But at his core, he knew that even if he had retained his strength, he could not fight an entire army on his own. His men were still statues on the field.

"I suppose you're here to gloat. Or to offer me another deal," he said without turning around.

"No," Nevina said, her steps pattering on the stone floor as she came to stand beside him, "not a deal." But she didn't go on. After a few moments of silence, Ever turned to look at her. He was the same height as the Tumenian princess now. But for the first time since they'd met, she didn't look proud or mischievous or angry or suspicious. She looked tired. She had no weapons drawn, and her shiny black hair was loose down her back.

"Then what?"

"I want to start again."

He quirked a brow. "So you brought your entire army and tried to sneak unnoticed into my home?"

"A girl has to take precautions." She shrugged, then sighed. "Look, Everard. We started off wrong as children. I never meant for it to become so–"

"You tormented me for years!"

"So you would see me! If I hadn't done something drastic, I would have been invisible to you."

Ever turned to her, incredulous. "You don't think I was curious when I was told there would be another like me at that tournament? What was I supposed to think when you gave me headaches and sent night terrors for the entire duration of the tournament? I never even had a chance to get to know the other children until it was too late."

"Curiosity is not the same as choosing a companion," she pouted.

Ever stared at her for a moment until the truth dawned on him. "You were singling me out for yourself!" He shook his head in disbelief. "You cut me off! Just like everything else, you tried to take what wasn't yours!"

"How else was I supposed to find someone who understood me? You were the only one, and my father had told me the Fortiers paid heed to no one but their own! I needed you to see me." She tried to lay her hand on his arm, but Ever jerked it away.

"With kindness. And goodness."

"Like you showed her?" It was Nevina's turn to look incredulous.

Ever felt his shoulder slump as he leaned against the window wall. "No," he said softly, rubbing his eyes, "not like I showed her."

"Exactly. You took her just as you accuse me of doing! And yet, she seems to have developed a sick infatuation with you." She paused for a moment. Through the silence, Ever could hear the clink of armor as her men fanned out into the halls. He threw up one last prayer for his servants, that the Fortress might at least spare them.

"Why her?"

"What?"

"Why a lame peasant?"

Why indeed? "Her heart... her heart is different," was all Ever could manage to say. How could he put into words the way she was changing him? The way she brought light and truth to everything around her? The way her touch sent a beam of sunlight through his bent and sickly body? How her smile made him with to be something he wasn't? "She sees pieces of me that I left behind long ago. The Fortress sent her to me." As he spoke, Ever realized what he was saying. He should have seen it all along. "The Fortress knew I needed her." What a fool he had been.

"You want to be pieced together like a broken pot of clay?" Her tone was acidic. Then it grew quiet, and he felt her hand on his back once more. "Everard, what if you could be something else completely?"

Ever turned to look at the princess. Her green and gold eyes were pleading, and for once, she looked... hopeful. The coyness was gone from her face, as was the look of scheming she so often wore.

"We could make you into something new altogether! Just the two of us! We could start over, and you would be a new creation all of our own!" Her voice had dropped to an excited whisper.

"You really think you could save me now?" He lifted his arms as if to show her the damage.

"If you let me, I could sodder you into a new creature entirely." Her hands came up before her, golden flames leaping from them.

Ever crossed his arms. "First you wanted the Fortress. Then you wanted the girl. And now you want me? Nevina, not even *you* know what you want."

"I want something new! I cannot live in my baby brother's shadow. Whether I gain a husband or a sister or a kingdom, I cannot go on like this!"

He stared at her for a long time before speaking, for once, carefully choosing his words for her. "No matter where you are or who you're with, your heart will blacken everything around you. You must change before your circumstances do."

Just like him.

"Then help me!" She grabbed his arm and wouldn't let go this time. "Make me better!"

"I cannot."

She backed up slightly. "So you're decided then."

Ever nodded once.

With tears in her eyes, the flame within them leaping wildly about, Nevina took one step back, then two, before turning and running for the tower door. "Then I will leave you to it!" Her voice grew cold. "For I have work to do."

Ever stood with the sword at his side for a long time as the Chiens did the Tumenians' dirty work for them. Smoke made the air putrid and thick as they began to set his beloved world ablaze. Ever imagined the intricate tapestries and exotic, crafted rugs going up in flames, the very ones he'd played upon as a child.

Following the Chiens came the men Nevina had managed to lure into her rogue forces. Their footsteps echoed up the stone stairs as he turned to face the door. A minute later, soldiers burst through.

They were far from Tumen's finest, just common hired swords who happened to stumble into the wrong part of the Fortress, from the expressions on their faces. And yet, there were at least a dozen that had come up together. Upon seeing him, they froze.

Ever knew that despite their princess's assurances of his weakness, they must still have still felt the fear for the Fortiers' legendary blue fire. Some of them had probably seen it in battle with their own eyes. When he produced none, however, only standing there staring back, they began to hesitantly advance towards him.

His sword was much heavier than it had ever been before, even when he had first received it as a boy. Still, somehow, he was able to throw his weight into the first swing. Small traces of blue flashed as he met his attackers. They came at him cautiously at first, one at a time. As he fought more and more like a man, however, instead of a legendary warrior, the soldiers became more confident in their strikes.

Sweat poured down Ever's temples, and his fingers trembled as he willed them to keep their grip on the sword's hilt. His bones jarred with each clash, and along with smoke, the stench of blood filled the air. Ever fought instinctively, without really knowing what he was doing, and as he moved, he wondered at the fact that none of them had managed to kill him yet. Even one of his newest soldiers would have gutted him by now.

The world had begun to blur when a voice interrupted his desperate attempt to focus. "Well, I didn't think you would last this long."

Nevina stood at the door of the tower, stepping over her soldier's bodies as she made her way towards Ever. It was only as he turned to face her that he realized the dozen men lay at his feet, the stench of death suddenly making the air noxious. A burning wave of dizziness set in, and Ever fell to his knees with a sickening crack on the hard stone floor. Gasping, he tried to raise himself off of all fours. He hadn't succeeded by the time cool fingers moved gently through his hair before grabbing a fistful and yanking back so that he had to look up.

Ever tried to ready himself for his death. She wouldn't make it easy. The princess was too ambitious, and her father had trained her well in the ways of torture. Her victory wouldn't be as rewarding if she didn't make him suffer first. The keen enthusiasm in her eyes made that clear.

Despite Ever's weariness, the small smile on her face sent a chill through him. Would they use fire? His own hearth was still lit, the poker resting temptingly beside it. The hawks were also an option, as the balcony outside would provide ample space to watch the princess's beloved pets tear him to pieces. He also knew from the battlefield that she was particularly fond of eyes. Then, of course, there was Nevina's wicked knife, the crooked one that never left her side. But nothing he imagined prepared him for the words that came from her mouth.

"Bring her in, Captain."

Ever panicked. He should have known she would try something like this. Isa was hot-tempered and stubborn. Where, he wondered, was Garin? Of all the people to get her out of the kingdom, it should have been the steward. What had possessed him to allow her to return? Or worse yet, he thought with horror, what might have kept him from his duty?

Nevina's captain walked through the door, dragging Isa behind him by the arm. As always, he said less than his mistress, but excitement burned brightly in his eyes. His dark cloak trailed over his men, but he didn't even attempt to avoid their corpses as the princess had. Isa let out a little yelp as the captain threw her hard against the ground. Ever tried to call out for her to run, but Nevina jerked his head back even harder, and the captain walked over and kneed him in the chin.

Ever was still gasping and spitting out blood when she looked up at him. Her eyes went wide, and they glazed over when the blood began to dribble down his chin. As she gaped, the captain walked over, grabbed her again, and held her tightly. She tried to struggle, but his arms, nearly as thick as her waist, might as well have been bonds of steel.

Nevina let go of Ever's hair and left him kneeling on the floor. Walking over to Isa, the princess softly tucked a stray lock of copper hair behind Isa's ear. "Really, Everard," she murmured, "I know I was never your first choice, but you chose *this* over me?"

Ever gritted his teeth as the princess lifted Isa's crooked wrist. She held it for a moment between two fingers as if it were a dead fish, then dropped it. "You've changed, my dear prince. You have grown soft. Your father at least had the good sense to see that a life with me would have been preferable to this kind of end. And what was it truly for? She lacks the strength you so desperately counted on." She walked back over to Ever and kicked him in the ribs. "Such a waste."

As Ever coughed up more blood, he saw a brilliant flash out of the corner of his eye. Isa's eyes suddenly burned with a ferocity Ever hadn't imagined her capable of. A bolt of blue shot down her right hand and traveled up the captain's arm. With a cry, he let go and stumbled backward. Isa turned to run to Ever, but Nevina quickly grabbed her by the left wrist and yanked hard. The blue fire ceased as Isa let out a cry of pain, and Nevina expertly twisted the girl's hand behind her.

The captain was quick to get up, his eyes bright with an eagerness Ever wished he could beat from the vile man's face. "No, Your Highness," the captain said to his mistress, "I don't think there will be any waste here."

Ever watched in horror as the captain took Isa from Nevina's arms. Nevina smiled and drew the knife from her belt.

"I used to dream of stealing your heart, Everard. But if I can't have it, at least I can steal your soul." Without pause, she buried the blade deep in Isa's chest.

Ever didn't hear his own scream. He no longer smelled the smoke that was beginning to make the air in the room unbreathable. He didn't notice when a soldier stepped in to tell the princess that the Fortress steward was making trouble downstairs. All Ever saw was the blood that stained Isa's dress as she lay on the floor where they'd let her fall. Slowly, he crawled over to where she lay, and with a shaking hand, he tried to wipe the tears that ran silently down her face.

"I couldn't leave you here," she whispered.

"Hush." He cradled her face in his hand. Though she tried to smile at him, he could see the shock in her eyes. "You have endured far too much pain at my hands to be forgivable. And yet," he coughed, "I must ask of you one more thing." Isa still watched him, but her eyes were beginning to look glassy. He didn't have much time left. "I simply ask you to remember me not as the monster I was, but as the man you taught to love."

"Why?" Isa whispered. "What are you saying?"

"I'm going to fix everything," he promised softly.

Her eyes grew a bit wider. "Ever, what are you doing?"

"What I should have done long ago." His fingers quivered as he pulled the crystal ring from his pocket and placed it on her bloody hand. Tenderly, he rested his lips on her forehead as he felt the strength within him begin to bleed out.

Garin had been right. The Fortress had never abandoned him. Rather, he had chosen to go his own way. To truly serve his people, he had to be willing to give it all, and to trust that the Fortress would make it right. But the vanity of who he was and what he was had kept him from acknowledging that truth. There was only one thing in the world that could break him of that pride. His men hadn't been worth such a sacrifice of self in battle. Not even Destin had been worthy. But the Fortress had given him Isa, and Isa was worth it.

As he pushed the power from his body into hers, he could hear the bones in her wrist reset, and then in her ankle. Her breathing began to deepen again, and he knew her wound had closed. When Isa opened her eyes, they once more burned blue, and Ever smiled as his own eyes closed. He felt the peace of his beloved Fortress cradle him as he welcomed death. He was willing.

23

QUEEN ALONE

*I*sa had never felt such pain in her life. Not when Ever's power had first touched her, nor when the horse had broken her wrist and ankle. Even the flaming arrows singeing her skin and the bird of prey gouging her leg couldn't compare.

She could tell immediately that the blade Princess Nevina had thrust into her chest was no ordinary blade, its dark power beginning to poison her blood as soon as it broke her skin. An icy fear seized her, and she couldn't think through the fog that suddenly clouded her vision. As the dark princess let her fall to the ground, her mind ran in circles. Ever was dying. She had seen it as he'd knelt on the floor just a few feet away.

Despair took her until she became faintly aware of a pleasant sensation on her face, a familiar one. The touch helped clear a way for her thoughts through the ringing in her ears. He was asking forgiveness. He was promising to make the pain go away.

The seconds seemed like eternity, but finally, Isa was able to open her eyes. Princess Nevina was shrieking as she ran towards them, but she stopped short. A blue cocoon of fire had encased both Isa and Ever where they lay upon the floor. Looking down, Isa realized she was gripping Ever's arm tightly with her left hand, something she'd not been able to do since she was nine.

For just a moment, she felt nothing but bliss as he softly kissed her face. His lips were still on her brow, but the longer he held on, the more she could feel him slipping away. Finally, he slumped limply to the floor, and she didn't have to touch him to know that he was gone. The chill had touched his lips just as he had let go.

"No!" Isa screamed.

The blue shelter that had hidden them dissipated, and its protection with it.

But that didn't matter. Isa rose slowly, and for the first time in fourteen years, stood erect. She hardly noticed, though. Nevina and the man beside her watched, their mouths agape and their hands slightly raised. The agony of loss washed through Isa like a raging flood, and blue flames tinted her vision as anger followed the pain.

Nevina's captain made the first move. Without hesitation, Isa raised one hand, palm out. Before he could take two steps, a bolt of blue lightning threw him backward against the wall, knocking him unconscious.

Nevina was smarter. Raising her knife, she began to walk towards Isa. Golden flames wrapped around the knife, spinning faster with each step. On an instinct she didn't know she possessed, Isa knelt and slammed her fists against the floor. She could once again feel the darkness trying to ensnare her as it had on the balcony when Ever had proposed, but this time, she was ready. The power that swirled around the knife was strong, but it was no match for the power that now dwelt inside her. And though she had struggled to push back against the weight of evil before, Isa now found it nearly effortless. The presence of the Fortress flowed around and through her, and for the first time in her life, Isa knew without a doubt what she had been born to do.

At Isa's first strike, Nevina stumbled, but regained her balance quickly and continued to approach. Again, Isa pounded the floor, and this time, the blue flame flew out from her hands and traveled up to the princess's knees, making her freeze momentarily. Still, after a struggle, the princess pressed on, a look of fury upon her face.

When Isa struck the ground a third time, however, the flame raced up Nevina's entire body. The dark princess writhed for what seemed like an eternity before letting out a shriek of rage. Finally, she fell limp.

Isa stood there, staring down at the bodies for a long time. Eventually, as the black sky began to turn gray through the wall of windows, footsteps sounded on the stone steps outside the door. A handful of the servants burst into the tower, along with a number of Chiens. They came to a halt when they saw her, however, and it was only the expressions on their faces that made her think to look in the mirror.

Her eyes blazed with a wild blue, as did the ring on her hand. She hadn't noticed the Queen's Ring until now. Ever must have placed it there. Looking in the mirror, she saw an expression on her face that she'd never worn before, feral and dangerous. Her hair had fallen out of its place, and was covered in sweat and blood, making her look even more menacing. That was when, out of her peripheral vision, she realized that Ever's body was gone.

"Isa." Garin finally made his way through the crowd. He approached her slowly with his hands out in front of him, as if she were a wounded hound. "You are going to be alright."

Isa looked up at him, suddenly terrified. "They stole him, Garin," she whispered.

"No, dear." The steward finally reached out and took her hands. Their warmth helped draw Isa back to herself. "The Fortress has taken him. He was its son, and it loved him. It will give his body a more fitting burial than we ever could." With that, Garin dropped to one knee before her, still holding the hand that wore the ring. "And now it is your burden and privilege to lead us into the next page of Destin's future, should you accept it. Are you willing, Isabelle? Are you ready to be our queen?"

24

YOU

The Fortress's purge was finalized when the dark princess was bound, gagged, and put to death according to the law of the land. Exhausted, Isa didn't want to attend the hanging, but Garin told her it was an unfortunate duty of the monarchs to oversee the deaths of the people's enemies.

Recovering herself was a little easier once that was done. By the time the sun rose, the dirt and grime were gone, and the Fortress's white marble walls glittered in the light of the morning. The gardens bloomed with new buds, with no sign of the charred dust they had been set to the night before. The Fortress looked as if there had never been a battle in the first place.

Similarly, according to reports, Soudain had been purged and healed as well. The stone army had apparently returned to its human state at the same moment Ever had healed Isa. After pouring through the Fortress and finishing off Nevina's forces, they had run down into the city and slaughtered the Caregivers as they had attempted to escape with as many townspeople, willing and unwilling, as they could find. By the time the sun had risen, however, all signs of bodies and blood were gone there as well. Instead of a war-torn landscape, gardens and farms were suddenly filled with the ripest produce the farmers had ever seen. Even the Chiens who had come with their masters were healed, and could speak again. Everything seemed not only as it should be, but better.

In the days that followed, people flocked to see their new queen, the once crippled dancer who was now the most powerful ruler in the land. Isa's own family ran to her with open arms, her parents sobbing with joy, Launce bursting with pride, and little Megane as happy to see her as ever. As they held her, however, their embraces still left her feeling empty. She held on to them tightly, but deep down, longed for the arms of another.

Garin and Gigi were really the only ones who understood her pain, and she realized quickly that she preferred their presence to all others'. Gigi didn't ask incessant questions like the rest of the well-meaning courtiers and servants. She would simply hold Isa, crying her own tears along with her. And though he was less expressive about it, Isa could feel the pain that Garin carried with him. Human or not, he had lost a son.

The coronation ceremony was to take place a week after Ever's death. Isa relied on Garin to take care of the customs and rituals she knew nothing about. She tried to smile and do as her royal tutors instructed her to, telling her when to sit, when to rise, when to speak, and when to refrain. But the emptiness inside was gnawing, and the weight of loneliness was more than she had ever expected it could be.

The morning of the coronation, Isa sneaked out of her new chambers, which had once belonged to King Rodrigue. She'd discovered quickly that her new powers allowed her to slip past people unseen if she so wished. Silently, she made her way down to the rose garden, and sitting on the bench within it, pulled the little rose stone out of her pocket. The last time she'd sat on the bench had been when Ever had sat beside her, just eight days before. That day seemed like a different lifetime.

Everything he had told her about the strength had begun to make sense to her in the past week. Although there was certainly much he had hidden, Isa was beginning to understand the cryptic words and strange riddles he had used when discussing his elusive power. When Launce had asked her about it the day before, she had been able to tell him little. There just weren't words for what now bonded with her lifeblood and made her heart beat.

She also understood why she hadn't been ready when Ever had asked her to marry him. She had been trying so hard to be strong that she'd missed the point of the strength completely. It hadn't ever been hers to be begin with. The Fortress's power was too great to ever truly belong to a single human. It was something completely other. The moment Marko had whispered that Ever was going to die, her heart had cried out. Without thinking, she'd run to the Fortress, the presence that had become her closest companion. Despite not being physically at the Fortress, she had somehow known it would follow her. And her cry had been answered. It was only the realization that she'd belonged all along which had opened her eyes and, it seemed, her strength.

"I took too long," Isa said, still staring at the little stone as Garin sat down beside her. "I should have known sooner that all I had to do was ask. I could have healed him."

"Whether you knew or not wasn't the point." For the first time since the battle, Garin had shed his black garments for his usual attire. Not that Isa cared what he wore. "You might have made a mistake, but it would not have mattered in the end. Our missteps aren't powerful enough to thwart the carefully laid plans of this strange place or the Maker. Ever had been searching for peace for a long time, and this end was the only way he could find it."

"I wish that made it easier," Isa whispered.

Garin laid a hand gently on her shoulder. "Ever would want you to rejoice for his end. He gave all that was left of him so you could have a life worth living. He wanted you to find joy, Isabelle." Garin looked up at the rising sun and tried to give her a teasing smile. "Now, if you desire to keep that life, I suggest we return you to the seamstress. She might have both our heads if your gown isn't perfect in time for the ceremony."

And before she knew it, Isa was standing outside the massive throne room doors. She attempted to stand as she had been instructed, chin high, shoulders back, taking small steps when the horns sounded so as not to step on her flowing white and blue dress. The pearls that dangled from her ears were cold against her neck, reminders that this wasn't a dream. She had expected to feel jittery and afraid during this ceremony, but oddly, she felt calm. This was where she was supposed to be.

If only she had not been left to do it all by herself.

"Presenting Her Majesty Elect, Isabelle Marchand, Chosen of the Fortress!"

The throne room was brighter than she had ever seen it, full of light and even more full of people. The draperies and chandeliers glittered with hanging diamonds that caught the light and threw it everywhere that the sun didn't directly reach. As she walked slowly down the red velvet aisle, the people bowed, falling row by row. Isa didn't understand the awed look on their faces until she glanced down. With each step she took, spiraling blue flame swirled around her feet faster and faster. It made her so dizzy that she had to look up to keep from stumbling.

Finally, Isa reached the holy man. He smiled kindly down at her, but she couldn't bring herself to smile back. In a low voice then, he began to recite the ceremonial ordinances before taking the ring from its pillow on the short pedestal that stood between them. She had given it back the day before so that it could be properly accepted in front of the people. Garin said it was all for appearance's sake, though, since her true coronation had taken place when Ever had placed the ring on her finger.

The holy man began by asking the people if they accepted her as their queen. The choral answer was loud and sure. Though Isa struggled to pay full attention to the holy man's words, she had the charges memorized. He was now asking her if she was willing to accept the life of sacrifice this ring required of her.

"I am willing." None of them would be sitting here now if she wasn't. How could the holy man or anyone else in the crowd truly know about the sacrifice that had already taken place for her to have this position?

"Do you bond yourself forever to the Fortress and what it demands of you, relinquishing your own ambitions and designs?"

"Yes." Isa felt a tear slip down her cheek. She was glad her back was to the crowd. Before the priest could ask the next question, however, he was interrupted by the sound of the enormous doors opening once more. When Isa turned to see who had interrupted the ceremony, she nearly fell to her knees.

A man stood in the doorway. His posture was straight, and his bearing was regal.

Isa began to tremble.

The man's hands were not misshapen, nor was his face gaunt or pale. Strong limbs were clothed in deep blue, but Isa could not bring herself to look at them for long. She stood still, frozen by the fear that she had truly lost her mind.

The crowd gasped, then quickly fell into an uncomfortable silence, looking back and forth between the ruler they had just accepted, and the one that should have been.

Their discomfort was nothing to Isa, however. All she cared about was working up the courage to meet his eyes. And when she did, she let out a cry of joy. Even from across the great room, they burned a fierce blue. She couldn't pull her own eyes away from them as he began to stride down the aisle. Before she knew what she was doing, she was sobbing, running to meet him.

He caught her in his arms and held her close. There were so many questions she had, but he allowed none of them. Bending down, he took her face in his hands and kissed her with a resolve that shot heat through her lips and all the way down to her fingertips and toes, and she clung to him for fear of collapsing on the floor in a heap.

Isa had never been so afraid in her life. This must be a dream. And yet, when he finally released her enough to look into her eyes once again, she didn't wake up. Her heart stumbled as she reached up to touch his face. The bridge of his nose, the shape of his chin, even the angle of his jaw line were completely familiar, and yet, he was a stranger to her. He, in turn, seemed to be memorizing her features as well, a hungry look in his eyes.

"You Highness... Prince Everard..." the holy man stumbled. "I am sorry, but the people have already accepted..." At a loss for words, he finally looked at Isa desperately. "Your Majesty! You are now the rightful heir to the throne, and you alone. Unless, of course, you choose to marry this man?" His anxiety in questioning Ever's claim to the throne was evident as he looked at the prince. The crowd leaned forward, looking both uneasy and fascinated by the predicament. But Ever simply gave her a gentle smile and touched her face with the backs of his rough fingertips before dropping to one knee.

"I was going to ask you the same question," he whispered, his voice husky. "Will you marry me, Your Majesty?"

Isa fought to answer with an even voice. "With all my heart."

With a smile that put the sun to shame, Ever led her back to the head of the throne room, where they finished the coronation vows side by side.

Their wedding vows were also said along with the vows of coronation, something Isa was immensely glad for, as she wished immediately to simply be alone in the quiet of dusk with him once more. At least they wouldn't have to have a separate wedding ceremony a well.

Immediately after that, the servants scurried to turn the coronation ceremony into a wedding celebration, with Gigi leading the fuss all the way, but Isa couldn't have cared less if they had all worn sackcloths and feasted on bread and water. Her mind was full of nothing but questions. How had he come back? Where had he been all this time? How had he been healed? She didn't get to ask him, however, until it was time for the dance.

Isa's heart leapt in her chest as everyone watched her walk away from her family to meet Ever on the crystal floor, just as the tradition demanded. Funny, she thought as she went, that her captivity in the Fortress should teach her the origins of the dance she had wanted so badly with Raoul. As they met in the middle of the crystal balcony, she curtsied.

"My lord," she murmured. "May my life strength be bound to yours."

"My lady." He took her hand and kissed it softly. "Never will I let them part."

As the familiar music began to play, Isa realized that just how different this dance would be from all the others. Tonight, Isa was wearing silken slippers without fear of going lame. She laughed as her groom swept her across the floor in a dance that felt more like flying than anything she had ever felt in her life. Glancing at the ground, she gasped as blue flames rose around them, encircling them as they moved. She looked up at Ever in wonder.

"Blue is a lovely color on you, my lady," he leaned down and whispered in her ear.

"Why didn't it do this before? All those times we were dancing, and I never saw it at all!"

"It was always there. You just had to see that you were the one the Fortress had chosen."

Suddenly, the Fortress wasn't the only one that wanted her, Isa sensed. That hungry look returned to his eyes, and Isa couldn't deny that she felt the same desire rushing through her.

"Can we go somewhere alone, just for a few minutes?" she pleaded.

A mischievous, boyish look came to his face. "With pleasure."

A few minutes more and the dance was over. The priest announced that the marriage ceremony was complete, and the crowd stood to cheer for its new king and queen. Isa knew she should be thrilled and thankful, but she suddenly wanted nothing more than to simply be alone with her husband.

True to his word, once they exited the dance floor, dozens of other couples flooded it, and he led them quietly down a dark set of stairs. A few minutes later, they were seated in the rose garden.

Isa opened her mouth to begin asking her questions, but before she could utter a word, his lips were pressed firmly against hers. The evening spring air was still chilly, but his strong hands, now ungloved, kept her warm as they gently explored her face, then her neck. Her breathing hitched as they explored their way down to her waist and the small of her back. She could feel his desire as he drew her even closer. Isa fought to get control of her thoughts, knowing that if she gave him just half a minute more, her chance to ask would be gone for the rest of the evening.

She had to push his shoulders back with quite a bit of force before he realized she wanted to stop, and she had to laugh a bit at his confused expression.

"I just need to know... How are you here?" She gazed at him in wonder, tracing the contour of his brow with her finger. "You gave me all your strength. How did you survive?" Suddenly, she felt ridiculously as if she might begin to cry, although she wasn't sure why.

Understanding lit his face as he took her left hand. Before answering, he gently explored her wrist where it had once been broken. "When I was little, I never wondered at the wisdom this place exuded. It brought me peace, and that was enough. As I grew, however, and followed in my father's footsteps, I forgot the truth I had known since birth. I deluded myself into believing that the strength was mine, and that I was responsible for it all. I failed to realize that such a responsibility is a burden far too great for any one man to bear." His face now solemn, he looked into Isa's eyes, and for a moment, she saw the sadness in them that had haunted him for so long.

"And you. What I did to you as a boy was more than I knew how to endure. Garin told me that I could be forgiven, but my father made it very clear that I was never to go near you again. I could have done the right thing at any time, gone to you, healed you, and asked your forgiveness, but my pride was too great. I simply couldn't stand to look at what I had done, and as a result, you haunted both my dreams and my waking moments. By the time you returned to me, I was so desperate to hold on to my dwindling power that I was too much of a selfish coward to give it up to you." He paused and took a deep breath.

"I spent so many days and nights trying to come up with ways to break the curse. I sought every action imaginable to redeem myself and my home, and yet, in the end, it was nothing I did that broke the curse."

Isa was confused. "You healed me. Wasn't that when the curse was broken?"

"Yes, but it was not my action that broke the curse. Rather, it was my heart."

Isa shook her head. "I still don't understand."

"A new strength had to be found. You, Isa, brought a new strength to the Fortress, one that had never been known even to me. Your strength wasn't military might or skill with a sword. You brought the power of the heart. You taught me once again how much strength lies in love.

"Second, what was broken had to be remade. Yes, I had broken you as a child. I, myself, had been broken in body, but even more importantly, I had been broken in spirit long before that. I had to have my trust in the Fortress, my relationship with it healed. Truths I had abandoned as a young man needed to be made real to me again. At the moment I happily gave of myself, I, too, was healed.

"Finally, I had to be willing to die. This was the hardest demand for me to understand. I thought I had been willing to die before, but what I risked in war was no true risk. I grew up on the battlefield where men die every day, but my strength allowed me to desperately cling to life. With my power, I could never truly know what it means to sacrifice for my kingdom, or even for you. The

Fortress knew that for me to truly serve my people, I needed to understand self-sacrifice. The only way I could learn that was for the Fortress to loosen my vice grip on my power."

Suddenly, Ever's breath shook as he spoke his next words, and his large hands gripped Isa's arms desperately. "Isa, the moment I thought she had killed you, my world lost its meaning. I had no reason to hang onto my power if it meant living without you. You had brought light into my darkness. You were the only reason I was able to truly hope, and if you died, it would be because of my own selfish ambition. Giving you the rest of my strength was the easiest thing I have ever done. I was more than willing to die. And in offering up my strength, I found a peace. I could die peacefully, knowing once again that I was forgiven and that I was loved."

With that, Ever stood, and Isa stood with him. Her head swam with his words, making him even more attractive than she had known him to be before. He had leaned in for another kiss when a throat was cleared behind her.

"What is it, Garin?" Ever growled, and Isa giggled.

"I apologize, Sire, but the people are beginning to wonder where you are. It is nearly time for the final ceremony."

"We will be there in a few minutes," Ever snapped.

Isa laughed again. His temper hadn't changed as much as his appearance, and it put her at ease to see so much of the old prince in the body of the intimidating new king.

"It's strange how the things that brought you peace and healed you were the same things that helped me as well," she said, wrapping her arms around his neck. "And yet, we were broken so differently. I always blamed my weakness for my lack of purpose in this world. And yet, it was my very weakness that allowed me to fulfill my role here." She gave a dry laugh. "If you had done what was right, I would not have been injured all this time, and I would be a dancer now, married to Raoul." She shook her head. Compared to what she had now, that existence was the last thing she could ever desire, the wisp of a future she never wanted to consider again.

"This place has a strange way of working things out like that," he said, hugging her to his side. They both looked up in wonder at the soaring white towers above them that glistened even in the dark.

"One more thing I don't understand," she said as they slowly began their walk back. "Why did you just disappear? And why did it take a whole week for you to return?"

"I'm not certain, but I have an idea." He gave her a sidelong glance. "If I had survived and defeated Nevina, would you ever have seen yourself as queen?"

"I'm not sure." Isa shrugged. "I suppose not. I probably would have looked to you for direction."

"Exactly. Without me, you had to admit to yourself, the Fortress, and to the people that this is truly your place. You were meant to be queen, with or without me."

Isa nodded as she thought about this. As she did, another question popped into her head. "Where were you though?"

Ever chuckled a bit. "I'm not really sure. The Fortress brought me to a place of healing and dreams. I have to admit that it was a relief. I haven't had a tranquil dream since I was quite young."

"What did you dream about for an entire week?"

"Some dreams were memories. Others were scenes of a life I'd never lived, a life of peace and children and gray hair." Ever laughed a bit. "I can't recall many of them, but I do remember one thing in particular."

"What was that?" Isa found herself breathless.

In response, he stopped walking, drew her to him, and leaned down to kiss her again.

"You."

BLINDING BEAUTY: A RETELLING OF THE PRINCESS AND THE GLASS HILL

THE BECOMING BEAUTY TRILOGY, BOOK 2

~

The Classical Kingdoms Collection, Book Two

To Danny, for always protecting your big sister and threatening to break the legs of any man who broke my heart. I forgive you for stealing my dolls and eating my cookies before I was able to finish decorating them. I now laugh in your general direction for calling me a nerd in high school. Engineers forfeit all rights to call other human beings nerds. Keep on truckin' and protect that big brain of yours because one day, it might just save the world.

1

THIS QUEEN

*I*sa's weapon lay uselessly on the ground just a few feet away. She threw her hands up to protect her face, but it was too late. The blue flame from Ever's sword hit her head-on, knocking her across the floor. Her head slammed against the stone tiles with a sharp crack.

Sheathing his sword, Ever was at her side before the ever worrisome servants could make it to the center of the training room's large floor. "I'm sorry," he groaned, gently lifting her head and examining the spot that had struck the ground. "I didn't mean to make that one so strong."

His wife gave him a weak smile, but winced when his fingers found the spot they were looking for, buried at the base of her thick, auburn braid. Pulling off his right glove, Ever placed his hand over the bump that had already begun to rise, releasing just enough power to draw the swelling down. As the blue light rolled back and forth between the knot and his palm, Isa's breathing evened and she let out a gust of air.

"I truly am sorry," he said again. Isa gave him a genuine smile this time, and as they often did, her large eyes caught him off guard, holding him captive in their midnight depths.

"It was my fault." She shook her head and accepted his help in standing. After dusting her clothes off, she went to retrieve her sword. "I don't know why I keep missing that attack. I see you coming, but I'm too slow to parry."

"Your wrist is too stiff." He moved to stand just behind her so he could put his hand over hers where she gripped the sword's hilt to show her the proper form.

Instead of fixing her stance as he demonstrated, however, she turned and leaned back for a kiss, and Ever couldn't help himself as he bent his head to meet her soft lips. Somewhere behind him, he heard the sound of retreating footsteps, and he smothered a laugh.

Before his wedding and coronation, the crowd that gathered to watch Ever's combat practices had generally been large. In those days, as their then-prince took on single, double, even seven or eight opponents sometimes, his spectators would watch in awe. Fathers would point out specific moves to their sons, and the women would whisper about how graceful and strong he was. Everyone agreed they had never seen the like.

Since his wedding and coronation, however, though he still practiced with his soldiers, the spectators had learned quickly that their king was not shy about flirting with his wife.

Even during weapons practice.

"I don't know what else they think they're going to see," Ever had once overheard Garin, the Fortress steward, remark with a chuckle. "It's only been five months since the wedding. They would do well to let the love birds be."

But in truth, Garin and Ever both knew what the spectators wanted to see from their new queen. And as time went on, everyone, Ever included, grew more anxious when it didn't appear. Today had been no exception, and the flirting wasn't to blame.

"That's enough practice for one day."

Ever cringed as Gigi's sharp words drenched the warm moment like a bucket of melted snow. He should have known the exiting footsteps had belonged to one of the kitchen mistress's spies. Grudgingly he stepped back to allow Gigi to examine Isa more thoroughly.

"I thought we discussed this," Gigi scolded him, lowering her gray brows when she found a rather large bruise on the back of one of Isa's arms. "What if she were with child? How could this possibly benefit any of you?"

At this, Isa let out a huff. "We *have* been through this, and I am *not* with child. Ever is right. I'm still not very good at defending myself."

"Well, you're done for the day," the older woman clucked, taking Isa's sword and handing it to Ever as though it were a dead serpent. "We have to fit you for new gowns."

"More? What in the heavens for?"

"I'll tell you on the way. Speaking of which, Ever, Garin needs to see you."

Looking defeated, Isa let the matronly woman lead her away, and Ever turned to find his steward smirking at him.

"You may be king, but that woman orders you about more by the day."

"She doesn't do it in front of the servants." Ever sheathed his sword. "I can't see any harm."

Garin didn't argue. Gigi had been more of a mother to Ever than Queen Louise had. Certain liberties were hers for the taking. She had earned them.

"How was practice?"

"I thought she would be more in control by now. But she just stagnates." Ever let out a gusty breath. "She's so unsure of herself as it is. I just don't know how to help her."

"I remember the day you first discovered your strength." Garin waved his hand at the servants to open the doors to the king's study. "You certainly never hesitated to use it." The glint in his steward's eye told Ever that he was remembering all the tricks Ever had played on the Fortress staff as a small boy. "You were quite imaginative, if I may say so."

"It came so naturally." Ever shook his head as the doors closed behind them. "I never had the problems she's having."

"There is quite a difference between discovering the Fortress's strength as a child and discovering it as an adult," Garin said as he lifted a stack of parchments from Ever's desk and began rifling through it. "Children accept life as they see it. But Isa has had to face an enormous amount of self-doubt and adversity. Her confidence is still shaky at best. I know you do not want to hear it, but give her time, Ever. The Fortress knows what it's doing."

Ever placed his hands on his desk and let his head sag, something he never allowed any of his other subjects to see, or even his wife, for that matter.

"In truth, did any of the other queens struggle this much with their powers?"

Garin's eyes grew very old, as they always did when talking about the Fortress's past. "Let me remind you that many of the queens never even gained the Fortress's strength at all. The Fortress never saw them fit to carry its power. As for those who did receive and master it, I've found it best not to compare. The Fortress will teach her in its own time. Her heart must be ready. Now, for other things to talk of." He handed the stack of parchments to Ever. "I think you'll find some of today's reports quite interesting."

Ever grinned a bit when he took the papers and noticed their broken wax seals. It was nothing new to Ever for his steward to read his messages first, but Isa's younger brother, Launce, had once seen it and gawked.

"When you've overseen the Fortress business for a few centuries, you too may read the king's messages," Ever had told him when he had seen the young man's astonishment.

Today, Ever glanced at the first few reports, mostly numbers on taxes and regional crop production. But when he saw the letter from the Lingean king, his heart beat uneasily, and as he read it, he found his gut instinct was right to be worried.

Everard,

I fear I have no pleasant tidings to bring you this day. Though you know me as the sort to keep order in my own realm, I have had reports of a most heinous crime committed along our northern border. Indeed, it was so outrageous I would not give it heed until I had seen it with my own eyes.

Ten of our region's priests were journeying to a small town that has recently been taken with a terrible illness. It is my understanding that their intentions were to assist the healers. They never reached the town, though. The day after they should have arrived in the village, a shepherd found their bodies strewn about in a nearby field.

I regret requesting your assistance, as it is three days' journey from your home, but I cannot fathom what kind of monster the murderer must be to cut down ten men appointed by the Maker himself. If you are at all willing, I implore you to help me solve this mystery. My people are more afraid by the day.

Your friend and ally,
*   Leon Tungsvara of Lingea*

"I want a military contingent to escort two of the Fortress healers to Lingea at once. Have them examine the bodies and bring their findings back to me."

"I thought you would find that odd." Garin's voice was tight.

"Ten holy men murdered in one day goes far beyond odd." No wonder his northern neighbor had reached out to him. No such atrocity had been reported in decades. Garin nodded and went to relay the order as Ever read the next parchment hoping to find better news. Garin walked back in just as he finished.

"This one *is* truly odd." He waved it at Garin. So that was why Gigi had wanted new dresses for Isa. "Since when do the Cobriens allow outsiders to compete to be the royal successor?"

"Since now, I suppose." Garin frowned slightly before smoothing his face. "Does that mean you're going to find out?"

"It does. Apparently, we're going to Cobren."

2

FIT FOR A QUEEN

"Remove the sleeves up to the shoulder," Gigi instructed the seamstress. "Now replace them with this." She held up a white roll of sheer lace.

Isa eyed it suspiciously. "That's showing quite a bit of skin for a wedding betrothal, isn't it?"

"I know you don't think so, but may I remind you that you are the most powerful queen in the northern kingdoms. It's only appropriate for the others to see that you are not like the other women." Gigi nodded once to the seamstress as she pinned the new fabric into place over Isa's bare arms.

Isa looked down at her new dress, and in spite of Gigi's confidence in the daring design, felt all the more self-conscious. To be fair, Isa was a far cry from the crippled woman with a bad ankle and crooked wrist who had hobbled up the Fortress steps the year before. She now stood tall and proud as her etiquette instructors had taught her to. Her once lame wrist and ankle, now healed by the Fortress's great power, no longer hindered her. But that didn't mean she was quite ready to be put on display.

After being healed, Isa had reveled in her new body. She had spent long hours out riding with her husband, practicing archery, learning swordplay, and trying to better understand her new powers as Ever had insisted she do.

"While being a ruler of the Fortress does provide special strength," he had told Isa when he had handed her a crossbow for the first time, "it also means many people will see your power. And there will be others that covet it as well. I need to know you won't be helpless when the time comes that someone tries to test you, to see how far you can be pushed."

Happily, Isa had agreed. And in truth, she had enjoyed the training. She just hadn't noticed until now how tan and hard her lean arms had grown during her many hours in the sun. This new gown made her look almost fierce, and she wasn't sure she liked it. Gigi, however, seemed delighted, despite her great disdain for all of Ever's *activities*.

When the seamstress was finally finished, Isa donned a plainer dress and cloak, and using what little control she had over her powers, she made sure no one saw her as she made her way down to Soudain.

Destin was full of many cities, but none were as impressive as its capital. Or at least, that's what Ever said. There were no dirt roads, as Isa heard other cities and villages had. Instead, every street was covered in cobblestones or wooden planks. Lamp posts lit every corner at night, lighted by small boys who ran from corner to corner with tiny flames on long poles.

Isa inhaled the scent of fresh bread and newly picked herbs as she passed through Soudain's largest square. People milled about, most moving from stall to stall while others called out their wares to the passersby, but nearly everyone looked content. Since Isa and Ever had broken the Fortress's curse, harvests were turning out to be more plentiful than ever, which meant full markets and happy citizens. Isa felt herself relax a little in the familiarity of the setting. It was almost the same sense of belonging she'd had here at one time.

True nostalgia was impossible, however, for she was suddenly aware of the two guards that flanked her. They weren't supposed to be visible in their commoners' clothing, but Isa knew her husband would never truly let her go into town alone anymore. She sighed a little. Perhaps she hadn't been as stealthy in her exit as she'd thought, just another reminder of how unreliable her powers were becoming. But as she finally reached her destination, she mustered up a smile before walking through the door of the corner mercantile.

"Isa!" Deline wiped her hands on her work apron and drew her daughter into a strong hug. "I didn't expect to see you here today. Megane, take over for me while I speak with your sister."

They moved through the back door behind the store counter into the main room of the house. Isa exhaled deeply as she sank down onto the long bench beside the table and watched her mother stir whatever was in the kettle over the fire. It was here, with her mother close by and her guards outside where she couldn't see them, that Isa could truly rest.

"So," Deline turned and sat beside Isa, "what is it that you want to tell me?" Isa gave her a wry smile, and her mother laughed. "I know you, love. What's bothering you?"

"I'm not sure if *bother* is the right word . . ." Isa said slowly, tracing the grain lines in the wooden bench with her finger. "We will soon be setting out for a betrothal ceremony in Cobren. Gigi says the travel itself will take two days, and the festivities could last up to a week, or even longer. Apparently, something about this betrothal ceremony is different from their traditional ones of years past. It will be a lengthy trip." To her surprise, Isa looked up to see a smile on her mother's face.

"Isa, this is exactly what you and your husband need."

"Truly?" Isa blinked. "I thought you would be upset. It's so far away."

"I am not saying that I won't miss you, but I trust your husband to keep you as safe as anyone."

At this, Isa had to smile and nod. Ever's strength wasn't only known throughout Destin, but all of the northern kingdoms. And he took her safety more seriously than anything else. The guards outside were proof of that. She wouldn't have been shocked if more were milling about, unseen as well.

"You need to get away though, and have some fun," Deline continued, pulling a lump of bread dough from a basket and beginning to knead it. "You and Ever have been so busy since the wedding, I think some time together will be good for you. You may be king and queen, but you are also newlyweds. The strains on marriage don't disregard couples just because they're royal."

"I have to admit, it will be nice not to hear the Fortress gossips for a few weeks." Isa stood up and took the lump of dough from her mother and began to knead it. Sometimes it was nice to have something to pound. They never let her knead dough in the Fortress kitchens.

"With that, I can't help you." Deline let out a short laugh. "All I can tell you is that when the good Maker intends for you to have a child, He will give you one."

"You wouldn't think that from the way people whisper," Isa grumbled, hitting the dough a little harder than necessary. "You would think it has been five years instead of just five months!"

Deline stopped stirring the kettle and took Isa's hands in hers, pulling them away from the bread dough. "What else is wrong?"

Isa took a deep breath. It was hard to talk with her family about the special strength the Fortress bestowed upon its monarchs. The way it flowed from her soul felt so natural, such a part of her that she didn't really have words to express what it truly felt like. Or didn't, as of late.

"I practiced with Ever today, and it didn't go well." She shook her head and glared at the floor. "He doesn't say anything, but I can tell he's worried. I just cannot understand what's wrong with me. It felt like everything fell into place at the wedding, but now I can't seem to do anything right. I feel like an impostor, like I'm just holding the throne until the true queen appears. I haven't produced an heir, and my strength refuses to grow, and there seems to be nothing I can do about it!"

Deline drew her into a tight hug. Isa held on, clinging to her mother like a small child.

"I know not what to tell you, but just to trust the Maker. The Fortress acts on His will, and the Maker never makes a mistake. The Fortress chose *you*, and no one else. That has to mean something, as do these." She pulled back and touched just below Isa's eyes, which Isa could feel burning with the rings of blue flame she'd received with her powers. Just then, Isa's younger brother walked in.

"Launce," Deline said, not looking away from her daughter. "Isa will be going to Cobren soon."

Launce stared at them for a long moment, his mouth full of the bread he'd just shoved in, before swallowing loudly. "Whatever for?"

Isa had to smile. It was no secret that Launce detested everything royal. It didn't help that Ever, with good intentions of course, was determined to make him into a respectable member of the court.

"We're attending a betrothal ceremony for Princess Olivia."

"I'm sorry." He shook his head and grabbed another piece of bread. "Being around all those snobbish royals sounds terrible."

Isa had to agree with that. She hadn't met many of the other royals since her own wedding. And while their introductions and smiles had been polite, many of them had seemed less than genuine, particularly those of the women. When Isa had asked her lady-in-waiting, Cerise, about this, Cerise had admitted sheepishly, "Most of the women were either vying for your husband's hand just last year, or trying to obtain it for their daughters."

Isa had immediately understood the rest of what Cerise was *not* saying. Not only had their efforts been in vain, but to add insult to injury, Ever had married a commoner. For women who had been primped and primed to do nothing less than marry a king, losing a conquest to a nameless peasant was unthinkable. And while the opinions of others didn't seem to bother Ever in the slightest, Isa found herself dreading the trip once again.

As Launce continued around the room, gathering whatever food he could find to feed his voracious appetite, Isa had an idea. "Launce . . ."

He looked up at her, suspicion in his eyes. "What?"

Isa hopped over to her brother and threw her arms around him. "I am going to ask you something, and I need you to *please* listen before you say no."

He stared at her for a minute before his eyes bulged, and he tried to pry her arms off of his waist. "No. No! Absolutely not!"

"Launce, at least listen to what your sister wants."

"I know what she wants! And I am *not* going to Cobren!"

"Launce," Isa whined, "you said so yourself! I'm going to be miserable up there as the only commoner! You're going to leave me alone with all of *them*?"

"You'll be with King—"

"Launce!" Deline cut him off. "I told you I don't want to hear that word in this house! And be respectful. Your brother-in-law is still your king."

Launce scowled. "It's still your fault," he grumbled. "You didn't have to marry him."

"You know that's not true. Besides, I love him." Isa sighed. "I just don't love everything else that comes with being queen."

Launce glared at her for a long time before huffing.

"Fine! I'll accompany you in your misery." Then an evil grin stretched out on his face. "But you still have to convince your husband to take me. I doubt he'll like it any better than I do."

"Leave that to me." Isa smiled as she stood up, suddenly ready to return to the Fortress.

~

"Your brother hates court affairs." Ever frowned. "Why in the world would he want to come along on this one?"

Isa shifted uncomfortably. It had been easy to assure her family that Ever would accept Launce's company, but it was another matter entirely to actually secure that acceptance.

"I might have asked him," she finally admitted. Her husband's gray eyes widened in surprise, and she thought she detected a small amount of hurt in them before he smoothed his features over.

"I thought we would have the time to ourselves," he said.

"We will!" she hurried to assure him. "I *want* the time with you! It's just that you tend to get rather ... occupied during official visits."

Ever exhaled heavily and gave her an unhappy look. Isa escaped his frown by moving over to stare out the window near their bed. It was one of her favorite spots, affording a view that stretched up the mountain side that the Fortress sat upon. From the balcony, it was possible to see almost all the way up to the summit.

"You'll have the court ladies to get to know," he finally said in a more subdued voice. "As queen of the Fortress, it's imperative to become familiar with all—"

"I will. But a week is a long time." She picked at a loose thread in her gown. "It gets lonely being the only commoner." In response, Isa felt him walk up to where she stood and gently lift her face up to his. Her breath caught as his fingers brushed behind her ear.

"You are no commoner." His deep voice was unusually soft. "You never were. The Fortress chose you before birth to be one of its keepers. Don't ever forget that."

"True as that may be, it doesn't guarantee that anyone will agree with you once we're there. Please," she searched his face for a sign of resignation, "don't make me do this alone."

"I wish you could see the truth about your place for what it is," he said. After taking another deep breath, he sighed. "But if it will make you feel better, your brother may come."

Isa put her head on his broad chest. "Thank you."

They stayed in the embrace for a long, rare moment. Isa wished she could keep him there forever, away from dignitaries, councils, and wars. Too soon, however, he gently pulled away and kissed the top of her head before lifting a stack of parchments from the table nearby, and sinking into a chair to peruse their contents.

"You know I don't dislike Launce, but life would be easier for both of us if he would just trust me."

Isa let out a short burst of laughter. "Can you blame him?"

"Actually," Ever drew his eyebrows together, "yes, I can. He should trust your judgment in marrying me."

"To be perfectly honest, he thinks you have me under a spell." Isa couldn't quite hide her bemused smile as Ever's head snapped up from his papers with a horrified look. She walked over and sat on the edge of his chair. "Try to see it from his perspective," she said. "He blames himself for allowing me come here in the first place. He didn't see all the months of change in you that I did as we broke the spell. All he knew was that you threatened to kill his family in the autumn, and then you married his sister the next spring. You know I'm trying, but it will take time for him to really know *you*."

"If he loathes me so much," Ever scowled, "then why does he insist on spending so much time here?"

"You never had a brother or sister." Isa shook her head affectionately, wrapping her arms around his shoulders where he sat. "The ties are . . . inexplicable. My brother is a part of me, and he always will be, whether I like it or not. He wants to protect me."

"How does he honestly expect to do that? He can barely lift a sword without injuring himself."

"You were powerless against Nevina," Isa reminded him quietly. "Yet you still tried to save me."

Ever stopped trying to read the parchments and stared listlessly out the window. He didn't like talking about the part he had played in the Fortress's curse, particularly not the last night, when the greedy Tumenian princess had nearly caused Isa's death.

"He stays because he loves me," Isa said. "Isn't that worthy of some respect?"

Ever stared at her for a long time before his eyes softened. "Yes, I suppose it is."

3

FLAT SIDE OF THE BLADE

"I don't want to do it," Launce frowned at his sister. "I am not a member of the court. There is no reason for me to know swordplay." Launce *had* been enjoying the second day of their ride east. They were traveling through an exotic canyon with walls made of red sandstone and small scrub brush bushes at the bottom. A river snaked down the canyon floor, filling the air with a constant rushing sound of busyness. Admiring the scenery and watching for rattlesnakes in this strange little canyon had done everything Launce had needed it to and more to help distract him from the thoughts that constantly plagued him back in the city these days.

That was, until Everard had announced to Launce that they were practicing swordplay that night.

Isa stared at her hands as she fingered her left wrist the way she always did when distraught. "I told you, he's just trying to help."

"Look, I don't want to! What is so hard to understand about that? Why do you always have to take *his* side?"

"I am not trying to take sides! I love both of you!"

A movement from the camp caught their attention when Cerise, Isa's lady-in-waiting, glanced at them in concern before meeting their eyes and quickly looking away. Isa took a deep breath before lowering her voice and speaking again. "I need both of you. I just happen to think he's right in this instance. It would be safer if you learned—"

"Why did you even bring me out here if you were just going to side with him?" Launce glared at her through the quickly thickening darkness of the evening.

"I wanted to see you." Then, in a smaller voice, she added, "You've been avoiding me lately."

"I've been busy with Blanchette." He folded his arms and stared out into the blue, orange, and red layered depths of the skies, hoping she wouldn't call his bluff.

"No, you haven't!" Then her tone softened as she looked up at him with a pitying expression that was annoyingly close to their mother's, something he'd seen all too often as of late.

"And how do you know that?"

"Mother told me . . ." her voice trailed off as she fingered her red riding dress. "All I want to do is spend time like we used to. I know things are different now—"

"Different is an understatement, Isa. He's done nothing but make you miserable your whole life! First he ruined your ankle and wrist. Then he threatened to kill all of us if you didn't come live with him all alone—"

"The servants were there."

"We didn't know that! He kept you there for months without so much as a message to let us know you weren't dead, or worse! And then you married him!" Launce didn't realize he was shouting until Everard looked up from where he was talking with his guards and stood. Launce thought he might lose his mind if he had to face his brother-in-law at that moment, but Isa shook her head at her husband. The king hesitantly sat down again, but not without glaring pointedly at Launce, a look Launce did his best to ignore.

"I've told you, it's hard to explain, but he's different now. And I didn't bring you along to talk about this. I want to talk to *you*. I miss you," she finished in a quiet voice that threatened to soften his heart.

"Well, that's too bad." Launce turned away from his sister's pleading eyes and began to walk away. "Because you made your choice." Part of him felt terrible as he left his sister standing alone. But he was too angry to apologize for his words. They sounded cruel, but they'd made perfect sense the countless times he'd practiced telling her exactly what he thought. He had waited five months to tell her what he thought of her marriage, so when the opportunity came, the words had spilled out of him like a bowl with too much broth, haphazardly and without order.

As he stomped over to his horse and pulled the waterskin from his pack, Isa silently returned to Cerise and picked up a set of knitting needles, which she began to use in exaggerated, dangerous motions. Everyone else seemed suddenly very interested in their own pursuits. The servants cooked supper over a large fire, the guards swapped what Launce guessed to be embellished feats of victory, and Everard was already examining his sword, a sign of the dreaded practice sure to soon come.

It was difficult for Launce to look at the king without suppressing the desire to sneer at him. And as far as Launce could tell, the feeling was mutual.

Everard had approached him the day before, just before their party had set out for Cobren. Though it had still been dark out at the time, the servants were already running about like frenzied ants to make sure the king and queen were well prepared for their journey, and Isa was busy exchanging goodbyes with their parents and little sister when the king had pulled him aside.

"I gather that joining us on this journey was not your idea." Everard had given him a hard look. "You're coming because Isa asked you to?"

"Yes," Launce had answered him evenly, trying to match Everard's unmoving expression.

"If it will make her feel more comfortable, then I am grateful for your help. But—" The king had fixed his burning eyes on Launce in such a way that Launce had to fight the need to squirm. "I need your word that you will obey me without question should the need arise."

It had galled Launce that his brother-in-law would treat him so. Launce wanted to reply that what he did was his own business, but he'd bitten his tongue just in time. Relative or not, Everard was still the king, something Launce's father reminded him often. The Maker had seen fit to make it that way, although Launce often found himself wondering why.

"If you need an incentive," Everard's words had been low and dangerous, "and you are not to repeat this to a soul, not even your sister, something is amiss in Cobren. I'm allowing you to come because I know you care for Isa, and I need to know someone is watching out for her when I'm not around. Can you swear to me that you will obey me for your sister's sake?"

The words had surprised Launce so much, he'd nearly let his mouth fall open. Everard had never given him a secret before. And though he still hated being ordered around like a child, he'd finally nodded, a sliver of unease rippling through his body at the disquiet in Everard's voice. If being near Isa might keep her safe somehow from whatever had the king on edge, Launce would endure it for her sake.

But that did not mean he had to like it.

While the others waited for supper to finish cooking, Launce walked past the clearing they had camped at to stand on a wide bank just beside the small, swift river they were following through the chasm. Everard was no longer watching him, talking quietly instead with his personal guard, Norbert, and Isa was still intent on stabbing the life out of whatever she was knitting. Launce almost felt guilty for making her so angry. She hated knitting.

As he stared up at the stars that were slowly appearing in the twilight sky, Launce had to wonder again at Everard's choice to use him to help protect Isa. Launce had seen the king's skill with the sword, as with other weapons, and he had to admit that no one he'd ever seen could compare. The only thing Launce could imagine himself doing to remotely protect Isa was saving her from herself. Of course, that alone would be no easy task.

Of course, a small, annoying voice in his head prodded, *it might be easier if you admitted you were just a bit jealous as well.*

Nonsense. Nothing could serve to make him jealous of his sister. And yet, the hole Blanchette's missing company had created was most assuredly there. Had she still lived in Soudain, he would have asked to bring her, too. Launce could imagine her sitting beside him, raising her head toward the blackening sky, saying all the right things, flipping her goldenrod hair from her face in that adorable way she did.

But she wasn't coming back, and Launce didn't even know where she was or what she was doing, aside from what the note had said. He was tempted to take it out of his pocket and read it again. It wouldn't do any good though. He already had it memorized.

Launce,

Blanchette is safe, but you need to know that my daughter is no longer to be your concern. You are living a new life now, but it is not the life best for her. Do not search for us. We have begun our own new life, and Blanchette is to be married in a week's time. He is the son of an old friend, and she is happy. Please do not dash her happiness by searching. You would only cause her heartache.

John Guerin

Launce knew that John couldn't read or write, so the letter had to have been written by Blanchette, which made it all the more painful. Launce had taught her to read and write, so reading the letter in her hand was like hearing the words directly from her. She could have written anything, and her father wouldn't have known. She could have given him some hint as to where she was or that she didn't want to be married. And yet she hadn't, so after two years of courtship he had naught to show for it but the yellow, wrinkled letter.

"Supper is finished," one of the servants called. Soon, everyone except the two guards on watch was huddled around the fire. Launce ate his supper quietly as he listened to the group's hushed conversations, which seemed to have recovered from his argument with his sister. Only Isa still looked unsettled. After finally giving up on her knitting, she'd snuggled up against Everard with his cloak drawn about her, exhaustion heavy on her face.

The savory food Launce had been enjoying felt dry as he swallowed. His intention hadn't been to make his sister unhappy. But just knowing that it was Everard she had chosen, who had caused her fourteen years of pain, felt like a stab in the back.

"Alright, Isa." Everard stood and looked down at his wife. "Let's have a round before we turn in for the night." A nervous smile lit Isa's face as he helped her stand. Launce groaned inwardly. He had been dreading this activity since they'd set off. His brother-in-law seemed incapable of missing a practice session no matter where they were . . . or who wanted to participate.

They had gone through such practice the night before, so Launce knew what to expect. It would begin with Isa, who no matter how tired she was, couldn't resist anything involving movement since her ankle and wrist had been healed. It would end, however, with everyone but the servants, and sometimes even them, having a round with the king. Launce had managed to edge his way out the night before, but he was sure Everard wouldn't let him off the hook tonight.

Everyone settled in to watch as the king and queen faced off. As they moved, Everard gave instructions, praises, and critiques. Isa began the match with the same look of weariness she'd worn since the argument, but as she got deeper into the movements, the fire in her eyes grew brighter, and she focused more. She was improving in form to be sure, but Launce couldn't help noticing that there was no blue light tonight that flowed from her hands. He wondered whether that was by choice, or if she simply didn't have any to give this time.

It wasn't a secret that Isa's power was flailing instead of growing as it should have been, but it was a topic that wasn't widely discussed either. Everard made sure to silence all idle tongues in his court when it came to Isa's abilities, and commoners in general didn't discuss their monarchs' power at all. Still, somehow, everyone knew that the queen was struggling. It didn't trouble Launce much, if he were honest. In fact, it made her seem a little more like the sister he knew. But she was obviously bothered by it.

"That will be enough for tonight. You did better on the second form this time," Everard announced. Launce watched incredulously as Isa beamed at Ever, in spite of his stern tone. How could she stand to be treated so callously? He didn't have much time to wonder at his sister's madness, however, because Everard was suddenly looking at him.

"Launce, it's your turn." Everard held out one of the practice swords. Launce had the urge to slap it away, but knew better than to even fully entertain that thought.

"I'll just watch today."

"Come now." Everard held the sword out even farther. "All young men of the court are expected to learn."

Launce felt rage bubble up inside his gut. He wasn't a member of the court, and he never had been. But Everard was the king, and he had promised to obey. Still, he and Everard shared a long look before Launce unhappily accepted the sword.

The weapon felt large and clumsy in his hands as he moved into the clearing they had made for the practice. Everard's body melted into a ready position, like a snake coiled to strike. Launce tried to mimic him, feeling foolish. How much humiliation would Everard heap upon him tonight?

Norbert declared match begun. Neither of them moved, however. When Everard stayed still for far too long, Launce realized that the king was allowing him the first attack. Raising the weapon high, he lunged. The king lifted his sword just enough to block the exaggerated movement, then touched Launce's back with the flat side of his blade. It didn't hurt, but if it had been a real fight, Launce would already be dead.

"You communicate your intentions with your whole body," Everard said in a tense voice. "Don't waste your energy on such full movements. Keep them short."

Launce had no desire to do anything his brother-in-law told him to do. It was bad enough that he'd ordered him out in front of everyone just to embarrass him. Everard knew well how Launce struggled with the sword. Countless forced rounds at the Fortress had already proven that. Anger coursed through Launce's body as he threw himself in for another attack. Again, it seemed Everard hardly flicked his wrist before disarming Launce completely.

"Slow your breathing!" Everard said as he circled a weaponless Launce. "You'll pass out before the fight is half done."

Launce just stood there, hoping the torture would be over soon. His hopes of being left alone, however, were dashed as Everard pointed with his sword at Launce's blade where it had landed in the sand across the clearing. Launce glared at him a moment more, but Everard's stone face never moved. With a huff, Launce slowly went to pick up his sword, wishing the whole time that his sister had not married the king. The punishment for trying to bloody his brother-in-law's nose would have been less severe. For now, Launce could only fantasize.

It didn't matter how many times he suffered defeat. Familiar shame filled him as everyone watched him fight once more without so much as ruffling the king's fine golden hair. How many times would his brother-in-law insist on humiliating him this way before he stopped demanding Launce's obedience and participation? How many times would Launce be able to stand there as everyone watched him flail about helplessly like a clumsy child? He didn't know if he could take it very much longer.

One more desperate attack, and one more infuriating stumble later, and Launce refused to stand or raise his sword any more. He crouched in the dirt where Everard had left him, pebbles cutting into his palms and knees. Only the fact that his sister and her maid were watching them kept him from turning and throwing himself at Everard in anger, the way he would have at any other man who would dare to treat him in such a way.

"Ever." Isa's voice broke through the tension that had suddenly filled the clearing. Everard didn't move, however, as Launce tried to calm himself. When he didn't respond at first, Isa called her husband's name again, warning thick in her voice this time. "That's enough." A moment later, the king stood before him, offering his hand to help Launce up. Launce looked up at him, but the gallantry of the act was overridden by the disgust written all over the king's face.

Launce stood on his own, ignoring Everard's outstretched hand, but Everard grabbed and pulled him in as if congratulating him. In Launce's ear, however, he whispered, "Acting like a child will do you no good. Try to learn something once in a while." When Everard finally released him, Launce shoved away from the king, perhaps a little too hard.

"I believe it's my turn for a beating." Edgar was quick to pop off the rock he had been seated on. As he walked between Everard and Launce, he good-naturedly tapped Launce's sword with his own. Launce nodded his thanks before going to sit by himself at the edge of the circle.

Eventually they all had their turns, and everyone was seated again as they stared into the embers of the fire. It was high time everyone was in bed, but the chill of autumn made it cold enough that no one wanted to get up and actually lie down. So instead, they sat around the fire passing around wine and ale, telling stories.

"I propose a toast." Norbert raised his wineskin. "In honor of our queen's first official outing. May she strike the ladies with jealousy and the kings with admiration, and then find it all terribly boorish and want to return home as soon as possible."

"I'll drink to that," someone chuckled. Even Everard cracked a smile and looked down at Isa, who was curled up at his side, with an expression that nearly convinced Launce that the king truly did love his sister.

Nearly.

4

A BROTHER NEVER FORGETS

*I*t had taken a good deal of Ever's self-control for him not to march over to Isa's brother and strangle him when she'd returned from their argument with tears in her eyes. He'd restrained himself, however, because he knew she would have been even more upset if he'd interfered. So instead, as he had listened to them argue, Ever had contented himself with imagining how miserable he would make Launce during the sword practice he'd planned for later that evening.

Isa's relationship with her family was a mystery to Ever. She was different when she was around them, more like a child, more comfortable with who she was. And for that reason, a part of Ever balked whenever she wanted to spend time with them. They were so cohesive. Everyone, from the father to the youngest daughter, had a place and a function. They squabbled and laughed and teased each other continually. And yet, part of him relished the chance to study her among the people that had produced such an unusual creature as his wife.

Though it had been five months since the wedding, and the curse on the Fortress had kept them together for the entire winter before that, Ever felt uncomfortable sometimes when he realized how little he truly knew Isa. And it wasn't for a lack of trying on her part.

Just a few weeks before, Isa had waltzed into his study with two goblets of wine and a basket of fruit and sweets. "I spoke with Garin, and I know your afternoon is free of politics, councils, and hearings." She had raised her eyebrows, daring him to challenge her. "We are going on a picnic, and Garin is not to disturb us unless the Fortress itself is on fire."

Ever had walked around his desk to properly greet his wife, chuckling at her scheming. "You've had this planned for a while, haven't you?" he'd asked, peeking under the basket to see his favorite meat pies. As she beamed at him, he noticed that she wore a new dress. Its midnight blue matched her eyes, just as the jewels in her curled hair matched their sparkle. The pink of her lips suddenly had him wishing it were proper to scoop her up and escape the Fortress entirely as fast as his legs could carry them.

"When you leave on all of these diplomatic visits, it does give me some time to think." Isa's tone was just a touch reproachful. Smiling, Ever had leaned down to indulge himself with a kiss, but she'd grabbed his right hand instead and thrust the basket into his other hand.

"We're going *now*, before Destin finds some other way to fall apart and desperately need you."

Laughing, Ever had allowed her to drag him toward the door. Just as they'd reached it, however, a knock sounded. Isa's face went white, and Ever had inwardly groaned as his favorite general stepped in.

"Your Highnesses." Acelet bobbed a bow at both of them. "I—" He stopped short, though, when he saw the basket Ever carried. "I am so sorry," he said in a soft voice, "but I fear I must interrupt."

"What is it?" Ever had growled in an attempt not to moan like a spoiled child, which was exactly what he had wanted to do at that moment.

General Acelet held up his hands apologetically. "The king of Siamji is here, demanding to speak with you."

Ever had felt his eyes nearly pop as he stared at his general and then at Isa. He knew what was coming.

Acelet looked at the ground again. "I honestly am sorry, Your Highness," he spoke, this time to Isa. It was exactly what she had predicted. "But you know how he is . . ."

"Let's just go." Ever had handed the basket back to Isa and stormed out the door. "The sooner we see him, the sooner he will leave."

And so their lovely escape had turned into an afternoon and then an evening of listening to the whiny king pontificate about how another king had slighted him, and Ever had been forced to sit across from his dutiful wife, watching her as she fought the tears she deserved to cry.

Ever was adamant that his marriage not end up like his parents', but finding that balance was proving to be a much greater struggle than he'd anticipated. He had desperately hoped this trip would give them a chance to step away from their normal duties, to simply enjoy one another. Then she had asked to bring Launce along.

His immediate reaction had been to tell her no. This trip was supposed to be for them. True, they would bring along a few servants and guards, but that was to be expected. Ever hadn't planned on bringing the insolent young man who seemed intent on provoking him every chance he got.

Still, he'd wondered if having Launce along might not open new doors to Isa's true self. It wasn't as if he thought she was hiding anything from him purposefully. But Ever sensed that deep down, there was much more to her that she had buried, perhaps even unbeknownst to her. And although Ever didn't like to admit it, there was something about being around her brother that brought down her walls. Perhaps, if Ever learned how to find the true way to Isa's soul, she might find her full powers and her peace. And if nothing else, having one more set of eyes on Isa couldn't be a bad thing, particularly when her powers at present were so unpredictable.

So far, however, no good had come of Launce's presence. After their long exchange, Isa had hardly spoken a word all evening. She didn't even attempt to use her strength during their practice. Every time he glanced at her now, snuggled up against his arm with the fire's shadows flickering on and off her face, it became more apparent how upset she really was. His attempt at using this journey as a time to break down her walls was off to a dismal start.

"Launce," Norbert said in his song-song fashion, interrupting Ever's musings, "queens like ours do not learn bravery overnight. Surely you must have a tale about your sister from when she was young." Ever kept his face smooth, but was immediately grateful to his eldest guard for the suggestion.

Launce hesitated as the others looked at him eagerly, his eyes flicking to his sister and then Ever. Ever made sure his nod was grave enough that the young man wouldn't think him desperate. Isa didn't look at him at all, just stared straight ahead into the flames as they licked the cool night air.

"Come now, lad," Norbert prodded. "Give us a tale for sweet dreams." Launce looked once more at Ever before finally nodding in consent.

"After the accident ..." Launce started.

Ever's jaw tightened at the mention of the *accident*, as they called it, though Isa's fourteen years of pain had been wholly his own fault. "My father wanted to give Isa a way to get around. We had an old mare, but Father used her for business, so he and Mother decided they would buy Isa her own horse.

"Father worked extra hard that year, driving bargains he'd never dared to before, and Mother went without a new dress that winter. Gifts were small on that Sacred Star Day, but we didn't mind. By spring, Isa had her horse."

Everyone sat, spellbound, as Launce spoke. Only Isa wore a distant look. Suddenly, Ever was uncomfortable. Something told him this wouldn't be a tale with a happy ending.

"Isa changed after the accident," Launce said quietly. "The other children used to wait for her at first, but when they realized she wasn't going to get any faster, they usually left her behind. Sometimes she would follow along—"

"Launce." Isa interrupted him, her voice unusually sharp. "You can skip that part." They shared a long look before Launce finally nodded. Ever suddenly wanted desperately to know what her brother had been about to say, but Isa seemed adamant, so Launce continued.

"Father got the horse from a neighbor who was moving to Bas Riviere. It was a spindly, brown thing named Doux, and he and Isa were inseparable. When she and Doux were together," he whispered, "they were invincible. She stopped worrying about keeping up or looking like everyone else . . ." He paused, then shook his head as if to clear it.

"Sometimes I would ride along on the family's old mare. I couldn't keep up when she galloped, but at least we had a way to go places together. We were out one summer . . . I think I was about eight, so she would have been twelve. It was late afternoon, and we were riding through an orange grove, one of those just north of the city. Isa decided to go for one more sprint when we reached the road. Doux kicked up a trail of dust, and the last I saw of them was when they rounded the corner.

"It took me a few minutes to catch up. The road wraps around the mountain so that it's impossible to see around the bend until one makes the turn."

Ever knew exactly the spot Launce spoke of, and by the looks on the faces around him, so did everyone else. It wasn't a good place for any young girl to be riding alone.

"Isa had come to a complete stop, and she was facing two large men on the ground. One held a bow, the arrow already nocked and pointed right at Isa. The other held a sword. He stood a bit closer to Isa, close enough to reach her with the sword. They both had light, thick hair, and when they spoke, had accents from the north.

"'Two horses!' the one with the sword called back with a smile. 'I told you the gods have smiled upon us!' The one with the bow didn't answer, just frowned more deeply and stretched his bow a bit tighter. 'Boy, I will tell you what I told the girl. Give us the horse, and you're free to go.'" Launce shook his head, his eyes full of wonder as he stared into the fire. "I trembled so that I nearly fell off my horse. But Isa just held their gaze, didn't even blink. Instead, she told me not to move. The two men stared at her in shock, and the one with the bow finally spoke. He said, 'You will get off those horses, or I will get you off myself.'

"'No, you won't,' Isa answered him. She was as calm as a breeze. The one with the sword chuckled. 'And why the blazes not?'

"'Because the Fortress is just a short ways up this mountain,' she said, 'and the king is there at this moment. If you kill me, the king will know, and he will hunt you down like the dogs you are. And believe me when I say his treatment of you will be anything but merciful.'"

Ever couldn't help but look down at his wife. She was a bit taller than most women, and since he had been training her, she'd certainly grown stronger than she had been before. But even now, in the light of the fire, she looked anything but fierce, with her shoulders slumped forward and her head against his arm. He suddenly burned with anger as he imagined anyone threatening to kill her. Launce's voice pulled him back into the story, however, before he had time to linger.

"The one with the sword stared at her as if she were mad. 'And how would a girl know such a thing?' he asked. 'I know,' she replied lifting her skirts just enough to show her ankle, 'because the power that flows from the king is the same power that crippled me.'"

Ever looked up to see Launce looking directly at him, and he knew why. Though all had been forgiven between Ever and his wife, shame still filled him with a sickly warmth. All along, the story had been for him. Isa's brother might be terrible with a sword, but he knew exactly how to use his words like a dagger in Ever's ribs, slowly carving his way to the heart.

"The thief with the sword seemed a bit taken aback, but the one with the bow immediately turned and pointed it at me," Launce continued, not bothering to break eye contact with Ever as he spoke. "'How about this,' he asked her. 'You get off your horses, or I'll kill the boy.' Without another word, Isa pulled herself off the horse. She landed on her bad ankle, as she didn't have a step to help her like we did at home."

Ever closed his eyes as he imagined Isa, the crippled child, trying to get off the horse by herself. The remorse that filled him was nearly painful.

"We walked home that night, Isa leaning on my arm. Father had to borrow a neighbor's horse to come looking for us. He didn't find us until it was almost sunrise." Launce shrugged. "That's the story. Isa nearly came to blows with two horse thieves, and she couldn't even walk."

Ever tried not to look as miserable as he felt. Launce was indeed skilled with words. He had pierced his king's heart in one of the only places it hadn't yet healed.

"How old are you, boy?" Norbert asked, rubbing his silver whiskers.

"Twenty," Launce replied.

"I think I remember those two." Norbert looked at Ever thoughtfully. Ever struggled to pull himself together so he could somewhat intelligently answer whatever his guard was about to ask. "We had gotten several complaints from the people in Soudain in just two days. Weren't you leading the contingent to find them?"

"It was the first contingent my father allowed me to lead on my own." Ever's voice felt tight as he answered, like a rope strained too far. The two horse thieves had been foreigners, unfamiliar with the Fortress monarchs' unusual abilities. He had simply had them chained and returned to the Fortress for his father to deal with. It was nothing too exciting, but now he found himself wishing he'd made them much more miserable first.

Everyone sat in an uncomfortable silence after Launce finished, not sure what they should do. It had certainly been a story that exemplified Isa's bravery, but it left a bitter taste, and whether he wanted them to or not, everyone knew why. Ever had been the one to injure Isa, and if it hadn't been for Ever, Isa never would have been threatened by such evil. It always came back to him, no matter what he did. Sometimes, it felt as though Ever would never be allowed peace with his wife. There was always the past of his actions to haunt them.

As they settled into their tents for the night, Ever looked at Isa as she began to slip into deeper breathing. The moon was covered by the clouds that had rolled in, but the fire was still burning, and he could just barely see the contour of her face. Her expression was finally peaceful as she slept, and Ever found himself wishing greatly to keep it just as peaceful when she awoke. One thing he knew for sure, however, was that no matter the past, it was now his duty to keep her safe.

No matter what the cost.

5

COMMONER

"*W*ould you hold still?" Cerise sighed as she readjusted Isa's sash for the third time. Instead of tugging on her sash, Isa decided to fiddle nervously with her jeweled necklace as she stared into the rose-tinted mirror that hung on the wall of her new chambers.

"Are you sure about this?" She touched the piles of curls that Cerise had heaped on top of her head. They felt unusually heavy in their precarious perch.

"Gigi gave me strict instructions." Cerise's own honey-colored curls bobbed as she finished braiding the sash into Isa's bodice. "She even made me practice on some of the other servants until I had it just right. Now," Cerise finally took Isa by the shoulders and looked her in the eyes, "*what* is the matter?"

Isa placed one of her hands on Cerise's and squeezed, glad to have her childhood friend with her.

Choosing Cerise as her head lady-in-waiting had caused no small uproar in the Fortress court. Unwittingly, Isa had offended the noble candidates who should have been her first choices when she'd requested Cerise as her lady-in-waiting, rather than choosing a traditional high-born lady-in-waiting. Ever, of course, hadn't given it a second thought when he'd said yes. As usual, he didn't care a wit about which of his odious cousins were offended, particularly if it made Isa happy.

"Have you seen those women? They're beautiful! All of them!"

"And?" Cerise pressed.

"They've been raised for moments like this! While they spent time learning which utensil to touch first, I was selling grain in my father's store." Isa shook her head, her massive pile of curls exaggerating her motions. "I don't want to shame my husband," she said quietly.

Before Cerise could respond, the door was unlocked, and Ever stepped through. The silver wolf stitched masterfully into his clothing glittered from his chest as he turned. His thick, midnight blue robe, cut to distinguish his broad shoulders and muscled arms, was drawn together by a thin silver belt that encircled his waist. A black cloak flowed behind him, accentuating the grace with which he moved. In his short, wheat-colored hair, he wore a thin silver circlet with flecks of gold.

It was moments like this, when he looked more imposing than ever, that Isa still sometimes found it difficult to believe he was the same man she'd fallen in love with while he was under the curse. Hoping to do at least some justice to their joined titles, she stood a little straighter as Cerise pulled her gown out so it draped properly. The silver shimmered every time the gown moved, and while it was excessively pretty, Isa had asked Gigi before they left if it wasn't too gaudy.

"I don't think you understand what a high rank you hold, my dear." Gigi had shaken her head as she'd looked at Isa. "It is no longer just about your husband. The law says that you are just as much a ruler of the Fortress as he is. The first night will be essential to showing all of the northern kingdoms that you, too, are a force to be reckoned with, that you're worthy of respect. No gown or ornament will be too much for that first banquet."

But as Isa stared into the mirror, the queen that everyone expected and the queen that now hid beneath the shimmering silver dress suddenly felt like two very different people.

"We need to be going," Ever announced as he rubbed his sword with his cloak. "They will be announcing us soon." Another wave of nausea hit Isa as he turned and looked her up and down with an appraising look, the same look he gave his soldiers during inspections. Then, with a cursory nod, he offered his arm. Just before she took it, Cerise cried out.

"Wait, Your Highness!" Running to the back of the room, Cerise thrust her arm to the bottom of a bag and pulled out a small red velvet pouch. She loosened the drawstrings and pulled out a delicate silver laurel wreath. Leaves were woven in and out of one another with such grace that Isa gasped as Cerise brought it closer. Just as she was placing it on Isa's head, Isa caught a glimpse of sapphires the size of rose seeds sprinkled all over it.

"There." Cerise beamed at Ever. "She's ready."

"That she is." Ever nodded.

"I'm confused," Isa whispered as they left their chambers. "Shouldn't we be showing deference to the hosting king and queen? I feel a bit . . . conspicuous."

"If we were at home, we would be in our ceremonial attire," Ever said, inclining his head at a bowing stranger. Isa envied the ease and comfort with which he accepted the attention that made her want to cringe. "We are, however, to be the guests of honor here. Seven years ago, my father and I helped King Rafael quell a rebellion that threatened to tear the kingdom in half."

"So many wars . . ." Isa couldn't help wondering aloud.

"There would have been many more had the Fortress not given us the ability to intervene," Ever said in a low voice as they walked. "Tumen is not the only kingdom that tends to test boundaries. It's important that the other monarchs see we are watching. Evil persists when unchecked."

As they rounded the corner and turned down another low-hanging hallway, she prayed that Launce would be ready by the time they reached his chambers. Ever had commissioned the Fortress tailor to create new, appropriate clothes for her brother before they'd gone, and Isa wasn't sure if Launce would know how all of the fancy pieces would fit together. And from the look on Ever's face, he wasn't in any mood to wait for a boy who couldn't dress himself. So when Launce came to the door disgruntled, but all in one piece, Isa sent up a prayer of thanks.

"You look very handsome," she whispered back to him as the three of them made their way toward the ballroom.

"I feel like a fop," he said, daring a glance at Ever. Ever's mouth tightened just a bit, but he said nothing in response. To Isa's relief and horror, they arrived at the end of the hall just then. The hall ended in a balcony, which looked out over a great ballroom, and on it stood a lanky herald dressed in what Isa guessed to be the Cobriens' colors, fire orange and red. He stood with a large pole, which he pounded upon the floor twice before declaring in a loud voice, "Welcoming His Royal Highnesses, King Rafael and Queen Monica's guests of honor, the venerable King Everard Perrin Auguste Fortier of Destin, Queen Isabelle Fortier, and Her Highness's brother, Launce Marchand."

Isa felt her face warm at the shortness of her name, and her heart went out to Launce when she saw a few people snicker at the common surname. Thankfully, after the assembly bowed and curtsied and the pole had been pounded twice more, they were able to make their way down the front staircase and into the crowd. Ever led them directly toward the thrones on the right side of the large room.

As they walked, Isa was struck by how very beautiful the smooth red floor stones were, and how carefully they must have been laid. *Head up,* she reminded herself, fighting the sudden desire to study the floor. Instead, she strained to hold her head with completely unfounded confidence as her etiquette tutors had taught her to do, smiling benevolently at those around her who bowed as the crowd parted for them so they could reach the thrones.

When paying homage to the kings and queens of other countries in their own lands, the shrill voice of her etiquette tutor echoed in her head, *you will curtsy, but only so much. Keep your head up so others will know your station. You are showing them respect, not subservience, for you are not their subjects. You are their peers. Head up, now. You're not a commoner any longer, Your Highness.*

"Ah, Everard." King Rafael stood and held his hands out to greet Ever as they stepped up onto the large, round dais. Ever took them both in his own and gave them one firm shake. "It is good to have you back under more joyous circumstances." He then turned to look at Isa, taking her hand and bowing to kiss it. Isa forced the most confident smile she could muster, inclining her head in return.

"Your bride is even lovelier than the rumors here suggested." He raised a bushy brow at Ever. "I find it hard to believe she was ever a commoner." Isa felt her face grow hot, and glanced sideways at Ever, unsure of whether or not she had just been insulted.

"The Fortress chooses those who are worthy." Ever's voice was velvet and dangerous. "It does not see commoners and royalty."

"Of course," the other king said quickly. "I only meant that she is striking. Please," he gestured with a meaty hand at the empty places closest to thrones. "Do stay near. We will be beginning the banquet shortly." Ever once again nodded, and Isa and Launce dropped a quick curtsy and bow before moving over to the right of the throne. The men and women standing near the spot he'd gestured to spread out even further so that the three Destinians were nearly alone, despite the sea of nobles and royals that filled the great hall.

As they stood waiting for the rest of the guests to be announced, Isa used the time to discreetly study the two women on the king's left side. Both shared the same lovely complexion as most of the people around them, fair skin kissed by the sun with just a tinge of olive. Queen Monica sat, but Princess Olivia stood. Neither of them were as tall as Isa, but both more fully proportioned. The deep-set hickory eyes of the queen appeared distant and somewhat preoccupied, but the princess looked the way Isa felt, her eyes wide and her face paler than the rest of her skin. Isa could only imagine her fears, knowing she would unknowingly meet her future husband that night.

The princess's prospects were mixed from what Isa could see. There was a large number of unaccompanied men present, and quite a few were a great deal older than the princess, some even older than King Rafael himself. Isa suddenly felt mildly repulsed for the princess's sake, and hoped she would be won by someone more fitting for her age at least, if nothing else.

The pole sounded three times, quieting the crowd, and the king stood and raised his hands.

"Let us adjourn to the banquet hall, where each of you has had a special place prepared." After the king, queen, and princess stood and began walking down the dais, Ever stepped into line and followed them. Isa found herself very glad that etiquette required her to hold his arm. She would have been terribly lost among the great throng of people, had she been left by herself. Launce walked behind them, and following him, the servants placed the people in the correct order, Isa guessed, so from greatest rank to the least. It was unnerving to think that she wouldn't have even qualified to stand at the end of the line just the year before.

King Rafael led the procession through a tall arched opening into a long room filled with a cedar table that stretched from one end of the room to the other. Isa followed Ever's lead, continuing to stand even when they had been brought to their places on the long bench on their side of the table. It was astounding how many people would have to crowd into the room, despite its enormous length.

The walls in this room were whitewashed just like the rest of the palace walls were, with great timber beams crisscrossing the low ceilings. Each wall had one large arched fireplace in the center, as only one wouldn't have been able to heat the entire room. Intricate murals were painted on the walls around each hearth, large images of women dancing in twirling skirts the colors of strawberries and limes and oranges and lemons. Each of the painted women had the same deep-set hickory eyes as the queen, and each wore a smile as she performed.

Isa's musings were interrupted when everyone was finally in the dining hall, and the king sat, gesturing for everyone else to do so as well. Ever was seated on the king's right hand while Queen Monica sat on his left, the princess sitting to her left, just across from Isa. Isa wished desperately that she could have sat beside the princess, for they seemed to be suffering from the same set of nerves. Launce also looked about the table with wide eyes, but said nothing, and Isa wondered if he was regretting his decision to come with her. She didn't have time to ask, because a holy man was brought to the room and asked to thank the Maker.

The first course followed the prayer, and Isa was very grateful to have something to do with her hands besides twist them nervously under the table. She was aware of the eyes of a number of men and even more women upon her as she began to eat, and she hoped her hands didn't shake too visibly as they watched her.

"So, I want to welcome you back from your rendezvous with the Maker," King Rafael was saying to Ever. Isa studied her salted fish with renewed vigor as she waited to hear what Ever would say. While the encounter between the Fortress and its once wayward prince had ended well, it was still a somewhat intimate matter.

Fully explaining to others what had gone on there during the curse, the way the Maker, through the Fortress, had brought about change in both of them, was next to impossible. Only Launce, to Isa's knowledge, had come even close to understanding it, and that was most likely due to the nature of their relationship. Her brother had always been able to read her. Not that any of that would matter to the curious King Rafael.

"Thank you." Ever's deep voice was steady, but Isa detected a note of caution in it. "It is good to be traveling again."

"I must ask, what were you doing all that time, cooped up in that great citadel?" The king took a great bite of his fish before leaning so close to Ever that Isa could hardly hear his next words. "Rumor has it that Nevina had put you under some sort of curse?" Isa glanced at her husband to see his jaw tighten slightly at the name of the Tumenians' late princess.

"You should know better than to believe in rumors, Rafael. They will get you nothing but trouble."

"How will I know what to believe then if no one tells me otherwise?" the other king pressed. His voice was polite, but his brown eyes gleamed with interest.

"Suffice it to say that when the Maker gives you a great deal of power, and you choose to use it unwisely, his servants, such as the Fortress, will have no choice other than to show you the error of your ways," Ever responded as he looked the king straight in the eye. His blue fiery gaze was so stern that the king held it only for a moment before looking down at his food again and changing the topic.

Isa lost interest in the men's conversation after that, something about a recent excess of rabbits in farmlands, and she began to listen to see what the other royals and nobles were doing without the attention of their host king. The cacophony of voices was lively, many of the others deep into various conversations by now. As she watched, she caught other eyes watching her as well. Most of the men smiled, as well as some of the women, but a few simply stared, no inkling of friendliness in their tight lips, despite Isa's attempt at smiling. One in particular did nothing to hide her displeasure, glowering openly at Isa so intensely that Isa felt her smile falter upon meeting the stranger's eyes.

Isa had noticed the woman earlier, and she was nearly as tall as Isa, maybe even taller. Her delicate white skin, fiery red hair, and green eyes made it obvious she wasn't from Cobren. Her oval-shaped face would have been lovely, filled with almond eyes and rosy cheeks, had it not been so full of wrath. Isa wondered if this was one of Ever's serious contenders at his own betrothal ball, the one that had ended in a war with Nevina. The hate in the woman's eyes made Isa long to shrivel behind her husband. It was also at that moment that Isa realized her ridiculous pile of curls was beginning to give her a headache.

"Did that woman eat a wolverine?" Launce leaned over and whispered in Isa's ear. Isa nearly choked on the bite of potato she'd just put in her mouth. As soon as Isa laughed, the red-haired woman scowled even deeper before turning to the woman next to her and whispering in her ear.

"This is why I wanted you to come," Isa muttered to her brother. "It's going to take me a while to get used to this." Launce's response was cut off when the second course was announced, candied beets with nuts and sprigs of mint garnishing the plate. Isa turned her focus back to using the correct utensils, and as she did, King Rafael's voice caught her attention once again.

"About time we found a new path to choosing a successor." He sounded proud as he dug into the beets.

"How were successors chosen before?" Isa asked.

"Like your Fortress, a child of either sex can inherit the throne here in Cobren," Rafael said, a piece of food falling out of his mouth as he spoke. "I don't know if you are aware of it, Isabelle, but our two kingdoms are the only ones in the northern realm that allow daughters to be crowned as sovereigns." When Isa nodded, he continued. "Anyhow, the hopeful successors, mostly royals, second born and such from other kingdoms, and nobles from our own court, would face a series of interviews, tests run by the king, queen, and their advisors. All tedious, trifling affairs, I can assure you."

"What changed?"

The king leaned forward eagerly, this time speaking again to Ever. "As much respect as I have for you, my old friend," he whispered gleefully, "the Fortress and its inhabitants are no longer the main instruments the Maker will be using in the world." Then, leaning in even closer, he said, "The Maker has sent us a special holy man to divinely appoint this heir." Alarm shot through Isa's body as the king sat back and grinned, although she wasn't sure why. Ever had frozen completely, the rings of fire in his eyes burning more intensely than Isa had seen since the Fortress curse had broken. Even Launce's jaw had dropped. It took a moment, but Ever was the first to recover his voice.

"And how is this new method to take place?"

"Ah, you'll have to wait to find out," the king answered mischievously. "The same as everyone else." Then the king's gaze fell upon Launce. "You should try though, lad! Anyone can enter." Launce sent a petrified look to Isa and then Ever, and Isa almost dropped her spoon when Ever responded that they would think about it.

As she looked in shock at her husband, Isa sensed that he was keeping something from her, something important, and she resolved immediately to find out what.

6

WHAT MEN WILL DO

$\mathcal{B}$y the time the king declared everyone should dance, Isa's head throbbed as though a mason had laid a stack of bricks upon it. Ever offered her his arm, but his eyes were distant. Launce looked sick, though Isa guessed that was due to the many piles of rich food he had just consumed, and not the dancing itself.

Despite her party's current state of mind, Isa was relieved to have reached the final part of the opening ball. In secret, she had looked forward to it, relishing the anticipation of dancing with her husband. Her desire to dance with him grew even stronger when she noticed just how many women's eyes were trained on his fine form. And though she often struggled to harness the strength from the Fortress within her, it was so strong now that she had to flex her hands a few times to keep it hidden, heat building, threatening to burst from them as many of the ladies openly gawked. Frightening them with a little display would do little to improve their opinion of her, she chided herself . . . even if they did deserve it.

Ever led Isa and Launce over to the far center of the throne room, the same one they had been introduced in. From the front of the crowd, near the two golden thrones, they had a good view of the dance floor, which had been cleared for the ceremony.

A large group of musicians set in a corner began to play, a melody of sweetness and sorrow. As the music began, the king led his daughter out into the center of the floor. The smile the princess gave her father was lovely, her dark eyes gazing into her father's face. Isa noticed for the first time that the princess's skirt was a bright salmon color, and unlike her own complicated gown, looked as though it had simply been made to twirl. With each step, the fabric fanned out gracefully, making the princess resemble a flower in bloom. A movement to

Isa's side made her realize Launce was watching, too, his eyes more unguarded than she'd seen them in a long time, and it made her smile.

The sweet dance was over soon, and Isa's stomach fluttered with excitement as she looked up at her own dance partner. The night before, as Ever had explained the order of events to Isa, he'd made it clear that this was to be an important dance.

"As we are the guests of honor, the second dance will be for the king and queen and us," he'd said.

"Everyone else will be watching?"

"It doesn't matter." Ever had smiled and tapped her on the nose. "Surely you've had enough practice." At that, she'd blushed a bit, and he'd gone on to explain. "This is the first chance most of our peers and their nobles will have to see us together. It's important for them to see a united front, and that you are truly the queen the Fortress has chosen."

When she looked up at him now, Ever seemed completely unaware that the people around him were staring. Even the musicians hesitated, waiting for the guests of honor to join the king and queen on the dance floor.

"Ever," she whispered, tugging discreetly on his arm. After a moment, his eyes finally rested upon her, and he gave her a polite smile as he seemed to realize what they were supposed to be doing. Even when they were out on the dance floor, however, as soon as the music began, his eyes resumed their search of the crowd.

The dance was slow, one Isa knew well, but it failed to bring the feelings of peace she'd look so forward to. His calloused hand held hers loosely, and his movements were just slightly behind the music, not enough for the spectators to notice, but Isa could tell. As they turned, she watched his face miserably, wishing with all her heart that he might look down at her just once. His fiery eyes were occupied, however, and his jaw was set tightly in a line Isa knew well.

For all Ever's talk of showing everyone the Fortress's chosen queen, it suddenly appeared to be of little importance. Isa didn't even bother to glance at her feet, for she could feel that no blue fire whirled around them now, though from her husband's lack of attention or her lack of ability, she couldn't tell.

As soon as the dance was finished, Ever didn't hesitate, but immediately led them off the floor. The crowd began to rearrange itself, some people going to dance while others formed clumps. Somehow, Ever found the very group of women that had stared at her during supper.

"Isabelle."

Isa nearly cringed as he used her full name. She hated that royals didn't use nicknames in public.

"This is Lady Beata, Lady Jadzia, and Princess Damira." He slightly bowed to the three colorfully adorned women. Each woman curtsied in turn. The one who had glowered at Isa earlier responded to the name of Jadzia, and her eyes never left Ever's face as he spoke, not even when he introduced his wife.

"I would like for you ladies to become acquainted with my wife. Isabelle, I have some business to attend to. Please enjoy yourself." Isa watched him incredulously as he stalked away. Was he really leaving her alone with them?

"Queen Isabelle," the one named Princes Damira began. Her hair was the color of acorns, and it was worn long and straight with jeweled pins scattered throughout it. Isa envied the princess as her own head throbbed worse than ever with the weight of her hair. "It is wonderful to finally meet the lucky queen."

"Luck had nothing to do with it," Lady Jadzia reminded her companion. "She was chosen." Lady Jadzia's pale eyes glittered as she spoke, and her ruby lips pulled up at one corner.

"How is your family doing?" Isa did her best to ignore the jab by looking at Lady Beata, suddenly very grateful that her tutor had forced her not only to memorize all of the royal and noble names of their neighboring lands, but their current affairs as well. "Has your family repaired the damaged wing of your home yet?" The young woman looked as though Isa's personal question had surprised her.

"They've started . . ." she began, her composure melting away a bit. "The fire did more damage than we had originally thought though."

"So how have you and Everard been spending your time since the wedding?" Jadzia asked. Isa noticed the woman eyeing her shoulders, and was immediately very aware of her own suntanned arms which, thanks to Gigi, were on display for the entire ball to see through her thin sleeves.

"We have both been kept busy," she began, wondering at the woman's audacity. Even her commoner parents had taught her such questions were beyond rude. But before she could finish her answer, however, a movement caught Isa's eye, and she realized she'd been unconsciously searching the crowd for her husband. Launce was off in a corner hiding behind a platter of dried fruits, but it took her a moment to find Ever, and when she did, she felt her heart beat unevenly.

He was talking animatedly to a woman in the clothing of one of the southern kingdoms. If her dress hadn't given it away, her appearance would have. The woman held a proud posture, the fine curve to her neck and straightness of her back exactly what Isa's tutors had been trying to teach her for the last five months. The woman's skin was the color of almonds, and her eyes were alight as she listened carefully to whatever Isa's husband was saying. As Isa was studying them, however, the woman's gaze shifted directly to Isa.

Immediately, Isa wanted nothing more than to hide, suddenly unable to add anything to the pointless conversation she was now a part of. She might have had the energy to handle the catty women that morning. But seeing the excitement on Ever's face as he spoke to the woman, whoever she was, was too much. He hadn't spent that much time talking with her in over a month. Besides, her head felt as though someone were beating it from the inside with a mallet.

"I am going to get a drink," she excused herself in a weak voice, not waiting long enough to remember that royals did not get their own drinks, but raised their hands for them instead. And at the moment, her faux pas didn't matter. She just needed to get away.

After grabbing a drink off the first servant's tray that she could find, Isa took a long sip and sighed. The wine was exceptionally good, and a rebellious part of her wanted to grab another goblet and just run back to her chambers with it. But she ignored that desire with the shred of self-control which she still possessed, and began trudging back to the group of women. As she moved through the crowd of wide skirts and swishing capes, she could hear the women before she rejoined them, and what she heard made her stop in her tracks.

"Did you see how little attention he paid her even during the dance?" Princess Damira's voice had an amused edge to it.

"He made his choice. Now he has to abide by it," Lady Jadzia said. She took a sip of her own wine, no doubt acquired through appropriate means.

"You don't think she broke the curse?" Lady Beata asked.

Lady Jadzia gave a delicate snort. "I've heard rumor that she doesn't possess any of that special power, if that's what you mean. It's really a pity."

"Why did he marry her then? I thought Everard wanted his queen to be something special."

Lady Jadzia's reply was icy. "I heard that the man was imprisoned in a building alone for months, according to my sister. It's amazing what lonely men will promise to anything with a pretty face." Then Lady Jadzia stopped and placed her hand over her upper chest. "Good gracious," she said in a faint voice. "I . . . I feel quite awful just now."

"Perhaps it was the beets," Lady Beata said, her brows knitting together in concern. "Take some more wine for your stomach."

"No. No, it's not that. I feel—" But before she could finish answering, Lady Jadzia broke down in tears. "I just feel terrible, as though a great weight has been placed upon my soul!" she sobbed. "Please make it stop!"

A strange sensation had come over Isa, but she didn't know what it was until someone cried out and pointed to her hand that clutched the goblet. Looking down, she realized bright blue flame was coming from her hand. People scrambled to back away, yet all Isa could do was stare stupidly at the fire in her own hand as her head pounded harder than ever, and treacherous tears threatened to spill down her face. All the while, Jadzia continued to blubber about how wretched she felt.

The blue fire began to climb, and was almost higher than the rim of the cup when two cool hands took hold of hers. It wasn't until Isa looked up that she realized Ever was standing before her, gripping her hands and saying her name out loud. The woman he'd been speaking with stood behind him, her eyes troubled as she watched.

"What are you doing?" Ever's voice finally drew her into focus. It took another long moment for Isa to find her voice and the words with which to reply. Finally, under his steady gaze and cool hands, Isa's head cleared enough to respond.

"I . . . I don't know . . ." her voice trailed off as she looked around to see the entire court watching her with wary eyes. Princess Damira, Lady Beata, and Lady Jadzia were all huddled in a group, staring as though she'd turned into a monster. Seeing them made Isa remember why she'd been upset in the first place, and once more, briefly, power pulsed through her. Ever's eyes widened as he felt it move, and quickly followed her eyes as they settled on the women he'd left her with.

"Isabelle," he said in a low voice. "What happened?" Isa looked into his eyes, but to her shock, where she had expected to see comfort and concern, she saw frustration and impatience. Suddenly, it was all Isa could do not to burst into tears herself, or shout at the top of her lungs that her head hurt, and this entire ball was a waste of time, and that Ever was in no position to judge her after leaving her alone with such vipers.

"Everard," the woman behind him said chidingly, her low voice melodic. "Your wife obviously is not feeling well." As she drew closer, Isa realized with a start that she sensed power seeping from the woman as well. Much to Isa's relief and annoyance, her husband finally looked concerned.

"Is it true?" he asked her in an even softer voice, his gray eyes searching her face. Almost too angry to speak, Isa could only bring herself to nod. She was fully aware that the people around them were still watching.

"I don't know why my power—"

"Not here," he whispered urgently. "You never know who might be listening." He pried the silver goblet from her hands and held it out to the nearest servant. "Launce," he called. There was no need, for her brother was already there. "Take your sister back to our chambers, then return here to me." As Launce took her arm, Ever leaned in once more and whispered, "I will join you soon. Try to get some sleep."

As Launce led her away, the music began to play again, and people chatted once more, but the sister and brother were given a wide berth as they made their way to the closest hallway.

"King Everard and Queen Isabelle's chambers?" Launce asked a nearby servant uncertainly. As they followed the servant back through winding halls and many turns, Isa felt herself relax against her brother's steady arm. She could feel him studying her as they walked.

"I'll be fine, I promise," she said. "It's this confounded hair that's been giving me a headache. I never knew I had this much hair." To her relief, they had finally reached the familiar arched door of the room she and Ever had been given.

"Something else is wrong," he said, crossing his arms and staring down at her after the servant had gone. "This isn't just a headache. What happened back there with your power?"

Isa sighed. "I don't know, Launce. I really just want to go to bed—"

"You drag me down here to this blasted ball, then you won't tell me anything—"

"I promise!" Isa's threw her hands up to her aching head. "I will tell you later!

Just let me go to bed!" She felt a stab of remorse though as his face fell and he looked at the floor. For a moment, he looked just like the little boy that had once faithfully followed her about on her horse. "I'm sorry." She reached out and grabbed his sleeve. He looked back, his eyes injured, and she sighed. "I really do have a headache, and it's hard to explain. I just don't have the words right now." At that, her brother looked slightly mollified, and he nodded once before leaving.

As soon as Isa was back in her room, Cerise was hovering over her, trying to pull the pins out of her hair. Apparently, news traveled just as fast in King Rafael's palace as in her own. Isa counted it a blessing though in this instance. In less than ten minutes, Cerise had changed her out of her silver gown, shoved a cup of tea into her hands, and had her in bed, Isa's long hair free and spread out wildly around her.

It would have felt lovely, had Isa not been so angry with her husband. After treating her like a soldier waiting for an inspection, then ignoring her their entire dance, he had left her with the cruelest women alive, all so he could search out the stranger from the south and speak to her . . . without Isa. And it was only because of the woman that he had noticed she was in distress at all.

And he hadn't even bothered to escort her back to their chambers himself.

7

THE KING'S MEAD

"You should go to her," Kartek murmured as they watched Launce lead Isa away. Her voice was kind, but there was a reprimand buried in the soft words.

"I need to talk with Rafael first. He's having his third round of mead now. Then I'll see how she's doing," Ever said, although he knew deep down that he was trying to convince himself as much as he was trying to convince his friend.

Kartek nodded thoughtfully, the large golden hoops in her ears jangling melodically. "I am surprised Rafael invited me at all," she said as they watched the couples on the dance floor twirl about. "Rafael rarely bothers to meddle in the affairs of the south."

"I'm glad he did, although I can't say I'm surprised from the tenor of his invitation. It seems he wants the whole world to know about this contest. I suppose he hoped you would spread the word to the rest of the southern kingdoms."

At this, Kartek raised her chin and snorted delicately. "If that was his desire, he shall be disappointed. I did not speak a word of his invitation to my neighbors. I could not see a reason to share such foolishness until I had seen it for myself." She shook her head at the king as he raised his goblet a fourth time. "Look at him. Have you ever seen him like this?"

"He's worse than I thought." Ever shook his head. "Someone else has a hand in this, but what I cannot work out is who might want to alter his temperament so greatly."

"Do you think dark power is involved?" This question was whispered, but Ever still glanced about to make sure prying ears weren't nearby. Kartek continued, "I can't feel any, but your senses were always stronger than mine."

"Not yet." Ever unhappily studied Rafael once more as he laughed raucously with one of his nobles. "But empty praise can do just as much damage as dark strength. And I fear we might have both at play."

"Here comes your younger brother."

As Launce made his way over to them, she lowered her voice even more and leaned in close, the scent of dates hitting Ever as she did. "I am serious though when I say you need to take care of your wife, Everard. You are right to be mindful of whatever is at stake here, but do not forget the woman the Fortress gave you. Something tells me she is not as delicate as you think."

"You saw how tonight went," he groaned quietly. "She may never want to come out in society again."

"And it would not be her fault." The southern queen arched a dark brow. "You threw her to the wolves without even an apology." She turned to shoot a glare at the three women that stood not far behind them, keeping eye contact long enough to make even Lady Jadzia look away. "The red-haired minx has not looked away from you since you arrived. It is as if she does not count you married."

"I know, I know," Ever said. "Isa's come so far . . . I was hoping that speaking with her in person would convince Jadzia to leave the matter be. I didn't expect that—"

"She has a headache, but she refuses tell me what else is wrong," Launce announced as he joined them. Though his voice was quiet, the resentment in it was obvious, and for once Ever couldn't blame him. Still, he wished Launce would at least attempt to follow formalities in the company of other royals, if not in his own palace.

"Queen Kartek." Ever frowned hard at his brother-in-law, willing him to remember even a vestige of his manners. "This is Isabelle's brother, Launce Marchand. Launce, this is Queen Kartek, ruler of the southern kingdom, Hedjet." Launce had the sense to at least color when he realized his rudeness before the queen. To Ever's surprise, however, she graced the young man with one of her rare wide smiles.

"You care much for your sister, do you not?"

"I do, Your Majesty," Launce mumbled, still clearly embarrassed. The queen took the young man's chin gently in her right hand and turned his face from side to side, examining him closely. Launce seemed surprised, but didn't resist. Whatever she was looking for, however, she seemed to find, for when she eventually let go of him, she nodded once to herself and smiled again.

"You . . . you have the strength as well!" Launce whispered.

Ever felt his own surprise reflected on the queen's face at the boy's statement.

"You can tell?"

"I'm around Isa—Isabelle-enough that I know what it feels like," Launce mumbled again, this time looking at the ground.

"Do not underestimate this one either, Everard." She turned to him. "He may be wild, but his love for his sister strengthens him." Then to Launce she said,

"Yes, I am gifted by the Maker as well. My power is not nearly as strong as your family's though. Now, I must speak with my guard. Both of you take care. I will see you tomorrow." And with that, she turned to go, her colorful skirt creating its own breeze as she moved gracefully away. Launce finally turned back to Ever, his eyes full of wonder.

"I will explain later," Ever said. "For now, I need your help with the king."

"The king?"

"I need you to accept his invitation to compete for the princess's hand in the contest."

Launce's eyes looked as if they might pop. "I'm not a royal! I—"

"Anyone can compete. Besides, I'm not expecting you to *win*. I just need eyes in that stable. I need to know more of what is going on." He didn't miss the scowl Launce sent him when he mentioned his lack of expectations for the boy, but he ignored it and continued in a lower voice. "Isa has enough to worry about with controlling her power and adjusting to her place as queen. If you do this, we will be sparing her one more worry."

Launce held his gaze unhappily for a few long moments before slowly nodding his assent. With that, Ever turned and led them up to the platform where the king lounged in his throne, his wife sitting stiffly at his side. Rafael was holding out his goblet for yet another round of mead when they approached him.

"It's a sweet variety, Everard!" Rafael raised his drink to his friend, nearly falling out of his chair in the process.

"It should be," Ever answered dryly as he helped right the king. "I brought it." At this, Rafael's eyes grew wide and even more joyous.

"Just one more reason you're my guest of honor!" He laughed and took another swig. Ever felt almost guilty for knowingly taking advantage of his old comrade in such a way, but in light of the change that had come over Rafael, exploiting his greatest weakness seemed the only way to save him from himself. Ever had packed the barrels of his best mead as a gift for the celebration, one he knew the king wouldn't be able to turn down. And he had been right.

"Launce has something he wants to tell you," Ever said, deftly moving to block the king's view of a young servant woman as she refilled the king's empty vessel. In his right mind, Rafael would never have considered such a conquest, but he seemed drunker tonight than Ever had seen before. Queen Monica sent Ever a grateful look as he gave Launce a slight shove forward.

"And what would that be, lad? I'm in the mood to grant all sorts of boons." Rafael laughed, his flushed face shiny with sweat.

Launce glanced at Ever warily before stepping closer to the king. "I would like to join the contest for your daughter's hand, Sire."

"Ah, that's fine! That's fine, boy!" The king leaned forward and surprised Launce by slapping him on the back. "My servants will bring your things down to the stables immediately!"

"He won't be sleeping in his chambers then?" Ever asked. Isa wouldn't be pleased.

"No, no. The contestants share quarters in the stables." He gave them a drooly smile and then gestured for Ever to come closer. As he leaned in, Ever had to keep his face straight as he was hit with the king's rancid breath. "That's what the holy man said they should do! So he could keep an eye on them!" Ever nearly smiled when the king uttered the words he'd been waiting for all night.

"So when did this holy man come to give you such good news?" he asked casually.

"The storm was so great the night he came!" The king held his hands out above his head unevenly to show the size of the storm, nearly falling over again in the process. "*Boom* went the lightning! I've never seen the like of it!" He stopped and rubbed his head before proceeding. "He says that the Maker told him He was watching the quarrels of the land, and it is this holy man's job to mend it!"

"If you're speaking of the rebellion in your own land," Ever frowned, "we ended that years ago." But the king waved his hand as though he were slapping away a gnat.

"Fa! Disloyal subjects and spies stay on. You know that!" His words were beginning to slur so badly that Ever had to work to understand them. He wagged his finger wildly at Ever with a rebellious smile. "You will see soon that our holy man's power rivals even yours." Then he laughed, as though he'd said something quite funny. "The holy man alone carries the plans for the great structure. And the Maker gave him the power alone to create it!"

"Plans for a structure?" Ever pressed, hoping Rafael wasn't uttering the gibberish some drunkards were accustomed to doing. Still, a part of him wished the king's chilling words were nonsense.

"Yes! For the trials!" Rafael moved closer, sending his foul breath toward Ever once more. "The impossible trial will be for only the one who miraculously receives the means to pass it! And only the holy man will know who the Maker chooses!" His eyes grew wide and he stretched his arms to indicate the size of the crowd present. "It could be anyone! Even a commoner!" He pointed at Launce in awe with a dramatic jab of his finger. "Even you!" Launce's jaw twitched in annoyance, but to Ever's relief, he said nothing.

After such a revelation, Ever knew they would get nothing else coherent out of the king. He politely bid the king and queen goodnight, pitying the queen and princess as they stayed behind with Rafael, not missing the look of disgust Princess Olivia was giving her father as he yelled for another goblet of drink.

"How long have you known him?" Launce asked when they were well on their way back to their chambers.

"All my life. He and my father were like brothers."

"Does he do that often?"

"No," Ever answered grimly. "Though he's always had a weakness for wine, he has generally been careful to guard himself." He shook his head. "Someone has been manipulating him, and I intend to find out whom. Now," they stopped before Launce's chambers, "the king will not remember to call a servant to show you to the stables, so call one yourself, and if the stable master does not allow you to bunk there, direct him to me." Launce nodded unhappily before opening his door.

"And remember . . ." Ever stopped the door just before it closed. "This is for Isa."

"I wouldn't be doing it if it weren't," came Launce's reply. Ever itched to remind the boy that he had promised to obey him, whether he liked it or not, but for the sake of peace, chose to let it go. Allowing the door to shut, he turned toward his own chambers, suddenly more than just a little apprehensive of what he would find there.

8

APOLOGIES

a single candle still glowed on the nightstand between the window and Isa's side of the bed when Ever returned, although the large floor mirror made it look as if two candles shone throughout the room. He immediately felt a stab of shame as his eyes adjusted to the dark, and he took in Isa's sleeping form. It was as far from his side of the bed as possible. Her auburn hair flowed around her like a sea of dark amber, and her face looked sad. Ever rubbed his eyes, guilt gnawing at him from deep inside. He hadn't meant to stay out so late.

As quietly as he could, he changed out of his ball clothes and slipped into the bed beside her. As he did, he could hear her stir. Ever paused, waiting to hear her breathing return to normal. Instead, he heard sniffles.

"Isa?" Reaching out, he gathered her hair away from her face, not entirely sure what to say. He hadn't expected her to cry, and wanted to kick himself for it. "Isa, please, tell me what's wrong."

The sniffling only grew louder. Then, after a pause, she asked in a shaky voice, "Don't you mean *Isabelle?*"

Ever closed his eyes in frustration. He'd known she was upset, but nothing to this extent.

"Isa, I'm sorry." He drew a deep breath. "I should have paid more attention. It's just been a long night—"

"You've had a long night?" At this, Isa sat up, angrily shaking her wavy hair out of her face. "You seemed to be just fine, spending our entire dance looking for whoever she was, before dumping me with that brood of vipers! And then, when I needed you most, you sent me to my room like an unruly pet!" Ever was speechless as she put her head in her heads and moaned. "And this blasted headache is *still* here!"

Thankful for something he *could* fix, Ever drew her drooping form toward him. She didn't curl into him like usual, but she did allow him to place his hands on her head. As he did, whorls of blue danced briefly over her, and he felt her body relax into his, as if being healed had taken the last ounce of energy she had. He shifted her into a more comfortable sitting position in his lap and held her there tightly with his left arm while stroking her hair gently with his right hand.

"Isa, you forget," he said into her hair, "being attentive to other people's feelings isn't—it isn't what I excel at. I truly am sorry for not noticing you were feeling distressed." He paused. "Can you forgive me?"

"Who was she?" The hollowness in her voice broke his heart, and for the first time, it occurred to Ever that Isa actually thought he was considering being unfaithful. This mortified him more than he could bear to ponder.

"Kartek is the closest thing I ever had to a sister," he said. "She, too, has been gifted by the Maker. Her power isn't as strong as ours, but as a child, she was one of the few people I knew who understood me. I haven't seen her in a while, as she is from the southern kingdoms. I only hurried to her because I needed to ask her something before I spoke with Rafael."

It was a moment before Isa responded, but she finally nodded, seeming at least slightly pacified for the time being.

"If it makes you feel better," he added, "she is married as well, and she and her husband are nearly ten years my senior. Now," he shifted the topic, hoping his wife's worries had lessened, "I know Jadzia and Damira are rather unpleasant, but you can't take anything they say—"

"They called me a whore." Isa's voice broke into a sob.

Ever felt as though his blood had frozen in his veins before melting into dangerous heat, and it was suddenly a good thing that his arms were wrapped around his wife, and he was not free to take off down the hall and right the matter himself.

"That woman's father will hear of this," he growled, but Isa stopped him, shaking her head.

"That won't do any good, Ever."

"But they cannot be allowed to speak of you that way!"

Isa pulled away to look at him, a tremulous smile on her lips. "Women do not make amends through rules and by force of righteous indignation, love." She paused before saying in a quiet voice, "But I have to wonder if they were right, at least in part."

"About what?" Had she lost her mind?

"I don't belong in this world." She shrugged helplessly. "All these rules and proprieties I am to pay heed to . . . Even just last year, had Lady Jadzia come to the Fortress and visited the city, she would not have been required to pay me notice. What has changed so greatly in me since then? What does that say about my ability to be . . . to be this?" She gestured at the deep purple sleeping gown she wore. Ever's eyes lingered on the way it fit her graceful curves before realizing she was still talking. "And that power in my hands tonight? I haven't even the slightest inclination as to where that came from! I never meant to hurt anyone!"

"Jadzia will be fine." He briefly smiled. "I'm not sure how you managed it, but it seemed to me that somehow, you helped her to feel the appropriate emotions that should have shamed her after she said such dreadful things. Your power surfaced because you knew they were lying." He gathered her in his arms once more, wishing he could smooth the lines of pain from her face with just the touch of his hands in the same way he'd banished her headache. "You knew the Fortress had chosen you, that this is your rightful place."

"Then why do I feel so wretched?" Isa's voice broke once more.

"I don't know," Ever whispered, wishing desperately that he knew what to do. Scheming kings, he could handle. Battles, he could fight. But this helpless feeling that filled him, the inability to fix whatever had broken inside of his wife was far beyond his ability or understanding.

"Can you sing to me?" Isa asked pitifully. Ever gave a small sigh of relief and thanked the Maker. That, he could do.

And so, as he gently laid her head back down on the pillow and pulled the covers over her once more, Ever began to sing, and he didn't stop until her breaths were deep and even, and a serene smile lay on her lips.

9

SLEEPING STABLES

"This is where you'll be staying." The stable master pointed at a bottom bunk in the corner of the already overflowing stable. Launce quickly thanked him and dropped his bag onto the rough, narrow mattress. Sitting upon it, though, revealed that it was stuffed with very stiff hay, and one look up at the bunk above had Launce praying the thin wooden slats holding his bunk partner wouldn't break during the night. "Breakfast at first light in front of the stables," the stable master grunted. "Better come as soon as the bell is sounded. This bunch doesn't leave much for the tardy."

Just as the stable master turned to go, Launce caught his sleeve once more. "When are the trials to begin?"

"Day after tomorrow." He looked back at Launce's small bag of belongings. "Have you got some armor of your own? The king won't be—"

"King Everard will be sending some," Launce assured him, hoping his brother-in-law had brought something that would fit his thinner frame.

"Good. And mind you, King Rafael doesn't want the patrons of the contestants snooping around here. That goes for King Everard too." Launce nodded once more that he understood, although Launce's very presence in the stables was, in fact, Everard's form of spying.

When the stable master moved on, Launce simply sat, watching the others warily. A number of the contestants were still back in the ballroom, late as it was, so it was surprising that so many men were still awake in the stables. Exhaustion had him ready to sleep, but the torches within the stables were still alight, so instead of laying down, Launce studied his new surroundings.

The stable, though nearly as large as the Fortress dining hall, was already filled with men, and it smelled just so. From the looks of those milling around, Launce appeared to be on the younger end of the spectrum, and for that, he

pitied Princess Olivia. Isa had told him that her marriage to Everard was somewhat unusual, that many of the male royals were quite a bit older than their
wives. And though King Rafael claimed anyone was allowed to compete, it
didn't appear as though any commoners were aware of this. Nearly everyone in
the stable wore velvet or silk with gold rings and silver buttons. His own
clothes, while hardly poor, were nothing as fine. Ever would not only have
provided nicer dressings, had he requested some, but would have been overjoyed to make him look proper. But, Launce had told himself and his sister, it
was pointless to pretend to be something you were not. You would only disap-
point others when they found out the truth.

Had Blanchette been disappointed? Had she thought his new connections
would change him?

He could see through the open stable doors that a large number of the men
stood outside. Some, like him, were returning from the festivities, but others
appeared to still be arriving from the road, looking weary from their travels.

Although patrons weren't allowed in the stables, servants were not in short
supply. Many of the finely dressed men had their own pages scurrying after
them. One caught his attention as his voice rose in pitch. It was a tall, thin man,
one who made Launce look hefty by comparison.

"This is not the saddle I wanted! Boy, what good are you? If I—"

"You!"

Launce was jolted from his musings when a heavy bag was thrown into his
lap. Shocked, he looked up to see who had tossed it. A burly man, probably at
least a few years older than he, was staring down at him expectantly. He was
dressed in red velvet with large puffy sleeves, and wore no small look of self-
importance. "Ask your master how much it would cost to borrow you. My page
is ill, and I need a new one for the contest." His wide face went from an expression of annoyance to one of outrage as Launce shoved the bag onto the floor
and stood to face him, exhaustion forgotten.

"I am no one's servant."

The man cocked a thick eyebrow at him as though Launce were daft.

"Well, who are you then, to act so high and mighty?"

"I'm Queen Isabelle's brother." They were nearly equal in height, although
the man had him beat soundly in weight. Everything about him was muscled.

"So you're the commoner," the man muttered, his voice smug.

"And what of it?" For a moment, Launce thought the stranger might throw a
punch, but after a moment of intense study, the man just smirked instead as he
bent to pick his bag up again, shaking his head with a small, mean smile on
his mouth.

"Nothing."

Launce glared at his back as he walked away. Deep down, he knew he should
be grateful. If it had come to blows, there would have been no doubt as to whom
the winner would have been, but instead of relief, this only filled him with
annoyance. He could hear Everard's voice inside his head, telling him repeatedly

how important it was that he learn to fight. It was in this foul mood that the servant found him.

"Might you be Launce Marchand?" Launce turned to give a terse reply, but found himself staring into one of the friendliest faces he'd ever seen. The man was older, probably older than Launce's father, and he had deep, permanent smile lines etched into his face. His graying hair had large curls sticking out in every which way, and his eyes were a pale blue. In spite of his bad mood, Launce found himself grinning back at the man.

"Yes, sir. That would be me."

"Ah, good then. If you'll allow me, I have a gift for you from King Everard."

When Launce nodded, the servant turned to go back out front. For lack of a friendlier face in the stable, Launce followed him. Outside was a horse, and though it was dark, there was just enough moonlight to see that it was one of Everard's finest. Upon the horse was a variety of items, from clothing with the green and blue colors of the Fortress, to weapons, to even a suit of armor. Launce swallowed hard when he saw the size of the pile.

"What's your name?" Launce asked as the servant began to unpack the horse.

"Call me Brokk." The lines in the man's face deepened as he smiled again, seeming pleased that Launce had cared to ask. "Forgive me if I'm being too forward, but are you not the brother of the lovely Queen Isabelle?"

"I am."

The man puffed a little as he struggled to lift one of the heavier pieces of armor off of the horse. Without thinking, Launce reached out to aid him. Together, they were able to get everything off the horse without damaging anything. It intrigued Launce that the man allowed him to help without protesting as the Fortress servants would have.

"I must admit, I have been curious to meet you and your sister. Word travels far of her great deeds, what with breaking the Fortress curse and all. And I thank you," Brokk said as they finished. "Most of these men wouldn't so much as look at me unless I accidentally scratched their property."

"It is my pleasure." This time, Launce's smile was genuine. "And my sister would be grateful to hear you say as such." He lowered his voice a bit, the memory of her face that night sinking his spirits. "She is in need of such encouragement at the moment."

"I can only guess that moving from your father's home to this . . ." He gestured at the royal bustle going on around them. "It must have been quite a transition." After a moment, he lowered his head with a look of slight worry on his face. "I apologize, sir. I say too much. It is not my place to speak of the personal lives of those above my station."

"No, please think nothing of it," Launce hurried to assure him. "I will admit that I don't feel anything at home in this place. I can only guess my sister feels the same." He studied the scuffs on his boots as he spoke again. "I cannot imagine what it must be like for her to *live* like this. I'm only here because she wanted me to come along."

"What, a young man like you has no sweetheart at home?" The servant gave a chuckle. "I find that hard to believe."

"I *had* one," Launce gave him a wry smile.

"Ah, I see."

They were silent for a moment, watching the goings-on around them as men continued to stream into the stables.

"Well, I suppose I should be off. It is getting to be *more* than a bit late." The short man straightened his green work vest and dusted off his brown trousers as he turned to go. "But please, let me know if there is anything I can do for you."

"Thank you," Launce said, truly meaning it. "And the same for me as well. I have enjoyed some honest conversation." With another deep smile, the older man gave a short, quick bow and left the stableyard. Launce found himself in a somewhat better mood as a bell sounded from somewhere in the distance.

The men that loitered outside began to gather their belongings in a hurry before suddenly streaming into the stable. Curious, Launce found himself at the edges of the throng that was trying to fit itself into the stable doors all at once. He allowed himself to be jostled and carried along with the crowd.

"With all the dignitaries attending, you would think Rafael have hosted something a bit more appropriate," a man to Launce's left grumbled. "If I'd known we were to be housed and fed like animals, I would have brought my own caravan."

"He wouldn't have let you stay in it and compete," another said as they shuffled forward, although Launce couldn't see the speaker. "I heard him say the visiting holy man wants us all in the same place to see which one the Maker considers worthy."

"I think he's lost his mind," the first speaker, a short, solid man, said mildly.

"Why are you here then?" Launce realized as the words left his mouth that they sounded rather impertinent, but he was genuinely curious as to why such self-important men would stoop to live in what they considered squalor.

"The same reason you are," the man said with more than a hint of annoyance. Lance sincerely doubted that, but he pressed no further. Eventually, after being pushed and stepped on more times than he could count, Launce finally made it back to his bunk. As moments passed, the men still trying to find their own beds, many of whom were more than a bit drunk, began to move at a more frenzied pace.

"What's wrong with them?" Launce asked a servant boy who standing nearby him.

"You must be new." The boy looked him up and down curiously."

Launce nodded.

"Midnight has come," the boy said, as if that explained it.

"So?"

"Just after midnight, something awful happens outside." The boy, probably twelve or thirteen, looked unruffled, but there was a slight tremor to his warbling voice that gave him away. "How long have you been here?"

"I arrived today."

"Then you have only been to the ball," the boy said. "The other nights, before you got here, were different." He smirked proudly. "My master arrived a week ago."

"But what happened?" Launce pressed, glancing around as they spoke to realize the men were running even faster to finish whatever they were doing.

"Every night, the king stations a guard outside to make sure the competitors don't sneak out. Since we arrived, we've found each night guard on the ground in the morning, dead as they come, pounded to death. I've never seen so much blood." The boy shivered, his brown curls shaking just slightly with him.

"No one hears anything?" Launce asked incredulously. These men were certainly not Everard, but he found it hard to believe that seven men could be pounded to death without the company of men in the stable hearing a thing.

The boy just shook his head.

"But what does the king say about the men who have died?" Launce felt a warm bit of unease slither through his body.

The boy shrugged, glancing over his shoulder as he began to fidget.

"But what if it's dark forces at work?" Launce prodded.

"Someone suggested that, but the king said that if one of you is going to be king, he'd better know how to deal with such anyway. Look now, my master will be angry if I'm not back with him soon."

Thanking him, Launce let the nervous boy go and settled into his own bunk. Before he could wonder at such a strange turn of events, however, his eyes grew heavy, and the bed was suddenly much more comfortable than he'd first thought. As though sharing his sudden exhaustion, a chorus of snores erupted throughout the stable. It was as though all work and bustling had come to a complete halt, and no one cared any longer if their personal chores were attended to.

This struck him as odd, but Launce had just decided he would be better fit to search for the reason in the morning, when he felt the bed tremor lightly beneath him. And then again.

Surprised at his sudden lack of will to get out of bed, Launce did his best to flip over, fighting the crushing drowsiness with all his strength. The competitors' snoring continued for the most part, although Launce did hear someone get up and relieve himself outside. Or at least that's what it sounded like. Try as he might, though, it was all Launce could do to keep his eyelids slitted open.

The tremors began to come faster and harder, and through his nearly closed eyes, Launce saw a strange dust floating around in the air, but only for a moment. The ground was now quaking so violently, Launce felt as though he might be thrown from his bunk. Fear gripped him as he tried desperately to free himself from the grasp of whatever force held him in the state of severe sluggishness, and the strange shaking only made it worse.

As the earthquake grew in strength, Launce could no longer see the room as his teeth jarred and his body slammed into the wall repeatedly. Terror gripped him as he realized someone had left candles upright on the table, but as he prayed to the Maker to keep them from falling, sleep kept him from finishing even that.

10

BRITTLE HINTS

*L*aunce wanted to cringe as Everard studied him with that infuriating, unreadable expression. Since Launce had awakened that morning, he'd been dreading the scolding he was sure to hear for allowing sleep to take him during the night's quaking. The pastries Everard had brought did lessen the sting, but Launce was a bit suspicious as to how his brother-in-law had known he would be hungry. He didn't ask though. It was best not to expect too much from the king, even on the best days.

To Launce's surprise, however, his brother-in-law slowly nodded.

"I believe you are right, particularly since no one here in the palace felt the quakes, and many servants were awake much past midnight without a problem."

Launce nearly allowed himself to gape, but managed to keep his mouth shut and his sarcastic comment in as well. Everard's agreement had been the last thing he'd expected when his brother-in-law had sent a note early that morning, telling Launce to meet him in the south corner of the outer palace walk.

"I just wish we knew where this power was coming from," Everard mused, turning to stare at the distant seashore that glistened a pearly white in the distance.

"One of the men said the king wants the competitors in one place so the holy man can see them and judge whom is worthy."

"Have you noticed anyone who stands out?"

"Just self-important royals and nobles and their servants."

"From the way you inhaled the pastries," Everard frowned, "I'm supposing they're the same self-important coxcombs who kept you from getting a decent breakfast this morning too." He let out a gusty breath and ran his hand through his short hair. "If you would just wear the Fortress colors I sent, they would treat you with more respect."

"I won't pretend to be someone I'm not." Launce kept his eyes on the hills behind Everard.

"Whether you like it or not," Everard's words were nearly a growl, "you are now attached to the Fortress. It would be easier on everyone if you simply accepted it."

"I am well aware of my attachments!" Launce spat out. His sweetheart's father had said as much.

Everard fixed his burning eyes back on Launce. "We don't have time for this. Isa will be awake soon. Today, I want you to look for any signs of power. See if you can find any residue from last night. Look in the food, the hay, even on the horses. Someone does not want you to see whatever happens to those guards during the earthquakes."

On his way back to the stables, Launce swore to himself that after this, he was done being Everard's errand boy. Being summoned and sent on whim left a bitter taste in his mouth. He would go home, help his father with the shop, find a completely ordinary wife, and leave Fortress matters be.

But then, that still left Isa alone with *him*.

The stables were separated from the main palace, but not far enough to fit Launce's taste. The palace, with its red clay roof tiles and whitewashed walls, spread out in twists and turns in such a complicated manner that Launce still wasn't even sure that they resembled any sort of organized thought. The stables, though, were simply long rectangular structures, single rooms with double bunks built into each wall across from the horses.

As he entered the main stable, where all the competitors were staying, he tried to slip in unseen. It wasn't hard, considering most of the men were otherwise occupied. Some napped, while others dueled or engaged in political discussions. He found the horse Everard had sent for him and began to groom him. Launce needed to think, and brushing the animal was relaxing, something familiar. As he found a brush and began to groom the horse, he couldn't help but notice how striking the creature was. As far as Everard could push him toward insanity, Launce couldn't fault the man's taste in horses.

"Fine charger you have there."

Launce turned to find the friendly servant from the previous night standing behind him. Ease washed through him as he returned the man's grin.

"It belongs to King Everard." Launce put down the brush and ran a hand down the animal's shiny coat. "But he is a fine one."

The servant held out a cloth bag. "I figured this lot," he waved at the crowd of competitors and whispered, "wouldn't leave you much to eat. Hungry?" Launce had inhaled the three sweet rolls Everard had brought him, but then again, Launce was always hungry. They moved outside to sit on a log at the fringe of the stable shuffle, where there was a bit more space for Launce to dive greedily into the bag of eggs, bread, and cheese.

"I have to admit," Launce said between bites of the bread, which was still warm, "while I'm truly grateful, I am a bit confused as to why you've shown me so much kindness."

Brokk smiled wanly. "I have a confession of my own to make, I'm afraid. I haven't been a servant for King Rafael for very long. I traveled before that, and I've seen more than I would like to recall." His smile melted into a fleeting distant look. But just as soon as it had fallen, he was smiling once again. "As soon as I learned of what your sister did at the Fortress, I wanted badly to meet her. I'm sorry if it seems I've used you . . ." The older man pursed his lips and stared at the ground.

"I'm sure my sister would be delighted to meet you." Launce tried to give the man an encouraging smile. "And I never turn down food." When he said this, Brokk's eyes crinkled up pleasantly, and Launce had to feel pleased himself.

As he finished the eggs, Launce suddenly found himself very curious. "If you don't mind me asking, where are you from, if not here?" Indeed, the more he studied Brokk, the more the servant stood out against the others. Where most of the native Cobriens had olive skin and dark eyes, this man's hair had once been red, or at least had carried traces of it. His eyes were a pale blue, and his skin lacked the hardy warmth of the Cobriens.

"North," Brokk answered, pulling an apple from his pocket and studying it. "I doubt you would know of it."

"What made you decide to leave?" Launce tried to keep from sounding too curious, but there was something different about the man, something knowledgeable. He couldn't explain why, but this servant seemed as though he knew much, much more than what many of the men surrounding them knew combined.

The older man looked down at his scuffed boots and then out at the distant sea to the south. "Sometimes decisions are made for us, lad," Brokk said in a soft voice. The sadness in his voice silenced any further questions Launce was tempted to ask.

They stared out at the ocean for a bit until in a more cheery voice, Brokk asked what Launce planned to do with the afternoon. As he started to answer, Launce paused, unsure of how much he should tell others about his errand from Everard.

"Have you heard of the murders outside the stables every night?" Launce asked cautiously, trying to guess at what the unusual little man knew.

"The servants talk of nothing else."

"I thought I would try and poke around." Launce tried to sound casual as he folded the empty bag, afraid that he looked at Brokk directly, his nerves would give him away.

"May I give you a piece of advice then?"

Surprised, Launce looked at his new friend. The older man's eyes were thoughtful as he gazed back. When Launce nodded, Brokk's smile nearly became a smirk. "Try looking from a different perspective."

"What do you mean?"

"Have any of them tried looking?" Brokk waved his arm at the men milling about the stables.

"I heard some of them whispering about it, but no one seems to do much more than that." Launce frowned as he realized this group, more than any, should have been avidly pursuing justice. The contest was full of knights, princes, and even kings, all raring to show the princess their might. And yet, last night they had cowered in their beds. "What do you know of it?"

"Oh, as little as you, is my guess. But," he leaned in and whispered, "take it from someone who has seen a big world and many peoples. I've been watching this bunch, and I knew as soon as I saw you that you are different." He nodded once and stood, gathering Launce's empty bread linens.

As soon as Brokk had excused himself to return to his duties, Launce decided to try searching for the magic. He had been unsure before, but comforted by Brokk's kind words, he walked purposefully toward the stables, ignoring as best as he could the looks of disdain others cast his way. He considered putting on the tunic that Everard had given him, but imagining the look of satisfaction he would see on Everard's smug face was enough to keep it tucked under the straw mattress and safely out of sight.

Considering Brokk's words, Launce decided to begin at the bottom, with the floor. He must look addled, he thought to himself, bending down just inches from the ground to stare at it. But it was all he could think to do. What was he even looking for? He'd convinced himself he would be able to sense it, the way he could sense Isa's power when she was nearby. When he was near his sister, it felt as if the air was charged, as though lightning had just struck, and everything around him stood on edge. Surely it would be the same way, or at least, similar in sense.

"It's kind of you to offer so readily. My boots do need to be shined."

Launce looked up to see the man from the day before, the one who had mistaken him for a servant. Launce's face flushed with indignation, but before he could respond, a new voice called out from behind him.

"Leave him be, Absalom."

The new speaker was somewhat shorter than average, but everything he lacked in height was made up for in muscle. Visible even beneath his fine tunic, the man had one of the broadest chests Launce had ever seen.

"Stay out of my affairs, Randolph."

"Do you think it really wise to provoke King Everard's kin?" The strong man, Randolph, stood beside Launce and crossed his arms. "You're being a fool. I am merely trying to keep you alive." He grimaced. "Our own king will have my head if I return without you."

Absalom glared down at Launce, who returned the expression. In the end, however, he said nothing more, simply stalked away as he muttered. Not waiting to be acknowledged, Randolph gave Launce a curt nod before moving on himself.

How did Isa stand living around these people? As he returned to searching the floor for he knew not what, Launce vowed again to himself that this was the last time she talked him into accompanying her anywhere.

Two hours later, Launce was hungry again, his eyes were sore from getting dust and dirt kicked in them, and he was no closer to finding an answer. Everard would just have to sneak into the stables against the king's wishes and search for it himself. Just as Launce stood and stepped into the afternoon sunlight, however, a sparkle caught his eye. Leaning down, where he'd seen it, he searched again, this time with gusto.

The particle of shine was so small he nearly missed it, and he had to search to find it again. Lifting up a small handful of the dirt, Launce examined it in the light. This time, not one but dozens of minuscule sparkles glittered as he turned his hand in the light. It looked almost like glass. When he rubbed the dust between his fingers, however, all doubt fled, and he knew he'd found exactly what he had been looking for.

A slight shudder moved through him as the power of the glass rippled out. It was small but strong. Another sparkle caught his eye on his shirt. And his trousers. And in his boots. The more he searched, the more he realized he was coated in the powdery glass. Rushing back inside, he yanked his bag from the wall and held it up to the window beside his bunk. Sure enough, it was covered as well.

How had he missed something that covered every inch of the stables?

It was only then that Launce remembered the footsteps from the night before. What if it hadn't been a contestant going to relieve himself? What if it had been someone else? Launce nearly broke into a run to find Everard, but stopped himself just before leaving the stable.

No. He would do this alone. Then, for once, maybe he would escape that self-righteous look Everard always gave before he barked out more orders.

Launce spent the rest of the afternoon planning. His greatest concern was with positioning. Where could he go that wouldn't be covered with the glass dust? Based on what Everard had said, the dust must have been what was putting everyone into such a deep sleep.

Try looking from a different perspective, Brokk had said. It had worked to help Launce find the dust. Now he needed some way to escape it.

But of course. The roof! He would just have to make sure no one else saw him take his place after night fell.

Finishing the day felt like an eternity without someone to talk to, but finally evening came. There was no ball tonight, only a simple supper served outside the stables. Once he'd pushed his way through the supper line, and inhaled what little food he did get, Launce made his escape.

Shimmying up the side of the stables didn't take him long. The roof was sloped, but not enough to make it impossible to lay upon. To his relief, there was no dust. Only once he was up, however, did it occur to Launce that he probably should have brought some sort of weapon. Not that he would have known how to do much good with it.

It wasn't long before the guard arrived. As twilight faded, however, into the warmth of a lazy early autumn evening, with singing cicadas and croaking toads nearby, Launce had to shake himself often. His hiding position wasn't very comfortable, nor was it ideal for rousing oneself, as he laid flat against the red tile shingles with his body on a decline and his hands clinging to their edges. Launce had hoped it would keep him hidden, but if he fell asleep, he wouldn't be doing anyone any good.

A movement caught his eye. It was too dark to see much, but it looked as though someone had come through the same side door as the one Launce had noticed opening the night before. He had little time to concentrate on it, however, because out of the corner of his eye, the largest creature he'd ever seen in his life was charging straight for him.

11

TEA AND TEMPERS

"*Y*ou could call on Queen Monica," Ever suggested after he returned from his early morning errand.

"Do I have an official invitation?"

"Well no, but it would convey Destin's good will," Ever said as he scratched his head. But Isa could see right through him.

"If my presence is not officially requested anywhere this morning," Isa replied firmly, "then I'm not going." And nothing Ever said could change her mind. Isa could see that her determination to hide in their chambers confused her husband, but her decision was simply something he would have to accept.

Being in public was easy for Ever, so easy that Isa often envied him the way it buoyed his spirits and seemed to fill him with even more of his endless energy. Explaining her need for quiet was impossible. She had tried. He just couldn't comprehend how exhausted she became by being surrounded by so many people, even when her unpredictable fire wasn't upsetting their fellow guests. But after her upset of the night before, venturing out to socialize, as Ever called it, was asking too much. She needed time to think.

Sleep had come a little easier once Ever had assured her that the beautiful woman he'd spoken with was like a sister to him. Still, Isa knew there was something her husband was hiding. If the southern queen had her own version of strength, then there was a good chance they had been speaking of Rafael's strange behavior. Ever was more unruffled than he had been since the Fortress curse had been broken. But why wasn't he telling her? Isa might be struggling with her strength, but she was still the queen.

And so Isa spent the day with Cerise, laughing about their childhood pranks and hiding behind the thick wooden door as they sipped tea, trying to ignore the absence of her husband. As she had expected, however, he was up before sunrise, and spent the entire day running about the palace, interrogating whatever poor courtiers he thought might aid his cause, and muttering about how base it was for Rafael to give himself such a hangover that he couldn't attend to his subjects. During one of his many quick stops back at their chambers for this parchment or that gift for a dignitary, she had asked where Launce was. His response that Launce was assisting him surprised her, but Isa decided to simply leave them be. If the two men were somehow getting along, she wouldn't stand in the way.

Everard's determination to help her enjoy the company of her fellow royals couldn't stay dormant for long though. Isa cringed immediately when he waltzed in that afternoon with a sealed note from Queen Monica, and a triumphant smile on his face.

Isa glared at him while she broke the seal, half expecting to find his handwriting inside. Written on the finest of parchment in a scrawling hand that was most decidedly not her husband's, however, the note read:

Queen Isabelle of Destin,

Queen Monica requests your presence at her tea on the morrow upon the ninth hour. Your addition to the queen's company will be most welcome, where our circle finds itself eager to know you more.

In the Maker's Blessings,
    Queen Monica

"You put her up to this," Isa said upon reading the note.

But Ever held his hands up above his head, a look of utter innocence on his face. "Upon my honor, I did not." He tried, unsuccessfully, to hide a smile as she read the note again in dismay. "Believe it or not, some women do actually meet together to become friends. Not every woman interprets tea invitations as insults."

"Not every woman has the ability to accidentally frighten her peers after they insult her," Isa said, scowling.

"Isa, it would be an insult not to—"

"I will go, Ever! But that doesn't mean I have to enjoy myself."

And so Isa awoke the next morning with no small amount of fluttering in her stomach. Memories of the crowd's faces at the ball as she struggled to put out her flame haunted her as she ordered herself several times to get out of bed. It was a good thing Ever had gone so early. There would have been no happy smile to greet him today.

"Which dress will it be today?" Cerise held the wardrobe open as she and Isa leaned in to scrutinize the mountain of dresses Gigi had sent. Isa bit her lip for a moment before annoyance and disgust from the ball's events made up her mind for her.

"Ladies Beata and Jadzia and Princess Damira will be there. Pick the most stuffy, uncomfortable, insensible dress you can find." Isa turned sharply and moved to the full-length mirror to criticize her reflection as Cerise rummaged through the wardrobe. She tried to avoid, however, looking directly at her eyes. She didn't need to see them to know their fire wasn't any brighter than it had been the day before when she had checked. Or the days or weeks before that. It had been her hope that after the incident with the ball, perhaps they might glow a little brighter. But it was not to be. They were as dull as ever.

"Those women must have done something awful to merit such a gown from you." Cerise's voice was muffled, but Isa could hear a smile in it. So Isa told her friend what the women had said.

"What?" Cerise popped her head out of the clothing, gray eyes flashing.

With a sigh, Isa related the ball's events again. The awful ordeal still didn't sound much better, but at least she could speak of it without weeping this time. No. Now she was angry.

When she finished, Cerise shook her head in disbelief. Then her eyes lit up. Hurrying over to a trunk in the corner, Cerise pulled out a small wooden box.

"Gigi gave these to me for the final ball, but I don't think it would hurt to use a few of them today." She opened the box to reveal a pile of hairpins with bright blue jewels at the top. Cerise scooped out a small handful and began to pin them into Isa's hair. Usually, Isa protested such finery. It still felt strange to wear jewels to daily occasions such as tea. There would be no complaining this time, however, as Cerise expertly pinned the baubles into the curls of her hair.

Not long after, a servant knocked on the door to escort the two women to the queen's tea room. Isa was disappointed to know that Cerise would be leaving her once she was properly settled in with the queen's party, but she was grateful that her friend could at least accompany her there.

Isa came to a stop just outside Queen Monica's tea room, and as she waited for the servant to announce her arrival, she wondered about the women inside. If Everard didn't believe in her, why should they?

The queen's tea room was an airy, lavish space filled with sunlight and flowers of every kind. Despite the lateness of the season, bright red and orange petals seemed to cover each surface, and upon a quick peek, Isa realized they were actually growing right in the room, rather than being cut and placed in vases. Sleek, curved chairs carved of a pale wood were placed in a large circle to accommodate the number of women already present. Sofas for lounging edged the room, one placed every few windows. The windows were tall, reaching nearly to the ceiling, and the floor was covered in red stone tiles, like the rest of the palace seemed to be. The furnishings, though, seemed different in taste. Her astounding variety held pieces from a vast number of lands, including a vase made by none other than one of Isa's old neighbors in Soudain.

Nearly a dozen women and girls were already seated in the circle with small tables of treats displayed between each individual. Most of the other women wore lighter gowns than Isa did, but that was fine. The dark blue Isa wore matched her mood. She painted a smile on, however, as she broke into the circle just between Lady Jadzia and another woman, whom she didn't know.

The servant led Isa to the chair directly to the left of Queen Monica's seat; it was an honor to be seated so close to the host. Isa curtsied to the queen, careful to keep her head up. Once she was settled in her own chair, Isa took a deep breath and nodded to Cerise, who curtsied formally before leaving Isa both surrounded and all alone.

"I want to thank you, Queen Isabelle, for joining us on such short notice this morning." Queen Monica's words were formal, but her voice had a quiet cadence to it that Isa found relaxing. "Please, allow me to introduce you to the rest of our company." She gestured, and as she said their names, each woman nodded her head in turn. "My daughter, Olivia, whom you met yesterday. Lady Carlita of Giova, Queen Zineta of Anbin, Princess Damira and Lady Jadzia of Staroz, Lady Beata of Vaksam, Queen Kartek of Hedjet, and Queen Anna and her daughter, Princess Daphne of Ashland." Isa smiled at each, hoping she wouldn't insult one of them by forgetting which name belonged to which face. At least half of them would be easy. Queen Monica, Princess Olivia, and Queen Kartek she knew. Unfortunately, Princess Damira, Lady Jadzia, and Lady Beata's faces would be carved into her memory forever as well.

"I must admit," Queen Monica continued as a servant handed Isa a delicate porcelain cup with tiny painted green leaves, "that I was unaware Everard had married until after the wedding had already passed. I apologize for the over-sight." Isa noted the familiarity with which the queen talked about Ever, and for some reason, it made her feel good.

"There is nothing to forgive," Isa said. "Everard told me you were in Giova when it happened. The wedding itself was quick." Isa thought she heard a titter to her left, but she sipped her tea and kept her face on Queen Monica. The queen looked as if she were about to say something else, but Lady Jadzia spoke instead.

"You are looking well, Queen Isabelle."

"Thank you," Isa said hesitantly. What an odd thing to say.

"Most women do not look as lively or keep their figures so well as you have in your fifth month."

Isa nearly dropped her tea.

"Lady Jadzia, whatever do you mean?" It was Princess Olivia who had spoken, but all of the other ladies looked as appalled as Isa felt.

Unabashed, Lady Jadzia widened her eyes. "I apologize if I was mistaken. It was only my impression that the queens of the Fortress always conceive within the first month of their marriage." The other women exchanged glances but said nothing as they waited for Isa's response. If there had been any doubt as to how much this woman had wanted to marry Ever, it was all gone now. She had managed to learn more about the queenship than most Destinians ever knew in their lifetimes.

Isa took a deep breath. "It is the tradition."

"I see. I had only assumed—"

"I think you will find, Lady Jadzia, that I am anything but traditional." Isa's voice was hard. She held Lady Jadzia's gaze until propriety forced the other woman to look away, her orange curls falling over her face to cover her eyes.

Suddenly, Isa was thankful she and Cerise had chosen such an uncomfortable dress. The stiff blue material kept her back perfectly straight, itching her if she slouched at all. She could not have looked defeated in that dress even if she tried.

"Queen Isabelle," Queen Kartek spoke up, throwing a withering glance at Lady Jadzia, who was suddenly too busy smoothing out her flawless silk skirt to notice. "Is your family well?"

"They are, thank you."

"What lands do they hold?" Lady Beata asked. "I've ridden through your countryside a few times in my life, but I've never seen any lands by the name of Marchand."

Isa didn't miss the trap. She hesitated just a moment before answering. Their determination was shocking, but Isa wasn't about to let them frighten her off. "My father is a man of trade," she finally managed to answer in a cool voice, taking another sip of her tea. "He and my mother own a store in the marketplace in our capital city, Soudain, where they sell goods and care for their children and personal livestock."

"Goodness! Are you telling us you have actually milked a cow?" Lady Jadzia placed her tea back on its saucer with a loud *clink*. Some of it sloshed onto her ivory gown, but she seemed too delighted in Isa's past to notice.

"Lady Jadzia!" Queen Monica began.

"It is quite alright, Your Highness," Isa said, before fixing her gaze on Lady Jadzia. "Yes, I have milked cows. I have also hauled grain, sold goods, groomed horses, and sewn dresses. I have worked alongside my parents until my hands bled so that we could eat. It is a good thing too, as they are strong and ready, now that my husband has decided that I should learn the art of war." Out of the corner of her eye, Isa saw Queen Kartek's sly smile. Princess Olivia made a poor attempt at smothering her giggles before being silenced by her mother's sharp look. The rest of the women fidgeted, however, and nervously nibbled the pastries set out for them. Lady Jadzia's red lips parted, but it was a moment before anything came out.

"I see. It's just that Everard was always so like his father. I had only assumed he would—"

"What my husband and I choose to do with our lives and our kingdom and our family is our business, and ours alone. I will be sure to make you privy to such information, however, when it is in your best interest to know."

"And that," Queen Monica spoke before Lady Jadzia could respond, "will be enough of that. Lady Jadzia, you have insulted my guest in my home more than I should like to admit today, and I will not have it. You may take leave of this company for the time being until you gain control of your tongue."

The blush in Lady Jadzia's pale cheeks and the humble nod she gave seemed to show for the first time that she realized she had indeed gone too far. Mumbling an apology, she dipped a quick curtsy to Queen Monica and the princess before fleeing the room.

As Lady Jadzia passed her, Isa was struck again with the realization that the noblewoman would have been very beautiful had it not been for her mouth. She had lovely curves, more than Isa could ever dream of having, and her skin was flawless. Isa was instantly glad that she hadn't been present for Ever's first betrothal ball. Watching Lady Jadzia throw herself at him would have been torture.

The rest of the tea continued without excitement, something which Isa more than welcomed. Queen Monica was an expert at asking each guest exactly the right question to elicit a response, and Isa began to learn a bit more about other women there. She decided right away that she would like to be friends with the queen and princess of Ashland. The lady of Giova was rather dry, and spent most of the time stuffing her mouth with scones. The others answered in turn, but offered little information worth knowing, Princess Damira and Lady Beata in particular. Queen Kartek was quiet, but sometimes took over asking questions, Isa noticed, so Queen Monica could sip her tea and eat. Princess Olivia, though she spoke little, seemed to Isa like she might be a lot of fun. Of course, she also seemed as though she could be a lot of trouble if she ever had the mind for it. In person, she seemed far different from the shy princess King Rafael had presented the night before.

The remainder of the tea was enjoyable, but Isa ultimately found herself rather tired after her encounter with Lady Jadzia. Not physically, but rather she felt as though her heart had been spent. Relief washed over her when Queen Monica finally declared it time for her to oversee the preparations for that night's supper. Isa stood and curtsied, murmuring her well-wishes to each in the circle until it was Princess Olivia's turn. Rather than curtsying, as everyone else had, however, the princess surprised her by pulling her into an embrace.

"Do not allow Jadzia to ruin your day," she whispered into Isa's ear. "Rumor has it that she emptied her father's coffers on fineries to catch your husband's eye at that ball." The princess released her, only to step back and take Isa's hands in her own as if they were already the best of friends. "But look who has him now," she added with a smirk. Isa felt herself smiling back. It was impossible to be unaffected by the young woman's spirit. And, Isa grinned to herself as she met Cerise in the hall, the princess was right.

Ever was hers.

ESCAPING THOUGHTS

*C*erise eyed Isa's leather skirt and trousers suspiciously as Isa dug both the clothes and her sword belt out of the wardrobe.

The combat wardrobe had been Ever's idea. As soon as they were married, he'd ordered the tailor to make her clothes practical for swordplay and riding. No good could come of anyone trying to move about in such stuffy gowns, he'd told the reluctant Gigi.

Isa hadn't been sure of the new clothing, though, until she had tried it on. The top of the set was a long-sleeved tunic made of supple red leather. The tunic was long enough to look like a short skirt that ended just above the knees of her trousers, which were made of the same thin leather but brown. The boots were similar to those she'd worn when she was crippled — strong with good support for her ankles. Though she felt scandalous for thinking it, there was such freedom in trousers! Of course, she would never admit such sentiments to her mother.

"I need some space," Isa answered Cerise's unspoken question. "The streets here are too crowded for a good ride, and most everyone in the palace will be preparing to watch the games. The practice rooms will most likely be empty." Isa's day in bed had given her ample time to indulge in self-pity, but now she needed to *think*.

"Just return in time to dress for the contest, since you're determined not to leave this gown on." Cerise shook her yellow curls indulgently as she picked the stiff blue gown up from the bed where Isa had tossed it. "And Isa," Cerise called out as Isa knocked for Norbert. "Please be careful. Something about this place makes me nervous."

Isa gave her friend a smile, trying to look confident. She used the same smile to assure Norbert that there was no need for him to accompany her. She was only going to the training room downstairs. As soon as she was on her way, however, the smile melted away. Cerise was right. Something felt very off and had since the moment they'd set foot in the palace. If only Ever would tell her *what*.

Following a servant's instructions, Isa climbed down several flights of stairs to the ground floor. After turning down a few hallways, which Isa hoped she could remember on the way back, she came to a large square room with twelve bright windows lining the southern wall. And to Isa's satisfaction, it was empty.

She unsheathed her sword and walked to the center of the large room. As she prepared herself to practice the form, Isa noted with appreciation how smooth the floors were in here too. The Fortress's practice rooms were rough and uneven, but Ever refused to have them smoothed down. The ground was never smooth in battle, he would always say. And while Isa knew he was right, the level, red stone floors would make her practice a bit easier.

Closing her eyes, Isa pictured the form in her head. Ever had taught her a number of combat forms, specific movements, blocks, and thrusts that followed one another in rapid order. Isa had struggled with them at first, until she realized they resembled a dance. Thinking of the movements as such had made memorizing them much easier. With her eyes still closed, Isa began.

Though she would never tell him, sometimes it was easier to practice without Ever present. She could move at whatever speed she wished, and it gave her time to ponder. This morning, she needed to understand what exactly had happened at the ball. The slow, steady rhythm of the steps would help her do that.

Ever's behavior at the ball had hurt Isa more than she wanted to admit. When he had returned to the room, however, she'd felt more comforted, more loved than she had in a long time. The idea of Lady Jadzia being chosen by Ever, cradled in his arms, dancing with him, practicing swordplay with him, although the latter image was rather unlikely, provoked Isa beyond reason. True, her powers were failing, but Isa had been the one to face the curse with Ever. Isa had fallen in love, not with the daydream of a king, but with a broken, twisted, and hollow man. Isa had been forced to watch him die, and then had to be willing to live on without him. And it had been Isa whom the Fortress had returned him to. No, Lady Jadzia could daydream and plot all she wanted, but the Fortress had chosen *Isa*, and Ever would be *hers* until the day she died.

A shock rippled through her as a wave of blue fire slid from her hand down her sword. How long had it been since she'd felt such pure power? Isa knew there was only one definite way to search for more.

Isa carefully placed her sword at the edge of the practice floor, near one of the windowed walls, then returned to the middle of the room. With a renewed vigor, Isa threw herself into a different kind of motion. Dancing, though far less practical than swordplay, was her surest way to find her power. Unfortunately, Isa had been kept so busy at home, that there hadn't been time for dancing in months. But she was here now, and no one was watching. Faster and faster she went. Her body was fluid, flowing like water into steps, leaps, and turns.

The power wasn't strong, but she could feel it as it churned its way through her. Like water to a parched desert, she drank in the presence of her beloved Fortress, despite being in another kingdom. In this state of joy, she could feel it, even from afar.

If only she could stay in this moment forever.

In the middle of one of her hops, however, the toe of her shoe caught, and she found herself stumbling. But instead of tripping forward as she ought to have, Isa began to fall to the right, directly into one of the windows. She placed her hand on the glass in an effort to steady herself, but when she tried to pull away, it stuck. Something was keeping her there, and despite her attempts to pull herself away from the glass, it held her fast. Her fingers might as well have been melded to the pane, and the oddest trickle began to move through her. Fear seized Isa as frigid air blew on her face. Gathering all of her strength, she pushed herself away so hard that she fell to the ground.

Her breath was ragged as she stared at the window. Nothing looked out of the ordinary from where she'd fallen. Through the window she had just been held captive to, she could still see the tall trees rising into the autumn sky with birds flying past them. The window itself looked absolutely commonplace. In wonder, Isa held up her right hand. It also looked as it should. It was as though nothing had been amiss. But she had most assuredly felt a new kind of power, and one that differed vastly from hers or Ever's.

"Would you like some assistance, Your Majesty?" A servant hurried toward her, but stopped just a few feet away. He seemed torn between approaching her and waiting for her approval, one arm outstretched, the other still hanging at his side.

Isa tried to stand, but was forced back down onto the floor when a dull pain shot through her leg. She tried to smile as she nodded. "Thank you. I seem to have twisted my ankle."

As he got closer, she studied his thick mop of tight, silver curls and his cheery face. He wasn't tall. In fact, he seemed a good deal shorter than Isa. As he helped her stand, however, she could tell that he was physically more than capable of helping her return to her rooms.

Gingerly, she tested her ankle, but could make it no farther than a few steps before she was obligated to ask for his help again. "I don't know what the matter with me is," she said ruefully as they began the tedious climb up the first set of stairs. "I never stumble when I dance."

"I don't mind a bit," he said in a singsong voice, which Isa thought to be quite pleasant. "My name is Brokk. Or at least, that's what my mother called me. And I must confess," he paused and gave her a shy smile, "I have actually been hoping to meet you, ever since I found out you were going to be staying in the palace."

"You have?" Isa felt a flutter in her stomach, though she couldn't say what for.

"Your Highness, there is such news of what you have done for the people of Destin, for your husband! It has traveled far, and your power has inspired many!"

"I wish I could accept such praise with a clear conscience." Heat gathered in her neck as Isa considered his words with shame. They walked in silence for a few moments before the servant spoke again.

"I hope I am not being too forward, Your Highness, but are you referring to the little stumble you had? Or rather, was that incident perhaps related to a greater problem?" When Isa couldn't bring herself to answer, he nodded slowly. "And what does your husband think of your struggle?"

"He's not sure." She sighed. "My power is different from his." As the words left her mouth, Isa found herself very grateful for the kindness of this unusually forward servant. But even as she thought it, Ever's warning at the ball about speaking too freely of her strength suddenly echoed in her mind. She hadn't meant to say so much to the servant. In her exasperation, it had just slipped.

"Yes, I heard about that. What is it that you possess differently? Strength of the mind, was it?"

"Of the heart," Isa whispered.

"Ah yes, now I remember. Well, here we are." They had stopped in front of Isa's door. Isa nearly asked how he knew where she was staying, but then remembered that at her own Fortress, Garin made it the business of all the servants to know who all their guests were and where they were staying. Thanking him once again, she held out her arm for Norbert to help her into the room. The older guard gave her a look that threatened violence to whomever had injured her until she assured him twice over that she had only tripped. As much as she loved Norbert, she decided not to tell him of the strange power that had briefly held her in its grasp. It was too confusing.

Once Norbert had left her inside, Isa lowered herself onto the bed, misery overtaking her once more. She had fled her room that morning in order to escape the thoughts she'd awakened to when she realized Ever had already dressed and gone. The way he'd kissed her brow softly and had fallen asleep holding her to his chest for not one but the last two nights, had been the sweetest moments she'd shared with her husband in a long time. Still, she should have known better than to hope for him to continue his attentions in the morning. If nothing else, Ever was dutiful, and whatever had him on edge now had called him away again.

If only he trusted her enough to tell her, she nearly moaned. So much for finding a distraction.

13

GAME OF GLASS

"*I* was hoping that was you," Cerise said, walking in from the small room that was attached to Isa's chambers. "It's time you began to dress for the games." Isa did her best to smile as Cerise pulled the cranberry dress from the wardrobe. This one had sleeves at least. Sleeves so sheer they were nearly invisible.

"Did Gigi have to order every dress to show my shoulders?" Isa grimaced. "For eternity's sake, it's almost winter!"

"I'm sure your husband won't complain." Cerise raised an eyebrow and smirked. "The last time you wore this he noticed." When Isa raised her own eyebrows, Cerise just laughed. "I may be a servant, but to miss that man's stare, one would have to be blind."

Doubts still lingered, but Isa did feel a little better. They continued in silence, which gave Isa time to think, although she did get a quick scolding about her ankle. Rather than give thought to her worries, however, Isa decided to think about how grateful she was that Ever didn't insist on her wearing tightened stays in her dress, as was high fashion. Not that she would have worn them even if he had.

The first grand gathering they'd hosted after the curse was broken had been an attempt to reestablish Destin's place with a few of their neighbors. There had been no ball held with the gathering, so most of the guests had been men, foreign ambassadors and princes.

As her tutor's female assistant had prepared her for the evening, hammering names and etiquette into her head, one of the servants had brought out a long piece of stiff fabric with dozens of thin metal rods running up and down its entire length. Without a word, the servant had begun to fasten it about her waist and chest. After tying it in place, she took the strings that dangled down Isa's backside and with a great heave, began to pull. Isa had nearly passed out as her chest seemed to collapse and her waist had nearly disappeared.

"Stop!" she had gasped, desperate to draw in air. "Please! I can't breathe!"

"You will learn, as all the ladies of the court do," her tutor's assistant had said with a shrug. "It will not be so bad when you become used to it." She had nodded at the servant to begin pulling once again, but Isa had quickly yanked the strings away.

"I am not wearing this! I don't care what the ladies of fashion do!"

What she hadn't expected was for her tutor to report Isa's obstinance to Ever. Sometimes it seemed no one could remember that she had just as much right to the throne as her husband did. His response, however, had been so enjoyable that it hadn't mattered.

"But all the ladies of the court are wearing it, Your Highness," Master Claude, her head tutor, had complained. "It will be expected!"

Ever had only rubbed his eyes. "Pray tell, what exactly are stays, Master Claude?" And so the tutor had brought forth the disagreeable contraption and had explained precisely how a fashionably tiny waist was gained. Ever's response, however, was not what the etiquette master had seemed to expect. The horror on Ever's face still made Isa smile when she remembered it. That anyone could be so daft as to restrain one's ability to breathe, much less run or duel, was beyond Ever, and Master Claude was instructed never to bring the matter up again. Gigi had taken over Isa's wardrobe soon after that, and to Isa's relief, the awful stays had never resurfaced. And yet, Isa thought with annoyance, the older woman's obsession with the see-through sleeves had brought her just one more way to stand out tonight.

"Are you nearly ready? They're beginning soon." Ever's voice came from the doorway.

"Almost," Isa called back, and for the hundredth time that day, resented the simplicity of men's fashions that allowed Ever to dress so quickly without assistance. Her vexation was slightly dulled, however, when she turned to catch him staring fixedly at her figure.

"First I need you to heal my ankle, then I need to talk to you." That broke his trance. A dark look came over his face as he went to her and bent to examine her ankle.

"Come sit." He drew up a chair.

"I stumbled in the practice room," Isa said carefully, doing as he'd directed and measuring his reaction. He didn't look up from her ankle, which he had laid in his lap. She waited for a moment as he twisted it gently in different directions, freezing when she winced.

"It's not broken," he said in a low voice. "How did it happen?"

"I'm not sure," she admitted. He raised his eyebrows skeptically, so she rushed to explain, hoping to avoid the overreaction she knew was highly likely. "I'd been practicing alone . . . and dancing some, when I stumbled and fell into a window pane." She glanced up at him again to see the blue fire blazing dangerously in his eyes, his lips mashed tightly together. "When I touched the glass, something touched me, as though it were trying to pull me into the window itself. It was a power somewhat like our own, yet different."

"Did it hurt you?" he asked in a flat voice.

"No, I only twisted my ankle when I stumbled. But it was strong. Perhaps . . ." she paused, knowing that what she said next could put her husband into one of his famous brooding moods, "stronger than Nevina's power."

A daring thought flitted across her mind. It was a subject she had long wished he would broach, but not a word had been said about her fledgling powers since they had begun to wane. It didn't seem to make a difference how many times she seemed to fail. Maybe, since they were in the right context now, she could finally draw out of Ever what he truly thought of her struggles. And even more, *why* he thought the fire was beginning to fade from her eyes.

"I can't help thinking," she whispered before her courage fled, "that I might not have fallen had my powers been stronger. What do you think?" She placed one trembling hand on his to stop him as he continued to test her ankle, and used the other hand to raise his face to hers. When their eyes finally met, she stared into his, praying he would see what she meant. That he would assure her everything would work itself out. Or even that he too was concerned, but they would overcome it. When he did speak, however, she found only disappointment crashing inside of her as her hopes were dashed to pieces.

"I think that we will be late if we do not hurry." Without another word, he placed his hands around her ankle. Blue fire briefly danced around it until he let go. Taking her hand and then placing it in his arm a little more firmly than necessary, he strode out the door, dragging Isa along with him.

He still hadn't spoken by the time they'd reached the stands, but Isa knew all she needed to know. He had seen her failure to grow, to thrive in her new position as queen, and the disappointment on his angular features was written as clearly as with parchment and ink. He also knew the fire in her eyes was fading. If he was disappointed in these things, how could she ever get him to share what was bothering him so with King Rafael? How could she prove she was worthy to know?

14

ONE AND THE SAME

*D*isappointed with Ever's disappointment in her, Isa sighed and studied the stands around her. The stands themselves formed three quarters of a full grand arena, with the fourth side missing completely. The palace guests had already filled the majority of the stands by the time Ever and Isa were seated. The men elbowed one another and pointed at the gathered competitors at the bottom of the arena, while the ladies made faces at the biting wind that blew in from the northeast and mussed their hair.

For once, Isa was thankful to have been singled out as a guest of honor, for that meant being sheltered in a tent-like covered box in the center stands with the royal family. She slipped the princess a small smile, and to her delight, the girl sent her one back.

Princess Olivia had also changed since the tea, and was now dressed in a sunset orange gown that matched her mother's. Isa nearly smirked to herself. The princess put up a good show of being timid and submissive, but after watching her up close, Isa knew that whatever her fate, Princess Olivia was unlikely to go quietly.

The queen was busy chatting in low tones with one of her ladies-in-waiting, and the king was nowhere to be seen. Which reminded Isa, neither was her brother.

"Where is Launce?" Her question seemed to briefly pull Ever from his dark musing, enough for slight misgivings to flick across his face.

"He's with the other competitors."

Isa stared at her husband blankly for a moment before his words sank in.

"Wait, he is truly competing in the games?" Panic and anger filled her as she stared at Ever in disbelief. "He can barely lift a sword properly! You said so yourself! What in the blazes is he doing in the games?"

It was Ever's turn to look startled as the salty language fell from her lips, but at the moment, Isa didn't care. "Isa, others can hear you. Please keep your voice down. You heard the king invite him last night—"

"And I didn't think you would be foolish enough to allow it!" She wouldn't have cared if the whole kingdom heard her, except that she knew her words could affect Launce. "And I know this wasn't his idea!" she hissed. "Everard, if he gets himself killed out there for the sake of your curiosity—"

"The games are not designed to kill!" Ever raised his own whisper slightly in defense, and Isa sent him her most withering glare in response. Ever ran his hand through his hair, a sure sign that he felt guilty. "I'm sorry, Isa. But . . ." he paused and closed his eyes, as though admitting something against his will. Still, his words were slow, as though he were choosing them with great care. "Something is wrong, but I do not yet know what. I needed eyes in the stables. He's already gathered useful information. As soon as we know what Rafael is up to, I will pull him out." He finally looked at her directly, his gray eyes probing her for any sympathy she might harbor. "I promise."

Though the look he gave her threatened to soften her heart, Isa couldn't quite voice forgiveness yet, or her blessing. If he would just tell her what was wrong, they might have avoided all of this. But for all the repentance in his eyes, Ever was clearly not ready to share all of his worries with her yet. Isa finally turned sharply to stare down at the competitors on their horses, searching for her brother. She couldn't find the Fortress's colors, and from a side glance at her husband, she knew he was thinking the same thing.

"So, Everard, are you ready to watch the Maker choose the heir to my throne?" the king's voice boomed and made Isa jump. Ever's only response was a grunt, but Rafael didn't seem to notice. Instead, he walked to the edge of the large wooden platform they sat in and made a flicking motion with his hand. In response, trumpets blared, and the chattering in the stands died.

"It's not every day that we get to see the Maker in action!" Rafael called out, his voice echoing through the arena. "But today we have one of the Maker's very own holy men to guide us through the journey of choosing my next heir, the future husband of this kingdom's precious flower, my daughter." He turned and threw Princess Olivia an adoring glance before turning back to the people.

"The contestants will be competing in three events. A joust, a melee, and the final contest, which will be announced at the end. The general regulations will take precedent in combat. May the Maker's man win."

The crowds roared as a herald announced the first contestants, and the king sat down with a thump in his chair between Queen Monica and Ever, a satisfied smile on his face.

"It seems you couldn't care less for the first two events," Isa heard Ever murmur to the king. "Usually you can't wait for the combat."

"And miss the fun of the holy man's challenge?" Rafael shook his head and clapped Ever on the shoulder. "Oh no, the first two events are merely children's play. The third event will truly tell me who the Maker has chosen."

"So my brother is fighting for no true purpose?" Isa blurted out, unable to conceal her disgust any longer. The king looked at Ever, his wide smile wavering on his face.

"Of course, it is important for me to see the combat skills of the future king as well."

Ever snorted at Rafael's mention of combat skills, and Isa took a deep breath to prevent herself from saying anything she might regret. The insincerity in the king's voice was thick, and Isa tried to satisfy herself with ignoring him and studying the competitors below.

Isa had never seen a tournament before. The Fortress never held them, not that she would have been important enough to watch one until recently. Still, she'd heard of the violence they often showcased. In Soudain, she'd had neighbors who traveled and witnessed them in other lands. The town boys would run through the streets reenacting scenes of bloody carnage as they pretended to run each other through with long sticks. As the first contest began, however, Isa realized with some relief that the boys had indeed been exaggerating.

"This is a joust," Ever leaned in to explain as the first round was begun. "There will be two men, one on each side of the divider. They will ride toward one another and each will attempt to knock his opponent from his hose. When a man falls from his seat, he is disqualified."

"This is ridiculous. I've never heard of anything so barbaric and pointless in all my life." Isa crossed her arms.

"They were once meant to help knights practice their battle skills, but I agree. To make them public makes light of war, which is why we don't host them at home. You need not worry though. They are not allowed any further combat besides the initial attempt."

"That doesn't guarantee someone couldn't make a killing blow."

"Their lances have been checked by the games keeper beforehand. Nothing sharp is allowed upon the field. This is simply a test of skill, to see who would be the victor in an actual battle." As Ever spoke, Isa grudgingly found herself slightly relieved that there were such rules. Still, the horses rode fast and hard, and even with the rules, the palace healer was called out onto the field often. Isa was thankful to see that Launce was not among the contestants during the first match. Not that it would make a difference when he fought. She didn't want him fighting at all.

Holding her breath, Isa suffered through joust after joust for Launce to ride out onto the field for his turn.

"Where is he?" Ever muttered. Just then, the herald paused as he read the names, looking confused.

"The next contestants are Josepha, Earl of Faunton of Giova, and . . ." He squinted at the parchment. "Armand."

Whispers moved through the stands. It was unheard of for a rider to list only one name. This contestant not only listed just a single name, but also claimed no place of origin, nor a family name. Just Armand.

Which happened to be Launce's second name.

Of the two men that rode out onto the field, neither wore the Fortress's colors. The first wore Giova's red and gold, but the other was dressed in the most peculiar armor Isa had ever seen. From Ever's expression, he thought it no less bizarre. The knight's armor, from head to toe, was made of a polished bronze, so bright it hurt to look at in the afternoon sun, and his horse was the largest and fiercest she had ever laid eyes on. Despite her anger, Isa was sure her eyes were failing her completely, so she leaned over and whispered to her husband, "Could that be—" Before she finished speaking, however, the knight in question fumbled his weapon so badly it fell into the mud.

"It is," Ever said, rubbing his temples in wide circles.

The copper knight now had the attention of King Rafael, who had until then been talking with the queen and ignoring the tournament in general.

"Who is this?" he asked Ever, his mouth falling open as he peered closer.

"He wears no kingdom's colors," Ever said, glancing at Isa. If the king had been paying attention, he might have realized that Launce was the only contestant who had not yet been announced, but from the way Ever had looked at her, it appeared that keeping this knowledge from Rafael would work best to Launce's advantage.

Isa's breath sped and anxiety made her stomach flutter as she watched the copper knight make his way to the end of his lane. Their mother would faint if she could see Launce right now. There was a reason her family had never apprenticed him out to the blade smith who had requested him as a boy.

As the signal was given, and the two opponents positioned themselves, Isa found herself fervently whispering prayers of Launce's preservation.

The signal was given. Launce's opponent sped forward, poised, sleek as a fish through the water as the two men approached one another. Launce sat straight up, and it was easy to see that he struggled to hold his weapon properly. As they raced forward, Isa fought the need to close her eyes.

The two met in the middle. Launce's opponent's weapon landed with a solid thud directly into Launce's chest. Isa cringed as his opponent's weapon splintered upon impact. Launce fell from his horse, landing on his shoulder at an awkward angle. He lay there for a long moment, but when he stood unevenly and limped off the field, Isa finally let out a sigh of relief and sat back in her chair, suddenly exhausted. She could hear the chatter around her begin about the unfortunate, unusual knight, as the king declared the winner, but she couldn't care less. He was alive, and that was all that mattered.

The next sport was ground combat with the sword, but instead of a duel between two men at a time, all of the contestants would participate at the same time, according to Ever. It was easy to pick Launce's bright copper suit out as the contestants tumbled around the ring. Isa sent up a prayer of thanks as Launce stayed near the outside of the ring, and the other competitors seemed to leave him alone. She wondered if they'd figured out early on just how helpless he truly was with a sword.

"If he would have just allowed me to train him, this might have turned out differently," Ever mumbled.

"My guess is that he had no desire to even be a part of this," Isa replied, pausing for Ever to challenge her assumption. But he did not. "So it should not matter whether he wins or loses."

"It doesn't," Ever said, "but he might have been a little less humiliated in the process."

To Isa's great relief, the king announced a winner soon after, and declared that it was time for the third and most important event. Guards herded the contestants out of the clearing, and the king raised his hands once again. Isa noticed a gleam in his eye as he spoke, one that seemed just a bit too bright.

"This will be the final and greatest challenge of them all! Three days, the contestants will have, to lay claim to my daughter's hand and to my throne. Three days and three of these!" He held up what three apples that appeared to be made of solid gold. "Whomever shall present me with all three of these apples, given by my daughter's hand, shall be my heir, chosen by the Maker.

"Before your eyes, you will see His hand working through the holy man as has not been done in thousands of years." Isa felt Ever stiffen beside her. His jaw was set like stone, and the gray in his eyes was nearly eclipsed by the blue flame that leapt inside them.

"Daughter?" Rafael held the three apples out to the princess. She paled a bit, but took them and gave a small curtsy before making her way down to the center of the clearing. It might have been Isa's heightened sense of suspicion, but the look of fear on the princess's face seemed no longer a mask. Princess Olivia looked terrified.

When she reached the center of the clearing, the princess just stopped and stood there. A tense, uncomfortable silence blanketed the stands for a long moment. Then, the ground began to quake. Women shrieked, and the men's hands went to their swords. The ground stretched, and with a sickening crack, a bump in the land began to develop. Isa watched the princess, wondering what insanity her father had bought into that would have him send his daughter into the center of this chaos. Still, the girl stood dutifully as the ground beneath her began to tear and swell.

Before she could whisper to him, to ask what was happening, a strange cold sensation crept through her. Quickly, she recognized the same feeling as the one she'd felt that morning when she'd touched the pane of glass.

The ground that should have separated with such violent shaking began to twist and turn, growing up, pushing the princess higher and higher with it. At first it was only a little mound, but within seconds, the mound was growing. As it moved upward and began to widen, the center began to darken into a deep blue. The higher the hill rose, the wider the blue spread, until nearly the entire mound was one solid heap. The grinding and cracking continued until it came to rest, nearly as high as the Fortress watch towers back at home. The mound had become a solid hill.

The newly born hill was so wide around that it nearly touched the lowest level of the stands. And at the top, the princess now sat, clutching her three golden apples to her chest.

"Is that . . . glass?" Isa whispered. Ever didn't answer. For the first time since she'd met her husband, he seemed just as confused as she was.

Rafael slapped Ever on the back and the gleam returned to his eye.

"You see, Everard. The Maker blesses *others* with wonders and signs too." He walked to the edge of the box once more and called out, hushing the fearful whispering of the spectators. "This is our sign that whomever can make it up to the top of the hill thrice will be our answer from the Maker, a sure promise to bless their union."

As he finished speaking, a flurry of sparkling light fluttered down upon the stands. The crowd exclaimed in delight as it floated down like little jewels in the sky. Isa felt Ever put up a shield around the two of them as the glitter came to rest on every surface, even the inside of their covered platform.

"You missed some," she told him wryly, brushing a few pieces out of his hair, only to realize she'd gotten some in her own eyes. From the way he was blinking, it appeared that Ever had done the same. Isa held her hand up when her eyes were clear, and examined it in awe. The sparkles looked like glass as well, but lacked the sharpness that Isa would have assumed them to have.

Instead of brushing the sparkling dust off like everyone else, the king was holding his arms out as he raised his face toward the sun. A smile spread upon his lips as he seemed to be whispering the words *thank you, thank you* to the sky.

Once the excitement over the glitter dust had settled, the contest was begun. The contestants were lined up outside of the arena, far enough away that their horses could gather speed for their attempts to ride up the hill toward the princess.

First up was a duke. He wore six feathers atop his helm, and when Isa asked Ever about their meaning, he scoffed.

"That's Duke Tareq. He's young, and after winning a few rounds of jousting in his own kingdom, has become convinced he's the Maker's gift to the world. He reeks of ale though, and would hardly give the princess a second look. He's usually too busy with the women from the back of the alehouse."

The duke's ride was dramatic, his feathers adding to the flare of his pose. For all the show he put into his speed, however, his horse only made it up the hill a few paces before sliding back down. It served him right though for all that pomp and show.

As the contestants continued to try their hands at winning the princess, it soon became evident that the first duke's fate would be the norm. One after another, they raced forward like dogs to prey, only to fall back down after a few steps. At least, Isa thought, Launce wouldn't be alone in his struggles here. He was a fair horseman. This time he might blend in with the other competitors in skill.

The sun was close to setting by the time Launce's turn arrived. Isa wondered if his placement was because he had come in last in everything else, or if he was simply too nice to shove his way to the top. Or because he was a commoner. Whatever the reason, Isa was glad it was nearly over. Her backside smarted from sitting for so long, and her stomach rumbled. She'd been too nervous to eat much when the midday meal had been brought out on platters.

The copper-clad rider sat astride his horse with nearly a pose of confidence. Beside her, Ever leaned forward in his chair as the signal was given, and just like the others, Launce raced toward the hill. The crowd had long ago also grown weary of watching riders. As the mysterious copper knight approached the princess, however, a hush fell upon the people.

As soon as the gigantic horse set a hoof on the hill, a slight ringing hit Isa's ears. The feeling of foreign power hit her once again.

To everyone's surprise, far beyond the initial steps of the other competitors, Launce didn't stop at the foot of the hill. Isa felt her mouth fall open as he ascended. Only when he was two thirds of the way up did the copper rider pause. Somehow, the princess had just enough time to snatch an apple from her lap and toss down it to him. Launce caught the golden apple and began his descent.

Instead of stopping at the bottom and returning to claim his first victory, however, the copper knight continued to race away from the hill, past the stables, and into the forest at top speed. Knowing Launce's aversion to crowds and attention, Isa might have considered his strange behavior understandable if it weren't for the one thing that was bothering her more by the second.

"Ever?"

"Yes?"

"Did you feel that?"

"Yes." He turned to look her in the eye. "Why?"

"Because that's the same power I felt this morning when I touched the window."

As soon as the words left her mouth, Ever stood. His jaw flexed and his right hand twitched. "Are you sure? It is exactly the same?"

"Absolutely." She paused, glancing around as the people surrounding them gossiped and tried to surmise who the mystery rider might be. "What do you think it means?"

"I don't know, but I shall certainly find out."

15

LIKE MY FATHER

*A*fter the contest, Isa and Ever returned to their chambers to prepare for that night's banquet. Isa was strangely quiet as they readied, hardly even talking to Cerise. That was never a good sign.

To make matters worse, once they arrived, still without speaking a word to one another, Rafael's banquet lasted much longer than Ever had hoped. The king was clearly enjoying the talk brought on by the glass hill, and was basking in the attention, answering the same questions over and over again with vague, cryptic cackles that made Ever want to strike the man unconscious.

Isa was looking lovely, but miserable. Of course, that didn't stop him from noticing her. The dress she wore draped around her tall, slim frame like red wine spilling down a steep, tightly curved staircase, and the gossamer sleeves displayed her bare, lean muscled shoulders enticingly. On much more than one occasion throughout the party he caught highborn men staring unabashedly like unpolished village boys. One glare from him though was enough to send most of them scattering.

Isa seemed to notice little of it though. She'd spent the whole evening at his side staring vacantly out at the other guests as they laughed and gossiped and drank. She plastered a smile on her face every time Ever introduced her to someone new, but none of it was real. Even her dancing was wooden.

"Isa," he finally leaned over to whisper. "Are you feeling well?"

"I'm fine," she answered too quickly. When he cocked his head, giving her a wry, knowing smile, she caved. "I'm concerned about Launce."

"Would you like to return to our room?"

Before she could reply, he could see the eager answer in her eyes, so he quietly excused them and escorted her back to their chambers, where he called her lady-in-waiting to attend to her before he returned. Given her distant mood all evening, she surprised him, however, with a request just as he was ready to leave.

"Can't you stay?" The misery in her plea was pitiful. Chagrin washing through him, he leaned down and stroked her hair once before shaking his head. As he stared into her eyes, simply retiring for the evening and spending it quietly with Isa suddenly sounded enticing, and he had to fight his own longing to do as she asked.

"I need to see what else I can learn about whatever strange power it is that's using your brother." He tried to soften his words so she wouldn't think he actually wanted to leave her.

"I thought we could do that together." Isa frowned. "That was actually what I had been hoping . . ." She let her words trail off though as she studied him, long and hard, and he wondered uneasily what conclusions her study drew her to. "Well, if you must," she finally finished, and with that she slipped into the bed. His hopes at being forgiven were neatly dashed when she curled into a ball on the far side of the bed. He did his best to noiselessly step out, but not before her near silent sniffles reached his ears.

Hot shame started along his back and arms and worked its way up his neck and face as he walked back toward the raucous party. For all of his power and riches, he couldn't grant this one simple request. *Or you won't grant it*, some part of his mind nagged at him.

Ever could count on one hand the number of times Isa had requested something of him since they'd gotten married. And her last request had been granted grudgingly at that, he thought with guilt, recalling how nervous she'd seemed as she'd suggested bringing Launce along. A far cry from the way he'd vowed to himself that he would keep her happy the day they were wed. To make matters worse, he got absolutely nothing accomplished, as Launce had returned to the stables before they had time to talk, and Rafael was too drunk to talk at all. The whole night was a waste.

If Ever hoped for anything different that night after he'd finally gone to bed, he did a fantastic job of dashing those hopes the next morning.

"Where are you going this early?" Isa stretched and yawned. It was hard not to see the dark circles beneath her eyes, despite the early hour at which he'd dropped her off the night before.

"I have some business to attend to." He paused, wondering whether if he told her any more, she would let him go without too many more questions. He decided it was worth a try. "I'm meeting with an ally who might have some insight into Launce's position."

"You mean you're going to meet with *her*, aren't you?" The way Isa's eyes narrowed for a moment, raking him up and down as though she could see through to his soul, was slightly frightening. She surprised him, however, by then hopping off the bed and moving to dress herself without even ringing for her lady-in-waiting. "I'm coming with you then," she announced as she began to pin up her runaway locks.

Despite his rush, Ever had to appreciate that Isa's status as queen hadn't ever gone to her head. Like him, she preferred escaping her servants and dressing herself as often as she could. Unfortunately, today was a day he couldn't afford the delay. Or the distraction.

"I want to hear what she thinks about this whole spectacle," Isa continued as she went over to the corner of the room and opened her wardrobe, staring at its contents, tipping her head to the side as she did. At first she chose a yellow dress, then a more practical brown one, perfect for riding. Ever inwardly berated himself for what he had to do next, particularly amid the stream of sweet and happy chatter she was somehow conjuring.

"I'm sorry, Isa." He took the dress from her hands gently and hung it back up in the wardrobe. Her expression immediately changed from amiable contentment to suspicion. "I need you to stay here where it's safe."

"You're just going to leave me here?" Out of the corner of his eye, Ever noticed her knuckles whitening as she held on to the mahogany wardrobe door. "No. No, I thought about it last night, and I decided that I need to help you with this. The Fortress didn't make me queen to sit idly in my room all day. Besides," the blue flames that had risen up in her eyes for just a moment lessened as she said in a more pleading voice, "I'll be with you. You can keep me safe."

"We'll be outside palace grounds, away from nosy ears. It would be more dangerous for you out there, even *with* me. I need you to stay here." And with that, he turned and began to walk toward the door.

"And who says I have to listen to you?" Isa shouted.

When Ever turned back to look at her in surprise, tears were streaming down her face, making the dark circles beneath her eyes stand out even more. For a moment, he was stunned. It didn't take long for anger and frustration to well up within him though as he stomped back over to where she stood with her fists clenched and trembling at her sides.

"What if I choose not to be treated like a commoner?" She held her chin high, and her eyes held his, defiant and provoking.

"I think you will listen to me because you know I am trying to protect you," he growled, glaring down at her willful expression. "And if it behooves me, I shall tie you to a chair if I must to keep you safe."

Shock slowly registered in her features, and she fell a step back. "You really don't think I can help you then?" Her voice shook so hard that it cracked, and so did his anger. Ever took a deep breath and closed his eyes.

"Kartek has been gifted from birth. I need her—"

"More than you need me. I understand."

"Now, Isa, that's not fair, and you know it!"

"You've made your point, Everard. Get on with it then and leave me alone." Isa slammed the wardrobe door so loudly it made the windows rattle. The red streaks in her hair stood out more prominently than usual as she threw herself down on the bed and crossed her arms.

Ever took in a deep breath before making his mind up about what to say. A million words of apology and regret coursed through his mind, the greatest of them being the truth. He hadn't expected such a reaction from Isa, not even in the slightest, and from the glower she was giving the ceiling, it was evident he had wounded her deeply. But the truth would hurt even more, he reasoned, and there would be no respite from it until he had things figured out.

"I'll make sure you get your meals," he said softly as he paused on the threshold. But he received no answer. She just lay there in her blue nightdress, her glare never once wavering from the ceiling. Sighing, he turned to go before stopping and adding one caution more. "Just don't touch the windowpanes."

~

"Someone is toying with my family." Ever glowered straight ahead as they walked. The red of the leaves waved to him, signaling like a ship in distress. There was no time though to bask in the unusually warm autumn sun or to enjoy the colors of nature that surrounded Rafael's palace. Ever could feel Kartek sending him a wary glance every few paces, but he ignored her concern. If Isa had been present, she would have teased him and called it his beastly brooding. A stab of guilt slashed at him, dangerously close to breaking his concentration. Isa would not be teasing him for a while if the words they'd just exchanged were any indication.

"Speaking of your family, where is your wife?" Kartek's low voice was smooth like oil, and the familiar cadence of it usually comforted him when she spoke. This time, however, it only worsened the guilt.

"In our chambers."

Kartek stopped walking and fixed him with a look of knowing disapproval.

"And did you leave her there by her choice?"

"I left her there for her protection," Ever huffed, exasperated with his friend, avoiding her gaze by staring over her head at the distant waves that crashed on the white beach.

"Everard—" she began in a chiding tone.

"You would have done the same for Unsu!"

"No, I would not have locked him in his room and left him there like a little boy. He is a man, and it would hardly be respectful of my husband for me to treat him as anything but a man." She raised her eyebrows as though inviting him to challenge her.

"You don't understand." Ever, still staring at the beach, suddenly felt very small. It was a moment before he could bring himself to say the next words, and they came out almost as a whisper. "Her powers are floundering." He paused, not wanting to utter any more. Saying them aloud suddenly made the truth seem more real. But aside from Garin, if anyone could help him, if would be Kartek. "The fire in her eyes burns a little less every day." He turned to her, hating the way his voice caught in his throat and made it warble. "You know what happens when our fires go out."

Kartek stared back at him for a long time. She no longer looked reproachful, just thoughtful.

"I cannot fully empathize with you, as Unsu has never held a power." Her lips curved up into the smallest of smiles. "With the exception of his love. My husband has the heart of a thousand men. Still," she took a deep breath and resumed a grave expression, "have you spoken to her of your concerns?"

"Of course not!"

"And why is that?"

"She doubts herself enough already!" Ever ran his hand down his face, fatigue suddenly seeming to overwhelm him. He hadn't slept well in over a week. "She questions everything she does, from her posture to the way she speaks to the way she chews. I've tried helping her, teaching her to use weapons, something to build her confidence, but her strength just continues to stall." He let out a gusty breath. "On top of all that, the Fortress gossip is ripe with talk. I try to intercede when I can, but you know women's tongues . . ." He stopped himself when he remembered with whom he was speaking. To his surprise and relief, Kartek let out one of her deep, saucy laughs.

"I know a little of that." She continued to chuckle after she was done laughing. "It took me seven months after my marriage to conceive our son. The women of our palace just knew I was barren." She patted her belly and raised her chin high. "Five children later, and the old toads have not gossiped in a long time! So yes, I know how terrible court gossips can be. Surely you at least warned her when you were on your honeymoon."

Ever shifted uncomfortably again. Time with his old friend was rare and precious, but like an older sister, from what he gathered of closely knit families, she knew just how to make him squirm like a punished puppy.

"In truth . . ." he gathered up his courage for the look she was sure to give him, "we never had one." When he finally dared to peek at her, the look Kartek was sending him wasn't quite as reproachful as he'd anticipated. It was worse.

"You did what?"

"We were going to go!" he hurried to assure her, but it didn't dull her cutting glare of disappointment.

"Let me guess. A war broke out. A famine struck the land. Some poor city was flooded. Everard, after seventeen years of marriage to a king, I can guarantee you this: something will always come. But you still cannot put everything above your queen!"

"I'm trying! The world just suddenly seems ripe with distractions."

"The distractions were always there. They always will be. The difference between then and now is that your father took care of them while he lived."

"He always knew what to do." Ever sank onto a fallen log on the side of the path, rubbing his temples and closing his eyes. "I just wish I knew how he did it all."

"It is quite simple. He left you and your mother behind. She was never allowed to share his burdens or know his heartache. And look at how that turned out."

Ever shook his head, staring morosely at the sand beneath his boots. "Isa worries about so much. I just wanted to let her be. I don't want to burden her with more than she's already struggling with." His jaw hardened as he remembered what she had told him the day before on the way to the events. "To make matters worse, she was attacked by the same source of power that created that spectacle yesterday."

"The same?" Kartek quirked an eyebrow at him.

"In a pane of glass in the practice room."

At his words, the southern queen fell silent, a dark look overshadowing her usually serene face. She stared out at the ocean, and it was a long time before she spoke again.

"I do not like this, Everard. I do not like it at all. It is too . . . familiar." Ever nodded, hoping his friend would not continue to judge his actions too sharply now that she knew the foundation of his fears. "But it cannot be." Her voice was a whisper. "It has been nearly three thousand years! Surely they could not have survived!" She shook her head again. "Rafael should know better, either way. Whatever this power is, it is no good. I can feel it. And its attack on your wife yesterday just confirms that."

"I told you, someone is toying with my family. My wife is attacked inside our host's home, and my graceless brother-in-law wins the first day's competition with a horse and armor that aren't his." He paused before adding, "And all of it comes back to glass."

"And you think keeping your wife locked up while you talk with me is the answer?" The sharpness of Kartek's question took Ever by surprise. He stood and looked down into her deep honey eyes as they stared coldly up at him. "You are a fool, Everard, if you think walking and talking with me is going to save your wife while you hide her away. And if Unsu could have come on this journey with me, you know he would say the same!"

"I didn't know who else to turn to!" Ever objected, hoping she couldn't see just how badly she had wounded him. As she always did, however, Kartek seemed to sense just that. Her glare softened and she patted his arm as she gathered her thin, golden skirts and turned to make the walk back to the palace.

"I will consider this puzzle of glass you have presented me, but you are not a lost little boy anymore." She smiled at him affectionately. "And it is not my job any longer to find you someone to sit with at the banquet. I think your wife, however, will prove to be a great dinner partner. But first, you have to allow her to sit with you."

16

THE WRONG COLOR

"*I*'m not supposed to be here, you know." Launce's voice was sour. "The stable master forbade any of us from leaving the stables without permission once the events began."

"I am well aware of that." Ever kept his voice cool as he glanced at his brother-in-law. The young man was back in his village clothes, despite the perfectly good raiment Ever had sent down to him on the eve of the first contest. The dark circles beneath Launce's eyes mirrored those of his sister's from earlier that morning.

"I think you know just why I wanted to meet you though," he continued, before Launce could interrupt him again.

"She doesn't like that color."

"What?"

"Whatever you've done, Isa doesn't like orange. You're not going to win any affection back with that necklace."

The smug smile on Launce's face annoyed Ever more than words could express, but he took a deep breath and handed the piece of jewelry back to the stall owner. It pained him to admit that there were many things about his wife that he still didn't know, but it wouldn't do to make the situation worse.

"If I may be of assistance, Your Highness," the stall owner mumbled, a nervous, short man that reminded Ever of a hedgehog, "what color does she like? I have many stones of all different shades . . ."

Ever opened his mouth to answer, but stopped. Embarrassment flooded him as he struggled to answer. How in the heavens did he not know his wife's favorite color?

"She likes light purple."

Ever was both relieved and livid when Launce finally answered the merchant for him. The smile in the young man's voice was about more than he could bear at that very moment. Thankfully, the merchant held up a silver bracelet that was inlaid with lavender-colored roses that had been carved out of tiny purple garnets. When Ever grudgingly looked at Launce, Launce just shrugged and gave a half nod. At least Isa wouldn't hate it.

If there was one thing the merchants in Cobren excelled at over the ones in Destin, it was curating foreign wares. Though he had never been one for collecting baubles himself, Ever had never been able to stay away from the markets when he visited Cobren. When he was very young, he would beg his father to let him find gifts for his mother. As he grew older, and realized his chosen gifts were not to his mother's personal taste, after finding them all hidden away in a dusty box, he began instead to bring gifts to Gigi. Her reactions to his presents had been much more satisfying than Queen Louise's tepid acceptances.

Perhaps, he wondered now as he scanned the rows and rows of tents and stalls, he would bring Ansel the next time he came. Isa's father would have loved this. The bright colors of the foreign tents, the shine and sparkles of the wares, and the savory smells of the unfamiliar dishes being cooked up right in the square could easily overwhelm someone who tried to take it in all at once. Cobren was known far and wide for its exotic markets. King or not, Ever felt the burning desire to please his new in-laws. Perhaps it was because his own parents were gone, or maybe it was because they were the kind of parents Ever had always wished to have.

He paused at another stall. "What would your mother think of this?" He held up a thin copper ring, centered with a delicate green stone. Launce studied it for a moment before shrugging again and turning away, and Ever had to remind himself not to smile. He had finally succeeded in making Launce uncomfortable. Now he could begin his real work. "Speaking of shiny copper things," Ever began as he paid for the ring, "you certainly found yourself quite the new prizes."

"So you know about that." When he spoke this time, Launce stared at the ground, all bravado gone.

"And I find myself enormously curious as to what you have gotten yourself wrapped up in." They stopped at another stall. The owner held out a plate of small pieces of meat, no doubt anxious to test the generosity of one of the many kings present in the city. The bits of meat were nearly yellow, sprinkled with red spices and smelling strongly of bay leaves. Ever wasn't hungry, but he allowed Launce time to sample it and consider his response. After Launce had decided to buy himself a full leg of the bird, they continued their stroll, and the young man finally spoke between bites.

"How did you know?"

"Aside from the herald announcing a mysterious man with your second given name? There aren't enough contestants for you to lose yourself that easily." Ever tapped his temple. "And you forget that we're more acquainted now. It's easier for me to sense your presence. And your sister is even more attuned to you."

Launce's face crumpled, as though his turkey had turned sour.

"But that doesn't answer my question. What happened?"

"I don't see why it's so important!" Launce said. "Is it that shocking that I might actually be good at something?"

That was it. Ever was done with this foolishness. He took hold of the young man's forearm and dragged him past the lines of bright tents and a little ways into the forest the market bordered. Launce looked for a moment as though he might protest, but when Ever threw him his most dangerous look, daring him to make a scene, Launce complied, however unhappily. Once they were a ways into the woods, Ever left Launce standing at the center of a small clearing, where mottled sunlight filtered down through the trees. Ever stalked around the little circle, listening for curious busybodies that might be in the immediate vicinity, before returning to Launce and pressing in until they were at an uncomfortable proximity.

"Stop acting like a spoiled oaf! You are far too old to be playing these games! Isa was attacked yesterday, just before the competition!"

At these words, the rebellion drained from Launce's face.

"Was she harmed?"

"She only twisted her ankle. But a strange power is at work here, and your mysterious garb and horse last night aren't making it any easier for me to understand." Ever ran his hand down his face for what felt like the hundredth time that day. What he wouldn't give for a nap. He pulled in a deep breath, asking the Maker for some self-control, if nothing else. The world suddenly seemed much weightier than he had ever lifted, and the thread of patience that he struggled to hold on to on any given day was about to snap.

Launce was silent for a long moment, staring first at the blanket of moss beneath his muddy boots and then up at the sky that peeked through the thick foliage above. When he finally did speak, his words came out in uneven bursts, and his tone was at least appropriately disconcerted.

"After I talked to you yesterday, I did as you instructed, looking for anything that felt like power. It took me a while. For hours, I had nothing. Then I realized the entire stables were covered in a shiny dusting. So I decided to spend the evening on the stable roof where it was clear, so I could see what was happening."

"You didn't fall asleep?" Ever asked.

Launce shook his head. "I nearly did, I think because I must have still had the dust on me from inside the stable. But I guess I managed to shake enough off." He paused. "It was a good thing I had, because the earthquake was much stronger on the roof than it had been in the stable. I nearly lost my balance and rolled off, but managed to cling to the roof tiles, pulling myself just to the edge.

"When I looked down to see the guard, however, I realized the shaking wasn't an earthquake at all, but a horse, larger than any I had ever seen, charging up the path from the thin forest that surrounds the palace. The closer it got, the harder its hooves pounded the ground. Every jolt moved the stable like a wave crashing upon the side of a ship. It was all I could do to hold on to the roof tiles.

"The horse came to a stop before the new guard. The guard seemed nearly frightened out of his mind, and kept waving his sword at the horse. Stupid fellow thought he might stand a chance against the beast." Launce paused and looked up at Ever, for once, without resentment in his face. "King Rafael doesn't spend much time training his men with horses, does he?"

Ever nearly smiled. "No, but it's something I've advised him to do a number of times." How many times had the two men had that conversation? But no matter how much Ever chided, Rafael would remind him that wrestling was their national pride. A lot of good that would do them against enemies with swords and bows. But Ever hadn't come out to think about Rafael's wrestling army. "Go on," he told Launce.

"The horse kept rearing, slicing the air with his hooves, each movement bringing them closer to the guard's face. I was trying to think of a way to save him, but before I could come up with one, a particularly hard slam of the hooves sent me sprawling off the roof, right next to the guard.

"He screamed at me to run, holding his sword as high as he could between himself and the horse. I told him to lower his sword, but I couldn't help, as the horse kept pounding the ground too hard for me to get up. He told me that I was insane, but when the next hoof barely missed his head, he finally listened." Launce gave a distant half smile.

"'If I die, my blood will be on your head!' he told me as he put it down." Launce looked at Ever, just a glimmer of resentment in his eye his time. "I may know little of swords, but horses . . . I know horses." Ever was aware of this. It was the reason he'd never added horses to the practices during the few days Launce had agreed to train with him. But for the first time, Ever wondered if perhaps it might have been better for Launce to have had the chance to perform well in at least one arena.

"When the horse quit bucking quite so hard, I held a hand out low and began to whistle a soothing tune that my horse at home enjoys. Slowly, I crept toward the animal. It took me forever, but he finally let me touch him just between his shoulder and neck. When I did, the horse shuddered a bit, but let me continue to rub him. I rubbed until I thought my arm might fall off. When I'd made my way down his back though, I realized his saddlebags were full." Launce frowned at this and paused, as though what he was about to say troubled him.

"And?" Ever prodded, trying not to sound too impatient. He had to go soon to meet with Rafael's soldiers, but Launce suddenly seemed lost in his own world. At Ever's prodding, he gave himself a little shake, but when he spoke, his words were still slow.

"A note fell out of the saddlebags. It said, 'Job well done. This horse is now yours. Treat him well, and he will carry you to your first victory.' When I looked in the saddlebags they were full of the armor."

"And let me guess," Ever said. "The same thing happened again last night." A look of surprise and then annoyance flashed across Launce's face.

"Silver this time," was all he said.

Ever studied him for a moment, trying to quell the maelstrom of questions that swirled in his head. Something was still missing. There was a piece of this puzzle that had been lost, or stolen, rather, but Ever wasn't sure who held it. To be sure, Rafael was teeming with secrets. But had Launce told Ever all that he knew? Did he really grasp the danger of the situation? Ever doubted it.

"How did you keep the other competitors from knowing your identity in the copper suit?"

"They couldn't care less about me, for the most part," Launce said. "I didn't show anyone the armor. Only the guard knew of the horse, and I swore him to secrecy with a few coins. I dawdled until everyone else was lined up and ready, and went into the woods where I'd tied the horse." His dark eyes tightened. "You don't want me to compete tonight, do you?"

"Actually," Ever chose his words carefully, "I think you should. It can't be an accident that your sister was attacked, and you were gifted a monstrous horse all on the same day. We need to know more about this entity. But," he leveled his sternest look at his brother-in-law, "you must take care."

"So you worry about me then?" Launce's eyes glinted mischievously in the yellow sun that slipped through the trees.

"I worry about myself," Ever responded dryly. "Your sister will have my hide if something happens to you. I would like to make it home in one piece." Ever had begun to make his way back to the edge of the woods toward the noise and bustle of the market, when Launce called out one more time.

"Everard?"

"Yes?" He paused, looking over his shoulder. Launce had begun to follow him, but stopped several paces back, all signs of mirth gone from his thin face.

"I don't know if it makes a difference, but the undersides of both saddles, as well as the bottoms of the horse shoes, are made of glass."

Ever had to use every ounce of his self-control to keep himself from sprinting to the palace. He and Rafael needed to talk.

WISDOM OF KINGS

"So who is this famous holy man that has such a talent for glass architecture?" Ever nocked an arrow as he awaited Rafael's response. He worked hard to appear casual after finding out about the glass in Launce's mysterious gifts.

"So that's why you dragged me out here." Rafael shook his head as he nocked his own arrow. "I knew it couldn't be simply for old time's sake."

"You know me too well for that."

"I suppose I do," Rafael sighed as they nudged their mounts into the shadowy greens of the woods.

The horses obeyed, but moved along at a leisurely pace, not suitable at all for hunting. This was fine with Ever, as he had no intention of actually hunting with the king. He simply needed to get Rafael alone. Hunting was merely the invitation that was sure to draw the king from his courtiers.

"You never had fun much as a youth either. You spent enough time in my courts disconcerting the men and driving the girls mad by refusing to look at them."

Ever snorted. "It's not practical to woo women when a rebel is lurking in every corner, waiting to kill you."

"'Tis true, but you have a way of unnerving people, Everard. And you know it. In fact, you're doing a wonderful job of it now. Have you forgotten completely how to smile? Half of my servants are terrified of you, and I'll wager at least half of the guests."

At this, Ever allowed himself a small grin. That had been his plan precisely. "Your court needs a bit of fear driven into it. Everyone is too complacent, including you."

"And you blame all of this on my holy man?" Rafael pulled his horse to a halt and looked directly at Ever. The breeze moved through the trees in quick darts and whirls, trying to find a way through Ever's cloak to warn him that winter was fast approaching.

"I simply do not see how you can trust him so implicitly after such a short period of time. The message you sent before last seemed as though all was proceeding as usual. Why the sudden change in allegiances?"

"There is no change in allegiance, Everard." Rafael shook his head and nudged his horse forward again at a slow pace. "And the holy man has been here for quite a while. I have gotten to know him well. Besides . . ." Rafael looked at him again, but this time, a strange gleam came to his eye, the same maddening look he'd worn since they'd first arrived. "He has shown me many signs. Too many to ignore."

"I could show you signs, and I'm no holy man. Even such," Ever said, fixing the king with his most intense stare, "don't his signs remind you of a certain dangerous character?"

"Rubbish!" Rafael waved him off, but refused to meet Ever's eyes. "He's been dead for three thousand years. Just because one enchanter used glass doesn't mean no one else can ever touch it. Now, are we going to hunt or not? We haven't even left the path yet, and my wife is expecting me back for the midday meal."

Frustrated, but knowing he would get no further at that moment, Ever nodded, and they turned their horses off the trail.

Ever heard the arrow before he could see it. With a sharp crack, it hit the tree behind them, missing Rafael's neck by inches. Rafael's horse reared, but Ever's had been seasoned with more battles than he could count. Another arrow missed Rafael as he tried to get his steed under control, this time it came from further to the left. While Rafael continued to wrestle with his horse, distant hoof beats told Ever all he needed to know. With just a touch to his horse's sides, he and his beast were off in pursuit.

Ever laid low so the trees wouldn't hit him as they sped through the woods. It wasn't long before Ever's horse snorted. Ever gave him the lead, knowing he would follow the scent much faster than Ever could track by sight. Soon, the rear hooves of their prey's ride came into view. It was a gray steed, and blended in well with the surrounding forest.

They moved up and down hills, and even forded a small creek before Ever was able to come up alongside the attacker. Anger coursed through him as he caught sight of the man's saddlebags. Seeing the familiar red crest was like being thrust back into his youth, when he had chased hundreds of the separatists from the Cobrien borders with his father.

Yanking his sword out, Ever pointed it at the horse, hoping not to spook the animal too badly, just to bring him to a halt. It was the rider he was interested in. Blue fire gathered around his forearm, swirling about it briefly before shooting down the tip of his sword and into the beast itself. It let out a whinny of pain as the blue fire engulfed it. The encounter was brief, lasting only long enough for the horse to stop so quickly its rider fell off. Once it was free, the beast trotted off, completely unscathed. Ever couldn't say the same would happen for its rider. Without pause, he was off his horse as well, crouching over the man and pressing his sword into the man's neck.

"Who sent you?"

"I act alone!"

"You're lying."

The man started to protest again, but stopped when the blue flame returned to Ever's hand, the one that held him down. The man's eyes grew wide as it flowed and swayed in place. Ever leaned down to whisper in his ear, "As you can see, my fire doesn't burn unless I tell it to. It can, however, leave a dastardly stinging sensation."

The man's cry was loud, and long enough that Ever hoped it would change his mind about his next answer. "Now, who sent you?"

"I... I was paid!"

"By whom?"

"You saw my crest! Who else?"

Just then, Rafael rode up, flanked by a dozen of his guards. "I see you haven't lost your touch."

"And I see you have." Ever sheathed his sword as the guards gathered up the unfortunate young man to take him away. "You've gotten fat, Rafael. And slow."

"We can't all be you or your father, Everard," Rafael sighed.

"Does this happen often?"

Rafael shrugged and made an impatient gesture with his hands. "The rebel attacks resumed not long after you and your father returned to Destin."

"Why didn't you say anything?"

Rafael shrugged. "They were very few for a while. But they've been steadily increasing in number."

Ever stayed quiet as he swung back onto his horse, and they began their trek back to the palace. Rafael spoke again, and for the first time his voice was tired, void of the jovial sound he'd kept since Ever had first arrived. His large frame sagged, and the wrinkles at his eyes seemed to double.

"Do you see now why I need someone here though? I appreciate your help. I always have. But you cannot be here all the time to rescue me." Rafael pulled at his beard as he stared out ahead. "I need someone here who can do more than I. I might be fair at trade, but we both know I was never that strong."

Ever didn't answer at first. What Rafael said was true. In fact, it was probably the first sincere admittance Ever had heard since arriving. Still, a needy king only made the situation direr, riper for an intrusion, and Ever had yet to find out who exactly had come to the king's aid, claiming to be a holy man with signs, no less. "Have my years of friendship at least equaled a sign in merit to you?"

Rafael turned and gave him a weary smile. "What is it you want, Everard?"

"Let me meet him. At least let me get to see him face to face."

"Very well. Tomorrow, after the games are done. Meet me at the naval dock."

As Rafael said the words, a huge weight was lifted from Ever's shoulders. He finally had an end in sight. The sooner he could see this mystery solved, the better. They could go home, and he could care for Isa the way she deserved.

The two kings rode in silence for a few moments, the only sound the crunching of dead leaves under their horse's hooves.

"Perhaps," Rafael finally said in a soft voice, "you will allow me more grace when you have a child of your own, one whose future depends solely on your strength and wisdom. Then, maybe, you will not judge me so harshly."

BOY INSIDE THE MAN

he rap on the door startled Isa so much that she jumped, not enough to fall over, but enough for the unruly fire she'd been attempting to wield to shoot off into a ceramic vase on one of the bedside tables. The crash felt loud enough to wake the entire palace.

"Your Majesty?" Norbert called through the thick wooden door. "Are you well?" It was a moment though before Isa could gather her dignity enough to answer.

"Well enough. What do you need?"

"Queen Kartek of—"

"Send her in." Isa knew she was being more than rude, but she'd had about all she could take of the southern queen. Isa had been grateful for her rescue on the night of the first ball and the queen's kindness at the tea, but Ever's constant talk of his old acquaintance was grinding on her nerves. Then the pointed looks he and Kartek had sent one another over supper the night before, and finally, his abandonment of Isa for their meeting had been too much. She was on the verge of telling her husband that if he was so impressed with the queen, he should volunteer to be one of her servants.

As she bent down to pick up the larger shards of the vase, Norbert opened the door and the southern queen glided in.

Even without looking at Kartek, jealousy filled every cranny of Isa's being. The woman was everything she was not. The natural ease with which she kept her posture, the confidence in her stride, and the calm intelligence of her dark eyes as she took in everything around her, including the unseemly mess Isa was attempting to pick up, were flawless. It was this kind of perfection that Ever and the rest of the Fortress staff kept pushing her toward. And she was failing at every turn.

"Pardon me," Isa managed to mumble as she shuffled the broken shards on the floor, anything to keep her from having to make pleasant conversation. If this wasn't the most uncomely way to welcome another regent, Isa couldn't imagine what was. To her surprise, however, she felt the queen kneel beside her and silently begin to gather the shards as well. The clinking of the white-blue pieces quickly grew too loud for Isa to bear though. She had to say something.

"My maidservant wanted to visit the market, so I let her go."

"And you chose to pass the time trying to escape."

When Isa looked at the queen, Kartek wore a knowing look, and Isa felt her face redden. She finally sighed, not yet able to enjoy her guest's company, but tired of being contrary. She already had enough annoyance stored up for Ever to last the rest of the trip and longer.

"He sealed the lock so that only Norbert's key or he himself can open the door. I was trying—ouch!" Bright red blood ran down Isa's thumb, thanks to a particularly sharp piece of porcelain. She reached down to her skirt to pinch the throbbing cut, but Kartek was quicker. She grabbed Isa's hand and gently but firmly held her own index finger over the wound. To Isa's amazement, a soft pink glow emanated from between their hands where they touched, and even though Isa knew the cut had been deep, the pain lessened until it was gone. Kartek examined Isa's thumb before releasing her.

"Everard probably told you, but my gift is healing."

"No," Isa said, her voice suddenly tight. "He didn't tell me."

Without word, the queen gently took Isa by the shoulders and led her to sit on the bed. "Your power is being tainted by your frustration."

"You can sense that?"

Kartek smiled wryly.

"I may have a different kind of power, but I can sense yours. And your power is troubled."

Isa shrugged helplessly. "I am at my wit's end. I don't know how to wield this power. I don't know how to be the queen Destin needs. I can't ask Ever for help because he's never around. I mean, he trains with me, and I know he can see it as well as I can, and yet he says nothing. He refuses to talk about it even when I bring it up." Isa stopped, unsure of how much she should share with this woman she barely knew. Although, she reasoned, she'd already allowed her into their chambers, and Ever followed the woman around like a drooling puppy. If something happened, she could blame him. Besides, she really did want to talk to someone about what was happening to her.

"I thought the power was supposed to be mine. I thought that as the queen, it was my right. But it stagnates, and I cannot master it." Isa paused. "Still, I could live with that, if it weren't for my eyes."

"Your eyes?"

She looked her guest directly this time so Kartek could see the proof. "I think I'm dying, Kartek. My eyes haven't burned brightly in months. And if I am dying, I have to wonder if it's my fault, if I'm neglecting some part of my duty that just can't be neglected any longer."

Minutes of silence passed after she spoke. Kartek's face was somber, her golden eyes distant as she stared at the window. Isa stood restlessly and walked the full length of their chambers, wondering why Ever couldn't have locked her somewhere else, like in a garden. The space was decently sized for guest chambers. Not as large as the Fortress's, perhaps, but long enough to fit two rooms, the one they slept in with the bed, bedside tables, a desk, its tall, blocky wardrobe, and a small, round table with two spindly chairs. The other room was where Cerise slept on her pallet. Isa had left that room unexplored, as she knew from childhood that Cerise liked her privacy.

"I wish I could help you," Kartek finally spoke in a husky voice.

"Have you ever had problems with your power?" Isa blurted out.

A small smile formed on the queen's cinnamon lips. "I did. They were different from yours, but . . ." She chuckled a bit. "They had everyone in my palace wondering what kind of joke the Maker was playing on them. I was sixteen when I became queen. My parents were killed in a carriage accident, and I was their only heir." Kartek looked down at the intricate blanket she sat upon and absently fingered the deep red silk that had been embroidered into it. The pattern wove in and out of itself to form desert roses, the kind that filled every corner of the city streets beneath them.

"My healing power had manifested when I was twelve, which is late by my family's standard. Most queens' power shows by the time they are ten."

"How did your family receive the power?"

"Our gift is not as old as that of your Fortress, but it is old enough. My ancestor was a wealthy woman. Jal was her name. She lived in a lovely home beside an oasis in the middle of a wide desert. It was a grand house, one her parents had paid to have built, purchasing the materials from many distant lands. Great columns made up the face of the home, which was all white plaster, and windows upon windows filled every wall. Jal could look out upon the duned desert that surrounded her, and the oasis which lay before her home. Dates grew wild, and her garden prospered, despite the harsh, sandy winds that threatened to tear the produce from the ground. People would come from far and wide to visit her oasis, as water was scarce for miles around. Over time, people began to stay and make their homes near hers, and she became the caretaker of the little village that grew.

"On the seventh year after the village was planted, famine struck, and even the oasis became dry. Jal had to let her servants go, though it pained her to lose them. They were as family to her. She also encouraged people to leave the town to find water elsewhere for their families. Some refused to go, or rather, they could not go. Too old and frail to make the journey to the next oasis, or too young and delicate. In order to keep them fed, Jal began to sell her lavish possessions to passing caravans in order to purchase food and water for the stragglers, but soon even all the possessions of her many-roomed home were gone. All except for her most prized possession.

"Jal's mother had given her a family heirloom, a jewel that had been passed down through the families that lived in the long, white-walled mansion in the desert." At this, Isa realized Kartek was fingering the jewel at her own neck. A deep pink, the jewel was round, nearly the size of a grape, embedded in a disk of gold that had the thickness of Isa's thumb. Kartek nodded.

"She had managed to get all of the families to leave with the exception of one, but the last family could not go. A young widow had just given birth to a daughter, and without her late husband, she was not healed enough to make the journey. Jal was torn. She did not want to leave her family home, but she could not watch the young woman and her child die. So with great sorrow, she told the first merchant who came their way that she would give him her jewel if he would take the three of them as far as the next city. The man agreed, and at the end of the four-day trek, true to her word, Jal handed over the jewel.

"When she did, however, the man smiled and said, 'You have given everything to care for those who had nothing. The Maker has seen fit to test you, to see whether you are ready to lead many, many more than you have yet. And you have passed His test. By this time tomorrow, you will have back all you lost and more.'

"True to the caravan driver's word, she went to sleep in a poor house that night with the young woman and her child, and awoke the next morning back in her palace home by the oasis. But instead of the small, empty village she had once overseen, an entire city was stretched out before her door, and the oasis was once again filled with life. The young widow's husband had been returned to life, and all of Jal's beloved servants were home once more. Even the jewel was returned. It has been passed down through every daughter in the line since."

"How did she find out she could heal?" Isa asked.

"The young widow had experienced great pain during her birth, and it did not go away after they left the oasis. In fact, she grew worse, nearly delirious. Before they went to sleep in the poor house that night, Jal helped the young woman lay down on her pallet. As soon as she touched her, the young woman was healed. And so it has been ever since for the women in my family."

"Is every firstborn child a girl in your line?" Isa couldn't help asking. Kartek nodded.

"Just as the Fortress kings always sire boys first, my line gives birth to girls. It is only the women in our family who have the healing powers, never the men."

"I wish . . ." Isa began, but did not finish the thought, just let the words hang in the air like the last leaves of autumn. What she wished would never be accomplished by wishing.

"Isabelle," Kartek's voice grew stern, "there is something you need to know about your husband."

Isa felt her throat tighten. For some reason, it felt shameful to have another woman telling her things about her own husband that she should have already known.

"I am sure you know what Ever's relationship with his parents was?" Kartek raised a dark eyebrow. Isa nodded, so the queen continued. "Good. Then you should also know that his father's determination to raise him as superior to his royal peers meant he was alone much of the time, even on the few occasions that he was surrounded by other children. His unusual strength only made their differences that much greater. I tell you this so you will know just how desperate he is to protect everything he has been given.

"Your husband, for all his faults, is one of the Maker's most loyal creatures, and he loves you with a potency that even he cannot understand. He is terrified to lose you, and if he does not gain control of his fear, I am afraid he might do something dangerous and irreversible in the wake of his determination. Everard is a good man, but a dangerous one as well. You cannot allow him to think he will solve this quandary alone, because he will do so by any means necessary. He needs you to balance him, to temper him."

But Isa was already shaking her head. "He won't let me in. I've tried! He refuses to even tell me what has him on edge here in Cobren."

"Then that, my queen, is the puzzle you must solve. There is a reason the Fortress did not leave him alone. Unbridled, he will destroy himself in his attempts to right the wrongs of the world. Your duty as queen is to be the partner he needs. You must find a way to save him from himself."

"But my power is failing," Isa protested. "How do I stop him?"

"That is your duty to find out. The Fortress queens have not always been weak as Ever's mother was. They had their own difficult choices to make. You are no different." With that, Kartek stood, her colorful wrapped skirts swishing lightly around her legs in the process. Just as she raised her hand to rap on the door to let the guard know she was finished, Isa had to ask her the question that had been burning inside of her for months.

"I know you spoke with Ever this morning. Does he think that I can do this? Master my power and fulfill my role as queen?"

"That is something you will have to ask him," Kartek said slowly. As she left the room, her footsteps echoing down the stone hall, a chill moved through Isa.

That was exactly what she was afraid of.

A MIDDAY MEAL

*I*sa was still mulling over what Kartek had told her when another knock sounded at the door.

"Midday meal for the queen!" a lilting voice sang out. Despite the many, varied accents Isa had heard at the palace during the last few days, Isa knew this one immediately. Sure enough, Norbert opened the door to let in Brokk, who was carrying a covered silver platter.

"Your husband notified the kitchen that the queen was in need of some food."

"Thank you, Brokk. That is very kind of you." Isa wasn't particularly hungry, nor was she really in the mood to entertain more company, but the servant's presence lit up the place like a chandelier. As he placed the platter on the table, he glanced about the room.

"Are you not getting a bit bored in here?"

Isa let out a burst of laughter. "Yes, but ..." She paused, not knowing how much to say about Ever's orders. As much as she resented them, it felt risky to make the world privy to their personal disagreements. Brokk seemed to understand, and to her surprise, looked remorseful.

"I fear I am not a very good servant. I tend to put myself up on a pedestal where I do not belong, with the palace guests as equals. But may I let you in on a little secret?"

Amused, Isa nodded. While Brokk certainly didn't act the part of a typical servant, she rather preferred his little quirks. It was nice to have a friend somewhere in this new, unfriendly world.

"I have only been serving here for a little while," Brokk said with an unreadable expression. "And I don't plan on continuing for very long, either."

"You sound as though you're on a quest." Isa smiled. A sad half grin crept up on one side of the older man's mouth, and suddenly, his typical joviality was all gone.

"I guess I am."

"What for?" Isa leaned forward, all thoughts of the meal nearly gone.

Brokk hesitated, throwing a slightly nervous glance at the door.

"Please," Isa pressed, suddenly in great need of a distraction from the tumult of her thoughts. "If they say anything, I will explain that you were assisting me."

His eyes crinkled kindly at the corners and he nodded. "Very well. But please sit and eat at least."

Sighing, Isa did as he asked. As soon as she was comfortable, and her steaming platter of chicken, seasoned corn, and rice was served, Brokk settled himself across from her as she ate.

"I was even a bit younger than you when my path to this end was set, and I met the girl of my dreams. Her name was Agatha." His voice was low, and the expression on his face affectionate, as though he saw her even now before him. "I was much younger back then, but I sometimes still awaken in the night, and it feels as though she could still be beside me." He stood mostly straight, but bent just enough to lightly twist the hem of his green uniform, and the troubled creases that filled his face made him look suddenly much older.

"Agatha was from another province. But she was so lovely, with skin nearly the color of milk, and eyes almost as dark as the night." He paused before adding, "It wasn't long before I'd begged her to marry me."

"What happened?"

"It's rather uncomplicated. A sickness swept the land. Thousands died." He sighed. "She succumbed after weeks of fighting, much longer than most other victims had to suffer. But she was determined …" He suddenly had to clear his throat.

"I'm sorry," Isa breathed. She looked down at her picked-at plate, wishing she could help. It felt so wrong to see Brokk's sunny face so full of sorrow. Before she had time to say anything else, however, the door swung open, and Ever strode in, carrying a full plate of food.

"I brought you lunch—" Ever stopped, unhappy surprise registering on his face when he saw Brokk.

In that moment, Isa realized that someone had lied. Ever hadn't sent Brokk with her meal. Someone else must have sent him. But who would lie about her lunch?

"Thank you, Brokk." Isa hurried to put the cover back on the platter, and shoved it all back into Brokk's hands. The servant took the hint, and after bowing to both of them, quickly excused himself from the room. As much as Isa wanted to know about Brokk's quest, she knew the look in Ever's eye only too well. Ever didn't say a word, just watched every move the servant made.

As Brokk left, Isa closed her eyes and inhaled deeply in order to calm herself. This was not a good way to start the conversation they needed to have.

After he was gone, Ever thrust the plate he held onto the little round table.

"You could have been a little nicer to him," Isa huffed. "He was only trying to help."

"The second competition will start soon," he muttered, ignoring her objection. "Where's Cerise? You need to be ready."

"I let her have a day in the town," Isa said. She went over to the wardrobe and began to go through her clothes for lack of something better to do as she tried to find the words she needed to say.

She had been so angry that morning when he'd locked her in her room. She'd contemplated every possible way to communicate her fury, everything from shouting to ignoring him completely. But when Kartek had come and shared his story, a bit of compassion had seeped into her. *Forgive him*, a voice in her head whispered. *He's just trying to protect you.* Unfortunately for that voice, however, every brusque word he uttered, and every abrupt move he made, made forgiveness just that much more difficult. Nevertheless, Isa took a breath and searched for words.

"Thank you for bringing me something to eat."

"What? Oh, you're welcome." He was still glaring at the door as she pulled on a more practical dress for the outdoors. When he ran his hand down his jaw as he spoke, Isa knew immediately that it had been the wrong thing to say. He turned to glare at her. "Isa, what were you thinking?"

"What do you mean?"

"Inviting someone in when I specifically wanted you to stay here alone? What good is it being hidden if you invite the world in?"

"He was told that I needed a midday meal!" Isa felt the anger stir within her once more. "How was I supposed to know you were going to bring me something? I assumed you were the one to send him!"

"I certainly did not send him! Why would I send strange men into our room after you were attacked?" Ever stopped, his eyebrows going up. "Who sent him?" he asked in a deadly tone.

"He didn't say! And I'm not a child, Everard! You can't dictate my every word and move!" Isa's resolution to forgive him dissolved as she held his furious glare, which grew only more intense when she used his full name.

"I will do whatever I have to—" he stopped, and cocked his head. It only annoyed Isa more when she realized he was hearing something she couldn't, something she *would* have heard had her powers been working properly. "We need to go," he said finally. "It's almost time."

Isa fumed as she struggled to pull on her dress. Despite it being less complicated than most of the gowns Gigi had sent her, she still needed Cerise to close the back. But Cerise wasn't there.

"Then I need you to help me with this," she spat out. With a huff, Ever stomped over to help her, but she could feel the tension rolling off of him as he did. "We will finish this conversation later," she added icily, spinning around to glower up at him when he was done. Ever said nothing, just turned and walked to the door. Isa followed, swearing to herself that he wouldn't get off that easily. They *would* talk about this.

Ever paused at the door and fixed a withering look at Norbert. "I will have a word with you later."

Isa tried to throw the guard a look of pity as she scurried after her husband. It wasn't Norbert's fault she'd let the servant in.

As they walked down the halls, she realized she was still quite curious as to what he had been up to all day. His visit with Kartek had obviously not lasted the whole time that he was gone. Isa found herself nearly skipping to keep up with Ever as he stormed towards the outdoor arena. She would have to be quick, before other ears were near enough to hear them.

"What did you find out?" She pitched her voice as low as she could. If she caught him off-guard, maybe he might let her in and tell her the big secret he was consumed by?

He waited so long to respond that it didn't seem as though he would answer at first, but just as she was adding this to her list of grievances, he said, "I got Rafael to agree to introduce me to the holy man tomorrow after the final contest." And for the first time that afternoon, Ever turned to look at her with something not akin to anger or frustration. Instead, he seemed to be measuring her response. "And I wouldn't be shocked if your brother ends up next in line for the Cobrien throne."

SILVER

*L*aunce tried to relax his taut muscles as he waited, imagining each one a piece of leather that was strong and supple. Though the humongous beast he sat astride seemed to obey well enough, every horse could feel fear, and that was the last thing he wanted as they prepared to climb the hill, which somehow looked twice as tall today as it had the first day.

The decision to ride under his second name had been, if he was honest, made on a whim. It wasn't as though he was doing anything wrong, he'd told himself as he'd written his second name on the herald's parchment. If through some fluke, he won, everyone would all know who it was in the end. But just this once, just for a few days, Launce would be riding as his own man. Not the Destinian queen's pathetic little brother, and not The Commoner. The moment Launce had seen the beautiful red of the copper suit shining up at him in the moonlight, he had known it was meant for him and him alone. For just a short time, he would be the mysterious copper-clad knight.

Blanchette might regret her choice if she could see him now.

Not to say that keeping the secret had been easy. In order to ensure himself the most privacy, he'd slipped the herald a few coins so that his name would be last for each contest. As soon as each event had finished, he had raced into the edge of the forest, where he'd first hidden his new steed and suit of armor, and waited for his next turn. No one had thought to follow him, and it had given him time to marvel over the beauty of the gifts he'd been given.

The armor was surprisingly light, and to his relief, Launce was actually able to put it on himself. He would have needed help from a servant with the armor Everard had given him. The strange horse *had* made him a bit nervous. Launce was certainly good with horses but, he reminded himself, this was the beast who had very possibly brutally trampled seven guards to death.

After sending up a prayer to the Maker, Launce watched from the edge of the wood until it was his turn. His new beast had stamped around, impatient to let go and run, but Launce delayed each time until the very last minute. For the third event, he waited even longer, until the herald was looking confused. One touch to the animal's sides sent him shooting out of the forest, straight for the hill.

Launce still couldn't believe he had actually made it even partially up the hill. During his preparations, he had noticed that the horse's shoes were not metal, but glass, just like the lacy underpart of the saddle that he rode upon. *Have I lost my senses?* he'd asked himself as he barreled towards the great blue hill that stretched up as high as the Fortress's watchtower at home. And yet, somehow, the glass shoes had held, and as he climbed, he realized that the princess was sitting on top of the hill, looking as confounded as he was, and in her hands she held a single golden apple.

As soon as he saw the apple, his nerves had taken him, and the animal slowed its ascent. Launce had cursed himself as the animal began to turn on its own accord, but just before he shot back down, the princess had managed to toss him the apple. In his fright, he'd nearly dropped it. Somehow, however, it stayed in his hands, and he raced out of the arena just as quickly as he'd come. Back to the forest they went, and by the time the rest of the riders had returned to the stable, he was back as well, brushing Everard's horse and wearing an expression that was as cowardly as he could muster.

Only Randolph, the short, muscled knight who had intervened on his behalf two days before, had given him an inquisitive look. Launce hoped the foreign knight wouldn't dwell on his questions, whatever they were.

While Launce had told himself that he was just being careful because of the strange power he was dealing with, the more honest part of him had to admit that part of his secrecy was purely due to vanity, and relishing the looks that would be on his competitors' faces when he brought down the rest of the golden apples.

Well, he had to get the rest of the golden apples first. After the events of last night, however, he was almost sure he would win.

After the first contest, as everyone in the stables had prepared for bed, Launce had noticed another film of glassy dust all over the stables. The dust looked different this time though. It was most decidedly silver in tint. This had piqued his interest enough to lead him to spend another night on the roof, and as a reward, he had received another horse, gray this time, and a new set of armor. Only this armor was silver, and the second horse was somehow even larger and fiercer than the first. Other than that, everything had happened just as it had with the first horse. Including the glass on the horse's hooves and the edging of the silver saddle.

Launce's musings were interrupted by the herald as he announced Launce's singular second name. He kicked the horse, for no gentle nudging would budge the beast, and they shot forward, like an arrow loosed from a bow. As they sped towards the stands, into the arena, Launce felt his heart drop into his stomach. He had been right. The hill was twice as tall as it had been the night before.

In his surprise, he jumped, and the horse immediately began to slow. Panic filled him as he tried to fix his mistake, kicking the horse once more and attempting to turn his heading back to the center of the hill. His quick actions seemed to work, for the horse's glass shod hooves hit the steep incline with a jarring crack, one that left a great web of white lines shooting up the glass. He didn't have time to see how bad the glass had been broken, for they were already farther up the hill. Launce's body felt strange as they raced upwards, like he was leaving his insides behind while his skin and bones continued to lift off the ground at an alarming speed.

The speed still wasn't great enough, for as they neared the top, coming even closer to the princess than he had the day before, the silver beast began to slow. They weren't going to make it. Again.

Anger and shame filled his breast as the horse began to turn, despite his urgings, but before he could berate himself for his mistake too much, an apple landed in his lap. If the suit of armor would have allowed such movement, he would have turned to look back at the princess, whose ability to toss apples at moving targets was unmatched in any woman he knew. And yet, it didn't matter, he smiled to himself beneath the helmet.

The second apple was his.

2 1

GAMES WE PLAY

"*S*ince our secret rider is too shy to sup with us tonight," Rafael's voice boomed down the length of the ridiculously long dining hall, "I will simply have to give someone else the honor of dining with my daughter. You." He waved at an older gentleman two table lengths down from the head of the table, where Launce sat with Everard and Isa, near the king. "How far up the hill did you get?"

The poor man balked as all eyes turned on him. "My horse refused to attempt it, Sire."

The king harrumphed and pointed at another competitor. This one was younger than the first, but still looked to be a good fifteen years older than the princess, at least. It was a man Launce already knew far too well for his taste.

"Absalom, how far did you get?"

"Two paces, Your Highness."

"Fine, fine then. Come. You shall sit with my daughter tonight."

Launce wanted to make a face. Now he would be forced to watch the horrid man sit across from him for the entire length of the meal, which was only just being served. Of course, he had little to complain about, when compared with the truly unfortunate victim.

At least he wasn't the one Absalom would be attempting to woo.

Launce snuck a quick glance at the princess, curious as to what she would think of the king's choice for her. Thus far, she'd seemed perfectly obedient, compliant down to the letter of her father's seemingly haphazard laws. But as she waited to be greeted by her dinner partner, she seemed to have paled. He couldn't tell for sure, for her head was suddenly tilted down as she studied her plate with the ferocity of a scholar. Perhaps even her obedience had its limits. Launce almost smiled as he watched her stab her dinner violently.

It wasn't polite to stare, he tried repeatedly to remind himself. And yet, he couldn't keep himself from it. It wasn't as though he could distract himself by listening to Isa and Everard talk. Despite Launce's dislike for his brother-in-law, even he had to admit that their disagreement, whatever it concerned, was making life most uncomfortable for everyone around them. Normally, Launce enjoyed baiting Isa to agree with him, trying to get her to acknowledge her husband's faults. But something was different this time. The silence between them was tangible, so thick it was nearly suffocating. Everard had stomped about all evening like a storm cloud trying its best to make thunder, and Isa … Isa was far too quiet. The look on her face was almost empty, and too close to the surrender he had watched her sink into after her first fiancé had left her on their wedding night.

Memories of that depression, the deep hole she'd fallen into for months, kindled a fire in Launce. It was a dangerous fire, for when lit it didn't take into account how strong Everard was, nor how he was the greatest soldier known to the northern kingdoms. It simply knew that somehow, Everard had caused his sister pain, and if Launce wasn't careful, he would act very fool-ishly upon that anger. No, it was far less dangerous to watch the foreign knight torment the princess. At least that situation he could have a bit of fun with.

The princess was stabbing at the final pieces of roasted fowl on her plate as Absalom talked incessantly. He was actually daring to whisper in her ear. Launce gawked, first at the odd couple, then at the king, then back at the odd couple. The princess was clearly uncomfortable, cringing when certain words were too loud, and particularly when he made the s sound. But the king was too busy to notice his daughter's discomfort, too busy boasting about the holy man's great plan to Everard, who wasn't even pretending to listen. Launce suddenly had a wicked idea. He hoped the princess would catch on.

"You know, Sir Absalom …" Launce spoke loudly. The princess and the knight both looked at him, her expression grateful, and his vexed. "The way to a girl's hand is through her mother's heart."

"Really? And pray tell, young man, how did you come upon such enlight-ening wisdom?" Absalom's voice was practiced and smooth, but it had an edge to it.

Launce widened his eyes innocently. "My brother-in-law." He gestured to Everard two seats over. "He always brings my mother a new baking spice when he travels to other lands. Perhaps, if this mystery rider chooses not to reveal himself, you might have a chance at wooing her mother." As he spoke, Launce kept an eye on the princess, and to his relief, she was already struggling to smother a smile. The knight, however, was staring at him. Launce could see him weighing his options, and in the end, it seemed that suspicion would win, until Absalom turned and looked at the princess.

Launce nearly pitied the man. It would be difficult for any male staring into those warm, chocolate eyes to deny her sincerity. And with a start, Launce wondered if the princess might not be a more practiced opponent than her father in a battle of schemes and wits.

"It's true," she told the knight with large eyes. "However," she turned to glance at her parents, "my father is the one who would most need to be impressed." She gave an adorable giggle before leaning in to say in a voice Launce could barely make out, "If you truly want to impress my father ..." She continued speaking, but Launce could no longer hear her. As soon as she was done, Absalom pulled back in surprise, his thick eyebrows knitting together as he looked back and forth from princess to the king.

Launce was dying to know what she had told him. As he couldn't ask from across the table, he had to content himself with watching the knight stare vacantly at his food for the remainder of the meal, occasionally glancing up at the princess now and then. Whenever he did, she would catch his eye and send him the sweetest smile Launce had ever seen. If it hadn't been for the amused, fiery looks she would flick his way every now and then, he might actually have been convinced that she was taken with the imbecile.

Supper was finally finished, which to Launce's great relief meant he was closer to escaping the silent battle being waged beside him. But first, they had to live through the same introductory dances he'd watched the first night they'd arrived at the palace. The king and the princess, followed by Rafael with Queen Monica, and Isa and Everard. Rafael and Monica were perfectly decent dancers, but Isa and Ever put them to shame. They moved as one, as though the music itself came from them instead of the musicians.

But they were too perfect. Isa's smile was overly brilliant, her eyes too bright, and Ever's powerful frame moved like a great animal's, savage and agile. The cheers at the end of the dance were wild and real. They had been flawless, but to Launce's surprise, an unexpected sadness filled him. As little as he approved of his sister's husband, it hurt Launce to see her like this. At their wedding, he had seen the blue fire that flitted upwards from their feet and swirled about them as they moved. It was wrong that the others, particularly the catty women present, couldn't see what his sister was truly capable of. What she had become. But then, not even she could see that.

Much to Launce's relief, other couples began to fill the dance floor, which meant he was free to move about the throne room. His first inclination was to hide behind the hors d'oeuvres tables again, but a flash of red caught his eye. The princess was spinning, to his dismay, in the arms of Sir Absalom.

"What are you waiting for?" Everard's harsh whisper made Launce jump. He turned to look at his brother-in-law with disdain. Did the man ever stop watching him? It wasn't as if he was without his own problems to solve. Everard inclined his head towards the princess. "You won't get anywhere with the girl by gawking at her."

Launce scowled at him outright. "I have enough problems with royals as it is. I don't need another one complicating my life."

"Cowards never—" But before Everard could finish his thought, Launce stormed off to stand somewhere else. Of course, that didn't mean he was done watching the princess. But he was merely interested in protecting her from the likes of the horrid knight, he assured himself. She seemed as miserable as he was at this event. Surely it was only natural to feel a certain camaraderie in such a situation.

When Absalom claimed his third dance, Launce's resolve to stay hidden dissolved. The princess's panicked look was more than he could stand, and the knight continued to move closer and closer with each turn. Launce just hoped his action wouldn't be interpreted as pursuance. As he walked out amidst the twirling couples, he knew his saving grace would be his status. She couldn't expect a commoner to aspire to kingship.

"May I cut in?" Launce tapped Absalom's fine silk-covered shoulder, interrupting the couple mid-twirl. Absalom glared at him, but stepped aside as etiquette required, and for once, Launce was thankful for the stiff formalities Everard had hammered into him during their preparations at the Fortress.

Launce took the princess's arms, but once they began dancing on their own, was shocked to find her frowning at him.

"Did I do something wrong?" He glanced back at the knight's retreating coat.

"I nearly had him," Princess Olivia sniffed.

"I'm confused. If you want me to go—"

"No, you ninny. I just meant that he's getting desperate to impress my father. I almost had him ready to try. Besides," she arched one of her perfect eyebrows, "what took you so long?"

"I was under the impression you were enjoying the sweet little nothings he was whispering so tenderly in your ear. Ow!" Launce's foot throbbed as the princess continued to move lithely through the crowd of dancers with an ease that made Launce wonder how often she had practiced stepping on her partners' feet.

"That's for taking so long." She smirked. Launce limped to keep up as she twirled away again.

"You certainly play both sides," he said, wondering how he had mistaken her for a pitiful, helpless damsel just the day before. Everything about her was spirited and lively. The ruffled dress she wore snapped back and forth as though it were stepping forth for a challenge with each sharp move she made. Her dark, shiny hair had just enough curl to fly upwards even when she was still. The flush of her cheeks and the red of her lips contrasted beautifully with her olive skin.

Actually, Launce realized, she was quite beautiful. He had to focus on keeping his eyes on her face while they danced, for her figure was graceful in its generous curves as she moved, and her dress had been cut to pronounce those curves quite expertly. As this revelation dawned on him, he also realized she still hadn't answered. A dark shadow had come over her face instead.

"What's wrong?" he asked, his voice soft enough to keep most busybodies unaware of their conversation.

"I wasn't always like this," she whispered, then let out a shaky chuckle. "Well, I mean, I've always enjoyed pranks, but ..." She took another deep breath. "It's my father. He's changed over the last few years. Ever since the holy man came—" With a start, she stopped dancing, clapping her hand over her mouth. Launce glanced around furtively, as he took her hand from her face and continued dancing. Hopefully no one had seen her slip. Well, Everard had, he noted, as his brother-in-law continued to watch them with eagle eyes. But when was Everard not watching?

"That's what my sister's husband tells me," he whispered in her ear. A small, smug part of him rejoiced when she didn't cringe at his words the way she had for Sir Absalom's. Instead, she stared up at him, dark eyes wide on her smooth face as she spoke.

"He never ordered me around so before. He was considerate, and always asked me what I thought. But now ..." She shook her head and lifted her chin a bit, defiance gleaming in her eyes. "He's obstinate, pompous, and doesn't listen to anyone but the holy man."

Launce opened his mouth to ask, but was interrupted by Rafael's shout.

"Sir Absalom, put your trousers back on this instant!"

Launce turned to see Absalom standing at the top of the main staircase. The foreign knight swayed a bit, but that wasn't what caused the gasps from the ladies or the shrieks of laughter from some of the children present.

"Your Highness!" Absalom shouted in a warbling voice. "I am bold! I am brave! And I am not afraid to stake my claim to your daughter! With or without trousers!" He hiccupped the last word.

"You *will* pull up your trousers, and you will *not* make any such claim! Now get back to the stables before I return you myself!" The laughs and titters that ensued from the crowd created a slight roar as two guards appeared at the knight's sides to guide him.

"Father is going to be upset the rest of the evening now."

Launce turned incredulously to look at the princess as she stifled more giggles and stared at the king.

"That was what you told him? To take off his pants?"

"I merely told him my father appreciates men who are brazenly bold. I just didn't expect so much wine to be involved." She chuckled. After a moment, she added more seriously, "I suppose your sister had an easier time finding her husband without interference from a father who was slowly losing his mind, as mine seems to be."

Launce laughed without humor, and it tasted bitter. "You really haven't heard how they met?"

"Rumors float." The princess shrugged. "I choose not to believe them until I find a source of truth though." She didn't ask the question aloud, but Launce knew what she wanted to know.

"Not here," he said. "Too many ears."

"Well then," the princess said. "I expect an answer when we're a bit more secluded. And," she sighed, "apparently that will have to be tomorrow or later. My father is calling for me."

Launce stepped back and bowed. "Until next time, Princess."

"One more thing. Call me Olivia." Then, with a nod and a twist, she was gone, and Launce allowed himself one small smile, although he couldn't tell whether it was more because he'd spent most of the evening dancing with the princess, or because she wanted to see him again.

Seeing no reason to torture himself any longer than necessary, he excused himself from the festivities and returned to the stables, hoping to get a little bit of sleep before curfew was called. With the final race the next morning, Launce had the feeling he would be up on the roof for one more night.

As he laid down and tried to ignore the straw that poked him through the rough mattress, he smiled to himself. It had been more than slightly brazen for him to imply that there *would* be another chance to discuss Isa's marriage. But the princess had not objected. *Cowardly* was a word Everard could never use to describe him again.

22

DOUBTS

*I*sa took Ever's arm when he offered it, but he could feel her stiffness beneath the lace that draped so delicately around her wrist. When he dared to peek at her face, her expression was tense, almost fearful, and the sinking feeling that had lived at the pit of his gut all night grew even stronger. Whatever she wanted to talk about must be a difficult topic for her to broach for her to appear so nervous.

And if it was difficult for her, it would be next to impossible for him.

Unfortunately for Ever, Rafael was still babbling on about his plans for the kingdom, how the holy man would make all the difference in putting a final stop to the rebels. Ever was trying to nod and comment in all the right places, but his growing dislike for his father's old friend was becoming nearly too great for him to stand. Still, he'd reminded himself all evening, it would get him nowhere to treat the ungrateful king as he truly deserved. It would be better to play along and see which webs Rafael had ensnared himself in. As a result, the entire banquet had been spent watching Launce unknowingly flirt with the princess, trying to guess at Isa's source of unhappiness, and putting up with Rafael.

All he wanted to do was go to bed.

Before he could finish fantasizing about sleep, however, the sound of a staff knocking on the floor brought him to his senses, and he realized Rafael had risen from his throne, and was standing behind the herald.

"His Royal Highness, King Rafael, wishes to make an announcement!" When the ballroom was finally quiet, the herald turned and bowed to the king before slipping off the dais so the king could step forward.

"My friends," Rafael said, a patient, rather irksome smile upon his face. "I have told you little by little of how the holy one, our builder of the glass hill, has plans for this kingdom. Now I can tell you that he not only has plans for Cobren, but for the good of *all* the northern kingdoms!"

Ever tensed. What did he mean all of the kingdoms? But the king continued.

"I know these new signs from the Maker can seem a bit overwhelming after being silent for so long, so as a symbol of promise to promote peace between all lands, the holy man has asked me to give you these gifts as a token of his good will towards you all."

As he spoke, he gave a little wave with his right hand, and simultaneously, a servant came to stand before each visitor or party of visitors, and removed the covers from the silver platters. When the servant standing before Ever and Isa lifted the cover from the platter he held, Ever felt his heart stop as Isa gasped in delight.

One delicate glass flower, the Isabelle rose, and a miniature glass fortress, exactly like the one he called home, rested on the tray, neither piece longer than the span of his hand. The rose was a light shade of pink, and the glass fortress was blue. They weren't cloudy, the way most glass objects in the markets were, but sparkled as clear as water and as detailed as their originals themselves. Ever looked up from the tray and searched the room until he found Kartek, and her look of horror mirrored the one he knew he must be wearing now.

"Each of these gifts has been made specifically for you," Rafael continued after the crowd's elated murmurs died down, "so that you will know the Maker knows exactly who you are and what you need. Through these, and the future actions of the holy man, you are to know that He is watching over you, always."

The servant held the tray up closer, and panic filled Ever as Isa reached for the rose. Before she could touch it, he snatched both the rose and the miniature fortress and ground them to pieces in his hand. As the pink and blue dust fell to the floor, Isa's face went from glowing to crushed, and he suddenly hoped desperately that she wouldn't make a scene. Remorse filled him as she stared at the ground where her rose pieces lay. When he'd touched the glass, he hadn't felt any power emanating from it as he'd feared he would. But he'd been so filled with fear in that instant, that the overriding need to protect her had pushed away all other thoughts.

Thoughts such as: was the glass truly unsafe, or was it simply something pretty?

"We need to talk." Isa's whisper was low and dangerous, and though she didn't raise her head to look at him, he knew the pained expression was long gone from her face. Without waiting for him to respond, Isa began to walk away from the king's dais, where they had been standing, and towards the hall that led to their chambers. Without a word, Ever followed her. Since they'd been married, she had never spoken to him that way before. Her silver cloak billowed out behind her as she walked. She held her chin up heroically, but he didn't miss the tremble of her jaw.

Before Isa, Ever had never struggled with being direct. His father, King Rodrigue, had been insistent about speaking the truth as plainly and candidly as possible. It disallowed confusion, he always said, making communication efficient and useful. Ever had learned to speak the same way with his generals and soldiers, and they with him. But since Isa had come into his life, Ever had struggled with words in a way he never had before. It wasn't that he wanted to hide the truth from her. He simply didn't know how to share it in a way that didn't sound callous or brash. She wasn't one of his military officers, nor was she a servant to be ordered about. She was good and kind and ethereal in a way he'd never known anyone to be before. Speaking boldly and directly with her felt as though it might break her, as though *she* were made of glass. It was the reason he had not been able to speak of her struggle with her power yet. It was why he couldn't bring himself to tell her how great a threat the enchanter was to them all.

Isa approached their door and stood silently as Norbert opened it for them, and the surprise in the old guard's eyes told Ever that the difference in Isa's countenance was not imagined on his part. As soon as the door was shut behind them, Isa turned to face him. Her eyes reflected the light of the single lit candle in the room, making them look like those of a large cat.

"Why would you do that?" Her voice was still pitched low and menacing, but the slightest quiver gave her away.

"It was dangerous."

"Was it really?"

Ever stared at her, carefully weighing his next words. He wasn't sure where she was going, but he knew he was in perilous waters. Even in the dark, her midnight eyes flashed, and her breathing was deep and unsteady. She stared back at him, the expression on her face pained and ancient.

"If you want another rose, I'll get it for—"

"It is not about the rose, Ever!" Isa's shout exploded from her like thunder from unseen lightning.

"Then what is it about?" Now he was shouting too.

"You never ask!" she cried. "You just carry on as though you have no queen, and I have no ability to make choices! You assume I am weak! Locking me in my room?"

"I am trying to protect you!"

"I am not a child!" Isa snatched the jeweled tiara off of her head and thrust it out at him. "In case you forgot, there is a reason I have this."

"If you were able to fulfill the duties that came with that crown, I wouldn't have to treat you this way."

"Perhaps, if you ever spent a moment away from the kingdom to actually see me, we would know why I'm failing. Sometimes ..." Isa shook her head and held her hands up helplessly, "I feel like marrying me was simply the easiest way for you to get everything back."

"What other choice did I have?"

As soon as the words left his mouth, Ever knew they were wrong. The silence that filled the room was stifling, and he wished with everything in him that he could take them back. But as he watched her drink them in, watched her face strain not to show the tears, he knew it was too late.

"None, Ever. You had no choice whatsoever."

The air was suddenly too thick, and Ever turned before he choked on an apology that would only make things worse, stomping out the door before Norbert could keep it from slamming. He could hear the echoes of the merriment down the hall, but in no mood for a party of any sort, Ever escaped through one of the servants' exits.

∿

The night was cool in a cutting way, hinting at a difficult winter to come. Ever drew his cloak more tightly around himself, unwilling to even consider returning to his chambers for his warmer coverings. That would mean seeing Isa's tear-streaked cheeks, and facing the depths to which he had cut her. What had possessed him to use such cruel words? He hadn't meant to say them. They had simply tumbled from his tongue, as though some menacing imp had discovered all his meanness and awful secret thoughts that he worked so hard to rid himself of, and dumped them out of his mind and into his mouth.

Of course he'd wanted it all back. Namely, he had wanted *her* back. *She* had become his world. She and the Fortress were all he had ever wanted. Marrying her hadn't been an option, but a necessity. It was like being asked if one wanted air to breathe.

Why the blazes hadn't he said that instead?

Ever paused as he reached the path split. The red pebbled path he was on now continued down to the stables. The thin dirt path on the right, however, led down to the beach. Though he was tempted to check in on Launce, as he was sure the young man had left the festivities early as well, the roar of the ocean called to him, offering to wash away the stain of his wrongs.

"What am I supposed to do?" he groaned. The Fortress didn't answer, but he felt the stirrings within his heart that told him he knew the answer. "I'm just trying to protect her," he argued back. "And the kingdom. I don't know how else to do this." When no audible answer came, he began his trudge down to the beach.

The Maker had seen it fit to bequeath the Fortress's powers on Isa in the beginning. Ever had seen the bright blue flames burning in her eyes as he'd vowed to love and cherish her on their wedding day. How marvelous those eyes had been as they'd sparkled with hope and joy. And they had continued to flame with vigor until about a month after the wedding. Twenty-seven days, to be exact.

Spring had ended early that year, and the hot season had jumped right in to take its place. The day was particularly sticky when he'd first noticed the difference in Isa.

As usual, Ever had awakened before the sun. Nothing had seemed amiss then as he'd leaned over and kissed his wife good morning. She had given him the same sleepy smile that she always did, not quite able to open her eyes, but doing her best anyways. The smile she'd shared with him upon waking, however, was the last true smile he would see that day.

When she had joined him to break fast later that morning, her steps were uncommonly slow, and she kept her eyes distant, focused only on the ground or the walls or the food which she pushed around on her plate. No amount of small talk could bring her from her reverie, and though Ever wasn't one for idle chatter, Isa's lack of words blared like trumpets at the table. The servants glanced at her nervously throughout the meal, and even the stuffy nobles who were visiting them at the time gave her wary looks.

Ever had wanted to ask then and there what the matter was, but they had two diplomatic meetings to attend, and a training session with some of his newer soldiers. It would be hours before they were free to talk alone. By the time the first meeting was over with, Ever had suggested that Isa looked tired, and maybe she should rest rather than attend the next session. Isa had glumly nodded and left without a word. As soon as she was gone, he'd summoned Garin.

"Do you know what's wrong with her?" he'd asked the steward.

Garin had nodded slowly, but to Ever's surprise and annoyance, had said in a soft voice, "This is a matter that would better be discussed between a husband and wife alone."

Ever had stared at him, incredulous. He knew Garin well enough, however, not to ask where he had gotten such delicate information. He had a feeling though that Gigi had much to do with that.

It wasn't until later that afternoon that he was miraculously free to check in on Isa, who he found still in their bedroom, staring at the ceiling from their massive four poster bed.

"Find anything new up there?"

Isa didn't laugh at the joke or even crack a smile. She just continued to lay there.

"Are you unwell?" He gently laid his hand on her forehead. She shook it off, and sat up with a frown, but a slight grimace gave her away as she moved. "If you're feeling sickly," he said, "I can—"

"There is nothing unusual about the way I feel," she had snapped. "I feel exactly the way I do this time every month."

Ever suddenly felt confused, watching her cautiously as she stood up and threw the pillow she'd been hugging back down on the bed with an excessive amount of force. He stayed still as she paced the room silently for a few minutes before placing her head on her hands and leaning against one of the pearl bedposts. Ever had felt as though he should go to her, but the strange temper she was in kept him seated. He had no idea as to what he was supposed to do.

Finally, she sighed. "I'm sorry, Ever. I shouldn't be angry with you. This isn't your fault. I just ... I thought things would be different. I was assured they would be." When she had finally looked at him, the confusion and pain in her eyes was piteous, and she suddenly looked very vulnerable. Slowly, he'd stood and walked over to her. He didn't embrace her, still unsure of what she wanted him to do, but he could at least better study her, so he stood beside the bedpost opposite of hers. For the thousandth time that day, he wished his father had spent less time training him in the art of war and a little more time teaching him about women. Not that his father knew much about them either.

When the silence finally became too much to bear, he began, "I'm sorry, Isa, but I still don't understand."

"I'm not pregnant, Ever."

Ever had blinked. Where had that come from? "Were … you supposed to be?"

"Master Claude said I would be by now."

"What in the heavens does Master Claude know of women or pregnancy?" Ever had never liked that man.

"He says every Fortress queen has conceived within a month of her coronation."

Ever had started to protest, but stopped. In truth, he had no knowledge on the subject. Women of the court would titter about such a subject, but never within direct earshot of the men. He had only ever picked up snippets of conversation now and then. He wanted to contradict Isa's snide tutor, but then he remembered the sadness in Garin's face that morning, and he knew immediately that Claude must have been right.

Understanding and fear had washed through him as he stood there looking at his wife. Was something truly wrong? Why would Isa be any different from the others? Apparently, even his mother had followed suit, and she'd never had the Fortress fire to begin with.

With no words to comfort either himself or Isa, he'd simply taken her and drawn her close, holding her to his chest as tightly as he could without hurting her. She had wept into him then, and he had to fight the desire to run down to the practice room and break something. Actually, he had realized, distraction wasn't a poor idea.

"I'll talk to Garin later and see what he knows about the old queens." He'd lifted her chin and forced her midnight eyes to meet his. "But for now, how would you like to go down to the practice room with me? You were getting rather good at the sword form I taught you yesterday." Isa thought about that for a moment before nodding, much to his relief. As he began to walk to the door, she caught his hand and drew him back to her, and without a word, took his face in her hands and pulled him down into a warm, soft kiss. His heart had thundered as she kissed him, and his breath was as fast as if he'd just sprinted across a battlefield. In that moment, he'd known they were exactly where they were supposed to be. Together.

A while later, as they began to practice, however, he'd noticed that while her form was neat, the power she usually wove into her thrusts and parries was rather weak. The blue flame that had always moved down her sword and whirled about her as she twisted in and out was lazy and thin. And since that day, it had only grown worse. Along with her diminishing power, the fire in Isa's eyes had begun to dim as well.

Ever had relived that day over and over again in his mind, raking over every detail, trying desperately to find some significance that might unlock the mystery of her failing power. Garin was solemn whenever they discussed it, but he always cautioned Ever to be patient, trusting the Fortress to know what it was doing with its daughter. Ever trusted Garin, and he knew more than anything that he should trust the Fortress, but time was running out. He couldn't bear to see her fire extinguished the way his father's had been.

In order to distract them both, to keep them from mulling over the problem day after day, Ever had thrown them both into their duties with more vigor than ever. Hardly a second was free for either one of them, always spent in study, work, or exercise. This would keep her from worrying, he'd convinced himself. But if he was honest, he had to wonder sometimes if the distractions were more for her or for him.

Now, in the cold of night, as he threw rocks into the waves, Ever wished that Garin were there. Garin would know what to do. Garin always knew what to do, even when there was nothing to be done. But he took a deep breath; as Garin was not there, Ever would have to make do with what he had. And at the moment, since he couldn't imagine what Garin would suggest, a piece of advice his father had given him long ago was all he had.

"Make a plan and stay the course," King Rodrigue had always said. "If you don't, you will wander about uselessly, solving problems for no one."

That, Ever decided, was what he would do. The greatest threat now was the enchanter. Ever might not know how to help Isa, or how to fix the cruel words he'd hurt her with, but he knew he could best this enchanter, and once it was done, Ever would focus only on his wife. He would take her away and dote on her until she hadn't a piece of her left that could question his need, his devotion to her. They would find a way to heal her, and she would never be able to doubt his love again.

2 3

DUTY

*I*sa didn't even realize she had fallen asleep until she awakened the next morning to see early purple filling the sky. It had been the longest night she could ever recall, the kind that trapped her in sleepless dreams, images and words that made no sense, but were frightening all the same. Over and over again, she'd had to relive the moment when Ever had walked out and slammed the door. The worst part of it was that even after she woke up, Ever had never returned, despite her tears and prayers. Shouting, Isa reasoned, would have been better than contemplating the meaning of his absence alone.

It was so early that Isa decided not to ring for Cerise. She loved her friend, but was in no mood to explain the dark circles beneath her eyes or where Ever was. Instead, she washed her face in the porcelain basin and opened the window. Ever had told her not to touch it, but she was suffocating. After staring at the walls for two days, she needed to get out.

The street below, despite the early hour, was bustling with the sounds of poultry clucking, horses' hooves, and merchants gabbing as they walked to the market to set up their booths. The breeze had the chill of early winter, but Isa welcomed it, leaning even farther out the window. The frozen bite made her feel alive.

But it wasn't enough. Isa needed to do more than simply lean out of a window again to breathe. She needed to escape. The cold water and crisp morning air had given her courage, and suddenly, Kartek's words came back to her.

She was the queen of the Fortress, and she would not sit idly by as she wasted away and Ever destroyed himself.

Excitement thrumming through her bones, Isa quickly dressed in a yellow long-sleeved dress, another training outfit that hid a pair of trousers beneath it. Gigi had ordered it in exasperation when she'd found out that Ever was determined to train his wife in the ways of war not once in a while, but every day. Isa hoped there would be no fight today, but she wanted to be prepared. If Ever wasn't going to tell her what was going on, she would find out on her own.

And now for the hard part. Isa needed to escape her well-intentioned guards, but as they had sworn to Ever to protect her, there would be no talking her way past them. She would have to use her powers. Whispering a silent plea to the Fortress, Isa gingerly placed her hand against the rough wood of the door. She inhaled, then gently pressed.

Nothing.

Again, she took a deep breath and pushed. This time, her hand began to disappear, beginning with her fingers, then traveling up her arm and down the rest of her body. When she looked down, much to her satisfaction, she was completely invisible. It was one of the first tricks she'd learned at the Fortress.

Once more, she pressed into the wood, and just as she'd hoped, began to melt through it. Pushing through the door felt strange, like moving through a rough, wool blanket. Just as she was halfway through, however, far enough to see the other side, Norbert's head jerked up. Though he didn't seem to see her, the distraction had done its damage, and Isa was now stuck within the door. Panic seized her as she pulled and pulled, but it was no use.

Calm, she struggled to focus, *I must be calm*. More slowly this time, Isa tried pulling her right leg from the door without bumping into him. The older man had seen enough of the Fortress's power to guess what she was up to if she tipped him off. As though freeing herself from quicksand, Isa had to be ridiculously patient. Finally, she was free from the door. Thankful to be done with it, she ran silently down the hall, glad to stretch her legs again. It was empowering to walk through the halls alone. Isa felt strong and confident, though she hadn't the slightest idea as to how she would discover whatever her husband was hiding from her.

Then it came to her. Launce. Launce was grudgingly obeying Ever, but she was sure it wouldn't take much convincing to get him to share what he knew with her. Isa felt a bit guilty about sneaking around her husband, but Kartek was right. Whatever scheme Ever was so obsessed with would drive him to distraction if he was left alone to it.

Besides, his words from the night before still stung more than she wanted to admit, and his absence even more. She would go to Launce's final competition, then she would explore on her own.

The final ceremony was one of excitement and chatter, not to mention much earlier than the first two contests. The roar of many voices reached her before Isa even arrived at the arena. She was both relieved and saddened when she saw that Ever sat in his usual post beside King Rafael. She would have to find a new place from which to watch the contest. Others couldn't see her, but Ever would sense her presence if she was nearby. Invisibility was one of the few skills Isa had ever had a decent handle on with her powers, but if she became too upset or flustered, it would fail her too.

"Presenting his Royal Highness, King Rafael!" The trumpets blared and the crowd hushed as the king walked to the front of his box.

"My friends, it is the time at last for us to see who the holy man, the architect of this feat, has selected to marry my daughter and be the next king of Cobren. Whosoever shall present the three apples to me today shall be our next king!" Isa wondered if Launce would have a third suit today. It still irked her that Ever had allowed Launce to continue in the competition when he discovered that the holy man was using him. But Launce had gone along with it, particularly after the first horse and suit had shown up, and between the two men, there was no stopping it. She only hoped her little brother wouldn't get hurt.

Isa found a spot just beneath the raised benches, on the far right side of the arena. From there, she could see the distant line of riders awaiting their signals to ride. She tried to pick out Launce by the gleam of his armor, but then she realized he might well have a new suit of armor today, if he had fared as well as he'd done the two days before.

Once the final game was begun, as usual, the other nobles, knights, kings, and princes attempted the great hill. It was apparent, however, that their numbers were dwindling. There were far fewer competing today than there had been the day before. It didn't seem to make a difference to the people, however, as the whole arena seemed to be waiting for Launce. No one even took notice when the hill lowered itself for the princess to walk upon its summit, then raised itself up again with a grinding creak to a height even greater than the day before.

"Do you think the knight will ride again today?" someone sitting above Isa asked.

"Of course, why would he compete in two and not the third?" someone else snorted.

"I told you, it's not one rider, but two from the same kingdom. I'll bet they are here to make a fool of Rafael by showing him up and giving three different people an apple so he'll have to choose."

"But wouldn't it make sense for the riders to each compete? Wouldn't they rather be kings than servants?"

"Unlike *some* people, not everyone's allegiance can be bought."

Heavy hoof beats could be heard fast approaching from outside the arena. Like the streak of a shooting star, a golden blur of horse and man burst past Isa and into the stadium. This horse seemed the largest of any he'd ridden thus far. Isa couldn't imagine how the monstrous creature could get three feet off the ground, let alone climb the sleek hill, which was now at least three times the height of the Fortress's Tower of Annals.

Gasps went up as the horse charged up the hill without hesitation from horse or rider. Yesterday, Launce had slowed, but tonight he rode as though demons chased him. Somehow, he moved closer and closer to the princess as though the hill were flat. Fear made Isa nearly sick as her brother neared the summit. The crystalline blue beneath him let out a sharp cracking sound. White veins splintered beneath the hooves, extending with each successive touch. Isa gripped the edge of the platform above her until her fingers hurt, praying desperately that she or Ever would be able to save him if something happened.

Just when it seemed the entire hill might shatter to pieces, Launce reached the top. Time seemed to stand still as he held out his hand to the princess, who placed the final golden apple in his hand, a look of amazement on her young face. Then, he was down the hill as if he'd never reached the top at all.

"Halt!" the king shouted.

It didn't seem as though Launce would be able to hear him, but the giant horse somehow slowed just before reaching the edge of the arena, and Launce turned him to face the king.

"Come here," Rafael ordered.

Launce paused for a moment, the gold of his magnificent suit nearly blinding in the light of the early morning sun. Isa wondered what he would do. What would Rafael do?

The horse began to slowly make its way back to the king. Isa's heart pounded as Launce neared the royal box. Surely when the king saw who it was, he wouldn't announce Launce as his successor. Ever had said Rafael was a man of honor, but that was before this strange holy man had filled his head with vain dreams and grand schemes. Launce had never actually expected to *win*, something he'd told Isa himself.

"Show me how many apples you possess," Rafael said when Launce's horse stood below the royal family's platform. "I have decreed that only the rider who possesses all three apples shall have my daughter's hand and inherit the kingdom."

Launce paused for a long moment before slowly reaching into the horse's golden saddlebags. A gasp went up from the crowd when he produced all three apples.

"I *told* you the rider was only one person," Isa heard someone whisper behind her.

The king walked down the steps and into the arena, where he held his hand out for the apples. "What is your name? I cannot pledge my kingdom to a man whose identity I do not know."

When Launce removed the golden helmet, the shock was palpable. Isa thought she heard a snicker from Ever as Launce stared warily at the king, and the king gaped back with his mouth open, clearly not pleased.

Surely, Isa thought, he would postpone his announcement. There must be some way to keep the most unwilling and unlikely candidate from being forced to take his throne. But to her surprise, the king swallowed hard and grasped Launce's arm before raising it high.

"I announce to you the chosen one of the holy man, Launce Marchand, brother to Queen Isabelle of Destin, future king of Cobren!"

Launce looked around wildly, and Isa guessed he was searching for her, his mouth open in horror as she felt him silently pleading for her to do something. But what could she do? None of this was supposed to happen. And yet, there they stood as Launce was declared inheritor of a kingdom he'd never wanted.

The holy man wanted something with her little brother, and Isa realized that if she didn't find out what, and very soon, that man just might get it.

24

SLIPPING THROUGH THE CRACKS

*I*sa felt terrible for leaving Launce alone as he was ushered away with the king. He would hate all of the court's attention, but he would survive. It was now or never, and Isa didn't know when she would get another chance to slip away. Launce would be free of it all if she could discover whatever this strange holy man had in store for him.

Isa hovered at the bottom of the arena while the people began to pour out. The king had announced that they would all have a break before their celebration luncheon began. With chagrin and relief, she watched Ever join Rafael and Launce as they made their way back to the palace. How she longed to be with him. With both of them. But since Ever wouldn't let her help him, she would just have to do it on her own.

Isa waited to leave her hiding spot until the arena was finally clear of all but a few servants left behind to tidy up. If she could only know that her invisibility would remain effective, it wouldn't have mattered when she ventured out, for no one would be able to see her anyway. Since her powers had been so unpredictable as of late, however, she preferred not to take the risk.

As Isa made her way to the glass hill, it began to look much steeper and slicker than she'd originally thought. Launce was a good horseman to be sure, but nothing aside from a special power could have moved a man and beast up such an incline for such a distance on a surface of glass.

When she touched it, the hill felt exactly as she'd imagined, like placing one's fingertips on the surface of a clear, frozen pond. The longer she left her hand against the glass, however, the more she felt a secondary sensation. Though the glass sat perfectly still, it hummed with life, and not just a little. Harder and harder it pulsed, until it stung like water that was too hot.

Isa yanked her hand off and rubbed it as she walked slowly around the hill's great base. It was at least as wide as the ballroom. A strange fear crept into her heart. She was used to being surrounded by power. Even when the Fortress's power wasn't residing in her the way it did in Ever, she could feel a wave every time her husband drew near. Even Garin had his own odd sensation that entered and left a room when he did. But this power felt . . . old. There was no other word for it. And in its age, it carried a weight too heavy for her to touch for very long.

A movement caught Isa's eye through the glass. About a quarter of the way around, a servant stood, staring up at the hill as she did. The glass warped the man's face a bit, but after a moment of study, Isa realized she was looking at Brokk. He didn't see her, of course, as she was still invisible, but Isa suddenly wished she could share one of his warm smiles. She could use one today.

She stopped walking and watched him as he studied the glass. He had been raking the dirt to level the arena, as some of the other servants were doing, but now his rake leaned against the hill. Placing his hand against the glass, just as Isa had done, he gave a small smile. She realized he was touching one of the cracks that had moved down the hill during Launce's final ride.

After looking to his left and then his right, a violet flare leaped from his palm into the glass. A sharp icicle of dread formed in Isa's belly as she watched the strange flame jump from crack to crack, sealing them up as though they'd never been there.

Then, as if he'd heard a sound, though she'd been completely silent, Brokk looked away from the crack and directly into her eyes. The look of surprise on his face told her that he could see her just as plainly as she could see him.

Dropping her invisibility, for it didn't matter anymore, Isa turned and began to sprint as fast her legs would carry her. She didn't stop to see whether he was following her. He didn't have to. The power she'd felt in the glass was far beyond the need to chase someone. Someone with that power could have stood perfectly still and caught her without a second thought.

Still, she pressed her feet onward until she had climbed to the top of the arena and down its exit, heading straight for the palace. As she ran, she was struck with the realization that she should have brought her sword. Her power wasn't great enough to use it the way Ever had been trying to teach her, but simply having the weapon would have made her feel a little safer.

In the sharp cool of the late autumn morning, her breath quickly grew ragged, and her chest ached, but Isa pressed herself on. Only when she was within the palace walls did she grab the first servant she could find.

"Find King Everard!" she gasped. "Tell him his wife needs him. It is of the utmost importance! Tell him to meet me in our chambers."

The young woman looked slightly frightened when Isa finally let her go, but Isa was too upset to care. The walk back to their rooms was frightening on its own accord. Each time she turned a corner, each time she spotted a servant or courtier, Isa nearly fainted with fright. Where was Brokk? Was he looking for her?

Isa berated herself for being so naive. Ever had been right to be angry when she had allowed Brokk into their room. It was careless, and, she thought guiltily, she had told him far more than she ever should have shared with anyone outside their trusted circle. It would serve her right if he did find her then and there. Not that he had to look. He already knew of all the places she could be.

"Norbert!" Isa nearly ran to him in her relief when she turned the last corner. The old guard looked immediately disconcerted, then fierce.

"You should not have left, Your Majesty!" he scolded her, his silver and black peppered eyebrows raised. "It is not safe—"

"I know!" Isa grasped his rough hand and took a shaky breath to steady herself. "The enchanter Ever has been whispering to you about is here," she said, not at all sorry she'd been eavesdropping. "He is the servant that brought me the midday yesterday. I saw him fixing the cracks in the glass hill! He will be looking for me, I'm sure of it."

Norbert's thin, weathered face turned to stone as she spoke. "We must summon your husband!"

"I've already sent a messenger to find him. But while we wait, I'll need you . . ." her voice trailed off as it dawned on her that she had just put one of her favorite guards in great danger as well. The older man wouldn't think twice about sacrificing himself to keep the enchanter from reaching her.

Norbert must have sensed her fear, however, because his harsh look softened just a bit. "No one will cross this threshold," he said gently, squeezing her hand. "I swear it."

Isa gave him the most grateful smile she could muster as he unlocked the door and ushered her in.

Once she was inside, she paced. Cerise had laid a scone and some fruit out on her little table, but Isa wasn't even slightly hungry. How had this happened? How could she have been so blind? It seemed impossible to have been so close to Brokk twice, and yet to have missed his incredible power completely.

Ever had disliked him from the moment they'd met. This annoyed Isa more than she could say. He had been right. Again. Her power, even her ability to sense power, must be failing faster than ever. It was the only conclusion she could reach for such an oversight. Isa ran to the mirror to study her eyes. How thin the blue rings of fire seemed! They had been so bright, so illustrious when she was first crowned.

"Are you truly leaving me? Am I that unworthy already?" she whispered. But the Fortress didn't answer. The silence that filled the room though was just as loud as a shout would have been. In spite of all the more important events taking place at that moment, Isa felt her heart break. Ever had grown tired and angry with her foolishness. The people of Destin were confused and rightfully asking what was wrong with their new queen. And now, it seemed, even the Fortress had grown tired of her ineptness.

Where was Ever?

Isa paced even faster as she wondered how it could be taking so long for the servant to locate her husband. At the Fortress, the servants were the ones who knew all of the comings and goings of the great citadel. It couldn't be that different here.

As Isa passed the rose-colored mirror in her pacing, something made her stop. Looking back at its glass, Isa realized it no longer reflected the room. Instead, it was just slightly beginning to glow.

25

MISSING

"*T*his is your fault," Launce glared at Ever as he paced.

Ever simply crossed his arms and stepped back so the young man had more space to walk off his frustration. The dock was long, jutting out into the sea far enough to fit a dozen boats on each side, or even two of the larger war vessels if they were fitted tightly enough, stern to bow. It was strangely empty today, however. Not even a fisherman was nearby. Ever wondered if Rafael had ordered everyone to a different port so he could keep his holy man's identity a secret.

"True, it was my idea, but I wasn't the one who won the contest. You could have thrown the results and no one would have been the wiser," Ever answer coolly. "Admit it, you liked winning. That's why you kept your second name. You wanted to take everyone by surprise."

"I didn't think Rafael would actually grant me the victory when he saw who I was! Who chooses a successor based on a game?"

"It was never about the game. This self-proclaimed holy man, whoever he is, has decided that you were the one he wanted to be king. There is something he wants from you that he thinks none of the others can give."

Launce stopped walking, and for the first time Ever saw understanding sink in, and the disgust on Launce's face turned to true distress. Before they could say anything else, steps sounded on the dock.

Finally, he thought as he turned to greet Rafael. But it was not Rafael who approached him, only a servant girl.

"Your Highness," she curtsied hastily, "I have a message from Queen Isabelle for you."

Ever couldn't keep the surprise from his face. He'd been certain he would have to be the first one to make amends. Which, he had to admit, was only fair.

"The queen says that she needs you, and that it is of the utmost importance."

"Was she hurt?" Ever demanded, but the girl shook her head.

"No, Sire. But she did say to meet her in your chambers. That was all." Ever expected the girl to go, but instead of leaving, however, she just stood there, twisting her fingers and biting her upper lip.

"What is it?" Ever had to remind himself to keep his voice calm and kind. "Is there something else?"

"Nothing she wanted me to say, Your Majesty. It's only . . ." she drew a deep breath. "She appeared to be quite frightened." Her voice trailed off, and she just stood there for a moment, staring at the ground, before she seemed to remember that she needed to be somewhere. Bobbing another curtsy, she skittered back down the dock toward the palace.

"Aren't you going to go see what she needs?" Launce asked.

Ever just looked at him, unsure of how to answer. His body was completely still, but inside he was at war.

If she were truly in danger, he would be there in an instant, but given the timing, she most likely had simply heard of Launce's victory, and was worried about it. Or perhaps she wanted to discuss the night before. If he left now, something told him he wouldn't get another chance at meeting Rafael's holy man alone again.

"Well?" Launce pressed.

Slowly, Ever shook his head. "If this man is who I think he is, Isa will be in greater danger than ever if I allow him to escape, given his sudden interest in our family. I need to know for sure who he is and what he is about. Norbert will keep her safe until we return." And if Ever was right, and the holy man was the enchanter he suspected, Ever would strike him down on the spot. Judging by Launce's expression, he wasn't at all happy with Ever's response, but before they could argue, two more sets of steps sounded on the dock.

"Rafael," Ever growled, "you're late." And, to make things worse, it was only a servant with a tray of goblets that accompanied the king. Fury burned in Ever's gut. The king had gone back on his word.

"You know how these things go," Rafael snapped. "I was busy."

"Your Highness." The servant bowed and held the tray of silver goblets out to Ever then Launce. After Ever and Launce were served, Ever gave the servant a curt, not-so-subtle nod that his presence was no longer needed. What he was about to say to Rafael wasn't appropriate for the palace gossips.

"So," he took a swig before giving the king his most displeased look, "I thought we had an agreement."

"I still do not see why you insist on getting to know him." Rafael stuck out his lip in a ludicrous pout. "It is not your kingdom that he's assisting with."

"But the man he has chosen is my subject," Ever said, ignoring the disgusted look Launce gave him at the term subject. "I want to know who I'm sending him off to before I let him go. Besides, my wife would have my head if something happened to her brother." When he finished speaking, the servant was still standing there. Annoyed, Ever finished off his drink as quickly as he could and then placed the goblet back on the tray. Perhaps he was simply waiting to take the empty vessels back to the kitchen. "Well, do I get to meet him?"

"Be my guest!" Rafael waved a meaty hand before stomping back down the dock toward the palace. Ever watched him go in confusion.

"Brokk." Launce nodded at the servant.

The servant smiled back, the crinkles in his eyes deepening with pleasure as though he'd just seen his own grandson. "Young Master Launce, I hope you are well?" The older man's eyes gleamed with satisfaction as he affectionately shoved Launce's arm. "How does it feel to win?"

Ever studied the servant more closely. Then it dawned on him that this was the very same servant he'd found in their room the day before, serving Isa her midday meal uninvited.

As if he'd heard his thoughts, the servant, Brokk, turned and looked at Ever directly. "How was the drink, Your Highness?" As he uttered the words, a blast of power punched Ever so hard he nearly stumbled backward. Strength, so ancient that his mouth immediately tasted of dust, emanated from the man, and Ever could only stare in horror. How had he missed this? Either the man had accidentally let down his guard, or he no longer feared being found out. From the appraising look in the small man's eye, Ever was assured that it was the latter.

Launce, however, seemed unaware of the wriggling streams of power that flowed from the man. "It was wonderful, Brokk. I don't think I've ever tasted anything quite so sweet."

"I'm glad you enjoyed it." Brokk didn't move his eyes from Ever.

A ripple moved down Ever's body.

"There's an intriguing history behind this drink. It's a nectar, you see. One found only in the deep forests of the north."

Ever's feet were still planted on the wooden planks of the dock, but his head began to spin. Brokk continued to speak, but Ever couldn't make out the words. Blinking rapidly, he tried to fight the fog that was rolling into his eyes as he squinted at the remnants of the thick, red liquid in his goblet.

Bleary-eyed, Ever dipped his finger into the chalice and pulled out a few drops. The bright sunlight, which had been so cheerful only a few moments before, nearly blinded him, but he was barely able to make out the tiniest pieces of a crushed herb, though he couldn't tell which one. Dread and anger coursed through his veins like fire. He had been right.

Isa.

She must have known. And now she was by herself. Ever turned to grab Launce so they could run to her, but when he tried to pivot, the world tilted, and the force which should have held him to the dock failed him. Down Ever went, flailing his arms like a newborn, thrashing uselessly as the sea swallowed him. Through the murky water, he sensed another body sinking beside him. It sank, still as a stone. Spots began to fill Ever's eyes over the fog, and he stupidly sucked in a mouthful of salt water.

Even as he fought the water, Isa was the only thought on his mind. She had called for him, waited for him, and if he couldn't escape soon, the enchanter would have her first. *Not this!* he called out to the Fortress. *For her sake, please don't let me fail! Not like this! Not without helping her first!*

As he cried out to the Fortress, some of his sense returned, and Ever was finally able to find the surface. His pleas were answered, to his great relief, as his eyes began to regain their clarity, and he coughed up bile and salt. As he clung to the side of the dock, he could barely make out the retreating figure in a servant's uniform. His first impulse was to pull himself out of the water and hunt the bastard down. But the memory of the sinking figure came to mind. *No,* he thought, shaking his head. *I need to reach Isa.*

Pulling himself from the water, however, he knew he couldn't leave Launce behind. With a cry of anger, he dove back into the depths, putting the remainder of his strength into aiding his eyes. Every part of him screamed to leave the water and run to his wife. But Isa's voice, the one that seemed to now reside constantly in his head, wouldn't allow it.

As he searched, it seemed that Launce had simply disappeared. The deeper he swam, the more leaden his limbs felt. Unnaturally thick and opaque, the water seemed to fight him. His searching was in vain, for he found nothing. But just when he was about to give up, a dull shine caught his eye. Ever's lungs burned as he swam closer to find the buckle of a boot. When he grabbed hold of it, Ever praised the Maker that it was attached to a leg. Once again, he turned and swam upwards, trying to ignore the feeling of knives slashing at his lungs as they demanded air.

It took every ounce of strength for Ever to heave himself back onto the dock and then to drag Launce up behind him. For a long moment, try as he might, Ever could not move a muscle. The effects of the drink were still lingering within him. The Fortress had removed much of them, but he wasn't quite free yet. A yelp of pain slipped from him as he thrust one hand palm down against the wooden planks, and then the other. Gritting his teeth, he pushed himself onto his knees.

Please, he asked the Fortress. *Don't punish her for my mistake!* A familiar heat, which started in his heart, began to warm his shivering limbs, and slowly, ever so slowly, he was able to stand. Launce, however, lay still, his chest moving so slightly it was difficult to see at all. Again, Ever wanted nothing more than to leave him there in the pathetic pile he'd collapsed in. But was that what the enchanter wanted? For him to leave Launce behind, unguarded?

Ever sucked in a deep breath and placed one hand on each side of the young man's head. His arms trembled with the effort, but finally a thin blue flame moved between each palm. As it did, Launce coughed up a lungful of seawater, and his eyes flew open.

"Isa!" Ever wheezed. But he didn't have to say more. The look in Launce's eyes told Ever that he understood. Launce, too, struggled to stand, and then they were off. At first, Ever's steps were nearly as clumsy as his brother-in-law's, but as he left the dock behind and crashed through the royal gardens toward the palace, a new determination filled him. The clean, crisp air of autumn cleared his mind, and soon, Ever had left Launce far behind.

"Move!" he bellowed as he sprinted down the halls, willing to trample whoever got in his way. His heart beat as though it might burst, but it wasn't from the exertion of running. Fear drove him on like a madman. Against his will, images of all the things the enchanter might do to his wife invaded his imagination. Still, it didn't matter how fast he ran, because to him, it would never be fast enough.

Relief threatened to wash through him as he rounded the final corner and saw Norbert still standing guard, looking as fierce as ever.

"Norbert, move!" he ordered. The old guard barely managed to step to the side before Ever gathered his wavering strength and moved right through the thick wooden door. Stumbling to a halt, he watched in horror.

The room was filled with a sickening, violet glow, swirling about at ever-increasing speeds. Thin streaks of lightning flashed within the thin cloud that hung over the rose mirror in the center of the floor. Inside the mirror was Isa.

"Ever!" She banged against the inside of the mirror, shrieking his name in a way that tore his heart. Placing his hands on the mirror, Ever closed his eyes and hunched his shoulders, drawing every bit of power within him. His hands grew hot and began to scald as he kept them against the glass. Willing it to break, he breathed in and out in deep, even breaths.

When he felt the resistance begin to lessen, he opened his eyes, only to see Isa still trapped. It wasn't the mirror's power that was giving out. Rather, it was Isa that was receding and being pulled right along with it.

He didn't know how to save her.

Tears begin to slide down his face as he placed his hands against hers on the glass. He could no longer hear her, but the pain and fear on her face was only too visible in the purple glow that lit the room. The midnight blue of her wide eyes burned into his as he struggled to hold on. Slowly, she began to fade.

"No!" he shouted, banging on the glass. When he did, a great *boom* sounded, and he was thrown back against the bed. The mirror shattered, and his heart leapt with hope. Upon opening his eyes, he could see that the glass was indeed broken.

But Ever was alone.

26

TAKEN

*I*sa called out his name until her voice grew hoarse, but it made no difference. The glass she was trying to cling to became rough like frost, and Ever was gone. She pounded her fists against the mirror, and when it didn't break, she reached for her sword, only to realize she had once again forgotten to put it on back in her chambers in Cobren. When she looked at where her sword belt should have been, Isa gasped.

The floor was made of light blue glass. And not just the floor, but the walls, the ceiling, even the door across the room. Where was she?

The room she stood in was high, three times the height of that which she'd just left behind. There were no candles or torches lit, but there really was no need. Everything held the same strange blue glow, as though a great light lay beyond the walls and illuminated it from the other side. A single round window sat above the bed across the room from the door. The window was also made of glass, but the clear familiar kind, not the rough, frosty surface that made up the rest of the room. The bed was small and simple, neatly made as though it were expecting company. The only other piece of furniture was an old wooden wardrobe that stood to the left of the door. The wardrobe was open, and Isa could see that inside of it were stacked and folded blankets, a few gowns, and a large fur coat, the kind the northern trappers often wore when they traveled to Soudain to trade their goods. Only this coat was far more elaborate, with intricate stitching on the body and along the sleeves. It had clearly been made for a woman.

Only as Isa noted the coat did she realize that she was cold. Isa walked over to the window, which faced east; she nearly fainted when she looked out. Whatever structure she stood in was balanced precariously on the precipice of a great cliff. Razor-edged mountains that rose up into the lake-blue sky like daggers encircled her. The sun was up, and though she couldn't see it directly, its light wasn't the friendly autumn light they had been enjoying in Cobren. It was the light of a winter sun, tired and old, and hinting of sunset. The mountains themselves were covered in snow and ice, and Isa sensed they hadn't been thawed in many, many years, if ever.

She turned back to the room, to the wall that she'd come through, and wondered what had happened. She remembered pacing in her Cobrien chambers. She had been waiting for Ever when a strange violet light had begun to pulse from inside her rose mirror. Knowing better than to touch it, Isa had only stepped forward a little to get a better look, but it must have been too close. Before she knew what was happening, she'd felt herself being sucked into the mirror. Piece by piece, she had begun to melt away from her room in Cobren, but even as each piece of her had begun to fit back together in this strange room, she had held on. She had tried to pull the power from her aching arms to fight. It must not have been enough though. By the time Ever had returned, it was too late, and she couldn't hold on any longer.

Still, she had hoped. She was gone, but not completely. Ever could save her! The Fortress might not have left her with enough power to escape, but his was strong. If only he could find her.

A knock at the door made her jump, then freeze as Brokk's voice called out, echoing as though in a great cavern.

"Your Highness, I have some food. I thought you might be hungry." He sounded meeker than ever, but Isa didn't care. He had lied to her, gotten her to trust him. Whatever power he used was deep, and she would have nothing to do with it.

"Please, Your Highness. I know you're angry with me. I would be too. But if you only give me a few moments, I promise there is the best reason for this. I would never take a woman away from her husband and family against her wishes if it were not for the direst of needs. Please, just listen."

Still, Isa said nothing. There was nothing he could say that would move her heart from the place it was in now. Instead, Isa walked over to the window, made a fist, and tried with all her might to push the blue fire forth from her soul to open the window. But it was no use. Her insides felt dry, as though all of her blood had dissipated into the air.

And, she realized, she was very, very tired, the kind of tired that no amount of sleep could ever cure. Months of feeling her power, and then Ever, slipping away from her had been almost too much. Now, alone and terrified, it seemed there was nothing left in the world that she had to give.

"I'm sorry I lied," Brokk called quietly from behind the door. "I needed your help, but it would have been impossible to speak with you alone at the betrothal celebration. Your husband is a good man, but I knew he would never, ever allow me to speak candidly with you under his watch. I just need a few moments. I promise."

Still Isa stayed silent.

"I didn't lie when I told you that Agatha died."

Before Isa could respond, the wall she faced suddenly lost its frosted blue color, and instead became a scene, like one from the stories her father used to tell her. Despite her anger, she was in awe. Lovelier than any painting she had ever seen, this picture was flawless. Lush fields of corn and barley covered a countryside, which rolled with hills that glowed green and yellow in the dying day's sun. A young woman wearing a style of dress Isa had never seen before walked along the road, carrying a bucket in each hand. To Isa's surprise, the picture began to move. It felt as though she were there with the girl.

"She's lovely, isn't she?" Isa wasn't sure how he was doing it, making the scene move and change, but she felt the ancient power flowing again around her.

The young woman in the scene was indeed fair, but it was the openness of her face that was most breathtaking. A kindness lay there, like a refreshing crystal pool just waiting for a thirsty soul.

"She is lovely," Isa heard herself whisper, in spite of her promise to ignore the wretched man completely.

"I met Agatha while on a journey doing business for my mother," he said as the scene on the wall began to change. "In fact, we first saw one another in a tavern, where my companions and I had stopped to stay for the night. She was easy to spot, in spite of the crowded room, for girls of her manner and dress were never found milling about places like that."

Mesmerized, Isa watched as an older man yelled something unintelligible, and Agatha nodded and darted over to the tavern keep. The old keep nodded and poured her three mugs of what looked like ale, which Agatha immediately brought back to the table, keeping her eyes on the floor the whole time. After she'd handed the loud man the drinks, he gave a raucous laugh before issuing another order. Again, the girl simply nodded and half ran out of the ill-lit room.

"I followed her out to see if she was in need of assistance." Brokk spoke again. "When I found her outside, tending to her father's horse, however, it was she who helped me." He gave a strangled laugh. "Instead of answering my question, she placed her hand on my head and informed me I had a fever. And she was right. Within an hour, I was so sick I was delirious. Days later, by the time I was coherent enough to tell my companions my name, I was informed that it had been she who had kept me alive, as my companions knew absolutely nothing of nursing a dying man back to health." The wall began to move again, quickly this time. Summer turned to autumn, which turned to winter.

"I sent word to my mother saying I had found a matter of the utmost importance, and that I needed to remain gone for a time. Being the good woman she was, I was given full allowance to remain for as long as I needed. While I was there, I did odd jobs for whomever needed them, chopping firewood, bringing in the harvest, even helping the village holy man care for the chapel. Agatha and I spent every moment together that we could find." Brokk gave a sigh, and Isa knew he must be approaching his unhappy ending. Again, the scene on the wall began to move.

"Her father demanded payment for her hand. The amount was much higher than was expected for young women of the region, but he had long discovered I came from a high place, and he was adamant that he get his fair share. Of course, I had no qualm meeting his payments, using my . . . gift to bring in more than he had even demanded. With the rest of the money, I had planned to hire a coach to bring us back to my home in comfort as soon as the winter was over. I could travel without trouble in any weather, but she was made of more delicate stuff."

Suddenly, the wall stopped moving, and the scenes of happiness and contentment disappeared. The young woman with laughing eyes and light brown hair was gone, as was the younger version of Brokk. Once again, there was just a wall of glass. Isa sank slowly onto the bed, too distracted to notice whether it was clean or not.

"My mother sent word, however, that I must return at once. There was a matter of urgency that threatened all the regions, including that of my wife. Because she had taken to sickliness that winter, I left her with friends, promising to return for her as soon as possible."

Isa waited for him to continue, but instead he stopped. Silently, for the young woman's sake, Isa mourned the loss that she knew was coming. Whatever had happened hadn't been her fault.

"What happened?" Isa finally whispered after a long pause, unable to bear the unspoken any longer.

"A plague had begun to ravage the lands," he said in a hollow voice. "Not just one or two regions, but nearly all of the northern lands had been touched. My mother needed my assistance in deciding what to do."

"What to do?"

"My mother's power was also a gift of the Maker's, as yours is. Her gift was glass too, but it was much stronger and more potent than mine." He paused. "I can show you better in person later if you like. For now, I will simply say that we could have rid the lands of the plague easily. All of them. But curing the people would have required each land's regent to allow us to briefly take control of his lands. Some of the regents agreed readily. But there were some who would not."

"Why would the kings not allow it?"

"I'm sorry," Brokk said politely. "I forget you are not as old as I am. You see, we didn't have kings, or even separate kingdoms in our day. Regents stewarded different regions, but they all paid respect to my mother."

"Who was your mother?" Uneasiness returned to Isa's stomach as she fingered the thick, brown coverlet of the bed.

"My mother was the most powerful enchantress who ever lived. Her name was Sigridur, but the people knew her as the Glass Queen."

LEGENDS

*I*t took Isa a moment to find her voice.

"So the legends are true?"

"If you come out, I will show you."

Her common sense screamed for Isa to stay put. This man, this lying enchanter, had taken her from everything and everyone she held dear, and was keeping her captive in a strange glass prison. It felt rather familiar, she thought bitterly. Must she go through this again?

Still, she hadn't broken the Fortress's curse by sitting in her room and moping, and it didn't appear as though the glass wall was going to open again for her to step back through. If he was so desperate for her to see something that he thought he needed to abduct her, then she might as well see it. And a small, childish part of her did want to see if the legends were true. So without a word, she went to the door and cautiously opened it, ready to slam it shut if she needed to.

Brokk stood in the hall. "It's a bit cold here." He gave her a hesitant, almost bashful smile, and gestured back to the wardrobe in the room. "I think you will be more comfortable if you're warm."

Seeing no reason to argue, Isa pulled on the fur coat from the wardrobe, and after a deep breath, left the room.

From the moment she stepped out the door, Isa knew she would be forever changed, if by nothing else, by the place itself. She had never dreamed such an edifice could exist. And yet, the longer she turned in circles, staring up at the vaulted blue arches and the ethereal light that seemed to be part of the glass itself, she immediately couldn't imagine a world without it.

They were standing in a hallway nearly wide enough across to fit three large beds. Her room stood at the far end of the hallway. The other end of the hallway was so distant it was impossible to make out, and the ceiling above them was high enough that its details were fuzzy. Even so, she could make out that every single wall, beam, and corner was made of the same frosty blue glass as she had found in the bedroom. Even though she stood on a dark purple velvet, silver edged rug that looked to run the length the entire hall, she could feel the hard glass beneath it.

"Where are we?" she breathed.

"This is my home." He raised his hands, palms up, in a simple, happy shrug. "Its true name is Galdur Gler, but like my mother's true name, it was never used. It was simply called the Glass Castle."

"How did such a place become forgotten?" Isa stopped turning in circles to stare at him.

"That depends on what you've heard." The slightest shadow of unease crossed his face.

But Isa shook her head. "I really don't know many stories, to tell the truth. Mostly . . ." She paused and tried to remember the nights when traveling bards would come to Soudain, and tell frightening stories to the children in the firelight. "Everyone claims that there was an old queen once who lived in a glass palace, but that she died unexpectedly. Some said she had contracted the plague, while others said she died of a broken heart when her husband passed." Isa shook her head. "The other children and I mostly made up adventures about the palace and the queen's knights."

At this, Brokk's shoulders relaxed, and his welcome smile returned. He began to walk down the hall, motioning for Isa to join him. She did so, but they didn't speak, and for a few moments, all she could hear were the swishing sounds of their long fur coats and the sounds of their boots' muffled taps on the rug. Isa tried to memorize all of the details around her. Still, neither all the intricate curves in the glass molding, nor all of the fine lines in the ornately carved walls, could distract her from the one question she needed answered most. She stopped walking and stood as straight as she could.

"Why did you bring me here?" How she wished she could sound as calm and collected as Ever always did! "And why did you use your power on me in the practice room?"

"For that," Brokk sighed, not meeting her eyes, "I'm sorry. Honestly, if there had been any other way, I would have taken it instead." Isa steeled herself, determined not to allow his sorrow to sway her good judgment. He drew a breath before speaking again. "I needed your help."

"That doesn't answer my question about the practice room."

"I hope I didn't frighten you too much there. I merely meant to test your sensitivity to my power. I never meant for you to fall."

"You could have just asked!" Isa knew she was taking a chance with such sharp words, as he was an enchanter of sorts and, it seemed, a very powerful one. But the annoyance of being taken against her will for the second time in one year was too much. Walking, against her will, down great, silent halls of an enchanted citadel was too fresh, too familiar for her to feel comfortable. And she was *not* going to fall in love with her captor *this* time.

"Please forgive me for being frank, my dear, but your husband is a bit . . . overprotective. He never would have allowed me to discuss my problem with you." Brokk finally met her eyes and held her gaze. "You know that."

Isa just turned and continued walking down the hall faster than he had been going. To her annoyance, however, he kept up unusually well for an old man.

"Please, listen first, then make your judgment!" His words, louder than any she'd heard him speak before, echoed up and down the hall. He stopped. "I have been searching for someone like you for two hundred years."

Isa came to a halt. "What for?"

He didn't answer at first, just studied her. As he did, Isa realized, he looked much different than the servant she'd first met in the practice room at Rafael's palace. He stood straight, his bearing very much as regal as Ever's. Though his hair was still silver, it seemed less unruly than before, and his eyes suddenly flashed with a determination.

"I told you that my mother called me back here from the cottage I shared with my wife. When I arrived, my mother brought me in to her meeting room immediately. That was when the regents of each region turned to my mother to ask what they should do about the sickness. As soon as I arrived, my mother and I worked day and night until we found a way to heal those who suffered."

Curiosity overtook her once again. "What did you find?"

To Isa's surprise, he put his hand in the pocket of his robe and drew out a small goblet. He held it out, so Isa took it, carefully turning it over in her hands. The entire goblet was made of a purple frosted glass, much like berries caught in an unexpected freeze.

"All they had to do was drink from the goblet. They could drink anything from it to be healed."

"What went wrong?"

"My mother and I were given much power, but there were limits to even our abilities. For our goblet to work, my mother asked that the regents of the different lands allow us to visit their lands personally, to serve the cure ourselves. Since there were no kings, only regents, it should have been simple. And yet," he sighed, "she gave them the choice anyway."

As he said this, he motioned for her to follow him again. They came to the end of the hallway, where the walls opened up into the largest room Isa had ever seen. Their path had become a bridge that hung suspended above the center of the room. Curved railings, much like glass branches of ivy, bordered each side of the walkway. One staircase spiraled down from the right, and one from the left, each on the opposite side of the path. In this room, the ceilings continued to vault up into soaring arches, but between the thick glass beams which lifted the lofty ceiling, giant, colorful windows painted the distant floors below. The windows themselves had to be at least the height of the throne room in the Fortress. Each one depicted a scene, though the scenes were too complicated for

Isa to comprehend at just a glance. She would have needed hours of study to see what they truly meant.

To her right side, two doors that were taller than the Fortress's highest tower stood gleaming in the rainbow sunlight let in by the windows. They were simple rectangles without design or color, but their sheer size held Isa awestruck. On the left side of the glass bridge was a dais as wide as her parents' cottage, with two glass thrones whose backs nearly matched the height of the doors. Rather than blue glass, however, these thrones had also been given color, and looked as though someone had shredded a rainbow and thrown the pieces wherever they chose. The chaos was surprising in what otherwise appeared to be such a meticulous design, but the longer Isa looked at them, the more she realized they were possibly the loveliest objects she'd ever seen.

She was so caught up in wandering back and forth to gaze down upon each side of the bridge that she jumped when Brokk spoke again, breaking the brittle stillness that surrounded them.

"My mother built this palace when she was just a young woman, even before she married my father. Her power was so great that the size of this place helped her bear the weight of her strength. And yet, to heal the people, she was willing to leave and carry the burden on her own." It took Isa a moment to remember what they had been discussing before entering the throne room.

"The regents said no?" Isa turned to him incredulously.

"Some said yes, but others were too afraid. For one person to bring so much power to their lands, they said, was too much a risk. She might try to overthrow the peoples she visited. If she couldn't promise them a cure from her own home, she had no right being in theirs." The older man paused and looked away from Isa, but she didn't miss the sudden glistening in the corners of his eyes. When he spoke again, his voice was husky.

"The regent of my wife's land was such a man. When I heard it, I planned to go in and get her out myself, ill or not. The regent's order was sent to his fighting men though, and they watched the border day and night for me. By the time I was able to bribe someone into letting me in, it was too late," he said. "I arrived to find that both my wife and unborn child had taken ill and died the day before."

Isa closed her eyes. She tried to imagine what it might be like to lose Ever in such a way, but couldn't. And a child? Her mind shivered away from that train of thought before it could even get close to imagining such devastation. She'd lost him once. Unlike her, however, Brokk had never gotten his beloved back. He had never even met his child.

"You don't know what it's like." A quiet sob escaped him. "To be one of the most powerful creatures in the world, but still stand there helplessly as you hold the lifeless bodies of those you should have saved first." Another sob, louder this time, racked his own body, and his hands shook as they covered his eyes. "I didn't even know she was with child when I left! I never would have allowed her to stay!"

Isa stood a few feet away from him, unsure of what to do. Her first instinct was to reach out and touch his shoulder, to try and comfort him in some way. And yet, she stayed still. Something, possibly a stray breeze from the Fortress, the kind it often loosed inside its own walls, whispered in her ear to be wary. Such sorrow could only produce powerful reactions. And these reactions, she sensed, had been building for a long, long time.

"I'm sorry," she finally whispered. "But I still don't see what all of this has to do with me, or why you've been searching for so long."

"I apologize." He sniffed, and gave her a sad smile. "I haven't spoken of this to anyone since it happened. I still miss her . . ." He gazed longingly out one of the colossal windows before shaking his head and heading toward one of the spiraling staircases. "A man came to the palace when my mother had finished visiting the lands who had allowed her to come. His wife had also died in the plague, and when he realized that she could have been saved, he went mad. He burst in, roaring about how things could have been different.

"My mother had lived over a thousand years before I was even born. She had seen much death in her time, but this was more than she could live with. In her sorrow, she placed a sleeping curse upon herself. She must not have realized, however, that it would take the entire palace with her. As soon as the servants realized what was happening, they packed as quickly as they could and left. I couldn't leave her though."

They came to the bottom of the staircase and turned left out of the throne room and down another hall. This one wasn't quite as tall as the first.

"So you fell under the curse too?" Isa asked. As they walked past countless more glass doors, she was suddenly glad for the coat. It was growing colder as the sun began to fade.

"I did."

"Why did you wake up then, if she is still asleep?"

He turned and looked at her, surprise in his wide, leathery face.

"My dear, my good mother is dead. Even sleep gives way to death eventually."

"I'm sorry," she murmured again, but he shook his head.

"It could only have been expected. As to why I awakened, I'm really not sure, to be quite honest. I can only believe the Maker has greater plans for me."

They reached a door near the end of that particular hall, and Brokk pushed it open. This room was more decently sized, and was filled to the brim with glass objects of every shape and size imaginable. Isa had to remind herself not to touch anything as she walked past little dolls, plates, baskets, even a pair of dancing slippers that were all made of delicate, colored glass.

"Which brings me to the reason I need you," he said, walking over to a small fireplace in the corner where a pot of stew was bubbling. As the smell of its contents wafted over to Isa, she realized she was famished.

To her relief, he ladled out two bowls of the stew and handed one to her, along with a pink frosted glass spoon.

"Use this spoon, and no meal which you use it to eat will run dry until each member of the household has eaten. Then clean it, put it away, and use it again for the next meal." Isa took the spoon and examined it, a bit afraid to put his honor to the test. Would there be a reason for him to use it against her?

He must have sensed her suspicion, however, for he gently took the spoon back from her, poured most of his soup back into the black pot over the fire, and began to eat from the tiny puddle that remained in the bottom of his bowl. Isa nearly gaped when she realized his soup refused to run dry. Without a word, he held his right hand over her bowl. Snapping his fingers over her soup, he caught something invisible in his palm. He brought it back to his face and whispered into his closed fist. When he held out his hand to her again, a new glass spoon lay there. Hesitantly, Isa took it and, unable to resist the mouthwatering aroma of spices and beef for any longer, began to eat.

"Unlike your gift, my power, which I inherited from my mother, lies mostly within the gifting of objects. The objects are given the ability to help the recipient in a way specific to them. People from all over the lands used to line up in the throne room to see my mother. For hours, she would sit, or sometimes stand, and listen to their worries. If their hearts seemed sincere and their needs true, she would give them something to help." Brokk gave her a distant half-grin. "She loved people like that."

He moved over to the work desk and picked up an item Isa hadn't noticed before. It was a small mirror, barely larger than the palm of her hand. It was made up of two layers of glass. The outer layer, which served as a frame, was opaque, and had miniature trees and stars carved into it. The reflective part of the mirror was flawless, like an undisturbed lake that had just frozen over.

"I am now older than my mother ever was," he said as he studied the little mirror. "I have seen more heartache and sorrow in the world than I will ever be able to describe. After waking up and recalling what had happened, I traveled as a poor journeyman. I went in search of a way to heal the world that has become so far gone since my mother and I fell asleep." He took the mirror back and stared at it. "I was young when my mother placed the sleep on us, barely two hundred. We slept for two millennia and seven centuries. Since then, I have been searching for more than two hundred years. And yet, for all my searching, I was in despair, until I heard about you."

Isa paused, her heart suddenly hammering within her as she locked eyes with him. Without warning, gone was the meek, gentle face she had thought she'd known, and instead, she sensed that she sat in the presence of a powerful, passionate enchanter.

"What about me?" she stammered.

"You were given a magnificent gift, Isabelle. The Maker gave you a purpose. You can do what no one has been able to accomplish in nearly three thousand years. With your power of the heart, you can help me bring peace to the northern kingdoms."

"How?"

He glanced up, and when he did, she noticed that the angelic light that had seemed to light the entire castle earlier was fading. The sun must be setting

"It is getting late. Tomorrow, I will tell you. For now," he paused, his hand on the door and a strange smile on his face, "simply know that no plague or pestilence or war or famine or disaster of any other manner will hurt the northern kingdoms again as long as you and I and your husband, should he choose to join us, learn from my mother's mistake."

Isa was still terribly confused as he led her back to her room, but something within her, that small breeze from before, silently screamed that the choice he offered her seemed to be really no choice at all.

BEFORE YOU GO

*L*aunce watched in a stupor as Everard knelt before the broken rose-colored mirror in Isa's chambers. Despite their long run, water still dripped from his clothing, and his head felt as though it were stuffed with goose down. He still couldn't quite remember how he had fallen into the sea to begin with, only that Everard had dragged him out of the water and tossed him up on the pier like a fish. Their sprint had something to do with Isa, that much he knew. But for the life of him, that was all he could recall.

Even now he wasn't wholly conscious. A strange sensation still clung to him as the water rolled off his body, as though another skin had been laid over his own. This invisible second layer, however, squeezed his mind and dulled his senses, and even though he knew Everard was shouting, nothing his brother-in-law said made sense.

"Rafael!"

Everard's bellow made Launce's already aching head throb even harder. By the time Launce had caught up to him, Everard was still kneeling on the floor, his hands, bleeding, pressed against the remnants of the mirror. The thought of glass made something inside of Launce squirm, but for the life of him, he couldn't get his head clear enough to know what was wrong, and why glass had anything to do with his brother-in-law's distress. A familiar voice behind him broke through the cacophony in his head, sounding quite put out.

"Will you stop terrifying my guests and tell me what you're going on about?" In two giant steps, Everard was off the floor, and had the portly man by the shoulders, azure fire encircling his fists. At first shock, then anger and fear mingled upon the big man's face as Everard shook him so hard his head snapped back.

"He took her! Your blasted enchanter took her!"

"Who? Who did he take?" It seemed the man, whoever he was, was wise enough not to try and fight Everard, considering the state he was in. Something inside Launce niggled him again, suggesting he should try to save the man's life, but a distant memory of the familiar blue flame kept him firmly in place.

"Isa! He took my wife! Now where is he?"

The mention of his sister's name burned a hole through the thick fog between his ears, and with sudden clarity, Launce began to recall everything. Being on the pier with Everard, the warm, sweet drink Brokk had given him. And falling. Falling into the depths of the green, murky sea as a foreign drowsiness consumed him. But none of that mattered as Everard's words finally sank in.

Isa was gone.

Launce suddenly had the urge to join Everard in beating the answer from Rafael, but he held back, more from his fear of Everard's uninhibited power than from a desire to see the older king safe and well.

"I do not know!" Rafael's face was the color of tomatoes, and his breathing was raspy as he struggled against the strength in Ever's hands. "But if you let me call my servants, I will have them search!" For a moment, the feral light that had filled Everard's eyes only burned stronger, and Launce fleetingly wondered if Everard just might kill the king then and there. Slowly, however, his hands began to loosen, and as soon as they were gone, Rafael stumbled out of the room, only looking back once he was on the other side of the door frame. Yanking his clothes straight, he stood as tall as possible, and raised his chin defiantly.

"Meet me in the throne room in ten minutes. I will let you know what I find out then. But I must warn you, I expect you to keep control of yourself in my palace, Everard. I will not allow such blatant disregard for order in my kingdom."

"You will do as you promised," Everard growled, "or I will kill you myself."

Launce let out a small sigh of relief as the older king paled and disappeared, if for no other reason than that the princess would keep her father for another night.

"What was his name?"

Launce looked up to find Everard's glare in his direction. Launce stared back stupidly. "Whose name?"

"The servant!" Everard shouted. "The one who nearly killed us just moments ago! You were friends with him! What was his name?"

"Brokk," Launce stuttered. Everard's gray eyes hardened into granite, and the blue flames nearly engulfed them.

"Bronkendol," he whispered. Without another word, he turned and stormed back out the door, and it was all Launce could do to keep up. Norbert stood outside, but looked more distraught than Launce could have imagined the old soldier capable of. "Prepare my horses!" Everard called behind him as they walked. "I want you to bring the servants back to the Fortress as quickly as they can move, but Launce and I will be gone as soon as the horses are ready."

Still shaking off the effects of the sweet drink, Launce was breathing hard by the time they made it to the throne room. He felt clumsy and dull as he stood before the king, Queen Monica, Princess Olivia, and a number of Rafael's advisers. Still, he didn't miss the way the princess's shrewd eyes continued to flick toward him throughout the hearing.

"I'm glad to see you've regained control of yourself, Everard," Rafael began.

Launce blanched as the words left the king's mouth. Even Queen Monica looked at her husband in shock. Was he really going to provoke the king of Destin after his wife had been stolen? Still, Rafael continued on, suddenly a very different man than the one Launce had seen shaking in his boots just ten minutes before.

"Where is he?" Ever's voice was cold and smooth, like a polished slab of stone.

"My servants do not know where he has gone at this present time. He is not a dog on a leash."

"Do you know exactly who you have been housing?" Everard asked. "And if you reply that he is just a holy man, I will cut your tongue from your mouth." Rafael looked as though he wanted to snap, but the queen leaned forward and spoke first.

"Who is he, Everard?" Her voice trembled just a bit, and Launce was suddenly impressed by the queen's self-control.

"The same day your invitation reached the Fortress," Everard said, "I also received a message from the Lingean king that ten holy men had been murdered in a field."

The queen went pale, and Olivia's eyes grew wide, but Everard continued to speak.

"I received word this morning from my own healers that the holy men had been cut with glass shards . . . from the inside."

"Just what are you implying, Everard?" Rafael crossed his arms as though he were talking to an impertinent courtier.

"I imply nothing! I am telling you that in your pride, your greedy desire for power and strength, you have opened your doors for none other than Bronkendol himself."

Gasps and whispers erupted from those surrounding them, but Everard ignored them, keeping his eyes bored into Rafael's.

"Nonsense! He's been dead for nearly three thousand years."

But Queen Monica's hand flew up to her mouth. Slowly, she stood, as though in a daze.

"Everard, how do you know?"

"Could you not see the signs?" Everard's words weren't as sharp for the queen, but he was still just as frank. "A glass hill? Gifts of glass?" He paused, his shouts finally over. "No one truly ever saw him die."

Rafael continued to glower, but everyone else stood frozen in silence. Finally it was the queen who first roused herself from the fear that seemed to paralyze them all. Launce was dying to know what Everard was talking about. He'd never heard the name before, and it obviously meant something significant, but he would feel much better if they were already on their way to search for Isa.

"What will you do? What should we do?" the queen asked.

"I am going to search for her," Everard said. "We will be riding fast, but if I were you, I would gather my horses and the court as quickly as possible, anyone who wants to come, whether it be peasant or noble. Take shelter in my kingdom while I hunt him down. The Fortress will protect you there."

"We will do no such thing!" Rafael slammed his palm down on the arm of his ebony throne with a smack. "You come into my home and threaten me, then blaspheme a man sent by the Maker to help us! I am warning you, Everard—"

But Everard had already turned to go. A strange sense of division filled Launce as he began to follow Everard. He wanted to go find his sister. And yet, he had the sudden desire to talk to the princess before they departed, although he didn't know what possessed him to think she would want to bid him farewell. The game was off, and he was no longer competing for the hand of the princess. He was still just a merchant's son, and would likely never return to her country again.

With regret churning in the pit of his stomach, Launce finally tore his gaze away from Olivia, and began walking toward the hall. Before he reached it, however, he heard the sound of padded footsteps following him. A cool hand grasped his arm and whirled him around. Olivia stood there, a determined look on her face as she ignored her father's shouts to come back that instant. Without hesitating for even a second, she took hold of his sleeves in both hands and drew his face to hers.

Her smooth lips pressed into his, and the tenacity in her kiss surprised him. He could have remained there for much longer, but all too soon she was pushing him away.

"Our betrothal might have been designed by a monster, but I like you anyway," she whispered, a coy smile upon her face. "Please attempt to stay alive." And with that, she turned and walked back to her father, her chin held high as he protested her audacity.

Somehow, Launce remembered where he was supposed to be, but as he ran to the stables, he couldn't help the grin he felt spread upon his face. He liked her too.

29

MINE FIRST

"*W*hat in the name of Gahfferon—" Launce woke with a start. "Get this off of me!"

But Ever continued to ride. Launce was more than capable of untying himself. "You were about to fall off of your horse. I simply made sure you wouldn't be trampled to death while you slept." Ever ignored the sneer that Launce sent him, keeping his focus on steadying their horses as they raced up the mountain bend. To his relief, Launce decided not to pick an argument. But then again, for once, Launce and Ever were in pursuit of exactly the same thing.

"Will we be there soon?" Lance asked, ducking low as they passed under a thick patch of trees that reached across the mountain path.

"We are almost to the pinnacle. Once we make it over the top, the Fortress will only be a little way down."

"I still don't see why we couldn't just head straight for Brokk's home," Lance said. "If you already know that it's in the north—"

"That is not his name, and you would do well not to use it," Ever snapped. "As for his home, I do know that it is to the north, however the castle itself has been hidden for almost three millennia. It would be foolish to run in blind only to get ourselves caught in a blizzard or something worse of his own making. Garin is our best hope in planning our next moves. Garin and the Tower of Annals. We will consult and make our decision there."

Launce seemed at least somewhat placated by Ever's answer, but Ever himself wasn't sure he was correct in his assumptions. Garin was old, but from what Ever had gathered over the years, even he hadn't lived long enough to see the days of the glass castle.

The journey that had taken them two full days to make the first time took only one day and one night in return. Ever had used every bit of his strength to push the horses on so that they ran harder while needing less rest and water. He had used so much of his strength in aiding their furious pace, however, that he had little left for himself or the young man beside him.

To Launce's credit, the young man hadn't complained. But his ability to remain awake had finally waned, and after nearly twenty hours of riding, Launce had been unable to go farther. Ever had allowed them one hour of rest during the night before, but not a minute more. When Launce had begun to doze off again as they rode on, Ever hadn't had the power to keep him upright. Thankfully, there was enough rope in his pack to secure Launce to his horse without waking him. Had they been in any other situation, he would have thought it great fun to tie up the young man, passive revenge for the stubbornness Launce had shown him since the day they'd met.

It had occurred to Ever more than once that he would have moved much faster without the young man. It would have been easier to leave him in Rafael's court, where at least he had a warm bed and a decent number of eyes to watch him. And yet, just as Ever could almost hear Isa begging him to save her little brother's life as he sank into the sea, he could now imagine her begging him to keep Launce safe with him. These imagined pleas were constantly at war with the need he felt to dash off alone and find her himself.

Dark thoughts of what the enchanter might want with his wife endlessly swirled about his mind. Intrusive images of what she could be suffering bombarded him with every breath that passed through his lungs. Up and down the hills, through the canyon, and up the mountain, Ever had prayed that the Fortress would strengthen her, that her power might be returned for even just this time.

And with those prayers surged the desire to leave his clumsy young charge behind. But if he knew anything about Isa, it was that she loved her brother, and that if Ever sacrificed Launce in his attempt to save her, Isa would never forgive him.

It was afternoon by the time they reached the mountain's summit and began down the other side. Ever had never used so much of his power so fast for so long, and everything in him ached. But he ignored it and pushed the horses on until nausea almost got the better of him. Eventually, however, they did make it through the servants' gate, taking a number of the servants by surprise by racing right up to the stables. Even before they arrived, Ever could see Garin waiting outside the stables, elbows out and his hands behind his back in his usual position.

"Norbert's message arrived last night." Garin's voice was as steady as ever, but there was an undercurrent to it. "He wrote only that you were returning home today, but nothing more. I assumed he feared the bird might be intercepted?"

"Isa has been taken." Ever swung down from his horse easily, but his muscles screamed in protest when he landed. Garin's eyes flashed and his jaw tightened as he waited for him to say more, but Ever didn't want to incite panic. He leaned forward and whispered, "Bronkendol." Ever watched his steward's face carefully.

The comprehension took a moment, but it was clear when Garin truly understood. His face turned to stone and ash, and his eyes widened in a way that made Ever more than uncomfortable. Immediately, the steward turned and began to head toward the Fortress. Ever followed without a word, dragging Launce along behind him.

The trek from the stables to the Fortress's highest tower had never seemed to take so long as it did this time.

"If you value your life," Ever called softly back to Launce, "you will do well not to touch anything. This is sacred ground. Only Garin, the kings, queens, and a handful of servants have ever stepped inside of this room." Well, Ever thought with chagrin, those select few, as well as a dozen dead Tumenian soldiers and their dead princess, Nevina.

"Perhaps," Launce puffed as they climbed the winding tower stairs, "it would be best if I just waited outside."

"No. You're a part of this now, whether we like it or not. Just mind yourself."

By the time Ever and Launce had crossed the threshold, Garin was already clearing a large mahogany table at the center of the room and covering it in maps. Before joining the steward, Ever made sure Launce was standing in a place where, if he fell from exhaustion, he wouldn't break anything too old. Then Ever threw himself into a deep search of the great tomes he knew so well, grabbing as many as he could from the old, wooden shelves.

"How was she taken?"

"Through the mirror in our chambers." Ever wanted to gut himself for forgetting about the blasted mirror in their guest quarters, the one he'd used every day they'd spent at Cobren.

"You are certain it's him?"

Ever looked up from a dusty page he was skimming and nodded.

"But nearly three thousand years?" Garin slumped against the table in disbelief.

Ever struggled to keep his demeanor calm as he watched Garin waver. In all his life, only a few things had ever rattled Garin, and all of them had happened while Ever was under the Fortress's curse, which had been brought on by his own foolish mistakes. Nothing outside of his actions or his personal mistakes had ever seemed to even bother the steward. Until now. Now Garin's face was taut, and his suntanned, slightly lined face seemed suddenly much closer to the age it should be, whatever that was.

"I don't understand," Launce called from the other side of the room, where he was now sitting against a wall. "What kind of man lives for three thousand years?"

"Bronkendol is the only child of the Glass Queen," Ever said as he grabbed the first book from his pile and began to skim through it. "And he has lived for nearly four thousand years. We've only assumed him dead for three thousand."

"Wait, the Glass Queen was real?"

"More than real," Garin snorted, recovering himself a bit. "The Glass Queen is the reason our kingdoms exist the way they do."

"No one knows where she came from," Ever added as he continued to skim the dusty pages, "but we do know that the Glass Queen was gifted from the Maker, much in the way the Fortress monarchs are. Her gift was incredibly potent though, even when compared with many in my line."

"She could conjure glass objects," Garin said, "that would fill specific needs. There were no actual kingdoms in the land of what we now call the northern kingdoms. There were simply regions with low-ranking overseers. If disagreements between regions arose, they took them to the Glass Queen. She either mediated, or, if she was able, created an object from glass that would help both parties."

Ever finished the first book with annoyance. Nothing. He had read nearly every book in the Annals, but suddenly nothing seemed to have the information he needed. Tossing it aside, he moved on to the next.

"Like the gifts we were given at the banquet?" Launce's voice was hushed, nervous. Still skimming the book before him, Ever nodded.

"When a plague began to spread throughout the lands, the regents asked Bronkendol and his mother to find a cure. Bronkendol had inherited many of his mother's abilities, and together, it didn't take them long to create a cure. In order to administer the cure, however, a great deal of power would need to be poured out upon each land, and not all of the lands wanted that power."

"Why wouldn't they accept it?" Launce had moved closer, and was frowning deeply.

"Power gifted by the Maker can be terrifying to those unfamiliar with it." Garin, who had been poring over various maps, looked at Launce with half-lidded eyes. "If the Glass Queen had attempted to invade the opposing lands, she would have faced local armies. Too much blood had been shed already, she said. She did not want blood on her hands."

"Bronkendol's young wife took ill and died," Ever spoke again. "Bronkendol blamed his mother because she had not forced the cure upon that particular region after they had refused her help. In his anger, he attempted take control of the Glass Castle himself. He planned to murder his mother and seize dominion over all the regions on his own. The queen found out just before he succeeded, and she knew she would have to stop him. She couldn't bring herself to end her own son's life, however, so she told the servants to leave, and in her sorrow, placed a sleeping curse upon every living thing left, which at that point, was only her son, herself, and the castle."

"How do we know all this?"

"Servants escaped the glass castle carrying their belongings, as well as words from the queen," Garin said.

"In truth," said Ever, "it's Bronkendol and his mother that we can thank for our kingdoms being shaped the way they are. Once the queen, who was mediator between the regions, was gone, the lands eventually solidified into their own kingdoms, which led to Destin's eventual rise." Ever closed another book and joined Garin in looking at the maps. "Now, Launce, when you spoke with him, did he ever mention any of his plans?"

At this, Garin turned his gaze to Launce as well.

"No," Launce said slowly, then his face lit up. "But he did say he was from the far, far, north! When I asked him what made him leave, he said something about some decisions being made for us."

"I don't understand it." Ever glared at the maps spread out before him. "The entire continent north of us is inhabited. We know the Glass Castle was here somewhere..." He traced the northern Lingean border, his voice trailing off as frustration filled him. Every moment they wasted, Isa was alone, but their efforts felt fruitless. The lands north of them, Lingea and all of its neighbors, were too populated for anyone to have missed an entire castle.

"What about the murdered priests in Lingea?" Garin asked.

"They were found in a meadow not far from here." Ever pointed to a mountainous region that was surrounded by small villages and many farms. During the winter, the land was treacherous. Only the hardiest farmers could grow crops there. But that still didn't explain how an entire castle could go unseen.

"How do we even know he brought her to his castle? What if the castle is gone, and only he survived?" Launce asked.

"The power he uses was tied to that castle the way my power is tied to the Fortress," Ever said. "He would need a safe place to plan whatever he has been scheming, as well as the source of power. No, his castle is still standing. If only we could find it."

"Ever," Garin said, staring out the window. "I might have an explanation."

Ever turned to Garin, curious, but with trepidation as well. The steward only used that tone of voice when his knowledge of deeper power was called upon. By practice, Garin never spoke of such subjects unless he had to, and the hesitancy with which he recalled it had always kept Ever from enquiring any further than necessary. Ever trusted Garin more implicitly than anyone else in the world. Garin had practically raised him. But when he spoke of old power, a dangerous glint touched Garin's eyes, and Ever knew better than to prod.

"There was once a race, long extinct now, that could cut paths between realms. They could create bridges between their world and ours, somewhat akin to the way you use your power to speed your horse between locations."

"Different realms?" Launce balked. And for once, Ever was as confused as the young man.

"It is difficult to explain if you haven't been there to see it," Garin frowned.

Did that mean Garin had seen such things?

"The Maker created our world as one of many," Garin continued. "Sometimes, those worlds touch, overlap, even. In fact, that is how individuals like you, Ever, and the Glass Queen and Kartek can foster power at all. The Maker has allowed just a little of His world to touch and spill over into ours.

"These beings from long ago had the innate ability to build roads directly between the worlds, rather than spend the years it would take to reach the distant lands by foot, sea, and air. But first, they had to possess an item from that world before they could trace it back to its place of origin. Sometimes the Maker would allow them to come across items from other worlds through trade or miracle. I wonder," Garin stopped and looked at Ever, "if Bronkendol might have created such a road of his own."

"But his world was once part of ours," Ever said. "We know the castle and its queen occupied a particular place and time." He gestured at the books before him, as though that might change things, but Garin was already shaking his head.

"We don't know what was in the spell that the queen cast. I would wager that she not only put a sleeping curse on the castle itself, but sealed it off into a world of its own. She couldn't kill her son, but she could not risk this world's safety. As long as he was breathing, even in his sleep state, he was dangerous."

"But how did he get back to us then?" Ever asked.

"Bronkendol has engaged in deep planning." Garin began to gather the books and pile them on the edge of the table, away from the maps. "And he is his mother's son. Obviously, her sleeping spell didn't hold him. If he was able to awaken after all these years, it only makes sense that he found a way to tear the veil between worlds as well. He would only have needed a single item in his palace that had been made in the old world."

"But I still don't understand why he would want Isa," Launce, interrupted.

"Your sister," Garin said in a grave voice, "was granted more power than any other queen I have ever seen. She simply doesn't know it yet." He paused. "It would only make sense for Bronkendol to want to harness her power."

Ever said nothing, wishing with all his might that Garin was right about her power, because if he was, Isa might stand a chance of saving herself from this ancient foe. But the dying flames that had barely lit her eyes haunted him. Even if he found a way to reach her, would he be too late?

"So," Garin looked at Ever, as though reading his thoughts, "what are we going to do?"

"We're going to study these maps more. I will also be sending out messenger birds to Lingea to ask more about their priests that were attacked. Launce will return to Cobren—"

"I'm going nowhere except with you." Launce crossed his arms and straightened his shoulders.

"You will do as I say, return to the Cobrien court, and send messenger birds to Garin about what Rafael and Bronkendol are up to."

"You are not my owner!" Launce exploded. "And I am not your dog to do your bidding! My sister is gone! Who gives a husk about the Cobrien court?"

"I am your king, and you will do as I say!" Ever thundered back, slamming his fist down on the table. When he felt the wood crack, he knew he needed to calm down before someone else got hurt, particularly the obstinate young man before him. Taking a deep breath, Ever lowered his voice, closing his eyes so he wouldn't have to see the insolence on Launce's face.

"Rafael is the enchanter's puppet. I need to know what the enchanter wants with him. Saving Isa would do no good if there were no home to bring her back to. Besides," he said more gently, "I believe there is one member of the court that you would like not to see harmed. Watch over her while you're there. She needs someone she can turn to."

Launce snorted. "As if I could save her."

"Why do you think I spent so many hours trying to teach you?" Ever felt exasperated. For once, would the young man ever simply do as he asked? "Did you think I was practicing with you just to make you angry?" The look Launce gave him was answer enough, and Ever had to take a deep breath again. They were past the time of pointless arguments.

"Life with the Fortress is one of possibility and danger," Ever said. "Now, I have another reason I'm sending you back if you'll listen to me. Look closely at my eye." Ever leaned close to the young man, ignoring Launce's look of disgust. "Do you see this?"

Launce glanced down and up as quickly as he could before shaking his head.

"Look closer," Ever demanded. "There's a rough spot, right in the corner."

This time, Launce sighed, but did as he was told. When his eyes grew bigger, Ever knew he had seen it.

"Are those ... splinters?"

"Slivers of glass," Ever said. "Everyone who was in the stands that first day at the arena has them."

"I don't," Launce said.

"You weren't *in* the arena when the opening ceremonies began, as you took it upon yourself to hide in the woods. But you were the only one. The other competitors have them. All of my personal guards who were there with us have the slivers also. Isa does too, although I don't think she's aware of it. When the enchanter rained down his bright show of glittering glass that first day, they became lodged in everyone's eyes." Ever looked at Garin, regret coloring his voice. "I tried to shield us, but I was too late."

"And you can't purge it?" Garin's voice was calm, but the look he gave Ever was too focused to be genuine.

Ever shook his head. "I've tried, repeatedly. But this power . . ." he faltered, not sure how to tell his mentor and oldest friend how lost he really felt. "It's like nothing I've felt before."

Turning back to Launce, Ever said, "I don't know what the enchanter is plotting, but since you are not under his control, you are safer than any of us in that court. Now please," he said, wishing his request didn't sound so much like begging. "Go, so I can focus on saving your sister."

Launce stared at him for a long time. Ever held his gaze, wondering what the young man saw. Like Launce, Ever's chin and upper lip were covered in tough stubble, but it suddenly occurred to Ever that Launce looked older than he had only a week before. Finally, Launce simply nodded and left.

∾

Ever didn't remember leaving the tower, but somehow he woke up in his own bed while the morning was still dark. A knock sounded at the door, and Ever realized that must have been what had awakened him in the first place.

"Yes?" he mumbled, rubbing his eyes. He still felt so tired he could hardly get his bearings. "What is it?"

"Master Garin says to tell you that your brother-in-law is ready to leave soon. He thought you would like to see the young man off."

"Thank you," Ever said. "Tell him I will be there." He couldn't stop the groan that escaped him as he pulled himself into a sitting position, and out of habit, was careful not to disturb the other side of the bed.

Just because his strength allowed him to push himself harder than most others, it didn't mean he never felt the pain. Very quickly, he was realizing that riding as hard and as fast as they had could bring some serious pain. Still, he pulled on the clothes someone had laid out for him, and headed to the stables.

When he arrived, Launce was already seated upon his horse. Ever wondered what kind of trick Garin had used to get the young man looking so well so quickly after Ever had pushed him so hard the two days before. Full saddlebags hung from the horse's sides, and for the first time, Launce was actually wearing the official colors of the Fortress.

"Would you walk me to the gate?" Launce asked him quietly.

Suddenly curious, Ever nodded.

As they left the stables, Ever wished he'd worn a thicker cloak. Autumn was leaving more hastily than usual, and winter was definitely in the air. A mischievous breeze moved in and out around their legs and arms, squeezing into every cranny that wasn't completely covered. Aside from the breeze, everything else was still as they walked quietly across the browning lawns behind the Fortress to the servants' gate. For official business, Ever always used the main entrance, but the servants' gate was farther up the mountain, and made the ride to the main path much faster.

Unsure of what Launce wanted with him, Ever waited. Sometimes, he knew from experience, more could be learned from silence than from unwanted questions. Sure enough, just a few minutes into their walk, Launce finally spoke.

"If you could see the enchanter right now, speak with him face-to-face, what would you do?"

"I would kill him before he could speak a word."

"Then would it be safe to say that you hate him?" Launce turned and looked directly into his face, and in the light of the full moon, Ever could feel the intensity of his gaze.

"Garin has taught me that hate never accomplishes anything, hate for others, at least. We can hate circumstances, and we can hate tragedy, but hating others brings us close to a place of danger within ourselves," Ever answered evenly. "But that said, yes. I hate him with every bone in my body."

"Then you finally understand."

"Understand what?"

"How I feel about you."

Something violent stirred within Ever. He felt heat pulse from his hands, and the desire to taste blood surged within him. And yet, as he stared up at the lanky young man who rode his horse with such infuriating serenity, Ever realized his fury wasn't for Launce. It was for himself.

"She is your wife now," Launce continued in a calm, resigned tone, "but she was mine to protect first. After you hurt her the first time, I was the one to help pick up the pieces. I was the one to talk her out of daring attempts on her horse. While you were off fighting your glorious battles, Isa was my responsibility. On the night you gave orders to kill her, I carried her to the cart so we could flee the city before your bloodbath ensued. And as if that weren't enough," Launce's voice grew hard, and he glared openly at Ever this time, "you demanded her, like chattel. You took her from us. My parents had planned to escape, but they didn't know her like I do. I knew that just as she had given up her horse for me, she would give up her life for the rest of us. I even caught her just before she reached your gate."

Ever felt sick as he listened. There had been a time when he thought his heart had been beaten to its very core, but that was nothing compared to hearing what Launce had to say now. Because he knew, deep down, that the young man spoke the truth.

"It was only for Megane's sake that I let her go," Launce said. "And until we received news that you had died, and that Isa would be crowned queen, I had to look at that Fortress on the mountain every day, and imagine what you were doing to her there, all alone. And I knew that it was all because I had failed to keep her safe."

They had reached the gate, and Launce pulled his horse to a stop, turning it so he could look at Ever head-on.

"The only reason I didn't go mad on the day you married my sister was because I could see that she truly believed in you. And I thought to myself, if anyone can save my sister from her own brave, foolhardy schemes, it would be you." And with that, he turned his horse and gave it a kick.

30

CRYSTAL TRUTH

$\mathcal{A}$fter walking her back to the room she'd first arrived in through the mirror, Brokk gave Isa a few candles to see by as the darkness continued to fall.

"The mountains surround us on every side, so the wind becomes trapped within them, and grows cold and strong. Use as many blankets from the wardrobe as you need. I have also added a few of my mother's old gowns for you if you wish to change. She was nearly your size."

Once he was gone, Isa looked doubtfully at the bed. It looked old, but when she sniffed it, it somehow smelled clean and free of dust. Grudgingly, she laid down. Sleeping was the last thing she wanted to do. Still, she wouldn't be able to go far if she found the chance to escape, but was too tired to do so.

As she gingerly tucked herself under the blankets, Isa looked up at the strange shadows the candles cast upon the glass walls. Ever would know what to do, she thought to herself.

But Ever wasn't there.

Suddenly, Isa didn't care if she was mad at him or not. Just having his warmth beside her would have done wonders to soothe her frightened soul. And he would come, she promised herself. If anyone could find her, it would be him.

Isa would have given anything to have him with her at that moment. It stung to think about the last words they had shared. The yellow firelight on the white-blue ceiling danced eerily as though it could feel the gales of wind that rushed and roared around the castle. The shadows seemed to leer at her.

What if he doesn't come? they whispered. Isa rolled over, as if ignoring the flames could quiet the fears that whirled around inside her head. *Perhaps,* she prayed to the Maker, *you could at least send me dreams of him rushing to my side. Just let me escape in my dreams for the night.*

~

Waking up was difficult the next morning. The Maker had answered her prayers, and sweet dreams had taken her during the night. Images of Ever, and the sensation of his touch had brought her to a deeper sleep than she'd had in months.

And yet, their disappearance made waking up all the more difficult. Instead, shock and fear rippled through her as Isa struggled to remember where she had fallen asleep. At least it wasn't dark anymore, she tried to comfort herself. The glass castle's opaque walls were bright with gray sunlight once again, but there was not a sound to be heard, aside from the constant wind. Isa lay in bed, shivering for over an hour before she was decently sure Brokk wasn't listening outside her door again.

Finally, she slipped out of bed, only to be greeted by the coldest air she had ever felt. She hadn't intended to touch the Glass Queen's gowns, but as soon as she saw how warm they really were, made of thin, soft leather, and lined with white fur, Isa changed her mind, and quickly changed into a warmer dress and covered it with the thick robe. Then she waited one more time with her ear to the door before cautiously peeking out into the hall.

"Brokk?" she called. There was no answer. Twice more she yelled out his name before concluding he wasn't nearby. She suddenly wondered if he had gone back to Cobren. If he had brought her here through a mirror, he must have been able to return through one as well.

Her suspicions were all but confirmed when she made her way to his workshop and found one steaming glass bowl of porridge set out on the table. As she ate, Isa hoped he would be gone for a while. Since the moment she had discovered where she really was, Isa had longed to explore the ancient castle on her own. Legends of the Glass Queen had been some of her favorites when she was a child. Even more importantly, however, she hoped to find some hint as to what the enchanter was truly planning. Then, when Ever came for her, she would at least have something to tell him.

Her boots made sharp clicking sounds against the frosted glass floor that echoed down the halls as she walked back to the throne room. As she went, she dragged her hand along one of the walls. Though her ability to produce the Fortress's fire seemed to be all but gone, Isa wondered if she would at least be able to feel the power of one room if it was more important than the others.

Just as she entered the throne room, Isa stopped. It felt as though someone had poured something thick, icy, and hot into her blood. Her heart began to race, and the sudden urge to sprint up one of the spiraling staircase nearly overwhelmed her. Her chest grew so tight she could hardly breathe, but as soon as Isa removed her hand from the rough glass of the wall, everything stopped. Her breathing returned to normal, and it was as if nothing had happened. Mystified, Isa tentatively placed her fingers along the wall again. Immediately, the draw to go upstairs consumed her once more.

Could this be one of Brokk's tricks? Might he be watching, waiting for her to follow? As she continued to hold onto the wall, Isa realized the power was different even from that which she'd felt in the glass hill. As ancient as Brokk's power was, this felt impossibly older.

When she reached the throne room, the urge to go forward grew even more urgent. Sucking in a deep breath, Isa let go of the wall and walked to the closest staircase, and decided to let the strange pull, whatever it was, take her. The urge to run overtook Isa, and as she flew up the shiny steps, a thrill moved through her. Suddenly, she felt as though she were a bird climbing higher into the clear blue sky.

Eventually, she had to reach the bridge she had walked upon the day before, and the exhilarating flight was over. Whatever had first yanked her along, however, did not allow her to linger. Instead, it kept her hand upon the rail, then the wall, before pulling her down the hall opposite that of her room, the side of the castle she hadn't explored the day before.

As she went, the walls began to change. Instead of ivy, the walls here were carved with stars and moons. The impulse to continue walking grew stronger until she reached the last door at the end of the great hall. Isa placed her ear to it and listened, but she heard nothing. With curiosity now nearly as strong as the force which compelled her forward, Isa began to slowly push on the door only to realize it was locked.

"You would think a castle this old would at least have loose locks," she muttered to herself. But no matter how hard she pushed, it wouldn't budge. Stepping back, Isa stared at the glass handle. If Ever had been there, a lock wouldn't have posed a problem at all.

Ever wasn't there, however, and her need to see what was behind the door grew more incessant by the minute. Isa huffed impatiently, knowing what Ever would tell her to do even if he were there.

Placing the palm of her hand against the door, Isa exhaled, trying with all her might. She imagined the little bit of fire left within her gathering in her hands. Groaning with the strain, Isa pressed her hands into the door until they hurt. The faintest blue aura lit up the glass around her hands, but only for a second. Then, nothing.

The pain in her hands was nothing compared to that within her heart. If the Fortress's fire continued to leave her at this rate, she would be dead in a week. It wouldn't even matter what the enchanter had schemed up for her. Isa sighed and leaned heavily against the door. The glass was cool, but warmed quickly under her touch, and that nagging sensation continued to dance throughout her body, biting her as she stood still. If only she could do something to quell it.

As if someone were watching her struggle, the door clicked open on its own. Without hesitating to wonder why the door had opened by itself, Isa darted through, hoping that wherever Brokk was, he couldn't see or hear her. Something, perhaps the strange urgency in the glass, told her that she was not meant to see whatever was behind that door.

As soon as she was through, Isa came to another flight of stairs. These stairs led up to a tower that was tall and isolated, much like the Tower of Annals at home. This staircase, however, was much, much steeper, and the glass walls were no longer opaque, but perfectly clear. So clear, in fact, that Isa nearly screamed.

For the first time, she could see the castle in its entirety. The whole structure was indeed made of glass, and it was balanced atop a single island in the center of a mountain range that encircled them entirely. Between the castle and each monstrous mountain was a gorge so deep that the bottom was completely hidden from sight. The only way to reach the mountains on the other side of the gorge was to cross a thin glass bridge that spanned the chasm. It must have been nearly as long as the castle was wide. The bridge might have been quite sturdy itself, but over the deep, black chasm, it looked brittle, as though the wind might smash it to pieces at any moment.

When Isa looked up instead of down, she found herself staring at the jagged, snowcapped peaks. Their height made her dizzy, and the brightness of the snow in the sun made her nearly blind. It all made Isa want to suddenly lie on the floor, clinging to it with all her might, never to move again. Only the incessant sting of the glass gave her the ability to begin slowly climbing the steps that were as transparent as air itself.

Finally, after what seemed like an eternal death march, Isa came to a door in the sky. One more room sat upon the tallest tower. Like her own room, this one had frosted walls, but they were a rich blue. Cautiously, Isa gently pushed the door. This one, to her relief, opened immediately.

Suddenly feeling exposed as she stood between the nearly invisible stairs and the room's dark, tapestried walls, Isa practically dove into the room, thankful for the privacy of its walls. Only when the door was shut and locked behind her did Isa turn around and truly look at what lay before her.

A beautiful woman was stretched out upon the widest bed Isa had ever seen. Her hands were folded upon her chest, as though she might be taking an afternoon nap. Hair so yellow it was nearly white lay strewn out around her head, glorious in its brilliance. Bone-pale skin covered a thin face with high cheekbones and bloodless lips. Her exotic gown, lined with fur the way Isa's borrowed gown was, shimmered sky blue with purple jewels scattered about it.

She was the most beautiful woman Isa had ever seen. As Isa began to look around to study the rest of the room, however, a movement caught her eye. When Isa looked at the woman once more, her heart nearly stopped.

Isa was not the only one in the room who was breathing.

GIFT OF THE HEART

*I*sa tried to imagine who the woman might be, but the urgent sensation that had brought her here prickled her skin, even though she was no longer touching any glass with her hands. Instead, the air was thick with it, archaic power, heavy and hard to breathe.

And Isa suddenly had the overwhelming urge to touch her.

With a will that wasn't her own, Isa stretched out her hand and rested it lightly upon the woman's ashen cheek. When she did, the tapestried walls around her began to fade into oblivion, and instead she was standing upon the dais of the throne room below. Courtiers dressed in an exotic fashion similar to that which hung in Isa's new wardrobe stood loosely clustered about the throne. Her gaze rested on the scant assembly of what looked to be wealthy nobles and several dozen commoners. Brokk, though much younger, knelt before her.

"Come, Son," Isa said, realizing immediately that though she said it, the voice wasn't her own. "We will not speak of this here." She glanced up at the people milling about her. There was a sadness in the air, an urgency that Isa couldn't understand.

The two of them left the throne room and walked at a quick pace to a smaller room down a side hall behind the throne. Isa nearly screamed when six giants encircled her, two in front, one on each side, and two more behind her, until she realized they must be her guards. She tried to study them without looking too obvious.

They almost resembled the ice sculptures some of the artisans in Destin would create in the town square every winter. Their movements were surprisingly fluid, and their steps as light as one of Ever's personally trained foot soldiers. Each one stood a full head taller than Launce though, and they wore no human clothes, but garments that seemed carved into their glass bodies. Their opaque, pupil-less eyes seemed to see everything and nothing at the same time, and each carried a long, sharp glass scythe, as though it were merely an extension of its hands. The gleam of the weapons made Isa shudder, and suddenly wonder if they had disappeared with the spell as well, or if they still lurked in the shadows unseen.

After walking in silence for a few minutes, Brokk at her side, chewing his lip and looking very much as though he might burst, they turned and entered a sunny room made only of glass windows. Though it shared the southern wall with the rest of the building, the other three walls and its ceiling were unfrosted and clear. The walls weren't smooth either, but made of many six-sided small panes. Together, they played with the room's reflections, some parts of the wall concave while others were convex. The non-uniformity was strange and beautiful.

The room itself was nearly the size of Isa and Ever's sleeping chamber at home, but it was stuffed so full of plants and tables and growing tools that one could scarcely move without knocking something over. And it smelled of soil. Isa immediately felt at home in that room of green paned glass. In the great citadel of glass perfection, this room felt homey and lived in.

Isa's host body knelt near a little lemon tree, which stood in a pot wider than Isa's shoulders, and lifted one of the tools. She began to prune it methodically. "You know why I called you," Isa heard herself say in that low, melodic voice. Brokk paused in his pacing briefly, the long, deep purple cloak swishing around his feet, gathering dirt as it scraped the floor. His eyes were wild, and deep bags hung below them. He glanced at her, but remained silent, so she spoke again. "This is not the way the Maker intended us to use our gift." Her voice was kind, but authoritative.

"Then He meant for us to rest while we watched thousands die before us, simply to placate the vain concerns of mere men?"

"We are not gods, Bronkendol. You are a man, and I am just a woman, the same as them. Possessing the ability to help does not mean we are to possess dominion over all other peoples."

"You have not seen what I have!" Young Brokk exploded, suddenly so close that Isa could feel his breath. "You sit in this sparkling citadel and see them one at a time, withdrawing for the day when you tire. But I have walked among them. This sickness is only the beginning of their struggles! They fight amongst themselves constantly, killing one other for gain! The poor eat scraps, while the rich flaunt their overabundance. Mothers cannot feed their children, because fathers abandon them . . ." His voice trailed off as he held his head in his hands. The body Isa occupied rose gracefully to wrap her arms around him, but he shook her off.

"It wasn't your fault," she said softly, putting down the tool and standing.

"No, it was yours."

Isa's borrowed body drew back as though he'd slapped her, and a sharp pang filled her heart. "You don't think I mourn the loss of a daughter I never met, and even more, my grandchild?" She shook her head. "Had there been time, I would have brought her here myself. But sometimes the Maker brings them home to Him for reasons we cannot explain, the way He took your father. We are strong, but we cannot prevent death."

"Because you never tried!" He backed away, glaring at her, his eyes too bright in the reflection of the dancing firelight.

"Bronkendol," she warned, "you think I saw nothing in the thousand years before you were born? You think I know not suffering? I have seen more anguish than you can ever conceive of! This gift of strength and long life has its blessings, but it also brings trials. Witnessing the hardships of man is part of our lot in life. They suffer, and thus, so do we." Isa felt the woman tremble. "I told you, the Maker never gave me dominion over the people. He simply told me to help them."

Young Brokk began to walk away, but stopped when she spoke again.

"I know what you have been doing." As she said the words, memories that were not her own crowded Isa's mind. Unfamiliar faces began to appear, begging her to remove something so small Isa had to squint to make them out. Tiny shards of glass, grains the size of sand rested in the corners of their eyes, nearly too small to see. Embedded in the skin, they looked like tiny crystals waiting to catch the light.

Isa gasped, and though she couldn't see her own body, her hands flew to her eyes. To her horror, she could feel them there in her face as well. Before she could dwell on the horrible discovery, her host spoke again.

"These people are not your puppets! I have seen the glass you have begun to inflict upon the servants. They came to me, begging me to remove them while you were gone! I love you more than anything in the world, my son, but I cannot allow you to finish this."

"I have inflicted nothing! By doing this, I will save them from themselves!"

"By controlling them, you will take away what makes them most human!" Isa heard herself shout back. They stood there for an immeasurable time, and as they stood, mother and son, Isa felt an unnamable pain fill her body, so intense it was nearly crippling, as though lightning had streaked across her muscles and lit everything on fire. It was a moment before she realized that sorrow was what plagued her, a sadness unfamiliar because it was one she hadn't yet experienced. Isa suddenly understood that the woman whose eyes through which she now looked was feeling the pain of losing her son. Though he stood before her, they both knew what he was about to do, and that she would be forced to stop him.

"Brokk," she pleaded, caressing his face with her hand the way she had every day when he was a babe. "I beg you, give yourself time to heal." As she held his cheek, a raw, vulnerable expression crossed his face, making him look very much like the little boy she loved so much. "Promise me you won't do this."

"Father always said that I should be a man of my word," he finally said.

"Yes," she whispered. "He did."

And without a word, he leaned forward to kiss her on the cheek before walking out the door. Tears rushed down her face as she watched him go, and the crippling pain that had begun in her heart moved outward until she was forced to kneel on the dirty ground. She stayed that way for a long time, unable to move.

"Vidar," she finally called out, her voice so raspy it was nearly inaudible.

An older manservant appeared. "Yes, my lady?"

"Tell the servants to leave. They shall not pack their belongings, nor shall they prepare for a journey. There isn't time."

"But my lady." The man's cornflower blue eyes were wide with fear. "What about you?"

"I cannot leave my son. But I can stop him."

As soon as her servant had hastened to obey, the Glass Queen had closed her eyes and raised her hands before her. The power the Maker had given her so long ago still rushed strong through her blood, and though Bronkendol's power had never equaled hers, he was strong enough that her last spell would require all that she had. Not that it mattered. She would never be able to live in a world without him anyway.

The Glass Queen pulled in a deep, even breath before she began her work. Her hands moved in slow, steady circles. The light they created was nearly invisible at first, but began to glow more and more brightly as she continued. Streaks of violet, like webs, began to fill the air, hanging brilliantly as she wove them together. As she worked, she hummed a haunting melody. It sounded to Isa like a dangerous lullaby.

"Sleep well, my son," she murmured, as though telling a child goodnight. Then she paused for only a moment before clapping her hands together so hard that it hurt. The web-like streaks collapsed, and when she opened her hands again, a glowing, purple orb rose and floated toward the door. The woman stood and followed it, pausing once before leaving the room to stroke her favorite cherry tree fondly. She would miss this place of sun and life.

As she re-entered the castle and began walking toward her destination, fewer and fewer servants filled the grand halls, and by the time she neared her son's room, she could feel in her heart that the magnificent glass palace was finally empty. But the only person that mattered, she tried to reassure herself, was still there.

She finally came to a door that was partly ajar. How many happy hours had she spent rocking and singing to him here? After his father had died, how many times had they wept together upon the hearth? She paused at the entrance, running her fingers over the glass carvings of elk and does, the first carvings he had ever attempted, and she smiled as she remembered how proud he was of the does with their stick legs and the elk with their disproportionate antlers.

Inside, the violet orb glowed softly and steadily above the young man.

Bronkendol was stretched out upon his bed, his hands peacefully at his sides, the forced sleep making breaths slow and even. She sat on the edge of his bed and gently pushed a copper curl from his face. Then just as she had done countless times all those centuries ago, she sat upon the floor, crossed her arms over the edge his bed, and nestled her head upon them.

"Sweet dreams, my son," she whispered. "I will be here, just as I have always been."

Heavy steps interrupted the bitter serenity of the moment, and Isa startled. The cool air made her realize that tears had been running down her face, but the vision wouldn't allow her to leave just yet.

"Isabelle? You must leave that room immediately!" Brokk called.

But still, she could only see the son through the eyes of the mother. The Glass Queen uttered a few words in a tongue Isa didn't recognize, and she, too, began to drift away. It occurred to Isa that the mother had fallen asleep at the bedside of her son, rather than in this dark, cloaked room.

"Isabelle!" Brokk shouted this time, losing the patience he had always kept before. "You cannot be in there! You don't know what you are seeing!"

Just before the vision faded completely, Isa heard the Glass Queen's voice once more.

"You must stop him, young one. Even if it means you must finish what I could not bring myself to do. I love him too much to let him commit such evil."

The Glass Queen had kept just enough strength to summon Isa. And now, with a final breath, she was gone.

As the vision left Isa, and she began to use her own eyes again, the large door flew open. Brokk, along with two of the glass giants Isa had seen in her vision, burst through the door. Before she could run, one easily managed to pin her arms behind her back.

"What did she show you?" Brokk shouted. When Isa didn't answer, he grabbed her by the shoulders and yanked her forward, making her cry out when the guard didn't let go. "What did you see?"

Though it hurt, Isa somehow managed to keep silent. One of the first lessons Ever had taught her after their wedding was that knowledge is power. So when she still didn't answer, Brokk grew even more agitated. "Take her to my work chamber," he barked at the guards. "Apparently, I have run out of time."

Panic filled Isa as the guards carried her down the glass steps, and suddenly the feeling of falling through the glass tower didn't bother her at all. "My husband will find me!" she shouted at him, struggling with all her might. It was no use, however, for the glass guards were as solid as the castle itself.

In desperation, Isa begged the Fortress, pleaded with it to give her just enough power to flee. But helpless she remained for the rest of the way down the tower, and then back down to the workshop where she had eaten.

Instead of dropping her at the table or in one of the chairs near the door, they moved to the back of the room, an area Isa had not seen before. The two guards sat her down in a heavy, metal chair that faced a large furnace as wide as she was tall. Heat blasted her as one guard turned to feed the flames, while the other shackled her wrists and ankles to the chair.

Isa wept as she struggled in vain against the chains, praying that Ever would find her. He had promised he would protect her.

He had promised.

I PROMISE

"*I* know what you want to do!" Isa warned the enchanter as the glass guards retreated to the door. "And I swear to you, I will not be a part of it!"

"My dear," Bronkendol said in a patient voice, as he studied a set of thin poles that leaned against the furnace. "You cannot even control the power that is within you. I advise caution when making oaths so easily." He glanced back at her. "Your struggle with the Fortress's legendary fire is not the secret you think it is."

"He *will* find me," she said, ignoring his jab. But the tremor of her voice was far less convincing than she had hoped, even to her. "Besides." She licked her lips, which had grown dry from the furnace's heat. "If my fire is dying, I cannot see how you plan to use me."

"You need not worry about such trifles." He finally chose the pole in the center. When he lifted it, she could see that it was hollow, a long tube made of steel. It looked unlike any weapon Isa had ever seen. There were no points or sharp edges on any part of it. "When I speak to the hearts of the people, there will be no more war. When they have sickness, I will come. Where there is hurt, I will heal."

He began to turn the pole over and over again in his right hand, while rubbing it against the palm of his left as it turned. As he did so, a thin layer of what looked like wet glass began to appear, thickening as he continued to turn the pole around his hand.

"You cannot touch everyone," she warned. "You have only seen a very few in Rafael's court. The monarchs may follow him, but the armies will never listen. They will fight you. Hundreds will die."

"Thousands," he said, continuing to spin the pole, the lump of molten glass nearly as thick as his thumb. "But in the end, mankind will survive." He glanced up at her for a brief moment, his eyes burning with intensity. "And from the way men plunder and kill now, nothing is guaranteed our children. At least I can save some." The glob of thick, gooey glass was now nearly the diameter of Isa's fist. He removed his hand, but continued to hold it inches away from the still-spinning pole. Then he leaned forward, his eyes suddenly kinder, bright as though he were sharing a delightful secret.

"You have the chance to give life to this world, Isabelle! Just imagine it!" His voice dropped to a whisper. "No one else's child must pointlessly die."

The words of his mother came back to Isa from the vision, and they were on her tongue before she could consider their wisdom.

"We're not gods, Bronkendol."

His ancient name felt strange as it left her tongue, and Isa suddenly wished she could take it back. If she had wanted to delay him, those were surely not the words to do it with. Where was Ever?

Bronkendol had frozen in place, and Isa couldn't tell whether his expression was one of fury or fear. She hurried to distract him, searching for something else to say. Sweat poured down her back and neck as the flames of the furnace continued to grow. Even the liquid glass was giving off heat.

"Just as well," she stammered. "I could not give it to you even if I wanted to." A stupid thing to say, but it was all she could think of.

In one last attempt at conjuring her strength, Isa's fingers dug into the sharp edges of the chair's arms until they burned. The air had grown disgustingly thick as the heat continued to build, and Isa pressed even harder into the chair. But her fingers wrought nothing

"The Maker has not abandoned you, child."

Bronkendol's words took her by surprise, and for a moment, Isa stopped struggling. He nodded at her shackled wrists. "I see your fear. You think the Maker and your Fortress have deserted you, withdrawing the power you should have commanded by now."

Tears stung her eyes as she stared at him, fighting back his words. The Fortress abandoned no one, Garin had assured her. The problem was with her. She had not fulfilled her duties. Somehow, she had overlooked something she was supposed to do. She shook her head so hard her vision swam, clumps of her hair sticking to her sweaty face.

"No, I do not believe that!"

"But you do," he said. "I can see it in your eyes. You wonder why you cannot control the fire, why Ever is not here now." He paused. "Why you are not yet with child."

Against her will, the tears began to flow freely, and with them, the pain she had been holding back. Anger, fear, longing, and confusion swept through her, and with them the memories of all she had dreamed for, and how all those dreams had died.

She was not a mother. Her husband had not come to save her. And worst of all, the Fortress, the home she had grown to love more than life, had somehow relinquished the life-giving fire that should have burned hot in her soul. And now she was weak, captive, and very, very alone. Not even the Fortress's little breeze had accompanied her into this sweltering room.

"I promise." He gently lifted her chin and stared into her face, a tear running down his own cheek. "Your purpose is not gone. He was only preparing you. Your purpose is here. Your gift will be to the entire world, not only to your husband or even to Destin. The power of your heart will be for everyone."

"How?" she whispered. She wouldn't be able to delay him much longer, and suddenly, Isa realized, she didn't have the will to do so either.

"With my help," he said. "Now, I'm so sorry, but this will hurt quite a bit." Without waiting for Isa to reply, he lifted the pole and placed the molten glass against her chest, just above her heart.

Isa's vision exploded as excruciating pain wracked her body. Blistering white heat made her blood pulse as tendrils of white lightning lit every muscle within her. Her fingers, wrists, elbows, ankles, and knees felt as though they had been smashed to pieces with mallets. *Please,* she begged silently as she wept, *give me strength one more time. Let me know I am not alone! You said you would never leave me!*

But there was no answer. The agony only dragged on. Anger flooded her enough that she was able to force her eyes open, and to her shock, the thin ball of glass that was pressed against her chest did not burn her skin. Instead, it was alight with streaks of violet that stretched out in every direction. As she watched it, willing herself not to pass out from the pain, the glass turned the color of blood. Then, to her amazement and horror, all of her anger was gone. Every last bit of it.

Instead, the glass began to change to gold, the color of the sun.

"No!" Isa cried as she realized joy was beginning to slip as well. Despite the terror of the last few days, it was still there, hiding beneath her sorrow and frustration. Sensations of pleasure took her as she felt the joy rise like cream to the top. The way Ever's lips had lingered upon her own at their wedding, the love in her mother's embrace, the way her brother watched over her, even from a distance. The hunger in her husband's eyes when he had seen her in Gigi's ridiculous ball gowns. The feeling of belonging when the Fortress had welcomed her home. The hope she had felt when Master Claude had told her she should soon expect a baby of her own.

An even greater despair took her as she watched the golden joy slide from her heart into the liquid glass. As soon as the gold had been devoured, more colors followed. Moss green for jealousy, Jadzia's attempted conquests coming to mind. Guilt the tint of mulberry, frustration the shade of rust, and even the cobalt of sorrow were painstakingly torn from her chest and devoured by the pulsing, molten glass. Finally, only one emotion remained.

"You can't . . . you can't have that one," she gasped. "Please . . . just let me keep it."

"I'm sorry," he said sympathetically, "but it won't be complete without them all. Besides, this is the one that gives you more strength than all of the others combined."

"No." She shook her head pathetically. "I will not let you take it!"

"Just let it go," he crooned. "Without it, no one will ever be able to hurt you again."

Isa considered that. It was true. Without it, she would never again have the cobalt blue of sorrow, the mulberry purple of guilt, or the blood red of anger born of pain. But then, she knew, she would never be able to give Ever the life she had vowed to share at their wedding; she would never again bask in the peace of the Fortress's glistening marble walls. Without it, she would never again be whole.

"He hasn't come for you," the enchanter said softly.

Something inside of Isa broke. At first it felt like the smallest of cracks, the kind that allowed trickles of water to drip through the walls, but nothing more. But the crack did not remain small, and before she knew it, had widened into a chasm within her. As the glass continued to turn in his hands, the other colors that mingled within the burning glass disappeared, washed out by the flood the color of a dusty rose.

It was done.

Isa watched stupidly as a sad smile came over the enchanter's face. Carefully he lifted the glob of burning glass from her chest, and Isa exhaled deeply as the pressure released her. She felt him cup her jaw in his hand the way her father used to do, and he softly kissed her hair. Without lifting his face, he said, "I am so sorry. But it will be better this way. I promise."

Then he righted himself and walked over to the only work table that was completely clear of all clutter, and began to roll the glowing ball of soft glass against its metal surface. As he continued to roll it back and forth with his left hand, he grabbed another long metal tool, flat this time, about the width of three fingers, and pressed it against the glob of glass.

Hours passed as he shaped it, but Isa found that she didn't care. She watched him until the daylight of the glass walls faded, and the orange of the giant furnace began to light the room instead.

Finally, he held up his workmanship. It was a little glass mirror, just like the one he had shown her the day before. There was no handle, just the circle of glass and its frame. Waving his hand over it, then whispering a few words, the enchanter watched with a fervor Isa couldn't understand. He sucked in a quick breath as it showed not a reflection, but another scene entirely. Ever stood before Garin in the Tower of Annals. Isa knew she should feel an overwhelming relief to know her husband was safe and back at home, but when she searched herself, she realized she felt nothing. The enchanter waved his hand over the mirror once more, and this time she saw Launce standing in Rafael's court.

"Oh my!" Bronkendol startled as though he'd forgotten she was there. "I apologize, my dear. You need to rest." With that, he placed the mirror in his belt, and helped her up to her room. Every bone in Isa's body screamed, but she found that she had no desire to tell him. As soon as she was tucked into her bed, still in her clothes from earlier that day, he left and returned with a steaming bowl of broth.

"It will be all better from here," he promised as he lifted the spoon to her mouth. Without thinking, Isa parted her lips and swallowed, the soup scalding her throat as it went down. "One day you will see that it was worth the sacrifice."

But Isa didn't care about seeing that it was for the best. All she wanted to do was sleep. Soon enough, he left her alone, and within moments, and for the first time since she could remember, Isa fell asleep without wishing for anything more than the very bed she laid in.

~

Isa awoke the next morning long after the sun had risen, but didn't bother to stir. She wasn't sure why it was so hard to rouse herself, but she didn't have long to wonder. The enchanter was back again, this time with a bowl of warm biscuits and fruit.

"Now that you're finished eating," he said as he rose and went to the wardrobe, where he pulled out the thick fur coat he had given her the first day and wrapped it around her, "we must get you warm. You have a long journey ahead of you."

Isa allowed him to lead her to a long set of stables that were directly attached to the castle.

"Up you go," he said, getting down on his knee so she could climb up. Isa's limbs still ached as though someone had beaten her with a bludgeon, but she said nothing, simply grimacing once as she mounted. As soon as she was firmly on, he took her horse's reins and led her to the main stable door.

"You are going home now," he said. "The horse knows the way. I've placed rations in the saddlebags, so you shouldn't go hungry." When she didn't answer him, he took her hand. It shook just slightly as he patted it and then held on. "I have been thinking, and I've decided that the fate of the others should not be your own. You have given far too much for that."

As he spoke the strange words, a wave of warmth moved from the hand he held to her face, and Isa felt a sharp pain that stretched from her already aching heart to her eyes. Eyes open wide in pain, she watched as two pieces of glass fell into his other outstretched hand, along with a few drops of blood.

"I promise," he patted her leg, "you will make it home. And I never break my promises."

33

MERCHANT'S SON

*I*t crossed Launce's mind more than once that he could vomit on the foot of one of the guards as they dragged him through the palace. Inwardly, he cursed Ever for sending his horse back at the same speed they'd left Cobren the first time. It wasn't natural for a man to speed along, racing the wind for hours on end.

"Sire," one of the guards bowed while the other held him tightly, "we found him in the border woods."

Launce braced himself for another round of the nausea that was sure to hit as he lifted his head. He was in Rafael's throne room once again, just before the dais. Rafael stood, but Olivia and Queen Monica stayed seated. Launce wanted to search the princess's face to see what she was thinking, but had to drop his head once more so he wouldn't be sick.

"Do you not recognize who this is?" Rafael's voice was indignant. "This is King Everard's brother-in-law, and my daughter's intended. Unhand him at once!"

Launce could feel the guards hesitate, but finally they let go. And though the drop was rough, laying on the cool tiles helped him get his bearings. As he rubbed his aching head, Launce wondered if he had heard correctly. Was he still supposedly the king's successor? Rafael had been livid with Everard the last time they'd parted. Why the sudden change of heart? And where was Bronkendol? Then Launce spotted him, standing placidly behind the throne.

"King Everard," Launce paused, wincing as he stood, "tasked me with acting as his regent while he is otherwise occupied." There, he'd said it. Everard had made him practice for hours the day before.

"Of course!" Rafael walked down the steps as he spoke, motioning to someone behind Launce. "Davin, I want you to accompany young Master

Launce to his old chambers. Bring him something to eat, and make sure you're available to him for anything he might need."

As Davin nodded and turned to lead him to his new chambers, Launce threw one last look at the enchanter, and then at Olivia. Olivia's eyes were wide, although he couldn't read her expression clearly. Brokk . . . or rather, Bronkendol, looked unnerved. His hair stuck out in different directions, and his expression, for once, wasn't utterly calm and collected. Actually, Launce decided, the enchanter looked exhausted.

Once he was in the room by himself, Launce realized that Everard's plan for him to send the messenger birds wasn't going to work. Launce was fully aware that Davin was only there to spy on him. He'd even heard the door lock after Davin had stepped out. Surely Everard must have expected some sort of precautions to be taken against him. What did his brother-in-law really expect him to accomplish by being here?

His spirits lifted a bit when a plate of rolls, fruit, and pastries was delivered. As he devoured them, Launce tried to imagine who he might turn to for help. With Davin following him wherever he went, learning more about the enchanter's plans would be impossible. But with a partner, he might stand a chance, even if it was only enough time to send a single messenger bird to the Fortress to tell Garin that the enchanter was back.

Who could he trust though? If Everard was right about the shards of glass affecting everyone, even Norbert would have been touched. Not that they knew exactly what the shards were for, but, Launce decided, he would prefer not to take the chance.

That's when it hit him. The hill. Everard had said that those in the stands had been showered with the glass, but there was one person who had not been in the stands because *she* had been on the hill.

He would have to find a way to get her alone, away from listening ears. That in itself would be a monumental task.

Although Isa was grown and married, she was hardly ever left alone at the Fortress. Between her lady-in-waiting, curious courtiers, Garin, the ever-present kitchen mistress, who was rarely actually in the kitchen, and Everard himself, Launce realized he'd hardly seen his sister unaccompanied since the wedding. And she was a grown, married woman. As a young, unmarried princess, Olivia would be the last person in the palace they would ever allow him to be alone with. Launce smiled to himself, for if anyone knew how to lose her escorts, it would be her.

Launce walked back to the door and knocked. Sure enough, Davin was right there to answer immediately.

"I have a message for the princess," Launce said. From the look on Davin's face, it seemed that he was just as pleased with the princess's pending betrothal to Launce as her father had originally been.

"Very well. What would you to relay?"

"I would like to meet her in the garden. I have an important matter we need to discuss." After making sure the message was given to a runner, Launce allowed Davin to shut the door again. He needed to think anyway.

Launce knew he was taking quite a risk. But he couldn't think of any other way to get the princess alone. It had only been one week since they had met, and they'd only really had one full conversation. He suspected she would pick up on his hints, he hoped she would at least. But there was no way of knowing until he tried.

The queasy feeling returned to his stomach. He didn't have long to wait at least. Within minutes, the runner returned to report that the princess would meet him down in the courtyard garden. Launce walked as quickly as he could, which seemed to annoy Davin even more. Launce didn't care what the stuffy servant thought though. With every moment wasted, Isa could be enduring hunger, torture, or worse. Later, he promised himself, he could explain everything to Olivia . . . if she gave him the chance. For now, he just needed her to fall for his cruel trick.

As Launce reached the courtyard garden, his stomach leapt into his throat. Could he keep a straight face while he hurt her? Self-loathing briefly heated his cheeks as he wondered how many more decisions he would have to make that were similar to Everard's. It galled him to think that there was a reason his brother-in-law was so callous. Launce didn't have time to mull on it, however, because the princess was approaching him with her entourage.

"Your Highness," he said as he bowed. When he looked up, however, he nearly forgot what he had come to do. Her dark, shiny hair was swept to one side, where an orange-red desert rose had been pinned expertly beside her chin. In the weak late autumn sun, her skin was the color of wild honey, the kind that could be found in the untamed forest that lay north of Soudain. The sunset yellow of her dress made her round face glow like a warm summer day, and Launce found himself imagining her cheeks feeling like sunbeams to the touch. Blinking to regain his focus, he tried to settle on an expression that matched what he was about to say. He hoped, prayed that she would take the bait.

"Launce," she said, her eyes wide. "I'm glad to see that you've returned so soon. Did you find your sister? I have been sending up prayers for her since you left."

Launce nodded, not quite sure how to proceed. He offered his arm, and she took it as they turned and set about for a stroll through the garden.

"Well?" she prodded when he remained silent.

Launce took a deep breath. "Everard thinks he has a way to track her, but that isn't what I came out here to discuss." He paused, wishing she weren't so distractingly beautiful. "I . . . I've been thinking. And . . . I'm not convinced this life," he gestured at the finery of the garden around them, "is suitable for me." As soon as the words left his mouth, he wanted to kick himself.

A brief look of bitter disappointment flashed across her face before she recovered her poise. As he waited for her reply, he decided that he wanted to kick Everard as well. If it hadn't been for all the time spent around his dogged

360 | BRITTANY FICHTER

brother-in-law, he would never have dreamt up such a plan on his own. Even without being present, Everard was still in his head.

"I see." The princess was quick to move from pain to anger. Her hazelnut eyes flashed as she turned to look directly at him. Out of the corner of his eye, Launce saw the princess's escort and their accompanying guard share a small smile. Apparently, many people here liked him about as well as he liked them. "And why would that be?"

Launce shrugged, trying to keep up the act. "I was born a merchant's son. The mercantile has been in my family for three generations. It would hurt my father to die one day, knowing he had no one to pass it down to."

"And you did not consider this before you asked to compete for my hand?" Her words were ice. Launce opened his mouth to answer, but glanced back at their escorts first. She followed his eyes. "You will remain here," she snapped at them. "We will walk alone."

"Your Highness," her escort protested, fingering the ribbons of her bodice nervously. "It is uncustomary for a young woman such as yourself to be unescorted."

"The garden begins and ends here. Where on earth would I go?"

"I apologize, Princess." The guard stepped forward. "But I cannot allow you to go unattended. I am under strict orders from your father."

Launce felt his stomach, still weak from his midnight ride, do a flop. If the princess couldn't lose her guard, his whole plan might accomplish nothing aside from angering her.

"Then at least give me the dignity of walking where I cannot see you!"

Launce felt both hope and shame when he saw the resignation in the guard's mouth and the hints of angry tears in the princess's eyes. She and the guard continued to stare one another down for another long moment before the guard finally rolled his eyes. "If that is what you wish, then you will not see me."

Without waiting for Launce to offer his arm again, the princess grabbed his right sleeve and began to walk as quickly down the path as she could, dragging him behind her.

"Olivia," he whispered, "I'm sorry for deceiving you, but there is something I must tell you."

"You should be sorry," she said, not slowing for a second.

Launce glanced up at the three white palace walls surrounding the court-yard. The palace wasn't very tall, only three stories, but the hedges were short enough to allow busybodies to see them from the third story, had they wished to. Launce hoped no one was watching them from above now. He didn't have long to wonder, however, because without hesitating, the princess lifted her skirts in her free hand, and deftly stepped through an invisible break in the hedge, pulling him along with her.

As soon as they were through, Launce realized that they had not only left the maze-like courtyard, but that they had left the palace proper entirely, and were standing at the edge of the forest that filled the land behind it.

"Keep walking," Olivia said. "And while we do, I expect you to explain your dishonesty to the fullest."

"They'll think I've taken you," Launce said, frowning at the backside of the hedge.

"If you cannot give me a satisfactory explanation as to why you've deceived me, then yes, they will. If you can at least pacify me, then I might know a way to get you back unnoticed."

Clearly, she had done this before. Launce stared, dumbfounded, into her eyes, wishing more than ever to know what she was thinking. She was truly one of the most confusing people he had ever met. Perhaps his plan had worked too well. Gathering his thoughts, he shook his head and determined to explain himself, even if it meant he would have to clamp her mouth shut.

"We're not safe in the palace," he blurted out. "I was trying to find a way so that we could have a moment alone to speak. I need your help." As he spoke, her face lost some of its anger. Encouraged by her silence, he continued. "We think the enchanter, or the holy man, as your father calls him, is going to use her for her power somehow."

"How do you know?"

"Our Fortress Steward says she's more powerful than even she knows. But he isn't just using her. Everard thinks the enchanter plans to use everyone here too." As Launce went on to explain the slivers, he was sure she would deem him a fool. It sounded ridiculous as he spoke it.

To his surprise, however, she was slowly nodding as she stared at the ground. Before she could answer, low voices could be heard. Launce could just make out the low tenor of the guard's voice and the mouse-like squeak of Olivia's escort. Olivia grabbed his hand once more and began to drag him toward the west wing of the palace.

"It makes sense," she said in a low voice as they walked.

"It does?"

"Some of the servants have been complaining about their eyes hurting. Then my mother said the same thing. When I looked at my eyes, however, nothing was there. But how does he plan to use them?"

"Not even Everard knows, nor does he know how to remove them." Launce shook his head. "All *I* know is that we need to get Isa back. And that's why I needed you to get us alone."

"Wait." She stopped walking. "You said all of that because you knew I would find a way to get us alone?"

Launce dared a tight smile. "You're good at getting what you want."

They held one another's gaze for an immeasurable moment. Birds late to fly south chirped here and there, and the quiet chatter of the forest filled the silence left by their voices.

"Yes," she finally said in a small voice. "I am. I've had to be since the holy man came. Here, come this way." She held up a low branch so Launce could see a clearer path as they skirted the northern edge of the palace. Launce marveled at how lightly she stepped, and how she miraculously kept her skirts from tearing on the dry winter brambles that littered the forest floor.

"My father wasn't always the puppet he is now," she called back in a low voice. "You would never know it now from the way he flaunts the holy man's gift, but when the man first arrived after the rebellion was quelled, my father was cautious, suspicious even. This foreign man promised my father great power and stability for his kingdom. He would make his line even greater than the Fortiers of the Fortress, he promised. My father was hesitant. He was fond of King Rodrigue and his son.

"It was the continuance of small pockets of the rebels that eventually drove him to accept the holy man's help." Olivia shook her head, causing a tendril of silky hair to fall into her face. "When the holy man assured my father that he, of course, wouldn't harm the Fortier family, simply make my father's line their equal, my father finally accepted." She sighed. "It is little-known, but my father's health has been rapidly declining since the war. I'm afraid to think that all of this might be his attempt at providing for me."

Olivia paused and looked up into the gray of the afternoon light before looking directly back at Launce, her deep eyes searching his own. "I'm frightened, Launce. This man has changed my father into someone I do not recognize, and I fear that by the time my father's soul leaves this world, there will be nothing familiar left in the man or this kingdom." Still holding his gaze, she moved closer to him. The worry on her face stirred up a burning desire in Launce that he could not understand. Never had he wanted so desperately to protect someone that wasn't one of his own. Not even Blanchette had ever brought forth such a need. And yet, all he could do was stare back.

"I don't know why the holy man chose you," she said in a quiet voice. "Still, I can honestly say that for the first time since he arrived, I'm glad he did." She stepped so close that he could have leaned down and kissed her. "But I need to know whether you truly mean to take up the mantle of the Cobrien monarchy, or whether your words back in the courtyard were true. Because if they were truly a ruse, and you mean to stay, then I want no one else at my side. You are different from the others, and I admire that. However," her eyes darkened as she spoke, "if you *did* mean that you have no intention of marrying me and being king, then as soon as we return, I want you to pack your things and leave, and I never want to see you again as long as I live."

Launce stared at her, his mouth open, but no words could come. *They were a ruse*, he wanted to assure her. *I simply needed to speak with you alone!* But the truth weighed heavily upon his heart. For no matter how much he wanted to help her, Launce was still only a merchant's son. He had never wanted to be a courtier in Destin's own court, much less a king in someone else's. And even if he desired a crown of his own, what did he know of being a king? How could a commoner rule a country he hardly knew?

The longer Launce warred within himself, the more understanding dawned in the princess's eyes.

"I see," she said. Swallowing hard, she opened her mouth once more, and Launce dreaded hearing the words he knew would come.

Before she could speak, however, a distant moan sounded from somewhere deeper in the brush behind them. Without hesitation, Olivia took off toward the sound, and Launce followed as quickly as he could. Their chase took them over three small, wooded hills and a thin stream before they reached the source of the sound.

"Queen Kartek!" Olivia shrieked as she rushed down into the ravine. Launce followed, but more slowly. As soon as he saw where the southern queen lay, at the bottom of another small hill, it occurred to him how easy one could be ambushed at the bottom.

As he drew nearer, he could see that the queen was covered in blood. Her olive-green skirt and light cotton tunic were soaked with a dark red, and Launce's stomach lurched when he realized the spots of red were still growing on the queen's right side just above her hip.

"What happened?" Olivia cradled the older queen's head while Launce watched stupidly, too stunned to know what to do.

"My . . . my necklace," the queen gasped. She pointed a shaking hand at Launce's feet, and when he looked down, he realized he was standing just above a round pink jewel, inlaid in gold. Slowly, he bent to pick it up out of the dirt and twigs, but Olivia was faster. She snatched it up and placed it in the queen's shaking hands. The longer the queen held the jewel, the less she trembled. Launce felt himself let out a sigh of relief as a bit of color began to return to the queen's face, and the red stopped seeping into her clothes.

"I was searching to see if Everard was right," she whispered. "To see if Bronk-endol truly was the one who stole your sister."

Launce only then realized that she was talking directly to him.

"He . . . he must have realized what I was doing, for when I returned to my chambers, a maid was there, holding a dagger of glass. She came upon me with it, and I was not fast enough to escape!" She paused to pant, and Launce was again aware of how easy it would be for someone to attack them in the low ravine.

"We need to get you to safety," he said. "Do you think you can walk soon?"

The queen flashed him the shadow of a patient smile before groaning once again as she held the necklace to her side.

"My powers are strong, boy, but not that strong. It will be days before I am ready to walk." She coughed. "If it were not for the sound of your steps, the girl would have killed me here. You frightened her away."

"I will call the guards!" Olivia began to stand, but Launce grabbed her wrist.

"Don't you find it odd that no one noticed her being chased through the palace with a knife? Something is wrong here." Launce recalled the strange slivers of glass Ever had told him about. It was quite possible the enchanter was already at work. He turned to the queen.

"Do you by chance have any pieces of glass—"

"In my eyes?" She cut him off and nodded. "I did, but after Everard sent me a message telling me about it, I was able to pull them out." Olivia looked at him as though he were mad, but Launce knelt in the dirt beside the queen.

"How?"

"With more pain than I ever care to suffer again. It was only because of my gift that I was able to heal enough to pull them out in the first place." It was only when he had drawn closer that Launce noticed the queen's eyes had just a bit of dried blood about their edges. He inwardly grimaced at the thought of what she must have done to get the glass out. It was better to focus on the problems at hand instead.

"Do you have any guards or servants you trust that could escort you home?"

"Yes. Call for Apu, my eunuch. Do not tell the servants what you need him for. Only bring him to me here."

Launce looked up at Olivia. For the first time, he saw real fear in her eyes. The confidence was gone, and she suddenly looked very young as she bit her lip.

"Olivia, I need you to go for help. Find Apu and bring him back."

"But I want to stay with Queen Kartek." Her words were as bold as ever, but there was uncertainty in her voice.

He shook his head. "It's not safe for you to remain here. I need you to go back where you'll be safer." She opened her mouth to protest again, but he stopped her. "I promise, I will explain later. But now I need you to go."

She studied him hard for a moment longer before grabbing one of his hands and squeezing it. "I cannot understand why you fear taking the crown so much. You are the bravest man I know," she whispered before darting back up the hill.

34

KING

*L*aunce heard the voices before he could see them, but there was no time to try and conceal either himself or the queen.

" . . .Still don't understand why you couldn't just tell us where he was from the beginning," Rafael said as he and about a dozen others crested the hill. Olivia sent Launce an apologetic look as she answered her father.

"I thought you would be busy with the banquet preparations."

"When you and Launce didn't emerge from the walkway, Alejandro came to get me." Rafael frowned at his daughter, then at Launce. Launce felt himself blush under the scrutiny of the king, but Kartek spoke for the first time. Her voice was still weak, but she looked much more confident than Launce felt.

"They came to help me, Sire. They heard me calling for help." As she spoke, a tall man emerged from the crowd, pushing his way through. He had darker skin than anyone Launce had ever seen, and he looked nearly as muscled as Everard. If his physique didn't intimidate, however, the glower he wore certainly would. As he drew nearer, Launce also noticed the dried blood at the corners of his eyes as well. Apparently, Kartek hadn't only removed her glass. Immediately, the big man knelt down and gently scooped the queen up in his arms.

"Who did this to you?"

"I was walking, and I tripped and fell upon a sharp piece of wood."

Launce exchanged a glance with Olivia. Surely the others wouldn't buy such a blatant lie, but it was obvious the queen didn't want to discuss what had happened in front of everyone. He wondered why until he spotted another familiar face in the crowd.

Bronkendol now wore an ice-blue robe lined with a thick fur trimming along the arms, neck, and bottom edging. He seemed to feel Launce's eyes, and turned to smile at him as though nothing was wrong, as though he were actually delighted to see him.

"I think it best if we return home, my queen," Apu said.

Kartek looked from Apu's face directly into Launce's, and he knew what she was telling him. Once she was gone, he would be alone. Everyone else, even Norbert, Cerise, and the other guards could not be trusted now that the enchanter was back and everyone had the slivers. Well, Launce thought to himself, all but one. He would not be alone after all.

"Now that we know the queen will be seen to," the king turned to his servant, "I would like you to escort my daughter and young Launce to the throne room. I have an announcement to make."

Everyone began to walk back toward the palace, including Olivia, who was now too surrounded for any more real conversation to take place. Launce, however, held back. He noticed the enchanter pausing as well. Bronkendol's eyes never left his face, and it more than unnerved him. Launce leaned over and whispered as fast as he could before the enchanter could make his way down into the ravine with them.

"Don't go home."

"And why not?" Apu demanded.

"I don't think they mean for you to leave the continent alive. Our guards and servants should have departed yesterday. If you follow them, you should make it safely to Destin's borders. The Fortress should protect you there while you heal." Knowing her guard wouldn't listen, Launce pleaded directly with the queen. "I know our steward will want your counsel to help find my sister."

Kartek looked at Apu for a long moment. Launce wished they would hurry. The enchanter was still watching them intently, and Launce knew they didn't have much longer.

"He is right," Kartek finally said. The look of resentment never left Apu's eyes, but when she spoke, he simply inclined his head once toward his queen. The queen looked back at Launce again, her eyes probing. "I have not known you as well as I should have liked," she said, "but I can tell you now that this enchanter is more powerful than anything you have ever seen or sensed. He is playing a game with you that I do not understand. Take care."

"Master Launce," Bronkendol called out from halfway down the ravine. "I was hoping we could converse on our way back to the palace."

Launce gave the queen a short nod and bow before standing and heading reluctantly back up the hill. Bronkendol opened his mouth, but Launce cut him off.

"I know exactly who you are, and I have nothing to say to you." Launce stalked by him.

"I am truly sorry about the wine incident," Bronkendol called as he began to follow him. Launce swung around to face the enchanter. In that moment, he didn't care how powerful the man supposedly was.

"You abduct my sister, and you think I care about being put to sleep?"

"I swear, you will have your sister back. I was only trying to help—"

"Trying to help?" Launce shook his head in disgust. "By stealing her from her husband and family?"

"Your sister is dying, Launce."

Launce stopped short. A sudden dizziness filled him, but he forced his hands to stay steady.

"You're lying," he said. The conviction wasn't there though.

Bronkendol shook his head, a small, sad smile on his face. "I wish I were. Your sister is a . . . a magnificent creature. She is more like my mother was than anyone I've met. But the light in your sister's eyes has been dying, and you know it."

Launce wanted to shout, to strike out at someone. His sister wasn't dying. But he caught the enchanter's gray eyes, and as he glared into them, he knew he couldn't deny the possibility at least. As much as it killed him to admit it, Launce had known it for a long time. Perhaps, he thought, it was the reason he had accepted such a ludicrous offer when she had begged him to come with them. Her eyes had dulled too much, and he wanted to see her just that much more. Of course, that didn't mean he trusted Bronkendol any more now than before.

"And what do you plan to do about it?" Launce asked, hoping the enchanter wouldn't mistake his question for enthusiasm.

Bronkendol opened a side door of the palace. They entered one of the winding, back hallways. He suspected Bronkendol had chosen this door on purpose to extend their time alone.

"It is already done. I cannot be sure that it will work. To be honest, it has never been done before. But if does," he looked into Launce's eyes, "I promise, she will be returned to your family soon."

"And Everard?" Launce wondered if the enchanter knew of his brother-in-law's scheme to attack the enchanter's own home. Probably. It wasn't as though anyone expected Everard to sit and wait for Isa at home.

To his surprise, however, Bronkendol only swallowed and said in a low voice, "I fear we will not have need to worry about that."

A cold feeling settled over Launce. "Why?"

"The king will make everything clear once we arrive."

They didn't speak again until they were in the throne room. Now that he wasn't feeling so ill from the ride, Launce noticed that all signs of the week's festivities had been taken down. Instead, the room looked now as Launce assumed it always did. Orange banners hung from the ceiling with the Cobrien royal crest upon them in gold. Under the largest banner, the king and his family stood upon the dais. Launce and the enchanter found places to stand at the dais's foot, against the wall that backed the thrones. Launce tried to see Olivia better, but she was facing the crowd.

The number of people in the room took Launce by surprise. As he studied them, he realized that they weren't just Cobrien citizens, but all of the guests from the betrothal celebration were still there as well. It was odd, considering the contest had been won two days earlier. But it seemed that most foreign dignitaries had simply stayed put. Some new faces had even appeared.

Rafael stood, and the noise of the people died down immediately. Compared to the pomp of the week before, everything felt suddenly very informal to Launce, and he realized it made him somewhat uncomfortable, though he couldn't say why. "I apologize for the strange turn of events. I had desired to see my daughter and her suitor ceremonially betrothed by now." Launce stiffened. It would have been nice for Everard to tell him the betrothal would be so soon, considering he wasn't supposed to have been betrothed in the first place. The king continued. "But put your fears to rest. Everything will be explained now.

"First, however, I have some tragic news." Rafael turned to look directly at Launce. "You may have heard the rumor that Queen Isabelle of Destin disappeared two days ago." How anyone could have missed the scene Everard had caused was beyond Launce. Many must have been unaware, however, for a murmur of unease rose up from the crowd. Rafael shook his head and held out his hands in what looked like an attempt to calm the people. "I have now confirmed that Queen Isabelle is indeed ill, but she is not missing. She is simply in the care of our holy man." With that, he gestured at the enchanter. Looking solemn, Bronkendol walked slowly up to the dais, where he joined the king.

"It is true. I have the queen in my care, but if it is the Maker's will, she will fully recover."

"I fear, though," Rafael spoke again, "that I do not have such good news of her husband."

The room went deathly still. So did Launce. How could the king have news about him already? Launce had only left early that morning. The silence began to stretch, and frustration welled up within him. He wanted to run up the dais and shake the king until the news spilled out. Why did Rafael look so pale and shaken? Why was he suddenly so still? Everard couldn't be dead. Launce wouldn't accept that.

"King Everard was a dear friend of mine," Rafael said hoarsely. Launce could feel the blood drain from his face as a tear rolled down the king's wide, weathered face. "I am sorry to say that in his fear, he set out to find his wife early this morning, before the holy man could tell him what he was about. I have just received word that the young king was found dead after riding into a blizzard in the upper pass of Destin's northern mountains."

Launce felt as though someone had punched him in the gut. He had not realized until that moment how much he had come to rely on his insufferable brother-in-law. Despite his awful sense of superiority and unrelenting fierceness of character, Launce had come to see that Everard undeniably loved his sister. The wild panic on Everard's face after Isa had disappeared had been proof of that. Launce had never seen such ferocity and fear mixed together in one. Surely there had to be a mistake. Garin would never use a bird messenger to announce such a thing, would he? And yet, a bird was the only way anyone would have received the news so quickly.

Launce's head was spinning. Unfortunately, before he had time to gather himself, he realized that Rafael and Bronkendol were both looking at him again.

"I have one more announcement to make," Rafael said softly. The crowd quieted again, but it took longer this time. When they were finally silent, the king gestured for Launce to join them. Launce didn't remember telling his feet to move, but somehow he found himself standing at the top of the dais just beside the king. Rafael placed a heavy hand upon Launce's left shoulder.

"Although Queen Isabelle should indeed heal, our holy man says that she will not be strong enough to handle the duties of a ruler for a long time, perhaps never again. It is with great sorrow and yet, with hope as well, that I wish you to meet the next two rulers of great Fortress of Destin."

Launce gaped at the king. Was he insane?

The king ignored Launce's look and instead, pushed Launce and Olivia to the front of the dais. "I present to you the future King Launce Marchand of Soudain, and my daughter, future Queen Olivia Edite Raquel Rocha of Cintilante Areia, Cobren. May their union be blessed with much prosperity and many children."

Strained conversation broke out amongst the people. Some bowed or curtsied, while others simply looked angry or afraid. Launce could only look over at Olivia, and for the first time, he knew exactly what she was thinking. Her wide brown eyes and strange pallor told him that she was just as terrified as he.

35

PRISON OF PRIVILEGE

*A*fter Rafael's bold announcement about crowning Launce and Olivia king and queen of the Fortress, the enchanter made an even more brazen statement to the crowd.

"As of now, if you would please be so kind as to return to your chambers and prepare to leave immediately. We all shall soon make the journey to the Fortress together in order to witness this momentous occasion of two countries joining blood."

The crowd erupted with protests, questions, and all other sorts of cacophony. Launce stood, still too stunned to move as he watched the chaos unfold.

"My men and women have journeyed far enough to come here! We will not be continuing on any further," one king called out.

A queen from one of the eastern regions also called loudly, "I have duties to attend to at home! This nonsense has gone on for long enough."

"My liege only allowed me time to come for the tournament. I am not at liberty to extend it!" When the third protester spoke, Launce realized it was Sir Randolph, the foreign knight who had saved him from Sir Absalom in the stables.

Neither the king nor the enchanter responded to their protests, only watched as though measuring the people's reactions. Sir Absalom also looked around them, and when he caught Launce's gaze, Launce knew exactly what the knight was thinking. Would more blood be shed here today? Launce wanted to speak with him, but it would have been impossible to leave the dais without Rafael or Bronkendol noticing.

As the crowd continued to protest, Bronkendol pulled something small from his robe. He brought it to his mouth and began to whisper into it. Launce couldn't hear what the enchanter said, but he could see the thin bursts of blue and violet light begin to glimmer in the eyes of those around him. Everyone but him and Olivia.

Launce watched in amazement as the people fell silent and looked at Bronkendol with trusting eyes. Light glimmered from the corner of each eye with an eerie glow, but that wasn't what Launce found so strange. Instead, he was hit with a strong sense of familiarity. As he looked around him, he couldn't find its source. Olivia wasn't far off, but this sensation went far beyond what he knew of the princess. In fact, it wasn't coming from a single person at all. It was coming from the blue light that shone from the people's eyes.

It was Isa's power. Everard had said the enchanter's power influenced glass, but Launce would have known the feeling of his sister's power anywhere. It was the power of the heart, Everard had said. Somehow, the enchanter was using Isa's gift.

A new understanding of the enchanter's true strength dawned on Launce. How did one steal the power of another? Isa wouldn't have given it to him willingly, of that Launce was sure. What did this man want? And why wasn't the Fortress stopping him? And if the Fortress wasn't, why did Launce think he even stood a chance?

As if there hadn't been enough confusion already, the room filled with black and orange coats as Rafael's soldiers dispersed into the crowd. Not a single party was without a uniformed body nearby.

"I have assigned an escort for each party." Rafael spoke again, his eyes also glimmering violet and blue. "Your escort will accompany you to your chambers and then guide you to our designated meeting place so we can begin our journey soon. We will take our leave on the morrow."

Before Launce could consider what this meant, a heavy guard stepped up onto the dais and addressed him. "Master Launce." He bowed, but the gesture was shallow, and his words were stiff. "I will escort you to your chambers now. We will be leaving shortly." Light glimmered in the guard's eyes as well.

Back in his chambers, Launce threw his last pair of trousers into his pathetic sack with as much force as he could. As he thought of his sister, a shiver ran up his spine. If the enchanter was back, where was Isa? What had happened to her? While Bronkendol had been right about the fire in her eyes dulling, Launce didn't for a second trust the man to keep her safe, nor did he believe that Everard had died in a storm. There had been too many half-truths already.

Launce was herded out to the clearing that surrounded the stables, just like everyone else. It was disconcerting to see so many kings, queens, diplomats, and even knights being ordered about. The majority of the western kingdoms were ruled by the people who surrounded him. Many stood outside their fancy carriages, though a few, such as the knights, stood beside their horses. Most of the servants looked as though they would walk.

Launce found his horse, and was directed by the guard to lead it to the front of the throng. Despite the chaos erupting around him, he was glad to have this horse beside him. The monstrous animals that had been gifted to him during the contest had seemed wondrous when they'd first appeared. But now that he knew their origins, he was glad to have a familiar piece of home, even if it was one of Everard's horses.

He could see Olivia and her mother being escorted to a fine carriage not far away. When the guard held out his hand to help her up the carriage steps after her mother, however, Olivia shook her head vehemently and pointed to a group of people on horseback. Launce wished he could hear what they were saying. After a moment of arguing, it seemed Olivia had won. She wore a triumphant look and crossed her arms as she watched the guard stomp off toward the stables. A few minutes later, the defeated guard emerged with a cream-colored horse.

In spite of himself, Launce nearly laughed at the scathing look Olivia sent her father. She didn't move though until she was sure Rafael had seen her. Then, her chin lifted high, she stepped up onto the carriage step and lifted one leg to mount the horse in the most unladylike fashion Launce had ever seen, fine silk dress and all. King Rafael looked as though he might say something, but only closed his mouth and shook his head before turning back to the servant he'd been speaking with.

"Let us begin," Launce heard the enchanter tell Rafael.

"Wait!" Olivia cried out. "I want to ride beside Launce!"

"Whatever pleases you, my dear," Rafael said, sounding dazed and tired. Launce looked at Bronkendol, but to his surprise, the old man was watching them, looking pleased, as though it had been his idea.

Why, Launce wondered, was Bronkendol so eager to get them together? As much as he admired the princess, and as much as his heart told him he was already falling for her, it made him nervous to think that their relationship was part of some plan that also plotted Everard's death and the exploitation of Isa's power. Why were they the only ones without glass? Why did Bronkendol so desperately want them to fall in love?

The questions continued swirling about in Launce's head. Even so, a part of him relaxed when Olivia pulled her horse up next to his. Her hand slipped inside of his own, and he gave it a squeeze. They said nothing to break the dreadful silence that hung over the strange company of travelers, but Launce gave her a meaningful look as wheels, hooves, and the sounds of many feet began to move forward. The warmth of her palm against his matched that of the sun as it hung low in the western sky behind them, and the tiniest seed of hope sprouted inside of him. The outlook seemed dire now, but it couldn't always remain that way. They were going home, to the Fortress itself. The Fortress would keep this invader out, and the Maker would surely have pity on them. And when He did, Launce would make sure the enchanter's hopes would never see the light of day.

BRING HER HOME

"I still cannot fathom how we never managed to receive a single relic from the Glass Castle!" Ever slammed another book shut in disgust.

"It's been twenty-seven hundred years since the castle was sealed with the curse, Everard," Garin said, picking up the book and moving it before Ever could abuse it more. Not that Ever was in the mood to care.

"Wait!" The steward looked up. "What about Launce's armor? Didn't you say it was coated on the bottom with glass?"

But Ever was already shaking his head. "The armor and horses disappeared after Launce was declared the winner. Either someone stole them all or they simply vanished." Ever rubbed his eyes and moaned. "If I hadn't been so stupid and broken Bronkendol's glass gifts, we may even have had a chance with that." Ever picked up another book, unsure whether he wanted to read it again, or hurl it through a window.

"There is something you haven't told me yet, isn't there?" Garin said. Ever just looked at him miserably, and Garin nodded. "I could tell from the moment you arrived. What is it?" When Ever still didn't answer, he added in a soft voice, "You know you can tell me anything. You knew that as a boy, and you should know right now."

"She sent a message, begging me to come to her." Ever looked at his hands, dry and cracking from arranging and rearranging the maps. "It was something urgent. I could tell from the way the servant relayed the message!" He shook his head. "But I was so dead set on carrying out my plans, that I missed what was right in front of me. If I had only listened, she might not have been . . ."

Ever paused and let out a gusty breath, placing his hands over the edge of the table and leaning on it heavily. He felt as though his body had been clapped in irons, and he was dragging his chains behind him. No matter how hard he tried, finding her simply seemed impossible.

They had been back at the Fortress for three whole days, and Ever was nearly beside himself. He had sent out messenger birds to all of the western kingdoms. Many of his peers were still away in Cobren, so many respondents had been stewards and ambassadors, who knew nothing of the Glass Queen's reign at all, and the few kings who had responded had nothing to help him either.

Even Garin was running Ever's patience thin. Ever had never doubted the steward's attachment to Isa. Once the spell had been broken, Garin had spent his every free moment ensuring that she was comfortable in one way or another. But for someone so devoted to the girl, he seemed to be dragging his feet more and more in sending Ever off.

"There is a reason you haven't found an answer," Garin said. "Trust the Fortress, and wait to see what happens. If you cannot find her, there is a purpose in your inability to go."

"And do what? Sit on my haunches? Or should I just wait for her to drop out of the sky?" As the sarcastic words dripped from his mouth, a small voice inside of Ever wondered what he was doing. Garin's voice was the one that Ever trusted most, after the Fortress. He had never let Ever down before. But his words of caution were just too much for Ever to bear at the moment.

Instead of waiting for Garin's response, Ever stomped outside for some fresh air. They were getting nowhere. Without thinking about where he was going, Ever found himself in a part of the fortress grounds he had not visited in what felt like a very long time.

Although their season of bloom was long past, the cherry trees somehow still displayed a surreal beauty. Their bark had grayed, but the shapes of the branches still resembled dancers reaching for the sky. Or at least, that's what Isa said. The grove wasn't large, but was deep enough to hide a weary soul who did not wish to be found by the outside world. Dead leaves crunched beneath Ever's feet as he closed his eyes and walked slowly to the grove's center. To his relief, the only sounds here were the chirping of a few winter birds, and the scampering of chipmunks as they hurried to finish their winter nests.

Falling to his knees, Ever kept his eyes shut as he leaned his head backward and waited for the presence he knew would be listening. "I don't understand," he said. "How do I continue to lose all that You give me? Even when I realize the error of my ways, why is it that I am unable to make it right?"

There were no words that responded, but then again, Ever knew there wouldn't be. Instead, he simply stayed upon the ground and listened to the rushing of the wind through the trees, knowing he was not alone. "Please," he said softly, "not for my sake, but for hers. I do not deserve her, but she deserves to be safe. I just wish I knew what You were doing." He didn't realize he had been weeping quietly until the breeze brushed his face, and he felt for the first time that his cheeks were wet.

"So it's true." A hollow voice came from just a few feet away. Ever's eyes opened as he drew his sword. As soon as he saw who it was however, the grief that he was sure could not grow heavier doubled. Isa and Launce's father, Ansel, stood there watching him, his own face a reflection of the despair Ever felt inside.

"Garin said that you were busy, but you have been home for three days, and I had to know . . ." He let his words trail off, the fear in his eyes saying more than Ever needed or wanted to know.

"Your family has all the right in the world to despise me," he said, sheathing his sword. "I have done nothing but bring you pain." Ansel didn't answer, just stood there staring at the leaf-littered ground, opening and closing his hands as though they searched for something to do. And yet another wave of failure washed over Ever.

They had come so far since his first meeting with the merchant, when, to his shame, he had demanded the man's eldest daughter in desperation, hoping she could be the one to save the kingdom from the curse he had brought upon it. By the time Isa had helped him break the curse that had held the Fortress in darkness, Ever had been changed, his soul cut and healed in a way that would never go back to what *he* had been, an insecure, self-reliant beast. His complete transformation, along with Isa's winning spirit, had coaxed her family, all but Launce, of course, into a sort of uneasy trust, one that had been deepening slowly with time.

As he faced Ansel now, however, Ever despaired of ever having any sort of relationship worth keeping with his father-in-law. Not that he deserved one in the first place.

For a long time, they stayed still, Ansel leaning against a tree, and Ever standing before him. Ever begged the Fortress once more. *If not for me, for him. For them. Show me where to go! Do not let them suffer this way for my mistakes!*

"I would die in a moment if it would bring her home," Ansel finally said. "But as much as it kills me to say, the fact of the matter is that she chose this life."

"I didn't give her much choice."

"You were dead for a week, son. Isa hated it, but she accepted who she was and what she had been chosen to do. She wanted . . . she needed this life. She would have met this foe with or without you." The older man let out a deep sigh and rubbed his eyes. "You are not a father yet. I pray to the Maker that one day you will be. But as of now, you cannot know the pain of having your child ripped from you again and again."

Ever flinched, but Ansel continued. "I have seen too much in the last year to know anything but that the Maker has used the Fortress to call my daughter to a higher purpose. I do not know what it is, but I do know that whatever it is, the purpose is hers. Nothing you do or don't do will break her of that purpose. Now, you can choose whether or not to help her bring that purpose to fruition, but I can assure you one thing." Walking up to Ever, he placed his hand on Ever's face and lifted his chin, as only a father could do. "I have not lost hope. And neither should you."

As though confirming Ansel's words, a sudden tug at his heart alerted Ever of the familiar presence before the shouts of a servant did, and without a thought, he found himself running as though a demon chased him toward the Fortress. His heart felt like it might leap from his chest. *Is it . . .?* He asked the Fortress, too afraid of the answer to finish the question. Up the field and across the gardens, he tore. His head pounded and he was nearly lightheaded from the delirium that drove him on. *How?*

His sensitive intuition had not failed him. As soon as he crested the mountain meadow upon which the Fortress sat, he could see the multitude of servants that was gathered round a single horse at the front Fortress steps.

"Be gentle!" he could hear Gigi order. "Watch her head! She can't hold it up!"

Despite his speed, his approach seemed painstakingly slow. "Hold back, all of you!" Garin ordered from somewhere above the din.

"Move!" Ever shouted. So loud was his call that the startled servants scrambled to clear a way for him. Finally he reached the crowd. Everyone watched solemnly as he slowed, gasping for air.

There she was. Draped upon the horse as though there was no life in her, Isa clung to the horse's mane with fingers that looked like they might break. Her auburn hair had fallen from its place, and spilled in tangled bunches down the horse's side.

"Isa."

She did not raise her head to look at him when he called her name. With unsteady hands, he reached up and pulled her limp body from the horse. As she fell into his arms, her eyelids didn't open, and her lips barely moved as her shallow breath went in and out. Cradling her to his chest, Ever began the long walk up to their chambers.

By the time they arrived, Garin already had an army of servants preparing the room. Blankets were pulled back from the bed, and curtains were drawn shut. A healer had a tray of potent poultices and herbs prepared beside the bed, and he was arguing in a low voice with Garin over their necessity, but Ever shook his head at all of them.

"Out!"

No one objected, and soon the room was clear of all but Garin, who paused to squeeze Ever's shoulder before leaving and closing the doors behind him. With more care than he had ever taken in his life, Ever laid his wife in the center of their bed.

Her cheeks were red and dry with the early stages of frostbite, and her fingers were even worse. No warmth emanated from her skin as he felt her head and then her neck. The only sign that there was still life in her was the ever-shallow rise and fall of her chest, and the sense of purpose that the Fortress now poured inside of him. He knew what he needed to do.

Before he began, he laid his lips on hers and lingered there. To think he might never have kissed those lips again.

"I'll make this better," he whispered. "I promise." Then, with all that was within him, he gathered his power and let it go. An ocean of blue light filled the room and lit the walls. He wondered how long it might take before she was healed enough to open her eyes, but then decided it didn't matter.

She was home.

NOTHING

*E*ven in the dark of the early morning, Ever couldn't take his eyes from her. The soft glow of the moon peaked in around the curtains, lighting her face in a dreamlike glow. Isa's eyes were no longer sunken in, and all sign of frostbite was gone. The Fortress's power had healed her body in every way. But, Ever wondered, what state would she be in once she awakened? She had not so much as stirred since he'd first laid her in the bed.

"I will never have the power to express how truly sorry I am," he whispered into the silence. "But I promise you that never will I fail you in such a way again. I do not know why I ever doubted you. You were the one who broke the curse, and you were the one who taught me to be alive once again." He tenderly brushed wayward strands of hair away from her face. It was easier to practice his apology when she couldn't hear him.

"I hope," he breathed, "that in spite of all my blind foolishness, you've never had reason to doubt my need for you." He leaned down placed his lips on her brow. "Or that place which you hold in my heart." He smiled into the darkness as the words which he should have said months ago now flowed with abandon.

"I cannot wait to begin the rest of our life after all of this is finished. You will make the most intelligent and wise queen the Fortress and Destin have ever seen. And," he leaned forward, as though telling her a secret, "when the Fortress so chooses, the most wonderful mother our children could ever ask for. Whether it is soon or later, I will be overjoyed."

As he spoke to her, Ever wondered how he would ever be able to let her out of his sight again. To think he had nearly lost her was unbearable. And yet, an unease wriggled within him. Unless she had escaped on her own, there was a reason the enchanter had allowed her to return. Her body had been pushed to the brink of exhaustion, and she had to been without water and food for a few days, but for Ever, those wounds were simple enough to heal. And the enchanter would have known that.

What Ever feared was not the injury done to Isa's body, but that which had been done to her mind and spirit. If only he could know what else had been hurt, he might be able to help her more. But such was impossible, as he was unaware of what had happened during her abduction. Without thinking, for the thousandth time that night, he leaned down and softly kissed her lips once more. What was he going to do?

"Ever?"

"Isa?"

Joy and fear and trepidation rushed through him as he lifted and cradled her to him, tears running down his face. Relief flooded him so entirely that it felt as though he might drown. But Ever couldn't have cared less.

"Isa," he whispered over and over again. "You're home. You're safe." He could feel her swallow hard, and loosened his grip so she might breathe more easily. He was nearly giddy as he felt her lean back into the crook of his arm.

"Where . . .?" She stopped and cleared her throat. "Where am I?"

"You're home," he said. "Do you not remember your journey here?"

Isa paused. "Not much, I suppose."

"What do you remember?"

"The . . . the enchanter . . . he took my power. He took my power, and placed it in a mirror."

"What?" Ever had never heard of such a thing. Alarm raced through him, but he knew that for her sake, he needed to remain calm. She was in no condition to handle more stress. "This is not something we should worry about now," he said. "We will talk to Garin in the morning. For now I simply want to be with you." He leaned down once more to kiss her, but instead of leaning in like she always had, Isa turned her head away instead.

Pain hit him, along with confusion. She had never turned away from his kiss before. Worse than her refusal though, was the realization that for her to move the way she just had, she must have opened her eyes. If she had opened her eyes, why weren't their blue flames piercing the darkness?

"I'm tired," she said. "And hungry. Is there something to eat?"

Ever shook his head and scrambled to bring her the tray that had been waiting in the room, just as she had asked. But as he did, panic threatened to overwhelm him. Isa's fire was gone.

~

"She never even asked about her brother," Ever muttered as he paced the floor in front of Garin, who sat more patiently in one of the great chairs pulled up before the fire in the king's study. "All she wanted was to be left alone."

"Patience, Ever," Garin said mildly. "We do not yet know how deeply she was injured. Perhaps quiet and solitude is what she most needs to heal."

But Ever was already shaking his head. "When she awoke the second time, she told me she wanted to go outside. I tried to warn her of the cold, but she insisted." He sighed and scratched his head. "I'm supposed to be getting our horses prepared as we speak."

"Well then, you can tell me more as we do just that." Garin stood and pulled one of the bell chimes upon the wall beside the grand fireplace. Moments later, a knock sounded at the door. "Prepare the king and queen's riding horses," Garin told the servant boy, and with a quick bow, the boy was gone.

Ever could see that his mentor was curious as to what had riled him so, but it was difficult to explain. He didn't yet have words to describe the disappointment that had filled him when she'd awakened the second time that morning.

"Garin, her fire is gone."

This time, there was no soothing calm in Garin's face. He put down the parchment he had been examining and stood straight.

"What?"

"It's just that. She has no fire left. The flames are gone!"

Ever had convinced himself he was wrong after she had first awakened. He'd been so relieved to simply hear her voice and see her move that he'd hoped that perhaps he had been wrong, distracted. The second time she'd awakened, however, had been different. She'd allowed him to kiss her quickly that time, but there was no warmth, no return. She had merely seemed to tolerate it, turning away from him as soon as he was done.

It was then, as he searched her face for some hint of affection that he realized her eyes were indeed as hard and cold in their blue depths as glaciers. The Fortress's fire was completely extinguished. And yet, she was still alive. Ever had never heard of such a thing in all his years of studying the Fortress's history. How was there breath still in her when the Fortress's life-giving fire was gone?

"What do you feel?" Garin's voice was strained. "What do you sense when you're near her?"

"Nothing." Ever hated the words even as he said them. "I feel nothing."

Garin's eyebrows rose, and Ever knew the steward was beginning to understand his state of panic.

"She shows no sign of joy at being home, no anger toward me for failing her, not even sorrow at what the enchanter did to her." He shrugged. "And whenever I ask her about what he did to her, all she does is repeat herself, saying he stole the power from her heart."

"My lord." A young voice came from the other side of the thick wooden doors. "The king and queen's horses are prepared." The two men left the study to fetch Isa for their ride, but Garin looked far from done with the conversation.

"Go with her," Garin ordered him outside the chamber door, his voice suddenly fierce. The fine lines at the corners of his eyes and on his forehead were more pronounced with worry than Ever had seen them before. "Do not let her out of your sight. I don't like this. I will see her myself later."

Ever gathered his courage as he knocked on the door. Garin gave him a curt nod and stalked off.

"Our horses are ready," Ever called through the doors. It felt foolish to ask permission to enter his own chambers, but for all Isa had suffered at his hand, he was willing to play the part of any fool if it would help her heal.

Isa appeared in her riding gear, but remained silent as they walked down to the stables. Her eyes stayed trained on the end of the hall. Not a word was spoken as they mounted their horses and left the servants behind. Only the early winter wind whipped around them, as though agitated with everyone and everything, threatening to send them back home. Dead leaves hit their faces, and the gray of the sky did nothing to cheer the somber mood. Ever had hoped that being outside would help him find the words he was looking for, but he didn't gain the courage to speak again until they were far from everyone and everything, way out on the far end of the back field.

"Isa," he finally said, clearing his throat twice before he could continue. "I wish you would tell me what's wrong. I want to help you, but I can't unless I know how."

"Nothing," she answered. "Nothing is wrong."

"Something is most definitely wrong." He pulled his horse in front of hers, forcing her to stop. "Have you tried using your power?"

Isa stared at him as though he were dim. As he waited, Ever decided he disliked the way she had told the servants to fix her hair. It was too tight, too severe for her young face.

"There is nothing left to use. I told you, he took everything."

"Well, at least tell me how you feel about it." He was grasping for smoke, desperate for some answers. "Surely you must feel something for me, if not for him. Anger? Sorrow? Hatred?" He took a deep breath, steeling himself for the answer he knew he deserved to receive. "Do you hate me, Isa?" For a moment, he was sure she would say yes. A brief flash of recognition lit her eyes, but then she only resumed the bored, impatient expression she'd worn all day.

"What part of *everything* do you not understand? My power came from my heart, little as it was." She sniffed. "He took what was left, and with it everything else in my heart as well. So when I say I feel nothing, I truly feel nothing. Not for you, not for my brother, not for my family, not even for Bronkendol himself. Now, if you'll excuse me, I'll go before I say something that will assuredly injure you more." And with that, she kicked her horse into a gallop.

What had he done?

3 8

AN ENCHANTER'S BLOOD

*R*emembering Garin's words of caution about leaving Isa alone, Ever pushed his horse to follow hers. To his relief, she simply returned to the stables and dismounted. Once he knew she was back inside the Fortress, Ever called one of his messengers.

"Go to Soudain and find Ansel and Deline Marchand. He's a prominent merchant with a shop in the main square. Bring them to me immediately."

Ever decided to go find Garin while he waited for the Marchands' arrival. As he climbed the curving stone staircase of the tower, he prayed that Garin might have found the answer. Never had Ever heard of anyone being able to steal a monarch's power. He wondered if Isa had truly understood what the enchanter had done. But then, he conceded, he had never heard of a strength like Isa's before he had witnessed it himself.

The Fortress monarchs had always possessed one form of strength or another. Most had exceeded the physical abilities of the average man. Others had the ability to discern lies from the truth. Still others could heal, and there had been one or two on record who could converse with the animals. Ever's own powers were unusual for even a Fortress king, according to Garin, in that he had most of the powers combined, animal communication excluded. But none were like Isa's power of the heart, and that made her current struggle all the more puzzling.

"Anything of interest?" he asked as he finally reached the tower. As Ever had expected, Garin was deep in thought, his head bent over a number of old books spread out upon the table.

"Nothing that will help us now," Garin sighed. "If this truly is Bronkendol, then his power is much older than I am, much older than our most ancient texts. The first kings gathered a few scrolls and such here and there, but even those were written after the kingdoms formed." He looked up at Ever. "Did she tell you anything new?"

"Only that it is Bronkendol." He paused. "And she says that when he stole her power, he stole everything."

"What do you mean everything?"

Ever shrugged. "Her feelings, her emotions. She says her heart is empty."

"Your Highness, the Marchands are waiting in your study, just as you requested," a servant called out. The look Garin gave him was not a hopeful one, but Ever only shook his head.

"It was all I could think to do. It can't hurt anything." At this, Garin inclined his head once and went back to searching his books. Ever began the long descent down the steps with a hope he feared was in vain. But if anyone could reach Isa, it would be them. If they could not find her, Ever worried that no one would. He put such dark thoughts from his mind and smoothed his face, however, as he entered his study. He would not give them false hope, but they still deserved their best chance too. Despite his intentions, however, Deline didn't give him a chance to even begin explaining. She ran straight up to him, her dark eyes hopeful.

"Where is she?"

"Resting in her room." Ever took a deep breath. "Before I bring you to see her though, there is something you must know." Deline exchanged a worried look with her husband, but let Ever speak. "Since she has returned," Ever began, "Isa has seemed . . . different." He stopped and bit his lip, trying to think of how to explain in a way that would not be too painful, but would prepare them for the daughter they would soon meet.

"Just tell us what the matter is," Ansel said softly. "She is our daughter. You know we will do anything and more that she needs. Now, what does she need?"

"That's just it. I wish I knew. Since she's returned, Isa has said she feels empty. She does not wish to be doted on, nor does she wish to speak of those she loves. She has not even asked of Launce's welfare since she's arrived." Ever felt his careful façade fall as he spoke. "She will not even allow me to touch her." The weight of what he was saying suddenly drained him, and Ever rubbed his eyes and allowed himself to sink into one of the chairs.

Ansel was a merchant, nothing like the father Ever had known, but there were times like this when he wanted so much to think that his father-in-law might see him as a son in some way or another. Part of the family, at the very least. "I need you to help her remember," he said, looking up at them wearily. "That is all I know and that is all I can ask."

"Then that is what we shall try to do." Ansel looked at his wife and with a comforting smile, gently took her by the waist and led her from the room. Before they left, Ansel placed a hand on Ever's arm. The gesture was kind and for a moment, Ever felt a little less alone. There were others who shared his grief, others who loved her nearly as much as he did.

When they were gone long enough to ensure that they wouldn't see him,

Ever followed their footsteps down the hall to his own chambers. He stood outside the door where he could just hear the conversation inside.

"I thought he might send you." The slight tremor of uncertainty in Isa's voice was the closest thing to feeling that Ever had heard since she'd arrived home. His heart leapt with a dangerous, uneven sense of hope.

"Ever says you're having a difficult time since you arrived home." Deline's words were as sweet and welcoming as an embrace.

"I am perfectly fine, and I cannot understand what all the fuss is about."

"Have you heard from your brother?" Ansel's voice was also kind, but more reserved than his wife's had been. He was testing her, Ever realized. *He wants to see what she does when I am not around.* A part of him both dreaded and hoped to find that Isa's strange behavior was simply born from resentment for him, but the longer Ever listened to the family speak, the less he dared to dream.

"Launce is a man now," Isa retorted. "I wish everyone would simply leave him be."

"Ever says your brother is alone in another country under the thumb of a king who despises him." Ansel's voice grew agitated. "And you don't wish to know of his well-being?"

"We are done here." Isa's footsteps quickly approached the door. Before Ever could move, Isa had opened the door and fixed him with a cold stare. "You may see them out." And with that, she whirled and began marching toward the hallway that led to the Tower of Annals.

"Everard." Deline was looking up at him, beseeching him with her eyes. Commanding him. "You must help her." She stepped forward and clutched his sleeve. "She would not be in this mess if you had protected her. Now help her!"

"If you don't help her," Ansel's voice was not so accusatory, but the sadness in his eyes was somehow worse than the anger in his wife's, "I don't know that anything or anyone can. Please." He held Ever's gaze for a long moment before turning and guiding his weeping wife out. Ever could only watch in misery.

"It's been three days," Ever growled. "I don't know how much longer I can stand this." He gestured at the lone form sitting in a chair on the south side of the Tower of Annals. Though Garin and Ever were on horseback at the edge of the field that bordered the mountain road, it was easy to see her small figure through the glass walls of the round tower room.

"Have patience," Garin cautioned him. It annoyed Ever to no end that his mentor seemed to know Ever's actions before he did. "Isa needs to find peace with the Fortress before she can find peace with anyone else. There is nothing you can do to make that happen faster than it will."

Ever shook his head. "We don't have time. I need to know what he did to her and what he plans to do with her power. This foolish mess is all intertwined somehow. I need to reach the heart of the matter. But I cannot do that without her help."

"Don't do anything rash. I know you want to help, but she is the Fortress's daughter. It is watching her just as it has been all of her life. It's best not to interfere." He eyed Ever suspiciously. "You might learn a thing or two as well by watching." They sat for a few moments longer, watching her in silence. But Ever knew, and he knew Garin knew as well, that there would not be much more waiting for him.

Once more, Ever promised himself and his mentor silently. *Once more, I will try, and even if it kills me, I won't hold back.* Urging his horse forward, he let his mount carry him with the wind, back to the cold, beautiful eyes he could feel watching him from above.

By the time he reached the Annals, Isa was nowhere to be seen. So intent had he been on his mission that the thought of speaking with her anywhere else made his heart sink within him. He let out a gusty breath before walking over and letting himself fall into the chair Isa had been sitting in when he'd seen her from the fields below.

The Tower of Annals was one of the few places the monarchs could escape to for true solitude. Since the Maker had so uniquely blessed the Fortress with a life of its own a thousand years before, the tower had been created as a place of sacred rest.

Constructed of only windows for walls, the entire room was one large circle, allowing a view of nearly the entire kingdom. Each of the floor-to-ceiling windows could open to the balcony that ran around the entire tower. A single large fireplace stood in the center of the room, surrounded by tall bookshelves and various pieces of sitting furniture. The air smelled of musty pages and sweet cedar from the logs they burned in the fire. As soon as one stepped from the stairs into the tower, a veil of solemnity and age hung in the air, making it just heavy enough to notice when one breathed.

It was in this room that Ever and Isa had nearly died, and in which they had been brought back from certain death to life. It was here he had hoped to speak not to the silent, mysterious stranger, but to the heart of the companion he missed so much.

"What happened?" he muttered, closing his eyes and leaning back, allowing the warmth of the sun to cover him like a blanket. "How did we end up here?"

"You failed."

Ever nearly fell out of his chair when Isa spoke. She must have known he would come. She stood behind him now, several paces back. The silk lavender gown she wore was simple, but it fit her frame well. The purple made the copper streaks in her hair more vibrant than usual. Everything in him yearned to close the distance between them and will her back to him. But he stayed still, and so did she. The expression on her face was neither hateful nor angry, but there wasn't a trace of warmth in it either.

"You asked what happened," she said when he didn't speak, "and the answer is that you failed. While you were traipsing off with Kartek, trying to find the answers all on your own, you failed. When you ignored my warning, he took me, and you failed." She shrugged. "It's as simple as that."

Ever knew everything she told him was true, but hearing her say it was so much worse. "No amount of victories in the battlefield can redeem me from the way I've neglected you." His throat sounded gravelly, too tight. "Everything you say is true."

Ever didn't realize he'd fallen to his knees until he looked up at her once more. The pain inside him felt as though he might split in two, but somehow her face was unmoved. Even in the few months they'd been married, he had come to rely unquestionably on Isa's forgiving nature, the grace she extended with a tired smile when he was back late from a journey, or when he had time and time again cancelled plans for picnics and special suppers up on the tower balcony. The softness of her sweet touch and the adoration of her eyes had always brought him through, even in the short time they had been together.

But this woman made of stone, this cold, unfeeling heart in the body of his beloved was more than he could stand. Anger, screaming, tears, anything would be better than this silence. "Can you forgive me?" he pleaded, his voice almost too quiet to hear. "I just wanted to protect you."

"Whether I forgive you or not makes no difference. You let him steal everything from me, and no words of mine or yours will bring it back." With that, she uncrossed her arms and began walking toward the door.

A feeling of wild angst overtook Ever, and in that moment, something told him that if he allowed her to walk out that door, the Isa he loved would never return. *I beg you*, he cried out to the Fortress, *let this work!* He was on his feet in an instant. In three long strides, he'd overtaken her. A feverish hope consumed him as he grabbed her by her waist and pulled her back into him.

How many times had he taken this embrace for granted? Ever reached up and gently but firmly guided her jaw up to his. All the pain and loneliness and worry and passion that he had been harboring poured into his kiss like oil into a flame. Never had he loved her more.

For one brief, glorious moment, his lips melted into hers.

But only for a moment. All too quickly she pushed herself from his arms. The shake of her head was nearly imperceptible, but it was still there. The all-too-familiar cool solidity quickly chased away the fleeting look of uncertainty that her eyes had held for that short second.

"I told you. I have nothing left to give." With that, she was gone. A hollow ache filled him as he watched her begin the winding descent down the tower steps. It was not long, however, before he became aware of the anger that had been simmering within him since Isa had returned. Common sense had cautioned him against allowing his desires to control him, but the loss of his wife was simply too much.

"Garin!" he shouted as he took off quickly behind her. Only a few steps down, and he had passed her on the stairs, but Ever didn't stop. "Gather my things!"

As always, despite the distance, Garin somehow heard him, and was waiting at the foot of the tower steps. He didn't work to conceal his disappointment, his mouth turning down on one side as it always did when he was displeased. He followed Ever, as Ever burst into his chambers and began to gather his belongings in a violent storm of purpose.

"And where might you be going?"

"I'm going to find that enchanter."

"How?"

In response, Ever held up the robe he'd taken from Isa when she'd first arrived home.

"All I have to do is follow this. It's from Bronkendol's castle. It should lead me between the realms."

"And then what do you expect to do?" Garin continued to trail Ever as he stormed down to the armory to gather his favorite weapons. "You still have the slivers of glass in your eyes. You don't know what he plans to do with those."

Ever paused on the threshold.

"It doesn't matter. I will find him. And then I will kill him."

39

BLINDSIDED

*I*sa watched as Ever's horse carried him down the mountain road. Only once did he slow to look back. Though she couldn't see his eyes, she knew they were searching for her. She thought about waving, but what would the purpose be in that? It would only encourage him in this foolhardy end he was racing toward.

It was so strange not to feel. Tears should have stung her eyes, and apprehension should have seized her chest, nearly suffocating her. As strong as her husband was, Isa knew now that Ever was no match for Bronkendol. He hadn't even been able to remove the glass slivers from his own eyes, let alone come rescue her. The Fortress's strength was old, but it was infantile in comparison to that which ran through the enchanter's blood.

Morbidly curious, Isa continued to dig down deep inside of herself. She had once felt as though words could never come close to expressing the connection she felt with Ever. But now it all seemed in vain, for her heart felt as hollow as the animal skin drums the soldiers used to signal battle.

"What was it?"

"What was what?" Isa kept her eyes on the distant figure below as she felt Garin move behind her.

"You kept something from him."

"I didn't lie, if that's what you mean." She swerved to face him.

"Omitting a fact of importance can be just as dangerous as a blatant lie, if not more so."

"He never asked for every detail of my time there, so I didn't give it. Is that such a crime?"

Garin scowled. "Your husband could hardly think clearly enough to eat once you were home. Now he's riding off into the jaws of the enemy for you, and you have the brazenness to sit here and play semantics?"

"I don't know what is so difficult for you all to understand." Isa looked him straight in the eye. "I have told you time and time again that the enchanter emptied my heart. I have tried, believe me!" Isa realized her voice was growing louder as she spoke. It was the closest she'd come to feeling since she'd been in Bronkendol's chair, and the feeling she drew near to now was exasperation. "I can't understand why he went at all. He cannot challenge the Glass Prince. No one can. I thought I'd made it perfectly clear that he would simply be wise to allow things to pass as they will. His decision to ride off for my sake was foolish and rash, and I had no part in it."

"Your husband will die if you do not do something! Look deep inside yourself, Isabelle! Do you truly wish him dead?"

Despite her lack of feeling, Isa had to fight the urge to cower. It was the first time she'd ever heard Garin shout in such a way. Worry lined his face, and the slight lines of gray in his dark hair stood out. And though the Fortress steward did not have the blue rings of fire in his eyes that the monarchs kept, Isa thought she saw a hint of the same blue emanating from around his entire being. Her heart thumped once in a strange, uneven way.

"I do not wish him dead! I wish to know why my fire is gone. I wish to know why I'm still breathing even though my fire has died! I wish to know why I was allowed to go through such pain and suffering if I truly am a daughter of the Fortress!" She was shouting now, although she wasn't sure why.

Garin watched her, his arms crossed and his eyes still flashing, but he didn't interrupt as she continued her tirade.

"I have tried to feel! But when Bronkendol emptied my heart, then placed me on the back of a horse with little water and even less food, and sent me through terrain which no one should survive, every bit of feeling I'd tried to hold onto was blown away into nothingness. I have nothing left!"

Garin simply stared at her. His eyes were not cruel, but they were determined, and his silence was suddenly worse than if he had shouted hateful words at her. A familiar yet foreign feeling attempted to enter her. She couldn't tell though whether it was anger or sorrow or worry or foolish, foolish joy. Instead, she took a deep breath and steadied herself on the corner of the solid cedar table that was littered with every kind of book and scroll imaginable.

"My husband did not listen to me, and he failed to keep me safe. The Fortress has failed me too. I simply don't see the point in trying to fight for or against this heinous fate any longer—"

"Now stop right there." Garin was suddenly so close to her that he had to tilt his head down to look into her eyes. It was a challenge she didn't flinch from. "Do you think you're the first Fortress queen to suffer? Have none before you ever felt pain, too?"

"The Fortress abandoned me! It let that monster steal all that was left of my power!"

"And?"

Isa stared at him in shock. What did he mean *and*? Isa had put all of her trust in the Fortress, and thus in Ever, and neither of them had kept her from the pain that had ultimately broken her.

Garin walked over to a bookshelf four shelves down and pulled an ancient leather book. "Queen Adeline." He flipped open the pages with a puff of dust that made Isa cough. "Lived four hundred years ago. Was stabbed in the chest by one of her handmaidens who had been paid off by an enemy. She was journeying to investigate the welfare of Destinian merchants who were disappearing." He slammed the book shut before laying it down and pulling another book from the shelf.

"Queen Dione, who lived seven hundred years ago, was abducted and tortured by a sorcerer who demanded to be shown into the Tower of Annals. When she told him she would not desecrate that which was sacred, he beat her for days on end until her husband arrived. By then, she was blind in both eyes." Placing this book on top of the other one, he folded his arms and began to rattle off more names.

"Princess Martine never married because her father and brother were killed by her betrothed the eve before their wedding. Queen Odile lost five of her sons in the War of Boars. Queen Mother Radelle was forced to take the throne again when her eldest son, King Aubin, was killed before her very eyes, and she did not have time to properly mourn until her youngest son was of age to be crowned, thirteen years later. Need I go on?"

Isa wanted to retort that none of those women had watched their hearts being ripped from their chests, but her throat was too tight. All she could do was blink rapidly while her eyes developed a strange sort of sting at the corners. Garin placed his head in his right hand and inhaled deeply. He stayed like that for a long time, as though the memories or stories, Isa did not know which, had overwhelmed him.

When he did speak again, his voice was kinder, and his eyes held something closer to the affection she was used to seeing. "You are not the only one who has been taken advantage of. As shrewd as he is, even Ever's power has been taken advantage of. Those who do not wish to solve their own problems call out in distress, and your husband, dutiful as always, rushes in to help."

Garin looked down at her left hand. Isa followed his gaze to the blue, crystal ring that hadn't glowed in quite a long time. "And yet," he said, "Ever's strength does not run dry. It cannot, for it is not his to run out of. The power comes from the Fortress itself, which is gifted to the Fortress from the Maker. So truthfully, the power was stolen from the Maker, not from you."

Isa swallowed, her throat suddenly dry.

"I still don't understand why the Fortress would allow me to be used in such a way, why it would allow my power to all but disappear, and then to have the rest, along with all my feelings and emotions, stolen away." As she spoke, a small smile suddenly flickered across Garin's face.

"I don't believe that Bronkendol stole all of your power or your heart. You say your heart is empty, but I think it's merely boarded up. You feel things deeply, Isa. It's part of who you are. But you make the mistake of allowing your feelings to be too tied up in your willingness to do what is necessary."

"I told you, I—"

But Garin held a hand up. "If you are truly without feeling, then why are you glaring at me with such disdain?" Again, that small, irritating smile crossed his face, and Isa swallowed what she had been about to say. As much as she hated to admit it, he had a point.

"I know you don't feel like helping your husband," Garin said in a soft voice. "But love isn't doing things when we *feel* led to. Love is doing what someone needs when they need it. Hang feelings, Isa! Good wine will bring feelings, but when the night is over, none of those feelings bear witness to the truth! Feelings can come and go any time. When the Fortress wants you to do something, it will give you the power to do it. And it will expect it of you, whether you feel like it or not."

Isa sighed and turned to walk out upon the balcony. The world below her looked still. Specks of animals grazed in distant fields, and patches of wood dotted the land from the mountain on down to what she knew was eventually the distant sea. Garin's words spun circles in her mind. What she wouldn't give for a way to put her thoughts in place, to know what she was truly thinking, for in that moment, she did not know.

"I'm not blind to the way Ever has treated you since the wedding." Garin placed a calloused hand on top of hers and squeezed gently. "He tries, but the boy still has much to learn. Sometimes anger manifests itself in strange ways."

"You think I'm angry with him." It was all Isa could do to keep her voice steady.

"If I'm wrong, then why are you so opposed to helping him?"

Something inside of Isa burst. Like a dam bursting from the surge of spring rains, what felt like scales flew violently from her heart. With a cry, Isa clutched at her chest and fell to her knees.

Loneliness from Ever's constant absence.

Pain from his doubt.

Fear, now that her fire was completely gone.

Sorrow for all she had done and seen flooded her and poured from her eyes in unending streams. Immediately, Garin was there, holding her shoulders as she wept.

"The fire is gone, Garin! I woke up here, and it was gone! And now Ever is gone, and Launce is gone, and I don't even know who I am anymore." She continued to weep as Garin pulled her gently to her feet and began to wipe the tears from her cheeks.

"That's the wondrous thing about the Fortress. Just because you have temporarily lost sight of who you are, that doesn't make you any less the

Fortress's daughter than it would separate you from your blood father if you disowned him."

At the word *disown*, Isa began to sob even harder. She truly had disowned the Fortress. If Ever had been unfaithful to her in his attentions, she had been unfaithful in the Fortress a thousand times more with her words and careless actions. But Garin lifted her chin so she was forced to look him in the eyes.

"And whether you feel like it or not, the Fortress chose you. You are its daughter. And you are Ever's wife. Never, in all my time here, has the Fortress ever taken that lightly."

"I still don't understand though. How is it that when I look in the mirror, I see nothing? My fire is gone."

"So your eyes can see all, can they?" Garin gave an amused snort. "You can see the birds in the treetops of the orange grove, from here? What your mother is doing at her hearth in this instant? Or the—"

"Ever can't see it either."

Garin chuckled. "Dear, your husband is gifted, but hardly infallible. Just because neither you nor your husband cannot see it doesn't mean it's not there."

Isa studied Garin for a moment more before looking down at her hands. Could he be right? Deep down, she knew he was. But fear of failure made her shiver, and her hands shook as she closed her eyes and reluctantly tried to conjure the blue fire that always came to Ever so easily.

There was not even a tingle in her fingertips. She started to protest again, but Garin shushed her.

"Do what you know is right," he said. "Feelings will eventually follow."

"Will my power ever return?" she asked, unable to keep the sadness from her voice.

"If the Fortress believes you need it, then the power will be yours when the time comes. Until then, trust that the Fortress will not leave you alone, ever. Even when you *feel* alone."

Isa looked out once more to the northern mountains. She had barely survived the journey through them. Was she really ready to risk another brush with death so soon, and without her power at that? Her heart told her that no, she wasn't.

"Ready my horse."

Garin grinned.

"It's already been done."

"And my sword? I think I left it in…" She let her words trail off as his smile grew even wider.

"After a few centuries, you learn a thing or two."

In no time at all, she was dressed in her warmest combat clothing and on her horse. Gigi hovered and fussed, as usual, but Garin was as calm and collected as always.

"It will take time," she admitted in a low voice. "I still don't feel the way I used to."

"Remember, do what is right. Feelings will follow. Now," he patted her knee, "go."

Before she knew it, Isa was thundering down the same road that Ever had taken less than an hour before. She shook at the thought of returning to the terrifying, white, blinding beauty she'd left behind.

Well, she thought to herself wryly, fear had returned, at least. And if fear was there, the other feelings were lurking somewhere as well. If only she could locate her courage before she faced the enchanter once more.

40

SACRED GROUND

*I*f Launce never traveled the road between Cobren's capitol and the Fortress again, he would be more than pleased. For the second time that week, Launce was on his way back to the Fortress, but this time, rather than racing along at Ever's pace, the royal company crawled. It had taken the multitude of royals and nobles and their entourages all afternoon and evening to leave the hill country behind, which should have taken only a few hours. Carriages, horses and riders, and caravans filled the road behind him so that Launce couldn't even see where the multitude ended.

Red sandstone pillars stood ahead of them, the same gorge Launce had stood in to argue with Isa not so long before. His heart ached as he thought of the unkind words he'd used to cause both Isa and her husband pain. Everard had been right. Launce did often act like a spoiled child when life didn't go his way. He would sacrifice much to go back to that day now.

"He doesn't look happy." Olivia interrupted his thoughts. Launce looked ahead to where she was pointing, to see the enchanter staring into the distance with a deep frown upon his face.

"He's probably upset about how long it's taking us," Launce said. "At a decent trot, we would have reached the Fortress by tomorrow night. At this rate though, we won't be there for *at least* another five days. Serves him right for bringing a bunch of royals along." As soon as he'd said it, Launce bit his tongue. Olivia didn't have time to answer him, for Rafael had stopped, and was gesturing for everyone to do the same. Even halting was painstakingly slow.

"We'll camp here tonight" Rafael called to the captain of his guard. "Tomorrow, we will resume our journey at a faster pace." Immediately, people began to dismount their horses. Servants scurried to piece together their masters' tents and prepare the cooking fires.

"Hello there." Launce hopped off of his horse and called to a passing boy. "Aren't you Sir Randolph's squire?" The boy nodded eagerly.

"Yes, sir!"

"Tell me, when was your master supposed to return home?"

The boy blinked a few times, as though trying to recall. Finally, he said, "I suppose we were to return once the betrothal ball was done."

"Well, why didn't you?"

"We just don't want to anymore. It's important we stay with the holy man." The boy shrugged. "Now, if you'll excuse me, I need to go." With that, he scampered off in his master's direction. Launce looked up at Olivia, who still sat upon her horse.

"They don't *want* to anymore?" she echoed, one eyebrow quirked.

"Your Highness." A servant came up and bowed to them both. "Master Launce, both of your tents are prepared. Princess, you are staying with your mother. Master Launce will have his own tent."

Of course, when the servant pointed, Launce saw immediately that they had placed him near the king's tent. Rafael wanted to keep an eye on him, no doubt put up to it by Bronkendol. But Launce knew better than to argue. He led his horse beside Olivia's as the servant brought them first to her tent, then to his. At her mother's tent, Olivia pursed her lips and simply gave him a weak shrug before going inside.

His own tent was surprisingly lavish and tall enough for him to walk inside without ducking. Thick, vibrant rugs of blue and orange covered the dirt floor, and silk pillows were piled up against the corners. A silver tray of artfully arranged dried beef, cheese, and herb bread was already laid near the biggest pile of pillows. Launce shook his head. How many pillows did they think he needed? Back at home, Launce had been famous for his ability to fall asleep anywhere since he was a small boy. But an excess of pillows wasn't his main concern right now. After gobbling down his supper as quickly as possible, he marched off in the direction of the king's tent. He was going to get some answers.

Before he reached Rafael, however, a gloved hand rested heavily upon his shoulder. "I'm afraid you won't be getting many answers out of him tonight." Launce turned to see Bronkendol himself. A rainbow of emotions colored his vision. Anger, frustration, and to his annoyance, fear. The fact that he was two heads taller than the old man steeled him a bit though as he turned to face the enchanter.

"Then where do you suggest I go?"

"I actually was hoping you would come speak with me in my tent." Launce was tempted to use words his mother didn't approve of, but instead he swallowed them and simply followed the enchanter inside.

Bronkendol's tent didn't look any different from Launce's, with the exception of a full-length standing mirror and a tray of tea. Bronkendol sank slowly onto one of the cushions and poured himself a drink.

"Tea?" He held up the second empty cup, but Launce shook his head. "Before you become too angry with me," Bronkendol continued in a soft voice, "I need for you to understand my purpose."

"Then you should know as well that I am aware of your little trick," Launce replied, his voice acidic.

The enchanter stared at him blankly.

"Isa's power?"

"Ah. Yes, that is an astute observation. Before I can explain that, however, I must tell you *why*."

"I'm waiting."

The enchanter took a long sip of his tea. "When I was placed under the sleeping curse, I slept for a long time." He sighed. "Twenty-seven centuries is a hateful amount of time to be gone, young man. Imagine now, waking up to find your home empty, your mother eternally still, and all of your friends and servants gone. Even the road which we used to reach and leave my castle by was gone. Wind and rain had carved my valley home into a place of isolation with deathly drops on each side. Every sign that I or my loved ones had ever existed had disappeared, with the exception of the castle and its contents.

"My shock was even greater when I emerged back into the word of civilized man to find kingdoms and boundaries, which borderless lands had once stretched on forever." Bronkendol shook his head. "I wandered like an addled vagabond. Indeed, that's what I was. I hadn't a penny to my name, nor in my state of loss did I think to bring anything with me but the clothes on my back.

"For years I wandered. Kindly folks here and there would take me in, and sometimes I would find solace in the corner of a church where I could lay my head at night. As I moved from place to place though, I began to relearn how to be a man. The local tongues became easier to speak and understand, and customs were no longer completely foreign. But the part of this new life that I could not grow accustomed to was the suffering." His eyes were wet when he raised them to look at Launce again.

"There is so much war here. So much selfishness, so much suffering! You must understand that when my mother was the mediator between men, this kind of evil did not happen. So many die, and so few care! I couldn't allow it to continue while I had strength in my hands. Then I heard of the Fortiers." He took another sip of tea.

"Launce, I have been watching your sister's new family for the last three hundred years. I even journeyed to the Fortress a few times myself in hopes of gaining audiences with the different kings."

"Did you?" In spite of his anger, Launce found himself curious.

"A few times. But more often than not, they were off on some war campaign. When I finally did have the chance to speak with them, I found they were not what I expected at all. The first time I'd heard of them, I had been overjoyed. Though much younger, their power was similar to my own, a gift passed down from the Maker through the generations, as my mother's had been passed down to me. But where my mother had kept the peace through gifts and wise words, the Fortiers did so through blood and battle."

"Perhaps they tried words first, and the others refused to listen." Was Launce *really* defending Everard's clan?

"Perhaps. But with time, I recognized the mistake that kept this land of kingdoms constantly at odds, despite the Fortiers' constant interference."

"And that was?"

"They would subdue the uprisings and evil when it came, but they would go no further. The strength I felt when I was in the Fortiers' presence was more than enough for them to have united these miserable kingdoms to bring them to a permanent peace."

Launce gave a start. "You mean overthrow the other kingdoms?"

"Don't you see, my boy? By not conquering the evil where they found it, they merely beat it down as a temporary solution. The same evil was able to return again in the future, even stronger! And it did, time and time again. After three hundred years of watching, I decided that I had only one choice. I needed to rectify this constant bickering between the peoples for their own sakes. In fact, I had already begun to prepare Cobren for this, but then I received word of your sister."

Launce had been gazing out the entrance of the tent at the people as they milled about, but at the mention of Isa, he looked back at the enchanter. Bronkendol's face was careful, and Launce knew he was measuring Launce's reaction. Taking a deep breath, he steadied his own expression so that it was unreadable. At least, he hoped it was.

"Just as I had predicted, the Fortiers' constant obsession with war had brought down a curse upon their own heads, and one ultimately from the Fortress at that. But when I heard of the work your sister had done, breaking the curse with her heart's strength, I knew she would be the one the Maker had chosen to save the western kingdoms."

Launce crossed his arms. "So you lied to King Rafael about being anointed directly by the Maker."

"No, not at all!" Bronkendol was on his feet, suddenly alive with energy. "How else could you interpret this power?" He held up his hands. "And the fact that I awakened from a curse of over two thousand years? The Maker might not have spoken to me aloud, but I knew what I must do. Your sister had the power to change others' hearts. What better way to keep people at peace?"

"So where do Olivia and I come in? And what about Everard?"

The enchanter blew out a breath and ran his hand through his curly silver hair. "I *am* sorry about your brother-in-law, truly. I hadn't expected him to go like that . . ."

"To be frank, I don't believe that he's dead. But even if he wasn't, you would still be scheming about his death somehow," Launce spat.

"If he was willing to be a part of this, then by all means, I wanted him to remain! But when it became clear that he was dead set on keeping her away from me—"

"So you do aim to kill him."

For the first time, Bronkendol's face darkened, and a flicker of purple flashed in his eyes.

"Before you go any further, do remember what happened the last time your brother-in-law lost someone that was dear to him."

It pained Launce, but he had nothing to reply with. It was true. Ever had been the one to plunge the Fortress into darkness after he'd lost his father.

The enchanter spoke again, but this time his voice was more sympathetic. "I wasn't expecting your sister to be so sick when I first met her. I have tried to help her in the best way I know how."

"I still don't see what Olivia and I have to do with all of this. We have no powers, and I'm the last person anyone would want as king, including myself."

"But that is what's so perfect about you. There are too many old bloods in the royal lines. I have searched far and wide throughout the lands, but when you spoke to me that first day in the stables, I knew I had to have you. You will make a good king because you are kind, and you have more common sense than the rest of these prigs put together."

He waved his hand at the rest of the camp that lay behind them. "The princess is young, and has a fire in her spirit." He paused. "I assume you've noticed that neither of you have the glass slivers."

Launce hadn't planned on discussing what he knew of the glass, but he reluctantly agreed. The enchanter put his tea on the tray and leaned toward him.

"As much as I know, and as well as I can advise you, I am still aware that it would be unwise to keep *everyone* under my influence." So he was intending to put the glass in even more people.

"You are of a kind heart and sound mind," Bronkendol continued. "I want you to be free."

"And if I don't accept?"

The enchanter's face grew hard.

"Then I suppose one of you shall not remain free after all."

It was all Launce could do not to shout every vile word he knew at the man before him. Before he could say anything, however, the ground began to shake. Launce was knocked off balance, and landed hard on his right side, while Bronkendol dove to catch the mirror. Screams rose from the camp, along with the sounds of objects crashing to the ground. And just as he had known the feeling of Isa's power when he felt it, Launce now recognized none other than the power of the Fortress itself.

The earth continued to tremble as Launce watched Bronkendol cradle the mirror, and suddenly he knew what to do. Getting on all fours, Launce crawled as best he could over to the enchanter. Bronkendol protested as Launce pried the wooden frame from his hands. With all his might, he threw the mirror to the ground. The shatter was satisfying, as was the look of injured betrayal on the enchanter's face. Launce wanted to skip with joy, but the earth still quaked so hard that he couldn't get off the ground.

Finally, the shaking stopped. Launce stood unevenly, but the enchanter remained on the ground, holding shattered pieces in his hands, looking stunned.

"Why would you do that?"

"We crossed over into Destin's lands just before we set up camp. That was the Fortress, telling you that are not welcome here. Nor are your schemes." With that, Launce turned sharply and marched out of the tent.

"Launce!" Bronkendol called out behind him. "Remember what I said about the glass. Do not force my hand!" But Launce didn't answer.

41

HONESTLY

"*L*aunce." Launce looked up from the rock he was sitting on to see Olivia approaching. As usual, her guard followed close behind, but this time he also carried her supper tray as well. "May I join you?" Launce scrambled to his feet to fetch a cushion for her. When they were both seated again in front of the tent, she spoke, but her voice was so low he could barely hear it.

"I saw what you did with the mirror."

"I think he's been using it to travel."

"He does. I saw him once, shortly after he came to our kingdom." She set her spoon down and squeezed his knee. "You have to be more careful! He fixed the mirror, but my father is furious. He says you might have derailed the Maker's plans. There are dozens of young men still vying for your place, and the moment this strange enchantment ends, they're going to be at your throat." She went back to eating. "Thankfully, the holy man likes you for some reason."

Launce rolled his eyes. "Bronkendol is no holy man. And he's deluded himself into thinking I actually *want* to be his puppet king."

"Am I so grim a future to be stuck with?" In the dying light of the red sun, tears suddenly glistened in her eyes. "So you were telling the truth back in the courtyard." Before he could explain, she handed her tray to her guard and stood to go.

As he watched her, Launce decided that he was possibly the dullest suitor ever to walk the face of the earth.

"Wait!" He bounded after her. She scowled at him, but allowed Launce to take her hand and drag her to the edge of the camp. Her two guards followed closely behind. Launce didn't stop until they had reached the edge of the first sandstone rise that stood as a sentry outside the red gorge.

Launce had the urge to climb up the little foothill and never come down. He could imagine seeing the entire country for miles. On one side lay the gently winding hills that led to the sea. They were covered in the yellow remnants of aged grass. On the other side stood the gorge. The sandstone was easy to climb. It felt nearly sticky to the touch, and yet wonderfully dry. But the red stone only went up so high, because right behind it was the mountain that held the Fortress.

Olivia instructed the guards to wait on the ground while she and Launce went up just a bit higher. The two men exchanged nervous glances, but she huffed, "You will be able to see us the entire time. I simply don't wish for you to be right on top of me."

Once they had gone high enough to sit above all the tents in the valley, they stopped. Olivia plopped down and arranged her skirts while Launce hovered awkwardly, unsure of how close she really wanted him. This was not a conversation he was ready for yet, but the only way to stop the prolonged pain, he decided, would be by getting it all over with at once.

"I'm going to be honest with you," Launce said.

"That would be nice." She glowered up at him.

Launce took a big breath. "I hadn't planned on even entering the contest until we arrived at your home. Once we were there, Everard could sense that something was wrong. So he convinced me to join the competition, simply so I could tell him what was going on in the stables. I never expected to win." He sat down a few feet from her and let his head drop between his knees.

"No one forced you to win." Launce could hear the resentment still in her voice. "What do you want, Launce? You don't seem to want me or my way of life, and yet you continue to seek me out. It's quite vexing. Actually," she said, "I'm not quite sure that *you* know what you want."

"I couldn't agree more," Launce scoffed, then paused. "My old sweetheart's father made it clear that he wanted her to have nothing to do with me after Isa and Everard married. I'm not common enough for the commoners anymore, but I have no place in courtly matters either." Launce prayed for her to understand. "I'm a man of two worlds now, and neither I nor the world knows to which one I belong."

The anger melted from Olivia's face just a bit, but Launce hated that she still looked sad. He hadn't wanted to bring up his former girl, but if they were being honest, she needed to know everything. "I swear," he scooted just a bit closer, "I never expected to love you."

"*Love* me?" Olivia's voice quivered.

Launce faltered. He hadn't meant to use that word. It had simply come out. And yet, as his father always said, if it escaped the mouth, it had to have been hiding inside of him somewhere. Launce spoke slowly this time, trying to choose his words with more care. "I'm not sure," he admitted. "I've only known you for a few days. But . . ." He caught her hand and held it, even when she tried to pull it away, silently begging her to look at him again. "If not yet, I will be soon if you keep dragging me around like this."

Olivia almost smiled, her lovely skin the color of brown sugar in the fading light of dusk.

"Do you love me?" he pressed. "Because a girl of your sensibility seems far too intelligent for that."

This time, Olivia laughed outright. "I suppose I don't know yet either." Then she sighed, all traces of laughter gone as she looked out at the multitude of campfires dotting the valley below. "All my life, I've been trained in what to say and told how to dress. And when my father told me we were choosing my husband through a contest, I was expected to go willingly." She shuddered delicately. "Until I saw who was competing for my hand. Many of them were older than my father, and most of those that weren't were vulgar, dim-witted, or desirous only of my father's lands.

"But you," she said, finally meeting his gaze again, "you saw me." Then she frowned. "If you entered the contest, how could you expect not to win?"

Launce snorted. "Were you paying heed to any of the games? I couldn't win a duel if my opponent begged me to run him through." Launce stood again and walked a few steps higher. He knew he was making their guards jumpy, but he didn't care.

"I was only able to speak with your sister once," Olivia said softly, "but I liked her right away. She seems kind."

"That she is," Lance said. "So now you know the truth. All of this began because I wanted to take care of her. But there's more now, whether I'm ready for it or not." He looked down at the girl. "I want to take care of you too. I may be a commoner, but I know a good woman when I see one."

"No one has ever called me that before . . . a woman."

Launce wasn't sure, but he thought he could hear a smile in her voice. A foolish sense of joy wriggled through him as he listened, but all too soon it was chased away by the sense of danger he had felt before.

"Your Highness," one of the guards called up. "It is growing dark. Your mother wishes for you to return to your tent soon."

"There is something that you must know, regardless of whether you decide to love me or not." He crouched before her and took her hands in his. "That earthquake earlier today? That was no accident. I have been in and around the Fortress enough to know its power when I feel it. And that earthquake was a warning. If we accept the thrones once we arrive at the Fortress itself, I have no doubt that we will die."

"And how do you know that?" Her voice was suddenly small.

"Only the Fortress chooses its heirs, and to assume we know better than the Maker who placed it there is nothing less than treason." He gripped her hands even more tightly. "At all costs, we must prevent them from placing *anyone* on those thrones."

"How do we do that? How do we stop an entire army that's under Bronk-endol's command?"

Launce grinned in the dark. Never had he liked the Fortress steward more.

"That's what Garin is for."

VENGEANCE

*I*t was tempting to push his horse even faster through the icy pass. But deep down, Ever knew that would be unwise. Using the stolen robe he had followed Isa's original trail to reach what he thought felt like a different realm, although there was no way to tell for sure. Isa's original passage from the Glass Castle to the Fortress was thin, but still present. Like the scent of another man's house, the string of power was similar to that of the Fortress, but was just different enough to stand out against the cold winds that burned his nose.

Ever had traveled the continent with his father numerous times even as a boy, but he'd never even considered that there could be other realms aside from his own. And yet, occupying the same lands that should have been Lingea, Destin's northern neighbor, the familiar territory was nowhere to be found. Instead of the fields of lavender, Ever and his horse were now braving beautiful, dangerous, jagged mountains that stretched for miles and miles, packed with snow that looked as though it had never melted.

Ever hadn't seen another human soul since he'd left the Fortress. Judging from how long Isa had been gone, he knew he should be approaching the castle anytime. Hunger gnawed at him, but he pressed on. The length of time it was taking made him uneasy, and he hoped the strange bridge between realms hadn't closed already.

Ever's horse came to a violent halt, and he was nearly thrown from his seat. "Well, boy, keeping me on my toes, are you?" He rubbed the nervous animal's neck and whispered soothing words in his ear as he dismounted. The horse had come to a stop just at the edge of a new mountain range that stretched from east to west as far as Ever could see.

Knowing the horse would not take him farther, Ever took the reins and began to lead the animal himself. The sense of power was much stronger here, and though his horse, Hugon, was familiar with Ever's own strength, it seemed he did not like the new power one bit. Ever somehow knew that the narrow pass through the towering heights was where he needed to go, so there was no sense in pushing his faithful friend past his limit.

Ever found a protected cave at the base of the mountain to his right, where he fed and watered the beast. "You know what to do," he crooned as he brushed his animal down.

On the day Ever had been presented with his first horse, his father had insisted he train the horse himself, and one of the first major lessons he was instructed to practice was setting the horse free in case of disaster. The practice had taught him to use his unique strength in an entirely new way, and now, as he spoke to his horse for perhaps the last time, he was grateful.

"One day," he told his old friend. "If I'm not back in one day, you need to go home as fast as you can." The horse tossed his midnight mane and nudged Ever's hand for sugar. With a heavy heart, Ever gave him another lump from his pack before checking his weapons once more, and then setting off on foot.

Ever drew his sword as he walked between the towering peaks. The road was notably easy to follow for one that had been used so little in the past three thousand years. The powdery snow crunching beneath his boots, and the warning moans of the wind as it bounced off the mountain sides were the only sounds he could hear. The farther he walked, the more the gusts pushed back at him as well, as though he weren't taking their warnings seriously enough to leave.

"I'm not afraid of death," Ever muttered to the worrisome wind. And it was true. Perhaps he'd feared it once, before he had known what it felt like to witness Isa dying. But this brush with eternity was different. He would give his last breath and more if he could be sure that it would return Isa to herself. No, he did not fear death.

But failure was another consideration entirely.

After a ten-minute walk, he came to the crest of the small hill between the mountains. And what he saw brought him to a halt. As angry as he was, nothing, neither stories nor dreams had prepared him for the beauty that lay ahead. On both sides of the little path he stood upon, a black chasm separated the towering, pointed, snow-encrusted cliffs from the island that they encircled. Only a narrow bridge connected the island of land to the world outside. It wasn't the island that took his breath away though. It was the castle.

Stories of the Glass Queen had been passed down for so many generations that few knew what was truth and what was myth. As a boy, Ever had searched the scrolls and books for anything and everything that even hinted at the mythical citadel.

"Why don't others believe?" he'd once asked Garin as the steward had tucked him in. Garin had patted his head and smiled indulgently.

"Others don't know the Maker's power the way you do. It takes a lot of faith to believe in something you can't see or feel."

"But I don't see or feel the Glass Castle," Ever had argued, "and I still know it's there." Then he'd leaned forward eagerly. "Do you think I will ever see the castle one day?"

"No one has seen that castle in three thousand years. But who knows? Perhaps you shall."

Ever had passed many hours of his early childhood dreaming of meeting the Glass Queen. Surely she would understand him, he'd thought. She would know what it was like to be powerful, to be different. And now, here he was, ready to visit the Glass Castle at last. But instead of meeting the Glass Queen, he had come to kill her son.

Drawing his cloak around him against the chill of the air, Ever steeled himself for what was to come as he began the treacherous journey over the chasm. The further out he went, the icier the path became. It narrowed as well, until it was too thin for more than two men to walk at a time.

The trip across the bridge covered in snow and ice took him much longer than he had expected, but finally Ever arrived at the base of the castle. Glistening blue and purple glass plates with frosted swirls like ivy and wind were etched into the solid gates. Again, despite his hatred for the enchanter himself, Ever had to wonder at the beauty of it all, and his soul ached just a bit. Why couldn't the son have died, and the queen have survived instead? There were so many things he longed to ask her. What was it like to have so much power? Had she always felt slightly deserted, the way he had growing up?

Was there a way to return Isa's power to her?

But he hadn't come to gawk. Ever removed one of his leather gloves and placed his palm against the right gate. Closing his eyes, he pressed firmly, and blue flame leaped from his hand. With a creak, the gate began to open. He stepped through, relieved. He hadn't been sure until then that the ancient castle would respond to the Fortress's power.

Four blue, sleek steps stretched across the entire entrance and led up to the castle itself. Two more great doors towered above Ever, and again, they opened for his power. A small flicker of hope warmed his heart. Perhaps he did stand a chance of surviving this encounter. After all, it was all the Maker's power, and his cause was the righteous one.

Vengeance isn't generally considered a noble cause, a blunt voice inside of him whispered, making him pause before passing through the gigantic door.

But he wasn't doing this for vengeance. The man needed to be stopped.

True as that may be, you know you wouldn't be satisfied if he simply fell over and died of old age after all he's done to Isa. You want to make him suffer.

And it was true. Never had Everard longed so much to shed one man's blood.

Just as he began to enter, something made him stop once again. It was faint, but it sounded like someone was whistling, an eerie noise in the empty halls. He followed the unfamiliar tune through the longest and highest throne room he'd ever imagined. The entire Fortress could have fit into this room alone. The whistling took him down a smaller hallway, out of the throne room and to the left. Ever's heart sped up to an alarming rate as he got closer. This was it.

When he pushed the door open, however, there was no one, only a large furnace in the far corner of a cluttered room filled with worktables and glass odds and ends scattered everywhere. He stepped in and listened harder. The sound was still getting closer. By the time he realized that the whistling was coming from behind him, however, it was too late.

"Ah, there you are. I've been expecting you."

43

READY OR NOT

*E*ver whirled around to find the short, curly-haired servant from Rafael's palace holding a steaming tray of tea and biscuits. Ever lifted his sword, but the small man only waved his hand as he walked on by. "You won't be needing that. I'll tell you whatever you want to know, so long as you allow me my nightly cup of tea. It helps me sleep."

If the little man had meant to make Ever more comfortable, he had done exactly the opposite. Knowing his enemy would tell him everything meant he had only one purpose for Ever. Death, or some fate even worse, where he wouldn't be able to utter a word of it to anyone. Still, as Ever warily watched the man pour, stir, and sip his own tea, the idea of discovering what the enchanter had planned was tantalizing. Ever didn't sheath his sword, but he did lower it enough to stand directly before the enchanter as the small man served himself a biscuit.

"You'll tell me anything?"

"Ask away." Bronkendol smiled and leaned back in his chair as though he were merely having a friend over to gossip. Ever wasn't sure where the question came from, but it was the first one on his tongue that didn't tempt him even more to kill the enchanter then and there.

"Why Launce?"

"He recently asked me the same question," the enchanter chuckled. "I like that boy. You see, I knew I needed someone new, unsullied by the world, hence the contest. I had hoped that of the many contestants, I might find someone that I could at least tolerate. And then you thrust him right into my hands."

"Launce hates the court."

"But he's also young and impressionable. And also desperate for some approval."

Was he? Ever tried to remember if he'd ever noticed that about the young man, but his mind was too cluttered to remember.

"I know what you're not asking though." Bronkendol placed his tea on a table's edge and stood up, all signs of joviality gone. "And I can assure you that I will never be able to express to her how sorry I am for what had to be done."

Ever tightened his grip on the sword.

"I know it must be difficult for you to understand now, but in time you will."

"You sent her back a shell of who she was before!" Ever exploded. "Her fire is gone, and she can no longer laugh! Why did any of that have to be done?"

"I saved her life." He crossed his arms and studied Ever. "Your wife was losing her fire already. Before it left her on its own accord, I took it from her so that she would continue to live at least in body." His voice grew softer. "I didn't want her to die the way your father did when his fire was extinguished."

Cold fear trickled into every part of Ever's body. What had this man done to her that was so bad that he still refused to tell him? As if the enchanter knew what he was thinking, he pulled a small mirror from his pocket and held it out to Ever.

"It would be easiest if I simply showed you instead."

Ever glared at him for a long moment before looking into the mirror.

He could see Isa bound to the chair that faced the furnace in the corner of the very room he was standing in. The fear on her face broke Ever's heart. Isa wasn't a warrior, nor had Ever trained her to withstand torture. She shouldn't have needed *that* training.

The enchanter's light hit Isa's heart with such a force that her chair slammed backward, straining against the chains that bound it to the floor. Her face went specter white as the glass which he held to her chest began to suck the life from her body. Tears of rage welled in Ever's eyes as he watched her suffer. The worst part was hearing her cry out his name over and over again. No wonder she believed he'd failed her. She had pleaded with him to come. And he hadn't.

Ever thought the scene would end soon. It must. But instead, it dragged on as Isa fought for every bit of her heart as it was wrenched from her. Despite knowing the outcome, panic slipped through Ever as he realized she was giving in. Her fight, valiant as it had been, had come to an end, and as her head rolled forward, Ever saw for himself what she had truly lost.

"That kind of pain should have killed her!" Ever's voice was not his own. It sounded strangled.

"I shared some of my own strength with her so she would last," Bronkendol said as the mirror went dark. "I promise, I made it as short and simple as possible. But it will be for the best."

"For the best?" Ever slammed his fist into the enchanter's temple. Bronkendol went flying backward, and Ever hated him all the more for surviving the attack. That kind of hit would have killed an average man. "You killed your mother for power, and now you've taken every sliver of happiness from my wife!" This time, Ever kicked him so hard he heard the satisfying crack of a rib. "Was it worth it?" he shouted.

The enchanter slumped against the floor, shaking with the effort, but at last, he raised his head to speak.

"The power to influence hearts and bring peace to the people? Yes." Bronkendol's eyes darkened. "It was worth it."

Ever raised his sword, but it didn't come down as it was supposed to. It felt like it had caught on something. Looking back, Ever realized that it had.

A glass man, taller than any human, had caught his sword with one hand. With a shout, Ever sent a bolt of blue flame up his weapon, and the glass giant shattered to pieces. Before Ever could turn back to Bronkendol, however, another glass man emerged from the far wall. This one had his own scythe, a piece of glass twisted to reveal hundreds of razor edges along its blade.

Each time a new guard came at him, it was no match for Ever's sword and flame. But his glass opponents began to come faster and faster, and Ever soon realized the enchanter was nowhere to be seen. The glass guards were coming too fast for him to go searching, as he had to take care to actually dismantle the warriors entirely. Cutting off an arm only made it a new weapon, a limb of broken glass that swung wildly about, sharp enough to shred his skin to pieces if he allowed it to touch him. He was getting nowhere.

With a loud cry, Ever exhaled and pressed every bit of fire within him out into a ring of blue flames. It was exhausting, but the ring rippled out, and this time no glass warriors emerged again. There was only Bronkendol, huddled in his corner, holding his precious mirror up in front of his mouth. Like a frightened babe talking to its doll, he whispered to it.

Ever moved toward him like a storm, but just before he was there, a thick red filled Ever's sight. Clouds of crimson smoke burned and made it impossible to see. But if the enchanter had wanted to stop him, he would have to try harder than that.

Ever had wanted to learn all of the enchanter's plans, but he would never have the patience for that game now. A crash sounded from behind him, and when Ever turned, much to his dismay, he saw the small form that had been huddled against the wall just seconds before had somehow made it to the door, and was watching him stupidly as though in a daze.

Ever launched himself at the figure. This time, he would hit him so hard that Bronkendol would never again open his eyes to see anyone or anything. The dance of war carried him to his foe, the taste of blood already on his tongue.

~

Isa shivered as the shining blue walls came into view. She didn't recall much of her journey from Bronkendol's castle to the Fortress. Her pain had been too great, and her mind too muddled. All she could really remember was wishing to fall asleep and never awaken again. Sometime during the first day, the bag of food and water the enchanter had strapped to her horse had been blown off by a strong gust of wind. It had been all Isa could do to stay astride the horse herself.

This time, pain and hunger weren't her sources of discomfort, but rather the ache in her chest. Yes, the feelings were there once more, but she still felt raw inside, as though the return of her emotions had chafed her heart until it was ready to bleed. Isa was going because she knew she should save her husband. But like the stark gray and white of the land that surrounded her, the sunbeam delight she'd possessed on her wedding day was nowhere to be found. She kept her heart blank, choosing not to remember all the ways Ever had hurt her . . . and all the ways she had hurt him. And like her joy, her strength was still gone too.

Now that the glass citadel was in view once more, Isa knew she would need to focus not on the aches inside, but rather the impossible undertaking ahead of her. Garin had told her how to follow Ever's path between realms, using the Glass Queen's dress that Isa had worn home, but she hadn't plotted out a course of action for what she might do once she arrived. For while she rode into the wilderness, that moment had felt like it would never come, and she nearly didn't want it to.

A whinny caught her by surprise. Shielding her eyes from the bright snow and strong gusts of wind, she found a large cave to her left. Inside, shielded from the elements, was Ever's horse, Hugon.

"You should stay here too," Isa said to her own horse, dismounting and rubbing his neck. It hadn't been hard to fall in love with her horse again at least. A few nuzzles and she was all his. If only Ever were so easy.

After leaving her mount alongside Hugon, Isa took only her sword and started toward the castle alone. When she got to the pass that cut between the two mountains, her stomach flopped at the sight of the icy bridge she would have to cross.

To distract herself as she crossed the bottomless chasm, she thought back to her conversation with Garin. Was he right, about gaining her feelings back in time? It wasn't that Isa didn't feel now, rather she didn't feel the way she once had. It was too easy to recall every instance when Ever had left her for some other business, particularly when it was to go see Kartek. She recalled every time he spoke with another woman who had once been one of his admirers; each time, she'd wondered if deep down he had wished for someone who was able to fulfill her duties to the Fortress and the kingdom. Someone to give him an heir and command the Fortress fire.

To be fair, he had been most attentive upon her return to the Fortress. His words and touches had seemed earnest. But had he truly missed her? Or was he simply feeling guilty?

By the time Isa reached the other side of the bridge, she had nearly convinced herself it would indeed be easier never to feel again. Still, she had a job to do. It wouldn't do to let her nonexistent emotions hinder her from protecting him. Isa drew her sword as she crept up the glass steps into the castle.

The fact that the gate and the doors were still open was at least a small comfort. It was unlikely they would have opened if Ever had died below the bridge before reaching them.

The throne room was empty, but Isa could just make out the sounds of voices. Anxiety squeezed her insides as she came to the end of the throne room and realized where they were coming from. She would have to go into that horrid room again. Every part of her cried out to go back. Isa paused halfway down the hall from the hateful door, which was ajar. Voices no longer spoke. Instead, collisions sounded as metal clanged and glass shattered.

The glass giants, Isa realized. Readying her sword, she crept to the door, wondering how she could help without her power. Perhaps she should just watch and see what had happened. When she peeked around the open door, there were no glass giants waiting for her.

Only her husband, with his sword raised and his body ready to strike. And his fiery eyes of steel were trained right on her.

44

BLADE'S EDGE

*I*sa stared in shock as Ever charged toward her, his sword blazing with blue flame. By the time she thought to run, it was too late. Their weapons met with a violent clang that jarred Isa's bones. Her movements were flimsy and weak against his. Still, even if they weren't empowered in the way Ever's were, the hours of practice had stamped at least the rudimentary skills of swordplay into her head. To escape their locked weapons, a contest she was sure to lose, Isa twisted and rolled. As soon as she was on her feet again, she took off running as fast as she could back toward the throne room.

Dismay hummed in her mind to the rhythm of her heartbeat. Why was he trying to kill her? No matter how confused her feelings were about her husband, Isa knew *this* was not what she wanted.

Halfway down the hall, Isa dared a glance over her shoulder. Ever was pursuing, but not at his usual speed. Pushing herself faster, she wondered what she was going to do when she got to the hall's end. There would be more room to run in the throne room, for sure, but there was no place to hide. The entire room was empty, with the exception of the two thrones. No, she decided, she needed to go somewhere where she could hide and catch her breath as she figured out her next plan of action.

When she reached the throne room, Isa was already out of breath, and she could hear Ever quickly coming up behind her. Without thinking, Isa darted up the closest set of spiral stairs that led to the bridge that overlooked the entire room. She wasn't more than a dozen steps up though when she felt the glass shudder beneath her.

Ever had reached the stairs. To her surprise, before he had gone three steps up, his foot slipped. As he tumbled backward, Isa caught a glimpse of the violet glow just inside his eye. And blue. There was also the glint of blue.

So that's what the enchanter was doing with her power. Anger rose within her as Isa realized Bronkendol was using her own power against her. Now, if only she knew how to break the hold.

As Ever struggled to right himself, Isa bolted once more up the steps. Whatever rage the enchanter had put Ever in must be making him clumsy. Everard was the most agile creature she had ever seen, but now his clumsiness was the only thing that was keeping her alive. Once she reached the bridge, she paused, not sure which way to go. She hadn't explored enough to know which ones would provide places to hide. Then she remembered the vision.

The green room. With the confused state Ever was in, the mirrors might make him pause. They certainly wouldn't protect her from his wrath, but the time it would take for him to find her within the room's strange reflections might give her time to form a plan.

Unfortunately, if Isa remembered correctly from the Glass Queen's vision, the room was downstairs, which meant she was running the wrong direction. There had to be someplace where Isa could turn around. With her decision made, she sprinted down the hall to her right, but she could hear Ever trailing behind her.

Please, she begged the Fortress, *I don't know what to do!* Without her strength, she was no match for him physically. Her only hope rested in knowing the castle better than he did. But when he found her eventually, which he would, what then?

She didn't want to hurt him, but she couldn't let him just kill her either. A strange sense, one that felt much like the power she used to have, warned her to look back. When she did, she found that Ever had closed much of the distance between them, and was continuing to gain on her. Desperately, she tried to choose a door, any door that might give her somewhere to hide. And hopefully, one that wasn't locked. As he drew closer still, Isa picked the closest room to her and threw herself against its door with all of her might.

To her immense relief, the door was unlocked, and she had just enough time to lock it after flinging it closed. Ever let out a shout of rage that echoed down the glass halls outside, and Isa knew she didn't have much time. Unfortunately, she realized, she had chosen what could only have been the worst room in the entire castle.

Weapons filled the room. Although the chamber was nearly the size of the servants' kitchen at home, it was so cluttered she received several nicks along her legs and arms in her hurried entrance. Hung on the walls, from the ceiling, and filling the floor in piles, there was little space to even turn around between the stacks of swords and axes, flails, and scythes. Even chains were strewn about. Some of the weapons were so ancient she didn't recognize them, but didn't need much imagination to guess how they could be used. She would never make it out of this room alive.

Then, out of the corner of her eye, she saw another door that was hidden behind a stack of pikes leaned upright against the wall. Everard had resorted to kicking the door, and it wouldn't be long before he knocked it in. Praying the door wasn't a closet, Isa crawled between the rows of razor edges that stuck out from all directions, and tried to push it open.

It seemed ridiculous that a glass door should stick in the same way a wooden one might, but this door was most definitely stuck. *Just let me open it,* she pleaded to the Fortress. But the door didn't budge. As she heard the glass lock on the door behind her shatter, Isa cried out in frustration.

To her amazement, the smallest streak of blue fire flitted from her fingers into the door. Unfortunately, it wasn't fast enough. The door behind her crashed to the ground with a sound that echoed throughout the empty castle. Isa barely managed to throw herself behind an ancient suit of armor just before he stormed in.

Because of the height of the piles, and the rage that seemed to somewhat blind him, Isa felt oddly well-hidden. As she watched Ever shouting and swinging his sword in circles, something warm dripped down her cheek. She put her hand up to her face, only to pull it down covered in bright red blood. Judging from the glass pieces all over the floor at her feet, she realized a piece must have flown out and cut her when the door had shattered.

The armor was just beside the second door, so when she thought he wasn't looking, Isa reached out and tried once more. Again, the blue glowed, but only just. This time, however, the door opened, and Isa nearly let out a cry of joy when she saw that it wasn't a closet after all. Before she could dart into the new room, however, she glanced back to see Ever standing over her, like a wolf regarding its prey. Instinctively, Isa kicked both her legs out, knocking the suit over onto him, and though her heart weighed heavy with guilt, she knew it was better than being gutted.

Scrambling through, she shut this door as well. As there was no lock, she would have to hide quickly. The room appeared as though the servants had left their work in a hurry. The room was full of bed linens. Most were folded and stacked neatly, but some had simply been tossed in a heap, most likely waiting for their washing. Just before the door behind her burst open, Isa ducked behind a tall pile, hoping it would hide her while she made her way to the room's main door.

She did no such thing though. Ever leapt to the center of the room and began kicking down piles of cloth. Isa froze, praying for him to just go away.

"I know you're in here," he bellowed. "I can see the trail of blood!" Isa instinctively put her hand up to her cheek. The cut was still bleeding. Before he could come any closer, she took her chances and bolted for the door, which put her back in the hallway once more. She didn't pause to look back this time. Instead, she dashed toward the back of the castle, where she knew the greenhouse lay.

Her strength was so spent from running down the stairs, through the throne room, and down the secret hall behind the thrones that Isa nearly gave up by the time she reached the greenhouse. The light outside was beginning to fade into twilight, and it was hard to see as she worked her way toward the back. She could hear Ever thundering down the last hall. Her progress was infuriatingly slow as she continued to bump into pots of soil and buckets for water. As she squeezed down behind a pot that grew something with thick, furry leaves, she began to plead with the Fortress.

Let him . . . But she didn't know how to finish. *Let him what? Let him get confused and give up? Let me best him in swords?*

Let him see.

Isa looked down at her hands in the dimming light. Though a bit of her flame could flicker, it was no more than that which might light a candle. She couldn't beat him in swordplay, particularly not without her full strength, and Ever's surrender was out of the question, unless the Fortress knocked him down on its own accord. Ever didn't give up even when he was his own self.

But how do I open his eyes? she whimpered, more out of habit than out of an expectation of an answer. The blue glow grew brighter as it moved down the hall toward her, its light already bouncing off the oddly angled windows.

Love him the way he tried to love you.

Isa gasped, nearly giving away her hiding place, when the Fortress spoke to her. How long it had been since she'd heard that voice! How she had yearned for it! *But it didn't work,* she stammered in her head. *And I can't go near him. He will kill me!*

Leave his heart to me. Just trust me and do as you know you should. I will bring about the rest.

Isa drew in a shaky breath. Ever had entered the greenroom. Just as she'd hoped, the light of the dying day cast eerie reflections upon the hundreds of concave panes, making it difficult to tell illusion from reality. She nestled even deeper into her hiding place.

"I can sense you in here," Ever hissed. "And I can smell your blood." Isa peeked out just enough to see him crouched, tightly coiled like a predator ready to strike. His face was unshaven, and his eyes burned with a hatred Isa hadn't known him capable of. Perhaps brightest of all were the blue-violet slivers at the edges of his eyes. All the courage Isa had gathered fled her again. How was she to conquer her own power?

Isa cringed as he passed her, circling the room. It was only as he walked away, still circling, that she realized that there *was* another power present besides her own and the enchanter's, one that she might use.

She would have to harness Ever's strength in place of her own. If she could hold it just long enough to slip past his defenses, there might be a chance. The Fortress *had* provided a way.

Ever had finished his first circle around the room, and was beginning his second. If she didn't strike now, she might lose her chance. Fear made her tremble, but Isa swallowed hard and silently laid her sword on the ground. She felt around her feet until her hands found a clod of dirt. She would do her best, but everything was up to the Fortress now.

As hard as she could, Isa flung the clod across the room, where it hit the window with a loud *thunk*. When Ever flipped his head to look toward the sound, Isa jumped up from her hiding place, landing before him. She seized Ever's cloak and pulled so that his face was almost touching hers.

As was his sword.

Somehow, he'd managed to bring his sword up to her neck in the split second she had moved. He had not only evaded her trap, but had set one of his own. And Isa had walked right into it. She could feel the edge of the blade beginning to cut into her skin. Her breaths were ragged and fast, as he held her there, neither of them moving. She still clutched his cloak in both hands, unable to move even if she'd wanted to.

"You stole her from me." Ever's breath was hot on her face. "Now I will do to you what you did to me."

"Ever!" Isa squeaked, but her husband only shook her with his free hand, so hard it felt like her head was rattling.

"Ever, it's me!"

"Silence!" Pressing the blade even deeper into her throat, Ever leaned down and whispered in her ear, "Now I will do to you just as you did to her. It will be meticulous and slow." A trickle rolled down her neck, though she couldn't tell if it was blood or sweat. She had no more time. Closing her eyes, Isa reached out the way Ever had taught her to.

And felt nothing. If she hadn't been able to see the blue light in her husband's eyes, she would have thought none was there. But it was there, and she was determined to find it. Or she would die.

Again she reached out, but still there was nothing. Isa reached further. She only had a little air left . . .

It was hardly even warm at first, more like a tingle than a flame. But the more she concentrated, the more Isa remembered the feel of Ever's strength. Whereas her own strength had often felt like a stream of joy, bubbling delight-fully as it danced along its banks, Ever's was more like a river that had exceeded its capacity to hold rain. Strong and swift, it moved to envelop everything it touched. And now, Isa needed it to envelop them both. After drawing in what might be her last breath, Isa pulled Ever and the blade closer.

Her lips met his, and they tasted of salt. Pain bit her neck, but Isa let it. He fought her. Instead of the predator, he was now the hunted, trapped in a net and wriggling in confusion. In her mind, Isa wove their strengths together, braiding them into a rope that could not be severed. Her weak light and his strong one. But the sword was too sharp. Too much blood was spilling down her neck.

Just when she could not hold the blade off any longer, Ever leaned in.

Dropping the sword, he crushed her to himself as he kissed her with a desperation he'd never had before. A wave of blue light exploded out from them with a *boom*, and with a cry, Ever let go and dropped to the floor, pressing his eyes into his palms.

"Ever!" she tried to scream, but her call was lost in the deafening crack that echoed throughout the entire castle. Isa hit her knees beside him, holding him as he clutched his head. Beneath them, the entire island shook.

Somehow, despite his pain, she felt Ever throw up a shield of light around them. Through the shield, Isa watched as the queen's tower gave way first. The cracks appeared in the center of the tower itself, then crawled both up toward the six-sided bedroom and down to the rest of the castle. Like the plague it spread. Even in the near darkness, splinters visibly worked their way loose from the cracks. The castle was collapsing.

Once the tower could no longer support itself, the queen's room fell. Hitting the main roof on its way down, it was as though the tower had claws, and used them to ensure it wasn't alone. Chunks of tower and rooftop and walls mingled as they sank. The castle groaned as it began to break apart.

Isa didn't have to watch the pieces plummet into the depths of the chasm that surrounded them to recognize that the cracks were moving toward them. Her ears began to hurt as larger chunks of towers and upper floors caved in on themselves.

Finally, it was their turn. Isa screamed and clung to Ever as the roof above them collapsed. The shattering glass was deafening. Isa wondered if the island itself might topple. The ground beneath them shook, and even the moon was blocked by the cloud of dust and debris as the Glass Castle crumbled. It felt as though it would never end.

Eventually, the ringing in her ears did stop. Isa dared to look up, and Ever let the shield fall. In the light of the moon, they crouched, surrounded by a sea of blue-green dust. What had been proud pillars and arches was now reduced to sparkling sand beneath their feet. After surviving myth and legend, time and spell, the Glass Castle was truly gone.

45

TREADING WITH CARE

"Shouldn't we have been there by now? They said it would only take four days." Olivia grimaced and shivered. Despite the thick fur cloak her maidservant had brought along, she was somehow still cold. How she was still cold under all those petticoats, Launce would never know. With the vast layers of clothing women had to wear, he was amazed they didn't sweat all the time. Launce knew better than to say such things aloud though. His mother and sisters had chastised him for pointing out such truths on more than one occasion.

As the mountain road wound higher, travel had become more difficult for the carriages and supply caravans. So difficult that the trip had so far taken eight whole days. Of course, Launce had anticipated this, reveled in it, actually, and had suggested they take the longer road around the mountain in order to extend their slow trek.

"We don't have the time to dally, but it is good of you to consider such things," Rafael had gushed. "That's kingly thinking for you already. Is it not so, Your Holiness?"

"Quite so," Bronkendol had replied placidly. From the look he'd sent Launce after that, it was clear he knew what game Launce was playing. Taking the longer road would buy Garin at least another week to prepare for what was coming. And since he'd not been able to send out any messenger birds, Garin must know by now that something was wrong. Had Rafael taken Launce's suggestion, it would have bought Garin at least three more days' time.

And yet, it was for naught. The mountain road it was. All Launce could do was pray that the caravans carrying weapons Rafael had ordered to be taken would roll back down the mountain and be dashed to pieces. Without their drivers, of course. But thus far, no such good fortune had come. Even the mirror, which Launce had hoped to dash again while the enchanter was gone on one of his many disappearances, was wrapped up tightly in bedclothes, and guarded fiercely by two soldiers. The soldiers had been added after Launce's first attempt at ridding them of the glass. Now, all he could do was pray and try to prepare Olivia for the difficulty that lay ahead.

Bronkendol's good mood had disappeared along with the last of the autumn warmth. After his last disappearance through his mirror, he'd returned with just a vestige of his easy mirth. Instead of watching Launce and Olivia with the contentment of a grandfather, he simply stared vacantly, or spoke to the stupid little mirror he kept in the pocket of his robe. Despite the unfortunate consequences this dark mood promised for Launce and Olivia, Launce found an immense deal of pleasure in seeing the mysterious bruises on the enchanter's face, as well as the way he kept an arm protectively over his side. Launce didn't know where the man had gone, or what he had done to earn himself such injuries, but Launce hoped they would hurt for a very long time. Launce also hoped they were one more sign that Everard was still alive.

Today, however, Launce had no time to dwell on such niceties. "Before we reach the Fortress, there are a few things you need to know," he told Olivia in a low voice. Olivia regarded him with a keen eye before nodding.

Thankfully, the narrowness of the mountain path had made it impossible for more than two people to ride side by side, which gave them at least a small bit of privacy. This would be the last part of the journey that would be safe enough for them to share secrets. Launce decided to make it good.

"You asked me how my sister and her husband met. Are you still interested?"

"As you can see, I am much too busy."

Launce nearly laughed aloud as she rolled her eyes at him. He sobered quickly, as the story began to bring about all sorts of memories that he would rather have done without.

"When my sister was just nine, our family went to see the annual parade that Everard and his parents were to participate in. She was shoved into the street right in front of his horse, and he helped her to her feet. My sister didn't know royal etiquette, and in her haste to thank him, grabbed his arm. He shoved her off, but didn't control his power." Launce drew in a breath, the bile rising in his throat the way it always did when he remembered. "Everard's force shoved her beneath a rearing horse. She nearly lost the use of a wrist and ankle. Then, for thirteen years, Isa lived as an outcast. He took everything from her, and he never cared to know it."

Olivia watched him with large eyes, but didn't speak. He could see from her expression that she hadn't heard this version of Isa and Everard's story before. It made him wonder how many people really knew.

"Then last year, when Ever's father, King Rodrigue, died," Launce continued, "Everard lost his temper and got drunk." The words flowed more freely the more Launce spoke, the desire to tell someone suddenly bursting forth like an overfilled wineskin. He hadn't realized how much he needed to share this story, the one that haunted him every night as he fell asleep.

"Everard ordered his soldiers to kill all the sick and crippled right where they found them, on the streets, in their homes, everywhere." The princess's eyes grew wide, but Launce shook his hand at her alarm. "His orders were never carried out."

"Why not?" she breathed.

"The Fortress cursed him, taking the very strength from his body. But not just him. Even the Fortress servants turn to phantoms, and the Fortress itself went dark for the first time in a thousand years."

A light of understanding lit Olivia's eyes.

"That's why he never chose a queen after his ball. I mean, we knew he had gone to war with Nevina, but everyone had still expected him to choose someone . . ." She stopped the train of thought abruptly and leaned forward. "So, how did he find your sister?"

"Honestly, it's still beyond me. Isa says it was the will of the Fortress." He still hated thinking about it to this day, even if it was of the Fortress. "My father was caught in a blizzard, and he decided to seek shelter in the Fortress, not knowing Everard was still living there. We hadn't heard or seen anything of the Fortress or its staff for months. But once Father was inside, Everard forced him to share all about our family. When Everard learned that my sister had a strong heart, he demanded she come to the Fortress alone, or he would send a sickness on us all."

"She went, didn't she?" the princess guessed quietly

Launce nodded. *Deep breaths*, he reminded himself. Remembering that day still made his heart race. When he was able to speak again, his voice was shaky.

"It was months before we heard from her. My father nearly lost his senses as we waited. And even after we heard that she was safe, even after she returned home, Isa was no longer ours. She belonged to the Fortress, and somehow, to Ever. But still, the curse would not break."

"What changed?"

"Everard's heart was so hardened that they nearly both died before the curse broke. In his fear and anger, my brother-in-law had decided that he knew better how to protect Destin. That decision to trust himself, rather than the Fortress, nearly cost him and my sister their lives."

"So that is the burden he carries," Olivia said.

"What?"

Olivia paused for a moment before answering, drawing her yellow cloak about her a little more snugly.

"King Rodrigue and my father were the closest of friends. I suppose you could say that Everard was always like a bit of a nephew to my father." She blushed a little. "When I was little, there was some talk of betrothing us from a young age, but Everard wouldn't have it. He always said he wanted the Fortress to choose." She gave a nervous laugh. "I was more grateful than you'll ever know. I trusted him, but the man frightened me, even from a young age. He was always so brooding . . ." Her voice trailed off as she stared up at the path ahead of them, her eyes distant.

It took everything in Launce not to think daggers at his brother-in-law, who might or might not be dead.

Finally, she shook her head and resumed speaking. "Anyway, I noticed as soon as you all arrived that there was something different about him. He was serious before, but now he stalks . . . I mean, he stalked around like a panther, guarding its prey. There was a feverish look in his eye the whole time he was there, as though he were desperately afraid of something. It all makes sense now, because he *needs* her." She nodded once to herself. Launce didn't miss the dreamy look in her eyes though. Isa had often looked the same way as a girl when she talked about true love. Launce had always scoffed at such things. Now, however, he found himself morbidly curious as to what she was thinking.

"But," Olivia looked at him, "why are you telling me all of this? I sense it is not a time you particularly like to relive."

Launce edged his horse closer to hers, hoping not to draw the attention of the others. King Rafael appeared to be lost in whatever world the enchanter kept him and the rest of the travelers in, but Bronkendol continually glanced back at the two of them.

"This scheme the enchanter has with your father is nothing short of suicide." Olivia's eyes grew wide, but she said nothing, so Launce continued. "There is a bond between Destin's Fortress and its monarchs. Isa has tried to explain it to me four or five times, and it's rather difficult to understand or talk about, but I'll do my best.

"A thousand years ago, a lower knight from Tumen happened to hear a cry for help from a woman that lived in what is now Soudain, just at the foot of the Fortress's mountain. He went to his liege and requested to bring some of his brothers with him to help the woman's family fight off the bandits that had been plaguing them. Tumen's king refused, however, as the woman wasn't wealthy or anyone of importance. So the knight said he would help her himself.

"The knight set out on his own, and nearly died helping the woman's family. But in the end, he was victorious, and when he was, others from the area began to ask him for help as well. They had been forgotten by the Tumenian king, and needed protection from the marauders who frequented their homelands. And while the king refused to assist him, even ordering him to return to Tumen's capital and to ignore the peasants, the Maker was pleased. As a reward for helping the helpless, He gave the knight his own crown, and Destin was born."

"That doesn't seem so hard to understand," Olivia said.

"It isn't. The difficult part is understanding the Fortress itself. You see, the Maker gifted the Fortress to the knight as a way to help protect the people. He imbued His own power into the citadel to aid the king and his descendants in protecting the people and providing shelter for the desolate.

"But the Fortress isn't just a place. It's..." Launce struggled for words. It didn't matter how many times Isa explained it. The Fortress was hard to comprehend. "It is as if the Maker placed a part of Himself within the Fortress stones. And not just there, but in the hearts of its monarchs as well. I hear Everard and Isa talking to it sometimes, even when they're not at home.

He paused, feeling silly for his inadequate words. "I used to scoff at the old stories, but since spending time there myself, I can't deny the feeling of power and awe that the place inspires." Olivia still stared at him, looking more confused than ever, so Launce tried another tactic.

"I'm sure you've seen Everard's eyes?"

"Everyone knows about the Fortiers' eyes."

"Well, it's said that when the Fortiers' fires go out of their eyes, they die. For those with pure hearts, who have been faithful to the Maker, it is of old age or during battle. But for those that forget whom they serve, the Maker takes them home sooner. Isa says it is because the Fortress holds too great a power for an unfaithful king to handle. If he cannot wield it correctly, the Fortress removes its light from his eyes, and the Maker takes him to eternity so the people will remain safe in the hands of the next monarch. As I said, it is not easy to understand."

He looked her right in the eyes, holding her gaze this time. "The reason I tell you this is because we are in grave danger." Olivia bit her lip, but said nothing, so Launce went on in a rushed whisper, for Bronkendol was watching them once more.

"The Fortress cursed Everard, its own son, in order to preserve the purity of its kings and queens and save the innocents of the land. How do you think the Fortress will respond when we barge in and declare we're putting ourselves upon its throne, the throne the Fortress alone has chosen for the last thousand years? Especially," Launce said, "after its queen was taken and its king was attacked." Even if Everard was still alive, Launce had no doubt Bronkendol had at least made some attempt on his life, or would soon, at any rate.

A delicate shiver danced across Olivia's shoulders. "I didn't think of that," she said in a low voice. Then she glanced up at her father and Bronkendol ahead of them. "What about them?" she whispered. "If we don't do as they say, they will do terrible things to us too."

"If there is one thing I've learned from my sister," Launce said slowly, "it's that the Fortress always knows what it's doing. The hard part is believing that, even when we can't see it."

And as much as it pained him to say it, Launce finally knew it was the truth. Isa had trusted the Fortress to see her through the curse. And it had. Now it was his turn to trust, and, he prayed, Olivia's. He didn't doubt Olivia's sincerity in the slightest. As they reached the rounded summit of the mountain, however, he hoped she could keep that faith, for he got the feeling that their current troubles were about to multiply.

46

RAW

*E*ver's eyes felt as though someone had ripped them open. The glass dust had settled, and the sounds of shifting debris were quieting, and yet he could only clutch his eyes. His arm shook as he looked down, half expecting to see blood gushing from his face, the pain was so great. To his relief, however, there was no great flow. Only a few drops sat on his hands where the slivers had fallen from his eyes. The shards of glass themselves were gone.

His relief was short-lived, however, when he looked up at Isa. His wife knelt beside him, looking around with the same dazed expression Ever felt on his own face. Copper strands of her hair waved in the dry, icy wind. Her right cheek was smeared with dried blood, and the wound on her neck was still fresh.

Who had done such a thing? And where was Bronkendol?

The enchanter was nowhere to be seen. Only the island covered in broken glass remained. Enough of the glass had fallen over the edges of the island, into the depths of the void below, that it was possible to see some of the objects that had been inside the castle through the remaining debris. Here and there, shining green and blue in the moonlight, bits and corners of objects and furniture stuck up out of the gleaming rubble.

Joy and alarm exploded within him as he realized that the fire was once again burning within her eyes. From the guarded weariness in those eyes, a terrible feeling as to what had just transpired began to build in his stomach as well. He tried to recall all that had happened, but had to sift through the haze. He remembered rage. Hate as pure and volatile as molten steel had taken hold of his body. The more he considered it, the more he did remember fighting someone. But that had been Bronkendol . . .

He filtered back through his memories, and saw only her. What had come over him? How could he have been so blind to do such a thing? Such things?

Slowly, so as not to frighten her, Ever reached out and gently took her face in his hands. She made no move to stop him, but watched him warily all the same. The wound just under the hollow of her cheek was easy enough to heal. The cut at her neck was much deeper though. Guilt roared in his ears. Had he pressed any deeper, it would have killed her.

As he worked to heal her, the blue fire thrumming between his fingers, Ever tried to come up with something to say. All he could think to ask, though, was the question that had drawn him to this forsaken wasteland in the first place. That Isa had followed him was enough to give him a shred of hope. But she wouldn't meet his eyes long enough for him to know for sure.

After five minutes of silence, Ever could stand it no longer. "Are you—"

"Yes." She still didn't look at him.

Ever longed to tuck the stray bits of hair behind her ear, but he knew better. So he focused instead on trying to keep her skin from scarring. When he was finally done, he hoped she would speak, but she simply stood up and wandered through the rubble, pushing the broken glass bits around with her foot. When she did speak again, her voice was practiced and distant, statesmanlike.

"Did you see what he did with the mirror?" She spoke without looking at him.

Ever tried to recall. The enchanter had spoken to a little mirror before the rage had overtaken him, but he couldn't remember what had happened after that. "Not after he spoke to it."

"He spoke to it?" She finally raised her eyes to his and lifted an eyebrow delicately, but not for long.

"What did he do to me?" Ever hated feeling lost. Even more so, he hated being out of control, and that, he got the feeling, was exactly what had happened to him.

"I think," Isa spoke slowly, "he is using my power to control the hearts of others. He placed the glass inside of you so that you only saw what he told you to see . . . or feel. I don't know. But it seems that he used my power, which was channeled into the mirror, to influence your heart so that you would do as he wished."

"Of course he did." Ever groaned and placed his head in his hands. He'd been so blind. It was Isa Bronkendol had been after. And by leaving her alone, Ever had practically handed his wife over on a platter. If only he'd listened to her. "But you can feel again now, even though he took your power?"

This time, she turned and looked right at him, her eyes piercing. "Yes," she said quietly. "I can feel again."

Somehow, that was almost worse than when she couldn't.

Ever pushed himself to his feet and began to sift through the glass. He found Isa's sword, and she took it without a word. Before she could walk away again, he grabbed her shoulder.

"I need to know." He searched her midnight eyes. "Did he touch you?"

Isa's gaze softened for just a moment. "No. Not in that way."

Relief filled Ever so that he nearly felt shaky. The question had burned within him since she'd been taken. Buoyed with the knowledge, he grew a bit bolder with his questions.

"Why didn't the glass shards work on you?"

"He pitied me after he took my power, so he removed the glass before he sent me home. He promised me I would never have to suffer the shards again." Isa stopped searching the debris below and smiled acerbically up at the frigid starry night. "He may scheme to the utmost, but the man has a strange sense of honor. He could have given me more glass anytime, and he didn't." Before Ever could ask anything else, she declared their search fruitless. "He most likely escaped before the castle fell, and I know for certain he wouldn't have left the mirror behind. Let's go."

Ever followed in somewhat of a daze. That she was speaking to him at all was encouraging. But her walls were up. Ever sighed. It was their early days at the Fortress all over again.

He didn't dare speak until they had crossed the bridge, which had miraculously survived the castle's collapse, and had mounted their horses. It hurt to watch as Isa dropped her stiff formality to lean over and whisper musical tones in her horse's ear. How long had it been since she had shared that same warm smile with him?

Hugon tossed his head and rolled his eyes back to glare at his master, as though demanding to know why Ever wasn't singing to him too.

As they set out for the Fortress, back into their world and out of the nightmare of snow and glass, Ever gathered his courage to broach the subject that would either save or break his marriage. They might as well get all of the heartbreak over with at once.

"Isa, I know that you're angry with me."

"You are right." Isa nodded amiably as though they were discussing one of Cook's new dishes. "But how well do you actually know me? How many hours have you spent with me to know with any confidence what I think or feel, or why I might be angry?"

"What about the time we spent practicing?" Ever stuttered. It was like trying to grasp a fistful of water.

"There was that. It was so kind of you to fit me into your schedule so that we could fight every day."

"What is this about, Isa?" Everard pulled his horse to a halt. "I am trying to fix this! But I cannot change anything if I don't know what you want!"

"What I want?" Isa's eyes finally met his, and though the rings of fire within them were thin, they blazed with heat. "What I want to know is why you are incapable of putting me first! Why I will always come second to your weapons and your allies and your schemes. Even on—"

"A war was about to break out!"

"On our wedding night? Twelve hours, Everard. You couldn't give me twelve hours before you galloped off to meet the first cry for help that reached your ears, off chasing that next glorious feat." With that, she urged her horse into a gallop, tears streaming down her face.

Ever followed along, but more slowly. It irked him to know that his ultimate failure hadn't been the enchanter's success, nor had it even been any of his idiotic words back at the Cobrien palace. No, this pain had been brewing since the beginning of their marriage. The chink in their relationship had been there all along, beneath every hopeful smile she gave him, each time he'd put her off for a foreign dignitary, or when he'd imprisoned her in her room so he could consult with another queen. As usual, it was his own pigheadedness that had threatened to dash the thing he loved most.

"I am so sorry," he said into the wind. The words were pathetic, but they were all he had.

Isa didn't even turn to look at him.

Ever pushed his horse to catch up to her. If his heart hadn't been contrite already, it shattered completely when he saw the way she now wept. Her cries weren't silent, as they must have been for so long, but were ragged and broken. Abandoned.

Ever wanted nothing more than to draw her into his arms and hold her until her tears were all gone. He would hold her until they were gone, he decided. Reaching over, he grabbed her horse's reins. Then, after hopping off his own horse, he pulled Isa off too, ignoring her weak protests.

"We will sleep here tonight."

"It looks cold." Isa sniffled as she glared at the snow-covered ground.

"It will be cold up on the horses too. Besides, we won't be in familiar territory until tomorrow. We might as well get some rest."

Before she could argue, Ever lifted his hands to his face, palms up. He blew gently but steadily into them until a small blue flame danced within them. Then, with the flick of his wrist, Ever tossed the flame to the ground. The blue flame grew larger and flitted to the ground, surrounding them, licking up all the snow in its path. It didn't die until they had a perfectly round patch of dry ground, large enough to fit both the horses, a campfire, and enough space for the two of them to stretch out fully and lie down.

Since they had moved into the lower country, evergreen trees were scattered about. They broke the plains of whiteness in small, uneven clumps. It didn't take Ever long to find and dry some firewood in the same fashion as he had dried the ground for their camp. Soon enough, a small but warm flame blazed in the center of the circle. As he worked to prepare their supper, he watched her out of the corner of his eye.

She no longer cried, but the emptiness in her face said it all, and Ever prayed for words to tell her what he felt. If only she could see his intentions, perhaps she could forgive him one day.

"I know it doesn't change anything." He handed her a bowl of dried cherries, honey-sweetened bread, and pork, then sat down beside her with his own food. "But I swear, I was only doing what I know best to prove that I love you." He looked at his bowl only to realize his appetite was long gone. "You had just saved me. I was eager to show you my own love in return."

Isa turned and looked up at him. The anger in her eyes had somewhat lessened, but it had been replaced with dark circles beneath her eyes, as though she hadn't slept in a week. "But you were never there. How was I supposed to know your love if you were never there?" She dropped her eyes and muttered, "I thought you were avoiding me."

"Avoiding you?" What on earth had possessed her to think that?

Isa nodded without looking up. "I hadn't fulfilled my duty to the Fortress. My fire was dying. I just thought that perhaps being gone on official duty was your way of avoiding the subject. If you were off being the king everyone expected you to be, then you wouldn't have to be embarrassed when someone asked about your inept queen."

"Is that what you truly think?" Ever put his bowl on the ground and grabbed her face with both hands, forcing her to look at him.

Isa bit her lip before nodding as tears came once again to her eyes.

Ever pulled her close, holding her as she sobbed quietly into his shirt. How had he muddled things so badly?

"Before we go any further, you need to understand something. My father rarely spent more than five minutes with my mother after I was born. The way he showed his family and the kingdom his devotion was by conquering those that threatened their freedom." Ever chuckled humorlessly. "You may think I'm gone often, but I am present much more than he ever was." He pulled back just enough to wipe her eyes with his thumbs. "I'm not strong enough to be without you for that long."

"As much as you're absent, you would never know it," Isa pouted.

"But that's what I mean! Isa, you grew up with a family that spent time together and built one another up! And thanks to you, I'm learning. But it's hard to show love in a way you've never seen it! Just because I don't know *how* to love you doesn't mean I don't love you at all." He gave her a cockeyed smile. "It just shows you what an idiot I am."

Isa let out a choked sound that seemed part sob and part laugh, and Ever was able to breathe once again. It was the first hint of a smile he'd seen on her face since she'd been taken.

He leaned over and pulled a thick blanket out of his pack, draping it carefully over them. It would be a long time before he was able to sleep, but the late night air was becoming exceptionally cold. After making sure his sword was positioned well beside him, he reached under the blanket and pulled her closer. Warmth flooded his soul as she snuggled her head in the hollow beneath his chin. *Teach me,* he begged the Fortress silently, *to show her how much I love her! I need her to know what she means to me.*

The only sounds were the snaps and pops of the fire as it slowly ate into the firewood, and the songs of the wind as it pushed through the trees and over the snow drifts. The yellow tongues of flame licked the wood, filling the air with a sweet earthy scent that rose and danced into the night, where it dissipated. A tired silence floated around them for such a long time that Ever was surprised when Isa spoke again.

"It was just so hard to be told time and time again that I was the Fortress's chosen. That I was the queen everyone had been waiting for. And then months passed. There was no child, and my powers drifted, and you were always gone. I suppose I never really felt the part of a queen after the coronation, nor did I feel like your partner. You were just so good at everything, and it felt like I could do nothing right. But worst of all, having what little power I had left ripped from my heart . . ." She shuddered. "It was like losing the air from my lungs. After Bronkendol sent me away, my heart simply decided it would be easiest to be without feelings at all."

She turned her face up to gaze into his, and Ever felt his breath catch. How he had hungered to see her look to him with that sweet adoration once more! "Forgive me, Ever?" she whispered.

Before she could say anything else, Ever had drawn her into the kiss he'd been craving for so long. It was pure bliss. There were no curses to be broken, no enchanters to defeat. Only wounds that needed to heal. And it would take time, Ever knew, to heal the wounds they'd inflicted upon one another. But that was alright. They had the rest of their lives to move past this place, and Ever swore then and there to never let her hide from him again.

He would have gone on kissing her forever, but Isa pulled away, a small frown on her face.

"I'm still not sure where to go from here. I mean," she stared at her hands, "a little of my power returned at the Glass Castle, but only just a little."

Ever placed his forehead against hers. "Honestly? I don't know. This is new for me too." He picked up her left hand and traced circles on her finger, around the crystal ring she always wore. "My father and I were close, but either he was king or I was. I've never had a partner before. And I mean it when I say I've never needed anyone so much."

He tipped her chin up, drinking her beauty in. Her hair was mussed and there were deep shadows beneath her eyes, but never had she been so lovely. "You may think I'm strong," he whispered, "but I don't know how to go on without you. I may be Destin's sword, but you are the heart. I cannot tell what the Fortress has in store for you, but you are too rare a woman for its choice to have been an accident."

For the first time, a wide, radiant smile shone from her face, and an all-too-familiar yearning filled Ever as her flame-rimmed midnight eyes stared up into his. He began to pull her in again for another kiss, but she gently placed her fingertips on his lips.

He must have looked pathetic, for Isa let out a laugh, her blue eyes sparkling.

"You can have all the kisses you want in a minute, but your queen needs something from you first."

"The king will do all that is within his power and more," he said somberly as he held her fingers against his lips and bowed his head. "For he is under your spell."

Isa giggled again, then looked as if she was trying to be serious. "If you truly mean it when you believe I was meant to be queen, I need you to trust me to be your partner. You can't keep hiding me away like a little doll."

Ever frowned. "I nearly just lost you. That is going to be difficult to do."

But Isa patiently shook her head. "I know I have much to learn, but if I'm truly meant to wield the Fortress's power, you must trust the Fortress to protect me." She sat back a little. "You also need to consider me your partner. I like Queen Kartek. She's intelligent and kind, but," Isa leaned forward with a knowing look, "she is not *your* queen, and she has said as much herself. In the future, I need for you to confide in *me*."

Ever drew in a sharp lungful of frigid air before letting out an annoyed huff. "You don't know how much you ask of me." He leaned forward also. "I can't lose you again."

"By ignoring my call, you nearly did lose me already."

They watched one another for a long time. She was right, but Ever hated to admit it. Allowing her to face evil by his side was going to be the most difficult challenge he had ever undertaken. His concentration was broken, however, when she slipped him a little mischievous smirk.

"If it's going to be that hard, I'll just have to convince you."

He started to ask her how she was going to do that, when her arms wrapped themselves around him, and her lips were suddenly on his. He pulled back enough to groan.

"That's not fair."

She smiled into his kiss. "It's not supposed to be. Now, hush. Your queen commands it." And before Ever could protest, she kissed him again.

.

47

IMPOSTORS

*P*anic seized Isa as she stretched her arms out and found nothing. Where was Ever?

Bolting upright, she looked around, and relief came over her when she found him stoking the fire.

"I'm sorry," Ever said. "I was hoping you would sleep a bit longer. I thought I would get the fire warmed up before I woke you."

Isa snuggled back under her blanket as deep as she could go. Morning hadn't yet broken, but in the early gray, the gently sloping hills of snow looked much less threatening than they had the night before. As she looked around, she realized she was clutching Ever's black cloak as well as her blanket.

It was so good to have his attentions once more.

Ever's posture was as straight as always as he knelt to feed the fire. The bags beneath his eyes were even more pronounced though than they had been the day before. He must have remained awake all night to keep watch. Isa felt a prick of guilt.

"I should have taken a turn on watch. It wasn't fair for you to take the entire night."

Ever smirked at her. "You wouldn't have been able to stay awake even if you had wanted to. Besides," his tone became more serious, "I may not know how to be attentive, but I can guard. Let me love you in the way I am able."

Isa couldn't help the smile that spread across her face. Pulling his cloak off the top of her blanket, she braced herself for the wave of cold air that would hit her as soon as she left the safety of her covers. As soon as she stood, the wind was so cold she nearly squeaked. She tiptoed to Ever as quickly as she could and draped his cloak over his shoulders before cocooning herself up again in her blanket beside him. Thankfully, the warmth of the fire soon began to grow, and as it did, Isa felt a little more awake.

There were so many things she wanted to say, an unending stream of questions she could ask. But as much as they'd rediscovered the night before, talking and laughing again in a way they hadn't in a long time, there was still a veil between them. Time would have to heal their marriage in some ways, she sensed.

"So what happens now?" She finally worked up the courage to meet his eyes again.

"We need to speak with Garin. Launce was supposed to send him word of what's been going on in Cobren."

If Isa had been sleepy before, she wasn't anymore. Shame and frustration slapped her as she remembered her callous words when Ever had first told her about Launce's dangerous intent. And yet she couldn't quite scold her husband greatly, as for several days, he had been more concerned about Launce's welfare than she had.

"I still don't understand why he had to go," she mumbled, not quite able to look Ever in the eye.

Ever appeared unruffled, however, as he handed her a warmed biscuit drizzled in honey. "If I hadn't sent him to Cobren, he would have insisted on coming along with me."

Isa shivered, and not from the cold. It was bad enough that Launce had gotten so tangled up in their business in Cobren. She couldn't imagine him squaring off against Bronkendol in the Glass Castle. At least there were others he could turn to in Cobren. She hoped. When she looked back at Ever, he was still frowning thoughtfully.

"What is it?" she asked.

"It's nothing."

Isa gave him a knowing look. "You promised. No more hiding."

Ever sighed. "It would be simple enough to take on an army, even an army of glass men such as those Bronkendol conjured. But if everyone else falls to his power the way I did, then he won't need an army." Ever picked up a pebble at his feet and chucked into the white wilderness before them. "We won't even have a choice. Once he sees we're alive, he will set them upon us. Shedding your enemy's blood is a grim enough matter, but fighting our allies, our friends, and our kin?" He pressed his mouth into a tight line, but didn't go on.

The thought of fighting against Launce chilled Isa to the bone. The enchanter hadn't given him the glass slivers before, but what was stopping him from doing it now? No. Isa shook her head to lose the thought. She had raised her sword to Ever only to survive, because she knew he would kill her, and ultimately himself, if she didn't stop him.

But Launce wasn't the killing machine her husband was. Against her weak blocks and parries, she had known Ever would survive. Launce's self-defense skills, however, were such that he might injure himself if the enchanter told him to use a sword. Ever was right. They needed to get to Garin.

Without saying it aloud, they both knew it was time to go. As they resumed their journey, the sun lifted above the horizon completely, just in time for the eternal hills of snow to melt away, and Isa was grateful to see the signs of late autumn still upon the ground. Had full winter truly arrived everywhere, it would make the journey back to the Fortress, and then Cobren, much harder.

"How is it that I've never seen those mountains that surrounded the Glass Castle on the maps before?" Isa asked. "Shouldn't Lingea be north of us?"

Ever nodded. "I do not think it's so much of a place, as a time." When Isa frowned in confusion, he continued, "Did you notice that the castle had no dust? Three thousand years go by, and the wood of the furniture hadn't crumbled, the linens were still clean, and the plants in that greenhouse were still alive. Even the newer houses in Soudain need their wood reworked on the years where snow and rain are particularly heavy. Let's rest the horses here." He clucked to Hugon, and Isa followed him off the road and into the brush. A gurgling stream ran right down at the bank's edge.

Though the snows had not yet come to these woods, it ran deep enough for the horses to drink heavily. Isa could tell they were getting close to Destin's northern border again, as the tall pine trees were looking more familiar. Soon they would cross the desert gorges that separated Lingea, Destin, and Tumen's lands. Not that Isa had any desire to visit Tumen, but at least the desert would mean they were only a day from home.

"I have a question for you this time." Ever interrupted Isa's thoughts. He was leaning back against a tree, sharpening a dagger as their horses rested. Isa let her eyes follow the fine lines of his arms and chest. "Isa?"

"What was that?"

He gave her a cockeyed smile as though he knew where her thoughts had gone, and she felt herself blush.

"I was asking you how you knew the kiss would break Bronkendol's hold on me."

"I didn't."

Ever raised his eyebrows, and Isa shrugged.

"It was instinctive. Like the way I stopped Nevina. I knew what I needed to do, and somehow, it happened. Why?"

He rubbed his neck thoughtfully. "The Fortress gave you the power you needed both times, and yet, we continue to worry about why it isn't there. I think it's been there all along though."

"I've failed so much!"

Ever held up a hand. "Your power of the heart is different than any the Fortress has on record. Even Garin hasn't seen anything like it before." He gave her a thoughtful look. "I think it's time we stop trying to judge your strength by the strength of others. The Fortress has given you the strength to defeat Nevina and Bronkendol at the exact moments you needed it. No more and no less." A small smile began to grow on his face. "I think that when we are all through with this mess, you're going to be just fine."

"But you're strong all the time."

"And see how far I've fallen." He gave her a sad smile. That wasn't exactly what Isa had wanted to hear. And yet, they had more important problems to solve than her erratic fire.

They led their horses back to the road before she dared ask the question she feared had no answer.

"So how do we stop him?"

"Simple," Ever said. "We break the mirror."

He bent to help Isa mount her horse, but she placed her hand on his face first. Her heart fluttered as he paused, their faces nearly touching. "Together?" she asked breathlessly.

Ever began to answer, but a bush rustled to their left. Before she could move, Ever had drawn his sword, and was crouched in a ready stance in front of her. Isa felt clumsy as she unsheathed her own sword and tried to hold it out just as he had taught her. As they waited, listening, Isa prayed it was only an animal. It would be absurd for them to die now at the hand of bandits.

The men who stepped out of the trees were no bandits though. Isa heard Ever let out a sigh of relief when ten foot soldiers walked into the little clearing, all wearing blue and green. She even recognized a few of them.

"Percy!" Everard reached out to clap the shoulder of the soldier closest to them.

Isa watched in surprise as the man did not bow or salute his king, as the soldiers always did at home. Instead, he only looked at his companions, confusion on his face.

"They cannot be—"

"Don't let your eyes deceive you, Percy. He said there would be no noticeable difference."

Ever watched them in disbelief as the soldiers conversed among themselves. "Could someone please enlighten me?" he shouted.

The second soldier cleared his throat. "You are hereby ordered to appear before His Majesty in court. He and His Holiness will know what to do with such impostors."

"Impostors?" Isa repeated. "Do you not recognize your king?"

"And if I'm here, who in the blazes is 'His Majesty?'" Ever roared.

"His Holiness, Bronkendol of the North, will deal with you. Now, if you will cooperate, we can keep this from being unpleasant." The soldier looked at them expectantly, as if he actually believed they would obey him.

Isa could feel Ever tensing beside her. Heat radiated from his body as he began to lift his sword, but she grabbed his arm and whispered, "Look at their eyes!" Indeed, the smallest fractals of blue-violet light pulsed from the edges of the soldiers' eyes, just as they had done in Ever's. "They're just as much prisoners as we are," she urged him. "Let's just go with them, and no one will be hurt." Ever glared at her, so she added, "Just as you said, we cannot fight our own."

"I will take those." The guard held his hand out and nodded at their swords.

"Over my dead body," Ever growled.

"No." An arm wrapped itself around Isa's neck and dragged her backward. Isa felt herself choking as her captor continued to tighten his grip. "Over her dead body."

The fire which had burned strong in Ever's eyes now threatened to kill each and every soldier present. Desperately, Isa shook her head as well as she could from beneath the man's tight hold. She wasn't ready to bear their blood on her hands just yet. For a moment, she wasn't sure he would listen. It felt like an eternity as he held her gaze. As he did, she pleaded him with her eyes. Not yet.

Finally, he lowered it nearly to the ground. "You swear we shall remain safe?"

"We are under direct orders to bring you to the Fortress," the soldier said. "The Holy Adviser wants to meet with you himself." The young man's eyes flicked down to the slight blue floating over Ever's hands. "He said there would most likely be sorcery involved," the soldier muttered. Then he nodded at another man behind him. "Pull out the talisman."

Isa's stomach twisted violently when he held out the "talisman." Instead of a gift to ward off strange magic, as they must have been told, it was a simple hairpin, decorated only with a thin, discolored rose made of painted wood. It was Gigi's.

Anger burned within Isa, and she felt Ever watching her curiously, no doubt sensing the sudden change within her mood. She could feel the fire burning in her eyes, as thin as it might still be. The soldiers might not know what pawns they were being played for in this game, but Bronkendol surely did.

"Take us." Isa had never issued a command with such authority. She focused so hard on the soldier's face that he began to look uncomfortable. Ever said nothing else, handing over his sword once and for all. Isa felt another set of hands take her own sword from her, but she didn't care. Soon they would be back at the Fortress, where it now seemed as though the enchanter was waiting for them. And soon, he would be sorry.

48

DUNGEON

*A*lthough she was perfectly aware that the soldiers were under Bronkendol's influence, Isa hoped the hard desert floor hurt their feet through their boots. Before they had left for Cobren, Isa had been planning on ordering the royal cobblers to craft boots with thicker soles for the foot soldiers, but now she was glad she'd never found the time.

At least they had allowed her to ride her horse. Her hands were bound, but it was still better than walking. Isa never would have made it through the night had they forced her to walk the whole way. Their captors seemed to be in a hurry, as they only ever stopped long enough for the horses to rest, then they were off again, riding all through the night. Isa's own muscles ached whenever she thought of how hard they were pushing Ever. He was not allowed to ride his horse. She'd overheard some arguments between the men themselves about this. One, with hair the color of the desert they now traversed, never lost his worried look.

"If we push that one too hard, His Holiness will be angry with us."

"We cannot risk his escape." Another man with a large nose shook his head. "He might be an impostor, but that doesn't mean he isn't powerful. His Holiness said the forests would be ripe with wizards trying to take King Everard's place." And so, Ever walked.

Isa glanced back to Ever again to see how he was faring. They wouldn't allow him to come any closer to her than thirty paces' difference. They were a rather strange sight, with two soldiers riding alongside Isa and her horse in the front, and eight soldiers on their mounts as they surrounded Ever in the back. After seeing her change of countenance back in the forest, Ever had allowed them to tie and hold him with four different ropes, but the look on his face had told her just how difficult the submission had been.

Still, he walked proudly with his head held high. Isa knew him well enough, however, to recognize the exhaustion on his face. Even Ever had a breaking point. She just prayed he could last a little while longer before reaching it.

The desert seemed to stretch on forever. This was the valley, Ever had once told her, where the Tumenians' late princess, Nevina, had killed his father, King Rodrigue. Their party had reached it a few hours after leaving the forest.

Isa couldn't remember the distance feeling nearly so long when she'd ridden after Ever toward the Glass Castle. Dry, powerful winds bounced down the bare, crusty cliffs above and rushed down into the arid valley below, covering them with dust.

Just then, Isa spotted the main road that led back to Soudain. Hope swelled, as she realized they might meet someone she knew on the path, someone who might be able to find Garin, or her parents, at the very least. Rather than heading toward the main road, the soldiers turned while still in the valley. They led her horse to a sandy slope, where a path barely visible hugged the steep incline. It was their own mountain, but Isa couldn't see the Fortress from the north side, or its wide, pristine fields and gardens. Why were they going up the mountain this way?

The slope eventually grew so steep that Isa could feel her horse straining beneath her when they were barely halfway up. Again, frustration and anger warred within her. She had never forced her animal to take such difficult terrain. She made sure to whisper encouragements to him, and eventually talked her guards into letting her walk beside the animal instead. That helped, but by the time they were nearing the top of the slope, foam began to appear on the animal's silken coat.

When the path split, one side going right and one left, Isa stopped her horse and refused to go further. "I do not know what your *holy man* has told you," she snapped at the guard nearest her, "but you are going to ruin my horse if you don't allow him to rest."

"We're nearly there." The guard with the sandy hair pointed and gave her a shove as they turned up the left path.

"What is this?"

The three of them turned as Ever shouted from below, where he and his entourage still hiked the trail.

"You're taking us straight to the dungeons?"

Isa's breath hitched. She had never been to the dungeons. Not even a part of the Fortress itself, a distant ancestor of Ever's had thought it necessary to hide the prisoners where no loyal friends or hired swords would know how to find them. She'd asked about visiting once, but Ever had said there was no reason to make herself uncomfortable. Now she was to be held there.

Isa's soldiers urged her along the top of the cliff until they came to the most out of place door Isa had ever seen. It was hardly visible, carved into the side of the mountain itself, little roots and grasses sticking out of the wood where soil had gathered in its cracks. One of the soldiers gave four sharp raps upon the door. It opened from the inside with a creak, and Isa was assaulted by the stench of stale air and soured dirt.

She leaned into her horse and wrapped her arms around his neck. Never had she seen such blackness as that which was down that hole of a hall. Just higher than Ever was tall, and wide enough for three to pass through at the same time, the hole belched forth its wretched stench as though a wind carried it from the dungeon's belly. *I can't go in there,* she silently screamed to the Fortress. *It's worse than You ever were, even under the curse!*

No saving grace appeared, as each of the soldiers firmly took her by an arm and began to pull her toward the hole.

"No!" she shrieked, falling dead weight as best she could while kicking her feet. "I can't go in there! I just can't! Please!" But no matter how hard she fought, she was no match for the men who held her. *I need Your power!* she told the Fortress. But no power came, and with a little effort, they were able to haul her inside.

A single weak torch hung on the wall. The third man, who had opened the door, removed the torch and walked before them as a guide. But the flame did little to illuminate the inky blackness. Isa continued to trip over her own feet as they led her further in.

After they'd been walking for some time, she could hear Ever struggling behind her, but when she turned to see if he was any more successful than she at her attempted escape, it was impossible to see through the dark.

Deeper and deeper they walked. The air began to feel different, as though it were pressing in on her from all sides. Panic sped her breathing, and it was all she could do not to break out into hysterics. They seemed to be moving upwards, though the incline was barely noticeable. She wasn't allowed to stop until the narrow passage opened up, and Isa could feel that they were now standing in a room of some sort, though she couldn't see how large it was or any of its other details. In the light of three more weak torches hung on the wall, she could make out the silhouette of a man, powerfully built. As her eyes adjusted, she realized the lines of his face were familiar.

"Acelet!" She nearly sobbed with relief. Isa lunged forward and threw her arms around her husband's favorite general. He would set things straight.

But Acelet didn't move a muscle. He merely waited as the two guards fought to get her under control again. Only then, after they'd pulled her back, did Isa see the faint blue-violet glow from the edges of his eyes. Bronkendol had gotten to him too.

Without a word, he began walking. Isa's guards followed, dragging her with them. Isa could feel resentment and hatred rolling off the general, and decided pleading with him would do no good. Whatever the enchanter had convinced him of, using her stolen power, she would not be able to turn his heart as she was pulled along behind him.

The soft planks of wood they'd walked upon since entering the cave gave way to metal. She could feel it echo with each step as they moved her into another area that was, again, too dark to see.

She wished so much for Ever's group to catch them. Earlier, she'd heard him put up a fight loud enough to echo down the hall, there was complete silence now. Either they'd moved him farther away, down another hall, or they had found a way to silence him. That thought rattled Isa more than anything else she had seen that day.

They came to a stop. "You will take three steps forward."

"No." She was shocked at her audacity as the word left her lips. But whatever he had in store couldn't be good.

"You will do it, or I will move you myself."

Isa glared into the darkness, wishing he could see the anger in her eyes. In that moment, she felt the slight heat of the blue fire glance her right foot. She froze, hoping for it to flare to life. Nothing permanent stayed though. It was almost as if the Fortress was telling her to trust. To go. With a sigh, she made three slow steps forward.

On the last step, her boot touched something soft, like cloth. As soon as both feet were down, the floor dropped from beneath her, and Isa shrieked as she fell into what felt like a giant sack. The cloth leapt up around her, catching her in midair. Slowly, the sack was lowered deeper and deeper. When Isa touched a hard surface, the sack twisted, and she was dumped out onto the ground. Immediately, the sack was taken right back up. Still on the ground, Isa stared up. In the distance, she could barely make out the light of a torch as a slitted metal cover was pushed over the opening of the hole she'd just been lowered into.

As she stood, trying to study the light above, Isa stumbled. When she tried to catch herself, she quickly realized that the floor wasn't even, and she tripped forward into a hard metal wall. When she finally caught her balance, Isa lowered herself to the ground again and began feeling her way up.

As if being buried deep in the mountain wasn't bad enough, the cell itself had no level surface. Even the ground was curved upwards, like a giant's bowl with sides that curved up all around her, narrowing as they moved to the top. The metal reflected dimly at first in the light of the torch, but that didn't last long. Distant voices murmured unintelligible words, but soon they disappeared, echoing footsteps carrying them away. And as they went, so went the light.

CHOOSING A LOSS

"*I* am sorry, Launce, but I am under strict orders to let Princess Olivia rest."

"But it's been two days!"

Gigi reached out from the doorway and patted his cheek affectionately. "I know. And you will see her soon enough." Her face grew somber then, as though she had just remembered something. "You should use this time for mourning, you know. You won't have the proper time once the coronation takes place." As she spoke, her eyes welled suddenly with tears, and Launce swallowed the frustration he needed to unleash.

"You know he might not be dead after all." He lowered his voice. "We have no proof Ever actually died." *Please, let her believe me*, he prayed. If he could get even one person to see sense, perhaps there was hope for them yet.

Gigi brushed a silver curl from her face and gave him a watery smile. "Always so hopeful. Do not lose that once you become king." And with that, she reached out and squeezed his hand before retreating back into the room that was now declared Olivia's.

Launce stared at the closed door for a long moment, wondering what kind of chaos would ensue if he barged in and seized Olivia. He would drag her to the farthest corner of the world, where they would settle as strawberry farmers, never to be seen or heard from again. Before his dreams took him too far, however, Launce gave a weak kick to the door, then turned back to his own chambers.

Well, technically they were the king's chambers, but no amount of gold could convince him to sleep anywhere but in the corner, on the floor. Perhaps the many connected rooms would afford him somewhere to plan, without someone stumbling upon him and asking his opinion on the smoked boar, or where else to house the hundreds of horses and carriages brought along by the unexpected visitors that now filled the Fortress to its fullest capacity.

They had arrived at the Fortress two nights before, whereupon Olivia had been immediately whisked away to be "prepared" for their upcoming nuptials. Launce knew what Bronkendol was up to though. Their constant whispering throughout the journey must have made him finally nervous, for Launce recalled Isa being allowed to leave her room during the week before her coronation. But the enchanter held the upper hand, and now he played it well, for though no one else seemed to suspect a thing, Bronkendol's threat was less than subtle to Launce.

Not that the servants or other royals were good standards to judge by. In less than an hour after they'd arrived, Bronkendol had somehow planted the shards in all of the Fortress's residents as well. And like Gigi, since then, none of them had made a bit of sense. Now, as staff hurried up and down the halls, preparing the Fortress both to mourn for Everard, and also for its forthcoming double coronation, Launce refused to look at the purple and blue glow of power each servant wore.

Garin was the only exception, of course. Because Garin was gone.

As though he'd never existed, the steward was nowhere to be found, nor did anyone remark on his absence. Launce could only hope that Garin was in hiding, waiting for the right time to emerge, for it was on Garin that Launce's plan of escape depended.

"It would appear that autumn has gifted us with one last day of sunbeams."

Launce didn't have to raise his head to see who waited for him at the window across from his new chambers. "What do you want?"

"Walk with me, lad." Bronkendol turned away from the window to smile amiably at Launce. "Let us enjoy this last day of good weather the Maker has provided for us."

Launce thought about giving him a smart retort and then locking himself in his chambers. But when he remembered Bronkendol's threat to Olivia, he silently fell into step alongside the enchanter.

The visiting guests from Cobren strolled by the two of them as though nothing were out of place, and the servants carried along as well as any servants might do whose good king had died after only five months of rule. No Destinian citizens crossed their paths though. Launce could only guess news had been circulated that there was a plague or some other sort of foolishness at the Fortress. Surely Bronkendol could not have placed the glass shards in all of Soudain's citizens already. He hoped not, at least.

As they walked, it galled Launce that someone so short could hold him in such a tight grasp.

"It would be simpler for you if you stopped trying to convince your friends that Everard is alive, or that all of this is an evil plot," the enchanter said. "They will not be able to see your version of the truth no matter how hard you try."

Launce kept his eyes trained forward. "And why is that?"

"Because it's incredible how blind we can be when our heart promises us a certain truth. Even when the facts before us point to another truth entirely."

"So you admit you're lying to them."

"I am allowing them to see the world through the lens of truth as I know it. Of course, that might demand a few embellishments here and there, but soon enough, it won't matter."

"And how is it that you've convinced them all so thoroughly?" Launce had a hunch, but if Bronkendol was in the mood to talk, he was by all means welcome. Listening could only aid Launce in the end.

"Let us venture outside, shall we? I feel the need for some fresh air."

Launce didn't argue as stepped out onto the northernmost balcony. It was an extension of the royal library. Not the sacred one in the Tower of Annals, of course. But its view was nearly as breathtaking. From where they stood on the white marble overlook, Launce could see the border deserts that began at the foot of the mountain. A thin trail he had never noticed before snaked out from some hidden spot below. When he squinted, it didn't appear the trail had any purpose at all. It simply ended midway between the Fortress and the desert floor at the bottom.

"This wouldn't have anything to do with my sister's power, would it?"

"You are sharp. I will credit you that. And yes, the power I drew from Isabelle to end her suffering is the power I harness now to keep the people from panicking while we transition here. It will make the change more palatable for everyone present. That, in turn, will make it easier for your citizens, as well as everyone else's."

Launce frowned. "I don't understand. The people are themselves . . . but they are not at the same time." So far, the enchanter had answered his questions. Launce hoped he would answer this one as well.

"Even your sister has never understood her power. In fact, she hardly ever tapped into its true potential. And yet, it is her power that holds every new thing in place here." Bronkendol leaned over the edge of the balcony railing, and Launce noticed his eyes training on the thin trail as well.

"Everyone has been waiting for your sister's power to blossom into a strength akin to her husband's. Everard was always fast, strong, and intuitive enough to use his power far beyond his years, at least compared to those of his ancestors that I witnessed. But Isabelle's power is something else entirely, and no one has been able to see it." He placed his hand in his robe pocket, as he seemed to do often. "Not even she can see it," he murmured.

"So Isa's power hasn't been dwindling?" Launce asked. If Isa somehow survived all of this, it was something she deserved to know.

"Not in the way everyone thinks. You see, Everard was bestowed with the strength of the hand, while Isabelle was given the strength of the heart, something you knew already. But what that heart power truly entails is far beyond what even your Fortress steward could understand." Bronkendol spit out Garin's title as though it tasted sour, and Launce nearly smiled. Garin must have at least posed something of a challenge to have ruffled the enchanter's feathers so.

But Bronkendol continued. "Your sister had the ability to turn people's hearts." He eyed Launce. "She's unwittingly used her abilities on you several times." Immediately, Launce recalled the night he had allowed her to go to the Fortress without him. And then, when she'd convinced him to join her in Cobren. That had been her?

"She doesn't force others to act against their will," Launce said, unable to keep the disdain from his voice.

"Oh, but I haven't done such a thing either!"

Launce looked at the enchanter in disbelief.

"All I had to do was introduce despair into their hearts."

"But you've given them no proof!" Launce turned in disgust to leave the balcony. The view of the thin trail made him uncomfortable for some reason.

The enchanter followed, but instead of wandering the enormous round room, filled to the ceiling with books, Bronkendol passed him and strode purposefully to the first set of stairs he could find. "I've told you," he said over his shoulder as Launce flagged behind. "When someone's heart whispers truths to him, his instinct is to trust the whisperings inside above all else. Your friends may not see any proof that Everard is dead, but they don't need it. Their hearts tell them it is so already."

They walked out to the edge of the northern lawns and had come to an old gate. He stopped, fishing around in his other pocket.

"Ah, here we are." Strangely, its bolt was strong and new, not rusted like the rest of the gate. As Bronkendol produced a large brass key and opened the gate to let them through, Launce wondered at how easy it had seemed for the enchanter to get whatever he wanted. Launce had seen that key only once. It had been tied to a leather cord that hung around Everard's neck.

"Launce Marchand, you are a clever young man, and I know you're probably wondering why I have been so free in sharing all I know with you."

Launce didn't respond, but it was the truth.

"I have told you before, and I was earnest, I am excited to see all the Fortress and the future hold for you. You are kind, you have a sharp wit, and you know what it is like to suffer. Most kings haven't lived half as much as you by the time they die. But you still have a choice to make, and I fear you are running toward the wrong one."

As soon as they were through the gate, they found themselves at another door. Only, this one led straight into the side of the mountain. Bronkendol unlocked it as well. As the door swung open, a blast of rancid air hit them, making Launce want to choke. A small torch hung from the wall before them, and just inside to the left, a set of narrow, stone steps led down into a darkness Launce had never before imagined. He wanted nothing to do with such darkness, but for now he decided to follow the enchanter. There must have been a reason the enchanter was bringing him to this horrid place.

Launce had to breathe deeply as they descended, to remind himself that the world wasn't caving in upon him. The stairs twisted and turned in different areas, to the point where Launce couldn't recall what direction they were traveling in. All he knew was that they continued to climb down.

After what seemed like an eternity, he felt the stairs give way to steel floors. He followed Bronkendol's torch, but he noticed that some areas beneath his feet sounded hollower than others. Bronkendol soon came to a stop, and a soldier appeared out of the darkness. After the enchanter whispered something to him, the soldier nodded and led them even further into the depths.

Finally, they stopped in a small corner. Again, the torch was lowered, but this time, Launce could see a large circle carved into the steel floor they walked upon. About four feet across, it had bars slitted through the middle. Bronkendol nodded at the floor, so Launce bent down to look through them. There, at the bottom, the form was nearly invisible against the blackness. But it was one he would know anywhere.

"Isa!" he shouted. His sister's name echoed throughout the wide steel chasm they stood in, but his sister's sleeping form didn't stir. Launce glared up at Bronkendol and the silent soldier that guided them. "What's wrong with her?"

"Nothing serious, just some sleeping herbs. She hadn't slept well in days."

As Launce leaned back down to try and see her as best he could in the dark, he knew exactly why the enchanter had brought him here, why he had been willing to tell him so much.

"Everyone has a choice to make in this world, even if he claims to have none." Bronkendol's lilting voice echoed off the stone walls that surrounded them. "Your sister and brother-in-law made theirs. If you choose rightly, however, I can spare your sister from her choice."

Fury heated his face as Launce stood and stepped as close as he could to Bronkendol. If he had only been as strong as Everard, he could crush this little man like the parasite he was. "I would hardly call extortion honorable."

"I'm showing you how dire this situation is."

"You mean how dire you've made it!"

"When you've lived as I have, then you can tell me what is and is not dire!" Bronkendol's shout echoed through the underground tunnel. Neither of them spoke for a long time, only glowered at one another in the dark. Finally, Bronkendol sighed, and when he spoke again, his voice was ancient.

"I promised you I wouldn't place a shard inside of you. And though I may bend the rules in other ways, I always keep my promises. But I needed you to see what is at stake here."

Launce's fist burned as hot as his face, and he longed to do nothing more than beat the enchanter to death. Where he had once abhorred Everard's ease with violence, he now hungered for it like a man on the brink of starvation. Launce racked his memory for something, anything he could do to make the man uncomfortable. Anything that would cause Bronkendol a portion of the pain and misery he was bringing down upon everyone else.

"Launce, look around you. You speak of doom and wrath, but the Fortress has not shown any sign that we are not welcome. There have been no more earthquakes, and no one has died since we arrived. No one has even been injured. Surely you can see that the Maker is with us, rather than against us. It should serve as a comfort to you."

Launce didn't answer. As he continued to search for the words to express the depths of his loathing, the soldier replaced the metal grate and led them back to the winding set of stairs. Neither Launce nor Bronkendol spoke again until they reached the top. As the enchanter locked the gate behind them and they stood on the Fortress grounds once more, Launce turned and said softly, "You cannot move through the Fortress's glass, can you?"

Bronkendol froze, the key still in the gate. "Why would you think that?" The words were casual, but Launce felt satisfaction wash through him as he watched the enchanter struggle. Finally, he had found a weakness.

"That's why you had to bring your own mirror. The Fortress will not let you travel within its glass. In fact, I will venture to guess that you've even tried on more than one occasion, but after you had failed enough times, you had to come up with an alternative plan." When Bronkendol still didn't answer, Launce allowed himself an acerbic smile. "You think you know the Maker's will, and you think you know the Fortress. But the Fortress never chose me. And, it would seem, it never chose you either." With that, Launce stalked away.

50

BRUISES

*A*s soon as Launce was able to leave Bronkendol behind, he hurried to the king's quarters. Frustration swelled inside of him as he knew he only had a few minutes before the enchanter sent someone to either interrupt or keep an eye on him.

Everard had to have blank parchment in his room somewhere. He was too preoccupied with his work not to have writing materials somewhere at hand.

After a minute or two of tearing the room apart, Launce finally found some parchments tucked behind a pile of books on the large desk in the corner. He snatched up the nearest quill he could find, but his hands shook at he tried to sharpen it, breaking the nib off completely. Disgusted with his clumsiness, Launce grabbed another quill and began to sharpen this one also, more careful this time.

He still wrote too quickly, smearing the ink beneath his hands as he held the paper, but at least his words were legible. After writing only the salutation, however, he stopped. He would have to choose his words with care. If this letter fell into the wrong hands, Bronkendol would not leave his family unpunished, of that he was sure. It would have to read like a letter any absent son might send his family. And yet, his parents would need to understand that something was indeed wrong.

Dearest Mother and Father,

Please accept my apologies for staying away for so long. I've had a series of unexpected, and yet delightful happenings that have gone on as of late. I am not at liberty to discuss them now, but I can promise you, they will be spectacular.

I must admit, however, that I am most sorely homesick. While on the way to Cobren,

I was talking to Isabelle, and we were laughing about our old escapades. We were wondering, though, if you could resolve a disagreement between us. Father, do you remember the place Isabelle used to hide in when she was small, each time you would return from trading? She believes that they did not bother to fill it in, but it has been my impression that the spot is now paved, and completely useless. If you can, end this disagreement we've had. Isabelle desires greatly to clear it for a place to picnic. I have told her, however, that such an idea is worthless if the place is no longer in existence.

Alas, I must remain absent for a little while longer. I am needed here at the Fortress. Isabelle has taken a bit ill, but we have high hopes for her recovery, so Mother needn't worry. The Fortress has been closed off from visitors until the sickness is gone, as it seems quite catching. It is midday as I pen this, but we hope by tonight's highest moon for Isabelle to be in better health and spirits. You know Everard will have her on her feet in no time.

Your devoted son,
Launce

The letter was rubbish, of course. Launce never called his sister by her full given name, nor in his wildest dreams would he have ever penned anything with the words *delightful* or *spectacular*. The Launce his parents knew would not have given Everard so much credit, even when it came to healing. At least, not in writing or aloud. And while there truly was a spot on the side of the road where Isa had liked to hide as a little girl, it would have made a ridiculous spot to picnic.

But Bronkendol didn't know that.

Launce just hoped his father would understand the hidden message, where Launce begged him to meet at Isa's hiding place so he could ask for advice. He was desperate for someone, anyone to talk to who wasn't bound by the enchanter's power. Had Garin been present, he would have been Launce's first choice, but at this point Launce would have gladly consulted even with Everard.

If his father could understand the meeting place and time, just before midnight, when Isa was supposed to be in better health and spirits, Launce could have just a few moments alone with him. Ansel might not have unique healing powers of Everard, or generations of experience with the Fortress like Garin, but he was the best man Launce knew and his heart was pure. Ansel would help him sort things out.

Launce went back to the door and peeked out into the hallway. To his relief, the enchanter was no longer hovering about outside of his door, at least for the moment. And to his surprise, no one else was there either. With the parchment folded neatly in his pocket, Launce began to walk toward the servants' quarters.

He wasn't sure who he might send. Everyone he saw had been touched by the enchanter's powers. The violet glimmer in their eyes signified that. But surely there had to be *someone* who had escaped!

After scouring the kitchens, the stables, and even some of his childhood friends' quarters, Launce had nearly given up when he spotted a small, bare-footed girl playing in the tomato garden, just outside the servants' kitchens, and he gave a sigh of relief. If anyone was likely to have missed the glass shards, it would have been her.

Launce had seen her enough times during his time spent at the Fortress that he'd taken a liking to her, perhaps because she reminded him a bit of Isa. The first time they'd met, Yasmina had placed a burr on his chair at the dining hall. Her mother had been horrified, but since then, Launce and the child had taken to trading pranks whenever he would visit. He prayed now that she wouldn't think this was a game.

He pulled a sugar lump from his pocket, the kind he often kept there for his horse. It wasn't the best payment, but perhaps for a child, it would do. As he stepped outside, he could see that again, to his relief, she was alone. He would have to be fast.

"Yasmina," he called softly. It took a few tries before she heard him, so deep was she immersed in whatever game she was playing in the mud. When she did finally turn and see him, her brown eyes lit up without any hint of a violet glimmer, and she bounced over immediately. "I have a job I need you to do for me," he said, holding up the sugar cube so she could see it in his palm.

Her eyes grew wide, but then she blinked and shook her head. "No. That's not nearly enough."

Launce frowned as he dug his hand back into his pocket for another lump. Was he truly negotiating with a child for the balance of the kingdom?

She looked at his new offering and pursed her lips for a moment before reaching for the treats, but Launce closed his hand.

"Hey!"

"You can have them, but I need you to agree to accept my job first. Only good workers get paid two sugar lumps. Do you understand?"

Impatiently, she nodded and reached for them again, but Launce kept his fist closed.

"I need you to deliver a letter to my parents back in Soudain. Do you know the way?" She raised an eyebrow, and he had to laugh. Of course she did. All children raised in the Fortress knew the way to Soudain. In his own childhood, his friends had shown him a number of ways to sneak in and out of the Fortress without even having to use the gates.

"Their names are Ansel and Deline Marchand, and they have a mercantile in the city square. If you get lost, just ask for the queen's parents."

"I know," she said with a dramatic sigh, tossing her stringy blond hair. "I've been to their shop before."

"Good. This is very important." He bent down to look her straight in the eye. "I mean it," he said in a softer voice. "This is so important that I need you to promise me you'll give them this letter. But you can't tell anyone else!"

When she had promised, he finally handed her the sugar. She tucked the parchment into her apron, and he watched her as she sprinted off toward the forest.

He allowed himself half a smile. No child ever used the road to reach the Fortress or the town when traveling between the two. He'd never questioned the oddity of children being able to come and leave the Fortress at will, when many adults tried and failed in the same way. But now that he was older and more familiar with the Fortress, Launce wondered if the children were given special permission by the Fortress itself, simply because it loved them. It appeared that way at least, which was why he had chosen a child to be his messenger in the first place.

"You've certainly been busy since we last spoke."

Launce jumped at the sound of Garin's voice. Turning, he found the steward leaning against the wall with his arms folded, as if he'd been there the whole time. Never had Launce been so relieved to see anyone in his life.

"Where have you been?"

"A certain someone sent me an invalid queen and her cheeky personal guard." Garin raised an eyebrow. "Apparently, sending a travel party was easier than simply sending me a messenger bird."

"I'm sorry. I tried, but Bronkendol wouldn't let me get near the birds. I'd hoped Kartek and Apu would explain what he was up to but . . ." Launce shivered. "I didn't know he had planned for us to come here."

Garin nodded once. "I had thought as much." He straightened himself and gestured toward the trees. "Come. Let's not linger where they might see you."

"See *me?*" Launce laughed, but he followed Garin anyway. "And where might you be?"

Garin only gave him a sly grin before heading quickly up the brown fields toward the edge of the Fortress land. Of course. Launce should have known Garin would be hidden from others. Little the steward did surprised him anymore.

They walked until they were deep inside the trees that edged the Fortress's back lawn. A wide assortment of fruit trees had popped up here, which, according to Garin, were due to the pieces of fruit Everard had loved to toss on the ground as a boy. Now, the two men settled under a grove of orange trees. The branches were bare, but the trees themselves were thick enough to shield them from prying eyes up in Fortress tower windows.

"I hear you will be gaining a new title soon," Garin said.

Launce blanched. "I have told Bronkendol repeatedly that I want no part in this!"

"And yet," Garin raised his hand, "here you are." The steward's tone was conversational, but Launce knew there was a purpose to Garin's visit. He hadn't sought Launce out to chat about orange trees.

"They have Olivia . . . Princess Olivia, from Cobren. My family is still in town, that I know of. And just this morning, I found out that Isa is being kept in the dungeons."

A flash of something dangerous crossed Garin's eyes at the mention of Isa, but he didn't interrupt.

"I need to be here for them. I need to do *something*. I just don't know what that something is." He sat down on a large boulder. "I know you aren't like Everard, but can't you just . . . make them go away?"

Garin laughed. "No, my power isn't like his. However, I do believe that *you* have a decision to make."

"What do you mean? I've already told you I won't accept Bronkendol's offer."

"So if this coronation I've heard about is still on by tomorrow, you'll refuse?"

"What am I supposed to do, Garin?" Launce was exasperated with the steward and with himself as the truth came spilling forth. "If I refuse, my sister, my family, even Olivia could die. If I accept, I will be defying the Fortress." Launce stood and began to pace.

"I think you know what you should do," Garin said quietly. "But your fears are telling you otherwise."

"Look, I am trying. I even sent Yasmina with a letter to my parents to ask my father to help." Launce paused, suddenly worried. "You'll make sure no one harms her along the way?"

"The Fortress will see to that. You have no reason to worry."

Launce let out a deep breath, greatly relieved he hadn't just sent a little girl to her death. He stopped pacing and looked up to ask Garin another question, but the steward was gone. Annoyed, Launce trudged back to the Fortress to wait for the night.

Perhaps his father would have some advice that was a little less cryptic.

~

Launce pulled the borrowed cloak tightly around him as he waited for the bells to ring the hour. Using Everard's clothing was hardly ideal, but Launce's cloak wasn't nearly as thick, and the night felt as though it would be exceptionally cold.

Just a little longer and he would be with Ansel.

Launce's years might have made him a man, but at the moment all he could do was think of how safe it would feel to be in his father's fierce embrace once more. Sometimes it would be easier to be ten than twenty.

Steps approached his room, and someone pounded on his door. Before he could answer, the door was kicked in, and Sir Absalom tossed a large bag into the room with a *thump*. The look he gave Launce was cruel, and though the purple and blue light glimmered in his eye, the hatred in Absalom's glare was real.

They stood there, the large bag laying between them for a long time. Finally, without saying a word, the awful knight left.

Launce considered looking at the bag's contents after he met with his father, but a rustling inside of it caught his attention. He stared for a moment, wondering if he should find some gloves or a weapon, just in case the bag contained something that might bite. There was no telling what strange prank Sir Absalom had played on him while he wasn't under the enchanter's direct orders. When another sound came from the bag, this time a very human groan, Launce didn't hesitate. Loosening the drawstring with fumbling hands, he threw it open.

Inside, Ansel's face was covered in dark, sticky blood, and his eyes were swollen shut. Launce's chest constricted as he struggled to yank the rest of the bag off of his father's limp, battered body. As soon as Ansel was free, Launce fell beside him and cradled his father's head in his lap. Tears made it hard to see as he tried with shaking hands to wipe the blood from his father's face.

"Father? Father, can you hear me?"

Ansel couldn't quite open his eyes, but after a few moments, swallowed weakly and opened his mouth.

"Launce?" When his voice finally worked, it was raspy.

"I'm here, Papa!"

But his father could say no more. His chest rose and fell in shallow bursts, and he could hardly open his eyes. The hands that had held, disciplined, and instructed Launce now trembled like an old man's.

"I'm sorry," Launce whispered, trying to keep the tears from blinding him entirely. "I'm so sorry." Part of him was dying, screaming to find a healer, anyone, even Gigi, who might know how to help his father. But with Bronkendol in charge, there was no assurance that anyone he asked would help him at all. The helper might harm Ansel even further if he or she was under orders.

Without the slightest knowledge of how to care for someone so wounded, Launce lifted his father from the floor as gently as he could and laid him in the king's gigantic bed. The thick, wide mattresses might be too much for Launce, but his father deserved the best.

A clean cloth and fresh water had been laid in one of the two porcelain basins for Launce to use before bed. He took the cloth and wet it so that he could try to get the worst of the blood from his father's face. Then he checked for stab wounds and broken bones. There appeared to be no punctures, but from the way Ansel cried out when Launce had lifted him, there was a good chance he had broken a few ribs at the very least.

Once he was done with that, Launce sat on the edge of the bed and watched his father. It was impossible to tell if Ansel slept or not, but he did stop trying to move as much. As he watched, Launce wanted to kick himself for ignoring the field wound treatments Everard had tried to teach him. What he wouldn't do to have his infuriating brother-in-law here now.

But, a small voice of hope whispered, someone else was nearby that might know how to help. As soon as the thought was in his head, Launce was off of the bed, and plowing ahead toward Olivia's room, barely remembering to lock the room and bring his key in the process. He couldn't have anyone else entering to hurt his father further.

Launce sent up a prayer of thanks as he met no one in the halls. Not even servants or guards were to be seen at the late hour. It struck Launce as odd but, he decided, it must be the Maker finally moving events in his favor. That revelation buoyed him on even faster until he reached her chambers. Once there, however, he slowed. The thought of entering a young lady's room without escort, or even knocking, heated his face. But he couldn't risk being discovered and thwarted by Gigi or any of the other women who constantly hovered nearby.

If the enchanter has his way, he thought, *you'll be sharing chambers soon anyways.* This thought made him flush even more, and he hurried to banish it as quickly as possible. His father's life was at stake.

Launce snuck into the room as quietly as he could. It only took him a moment to find the bed, and when he did, he was overjoyed to realize there were no other women sleeping in the room as well.

The moon spilled through an open window and onto the girl's face as she slept, her face more peaceful than he had seen it since they had met.

"Olivia," he whispered as loudly as he dared. She stirred but didn't wake, so he tried again. "Olivia! I need your help!"

"Launce?" she mumbled. Slowly, she rolled over and sat up, rubbing her eyes. When she did, however, he froze, panic squeezing his chest.

"Launce, what are you doing here?" She pulled the covers up higher against her chest, suddenly more awake. "This is highly improper!"

Launce struggled for words as he stared at the blue and purple glimmer in the corner of each of her beautiful, almond eyes.

"I..." He swallowed, not sure what to say. He could hear footsteps approaching in the hall, so he had to try. Perhaps her feelings for him would show her the truth. "My father was injured! I need your help to take care of him!"

"Master Launce!" Gigi stormed in, holding a candle and looking quite shocked. "You must leave this room and return to your own chambers at once!"

"Please, Olivia!" Launce yelled, not caring anymore who heard him. "My father might be dying!"

At this, Olivia's eyes softened, and a look of compassion came over her face. Maybe, just maybe she had heard him, even through the enchanter's lies.

"I'm sorry, Launce," she said gently. "But it's better this way."

Shock paralyzed him and rendered him powerless as Gigi fussed and pushed him from the room. Olivia's cruel words echoed in his mind as the door was shut in his face. Deep down, he knew the words were not Olivia's, but the enchanter's. Still, his hope of swaying her heart with his affections had been dashed. Launce had failed, and because of him, his father might die.

Somehow, Launce made it back to his room, although he couldn't recall actually directing his feet to carry him there. Curling up at the edge of the bed, he allowed himself to weep, holding his father's limp hand as tightly as he dared.

He didn't realize he had nodded off and let most of the candles die until a light knock sounded at the door. Sitting up, Launce rubbed his eyes as a shadow stepped in to the edge of the room, light from the torches in the hall spilling through the gap.

"I'm sorry this had to happen." Bronkendol's voice was low and soothing. "I told you, though, that you need to think carefully about your choice."

"You think you're helping the world," Launce snapped, wishing desperately that tears were not running down his face as he spoke. "But everywhere you go, only pain and death follows!" He stood and began to stalk toward the short figure in the corner. He was going to kill this evil little man. There would be no one to hear him scream if he shut the door first.

"Your sister will be at the coronation tomorrow."

Launce froze.

"You should also know that I cannot be so forgiving next time." The shadowy figure crossed back into the light, but before he stepped out, turned back once more. "If you cross me again, I swear to you that there will be death. And it won't be yours."

Launce collapsed on the ground and beat his fists against the stone floor until they were bruised. Angry hot tears drenched his face.

How dare this man threaten and hurt his family? And how dare the stupid guests do his bidding? He didn't care if they were under a curse. He hated them all.

But most of all, how dare the Fortress allow such evil to endure?

"I tried, Garin," he choked out into the darkness, wondering if the steward was near enough to hear. Part of him hoped he wasn't. "But I can't lose anyone else."

51

THAT NO PRISON CAN HOLD

"There now, some of this will do you good. Drink up."

Isa tried to open her eyes, but they felt stuck. And so did the rest of her body. When she tried to move one arm at a time, she found she could barely wiggle her fingers. What was wrong with her? She felt as though she'd been sleeping for years. And why was it so dark?

"There you go," the voice said. "Now swallow."

Isa did as she was told, and a hot liquid slid down her throat. As it moved, her body began to remember itself, and her memories began to return one at a time.

A broken glass castle.

Ever's promise.

The dungeon.

Isa opened her eyes wide when that memory returned. Wildly, she looked around, but after a moment of blinking the sleep from her eyes, she realized she was still there. Instead of being down in the metal pit, however, she was laying on the metal floor beside a large hole. In the dim light, she could see Bronkendol leaning over her with another spoonful of what looked to be soup. He held the spoon out even closer, but she resisted, licking her lips instead.

There was another taste on her tongue, and it wasn't from the soup. It was older, as drops of it had dried on her mouth. First, she tasted the sweet tang of a nectar, but very quickly recognized the subtle bitterness beneath. Isa couldn't remember the name of the plant that made such a wine, but she did remember learning that it could put a full-grown horse to sleep in minutes.

"How long have I been asleep?" she asked, rubbing her head, which felt as though someone had laid a pile of bricks on top of it.

"Just one day and night, my dear. You were distressed, and I didn't want you to hurt yourself."

Ah yes. Despite the impossibility of escape, Isa vaguely recalled trying desperately to do so. She had even managed to work the bindings on her hands loose somehow. It had felt as though the walls were closing in around her, and the voice of reason that usually resided in her head had snapped. Then the enchanter had come with his drink and forced her to sip it, and suddenly, her unbound hands had made no difference as she had been lowered, unable to move, back down into the pit.

"Please, eat a bit more," Bronkendol said, pushing the bowl toward her.

Isa lifted the bowl and sniffed the soup. It smelled like any chicken soup, but how was one to tell whether or not he had hidden more herbs?

As she hesitated, Bronkendol sighed. "I promise, it's just soup."

Isa studied him, refusing to let go of her suspicion. How could she know for sure that she wasn't under the influence of the glass slivers even now? What if he had placed some inside of her while she'd slept? She touched the outer corners of her eyes, but felt nothing unusual. Still, would she be able to tell if he had hidden them there?

Isa came to the conclusion that the only way to know whether or not he had her under his influence was by asking herself one question. How did she feel about him? After a moment of thought, Isa decided with satisfaction that she still loathed him. The fact that she was still imprisoned and desired to escape only further convinced her that he was telling the truth.

Reluctantly, she began to feed herself. He smiled a bit, his boyish grin reminding her of why she'd been so taken in at first by his sweet, enthusiastic ways. How things had changed.

"I've come to ask for your help."

"My help?" Her voice sounded like a bullfrog's. She took another sip.

The enchanter nodded. "I want you to know that though your power is gone, you're still more valuable than I can express." He took a deep breath and looked her in the eyes. "The people love you. You could still be great."

"And why would I help you? You turned my husband against me. You've imprisoned me beneath my own home. You even threatened those I love!" Strengthened by the food, her voice began to rise as the familiar anger returned. "Why, for the love of goodness, would I want to help you?"

"In just a few hours, I will be crowning your brother king of the Fortress. I—"

"You can't do that!" Isa jumped to her feet, every ounce of energy returned. "The Fortress hasn't chosen him! He'll die!"

Bronkendol stood, too, so that they were nearly nose to nose, and his voice was no longer patient.

"You've been queen to a holy place that rejected you after only a few months, and you think you have enough understanding to tell me what is not acceptable?"

His words stung more than Isa wanted to admit, but if there was any truth, any knowledge left in her, she knew without the shadow of a doubt that Launce would die if he accepted that crown.

"For our world to move on from these wars and disagreements," Bronkendol continued, his voice quieter once more, "we must learn unity. I pray to the Maker that you choose rightly." He snapped his fingers, and two guards appeared. Each took one of Isa's arms, and though she fought them, they managed to wrestle her back into the giant sack once again. As they began lowering her into the pit once more, Bronkendol's curly head appeared over the hole's mouth. "I am ready to make difficult decisions. The question is, are you?"

Isa didn't answer as she went deeper, only watched until the light disappeared again. Once she was at the bottom, she folded herself up in the most comfortable position she could find and buried her head in her hands.

Was there a chance the Fortress might accept Launce? He had a good heart, and he'd spent enough time around the Fortress with her that he wasn't a complete stranger to its unusual ways. Perhaps it would overlook the insubordination of those who were pushing him to accept the position, and focus only on the young man himself.

But what about Ever?

Bronkendol was too much of a schemer to have killed Ever yet. By using her to ensure his cooperation, the enchanter had a great deal of power at his hands, even more than usual. Of course, the enchanter could work the other way too, threatening Ever to gain Isa's cooperation. And as much as she hated to admit it, the tactic would probably reap significant results. She knew better than to make any deals, but a tiny voice inside of her wondered all the same whether she would be strong enough to withstand his threats.

Was there a chance that her agreement to help Bronkendol might ensure her husband's freedom? He would hate that so much. But Isa had lost him too many times already. She really didn't think she could lose him again.

Tears rolled down her cheeks as she pressed her face against the cold metal beneath her.

"Why are You allowing this?" she sobbed softly. "What are you telling us that we just can't hear?"

But no one answered. There was no friendly breeze ruffling her hair. There wasn't the slightest bit of a whisper. But the truth already in her soul was nearly deafening inside.

If the boy hadn't pushed her, she never would have fallen in front of Ever's horse. If Ever hadn't injured her, she would have married Raoul instead of Ever. If the curse hadn't been cast, she never would have known the strength the Fortress had given her at birth. If the enchanter hadn't given Ever the slivers of glass, they never would have moved past the brokenness that had been haunting their marriage from the start. If she had conceived as early as all of the other Fortress queens did, her baby would be in grave danger now.

As Isa lay huddled at the bottom of the dungeon, she didn't feel strong, nor did she feel brave. And yet, she knew what she had to do.

LETTING GO

*I*sa awoke to the scraping of the metal cover being removed from her pit. As usual, the light was low, though she was getting used to it now. A rope with knots and a loop at the end was lowered until it hit the bottom of her pit with a soft thud.

"Get on," a man ordered from above.

Isa obeyed, not caring who waited for her at the top. Whether it was friend or foe, she would be out of the pit. Staring into the darkness, wondering whether or not she would die there, feeling helpless to save the ones she loved, had been maddening. Once she held on tightly and had her foot through the loop, the rope began to rise.

Still, she wondered, who was pulling her out? Her heart leaped before she could quell the hope. Had Everard somehow escaped? Could Garin have staged an escape? As the circle of light neared, she strained to see who was awaiting her. Disappointment set in though when the enchanter was the one who appeared over the edge.

"How did you sleep?" he asked, as though he was the host and she were his guest. Isa decided not to answer, but he carried on as if she had. "Have you thought about my proposition?"

Isa glowered at him in response, and he nodded.

"I see. Well, your mother will be disappointed."

Even if Isa had wanted to talk after that, it would have been impossible. She was too busy trying not to imagine her mother's face. Traitorous tears rolled down anyway.

The guard who had pulled her up took his torch from the wall and set off to their left. It was the direction opposite from which they'd entered the first time.

Or at least, that's what Isa thought. She wasn't able to recall just where they had come from or how much time had passed since she'd been imprisoned. All she knew was that any time spent in this hell had been too much time. And amidst all the more important worries, what she wouldn't have given for a bath.

Her legs felt wobbly after so many hours of sitting in the cramped, bowl-shaped pit. Walking quickly was impossible, so she was forced several times to stop and stretch her legs. Bronkendol waited patiently each time, though the guard sounded a bit irritated. She wondered where they were going through such a maze of tunnels, but she refused to ask and give Bronkendol the satisfaction of having the answers. So she simply walked. And stopped. And walked again.

On and on they went, through the halls, and up more flights of winding stairs than Isa could count. Finally, they came to a door, and the enchanter removed a golden key from his sleeve. Isa recognized it immediately as one that Ever never let out of his sight. He'd even worn it to bed each night. The only person it had ever been entrusted to was Garin, whenever Ever left the Fortress.

So if Bronkendol had the key, where was Garin? This thought brought her more apprehension than she'd thought possible.

"Are you quite sure?" Bronkendol paused, his hand on the door and the key in the lock. "Even if it meant possibly saving your husband?" This time, Isa couldn't help but meet his eyes. Even in the dim light, she could feel them probing her, hoping. And with good reason. Was there a chance that she could save him? It had been five months ago, but Isa remembered how her heart had torn as she watched him breathe his last to save her. The Fortress had brought him back then. But what about now? Isa knew the response she *should* give, and yet, she couldn't get her tongue to utter the words.

What would Everard say?

The whisper floated through the air. But even without the Fortress's prompting, Isa knew the answer.

"I have nothing more to say to you."

"You don't know how sorry I am to hear that. I'm also sorry that I must do this then as well." He passed his hand over her face, and in turn, something cold and hard began to grow over her eyes.

Isa rubbed her eyes until they hurt. She could still see, but it felt as if she were looking at things from a distance, as though there was a window between herself and the world.

"I thought you said you weren't going to give me the slivers!" she protested.

"I won't. But if you refuse to be a part of this new world, I can't have you confusing those who need to enter it as well." He reached into his cloak and removed a large, round glass pendant. It was a deep red, the color of wine, and he placed its gold chain around her neck. Bright flashes of light emanated from the glass, but Isa couldn't feel any deep power from it. It was just a trick. But what for?

Before she had time to wonder too much, Bronkendol had also removed a knife from his robe. He stepped back and studied her for a moment before grabbing her messy braid and cutting it off just below her shoulders. Then he gave her one more thorough look up and down before turning the key and opening the door.

Isa gaped at the length of braid in the enchanter's hand as she stepped into the sunlight. The locks that had reached nearly to her knees when loose and unbraided, now swung carelessly from the enchanter's hand, glinting copper in the sun's rays. Ever had always loved her hair. He'd even admitted once that though he had first hated her while they were under the Fortress's curse, he had always thought her hair was beautiful. A new anger heated her cheeks along with the morning sun, strengthening her resolve all the more.

She would die before Bronkendol had her allegiance.

Once they were outside, two more guards joined them. Bronkendol handed Isa off to them before taking his leave, and Isa was herded through another gate that led onto the northern lawn of the Fortress, and then into the Fortress through a side door. She could tell that careful attention was being paid to keep her hidden from sight, which meant someone was here that wasn't under the enchanter's thumb.

As the guards pushed her along, Isa spotted a mirror hanging on one of the walls ahead. She managed to stumble just in time to pause before the mirror as she stood back up, and when she did, she understood what Bronkendol had done in the dungeons. Her eyes were no longer a deep blue, but blood red. He must have placed colored glass inside of her eyes to alter her appearance. Even her own mother would have been frightened.

She didn't have time to dwell on the change in her eyes, because her escorts didn't let her rest until they were standing just outside the throne room's main doors. Before she could get too comfortable, something passed over her head, and Isa's throat tightened as she reached up to find a rope, nearly as thick as her braid had been, that now sat loosely around her neck. She turned her head just enough to see a hooded guard holding the end of the rope in one of his hands, and a tremor snaked through her as she recognized the executioner's hood. Another guard, who was also hooded, roughly slipped another, thinner rope around her wrists.

Where are you? she thought to the Fortress. But the only sound she heard came from inside the throne room doors. Hundreds of voices drifted in and out, and Isa wondered exactly who the enchanter had invited to witness this horrendous occasion.

How she wished for her sword!

A ruckus drew her attention as a clump of guards approached from her left. Surely they weren't for her. But when she saw the terrifying figure they led, Isa understood her own noose and bindings.

Ever had never looked more like an animal than he did now. His eyes had been made blood red as well. He wore a thick black cloak with a heavy hood, and an even larger red glass amulet around his neck. Thick black lines had been traced with charcoal around his eyes, the way dark sorcerers blackened theirs for incantations.

He had been walking along with the guards submissively until he saw her. His eyes widened as he took in her noose, and Isa could see him struggling with himself. She knew he could have taken those guards in a fight without question. Why didn't he?

Before Isa could say anything, however, she winced as the rope tightened just slightly around her throat.

That was why he didn't fight. Again, they were using her as a safeguard to make sure Ever cooperated. Isa wished more than ever that she, too, could have colossal strength. Then neither of them could be used against the other. But she had little time to wish, for the crowd on the other side of the throne room doors hushed, and the herald began to speak.

"Presenting King Rafael of Cobren." The herald interrupted her thoughts.

"Welcome," Rafael's voice boomed. "Most of you know who I am by title, but I doubt most of you know that I considered your king as a part of my own family. He and the late King Rodrigue, may the Maker eternally guide his soul, came to our assistance many times, and for that, I will always be grateful." Then Rafael sighed so deeply that Isa wondered if he truly thought Ever was dead. When he spoke again, his voice was gentle.

"Everard was just and fair and good. And he loved your queen with the tenacity of a thousand men." A sob broke through, and Isa glanced at Everard. To her surprise, however, he wasn't looking toward the door, or even at the guards surrounding them.

He was looking at her. And despite the frightening intensity of the ghoulish red in his eyes, the tenderness in Ever's face was unmistakable, deeper than she had ever seen. Unable to look away, Isa drank it in like a soul dying slowly in the desert. Never had she needed him more. Never had she loved him so much. If given the chance, she would do it all over again. Every single day. Every single hour, Isa would love Ever until the last breath had left her body.

"Only the most unrighteous of souls could have stolen two such gems from our world," Rafael continued, his voice growing steadier and more determined with each word. "And I take it upon myself to see them brought to justice! Bring in the impostors!"

Gasps broke out as the doors were opened, and Isa and Ever were prodded down the aisle like cattle ready for the slaughter. The fear in the room was palpable, and Isa wondered how many would see through the impostors' work, if any. If the glass amulets that hung about their necks didn't convince, and neither did her shorn hair, the terrifying, crimson-eyed man beside her would surely do the job of convincing everyone in that room that they were indeed impostors.

Rafael stood at the front of the raised steps, a few feet in front of the gilded thrones. Bronkendol stood close to the back, partly in the shadows. Soldiers were everywhere, some even on the steps of the dais itself. But where was Launce?

When they had reached the front of the room, Isa and Ever were turned to face the crowd. Isa scanned the people to see who was there. The kings, queens, and nobles who had been visiting Rafael's court hissed and shouted for the impostors' deaths. The Fortress nobles and servants openly wept, but there were faces from Soudain that showed neither anger nor sorrow, but rather frightened bewilderment. Friends and acquaintances looked back and forth from Isa to Ever. They had no purple light in their eyes, and their uncertainty was clear. Isa wondered if Bronkendol would be able to fool everyone without the use of his shards. From the looks on the Destinians' faces, it seemed highly unlikely, and Isa suppressed a smile.

"These sorcerers infiltrated my castle with their dark powers," Rafael said. "They took it upon themselves to imitate your king and queen, before brutally murdering Everard and Isabelle in their room at night, even after I had helped Isa recover from her illness." Another gasp went up from the crowd, and several more people started to weep. Still, most of those from Soudain continued to only look confused.

Finally, one man stood. A cobbler. Isa's mother used to take Launce to him for shoes because he was the only cobbler who could keep up with the feisty young man. He was also on the city council with her father. Twisting his hat in his hands as he spoke, the poor man looking everywhere but at Rafael himself.

"The king and queen were strong . . . The Fortress made them that way. I don't . . . I don't think they could be killed so easily." He swallowed. "Besides, if these two were strong enough to overtake our king, then how is it that you have them captured here?"

Isa both rejoiced and feared at the same time. Would Bronkendol or Rafael punish the cobbler for such questions?

"Good questions, good sir," Rafael said in a kind voice. "That brings me to my second announcement. I want to introduce you all to the holy man who has succeeded in subduing such villains."

Bronkendol stepped forward. Unlike when he went to visit Isa in the dungeons, he now wore a silk robe of ice purple. It was an unusual cut, but it reminded Isa somewhat of the ancient statues in the gardens, the earliest ones of the first Fortress kings. Without speaking, he merely gave a slight smile and bow to the crowd, before flicking his wrist. Glass spikes grew up around the two of them until the spikes reached two heads taller than Ever, imprisoning them both. Exclamations broke out, and the crowd shifted uneasily. Bronkendol moved his wrist once more, and the glass spikes disappeared.

The cobbler, visibly shaken, said nothing more and sat down.

"Because Everard was so dear to me," Rafael said, taking control of the situation once more, "I feel as though it is my responsibility to bring a new king to

Destin's throne, as there is no heir. He is new and young, and yet, not an unfa-miliar soul. One I believe your late queen could not have approved of more. And by his side, I present my own daughter." Looking back with a proud smile, he raised his hand.

Isa looked back as well, and her heart fell as Launce and Olivia stepped forward. She hadn't seen them in the corner before, but now they were impos-sible to look away from. The Fortress's ceremonial robe was too big on Launce's thin shoulders, and his face was a sickly pale, but he stood beside Rafael never-theless. Olivia was dressed in Isa's ceremonial gown, but her eyes also showed her to be under the enchanter's control.

Despite her resolution to wait, Isa felt like screaming inside. *Don't allow him to accept*, she begged the Fortress. *Let him know You're watching! Please don't let my brother die!*

"Your queen's younger brother, Launce Marchand of Soudain, has proven himself a worthy successor in my own country at my daughter's betrothal cere-mony." Looking back once more, he smiled indulgently.

In a movement so small she nearly missed it, Isa saw Bronkendol place his hand inside of his robe pocket at his side. Something small and silver glinted from inside, and as soon as he rubbed it, Isa knew what it was.

She had to get that mirror.

As soon as Bronkendol's fingers touched the mirror, Rafael's expression changed back to one of ceremony.

"And so, to bring justice to the needless deaths of King Everard and Queen Isabelle Fortier of Destin, your future king shall be the one to put these traitors to death."

Bronkendol stepped forward once more and handed Launce a sword of pure glass. Launce looked at the weapon in his hands with wide eyes. The two hooded guards reached out and turned Isa and Ever roughly so they faced the dais.

No. No, no, no. Surely the Fortress would not allow this. Being slaughtered with her husband as criminals was a fate harsh enough. But to expect Launce, her gentle-spirited brother, to be the one to spill their blood? What kind of hold did the enchanter have on her brother? Who had he threatened for Launce to be considering such a sin?

"And who has authorized such a change?" Ever's voice was loud and strong. Launce froze and stared at them, but Bronkendol glided forward and answered in a steady voice.

"Who can speak for the Maker? For the Fortress?" Then he turned to the crowd. "My power may not be as impressive as your former king's was," the enchanter said in a calm voice, "but it is a power from the Maker no less."

"And I suppose that is what you told the holy men in Lingea?" Ever threw off his robe and broke his shackles in the same movement. Hushed whimpers sounded from some in the crowd, but Ever stared only at the enchanter, his red eyes flashing even without the blue fire that was hidden beneath them.

Several of the guards pulled their swords, including the hooded guard nearest Ever.

"Ever!" Isa squeaked as the rope tightened around her neck.

But Ever kept on. "All ten of them, found dead in a field with glass spikes in their hearts! What did they do to earn such horrible deaths? Did they dare question your claim to the Maker's words?"

"And what proof do you have of this?" Bronkendol asked in a cool voice, his hands folded in front of him.

Ever reached into his cloak and drew out a glass spike the length of a grown man's arm. How had he gotten such a thing? Isa wondered. Hadn't he been stuck in the dungeons as well?

"How did this find its way into one of my messengers?" Ever hurled the spike at the enchanter's feet, where it shattered. Bronkendol stared at the broken pieces below him, while the crowd began to make uneasy sounds. Isa turned as well as she could in the noose, and she could see the people moving about as though they were wishing to run.

What was Ever up to? Clearly, he thought he had the upper hand. If so, then why was he waiting so long? And, Isa thought, why hadn't he freed her yet?

"They discovered you, didn't they?" Ever shouted. "When you traveled between realms, the true holy men saw through the tear in the worlds. And you saw fit to silence them before they could leak news of your little secret to others. What you forgot, however, was that the Maker does no look lightly upon the murder of His children. And you, sir, have more blood on your hands than any of my ancestors ever had!"

Then, as Bronkendol shifted uncomfortably throughout Ever's rant, Isa saw the glint of silver in his pocket again. The mirror. That was why Ever hadn't struck yet. He needed to get the mirror to free the others from the enchanter's grasp. She recalled his words on the road, about how hard it would be to fight friends and loved ones who were under the direction of their enemy. It would be a blood bath. Ever was stalling.

"Launce," Ever called up to her brother. His voice was kinder this time. Launce, who was still gaping at the glass weapon in his hands, had to be called three times more before he looked up to meet Ever's eyes. "I know he's threatened your family. But you must trust the Fortress. Do not commit a sin that will haunt you forever. No matter what he's promised you."

Once more, the rope tightened around Isa's neck, causing her to make a small choking sound. Launce watched her with fearful eyes.

"Launce," Ever's voice had a warning tone to it. "Remember what happened to me when I tried to shed innocent blood!"

But Launce didn't answer. Closing his eyes, he gripped the hilt of the glass sword until his knuckles turned white. Isa watched in horror as her brother walked slowly down the steps toward her husband. *Please!* she pleaded. *Don't let him do this!*

As she cried out inside, a movement caught her eye. Her hooded guard had moved up so that he was beside her, and Isa was able to glimpse just enough of the face beneath the hood to recognize Garin's slightly cleft chin. He gave her the smallest ghost of a smile before turning his attention back to Launce.

As Launce continued to move forward, Bronkendol walked forward as well, staying in line with the young man, and Isa decided not to wait and find out what would happen next. She didn't know what Ever and Garin had planned, but she was done watching her brother try to kill her husband. Whirling around, Isa knocked the rope from Garin's hand and stumbled into Bronkendol. She clutched the bottom of his robe.

"Your Holiness!" she begged as pitifully as she could, clawing at his robes. "Just let him be! Don't make my brother do this! I beg you!" She allowed herself to collapse at his feet, sobbing.

Bronkendol bent down and whispered, "You had your chance. Now let him have his." With that, he motioned to Isa's guard, and Garin hurried forward to take charge of his prisoner. Isa went willingly, but wanted to sing and dance with rejoicing as she tightened her fingers over the little mirror in her hand.

In one smooth movement, Garin's hood was thrown back, and he tossed Ever's sword over Isa's head. At the same time, the hooded guard keeping watch over Ever threw his hood back as well. Apu, Queen Kartek's personal guard, maneuvered to cover Ever's back. Garin grabbed a stunned Launce and Isa, who was still bound, and the group of five began to run toward the doors. Launce paused. Isa guessed he was looking for Olivia, but she was nowhere to be seen in the chaos that suddenly erupted from the crowd.

Unfortunately, even without the mirror, it seemed the enchanter's orders were still in effect. The soldiers, and even the kings and nobles from the other lands took up their weapons and gave chase. Isa ran as fast as she could, but the question plagued her even as they moved. How would they destroy the mirror?

"Isa!" Ever's shout came just in time. Isa ducked, just missing the swipe of a club from above. Men, and even some women, came from every direction, and somehow, they had all found weapons. Ever's blue fire was a blur as he moved from side to side. Apu wasn't much slower. Even Garin fought with increasing speed. Launce and Isa stood between the other three, although Isa wished to the heavens that *someone* would give her a sword.

"We can't stay here forever," Garin called out over his shoulder. They had been shoved up against a marble column, their progress stalled as the three men tried to hold off their attackers without drawing blood. "Where are we going, Everard?"

"To the tower!" was Ever's reply. He stepped out just enough for Isa to move behind him. In that instant, she saw the clearance to the stairs. Miraculously, there was a break in the waves of men, and Isa took it. Ducking beneath Garin and around Apu, she grabbed Launce's hand and dragged him toward the stairs. He fought her though. When she looked back, she could see him staring above the chaos at the room where Olivia still stood.

"We can't help her until the mirror is gone!" she shouted at him. When he didn't respond, she yanked on his arm. "Launce!"

As if waking from a dream, Launce slowly nodded and began to follow her. It was just in time too, for the brawl was nearly to the base of the tower stairs.

If they could destroy this accursed mirror anywhere, it would be in the Tower of Annals.

5 3

SHATTER

*L*aunce finally awoke from his stupor and grasped her hand tightly, even surpassing her as they ran up the winding stairs of the tower. Ever, Apu, and Garin were following after them, but as Isa and Launce left them behind, she could hear from the men's terse exchanges that the fight wasn't going well. Angry shouts echoed from further down the tower stairs as they ran, and her heart ached. Whose blood would be shed first? Her husband's? Apu's? Or one of their friends being used by the enchanter?

Isa stumbled a few times in the darkness of the tower, as did Launce, dropping the glass sword somewhere along the way. But the sounds of clashing metal behind them left no time to stop and look for it. And so they ran. For the first time, Isa questioned whether the tower really needed to have been built so tall.

They didn't reach the top until Isa's lungs felt like they might collapse, and her vision was spotty. Launce was first to reach the top. He yanked her into the tower behind him and then immediately shut the door. Isa stood beside him, waiting for the others to come through the door, but Launce locked it instead.

"What are you doing?" Isa darted back to unlock the door, but Launce grabbed her and held her tightly so she couldn't move.

"They're too far behind. If we let them in, the others will follow! Isa! Isa, look at me!"

Isa stopped struggling, and she stared up at her brother. Launce's hair had been cropped short for the coronation, and his eyes were lined with a stress she had never seen before. He looked older, and for the first time, to Isa at least, like a man.

"You know this is what Everard wants."

Once she was still, he carefully let go, and she stepped back. He was right. This is what Ever would want.

Which meant they had no time to waste. Isa raised the mirror as high as she could and threw it down upon the floor with all her might. Instead of cracking, it just rolled away. Isa grabbed it again and brought it down hard against the edge of the table this time. But the table only dented.

"How do we break it?" Isa cried, racking her memory for something that might stand a chance against the enchanter's magic. She searched the room desperately for something sharp or heavy. Books would do them no good, and the furniture was too heavy for her to lift.

"Hurry!" Launce had his ear to the door. "They're coming!"

Isa spotted the rack of swords that hung above the fireplace. Four of them were displayed against black velvet, the fourth one looking as if it were just low enough to reach. She hopped on a chair and leaned over the mantle, trying to pull it from the bottom rung. As her fingers touched the sword, Isa's boot slipped from the arm of the chair she stood on, and both Isa and the swords crashed onto the stone hearth.

Her left elbow came down painfully upon one of the stones, but when Isa opened her eyes, she was amazed to find that nothing was bleeding, and only two of the swords had broken. She grabbed the two remaining weapons and ran over to Launce.

"Here!" She handed him one sword and then moved back to the center of the room. Placing the mirror on the floor, Isa raised her sword above her head. Before she could bring it down, she was distracted by the sound of splintering wood.

The door shuddered as something beat against it from the outside. Launce adjust his grip on the weapon Isa had given him, and Isa realigned her sword with the mirror. But she couldn't focus enough to aim. Her breath was coming too fast, and her palms were sweaty, so the sword kept slipping.

"That's not Everard." Launce looked back at her.

They stared at one another for a long moment. If one of their enemies was here, where were Ever and the others? Cold panic pooled in Isa's belly. Had Ever's fear of killing his friends allowed him to be overcome? Had Bronkendol killed him? *Fortress*, she thought, *where is my husband?* The only answer she heard though was the hacking at the door.

Isa shook her head and tried once again to steady the sword. *Please let it break!*

The swords above the mantle had belonged to the first kings, Ever had once told her. That meant they would have been forged within the Fortress walls, imbuing them with the Fortress's power and strength. If any weapon could stand against the enchanter's charms, it would be one of these. Isa swung the sword downwards, but just as it hit the ground, the hilt slipped from her grasp and missed the mirror. Frustrated, Isa wiped her hands on her dress and raised the sword to try again.

"Isa."

She stopped and looked up at her brother. He wore a torn expression. "When he gets through, I will have to take him."

"No!" Isa immediately shifted into a ready position, mirror all but forgotten. This was what Ever had trained her for. "I can hold him longer than you can. If we can just wait until—"

"They're not going to make it in time."

"No! Don't say that!" Isa tried to run to his side, but Launce held out his sword to stop her. Isa began to protest again, but he interrupted, and when he spoke, his voice was resolved.

"I made the wrong choice by not trusting the Fortress before. Now please just let me make this right."

"By killing yourself?" Isa shouted. As if in agreement, the edge of a glass axe made its first hole all the way through the door, sending chunks of wood flying toward them.

"No." Launce gave her a small smile. "By trusting the Fortress will help you stop him."

"But how? I can't break it!"

Launce stared in frustration at the mirror on the ground, before a look of understanding lit his face. "Maybe you don't have to."

"What?"

Launce spoke quickly as the axe gnawed away at the hole, making it larger with each blow. "Bronkendol told me that your strength isn't like Everard's, that it's not like anyone else's! He said you have the strength of the heart, not the hand."

"What is that supposed to mean?" Isa tried to dart toward Launce again, but Launce held his sword in front of the door once more. "I can't let you do this!" Isa protested, her voice breaking at the end. "You're my baby brother!"

"Then don't let me die in vain. Let me be the hero, just this once."

As he spoke, the rest of the door gave way enough for Bronkendol to drop his axe and step through. His silver curls were matted, and sweat rolled down his face and neck. He pointed the glass sword straight at Launce's heart.

"Give me the mirror, Isabelle. This sword is poisoned, and though I don't want to kill your brother, I will if you don't give me what's mine." He held his left hand out to Isa as his right forced Launce against the wall with the glass sword.

Isa looked at Launce, then down at the mirror.

"Don't do it, Isa! The Fortress gave you the mirror for a reason!"

"Give it to me, or he dies! None of your Fortress's power can heal the poison this weapon was forged in!"

Isa looked back and forth between the mirror and her brother. How could she destroy it even if she had all of Ever's strength? Even now, away from its master, the mirror's power pulsed through her hands to a rhythm, like the beating of a heart.

"I don't know how," she mouthed to her brother, tears streaming down her face. Without hesitation, Launce launched himself off of the wall. Isa cried out as the sword bit flesh. Even Bronkendol stared in horror.

"Now you have nothing to lose," Launce gasped as the enchanter stepped back. "Do what you were made to do!"

Panic and sorrow clouded Isa's mind as she stared once more at the mirror in her hand. If only Ever were here!

Who is holding the mirror, Daughter?

The familiar voice Isa had waited so long to hear whispered now.

I am, she cried. *But I don't know how! I'm not my husband!*

A memory flashed before her eyes. Nevina, lying unconscious upon the floor before her. *How did you know what to do then?* the voice prodded.

I didn't! I just knew . . .

That she belonged. That she was wanted. That she was the Fortress's. That she had been chosen.

I chose you then, and I choose you now. And I didn't give you strength of the hands, but strength of the heart.

Isa could somehow feel the Fortress smile.

Now use it.

Without thinking, Isa lifted the mirror to her mouth.

"No!" Bronkendol lunged for her. "I took your power! You have none left!"

But Isa knew her power wasn't gone. It had never been hers to begin with. It was the Fortress's, and she was merely the heart to hold it, a vessel. Isa closed her eyes and focused on what she knew within. Not on what she felt, but on what she knew in her heart to be the truest of truths.

"Peace," she whispered.

AN OATH FULFILLED

*H*undreds of voices cried out in agony as the glass shattered between Isa's hands. Their shouts of pain echoed all the way up to the tower, where Launce laid on the floor bleeding and Bronkendol stood, a look of disbelief on his face. It didn't last long though.

"Do you know what you have done?" He raised the bloodied glass sword and began to stalk toward Isa.

Before he made even three steps, however, he stopped. A choking sound gurgled from his throat and his eyes bulged before he slid limply to the ground.

Behind him, Ever stood, his own sword bloodied as he let the enchanter fall from it.

"I swore I would kill you," Ever snarled.

"Ever!" Isa thrust herself into his arms, and held him with all the strength that remained in her worn, ragged body. He drew her in and silently stroked her short hair. She hadn't lost him again after all. As he rocked her from side to side, Isa caught a glimpse of her brother.

"Launce!" She tore herself from Ever's arms and collapsed on the floor, wrapping her arms as gently as she could around her little brother. Ever quickly joined her and turned him so that he was facing up. To Isa's dismay, his face was pale, and his eyes were lifeless, staring blankly at the ceiling. "You have to heal him, Ever!" Isa said frantically. "You have to stop the poison!"

Ever inhaled and laid his hands upon the young man. Isa held her breath as the blue flames licked Launce's wounds. But as seconds passed, nothing changed. Ever set his jaw and pushed hard. When still nothing came, however, Isa lost patience.

She placed her own hands on Launce as well, but before she could try her own strength, Ever shook his head and gathered her in his arms.

"It's too late for me to help him," he murmured into her ear. "I'm so sorry, Isa." Isa was about to protest. He had given up too easily, she wanted to shout, when another voice spoke.

"I might be able to help him though."

Isa looked up through tear-blurred eyes to see Kartek standing at the door. Her sun-kissed face was paler than usual, and she held one hand over her side protectively, but she gave Isa a weak smile.

"Garin." She turned to the steward, who had just walked up behind her. "Can you take this young man to a dark, quiet room?"

Garin stooped and lifted Launce's long, thin body as though he weighed nothing. The steward's hair was mussed, and his clothes were torn in several places, but aside from some sweat, dirt smudges, and the fact that he was wearing the executioner's uniform, he looked as much like himself as he ever did. As he turned to leave with Launce's body, Isa leaped up to follow, but Kartek held out a hand.

"I am sorry, but I will need to be alone for this. I will call for you when I know his fate." The queen's brown eyes softened, and she kindly took Isa's face in the hand that wasn't holding her side. "Do not despair, young one. The Maker's gift to me might yet bring him back from the dark."

Ever pulled Isa back to him as Garin and Kartek began down the stairs, and Isa let him, drinking in every second as though he'd never held her before. The warmth of his arms, the familiar smell of leather and the forest were as intoxicating as a fine wine. Isa gazed up at him and shuddered at the thought that she might have lost him again.

"What happened?" She frowned and reached up to touch the red gash just above his left brow.

Ever made a face. "An earl managed to throw a frying pan at me. I must have blacked out long enough for them to think I was dead, and for Bronkendol to slip by me." He shook his head. "Fighting in battle is nothing new, but not fighting my friends and those who have sworn to serve me . . ." his voice trailed off, and he looked away from her.

"How many?" She could hardly hear her own voice.

"Too many." He closed his eyes, but they glistened at the corners. "A few dozen of my own men, three servants, and a Cobrien duke." He opened his eyes, and a tear escaped as his face crumpled. "I tried so hard just to hold them off, but—" A ragged sob escaped him, and his chest heaved violently.

Isa felt tears running down her own cheeks as she reached up with both hands and gently pulled his face down against hers. In turn, Ever took her shoulders in his large hands and leaned against her as the sobs came faster and harder. Isa ached for him as he wept in her arms. Ever was always in command, always had a plan to fix what had gone askew. It was wrong for him to be this broken, as if the sun had risen in the wrong part of the sky.

She couldn't tell how long they stood there as he let her hold him, but it was, in a strange way, the closest to healing she'd felt in a long time.

"You don't always have to be so strong," she whispered to him as she wiped the tears from his face, ignoring those on her own. He opened his eyes and looked into hers. As he did, she realized that the red glass was gone, and wondered if her own eyes were clear again as well.

"But if I'm not—"

"I will be." She smiled and caressed his cheek. "I made that vow before the people, this Fortress, and you. I'm not about to break it now."

Ever stared hard at her for a long moment before wrapping his arms around her and kissing the top of her head.

"This is going to take a while to clean up," he said in a hoarse voice. And Isa knew he wasn't just talking of Bronkendol's doings.

"It will be worth it in the end."

"Yes. Yes it will."

All too soon, it was time to face the chaos that awaited them below. Ever shed the ludicrous, heavy garb Bronkendol had forced him into, and Isa changed into a practical gown that wasn't tattered and grimy. It was difficult to look in the mirror and see her hair so ragged, but at least its new length would keep it out of the way as they worked.

Garin had directed the servants to gather everyone to the throne room so Ever could address them, but it took a little longer than usual, as most of the servants were recovering from the enchanter's influence as well. The enchanter's power had taken a toll on many, and some of even their most reliable servants needed assistance.

When they were finally all gathered, Isa stood tall and proud beside her husband. The timidity she'd known was gone now. She was done comparing. This was her place, and these were her people. This was her Fortress, and never again would she doubt its love for her.

The kings, queens, dignitaries, and other guests of high standing were all unhappy to have been manipulated so easily, but they listened to Ever with respectful humility. Isa watched as Ever explained the enchanter's wiles. In the middle of his speech, Isa caught the eye of Lady Jadzia, but the woman refused to hold her gaze. Isa didn't miss the little daggers Jadzia still sent her throughout Ever's speech, when Isa pretended not to pay her heed. Would the woman ever give up?

After the address was made, Isa was standing beside Ever, when she spotted Jadzia primping herself before beginning to walk toward them. Anger flamed inside her, and her hands grew slightly warm as she felt her power rise within her. Before Isa could say anything, Ever surprised her by grabbing her around the waist and kissing her with such a passion that Isa felt her cheeks flush.

"Um . . . thank you?" Isa breathed when Ever finally let her go. He gave her a mischievous grin and wiggled his eyebrows.

"Perhaps Lady Jadzia will think twice next time she's tempted to try and play for a married man."

Isa turned, and sure enough, Lady Jadzia was staring at them, open-mouthed with a look of shock on her face. Isa allowed herself a wide grin for the woman.

So Ever had noticed. The thought made her nearly giddy.

～

Lady Jadzia and her father finally left a week after the enchanter's death, along with a few of the other royals. Progress was slow, as most of the servants and guests were still recovering, so Isa suggested that they bring in some of her old friends from the village to help, a suggestion which Ever readily agreed to.

Isa was glad to make the trip down the mountain alone. She didn't even mind the guard that trailed loosely behind her. While she had spoken the truth about calling on old acquaintances for help, there was a visit she needed to make. As soon as all of her requests for assistance at the Fortress were made, Isa wound her way through the main marketplace to the familiar little shop that sat on the northeast corner of the square.

Megane squealed when Isa walked through the front of the shop into their kitchen, and Deline was overjoyed as well. But there was one face in particular that Isa had come to see.

Ansel's face broke into a wide smile when she let herself into her parents' room. It hurt to see his eyes and cheeks still mottled and purple from Bronkendol's cruel orders.

"How are you?" She sat at the edge of the bed and looked anxiously at his legs, which were covered by his blankets.

Ansel shrugged as though it were nothing. "The healer says he's not sure if I'll walk again, but—"

"Father!" Isa cried. "Why didn't you tell me? I'm sure Ever can help you somehow!"

"Considering the chaos of that place after your enchanter died, it was good of the servants to simply bring me back here." When Isa continued to glare at him, he gave her a placating smile. "But perhaps I will, in time. For the time being, though, I would feel more comfortable if that husband of yours stays right where he's at."

Isa sighed and sat back down. Her father was right, as usual. Ever was busy, but he never failed to check on her brother whenever he had the chance. Kartek and Apu had gone home finally, so Ever was the main physician of the Fortress.

"It is up to the Maker now," Kartek had told them. "I am sorry I cannot do more, but now the best medicine will be for you to wait." And so they'd waited. Ansel, Deline, and Megane from the city, and Ever and Isa from down the hall at the Fortress.

"Your Highness," Isa's guard called from behind the door. Isa and her father looked at one another in surprise. Isa's guards always waited outside. "The king has sent a messenger to request that you return to the Fortress. It's about your brother."

Isa was off in a flash. As soon as she was on her horse, they flew up the mountain road until the incline made it impossible to run. Isa's heart pounded with impatience as they plodded along. Had Launce awakened? Had he taken a turn for the worse?

She didn't even pause to unbridle her horse at the stables. For once, she would let the servants take care of that. Once she had vaulted herself off the horse, she sprinted through the Fortress, not stopping until she reached Launce's room. As she approached, Ever was just shutting the door behind Princess Olivia and her escort. The princess curtsied, but didn't meet Isa's eyes.

"I cannot express how sorry I am for playing the part I had in all of this," she said. Isa could hear the tears in her voice. "We tried to hold him off, but it was just too much—"

Despite Isa's need to see Launce, she could only assume he was improving if Ever had brought the princess to see him. Isa didn't let Olivia go any further, wrapping the young woman in her arms and giving her a good squeeze.

"You did well to hold out for so long," she whispered. Then she laughed. "You have seen more of the Fortress at work in just a few short weeks than most Destinians see in their lives!" She pulled back to look the girl in the eyes. "The Maker has given us a new day. We've mourned the past. Now let's not dwell on it any longer."

Princess Olivia pulled back and gave her a tremulous smile. "Will you come visit me sometime? I should like to know you more without an enchanter trying to take over our kingdoms."

Isa laughed told the girl yes, giving her one more quick hug. Then Ever placed his hand on the small of her back and gently pushed her toward Launce's door. In spite of Ever's reassuring smile, Isa felt her heart pound as she entered her brother's room.

Launce was propped up against a mountain of pillows, which somehow made him look even scrawnier than usual. His head was leaned back and his eyes were closed as he lay there, but as she approached, he slowly lifted himself up to see her.

"Launce," was all Isa could say. The young man before her looked like her brother. And yet he didn't. There were thin lines of exhaustion at the corners of his eyes, and his skin was unusually red, as though it were thinner than usual. He looked as though he might faint at any minute, and yet she could still see a bit of life in the half smile he managed to give her.

"So you did it," he croaked.

Isa rolled her eyes. "As much as it pains me to admit it, you were right."

"I don't think I've ever heard that one before." His dark eyes gleamed with mischief. "I will be sure to bring that up now whenever you doubt me."

"I'm sure you will." Isa stuck her tongue out at him, then sighed. Even their childish games were difficult when he was lying in bed looking half dead. "But truly, how are you?"

Launce looked down at himself. "Everard seems to think I will be at least a few months in recovery. Apparently, Bronkendol's poison has proved to be the most difficult healing Queen Kartek has ever attempted. Still," he paused, "it seems I should be well enough to travel by summer."

"Travel?"

Launce looked down, studying his hands with sudden interest. "King Rafael has asked if I am willing to consider being Cobren's next king."

"And . . . you're accepting?" Isa frowned. "You hate court life."

"Of course I do. But I spoke with Everard and I think . . ." He drew in a deep breath and blew it out before finishing. "I can see a little better why your husband makes the choices that he does. The Fortress has given him many lives to be responsible for. And now, Cobren has lots of healing to do as well. Olivia thinks I can help with that somehow."

Isa smirked. "Ah, and the truth comes out."

Launce grimaced at her. "You know what I mean. It's just that I feel like the Maker, for whatever reason, has put me in this place now. I don't fit into the life I had before, thanks to you." He swatted Isa's arm, then doubled over in pain. "I keep forgetting about that," he grunted. "Anyway—Ouch!—I think it would be best to give this a try. They think they need me, and I think I need a new start."

"I still don't understand this life entirely either," Isa said. "And to be honest, I don't know if I ever will. However," she scooted closer so she could take his hand, "I do know that you and I make a terrific team. How about we just enjoy being lost together for a while?"

Launce smiled back. "Sounds good to me. Just don't go running into any horse thieves or glass enchanters or evil Fae until I'm walking at least."

"I will try." Isa grinned at her brother. "But I'm not making any promises."

EPILOGUE

NEW BEGINNINGS

"*Y*asmina, please hand me that spoon." Isa smiled as the little girl handed her the spoon with a shy look. "Then as soon as your mother is done eating, I think we're going to brush your hair."

"My hair doesn't need brushing," the little girl said, holding her stringy blond hair up for Isa to see.

"Oh, that it does," her mother said. Then she smiled at Isa with tired eyes. "I can't thank you enough, Your Highness. I couldn't stand watching her run around like that for one more day." The woman laid back into the pillows and sighed slowly as she rubbed her temples. "How are the others?"

"You're all getting along quite nicely." Isa reached out and squeezed the woman's hand. "I suppose that in a way, it was best that you were all down here to begin with. You would have gotten the glass too, had you been working in the upper levels with the others." The thought of the invalids under the orders of the enchanter made Isa shiver. There had been too much blood shed at the Fortress as it was. No, it was better that the infirmary had been forgotten, even if it meant more work for Isa and the few other women who were well enough to help.

"It has been two weeks." The woman shifted uncomfortably. "When will you be relieved? Surely the other servants will be recovered soon enough to return to their duties."

"Some are, but many of them were injured in the fight, and others are grieving . . ." They were silent for a moment, reflecting on their losses, before Isa cajoled the woman into eating. "You need to keep up your strength." Isa nodded at the woman's burgeoning belly. "Soon enough you will have two to keep up with."

Isa couldn't help the slight jab of envy as the woman smiled and rubbed her belly. And yet, Isa was the closest to feeling content that she had felt in a long time. The desire was still there, but at least she now saw a purpose in the wait. She sighed as the woman ate. The Fortress had known what it was doing all along, even though she hadn't seen the purpose at the time.

As soon as the woman finished her meal, Isa chased down the little girl, and was just finishing with her hair when Gigi came in.

"There you are. I'm sorry for interrupting, my dear, but the king has requested you meet him at the stables."

Isa patted the little girl's head once more before standing and gathering her things. "We were just finishing anyway." She gave the room another look before she was satisfied that things were in order. Hopefully, the woman and her daughter would be back in their quarters before long anyway. As she walked up the steps from the bottom levels to the main floor, Isa glanced at the other rooms along the way, making a list in her head of the items she would need the next time she came down.

"My mother saw her yesterday," she told Gigi, "and she says the child will come any day. The man in the next room over, though, will need to stay quite a while longer. His leg will take longer to heal than her convalescence will last." Isa sighed. "I wish we had more rooms down here, instead of having to keep so many in the greeting hall. Ever suggested using some of the guest rooms, but they're too far apart to see to everyone's needs."

"You leave those worries to me and the healers." Gigi took Isa's arm and guided her elbow so that they were heading toward Isa's own chambers. "You have done far enough and more than what could ever be expected from you."

"It was a nice change from Bronkendol's chaos. Now, what exactly am I doing? I thought we were going to the stables."

Instead of answering, Isa was hurried into her own chambers. Two voices sounded from the connecting sitting room, and it was impossible not to overhear.

"Do you think she'll need any looser clothes?" A young woman's voice gushed with hope, and Isa felt her cheeks turn pink.

"Of course not." Cerise's words were sharp. "They'll only be gone a week. Now please focus on what you're doing. You've just rumpled that gown."

"Are we nearly finished?" Gigi let go of Isa's arm as they rounded the corner to find the two young women filling a travel bag with Isa's things. Isa didn't miss the look of rebuke Gigi sent the younger servant.

Before she could get a better look at what was in the bag, however, Cerise dragged her over to her mirror, where she was bathed and dressed in a new riding outfit. The gown was trim and easy to move in, and there were only a few layers of petticoats beneath the skirt, something Isa would have liked for most of her gowns. The deep green was exactly the color of the rose stems in her favorite garden, and her boots were new as well.

"When did you have time to make these?" Isa was in awe.

"We didn't." Gigi grinned. "I had them made five and a half months ago."

"Whatever for?"

"For the night that should have been ours." Ever's deep voice came from the door. When she turned, Isa caught her breath. Ever walked toward her, also in a new outfit of dark red and brown. Red was a color he didn't wear often, and Isa thought it looked quite dashing on him.

"You were right when you said I chose others over you." He came to a stop just before her, and took her left hand in both of his, examining the blue crystal ring that burned brightly from her finger. "I cannot change our first night, as much as I'd like to, but I can offer you a new beginning in its place."

Was he being earnest?

Ever seemed to sense her doubts and fears. With a small smile, he pulled a delicate bracelet from his cloak. Isa gasped as he placed it on her wrist. Purple stone roses glittered from a gold chain. In awe, Isa looked up to thank him, and to her surprise he reached up and gently tilted her chin back. Before he could lean all the way in, Gigi squeaked and pushed them apart. "There is a reason your horses are loaded down with clothes and food and wine. Now go, before you forget where you are!"

Ever sent Gigi a scowl before leaning down and kissing the top of her white head. Then, in a flurry of people and horses and last-minute instructions, Isa and Ever somehow made it down to the stables, where Garin was waiting with their horses' reins in hand.

Isa hadn't seen much of the steward in the last few weeks, with the exception of quick exchanges about Launce. It was good to see him looking less harried and back to his typical calm.

"Thank you, Garin." Ever helped Isa up onto her horse before climbing astride his own.

"You'll watch out for Launce, won't you?"

Garin smiled knowingly. "Of course, my queen. Now, both of you, go!"

Finally, they were on their way. Isa was bursting with questions, but Ever was strangely silent, so she decided to hold back. Besides, it was too beautiful a day to clutter the air with words. The first powdery snow of the season had fallen the night before, and the wind was nowhere to be heard. Scarlet cardinals sat on bare branches, and the sun glistened off the snow until it nearly hurt to open her eyes. There were few sounds, aside from an occasional seasonally late chipmunk.

Isa wondered how Everard knew his way without the visible trail, as they had seemed early on, to veer from the usual road, into the forest itself. But Ever rode confidently, as usual, so she didn't ask. Although the more she studied him, the more she realized he looked . . . nervous. Every few minutes, his eyes would dart to her, but they wouldn't remain long enough for her to catch them.

After about an hour of riding, they came to a little wooden cabin that looked like it was dusted in sugar.

"It's beautiful!" Isa exclaimed as Ever helped her off of her horse. When he didn't respond, she turned to find him staring at her. A strange mix of emotions swirled about in his fiery, gray eyes. And Isa stared back. What was he thinking? Was he sorry they were away from the Fortress after all? But she didn't ask as he returned to unloading the horses in silence, confusion and sorrow and curiosity lingering in his eyes.

Still, Isa's patience had nearly worn out by the time he'd finished putting the horses away. Before she could say anything, however, his face broke into the most beautiful smile she'd ever seen. After throwing their supplies over his shoulders, he bent and lifted her so that his arms were beneath her shoulders and under her knees. Isa squealed with delight as he carried her over the threshold and into the cabin itself.

The inside was just as idyllic as the exterior. A wooden headboard carved with roses and ivy overlooked the bed that took up nearly half of the room. Across from the bed was a large hearth with a fire already lit, two plush chairs, and a small table with four books stacked on it. Two windows filled each wall except the one the headboard stood against, and each window had twelve panes, which could be covered or uncovered with curtains of red lacy gauze. Even the planks of wood were a light, cheerful maple wood.

"Oh, Ever!" Isa sighed. "It's perfect!" Then she laughed. "You can put me down now."

"I don't think I want to."

Isa laughed again at his ornery expression. "How did you find this place?"

"It's a little-known secret that Fortress kings and queens need rest too. My great-great-grandfather had this cabin built so he and his wife could escape for even just a few hours from time to time." He finally set Isa down, and she began to wander.

"Do the others know where we are?"

Ever made a face. "If the kingdom decides to go up in flames, Garin can find us, but I will wring the first person's neck who seeks us out with a declaration or a treaty that needs signing." He shrugged off their supply bags. "I also knew I could never convince you to stay away from your brother for too long."

Isa, who had been walking slowly through the little room, touching things to try and convince herself that this wasn't a dream, walked back to him as though in a daze. He placed his hands in hers and led her over to the warmth of the fireplace.

"I need to tell you again how sorry I am." He shook his head, a look of disgust on his sharp features. "The Fortress continues giving me chances to learn, and I continue to throw them away by thinking I know best."

"Ever, you really needn't—"

"No, I mean it. If I had allowed you to develop your own strength instead of trying to force you into mine . . . who knows how much sooner we might have stopped Bronkendol?"

"You weren't the only one." Isa placed her hand on his chin and lifted his face so he had to look at her. "I thought the same." She chuckled, although there was little humor in it. "Can you imagine me doing all of that running while pregnant?"

Ever's eyes flashed. "That's not funny."

Isa just shook her head and smiled. "But the Fortress knew better. It knew what I needed, and it pushed us so that we *had* to learn. You had to see that I was meant to be beside you, not behind."

"And what did you have to learn?"

"That Garin was right."

Ever smirked as he played with a lock of her short hair. "He usually is. But about what?"

Isa pressed Ever's shoulders down so that he sat in one of the chairs, then she sat in his lap and wrapped her arms around his neck. "I had to learn that it doesn't matter what I *feel*. Whether I feel like the queen or not is insignificant. What is most important is *knowing* the truth. I think that was why my fire disappeared. At least, from our sight. It was there all along, but as I lost faith in my place, my fire dipped lower and lower, until only the Fortress could convince me to believe I belonged once again."

To demonstrate, she held out her hand, and a small tongue of blue flame sprang up inside her palm. Gently, she placed her palm over his heart. Ever's mouth dropped and his eyes widened as the flame moved into his chest.

"What was that?" he asked breathlessly.

"Bronkendol was wrong about many things, but he was right about my power. That means that my power works in ways I'd never even imagined. I just took the love I hold for you in my heart, and I sent it straight to yours." She paused, watching him carefully. "Now you cannot doubt how much I love you. I promised to love you forever, and even if we don't always feel it, the love is still there, waiting."

"Do you know that I love you?" Ever's voice was suddenly throaty, and his breath came faster on her face.

"I don't know." Isa grinned and looked deep into the fiery rings inside his eyes that burned with a sudden intensity. "I might need some reminding."

"And how would I do that?" His lips brushed hers as he spoke, and his hand was buried beneath her hair, bringing her face close to his.

"As everything good and worthy is best begun."

"Which would be?"

"Simple," Isa whispered. "With a dance and a kiss."

Ever didn't answer. He was too busy following her advice.

BEAUTY BEHELD: A RETELLING OF HANSEL AND GRETEL

THE BECOMING BEAUTY TRILOGY, BOOK 3

~

The Classical Kingdoms Collection, Book Three

~

To my littlest brother, the baby we called General. It makes me proud that even with your ridiculous number of accomplishments, you still look up whenever you hear, "Squirt!" yelled into a crowd. It's like I preconditioned you or something, which is particularly impressive considering the number of times you ~~outsmarted me~~ took advantage of my sweet and loving nature. Though I wouldn't at all be surprised to one day see the actual title of general attached to your name, you will never cease to be my baby brother. And that's not a bad thing. Even generals need older sisters who still scold, hug, and occasionally buy them gummy worms and Twizzlers.

1

SICKLY SWEET

"Genny, would you stop crying?"

But Henri's sister only grew louder, her sobs turning to wails. Over her noise, Henri could hear thunder beginning to rumble in the distance, and his heart beat a bit faster. The way the bare branches swayed against the ash-gray sky made him nervous, and he knew without a doubt that a storm was brewing.

"Genny!" He took her by the shoulders. "I can't focus when you're so noisy! Just stop crying and I'll find a way home!"

"But Father said he would come get us!" she protested, wiping her little nose on her arm. "If we can't go home, then why can't we go get the sweets?"

Ah, there she went about the sweets again. And Henri had been doing so well to ignore it.

For the last few weeks, the woods had smelled much like the baker's shop in town. Genny, as most children of four years would, had begged incessantly to follow the scent. And to be honest, Henri had nearly given in more than once. Unlike Genny, however, he'd lived long enough in the southern woods to have learned the hard way that imaginings, such as sweets in the woods, were always far too good to be true. As this one was sure to be, despite the draw of its delectable smell.

"Henri, we need to find it!"

With that, Genny grabbed his hand and began to pull him in the direction of the smell. One glimpse of the green mist in her eyes sent him into a full panic. If he didn't get her back to the cottage soon, she just might escape him and scamper off into the woods alone, something that wouldn't bode well for either of them. That only left him with one choice.

With the snap of his fingers, the stones that Henri had been dropping ever since they left the cottage began to flicker in the dark, little tongues of flame lapping at the quickly deepening night. His stepmother would be sure to box his ears for such a deed if she saw, but if he was ever to get Genny home, it was a punishment he would gladly endure.

He heaved a sigh of relief when the little blue flames caught Genny's attention, and she quit tugging his arm in the direction of the rapidly falling dark. Instead, she allowed him to lead her back along the path of scattered stones, giggling when he put out each flame they passed.

"Where do you think Father went?" she asked for the tenth time that night.

"I don't know." Not only did Henri not know where precisely his father had gone to cut wood, but the fact that he had never come looking for them niggled at him, like a bug beneath his skin. Genny continued to prattle on with questions about every rock and tree they passed, seemingly brave and happy now that they were walking, but Henri's thoughts were too full for him to answer her.

His father had grown up in these woods, as Henri had. How had he lost them? Surely something must have happened. Perhaps a tree had fallen on him, or he had been attacked by an animal! Henri grasped his sister's hand more tightly as he hurried them through the trees, which were still bare from the vestiges of winter. It was getting colder by the minute, and if there were a dangerous animal nearby, he needed to get Genny inside.

They followed the little trail of lighted stones, and as they walked, Henri hoped again that his stepmother wouldn't notice their path. Whether they were lost or not, she wouldn't approve of him using his *trick*, as Genny called it.

"Blasted evil," she would mutter whenever she caught him creating the flames. "Unnatural, and sure enough to send you to damnation." Henri honestly didn't know if what she said was true, or even exactly what damnation was, but on a night such as this, he could think of no other way to get himself and his sister home.

Even with the path of stones to follow, the boy was beginning to get truly worried by the time the little cottage emerged from the trees and the last flickering stone was put out. The glow of the fire lit the gaping cracks in the wood, and a shudder of cold and dread rippled through him as he pulled the large door open. He wanted to stop and fill his pockets with stones again, as was his habit before he ever went in or out, for one never knew when he might need stones to light, but he didn't have time. It was already too dark, and Genny's teeth were chattering.

"Henri!" Helaine looked up at him from the wooden table that she was setting, her mouth hanging open as though she'd seen a ghost. "What in the blazes are you doing here?"

"Something must have happened to Father," Henri said as he closed the door and began to unwind Genny's thin shawl from her shoulders. "He never came back to get us." As he spoke, the door opened again, and a gust of cold air rushed in.

"This should be enough to keep us for—" Henri's father stopped and stared at Henri with nearly the same expression that Henri's stepmother wore, his arms still full of chopped wood. They all stood there like that for a very long moment before Henri's father glanced over at Helaine. Henri's stepmother said nothing but glared as though she were about to strangle someone.

What exactly had his father been up to, leaving them out in the forest like that after dark? Frustration simmered within Henri, but the question died on his tongue. Something was definitely off. His father hadn't come back to get them. In fact, it appeared now as though he never even meant to try. Why, Henri wanted to know, would he do such a thing? And yet the way Helaine was slamming the wooden plates upon the table shut Henri's mouth for good. In his heart, he had a sinking feeling that he knew exactly why his father hadn't come back to look for them.

Supper was meager that night. Helaine had only cooked enough for two, it seemed. And though stores were running low, as winter had been long in departing this year, Henri knew there should have been enough for them all to have their fill. Genny opened her mouth to complain, but before she could, Henri dumped the rest of his food on her plate. Going hungry was better than watching his stepmother take the switch to his little sister for talking back, and, if pressed, Genny would have no reservations about doing exactly that.

"If you make so much as a peep tonight," Helaine whispered above the children as they huddled together under the single blanket on their straw pallet, "I'll get the whipping stick for both of you!" Her thin, mousy hair stuck to the sides of her face, and the anger in her eyes made her look rather like a mole rat. But these thoughts Henri kept to himself, hoping very much at the same time that his sister would keep her thoughts to herself as well. Much to his relief, however, she fell asleep almost immediately, seemingly unaware of the strange goings-on that Henri was still trying to understand.

That his stepmother and father had not expected them back was obvious. But why would they try to lose them? Henri was well aware that his stepmother didn't care a mite about his well-being or his sister's, but his father surely wasn't that cruel.

But what if he is? Henri wondered. *And what if they try again? What will I do then?*

If his parents didn't want them at the cottage, then he and Genny would need to find somewhere else to go. No one in the village would take them, of that he was sure. The township had never liked his family much to begin with. The woodcutter's family, as well as others like them, who lived outside the village, were suspected of all sorts of wrongdoings. Why else would families choose to live outside the protection of the town?

Perhaps Father Lucien would take them in. Henri was sure the holy man would at least let them sleep in the church for a night or two until Henri could find a new home. But Father Lucien hardly received enough food now. There would certainly not be enough for three. So where would a boy of nine years find food and shelter for not only himself but his sister of four?

Henri's thoughts raced in circles until they were too worn to continue. Drifting off into an aimless sleep, Henri's last thoughts were a prayer to the Maker, asking, if for nothing else, that the Maker find them a home. It didn't seem like too much of a request. And yet the task seemed much too great for Henri to carry on his shoulders alone.

For the first time in a long while, Henri, who was far too old for tears, cried himself to sleep.

∾

"Get up."

Henri groaned and rubbed his eyes. How had morning come so soon? A light shove to the chest from his father's boot, however, roused him enough to realize that morning had not yet come. At least, there was no sun.

"Why are we up so early?" Henri yawned, wanting nothing more than to roll over.

"Long day's work. Now get your sister. We're goin'."

At this, Henri stopped stretching and squinted up at his father. As he did, all the events from the day before returned. Immediately, he knew that whatever this errand was, it would probably have the outcome his parents had wished for the night before. "Genny doesn't need to come with us," he said in a small voice. "She's too little to carry much wood. She'll drop it when she gets cold." It was a foolish thing to say, but his foggy mind couldn't come up with any better reason to keep Genny at home and warm. Perhaps, if Henri disappeared and his trick was gone with him, Helaine and his father would be kinder to his sister.

"Nah. She's coming too. Now up, both of you, before your mother wakes up."

Henri fumbled in the darkness for his sister. Curled in a tight little ball, she was a mess of yellow curls and blanket in the thin light that came from the orange embers in the hearth. Anxiety bubbled in Henri's stomach as he gently shook her awake. "Come on, Genny. It's time to get up."

"No. It's cold."

"Genny, I mean it. Father says—" As he spoke, a brilliant flash of light briefly lit the room brighter than day. The crash that followed was loud enough to send Genny into his arms with a shriek. Henri took the opportunity to drag her out of bed and tie her shawl around her shoulders, trying to ignore the piteous whimpers she was making about getting out of bed in a lightning storm. Whenever he could, he tried to throw a glance up at his father, begging silently against hope for mercy, but the room was too dark, especially after the flash that had just blinded them all. The air was heavy, its warning thick. This storm would be bad. Why was his father so insistent on taking them out *now*? If he was so determined to lose them, as Henri feared, couldn't he at least do it when the weather was less violent?

"Here." His father shoved a loaf of bread into Henri's arms. "We'll be working a long time today."

All too soon, they were dragged outside, his father's axe upon his shoulder and Henri clutching the bread in one hand and his sister's hand in the other. "Wait!" Henri called, stooping and desperately clawing the ground for pebbles. But his father gave him no reprieve.

"We don't have time for your foolish antics, boy!" His father turned and marched back to the children, grabbing Henri so hard by the shoulder that it hurt, yanking him back up from the ground. Another flash of lightning revealed a resolve on his father's face that Henri had never seen before. The look was more like one Helaine often wore, full of loathing, than his usual grave countenance. And it frightened Henri. No, his father would not allow any more antics.

When his father seemed satisfied and assured of Henri's obedience, he turned and stalked off in a direction they didn't usually go. South, where the trees were thin and crooked, and Henri wasn't nearly as familiar with the landscape. In desperation, Henri began doing the only thing he could think of. Breaking off small chunks of the bread, he began to drop them on the ground behind them as they walked. He would have preferred stones to the bread, but it was the only way he could think to mark their trail.

For once, Genny was silent, clinging to his arm as they walked. Keeping up with their father became more difficult as the forest around them grew soggier from the rain. Genny's legs were short, and as the mud became deeper, she struggled to keep up.

"Father!" Henri called out as he paused to pull his sister's feet out of a mudhole. "Wait!" When he looked up, however, all signs of his father were gone. "Father!" Henri cried again, tears pricking his eyes, mixing with the nearly painful raindrops that were beginning to pelt them.

He had known this would happen, he tried to tell himself. That was why he'd been dropping the bread crumbs. He had known his father was going to leave them. He could see it in his face. And yet, deep down, he had hoped his father might find a shred of pity in his heart, if not for him then for his little sister. But here they were. The bread had run out a long time ago, and Henri had no idea as to where they were. Worse than that, though, he knew now what he had feared for so long.

They were unwanted.

"I want my mummy!" Genny sobbed as she began to kick and thrash against him. "I want to go home!"

"Genny, stop kicking!"

"No! I want to go home!"

"I mean it! Stop it right now! No one is coming for us! No one wants us! We don't have a mummy!"

Genny stopped struggling and looked up into his eyes, their whites lighting up more as each flash of lightning drew closer. "But you said—"

"I lied. I lied so you would think we had a mummy. But we don't, so stop screaming and let me think!"

Genny did indeed stop fighting him, but the heartbroken sobs that she now heaved hurt his heart even more. He had never been that cruel, and he hated himself for it. But the lightning was growing nearer, and he needed to get them to a safe place before the savage storm was fully upon them.

After a few minutes of turning in circles, waiting for the lightning to strike so he could see the landscape, Henri spotted a little ravine with a hidden alcove beneath it. They would be squeezed tightly inside, but it was better than being out here or beneath a tree. Henri shivered. As the son of a woodcutter, he had learned early on what lightning did to trees.

Henri took a deep breath and began to drag his still-crying sister over to the alcove. It took a few tries, but he was finally able to shove her down into it and then follow along himself. The soil that they were pressed into was slimy and thick and smelled of swamp gas, but Henri wriggled himself as deep into the bank as he could, holding his sister tightly so she couldn't escape. And none too soon, as they had only been there a moment or so before the world outside of their shelter began to explode. Genny screamed with each boom of the thunder, and Henri screamed right along with her. Never had he seen such a storm. But then, never had there been such a night.

∾

"Henri!"

Henri moaned and tried to turn, only to realize that he was not on his straw pallet but squished up against a muddy ravine with his neck cranked uncomfortably. It took him a moment to remember where they were and how they had gotten there.

"Henri! I smell it!"

"Smell what?" Henri slowly pulled himself from the little hole in the earth to where his sister was standing, pointing with all her might to the east. The storm had finally passed, and weak sunlight made it through the thin clouds and crooked trees down to the riverbank on which they stood. Everything looked pale and tired.

"The sweets!" Genny looked at him as though their parents hadn't just lost them in the forest on purpose during a lightning storm. Instead, her pale blue eyes were alight, green shimmering ever so slightly through their depths.

Before he had a chance to ready himself, Henri was hit by the smell as well. He didn't just smell it, though. A hunger so strong it was nearly nauseating hit him like a stray kick from his father's foot, and it was hard to think of anything else but the delicacies that beckoned them to come and partake. Why had he resisted this call for so many weeks?

"Let's go find them!" Genny grinned. "Let's go find the sweets!"

2

WELCOME INTERRUPTIONS

"*I* don't think I want to go to the banquet tonight after all," Ever breathed into Isa's ear, his arms encircling her waist. "I would much rather stay up here with my wife."

Isa laughed as Ever held on to her, swaying her from side to side while giving her his most pitiful look through the mirror. "If you don't hold still, I'm going to drop this earring."

"You don't need earrings if we're staying here."

"Ah, but we cannot stay here, my love. What of our guests downstairs?"

Ever threw his head back and let out a huff before walking to the bed and falling on top of it. "I am tired of people."

"Since when do *you* tire of people?"

"Since my wife looks ravishing enough to keep to myself and away from prying eyes forever. Why don't you wear that color more often?"

Isa shook her head with a smile and walked over to the bed, where she gently pulled her husband up into a standing position. "But you look so handsome," she said as she straightened his cloak and tunic. "Don't deny me the pleasure of showing you off tonight."

Handsome was an understatement. The black tunic with silver stitching made Ever look even more imposing than usual. The strong line of his jaw and the erectness of his shoulders made her stomach warm, even after four years of marriage. A few flecks of gray peppered his golden hair here and there, much too early, Isa thought, for his thirty-one years. And yet, what could one expect with the many burdens Destin's king was forced to carry? Softly, she ran her fingers through that short hair and drew him down for a kiss. Even the gray hair she loved, for it was a constant reminder of her husband's love for his people. And his love for her.

"We need to go now," she said somewhat breathlessly, as she managed to pull out of the kiss. "They're waiting for us."

"Let them wait," Ever said in a gruff voice.

"They might not need us," she rested her forehead against his, "but the children do." Even as she spoke, Isa could feel the tension return to his shoulders, and she briefly regretted saying such a thing. Already, his storm-gray eyes had become resolute, and he leaned in for one more passionate kiss before walking to the door and holding it open for her.

"As usual, you are right," he said, his voice steeled and commanding once again. "It is time."

Once they had stepped outside, Ever offered Isa his arm, which she took most readily. Being on the arm of the most powerful, not to mention the most attractive, man in the realm still sent shivers up and down her back. Tonight, however, she felt as though she actually might match his regality, thanks to Gigi's hard work.

The red gown that Isa wore tonight was not comfortable in the slightest, its stiff material covered entirely with embroidered miniature white flowers, and it was already making her back ache with the formal posture it required. The elegance of the dress, however, made it one of her favorites. The bodice was fitted, with dozens of small ivory buttons laced up the front, a style taken from the far east, Gigi had said. The skirt was a fashion taken from their own tailors, with layers of cloth cascading in a red waterfall down her legs, much like the petals of a tight, slender rosebud just beginning to unfurl. Though intricate, the gown itself was far from soft. Its sharp angles at Isa's neck and wrists and the fierce color of the dress created an imposing combination, which was something Isa would need more tonight than ever before. This meeting of kings and queens was important, and choosing to call such an assembly had not been an easy decision to make, for they had much to ask of their neighbors.

"Your Majesties." Garin greeted them just outside the crystal balcony's doors with a smile and an appraising look. "You look ready to enthrall the world." He took Isa's right hand in one of his and placed his other hand on Ever's left shoulder. "Are you ready?"

Ever, his face set in the dutiful, vigilant expression Isa knew so well, nodded once. Garin gestured to the servants, who opened the doors to the crystal balcony.

A hush fell over the crowd as Isa and Ever cut across the spacious balcony and came to stand in its center, waiting for the music to begin. As they waited, Isa scanned the crowd. Most of the border lords were there, as well as the Tungean and Tumenian kings. A fair group of nobility who also kept lands on their borders surrounded them, along with the kings and queens of Kongretch, Pearlamar, and Anbin. But where were Launce and Olivia?

Before Isa could search more, it was time for the ceremonial dance to begin. Isa turned back to her partner to find Ever studying her face with a soft intensity, the blue fire in his eyes dancing in time to the music.

"You look breathtaking tonight," he whispered as they began the first slow spin.

"Why thank you," she murmured. Why did her cheeks still flush when he spoke to her that way? She hoped they'd never stop. "Don't get used to it, though. It took Gigi and three other servants four hours to piece me together like this."

"It's not the dress." He pulled her into a more dramatic twirl. "Your eyes sparkle when you're happy."

"And how would you know I'm happy?"

"Look." He glanced down at their feet, and Isa's heart leapt as the blue spirals of fire danced and twirled right along with them, encircling their feet as the flames rose out of the azure crystal. It didn't matter how many times they danced on this floor. The sight of the crystal's fire would never fail to steal her breath. How many dances had they shared here beneath the light of the moon?

All too soon, the dance ended, and it was time for the real work to begin. Servants ushered everyone into the grand dining hall, alight with a thousand candles hung from crystal chandeliers that reflected off pearlescent floors so that the room shone like a beacon even in the night. As soon as everyone was seated, Ever stood and gave thanks to the Maker for their bounty. Servants appeared, and platters full of steaming beef, sweet corn, honey-dripped hams, fruit so plump it was nearly bursting, and dozens of other delicacies filled the tables. The tables themselves were laid out to resemble a horse's shoe, with Ever and Isa at the front and center where they could see all of their guests before them.

Just after the first course, as the sugared rose petals were being served, a movement at the dining hall's door caught Isa's eye and she allowed herself a sigh of relief. They had made it.

"Presenting," the herald called, "Launce Armand Marchand, of Soudain, Destin, crown prince of Cobren, and his wife, Princess Olivia Edite Raquel Rocha of Cintilante Areia of Cobren."

Despite his three years in the Cobrien courts, Launce's cheeks still burned visibly as he let the servant lead them to their seats of honor at Isa and Ever's table. As they drew closer, Isa could immediately see that Olivia's face, however, was an unhealthy shade of gray. Isa's first reaction was to think the poor young woman had grown ill sometime on their journey, but as Olivia drew nearer, it became quickly apparent that no such thing had happened recently.

Olivia had never been slender like Isa but had always kept a lovely soft shape with generous curves and a wide face that was quick to share a friendly smile. But as she sat down heavily beside Isa, the sort of change that had come over Isa's sister-in-law was undeniable.

"Olivia!" Isa stood and leaned over to give her a quick, tight hug. "How... how wonderful! How long...?" Isa glanced up at Launce, who uncharacteristically ignored her as he sat beside his wife. The set of his mouth and the way he tucked into his supper made Isa realize he wasn't going to tell her anything easily tonight, so she reached out and gently probed his heart with her own. *Guilt*. He was full of guilt, as was Olivia. But at least Olivia was returning her gaze, albeit reluctantly.

"Please forgive us for our lateness." Olivia groaned as she leaned back in her chair. "I thought the carriage ride would be well enough, but I have had to stop more times than I can count."

"No, of course, we don't mind!" Isa hurried to assure her, trying not to sound as flustered as she felt. "But, Olivia, how long?"

"Five months." Olivia sent her a weak smile.

Five months. And they hadn't bothered to send word that they were expecting? That her own brother had hidden such a secret from her irked Isa more than she cared to show. She swallowed and sought to control her emotions. "But why didn't you tell us?" she asked as kindly as she could. "Mother and Father will be thrilled!"

"They know." Launce spoke for the first time, taking a deep swig of his ale.

They knew. Of course they knew. Launce might be crowned prince of Cobren, but no title would have saved him from Deline's wrath had she found out her son had hidden such a thing. Which meant Isa's parents had hidden it from her too. But why would they do such a thing?

"You are to be congratulated." Ever's deep voice rang out from behind her, and Isa was immediately grateful for the distraction as she fought to keep tears from streaming down her face. She knew exactly why they hadn't told her. It was the same reason the expecting women, servants and nobles alike, at the Fortress tended to avoid her until their babes were old enough to toddle around on their own. It was the same reason that Cerise, one of Isa's oldest friends, had suddenly taken her leave of the Fortress soon after marrying and had not returned.

The food on Isa's plate suddenly looked dry and unappetizing, and Isa wanted nothing more than to do what Ever had suggested before the banquet, to run back to their chambers and hide there for a very, very long time. But for now, she reminded herself, it was her duty, as a queen and a sister, to do what her heart wished most of all not to.

"I'm so happy for you." She turned to Olivia, hoping her voice didn't waver too much.

"Truly?" Olivia watched her through large, brown, careful eyes, so Isa nodded.

"It will be so wonderful to have a niece or nephew to play with. We need someone around here to spoil."

Just then Ever stood, much to Isa's relief, and waited for the talking to die down. When the grand hall was quiet, he looked at Isa, who rose and stood beside him. They had work to do.

"I want to begin by thanking you for coming to us," Ever began in his reverberating voice. "I know it is not an easy journey for many of you. But there is a matter of grave importance that we must discuss, and I'm afraid it is one that cannot be done through quill and parchment."

Their guests watched them silently. Even Lady Jadzia, one of Isa's least favorite people in the world, wore a look of alarm.

"We have discovered a great evil within our borders," Ever continued, "and it is stealing our children."

Gasps went up from a few in the crowd.

"In the dead of night, children from all over the kingdom have been disappearing from their beds, but when morning comes, no one can find a way or reason for their disappearance. Common children, noble children, there is no discrepancy. Boys or girls from every station of life, from three years of age up to the age of ten have gone. We have had our soldiers searching for the responsible party for weeks now. I, myself, have ventured out at least a dozen times. And yet we cannot find where the children are going, nor do we know how they are getting there. All we know is that somewhere at the core of this crime is a magic of the blackest kind."

Ever paused, Isa knew, to allow such dour news to sink in. Throughout the western kingdoms, there were little bits of magic here and there, often kept hidden by kings and lords to secretly further their own interests. But few kingdoms used the deep magics. For magic was far different from what Isa and Ever and other gifted folk wielded. Theirs was a gift from the Maker, a power that lived in their bones, and was as much a part of them as their hair color or the length of their fingers. Deep magic was conjured, dragged up from the dregs of the earth, substances and powers that no man should ever touch, according to Ever. The only kingdom to use such power in recent years had been Tumen. But even they had sworn off such power in order to promote peace within the realm.

"What is it that you could want from us, Everard?" King Leon of Lingea called out.

"I would like to position groups of my soldiers along all the borders of Destin," Ever replied. "I have the feeling that we will be smoking the offender out very soon. Should he escape, I would like my men, with your permission, of course, to have the right to chase him down, no matter which territory he crosses into."

"How do we know this isn't simply a step toward handing over our lands to you now?"

Everyone turned to see Lady Jadzia stand. Even taller than Isa and decked in emeralds that made her red hair look even redder, the woman sniffed and tilted her head with a look that made Isa want to smack her. Instead, Isa stood as straight as her own back would allow and fixed her most dangerous gaze upon the noblewoman.

"Would you prefer for the thief to run about your lands unchecked? Because I can assure you, Lady Jadzia, that such a thing would be perfectly possible."

The two women stood for another long minute, glaring at one another until

Lady Jadzia finally sat down with a thump beside her snoring, portly husband. If the woman wasn't so infuriating, Isa might have felt sorry for her. To be forced to marry such a man twice her age could not have led to a pleasant life. But the sneer on Lady Jadzia's face kept Isa from feeling too sorry for her.

"Losing the guilty to a man-made border seems a complete waste of time and resources." Ever resumed his speech as Isa and Jadzia continued to glare at one another. "I would like to personally ensure that he never produces such darkness in another kingdom again."

"You have our cooperation, of course." Launce spoke up, carefully keeping his gaze directed at Ever rather than her, Isa noticed. As the other kings and nobles began to talk amongst themselves, a soldier slid through the door and approached them at a quick pace.

"Your Highnesses." He leaned in to whisper to Isa and Ever, "Another informant has been brought in. General Acelet thought you would be quite interested in this one."

"Very well," Ever nodded, "I will be down in—"

"No." Isa was already on her feet. "I will take him. You finish here."

"Are you sure?" Ever quirked a brow at her, and Isa gave him a sly grin back. "I've been itching to get my hands on another one."

At that, Ever flashed her a knowing smile before turning back to his guests.

Isa followed the soldier as quickly as her legs could carry her, thanking the Maker all the way out of the dining hall and down to the examination room. While interrogating their newest informant would have been an intriguing task on any given day, now more than ever she was grateful for the escape. Anything to keep from having to sit beside Launce and Olivia as the object of their pity.

3

SORTHILEIGE

*T*he examination room, as it had come to be called, was located on a lower level of the Fortress. It had no windows and only one door. Ever had argued that interrogating criminals in the dungeon would have been more effective, but Isa refused to go down there. Dungeons of any sort held too many memories for her after the war with the glass wizard, even the upper dungeons that she'd never been imprisoned in. Besides, she'd told Ever, her talent didn't rely on darkness or his terrifying blue flames. She would be better able to focus in a simple room, one that allowed her to focus on the core of her victims' hearts. To that, Ever could not argue.

As Isa entered the examination room, a shiver moved across her shoulders and down her back, and she was suddenly thankful for the presence of the two soldiers that flanked her. They were two of Ever's best. *Can they feel,* Isa wondered, *the same cold blackness that surrounds their prisoner?*

Before the children had begun to disappear, Isa had had little experience involving those with the dark arts. The practitioners of Sorthileige had been well enough hunted down by earlier generations of Fortiers that there were few left in Destin. Even so, whenever word came in of Sorthileige activity, Ever had never wasted a second in tracking it down and cutting it off wherever he found it. When Isa had once asked why she should not accompany him, Ever had turned to give her a look that had chilled her to the bone.

"You will... someday. But the darkness will change you..." He'd paused, his eyes troubled. "It took me years of practice before I was ready to take the Sorthileige on without my father's guidance. One day, when I know how, then I will teach you."

Isa might have pressed harder if it hadn't been for the extreme weariness she had seen on his face every time he and his men returned from such an expedition. When she had asked Acelet, Ever's favorite general, the man had worn a haggard look very similar to Ever's.

"Such activity is not a place where we can help him. We simply clear the area so no one stumbles upon us while he is at work."

"What does he do with it?" Isa had asked.

"Burns it... all of it. Everything the Sorthileige practioner has touched or owned must be destroyed."

"Can you not set such items on fire?"

Acelet had shaken his head sorrowfully. "No mere fire burns such relics of darkness. Only the Fortier fire can engulf it."

"And the people?"

"I continue to await the day when one runs to him, begging for forgiveness, but no such thing has ever happened. They all try to escape or resist him. Every single one dies with a shriek of rage on their lips."

After that conversation, Isa had decided that Ever was right, and that she was not ready to face such an evil. Not yet. The Fortress was changing her, making her stronger to be sure, but she was still learning her own power.

That resolve had changed for both of them, however. When the children began to disappear a few weeks before, the work had become too much for Ever to handle on his own. Even then, Ever had not wanted her to touch the witnesses they were bringing in, but Garin assured him that he would be there with her as long as she needed it. Only Garin's presence convinced Ever to let her try. And to be honest, Isa hadn't really wanted to try at first, either. As always, however, in his own gentle way, Garin had guided her and protected her. Under his tutelage, her particular strength proved to be a great asset in the interrogations as they tried to track down the source of the disappearances. It had not been long before Isa was able to handle the interrogations on her own. Of course, that didn't mean she enjoyed the darkness any more than Ever had.

Still, it gave her something to do, a purpose she knew she had been made to fulfill. So now, Isa steadied herself as she faced the man who was bound to the chair in the center of the room. Chains, rather than rope, had been used, as Ever said rope was rarely effective with even the most basic of Sorthileige users.

Upon studying him, however, Isa realized that this particular man was somewhat unusual compared to their more recent prisoners. He reeked of the dark arts, as the rest of them had, but unlike the others, he wore no talismans or charmed stones. In truth, he much resembled a tavern regular, the kind one might find on its steps after having a drink too many and causing a ruckus. His stringy brown hair was long and tied poorly behind his neck. Along with the scent of darkness, his ragged clothes reeked of ale, sweat, and bodily parts that Isa preferred not to think about. As she studied him, the man stared right back at her. His dirty, matted beard covered most of his mouth, but what was visible was turned up in a cocky grin. Not that such looks bothered Isa. She had dealt with arrogance like his before, and worse.

"So," Isa began in a quiet voice as she fixed him with her most unnerving stare, "I am told you were found boasting of selling a book of the Sorthileige." She paused. "You do know that to possess such an item and not relinquish it immediately to the crown is a crime punishable by death, do you not?"

The man stuck his bottom lip out and shrugged. "I'm just a simple trades-man, Your Majesty. I don't care to make deals with the king. But you," his eyes raked her up and down, unabashed, "I might certainly be willing to make a deal with you... for the right price. We could—" The smirk melted from his face. "What are you doing to me?" He gagged.

"That is for me to know. What I need from you is the truth. Who purchased that book?"

"I don't like this!" The man shook his head violently and flexed his hands within their bindings. "Make it stop!"

"Then tell me to whom you sold the book!" Isa shouted.

"It wasn't recent! Four years ago... maybe five?"

Isa pressed harder. It was amazing how agonizing the truth could be when one had managed to suppress it for so long.

"A woman! It was a woman! She was new... I'd never seen her before that night! She simply showed up at the tavern one day."

"What tavern?"

"The one in Sansim. I don't even know how she found me. She asked if I knew where she could find a book of the Sorthileige, and I did. Picked it up off some dead hermit a few years before that. She paid me and left, and I haven't heard from her since!"

"And what, precisely, did that book detail?"

The man shrugged, his body shaking as she released him from the agony just enough for him to think. "I never read it. I told you, I'm a merchant. I have a few talents here and there, but I deal talents more than I practice them. Talismans, individual spells, even large items like the book, when I can find them." He sat up straighter. "It had something in it about fire."

"Did it never cross your mind," Isa leaned in close, "that she might use such an item poorly?"

"My lady," the man gave her a strained smile, "do you think such an object would be used in any other way?"

Frustrated, Isa stepped away to think. Of the dozens who had dabbled in Sorthileige that she had interrogated in the last three weeks, none of them had been as openly unguided or unrepentant as this fellow. Often, they would say nothing, or would try to find excuses, trying to hide their deviances in her presence. They had mistakenly seemed to believe that she would be more merciful than her husband, whom they had openly defied. They had been wrong.

Just as this man was wrong to underestimate her. He screamed as she fixed him with her most focused stare.

"You asked what I was doing, so I will tell you. I, sir, have the strength of the heart. That means that I can make you feel the truth as it is. Not the convoluted, twisted truth that you have convinced yourself exists. The real, visceral truth, the one you ignored when you sold that woman the book for enough coin to purchase a few more drinks." Isa leaned over him so that she could grab his chair and tilt it back to an uncomfortable angle. "I thought you should know that the book you sold the woman just might have aided her in luring away hundreds of children over the last few weeks, and if any of them should die, their blood will be on your head."

Isa stepped back, letting his chair crash to the floor, but she didn't release the grip she held on his heart as she sent barrage after barrage of images at the man, images of the distraught parents' faces who had come to the Fortress, begging for help. Their wails and screams and agony. This man was proving to be more difficult than most, despite his careless appearance. And yet, Isa could feel him beginning to soften as he started to quietly weep. Silently, she allowed herself a breath of relief and thanked the Fortress and the Maker.

"The southern forest," he finally said in a ragged voice, "past the Shadowed Chasm and the oak trees."

"That's nearly on the border of Kongretch!"

He nodded, still staring at the ground. "She headed south from the tavern after we finished our deal. But I must warn you," he said hastily as Isa took a step toward him, "something is happening there, though I know not what! But the Sorthileige is even stronger there now than it was back then." He looked up at her piteously. "What will you do with me, now that you know?"

"That will be for my husband to decide," Isa said softly before turning and nodding at her guards. But as she headed for the door, the man grunted behind her. Isa's sword was out in a flash. The man's chains burst as he let out a cry of anger, but Isa was ready. He took a step back, then two as she held her sword against the flesh of his throat.

"Are you harmed, Your Majesty?" One guard wound a new set of chains even tighter around the man's wrists, while the other guard began to examine her for blood. "We need to bring you to a safer place," the guard began, but instead of answering, Isa grabbed their prisoner by the collar and tormented him in the most agonizing way she knew how.

"May the evil that you have inflicted upon others visit your soul every waking moment until you die," she whispered in his ear. "And when it does, just remember that truth is only as painful as you have made it." She looked up at the older guard. "You will have no problem with him now." Then she nodded for the other guard to walk her back up the steps and into the main hall once more.

"If I may say so," the younger guard smiled shyly at her when they were finally on their way back to the banquet, "that was quite impressive, Your Majesty." Then his face paled. "I apologize for my forwardness. I have only just begun here. I fear my mouth—"

"Your compliment is kind," Isa interrupted him with a smile. "I could not be more honored. Now," she sucked in a deep breath, "pray tell, do you know what hour it is?"

With the enthusiasm of a small child, the young man dashed over to a passing servant, before dashing back over to her. "It is just past the ninth hour."

Isa thanked him but couldn't help the deep sigh that escaped her. She was grateful, of course, to have the information they needed. And yet she couldn't help wishing the interrogation had lasted just a bit longer.

4

IN WHICH MUCH IS SAID

"I must say, Your Highness." The Duke of Sud Colline leaned forward, a piece of beef sticking out of his mouth as he spoke. Ever tried to ignore it, but he had never much liked this cousin. "Either she failed miserably," his cousin continued, "or she is back very soon. If it is the latter, I am quite impressed."

Ever followed his cousin's gaze to see Isa reentering the room. A small wave of relief broke over him as she met his eyes and gave him the smallest of nods. He knew that Isa was safe within the Fortress walls, and yet the thought of his sweet wife standing within spitting distance of those who practiced darkness made his skin crawl. Not that there weren't monsters here in the dining hall as well. Ever didn't miss the way his oafish cousin studied Isa as she approached, and Ever was considering setting him straight when Isa seated herself again beside him.

"We have our heading," she announced in a small, triumphant voice. Despite her calm appearance, Ever could tell she was nearly bursting with excitement.

"You must have beat him with a weapon fierce," the duke's youngest daughter called out, her eyes bright with interest.

"Oh, of course not!" Isa smiled and smoothed her crimson skirts. "I am a lady! Striking a man with a weapon would be highly inappropriate."

"That is not what you seemed to think this morning during swordplay," Ever teased his wife.

She blushed prettily and began to eat her meal as if nothing out of the ordinary had just taken place, and she hadn't just found a lead to their kingdom's disappearing children. In fact, Ever realized with a pang of unease, she seemed far *too* happy.

"So how do you do it?" the duke pressed. "If you don't torture them with a weapon, surely they do not give up their information on their own accord."

Isa put down her fork, having not yet gotten a bite to eat, and fixed her sweetest smile upon him. Ever nearly grinned, for he knew what treatment his cousin would now be subjected to.

"There is an undeniable truth in this world, as sure as the Maker lives. I cannot make them agree with it, but I can use the truth to make them uncomfortable, for they know deep down that they are suppressing that truth. If they are not completely on their guard, or are not very strong, the truth can twist their hearts and alter their actions."

"So you make them change their minds?"

"Oh no. That is the work of the Maker. The Fortress simply gives me the power to show them the Maker's truth. Limited insight, you could say, into the lives of those he sends my way. In this case, I just showed the man the truth about the damage he has done to so many through his selfish, careless actions."

"It must be terrible to be a weak-minded person around you," the duke chortled. "I must be grateful that such is not my lot in life."

Isa didn't answer, only frowned ever so slightly, and just as Ever had expected, the duke's face went from its usual shade of puffy red to nearly a deep purple, and his grin disappeared completely.

"You really should pay more attention to your wife, sir," Isa said. "It is a shame to waste time pining for those that the Maker did not give you."

So the duke's attentions had not been lost on her either. Ever enjoyed watching the man squirm as he looked guiltily at his wife for perhaps the first time that night. Disgusted, Ever shook his head.

After that, Isa's other admirers hurriedly found other topics of discussion. That, of course, left Isa in the same position she had been in to begin with. Ever's heart hurt as he watched her give Olivia and Launce her kindest smiles and sweetest words. When Olivia felt ill again, Isa called Gigi immediately to tend to her in the guest chambers that Isa kept prepared for her brother and his wife. Not a moment too soon did the hour eventually strike eleven, and Ever stood and thanked his guests for their cooperation and attendance before turning them over to their prospective servants to be led to their guest chambers.

Finally, he was on his own with Isa as they made their way back to their room.

"Did most of them agree to allow men to be stationed at the borders?" Isa asked as he took her arm.

"Yes. Tumen wasn't very happy about it at all, but I think even they do not relish the idea of a child thief tramping about their kingdom."

"Good," Isa nodded, "then the evening was a perfect success." She continued prattling on as Ever held the chamber door open for her, talking too fast like she always did when she was uncomfortable. "And isn't it wonderful that Olivia and

Launce are having a baby! It will be a beautiful child, with her complexion, of course."

Ever folded his arms and watched her with sad eyes as she stood before her vanity and removed the piles of jewelry that Gigi had heaped upon her that afternoon.

"We'll have to get them a special gift, of course..."

The moment that Ever had been dreading all evening finally came as Isa's voice trailed off, and she laid her head in her hands. Quiet sobs shook her thin shoulders as Ever went to her and drew her into his chest. Desperately, he tried to find words that would lift the weight off her shoulders even just a little. But no words came. For really, what could he say?

"It hurts, Ever," Isa whimpered as tears continued to stream down her face.

"I know," he whispered as he lifted her and carried her to the bed, where he laid her gently in his lap. "I know."

"My duty is to show everyone else the truth," she continued between sobs. "But that means I have to see the truth as well. And the truth is—" Her voice broke. "The truth is that the Fortress doesn't want me to have a baby." She pulled back and looked up at him with her piercing midnight eyes, reddened and wet in their grief. "Why, Ever? Why is the Fortress doing this to me?"

"I wish I knew." Ever shook his head slowly and tucked a strand of loose hair behind her ear. Upon seeing his wife in the lavish red dress earlier that evening, Ever had hoped to spend the rest of their night in a way that hadn't involved tears. But the damage had been done, and with a sigh, he knew that what she needed most right now was simply to be held. And though it had taken much heartache on her part, and even more stupidity on his, Ever had learned through the last few years that sometimes his arms were most powerful healing he could give his wife.

They lay that way for a long time, shudders and tears still occasionally shaking Isa's shoulders. Not that Ever minded, of course. But, he suggested finally, she might feel better once she was out of her stiff red dress and into some proper nightclothes. Nodding, Isa stood and went to change. Ever briefly mourned his loss as she went from the striking red gown into a shapeless night shift. But, he reminded himself, he had one duty this night, and that was to be what Isa needed. And so, after they had both shed their formal clothes, Ever drew Isa back toward him beneath the covers and carefully tucked the blankets in around her.

Let me know what to say, he asked the Fortress silently. *I do not know why you have chosen to withhold a child from her, but at least tell me what to do.*

As if in response, a little warm wind moved from the hearth over to their bed, warming them just a bit more in the cool of the early spring night. *Alright then,* Ever thought, taking a deep breath. *If this is what you wish for now, then that is what I will do.* Ever pulled her close until she was curled up perfectly into him, her head tucked beneath his chin, and he began to hum one of her favorite songs into her ear. Little by little, he could feel her begin to relax.

"Oh," she said sometime later after he thought she had fallen asleep, "I forgot to tell you about the prisoner."

"It can probably wait until morning."

"Actually," she propped herself up on her elbow and looked him, her heart-shaped face lovely in the flickering shadows of the fire, "I think we should leave tomorrow. He said the woman did indeed buy the book from him and that she left toward the southern forest."

Ever tapped her on the nose. "You mean *I* will be going in the morning. I think it would probably be for the best if you remained here."

"Ever," she grumbled pathetically, "I want to go. We've been through this how many times?"

"That's *not* what I'm referring to." He pushed himself up to face her. "I am referring to the fact that this particular case has had you rather... emotional. I don't know if it's best for you to come until you're more settled internally."

"You know you need me."

"I'm not disputing that now, nor will I ever."

"So?"

"So I just don't want you to put yourself at unnecessary risk because you're too wrapped up in the moment. I think some distance would do you good."

"I do need distance." Isa somehow managed to crawl even closer. "Launce and Olivia won't be leaving for several more days at least. Olivia's not feeling well enough. If I need distance from anyone, it's from them!"

Ever groaned as Isa watched him with her most pleading look. He knew she was using her power on him, although he was rather sure she was doing it unconsciously, as she often did when she felt strongly about something. And as much as he wanted to deny it, she spoke the truth, for he knew that her gift would be most useful in the forest if they found anyone of interest. "Very well, we'll talk to Acelet by first light."

Before he could roll over to go to sleep though, Ever found his wife's mouth suddenly on his, and immediately, all thoughts of sleep vanished. He didn't need to be asked twice.

5

HIS FATHER'S EYES

"*A*celet," Isa called out to the general, who rode ahead of her, "how many at last count?"

As he thought, the general rubbed the back of his neck, which was probably stiff, Isa guessed, from the furious pace Ever had set since leaving the Fortress that morning. "My scouts brought in reports last night of two hundred and six, but I believe it might be higher than that."

"Why is that?" she asked.

"The woodland towns haven't reported losing any children, but I'm assuming they've had children go missing as well. They just don't like to send messengers up our way very much. The fools would rather handle their problems themselves." He looked at Ever. "And they don't much like you, Your Highness."

Ever gave him a sardonic look. "I think I shall survive."

Acelet smiled wryly before turning back to Isa. "Anyhow, I simply think there are a number of children who have probably gone missing and their parents have not come to us to tell of it. Hold now, is this it?"

They had come to a stop, and Ever was too busy studying the forest before them to answer, so the party simply waited. Isa had never been to this part of Destin before, and now that she was here, she was rather sure she hadn't missed much. The forests weren't thick and tall the way they were in the woods closer to home. Rather, the trees rose out of the ground like long, thin snakes with their heads turned toward the skies. The ground itself was wet and resembled a marsh much more than a forest. Isa was suddenly also sure that it probably hid an assortment of animals she would prefer not to meet. As she drew quick breaths in and out, the sickly, moist air clung to her lungs and made breathing more labored. No, Isa decided, she did not like the southern forest at all.

But it was better than staying at home to face Launce and Olivia's constant looks of guilt and pity.

"We'll walk slowly from here," Ever said as he dismounted and took his horse by the reins. "There is a source of power nearby. I can feel it."

"Thank the Maker," Isa heard one of the young soldiers behind her remark to one of his comrades. "I was going to puke if we ran another mile at that pace."

Isa didn't mind the speed that resulted from Ever's use of his power to hasten their travel. What should have been a three-day journey had taken place in less than one. And the view had been incredible. Isa had seen everything in one day, from their own mountain to valleys and plains to a great chasm of dark blue granite, which could only be crossed using a bridge wide enough for one horse to pass over at a time. But now that they had arrived, the sobering reminder of why they had made such a journey settled upon her once more.

"So many broken hearts," she murmured.

"What was that, Your Highness?"

"Oh," she shook her head, "only that I can feel the heartbreak." She looked up through the trees into the gray sky overhead. "Even here, the sorrow of their parents is thick in the air." Ever had been right. They were getting close.

At such a statement, an air of solemnity filled the group, and they passed on quietly, following Ever as he led them forward. Isa tried to focus, but as they moved deeper into the forest, and the despair of the many families wrapped about her like a hot, stuffy cloak, Isa's thoughts turned, as they had so often of late, to the child that by past Fortier standards she should have had by now.

If all had gone as tradition had led them to believe it would, Isa would have conceived the month they had been married. It would have been a boy, as all the Fortiers had boys first, and he would have been three years old by now. She knew what he would have looked like, too. His eyes would have been the same shade of stormy gray-blue as his father's eyes, and his hair would have been darker than Ever's, probably with just a hint of her own copper red. He would have had his father's stubborn jaw and might have ended up being even a bit taller than his father.

Not that any of that mattered. What mattered was that whether he had golden, red, or even white hair, he wasn't there for Isa to kiss to sleep at night. There were no chubby arms or legs or cheeks to squeeze and no little hand to hold. And though Isa knew the Fortress made no mistakes, she couldn't help feeling that she had been robbed of something very precious, for her arms were still empty.

And so were the arms of hundreds of other parents, Isa scolded herself. Now was not the time for a good cry, though she suddenly wanted very much to have one. Even the thought of her imaginary son being stolen from her in the dark of night angered Isa to a place of danger, and if she couldn't have a child of her own to keep safe, Isa swore to herself, she was going to do everything in her power to return these children to their families. No one should have to suffer such a terrible fate as to live wondering where a child had gone and what had become of him. Then she felt it.

"Wait!"

Everyone stopped and turned to look at her, but Isa only dismounted her horse and handed the reins to one of the soldiers nearby.

"Isa?" Ever asked warily. When she didn't respond, he drew his sword and began to follow her, but Isa didn't stop. Her fingers and toes and even her chest felt alive, humming like a hive of bees. Never had she felt such a powerful pull before, and without knowing where she was going, her feet carried her toward the source. Heartbreak. So much heartbreak. Loneliness, curiosity, and terror. The terror was thicker than any other feeling Isa could sense in the air. But this terror was different from that of the parents that she had felt earlier. Unable to utter a word, so filled was she with the need to find the children who were producing such emotions, Isa broke into a run.

"Isa, slow down!"

But Isa couldn't slow down. The feelings were too strong for her to ignore or break away from. It was as though they had stitched themselves right to her own heart and were pulling her in without her permission. Ever had been right. She was too wrapped up in this struggle. It was too personal. She should have stayed behind. And now she was letting her heart lead her rather than her head. Still, the vine-like trees continued to fly past her as she raced into the heart of the sickly wood.

Until she came to the house.

"Here," she said breathlessly as Ever came to stand beside her. "The children are here."

"All two hundred and six?" Ever cast a doubtful look at the ramshackle little cottage.

Even with the second story, there couldn't have been more than three rooms in the entire house, certainly not enough space for a quarter of so many children. And yet, the pull of terror was stronger than ever.

"Do you smell that?"

"Smell what?"

"It's sweet," she said, approaching the house. "Like... the scent of sugar." For a brief instant, a vision flashed through her mind, and instead of the crumbling stone house that stood before her, Isa saw a house made of every kind of candy imaginable. Red-and-white striped sugar stick columns supported the roof, rather than the collapsing wooden beams she had seen just a moment ago. Bright lemon drops, dark green mint drops, and even brown honey drops made up the walls, rather than gray, round stones. Roses made of chocolate, a rare delicacy Isa had only tasted after she'd come to the Fortress, lined the path up to the door, and unfamiliar blue truffles were arranged alongside them. Dozens of other sweets unknown to Isa made the house into the most lovely and inviting sight she had ever seen.

But then the vision was gone, as was the scent, and Isa was left touching one of the dirty rock walls. "Whoever did this lied to the children." She turned to Ever.

"Lied to them?" Ever frowned at her.

"I think... I think I know what they saw!" she exclaimed. "The thief used an illusion of sorts to draw them here, making them think the house was made of sweets."

Ever looked at her as though she'd lost her mind but said nothing as he moved closer to the house to examine it for himself. "Perhaps that would explain why no one saw these children leave," he said. "If the thief had the ability to create such a grand illusion, perhaps he had the ability to also cover the children with an illusion while they walked here." He turned to Isa, the blue rings of fire burning intensely in his eyes. "They must have walked for days," he said, wonder and horror mixing in his voice. "Some of the children were reported missing from near the border of Tumen, and others from the coast!"

Isa was about to respond when another wave of fear crashed through her. Again, she felt the immediate, driving need to find its source. As she began to open the cottage's door, Ever blocked her path.

"Isa, I know you are excited about this, but you need to take care," he said. When she didn't respond, he grabbed her arm. "I am serious. You need to unsheathe your sword and walk cautiously, or I will pack you up myself and send you home."

"You wouldn't—"

"I would, just as I would do to any of my soldiers unfit for duty. Something is very wrong here. Now, I need you to focus—"

"Mummy!"

The cry had come from inside the home. It was a little girl's cry, and the sorrow and fear within it touched Isa in a way no other voice had moved her before. In a moment, she had torn away from her husband's grasp and had burst through the slanted front door. She could hear Ever shouting to his men behind her, but there was no time to wait. The cry came again, and Isa darted deeper in. As she did so, however, her foot caught on a loose stone, and sent her sprawling across the dusty ground, where her head came down on the floor with a very painful crack.

6

TOO CLOSE

"Well, where is she?" Acelet squinted into the darkness of the dilapidated cottage.

"Wherever the children are, I assume." Ever stood and shoved his sword back into its sheath with more force than was necessary. What had she been thinking, taking off like that?

"What do you wish us to do?" Acelet looked more than a bit unnerved, shifting his weight back and forth as he awaited Ever's answer, and Ever couldn't fault him for it. Acelet had ridden, unblinking, into every battle Ever had ever waged and had seen more than his fair share of strange goings-on in the world. But the evil in this place was nearly tangible. Though it was decently humid outside, the cabin itself was dry and chilly with the kind of cold that raised bumps on one's skin. Each strange little breeze that wafted from darkened, cobwebbed corners was one that shouldn't have been, as there was no wind outside. And just inside the horrid little cabin, the queen had disappeared.

"Set up a watch around the cabin. I want no fewer than five men surrounding it at all times. And notify me of anything that moves. I don't care if it's a chipmunk. I want to see it myself." He walked back to the entrance and gestured at a clearing just before the cabin. "Set up camp, for the time being, just a small way from the entrance. I want another look around."

Acelet hesitated, but Ever only waved him on. When he was finally alone again, Ever let out a deep breath and rubbed his face before he began to explore. It had taken all of his self-control not to explode when Isa had disappeared, just as his hands should have closed in around her waist to yank her back.

This was exactly why he hadn't wanted to bring his wife.

Since they had been married, Isa hadn't been vested in any local disturbances the way she had been in this one. From the first report of a missing child, however, Isa had poured her heart and soul into finding the girl. And then the second child, which was a boy. And then the third. And on the pursuit had gone, a piece of Isa's heart becoming further wrapped up with each child that was reported gone. Of course, it didn't help that Launce and his wife had shown up the night before with their little surprise.

"I'm not sure it's fair to be upset with them," Garin had warned him early that morning as Ever had prepared to leave. "Having a child is not a crime."

"They gave Isa no time to prepare," Ever had huffed as he'd rolled the maps they would need and placed them in a pile. "They could have at least written, instead of springing it upon her publicly."

"True," Garin had said as he'd watched Ever make his preparations. "But they are young and were obviously quite uncomfortable telling her. They weren't callous, at least."

"Have you ever wondered," Ever had turned to his mentor suddenly, forcing out the question that had been eating away at him for years now, "if it might not be my fault?"

Garin had sighed and laid a hand on Ever's shoulder, forcing him to be still. "You know there is no one to blame here. The Fortress can change your situation at any time it chooses. Apparently, it thinks that now is not the right time."

"But what happens if we never get an heir? Does the bloodline simply die?"

Garin had shrugged and begun to place Ever's maps into a saddlebag for him. "I suppose, from a human standpoint, the Fortress's holy man might try to find a distant descendant, someone from another country who had a grandparent or great-grandparent that was Fortress-born. But," he arched one of his eyebrows knowingly at Ever, "I do not think you need to be worried about such things. The Fortress knows how to care for its own. Just live in the now, Ever. Do not borrow trouble."

Now Ever walked through the cabin softly, examining all of its holes and crannies. With the number of disintegrating beams and missing stones from the walls, it was a miracle that the house hadn't collapsed yet. As he moved about the little rooms, he noticed that there was no furniture. No one had lived here for a very long time, judging by the dust that had gathered in deep layers upon the floor. There weren't even footprints, aside from his own, Isa's, and Acelet's. And yet the sensation of power was everywhere, filling the air and making it strange to breathe in and out. But where was it coming from?

Frustrated, Ever finally stomped back outside to the fire Acelet had built nearly thirty feet from the cottage's broken front door. Aware that if he continued to stew on Isa's disappearance, he would most certainly lose his composure, Ever ladled himself a bowl of meat and apple stew that someone had put on the fire.

"So how exactly did you bring that one in last night without my help?" Ever leaned forward over his cup. "I'm quite impressed, of course, but I would have thought that one with *his* abilities should have been rather dangerous." It was nearly a rebuke, for Ever hated to have his men put themselves in danger unnecessarily, particularly when the problem dealt with the Sorthileige.

But Acelet only laughed and rubbed his chin as he also took a bit of the stew. "I know what you are not saying, and you need not fret. He was so drunk when we finally tracked him down that he was unconscious on the floor of the tavern he'd been visiting that day. It was less than a day's ride back to the Fortress, so we borrowed a coffin from a nearby casket maker, nailed the top down to be safe, and carted him back." He shrugged. "Garin took him off our hands as soon as we got back to the Fortress."

"A coffin?" Ever nearly spit out his food as he laughed. Acelet was creative if nothing else. "Still," Ever tried to look stern, "what you did was dangerous. In the future I would still prefer to be called for such errands. But... thank you."

"Pardon me, Your Highness," one of the newer soldiers called out in a timid voice, "but I cannot quite understand just how this Sorthileige can do such damage, especially..." he paused, "... when it is done within the Fortress's domain."

Ever studied the young man for a moment before answering. He was one of their most recent additions, one Ever had only finished training a few weeks before. Barely old enough to have left his parents and home, Eloy had impressed Ever with his desire to serve as a soldier. Eloy still had improvements to make with his swordplay, but the young man's skill with the bow was nearly unrivaled. And though he had handpicked Eloy for this particular venture, Ever couldn't help but hate what he knew Eloy, as all of his soldiers, would eventually touch and see and experience. Such was the role of his men, but the innocence in Eloy's face now, its openness, would not always be so. And it pained Ever to know that he would be the one to steal that innocence from him.

"The Fortress with all of its power was a gift from the Maker to the people of Destin," Ever finally said. "Such power is mostly unheard of in the other kingdoms of the western realm. Of course, the Maker also gives individual gifts to people throughout the lands, common, noble, and royal alike, but only the Fortress and its monarchs have been blessed with such a concentration of enduring power throughout the generations.

"Not all powers in the world are from the Maker though." Ever stood, suddenly restless. He had never been any good at sitting still. "Many strengths are born of evil, stolen from places in the earth that should never be touched. For example, until recently, the Tumenian monarchy ruled with a dark power of their own, which was originally molded and shaped by greed, greed so intense that it began to aid the hands of its wielders. Others are gifts—or curses, rather —from the enemy of the Maker. Of course, none are as potent as those from the Maker himself, but," he stopped and looked at the young man directly, "underestimating our enemies has gotten us into trouble more times than I can tell."

"That is why we take these individual witches and sorcerers so seriously," Acelet jumped in. "Even a single person dabbling in powers he should not hold and cannot understand can do a great deal of harm."

"I've heard stories..." Eloy said. "My mother told me once of the Glass Queen as a child, before the queen's son came here. And trolls. And the Fae! Were the Fae such a people?" His eyes were huge, making their whites stand out against his skin, which was the color of dates.

"Yes and no," Ever said. "They were an imaginative people, and the Maker gave them the ability to create wondrous worlds of their own from only their minds. He even allowed their homes to be temporary, so they could continue to build and rebuild again to their hearts' delight. In addition to that, they had the ability to build temporary bridges between their home and everyone else's so that they could hop between realms and travel the world, taking new ideas with them wherever they went."

"What happened?" Eloy asked, so enraptured that he seemed to have forgotten the food he was still holding.

"They got greedy. During their first exploration of Destin, they came upon the Fortress and decided it should be their own. The Fortier line was nearly ended during the battle, and as a result, the Maker sealed the veil between worlds, and the Fae were banished to their own land."

"But it was through these forests that they were said to have made the original visit," Acelet said as he stirred the stew, his eye glinting with a wicked enjoyment as he watched the young man shiver. "Of course, they're not the only ones who have haunted this region. In the five hundred years since their disappearance, other evils have taken up residence. Witches, sorcerers, trolls." He paused and lowered his voice menacingly. "We even found a band of blood seekers here once, a group driven mad by their excess dabbling in the Sorthileige."

Ever frowned at his general, for he was enjoying Eloy's discomfort a bit too much for Ever's taste.

"But why would someone want a bunch of children?" Eloy asked, slowly taking a bite of what must have been very cold stew.

"I do not know," Ever said. "We can only guess that the thief intends to use them for a spell, to threaten the people of Destin, or to lure us into the forest."

"So this might be a trap?" The young man's dark skin seemed to pale in the thin moonlight that was now shining down through the trees.

"It probably is."

"Then why are we here?" Eloy glanced around as though he might see the abductor step out of the shadows right then.

"We need to find these children, regardless of the reason for their disappearance. Besides, the Fortress and its power are with us. Don't ever forget that this light," Ever held out his hand and a blue flame appeared suspended above his palm, "is far greater than the darkness through which we now walk." As he spoke, the blue light flooded the campsite and all of the trees around it.

"So," Eloy swallowed, "what do we do now that the queen is gone?"

"We wait."

But in truth, waiting was the last thing in the world that Ever wanted to do.

7

HENRI AND GENEVIEVE

*I*sa groaned as she reached up and felt the tender spot on her forehead, just above her left eye. That would leave a pretty bruise. What had she been thinking, dashing off alone into the house? Guilt pricked at her conscience as she remembered Ever's warnings. When she opened her eyes, though, Isa was reminded why she had run into the broken house in the first place.

A little girl, sitting not four feet away, stared at her unashamedly with eyes the color of morning glories and hair as yellow as the sun. She couldn't have been any older than five. Behind the girl lounged a boy. His eyes and hair were the same color as the girl's, but he was a good deal older and wore an expression that was far less open.

"Well, hello there." Isa stopped rubbing her head and reached down to seat herself more properly on the ground. The sun was so bright that she had to squint, and when she was finally able to look around her, she nearly fell backward in surprise. She and the children were sitting on a small patch of sand in the middle of a great body of water. Isa had never seen the sea before, but that was all she could imagine this unending water to be as it stretched to the horizon in all directions. The sun beat down upon them, and the only shade in sight was cast by the two strange trees in the center of their little island, trees that climbed up into the blue sky with only a few wide, fan-like leaves at the top. The oddest part of the scene was that their island was not alone. Hundreds of identical islands floated around theirs, each island holding two or three children as well.

And the air that surrounded them was rife with fear.

"Where are we?" Isa whispered, more to herself than the children, but the girl answered her anyway.

"We're in the Boggart's land."

"We are not." The boy, who was leaning back against one of the trees, crossed his arms and huffed. "I told you, the Boggart isn't real."

"If he isn't real, then why does everything change when we're asleep?"

"I don't know, but it is *not* the Boggart!" He looked at Isa again. "Who are you? You've been asleep a long time."

"My name is... Miss Isa." Isa decided to forgo her title so the children wouldn't be even more hesitant to speak with her. Not that being without a title had ever bothered her.

"You're the first new grownup in the Boggart's land," the little girl said matter-of-factly. "All the other grownups just bring us food. They won't even talk with us even though I tell them I'm bored!"

"And what might your name be?"

"I'm Genny. Well, Stepmother always calls me Genevieve, but I like Genny."

"Genny it is then." Isa smiled at the girl, then looked at the boy, who still lounged against the trunk of the smaller tree. He seemed to be all elbows and knees, but there was something about him that was oddly familiar. "And what is your name?"

"That's Henri," Genny piped. "He's mad because he don't want to be here." She paused, and the smile suddenly melted from her face. "It's my fault," she whispered as she began to twist a lock of her long yellow hair around one of her fingers.

"What's your fault?"

"That we're here. We were lost, and Henri told me not to go to that house of sweets. But I did. And just when I was about to eat it, we came here."

"We weren't lost. You're gettin' it all wrong. And come here. You're mussing your hair again." With an expertise Isa had only ever seen in mothers, the boy lifted the girl and placed her in his lap, where he began to nimbly braid her hair. "Our parents sent us into the forest," he said in a quieter voice. "Actually, our father and our stepmother. She was *never* our mother." His voice grew even quieter.

"What happened?" Isa asked softly.

Henri didn't answer at first, just kept braiding. Just when Isa thought he might not answer at all, he finished the braid and sighed. "They sent us into the forest. While we were in the forest, a big lightning storm came. We smelled the sweets when it stopped. While we were out looking for the sweets, we accidentally found our way back to our house, where a tree had landed on the roof."

"That's when I asked him to come here," Genny said. "He smelled it, too, but he wanted to see the house first."

"We were already looking for the sweets," Henri mumbled, reddening a little. "We just found the house by accident along the way."

"I am so sorry," Isa managed to say. While most of the missing children had parents who had come to the Fortress begging for help, these children, it seemed, had been unwanted to begin with. How any parent, or even stepparent for that matter, could abandon children was beyond Isa. It might have been a providential thing for the horrid people that the tree had killed them, for if it hadn't, Isa would have made sure their punishment was swift and severe.

Ugh. Isa shook her head again. *Such dark thoughts!* Ever had been right. She was far too close to this problem to solve it without bias. But then again, she was too deep now to give up. Besides, Isa had absolutely no idea as to where she was or how she had come to be there. Or, most importantly, how to get out.

"How long have you been here?" Isa asked the boy, who was now tying a worn leather cord at the bottom of Genny's new braid.

"Five days," Henri said.

"Every day is different," Genny added, leaning toward Isa and getting a reprimand from her brother, who was still trying to tie her hair. "Yesterday we were in a meadow of poppies. The day before, we were next to a big puddle."

"A lake," Henri corrected her.

"A lake." Genny rolled her eyes dramatically, then she looked at Isa with a sudden intensity. "There is lots of power here. I can feel it."

Isa frowned, examining the children once again, more closely this time. How was the girl able to sense the power that surrounded them? Most humans could feel dark power in some sense, but to them, it was merely uncomfortable. Genny, however, not only felt the darkness but knew exactly what it was.

Before Isa had time to ask, a shadow rose out of the water behind her. Isa spun to face it, hand on the hilt of her sword. A woman stood before her, oddly dry though she had just risen out of the lake. She held her hands out in front of her then slowly put a finger to her lips.

"Please," she whispered, "you must come with me. Quickly!"

"What for?" Isa asked, hand still on her sword.

The woman glanced over her shoulder, though Isa could see nothing but more water and islands behind her. "They will be angry if they find out I'm helping you! Now come, before they realize I have gone!"

Isa looked back at the children. Genny looked worried and stuck her thumb in her mouth. Even Henri seemed disconcerted. "What do you want of me?" She turned back to the woman.

"I promise you will be returned to them. I need your help, though. I am trying to get you home!" The woman glanced around again.

Still, Isa hesitated. Something felt very wrong. In fact, everything about this situation felt wrong. But, she decided, what more damage could she do by following along and seeing what this woman wanted? Finally, Isa nodded.

Without a word, the woman took her by the wrist and pulled Isa into the water. Isa fought to grab a breath before being pulled under, but to her shock, as soon as she was underwater, she sucked in a breath only to realize that she could breathe.

"How—"

But the woman held up her hand and shook her head before turning and beginning to swim. Unfortunately, Isa had never been a very good swimmer, and after only half a minute was lagging behind. Her long dress made it hard to kick, and the muscles she strengthened in the practice room were far different than the ones used to swim.

Just when Isa's arms felt like they might fall off from all the swimming, the woman stopped. Isa stopped, too, but couldn't see what the woman was looking at. The pile of sand at their feet looked just like any other. And yet when the woman touched it, a hole opened up, barely wide enough for a single person to fit through. After one more careful look around, the woman dove into the black hole.

Fortress, Isa silently prayed, *that looks like a terrible way to die. Please let me come back out alive.* Then she grabbed at the edges and pulled herself through.

As soon as she was inside, Isa heard a thumping sound. The hole was covered, and for a moment she stood in inky blackness. It didn't last long, though, for much to Isa's shock, a candle was lighted, and the woman sat upon a rock, facing her. They were in a cavern of sorts with walls made of a black rock riddled with holes.

"How are we..." But Isa couldn't finish the question as she stared at the underwater candle. It was all too much.

"I am sorry for the... unusual method of bringing you here," the woman said in a rich, low voice. "But my people will not look kindly upon an assisted escape, and that is exactly what I am trying to help you do. They won't think to look here." She stretched out a hand, palm up. "My name is Sacha."

As they briefly grasped hands, Isa realized that the woman, whom at first she had thought to be young, was quite a few years older than herself and probably even older than Ever. Her long goldenrod hair was pulled back into a convenient twist at the back of her neck, and the thinnest of lines edged her eyes and neck. Her face had a certain undeniable handsomeness to it, though, with its angular shape and even proportions. Her gray eyes watched Isa just as curiously as Isa studied her. Isa suddenly had the sensation of having seen this stranger before. It was the same feeling she'd had with Henri, although she knew without a doubt that she would have remembered someone with such specific features. Who was this woman? Or rather, what was she? Was she a human, or something else?

"I thank you," Isa said cautiously. "I must admit, though, that I am a bit confused. Where are we, and how did we all get here?"

"I will be frank with you. You and the children have stumbled into the world of the Fae."

"The Fae!" Isa gasped. "But our worlds were sealed off after—"

"After my people attempted to take control of your kingdom." The woman nodded. "Yes, I know. But somehow, the veil has been reopened."

Isa frowned. Ever had told her once that the veil between the worlds had been sealed by the fire of the Fortiers. Such a seal could not have torn easily.

"I do not know how." The woman shook her head. "All I know is that a few months ago, the children began to appear in our world. As soon as my people realized they were human, they began to capture and keep them."

Isa nodded. "But I still don't understand how we got here." She waved her hand at the underwater cave. "And Genny said something about the world changing every night?"

"I'm afraid that in order to understand that, you will need to know a little more of our world." Sacha squirmed. It was so odd to watch her hair move up and down with the currents of the water, but to be able to breathe and speak as though they were above ground was even stranger. "My people live in a world of constant change," Sacha said. "Unfortunately, it seems your human children are more sensitive to the tear than most of your human adults. That is, except for you, of course. I hope this isn't too forward, but I must ask. However did you find us?"

Isa had many, many of her own questions to ask before she wanted to answer any of Sacha's, such as how they spoke the same language when they were from such different worlds, or about the house of sweets, which Isa knew the children had seen before entering the little cottage, or how the woman appeared to be so familiar with their customs. So she decided to indulge this request as simply as possible and see what results it bought her. "I came in search of the children."

At this, the woman's gray eyes grew large. "You don't have a child of your own who—"

"No," Isa said quickly, trying to quell the pain as it grabbed at her.

"Oh," the woman said softly. "I only meant to reunite you should you have had children here. No mind then." They were quiet for a moment as Isa put herself back together. Finally, Sacha spoke, placing her hand in her hair twist absentmindedly. "The two children in your pod seemed to like you well enough. It's quite curious. None of my attendants can get the boy to speak."

"My pod?"

"At the moment, it looks like an island. But really, it's the way my people are keeping the children in their places."

"As in cages?" Isa frowned.

"I suppose you could put it that way. They look less intimidating because we can make our world look just as we want it. Islands, coves, clouds." She shrugged. "They all look better than cages. I opened yours quickly enough that my people shouldn't have noticed."

"So what do you need me for?" Isa stood and walked nonchalantly to the nearest cavern wall. She touched it. The wall was solid, but at the same time it felt as though her hand might pass right through.

"I need your help to find the tear in the veil. I want to send you all back before I try to reseal the veil once more."

Isa turned to study Sacha, trying to probe her heart as she did. But to her surprise, the woman's heart was as hard to reach as the strange hole they'd climbed down into. Was that simply because Sacha was Fae? For a brief moment, Isa closed her eyes and pressed harder, until she was nearly shaking with the effort. Finally, she felt something. It wasn't much, but Isa suddenly felt sure that whatever her reasons, Sacha truly did wish to help them find the opening in the veil.

"I'm grateful for your help. Truly. But I have to ask... why are you risking so much to help us?"

Sacha looked at Isa for a long moment. Sadness flitted through her eyes and heart. "This tear isn't new," she finally said. "I don't know why the children have begun to come just now. No one has been here for years. They aren't the first, though." She shook her head. "There was a man who moved through the veil and into our world long before the children."

"Who was he?" Isa realized she was leaning forward in anticipation.

"My father." Without another word, the woman reopened the hole in the ceiling and swam out. Isa followed at a much slower pace. They didn't speak again until Isa was returned to the island.

"I will come get you when it's safe," Sacha told her quietly before turning and walking back into the water.

It had been such a strange meeting. Genny immediately put Isa to work shaping a baby doll out of sticks, but Isa couldn't focus the way she knew the little girl wanted her to. Somehow, she had come back from the swim with more questions than answers. The woman's heart had been heavily guarded, but Isa couldn't know for sure whether or not that was simply because she came from another world. Perhaps hearts didn't work the same way for this people. But was the woman trustworthy? And why, if the tear had been present for years, were the children only being drawn here now under the guise of a house of sweets?

Tomorrow, she thought to the Maker, she would get some answers. *But most of all*, she prayed, *let me get them home!*

8

TORN WORLDS

"How old are you?" Isa asked the little girl as she helped her skip rocks.

"Henri says I am four summers," Genny replied as she heaved another pebble out into the pond. "But Henri is more. He says he has nine summers." She stopped and looked at Isa, her clear blue eyes wide. "How many summers are you?"

Isa laughed. "More than that." For the thousandth time that day, she looked out over the rolling hills they were now occupying and wondered if Sacha would come. It was Isa's third day in the Fae world, and each day, the woman had snuck over to tell Isa that she was not yet ready to look for a way to send the children home. While they'd waited for the right time, Isa noticed at least ten more children arrive.

As Genny had predicted, each day brought new surroundings as well. The sea and islands were gone the morning after Isa stumbled into the Fae world, and instead, she and the children had awakened to find themselves atop a cliff so high that they were hidden within the clouds. Throughout the day, the wind blew enough of the clouds away to reveal the other children on little cliffs of their own. If Isa hadn't known they were encaged, she might have collapsed from anxiety. The day after that had been a vast desert with yellow, blowing sand. At least today's surroundings weren't as hot as that desert had been.

Standing up, she walked casually over to the edge of their little spot where Genny played and Henri sat against a rock. It hadn't worked yesterday or the day before that, but she might as well try. Raising her hands ever so slightly, she pressed into the air that surrounded them. At first, she met no resistance. But the harder she pressed, the greater the force that came back to meet her. Even when pushing her hardest, Isa could move her hands no more than a hand's span deep into the invisible wall. Frustrated, she let her hands drop once again.

"Are you ready?"

Isa looked up to see Sacha striding down the hill toward them. She wore the same simple violet work shift she'd worn every time she had come to see Isa, but her blonde hair was pulled back tightly against her head this time. She glanced at Isa's hands, which, to Isa's embarrassment, were still in the air from her experiment.

"I've found a place we can begin searching where they shouldn't see us. Are you ready?" the woman said, a slight smile tugging at the corner of her mouth.

"Of course," Isa said as she joined the woman. Sacha paused briefly, to unlock their invisible door, Isa guessed.

"You're leaving?" Genny cried. And to Isa's satisfaction, even Henri stood up, a slight frown on his face. She hadn't been sure whether the boy had really come to trust her yet or not, as quiet as he'd been, but it seemed that perhaps he was on the way.

"She will return, I promise." Sacha smiled sadly down at the children, her gaze lingering on the girl for a long moment. Then she turned and led Isa out. Up and down hills they went, toward the edge of what looked like a distant wood. As they walked, Isa wondered at how real the grasses felt as they brushed against her legs. The sky here was blue, as skies generally were, unlike their sky of orange from the day before.

"I apologize for taking so long," Sacha called back in a low voice as they moved briskly toward a thick line of trees. "The children have continued to arrive, and I haven't been able to get away much."

"How many Fae do you have?" Isa looked around at the other little pods of children scattered over the gently rolling hills.

"Around two hundred. Our people are not numerous. Now, this is it. If you would be so kind as to feel around here for the break in the air. I've felt it here before somewhere..."

Isa froze as Sacha continued to search. How did this woman know she could feel such changes in power and worlds? In previous meetings, Isa had not told Sacha of her abilities. Her heart thumped wildly in her chest, but she decided it would be best to go on as usual and to conceal her surprise. As Ever always said, keeping her own knowledge secret might teach her more than asking many questions.

With her hands raised and her eyes closed, Sacha looked different than she had before. When her eyes were shut, it opened up her face, making it look more youthful and less austere than it had before. Slowly, Isa raised her own hands and began to feel around for a disturbance the same way Sacha was. Though she had never dealt with tears in realms before falling through the one in the cabin, she had been at the Fortress long enough to know what it felt like when power was interrupted. And as she moved along now, she could feel the ripple somewhere nearby, although where it came from exactly, she couldn't say.

"What will we do once we find the tear?" Isa asked. How glad she would be to get back to her world where oceans didn't move and invisible walls didn't keep her holed up like an animal. And what she wouldn't give for a bath.

"We'll mark it so we can find it again tomorrow. I've planned a disturbance that should keep my people occupied for a few hours. Enough time to get them out. As soon as you are all gone, I will seal the tear from this side. I'm assuming you can help them once they are returned to your world?"

"Of course," Isa said. "Actually, my husband and some of his men are waiting there now."

"Your husband?" The woman turned to look at Isa, her eyes suddenly burning with an excitement Isa hadn't yet seen in her solemn face. Then she paused. "I feel the pull a bit stronger over here to the right. Let's move that way, and perhaps you can tell me a bit more about your husband."

Isa must have looked surprised, for the woman let out a short chuckle and closed her eyes again.

"My people don't keep one partner for life, the way my father told me most humans do." She smiled, almost shyly. "Please, if you wouldn't mind, you could tell me about him while we work?"

"He's a good man," Isa began, but as she spoke, a little wind swirled around her, and Isa knew immediately that the Fortress was warning her to be careful. "He is from a long line of respected protectors of our people." She tried to sound casual. "We live together in our home on a mountain."

"Oh, surely you must have something more to say about him!" The woman pressed just a little too enthusiastically, pausing her search efforts. "Is he an avid rider? Does he enjoy executions? Come now, you can surely spare a few more details." She laughed, but Isa suddenly felt nearly queasy with angst. How did this woman know so much about their world? Had her father taken her there? And why was she so interested in Ever?

By the grace of the Maker, Isa's arm went through a hole in what should have been an ancient, gnarled tree. "I've found it!" she cried, leaning over to stick her head through to look. Before she could, however, the woman grabbed a handful of her dress and yanked her back.

"No! You must wait until we are all ready! If you go through too soon, you may cause the bridge between worlds to collapse, and you will all be stuck here!"

Isa had not appreciated the yank, but what the woman said made sense, so she held her tongue.

The woman removed a red-jeweled pin from her hair. "This," she waved at the hills behind them, "will have changed again by tomorrow morning." She drove the pin into the soft wood of the tree, a few feet below the hole. "We will use this to mark the place. It is from your world, a gift from my father. So when this wood changes, the pin will remain. Now," she turned to Isa, her gray eyes gleaming again, "would you like to help me bring the children a little treat?"

Isa needed to learn as much of this world as she could before returning to the cage, but she couldn't help but feel confused at Sacha's sudden changes in mood. For all of her trepidation and solemn words on that first day, this quick light in her eyes didn't fit with the person Isa had believed the woman to be. If only she could see into her heart more clearly!

As oddly as her host was behaving, Isa had to admit that she did enjoy their next activity. The woman, apparently, had learned to bake a little from her father, and deep in the forest in a place Sacha claimed she had created that would be hidden from the others, she had prepared mountains of cookies for the children.

"I get little chance to practice my baking," Sacha said as she handed Isa a cookie that was larger than the others. "Hopefully, it's not terrible." She chuckled to herself, then sighed. "I know my people have caused the children much fear, but I hope they will go home to happier days."

When she was finally returned to her own little spot with Genny and Henri, Isa lay back against a large stone just as Henri had been doing all day. As the children devoured their treats, Isa turned her own cookie over in her hands, wondering if it were real or just another illusion. So many illusions existed here. And though Isa still couldn't see into Sacha's heart, she could sense the presence of half-truths.

Half-truths were the worst.

Isa put the cookie in her mouth and was surprised to taste its warm, buttery sweetness. If this was an illusion, it was a masterful one. Everything about it felt and tasted perfect. And yet, so had the tree and the ocean and the desert and now the hills. How was one supposed to find truth in a land of so many false appearances? It made Isa's head hurt.

That night, when one of the Fae came to deliver their simple supper of bread and cheese, Isa dared to move closer than she had before to study the other-worldly creature. It appeared to be a woman, but as Isa searched for details in the being's face, she realized it was almost impossible to find them. When she saw the woman out of the side of her vision, the face appeared to have two eyes that slanted out, a nose, and a mouth. But every time she tried to pick out any more individual features than that, it was as impossible as focusing direct-ly upon a star. The eyes and nose and mouth blurred into an oblong face, some-thing vague and strange.

Finally, Isa and the children prepared to sleep. During her first night in the Fae world, Isa had awakened to find Genny burrowed into her side as though it were the most natural thing in the world. Henri had kept to himself, but as the days had gone by, he had stopped watching Isa as though she might eat his little sister. Tonight, as it was unusually cool, Isa gathered a few sticks and grasses and started a tiny fire in their circle, one that would be easy to put out should some Fae object. No one came, though, and as had become her habit, Genny happily settled herself in Isa's lap and promptly fell asleep while Isa and Henri stared into the little yellow flames.

"She calls out for her mummy at night." Isa finally broke the silence, hoping not to scare the boy off with too many questions. "Was she close to your step-mother, or does she remember your real mother?"

Henri scoffed, his thin face scowling into the growing dark. "No. Our real mother was gone before Genny reached her second summer. And Helaine never liked us. She made me learn to dress and feed Genny and brush her hair so she wouldn't have to."

Isa looked down at the little girl lying in her lap. How one could reject such a child was beyond her. No wonder Genny was so desperate for love.

"Why then," Isa croaked, trying not to cry in front of the boy, "does she cry out for her mother?"

"She thinks our mother is coming back for her one day." Henri shook his head, then brushed a patch of his yellow hair out of his eyes. "I told her that our mum was coming back one day. I only did it so she'd stop crying one night after Helaine grew angry with us. I didn't think she'd remember the next day, but she's done it ever since."

I'll need to have his hair cut when we get back to the Fortress, Isa thought to herself. Then she realized what she had just assumed, and somehow, what she had been assuming all along.

Can I take them back with me? She looked up at the false sky as she begged the Fortress, suddenly desperate for a reply. Somehow, in the last three days, she had come to assume that they were hers. Isa didn't know when it had happened or how she had begun to believe she could keep them, but now it was as plain as day. Isa had undeniably begun to think of the children as *her* responsibility. Surely it wasn't her fault, she argued with herself. No one could leave them all alone, particularly as their parents had just died. That would be irresponsible, and Isa had more than enough resources to keep them well and fed until they could find someplace else that was suitable for children.

But then again, for the truth still reigned in her heart, Isa really had no desire to find someplace suitable, either.

9

OBJECTIONS

"Someone is coming!"

Ever leapt to his feet at the sound of the soldier's cry. He and his men fell into a semi-circle around the front door of the cottage.

"Hold for the signal," Ever reminded his men, looking in particular at Eloy. The young man seemed particularly jumpy today. Not that Ever could blame him. The four days they'd waited had been more than enough to try his own patience.

The shudder of power that came from the cottage was nearly enough to knock Ever off his feet. Acelet gave him a questioning look from across the half-circle, but none of the other men seemed to notice his trembling. Ever shook his head at his general and turned his attention back to the door. Some great power was moving within the old house. He only prayed that it was his wife returning, for he could allow himself to imagine possibilities no further than that.

The ripping sensation continued, and still no one appeared. What was taking so long?

"The children are coming!" Acelet called. Sure enough, dozens of children came pouring out of the little cottage, two by two. And they continued to come. Ever couldn't believe how many children there were. It seemed as though more might have been added right under their noses! *But where is she?* he asked the Fortress. Then, to his inexpressible relief, Isa appeared at the back of the great throng of children, holding the hand of a small girl. Ever sent up a prayer of thanks. Then after giving the nod to Acelet, who set the men to the task of rounding up the children, Ever ran to Isa. Before he got there, however, she stepped back and peered into the cottage.

"What is it?" he asked as he came to stand beside her.

"I was wondering if she was able to seal the tear," Isa said absentmindedly, still squinting into the dark, musty house.

"Who?"

"Sacha, the woman who helped us."

Ever strode into the dusty room once more. The shuddering he had felt was all but gone. Whatever tear Isa spoke of, it certainly wasn't there now. The feeling of evil that had pervaded the little place was entirely gone.

"Don't you ever do that to me again!" he growled, stomping back out to Isa and taking her by the shoulders. "You frightened me!"

"I'm sorry, Ever. I didn't mean to rush off like that. But..." She looked down, and Ever realized the child was still clinging to her hand. "I heard them calling for help." She looked back up into his face, her midnight eyes probing his. "I couldn't leave them like that."

"I know." He pulled her into a deep hug, only to be interrupted by a shout from one of his men. They turned to see Eloy chasing a boy no taller than his knee.

"Come back! You must stay here!"

Isa gave Ever a knowing smile and bent down to the little girl and a boy, whom Ever had not noticed earlier. "I need to help with the other children. You stay here with my husband until I come back."

The little girl looked up at him with the biggest, bluest eyes he had ever seen in such a small person. Isa smoothed the girl's hair and then smiled at Ever once more before heading off to help his men, who seemed completely inept at getting the children into any semblance of order.

"Who are you?" the boy asked, taking the girl's hand and pulling her closer to him.

"I am the king."

The boy's eyes grew even bigger before he ducked his head down and whispered something to the girl, who giggled and shook her head.

Ever looked again for Isa amidst the chaos of soldiers and children. He had brought twenty-four men with him, but even so, the children had them tremendously outnumbered. How did Isa do it, calming the children and organizing them so? And what did she expect him to do with these two?

"So," he cleared his throat, "where do your parents live?"

"They're dead," the boy said.

Well, this was going to be more difficult than he thought. "I am sorry."

"They didn't want us anyway," the boy said, watching Isa as she moved the other children into groups.

How did one respond to that? Ever sighed. Leave it to Isa to find the most pathetic, lonely children in the land. And then hand them to him to take care of.

An eternity later, Isa had not only rounded up the children, but matched their names to the lists of the missing. Then she'd placed them in groups that needed to be returned to different parts of the kingdom. There was also a number of children who were neither on the list nor did they know where they were from. That bunch would be taken back to the Fortress to be sorted out and delivered home with the help of Garin and the messengers. After instructing both the children and the soldiers on how to behave, Isa sent them in their respective directions, and finally it was just Ever, Isa, three guards, and the last batch of twelve children.

"What about—" Ever began to ask when he realized the two blue-eyed children weren't going to be grouped, but Isa stopped him.

"They're coming with us."

Ever raised his eyebrows in question, but Isa ignored him. Very soon, the smallest children had been placed on the horses with the guards, while the older children walked alongside Isa and Ever. Ever wanted to ask Isa about what had happened in the other world, as well as what exactly she was planning to do with the orphans, but he knew better than to question her when she wore that expression. Besides, it took all of their time and energy to keep even their little flock of twelve under control.

Ever couldn't push their horses back home as fast as he had before, thanks to the children. So even with the aid of a small amount of his power, they were only halfway to the Fortress by the end of the first day. Only after all of the children had been laid down and wrapped in spare blankets did Ever get to finally talk with Isa.

"So?" Ever threw his cloak over her shoulders as she stood watching the children, her arms wrapped around herself and her shoulders hunched. "What happened?"

"I'm not sure." She shook her head, still looking at the children. "I mean, I know what she told me, but I still cannot decide whether I believe it or not."

"How about you tell me, and we can choose to believe or not believe it together."

"How long has it been since the Fae world was sealed off?" She finally turned and looked up at him, the blue fire in her eyes moving in uneven bursts.

"Nearly five centuries. Why?"

"If we are to believe her, and I really can't find a reason not to..." she drew in a deep breath, "then the children and I were in the world of the Fae."

Ever was speechless. He'd known they were in some other world, but he'd never guessed it to be that one.

"I know the veil between worlds was sealed by a Fortier. So it couldn't just tear on its own." She looked up at him with frightened eyes. "Could it?"

He frowned down at her, unable to form any sort of coherent answer himself. "We need to talk to Garin," was all he could finally say. To this, Isa nodded and leaned into him. Ever wrapped his arms around her and pulled her close. "Aside from breaking every rule in the book," he said into her hair, "you did well. I would never have been able to do this without you."

"I only hope we haven't poked a hornet's nest."

Ever was hoping the exact same thing.

~

Despite their somber words the night before, Isa was nothing but smiles and sunshine the next day. She moved between the horses, talking to each child in turn. Little giggles would be shared with the younger girls, particularly the one with big blue eyes, whose name was Genny, Ever found out. To the boys, she would assign all sorts of tasks, such as watching for bandits and dangerous animals, which miraculously kept many of them occupied for hours. To the older children, she would move about asking more direct questions about their homes and families. Always busy, always moving, Isa seemed never to stop. And Eloy, who appeared nearly as enthralled with the children as Isa, was little better.

Part of Ever was a bit put out. He had more questions that he wanted to discuss without the children hearing them, but every time he tried to get her attention, one of the children stole it. And yet, he couldn't bring himself to be angry. She was happier with them than he had seen her in a long time. Caring for the children appeared to be the most natural calling in the world for her. Isa acted as though she had been born to mother them.

And that's when it hit him. She finally had someone to mother.

This was all well and good for the children, but it wasn't long before Ever was ready to have her back to himself. By the end of that second day, he was exhausted and felt most out of sorts. The sight of the Fortress's front steps, however, cheered his heart to no end, as did the sight of his steward, waiting with a smile to receive them.

"Garin!" Ever dismounted and clapped the older man upon the back.

"I heard reports that the outing was successful." Garin smiled, his eyes crinkling at the corners.

"The last three groups shouldn't reach their destinations for a few more days at least," Ever said, handing children down from the horses to surprised servants. "But all reported missing are accounted for. This group didn't even have time to be reported missing."

"Gigi," Isa called, "please help me find these children places to stay until their parents arrive." Immediately, Gigi, as well as a horde of servants beneath her, were out on the Fortress lawn, each taking a child and fretting over him or her and immediately dragging them back to the Fortress for what Ever guessed to be baths, new clothes, and cider. Soon only two children remained, half hidden behind Isa's skirts.

"And who are these—" Garin was staring at Genny and her brother, Henri. Before he finished his sentence, however, Garin's eyes went flat. "What are *they* doing here?"

Ever was taken aback at the poison in Garin's voice. Surely he didn't mean the two orphans. And yet, the steward was outright glaring at the children with a look that would wither any adult. Henri's eyes grew large, and he pulled his sister as close to him as he could. Even chirpy little Genny looked frightened.

"These children have no parents," Isa said, her voice suddenly as icy as Garin's glower. "They were taken as well and need someplace to stay."

At a loss, Ever looked back and forth between Garin and Isa. For the first time in his marriage, he was stuck between his wife and his mentor. And, he decided immediately, he wanted out. "Let us take a moment and then continue this in the study," Ever said cautiously, aware that there were servants also watching the scene.

"That is a masterful idea," Isa said, her voice still hard. "I am tired, and in horrible need of a bath, as are the children." She took Genny and Henri by the shoulders. "We will talk about this after everyone has been fed, bathed, and changed. I will take Genny. Ever, would you take Henri?"

"I will take the boy," Garin grumbled. When Isa fixed him with her deadliest stare, he rolled his eyes. "I will make sure he's taken care of. You have my word."

To this, Isa finally consented, and before Ever knew it, they were all off on their own separate ways. As he walked, Ever decided that he wanted nothing more than a hard drink and his own warm bed. He had a sinking feeling, however, that those two desires would not be granted for a while, considering the daggers Isa and Garin had been sending at one another through their glares.

What had just happened?

10

WHAT YOU ARE

"What is that?" Henri stared at the gigantic basin before him as the servants filled it with buckets of steaming water.

"A bath," the tall, grumpy man answered in a dry voice. "Have you never taken a bath?"

Henri scowled up at him. Of course he had bathed. But never inside the house. Instead, his father would take him to their nearby creek. Did this man expect him to undress in front of so many people?

"Where's Genny?" Henri asked, hoping the man might forget the bath if he could distract him with questions. He was to have no such fortune though.

"The queen is giving your sister her bath, but she will join you here when it is time for bed, should the king and queen decide, for the time being, to keep you. Now, I will be waiting outside this door." The grumpy man seemed to read his mind. "When you are undressed and in the tub, let me know."

Henri certainly did not intend to let him know. As soon as he was stripped and inside the warm water, which did admittedly feel rather good after their long walk, instead of calling the man, Henri set to examining the room. It was the largest room he had ever seen, big enough that his entire cottage could have fit inside, woodpile and all. There were two tall beds, draped in thick layers of coverlets and pillows, rather than straw mattresses laid upon the floor. A fireplace nearly as tall as Henri roared not far from his tub, and tall, rectangular windows stretched all the way up to the ceiling, which must have been nearly the height of four men.

He didn't have long to enjoy the richness and splendor of the chamber, however, for just then, the door opened. The grumpy man and a plump woman with ringlets of snow-white hair waltzed in.

"Hello there, love. My name is Gigi. Now, let us get you clean!" Without hesitating, she plunged a brown, squishy blob in the water, lifted Henri's arm, and began to scrub it with the blob. "Oh now, no need to howl like that," she said with a smile.

"I can wash myself!"

"Psh, I doubt that, love. You have dirt caked behind your handsome little ears, and your face looks as though you've been rolling in it."

"You had better listen to her." The grumpy man wore an annoying grin, as though he was enjoying Henri's discomfort. "She won't stop until she's finished."

Gigi was surprisingly strong for her age. The more Henri resisted her scrubbing, the more determined she seemed to do it, humming happily the whole time. "Now, Garin, why do you look as though someone's fed you a lemon? Goodness, the king and queen come home and everyone is a wreck! There, love," she turned back to Henri, "you sparkle like a newborn babe. Here's your drying cloth."

Henri did not want to sparkle at all, particularly not like a baby, but before he knew it, she had him out of the tub and wrapped in a thick, warm cloth. As he dripped water on the brightly colored rug that had been placed in front of the fire, Henri stared in wonder at his own arms. Had his skin always been that shade of white?

"I hope these fit you. Of course, we'll have to have some made up, but I was able to find some of the king's old clothes from when he was about your size." She stopped and pursed her lips to the side for a moment. "You do seem ever so much skinnier than he was, though. I shall have to fatten you and your sister up a bit. You look as though you haven't eaten a day in your life."

At the mention of food, Henri's evening suddenly seemed a little less dismal. If this woman wanted to feed him, surely she couldn't be so bad. As soon as she had him dressed in the brown trousers and white, long-sleeved shirt, she scurried off. Henri hoped it was to find him some food. When she was gone, however, the grumpy man, or Garin, as everyone called him, closed the door and approached him, stopping only when he was very close.

"I do not know your history," he said in a menacing voice, "nor do I know how you were raised. And for that reason, I shall abstain from making a final judgment of your character... for now, at least. But know this. The king and queen might not know what you can do, or what you are, but I know. And I will be watching you carefully."

Henri swallowed, and his hunger melted. Suddenly, he found himself wishing for Miss Isa or even Gigi. "What are you going to do to us?"

"Nothing, so long as you behave and act as any boy should who is a guest in the king's home. But if you try to hurt them, even the smallest bit, I will have you wishing you had never laid eyes on the queen. Do you understand me?"

Henri glared back at him, but worry thrashed about in his gut. Maybe he should have tried to slip away rather than allowing Miss Isa to bring them here. He hadn't realized she was the queen until they were on their way out of the forest. And how did this man know about his trick? Henri hadn't used his fire since the night he got lost. But Henri had no answers.

The man finally stood and went back to the door. "Gigi will be back soon with your supper. When you are finished, I will come and fetch you."

"Where are we going?"

"To see the king and queen. They need to know exactly what you are."

11

BEHIND CLOSED DOORS

*T*hough the hot bath and clean clothes relaxed Ever's sore muscles, they did little to clear his confusion and dread. It was already growing dark outside, and if the choice had been left to him, he would have been in bed an hour ago. Instead, however, he was on his way to his study, although he got the feeling it would become less his and more Garin and Isa's domain if the evening continued the way it had begun.

Isa, Henri, Genny, and Garin were already there by the time he arrived. Garin hurried him inside and then immediately began to plug the keyholes with cotton pieces. From Isa's expression, it was clear that she was just as dumbfounded as Ever at the steward's behavior.

"Did either of you," Garin asked as he checked the windows and closed the tapestries, "see any other being leave the Fae world as the children left?"

Isa and Ever looked at one another with raised eyebrows.

"How did you know I was in the Fae world?" Isa asked. Ever wondered the same thing. They hadn't had the chance to tell Garin anything of their journey.

Garin ignored her question and asked again. "Did you see any other creatures leave that world?"

"Uh...n...no," Isa stuttered. "It was only the children and me."

Garin walked back to them. "But you swear, you saw nothing leave with you?"

"Garin, what is this about?" Ever finally broke in. Since when had the steward become so paranoid?

"What I am about to tell you has not been uttered to a soul in five hundred years."

Ever's heart nearly stopped. How he had longed to know Garin's origins!

And yet, something told him this would not be the exciting adventure he'd dreamed as a boy it would be.

"Are you speaking of the Fae?" Isa asked.

Garin nodded, his silver-and-black hair glinting in the firelight. "I know that you've read what little the annals have to offer on the subject of that people." He looked at Ever. "I made sure of that myself when you were a boy. There is still much you don't know, however, because it was never written down. So few survived the battle with the Fae that no Fortress scribe was left alive to record it." He turned and faced the fire, cutting off Ever's line of sight to his face.

"The Fae were a race capable of greatness," Garin said in a low voice. "They could not only create temporary bridges between worlds, but they could also create temporary worlds within their own. When the Fae happened upon Destin in their travels, King Nel and Queen Chantal invited them to the Fortress in order to discuss new diplomatic ties." He turned to Ever. "I do not know if even you are aware of it, Ever, but the Fortress's cornerstone and inner walls are made entirely of blue crystal, rather than common stone."

"I didn't know for sure," Ever said slowly, "but I had always guessed as much."

"Well, you were right. As were the Fae. As soon as they entered the Fortress, they could sense its power."

"Did the power affect them?" Isa asked.

"No," Garin said, "they simply liked the way it felt."

"They could sense it... unaided?" Ever asked. That a whole race might feel the power of his beloved home was more than a bit unnerving. Only humans with gifts or the Sorthileige could do that.

"Without giving the king even a warning to leave, the Fae decided to claim the Fortress as their own. The slaughter began at midnight and lasted until the first rays of morning. The king's entire army was nearly wiped out, while most of the Fae remained untouched."

"How so?" Ever broke in. "Surely Nel's power would have been strong enough to defeat them."

"Oh, I'm sure it would have, had he known how to use it. The Fae's bodies are like their creations, only temporary. Every so often, they must dissolve into the mist they are and then recreate themselves in the same way they create their temporary worlds. When their emotions get the better of them, which is often, or they've waited too long to rebuild, they become a mixture of hot green light and wind.

"You can only imagine what kind of damage such an army could inflict on human soldiers. Disappearing then reappearing, the Fae moved across the soldiers in their sleep like a plague."

"And the servants and families?" Isa asked, her face taut.

Garin only shook his head sadly. "The Fae had all but taken the Fortress completely when one of the Fae soldiers found the infant prince..." Garin's voice suddenly broke.

Ever glanced at Isa, who looked very much as though she would like to go and comfort him, but neither of them moved until Garin seemed to recover himself.

"Before I go on," he said, drawing in a deep breath, "you need to know that in addition to their ability to create temporary works of beauty and intrigue in both themselves and their surroundings, they seek power of any kind, like moths to a flame. The Maker gave them the ability and physical substance to travel wherever they want, to see the world and not worry about hunger or shelter. They did not need such hindrances. For when the weather got bad or they ran out of food, they could simply transform and wander the earth as air and light until they found the next place they wanted to live."

As he continued to speak, Garin's voice began to harden, and he stood taller. "They are beautiful creatures, but when they reached the Fortress, the power here changed them, or rather, their desire for it did. Covetousness twisted their vision, and jealousy so warped their spirits that they became new creations entirely. Their innate vanity and their inability to see the world from others' points of view prevented them from living with men. Their greed rendered them incapable of love. They forgot all that they were and strove to hold what wasn't theirs to begin with."

"How do you know this, Garin?" Ever asked, dread making it suddenly hard to speak.

Garin turned and looked straight at Ever, his eyes hard like flint.

"Because I am one of them."

~

Ever looked as though he might pass out, but to Isa, Garin's story made perfect sense. "Back in the alley," she whispered, "when you saved me from Marko..."

"Yes," Garin said as he took Ever by the arms and eased him into a chair. "Although what you saw wasn't my complete Fae form. Here, Ever. Drink this." He held a small flask out to Ever, who downed its contents in one swig.

"But you use the Fortress's power," Ever finally said when he was done, grimacing slightly as the drink went down. "How?"

"The boy prince lived, even though his father, King Nel, died. And it wasn't for lack of trying on the part of the Fae." Garin's voice grew low again. "When I found the child all alone in his nursery, it should have been a simple solution. His mother and nanny were dead. His father, dead. I knew what I needed to do to ensure the happiness of my people. And yet, as I raised my sword, I was blinded by a barrage of images that flooded my mind. What the child could do, would do... what he would grow up to be. It was a miraculous gift of the Maker, an understanding of the situation's reality, how we were trying to take what wasn't ours. He showed me the truth, much like Isa shows others."

"What did you do?" Isa asked in a soft voice.

"I protected him from my own." Garin shrugged helplessly. "I even killed a young Fae who tried to kill the child while he lay in my arms." A darkness touched Garin's sharp features briefly then vanished, although Isa could feel the bitterness and sorrow lingering beneath his controlled expression. "Soon after that, as I held the babe in one hand and my sword in the other, the Fortress expelled the remaining Fae and pushed them back to their world. And when the boy was old enough, the Maker led both of us to the southern forest, which was much smaller back then.

"Before the Maker bid the prince to seal the Fae out of our world forever, I was given the choice of whether to return to my people or stay with the Fortress and guard the young man. 'If I return,' I told the Maker, 'I will surely be put to death. But if I stay, I am too broken in body and spirit to be a keeper of anyone.'

"'Leave your body to me,' the Maker told me. 'It is your heart I see of import. Do you trust me?' He asked."

"What did you say?" Isa asked.

"It was simple. I had tasted of the Maker's goodness for the past fifteen years as the boy had grown, and I knew I could never survive without it again. And so He made me a new body of two peoples. I no longer needed to dissipate and rebuild myself as Fae do, but I was allowed to retain a few of my Fae qualities. In addition, I was gifted certain powers of the Fortress itself. Over time, though," Garin murmured, "He did the greatest healing to my spirit." He briefly closed his eyes.

"Are all Fae five hundred years old?" Ever finally managed to choke out.

"No. We do not live that long alone. I can only assume I am still here to finish some sort of work, though how long that work should be, I do not know."

"Thank you for telling us," Isa said hesitantly. She did not wish to bring more pain upon the steward after all he had just shared with them, but she was still confused. "I still don't understand, though, what all of this has to do with the children."

Garin fixed a hard gaze upon Genny and Henri. Isa instinctively tightened her grip on their shoulders.

"These children," he said, "are no mere children." He walked back to the king's desk and pulled out the ceremonial scepter. Its sphere of blue crystal, which was fixed at the top of the golden twist handle, was as clear as water with thin, feathered lines that crisscrossed the crystal's interior like miniature spears of lightning.

"Come here," Garin told the children. Both of them looked up at Isa. Part of her wanted to take the children and dash off so she wouldn't need to see whatever Garin wanted to show her. And yet, she knew it was only right to see what he had to say, so she nodded, and they both took a hesitant step toward Garin. The steward turned the children to face Isa and Ever. Then he held the crystal out before them. "Fae are sensitive to power of any kind. Even if it is one they can't use, they can still feel it. Just as I can."

With that, he placed the crystal in Henri's hand, and to Isa's dismay, the black center of the boy's eyes began to shimmer with green.

"Just as these children can."

Isa felt sick to her stomach. The green light swirled about the boy's irises as his gaze stayed fixed on the crystal. Even worse, Isa realized, Genny was staring at it, too, a blank look on her face and the treacherous green inside her eyes as well. That's when Isa remembered Genny's claim about the Fae world being full of power.

How? Isa cried out to the Fortress, paralyzed as she watched. *How are these children Fae?* How had she managed to fall in love with the only children in the world that might be a danger to her kingdom? Her first desire was to scream. Instead, however, Isa swallowed and whispered, "How, since they were living in our world first?"

"Their bodies are too stable for them to be full Fae, which means they must only be part Fae."

"The Fae have been exiled for five centuries! So what do you mean, *part* Fae?" Ever scowled at Garin from his chair.

"I mean that someone found a way to tear the veil between worlds and sire children."

"Sacha," Isa whispered. Ever and Garin both gave her a strange look. "Sacha was the woman who helped us escape," Isa explained, looking back down at the children. "She said she wanted to help us because her father was human."

Garin began to say something, but Isa didn't hear it. Instead, she watched as Henri began turning the scepter over in his hands. And as he did, the crystal began to glow blue. It was the same light as that in Isa's ring, the one meant only for the Fortress's queens. And in Henri's hands, the scepter was glowing just as fiercely as Isa's ring ever had.

Ever pushed himself up in his chair, and even Garin seemed, for once, to be at a loss for words.

"Show them your trick, Henri," Genny said, taking her brother's arm.

But Henri just shook his head, fear filling his face as he stared at the scepter.

"Come on, Henri! Do it!"

Henri looked nervously from Isa's face to Ever's before shaking his head even more vigorously, his wide eyes making his young face look even thinner. Then he looked pointedly at Garin.

"Come on, now," Genny said, sticking her little hands on her hips. "You always do the trick for me."

Henri glanced up at Isa once more.

"You will be safe," Isa said, giving him the warmest smile she could muster. "I must admit, I am very curious to see your trick, especially if it is as wonderful as Genny says." But inside her heart thumped wildly as she prayed that his *trick* wouldn't result in something terrible.

The boy stared at her for a minute more before taking a deep breath. As he exhaled, the scepter not only continued to burn blue from within, but a tongue of blue flame rose from its surface as well.

Garin looked like his eyes might fall out of his head, and Ever, his voice flat, called out from the chair, "What is that?"

"That's his trick," Genny chirped. For a moment, no one moved. Not even Isa could bring herself to speak. Only Genny clapped delightedly. "Isn't it wonderful?" She beamed.

"Yes." Isa made herself smile reassuringly as Henri looked up at her with fearful eyes. "You can be finished now, Henri. You've worked hard enough for one day." When his fire finally went out, and Isa gently took the scepter and handed it back to Garin, however, she realized that Genny was right. It was wonderful. For though the boy's eyes certainly marked him as something other than human, his fire set him apart as well. She wasn't sure how he had miraculously received such a gift, but she did know that it just might save his life.

FIRE OF THE FORTIERS

*E*ver felt numb as his wife finally left to put the children to bed. She paused briefly by his chair and gave his shoulder a squeeze before leaving. But he was going to need something stronger than a shoulder squeeze to clear his mind of what he had just learned.

"I will be needing more of that." He leaned forward and pointed to the bottle Garin had placed on his desk.

With his usual efficiency, Garin went to do as he was asked, but it felt as if Ever watched his mentor through eyes that were not his own. Never had there been a soul he trusted more, with the exception of Isa, of course. Not that he had ever known what Garin was exactly. Garin had always simply been a part of the Fortress to Ever, much like the shining white marble halls and the crystal dance floor. Garin simply belonged. And now Ever was to believe that Garin was, or had been at one time, the enemy.

"Will Isa be safe with them?" Ever managed to choke out.

"She will be fine for the time being," Garin said evenly as though he hadn't just shattered Ever's world. "I will keep a sharp eye on the children while they're here, but they seem to be innocent of schemes for the moment." Then Garin leaned back against the king's desk and folded his arms. "But there is something I need to discuss with you before you go off to bed too."

Ever shrugged, out of words for the remainder of the night. Or possibly for the rest of the decade.

"Tell me everything you know about those children."

"Well," Ever pinched the bridge of his nose as he tried to recall what Isa had told him, "the children say their father was a woodcutter not far from the cottage where we found the veil's tear, just beyond the border of the southern forest." Ever's senses returned a bit as he remembered the wretchedness on the boy's face the morning before. "Their parents turned them out and then were killed later that night during a lightning storm."

"And what led them to the Fae world?"

"Isa says that someone created an illusion of sweets in the forest. The illusion made the air smell sweet to the children, and they followed the smell. Henri and Genny followed the smell, too, and stumbled upon the house." He frowned, remembering how little Isa had whispered to him over their long journey. She'd said there was really little to tell. Most of it had been an illusion. "The woman that helped them escape told Isa that the Fae had decided to keep the children, and they would have if it hadn't been for her. The Fae must have known of the tear and used it to lure the children in. But why now," he asked Garin, "if the tear has been there for years?" It still didn't make sense.

Garin wore a pensive look on his long, thin face.

"If the Maker had King Nel's son seal the bridge between the worlds," Ever continued, "then who could have torn it? And why does that boy have the Fortress's fire?"

"Only a Fortier could have torn what a Fortier sealed," Garin said bluntly. "So one of your ancestors must have reopened the veil. At least several decades ago if an adult half-breed is running about." He raised one black-and-silver brow. "As to the boy's powers, I was going to ask you the same thing."

Ever stared at him blankly.

Garin shook his head, a look of impatience on his face. "The green you saw in those children's eyes today proved that they do have Fae blood within them. But the fire proved that the boy isn't pure Fae at all, and neither is his sister, provided they are full siblings."

"I am too tired for this, Garin. What are you getting at?"

"That fire that the boy created on the crystal? That flame can only be created by someone with the blood of the Fortiers."

Ever managed to pull himself out of the chair so he could get some fresh air. Garin didn't stop him when he unlocked the balcony doors and stepped out to feel the late spring's cool breeze upon his face.

"Isa created fire before she was a Fortier," he pointed out to Garin, who had moved to stand beside him.

"But not that easily. The boy clearly doesn't understand what a great power he holds, and yet he created a flame as easily as you ever did. What's more, the girl said he's done it before, without the crystal we can presume."

Ever turned to his mentor, too tired to guess anymore. "What are you saying, Garin?"

"How old is the boy?"

"Eight? No, nine years, Isa said. Why should that matter?"

"Nine years ago you would have been twenty-two—"

"Wait." Ever took a step back. His stomach suddenly churned. "Are you really asking if *I* fathered those children?"

"I certainly hope not. But yes, that is what I am asking you."

"No! No, how could you ask such a thing! You would have known if I had done something so audacious!" Ever began to pace the balcony, running his hand through his hair. He could hear his voice crack as he faced his mentor. "Many things I have done in my life that I regret, but never that. *Never* that!" He was shouting now, but he didn't care.

Garin sighed and rubbed his eyes. "I am sorry, Everard. You are right. I would have known—"

"No, truly! You tell me that you are...were one of the enemy, then you accuse me of sneaking out like a street urchin, finding a secret tear within the veil, then siring not one, but *two* children. Then abandoning them with a good-for-nothing woodcutter?"

"I know, I know," Garin said, his voice subdued. "Forgive me. I just... I didn't expect any of this." He looked at Ever, his eyes suddenly sad. "I haven't seen another of my kind in five centuries. I am trying to understand how this could have happened. Of all the children there with Isa, she found the two with Fae *and* Fortier blood." Garin's expression moved from one that was incredulous to one of pain. "You know what this means, though. If it was not you, that leaves only one—"

"No." Ever slammed his fist against the wall so hard he could hear the stone within it groan.

Garin stopped, but still gave him a knowing look.

"I will not even entertain that thought," Ever said, breathing hard. "My father was a good man."

"Good men can run foolish errands, my boy." Garin took a deep breath. "Isa mentioned the woman was also half human. It would seem that more than one Destinian has found the tear. There's no way of knowing how many half Fae are running about in our world or theirs."

Suddenly, this day had become more than Ever could handle. Shaking his head, he waved his hand and shuffled toward the door. "I'll dispatch men in the morning to search for reports of Fae activity in the southern forests. But now I am going to sleep."

Unfortunately, as soon as Ever took a single step out of his study he was nearly trampled by a runner. "What is it, Edgar?" Ever asked, though he was sure that he really didn't want to know.

"I apologize, sire, but there is a large group of citizens here from Soudain."

"Now? It's the middle of the night!"

Edgar bowed his head as though he had been the one banging on the Fortress gates. "I know, sire, and I am terribly sorry. But they are insisting that you must come now. They claim," he paused before meeting Ever's unhappy gaze, "that the children you returned to them are cursed."

"Cursed?" Could this night get any worse? "How many?"

"That is just the thing, Your Majesty. All of them."

13

A GOOD MAN

*W*henever Ever felt as though the burdens he carried were too great, his father's voice would pop into his head with its vast number of admonishments, particularly on the topic of lazy kings. On nights like this, as Ever trudged to the throne room with Garin in tow, he sorely wished that his father's voice would sometimes just shut up.

When he stepped into the throne room, he was taken by surprise at the sheer number of villagers present. He did his best to look composed as he made his way to the throne, but inside, an uneasiness slid about in his stomach. When the runner had first come to him, Ever had hoped that a few villagers had caught a random illness, and they were only jumping to conclusions when they claimed that there was a curse. But there were far too many people for that. At least two dozen families stood in his midst and more were coming in the back.

"Alright, let us begin," Ever said, not in the mood for the usual hearing traditions. "What is it that ails you all at such a late hour?"

"Your Highness." A thin man with a graying beard and faded clothes knelt before him. "My name's Emile. I'm a baker in Soudain. We sincerely 'pologize for comin' at this time, but the need was too great to wait until mornin'." He turned and looked at the people behind him. Some nodded. One woman in particular, however, made dramatic sweeping movements with her arms, a scowl chiseled into her bony face. He turned back to Ever. "We want to thank you and our queen for returnin' our children to us, but..." His voice quivered and faltered.

"I understand this is about the children?" Ever prodded.

"Yes. Uh... yes, Your Majesty. You see, every child in Soudain that was returned to us has been struck with maladies o' the worst sorts."

"Maladies?" Ever leaned forward. All of the children had appeared healthy to him when they'd left the forest.

The man bobbed his head. "Yes, Your Highness. They're injuries and illnesses like our healers have never seen before."

"Well then, let me see these children."

"We didn't bring them here!" the woman who had been waving her hands called out. Her tone was not nearly as respectful as the man's had been. "They're all laid up in a sick tent. You need to see them now!"

"I see," Ever said. "None have died, though?"

"No, sire. That is the strange part 'bout it," the man said, shooting the woman an irritated look over his shoulder. "Some complain o' sore aches in their arms and legs. Others've broken bones. One has lost her voice! But they all have somethin'!"

Ever sat straighter and rubbed the back of his head thoughtfully. He was greatly relieved to hear that none of the children had died, but it made no sense. Then again, his day had made little sense to begin with.

"This is what I propose." Ever stood. "As we have only just returned from the rescue, I have not yet had the time to consult with Queen Isabelle. She was the one who was with the children in the other land. Since none of the children seems to be in mortal danger, I will take this night to talk with my wife and consult with the Fortress. Perhaps the queen can shed some light on the situation. First thing tomorrow, we will visit your children ourselves."

A quiet murmur arose from the men and women present, but one voice screeched out above the rest.

"The king cares for his sleep more than our children!" It was the same woman who had interrupted them earlier.

Ever marched down the dais and over to the woman. "And would you, madam, prefer me to travel there now as I am and perhaps injure your child even further? For I can assure you, such things do happen!"

The woman still glared, but she took a step back. "I find it hard to believe the Fortress's celebrated king could be so careless," she muttered.

"Come now, Agnes." A woman with a small babe tucked snugly in her left arm gently pulled on the rude woman's hand. "You have his word. There are only six hours left until the morning light. The children will benefit more if the king is rested." She looked at Ever, her gaze similar to that which Isa wore when she looked at Genny and Henri. "Your Highness, do whatever you must to help them. I know the Maker will watch over them as we wait."

Ever's heart softened at the kindness in her voice, for he was very weary indeed. "Thank you, madam. As you have said, I will see you early on the morrow."

Garin followed Ever out of the throne room, but neither of them spoke until Ever stood outside his own chambers.

"She was right," Garin said softly. "The Maker is watching over those children tonight, and you will need your strength tomorrow. Good night, Ever."

Ever paused, his hand on the door, but as he went in, for the first time in his life, he didn't wish Garin a good night in return. He could not bring himself to pretend that everything between them was as it had been.

As he shut the door, he expected to see Isa's sleeping form in their bed, but to his surprise, she was standing out on the balcony with a blanket pulled over her slumped shoulders. He went to her and wrapped his arms around those shoulders. She leaned her head back against him, and for a long time, they stood still. If nothing else, Ever told himself, he was thankful for this. His wife had been returned to him safe and sound. For though he had told no one else at the camp, he had feared the worst when she didn't return after that first day. Only the power of the Fortress had kept him from tearing the cottage to shreds with his bare hands.

"We are needed in Soudain early tomorrow," he finally mumbled into her hair. "The children who were returned have come down with a mystery illness of sorts."

In response, Isa briefly stiffened, but then she relaxed into him again. "That is strange," she said. But something in her voice gave Ever pause. She didn't sound like it was strange, or that she was even surprised by it.

Ever wanted to ask, but instead, he decided that he had another topic he needed to discuss. It might just drive him mad if he didn't. "Garin and I spoke after you left," he began, suddenly very afraid of what she might think. Should he even be telling her this? "It's about the veil."

She finally turned to look at him. "What about it?"

"Garin says that because a Fortier sealed the veil between the two worlds, only a Fortier could have torn it again." He took a deep breath. "He also thinks that a Fortier must have fathered those children."

Isa's eyes widened a little, but she turned them on the darkened mountain. "He thinks it was you."

"Well, at first, yes," Ever hurried to explain. "But he would have known if I had done such a thing. I swear Isa, those children are not mine!"

Instead of crying or looking suspicious or even studying him as Ever had expected her to do, Isa gently took his face in her hands and gave him a tired smile. "I know."

"You know?"

She smiled and lightly touched his chest, sending ripples of warm relief through the rest of his body. "I will admit that Henri does have moments when he reminds me of you. I thought that the day I met him. But," she turned her lovely moonlit face up to him, her pink lips parting softly, "four years have passed, and you still forget my gift sometimes. Ever, I know that you have only ever been faithful, even before you knew me." She gave him a meaningful look before taking his hand and leading him over to the bed. "I don't need my gift to know that."

"But how?" He wanted so desperately to believe her, but it seemed too good to be true.

560 | BRITTANY FICHTER

She pulled the covers over herself and leaned back into the pillows, looking suddenly as exhausted as he felt. "Because I know who I married. And you, Everard Fortier, are a good man."

Tired or not, Ever leaned over to give her the kiss she deserved. How he had survived without her, keeping any semblance of sanity, he would never know. For though the world was falling to pieces around him, the look his wife was giving him now made him feel as though somehow, everything would be made right.

14

PANIC

*A*lthough she'd lived in Soudain her entire life, it occurred to Isa that she had never visited this quarter of the capital city before. The houses were small and cruder than those in the main city blocks, patched up with straw thatch and mud. The people looked haggard as well. Such an area was no place for a young lady on her own, her father had sternly warned her once when she was seven. And now she understood why as she glared back at some of the men who were making not-so-subtle examinations of her person.

"Why would they put the tent here?" Ever asked her as he stopped his horse before a flimsy canvas structure. "The children were taken from all over the city, not just the outskirts."

"Because the well-off said they were too good for such commons." A scowling skinny woman appeared before them, wiping her hands on her apron. Her wiry hair was pulled back beneath a dirty rag. "Said they would keep their children in their own homes and buildings, rather than have them mingle with the *riffraff*. It took you long enough, Your Highness."

Isa stared, shocked at the woman's audacity, but Ever just shook his head ever so slightly.

"Sires," a man hustled out of the tent and stepped in front of the rude woman, "we're so thankful you've come. Please, follow me." Ever helped Isa dismount before nodding at his guards, three of whom followed them into the tent. The other two stayed outside with the horses to ask questions of those who lingered outside.

As Isa's eyes adjusted from the brightness of the morning sun to the dark of the tent, she made out ten little mattresses lined up in a row, each with a child lying upon it. When she drew closer she was surprised to find that none of the children shared symptoms as she had expected to find. One child had large brown boils covering his face, neck, arms, and legs. The next little girl had a broken arm. The boy after her appeared fine, but his parents stood over him looking anxious.

Isa knelt down beside the mattress closest to the door and laid her hand upon the boy's forehead.

"I remember you," she whispered to the little boy, forcing a smile upon her face. The little boy gave her an ornery little smirk. He had given the guards particular trouble before returning home. "Tell me, does this hurt?" She pressed gently against the child's arm, just above a boil.

He gave her a slight nod.

"Poor baby," she murmured. "You're burning up. Do you feel hot?"

At this, he shook his head and gave her another grin. "Only my skin hurts. I feel good enough to climb a tree, but Mummy says I must stay in bed." He crossed his skinny arms, a disgruntled look coming to his face.

Isa smiled. "I am thankful you feel well, but I think your mother is right. You need to stay in bed until your skin stops hurting."

"My papa is a healer," he said as she continued to examine him. "But he can't heal me. Can you?" The hopeful look he gave her made Isa's heart ache.

"We'll do our best." Isa felt her smile falter just a bit. "Now, I have a question for you. Did you talk to anyone while you were in that strange world? Anyone besides your friends?"

The boy immediately shook his head.

"Are you sure? I need you to think very hard and really try to remember."

He bit his lip for a moment, then his face lit up. "I talked to that woman with the yellow hair before she brought us cookies. She asked me about my mummy and papa."

Isa's heart sank as she looked up at his parents. "You say that this began after the soldiers brought them home?" His mother and father stood behind the bed with pinched faces and clasped hands.

"Not even an hour after," the mother said, her eyes never leaving her son. "We sent for help immediately. The fever came so fast. I didn't think he'd make it through the night..." Her voice broke as she leaned down and gathered the little boy in her arms, who promptly began to squirm.

"But after we were told your husband was otherwise occupied last night," the father dared a fierce glance at Ever before turning back to Isa, "we realized that he wasn't being affected by the sickness. At least, not in the way such fevers usually go."

"And he has remained like this since then?"

"Aye."

Isa thanked the parents and ruffled the little boy's hair once more before moving on to the next mattress, and then the next. Before long, she had talked to the parents of every child. Determined to leave no stone unturned, she then went to visit the eight families who were keeping their own children at home. Each story was essentially the same, but Isa grew wearier with each home she visited. The weight of helplessness was in each parents' heart, and as a result, in hers as well. The skinny woman, Agatha, whose daughter had blisters covering her hands, at one point accused Isa of being apathetic. If only she knew. If anyone understood their plight, it was Isa. Not only because of her gift but because Isa had a story like theirs all her own.

Something deep down, possibly the Fortress, warned her that theirs might not be a plight Ever's fire could easily fix. For there was a new power here that she felt slipping through the blood of each child. The strength was foreign but also familiar. It was the same power she had felt back at the torn veil, and the same strength that now moved through her blood as well. Ever hadn't been able to feel the tear in the veil as she had. And now she wondered if he would be able to heal a malady that seemed to come from the same source. And yet he had to try.

"I need her away from the other children," she told the father of the girl on the last mattress. Ever sent her a questioning look, but she gave him the slightest shake of her head. If this didn't work, she didn't want it to incite panic among the people.

As soon as they had the girl by herself in a corner, Ever took the child's throat gently in his hands. Her voice had disappeared, her parents had told them. She couldn't even whisper. Isa relaxed a little as her husband's familiar blue light moved from his hands into the child. The Fortress's fire was always comforting. They stayed that way for a few minutes, Ever kneeling before the girl's pallet with his eyes closed in concentration, and the child watching the ceiling with wide eyes as she waited.

But something is wrong, a voice inside her whispered as Ever's face tightened infinitesimally. *He should be done by now. Please, Fortress, let him heal her!* But as seconds stretched to minutes, Isa could see the parents beginning to shift nervously as well, and she could feel Ever becoming agitated. Finally, he let go, but she could see from the tightness in his eyes that he was not at all confident in the work he'd done.

"Well?" the father asked his daughter. "Did it work?"

The girl opened her mouth, but to Isa's dismay, nothing came out.

"I need to speak with you." Without waiting for the parents to respond, Isa took Ever by the hand and led him over to another corner of the tent.

"I don't understand," Ever said, looking at his hands. "I had hoped it was simply an effect of spending time in the Fae world..."

Isa shook her head, looking at her feet. This was not a conversation she'd planned on having here in front of their subjects, but she needed to tell him.

"Last night, when you were talking with Garin..." She stopped and drew a deep breath, willing her voice to stay steady. "While you were talking to Garin, I fell asleep and had a dream."

"A dream?" He raised an eyebrow, and she nodded.

"I dreamed that everything in me was emptied. I felt dry, parched, as though I'd walked for miles in a desert. Then I realized I *was* in a desert. I came upon an old orchard, where trees grew in the sand. But none of them bore any fruit. I woke up then and had the most terrible pain." She closed her eyes.

"Where?" Ever's voice was strained.

"Here." Without thinking, she placed her hand in the same spot that had kept her doubled her over the evening before. "Ever, I know I haven't conceived yet, but there was always the possibility. I could feel it. But now..." She shook her head. "I'm barren."

Ever's heart was more unreadable than usual. He opened and closed his mouth twice before simply staring outside the tent for a long minute and rubbing the back of his neck the way he did when he was unsure of what to do.

"It was her," Isa continued before she lost her nerve and her self-control. "It was Sacha. It had to be!"

"But how?" Ever finally looked at her, his eyes still indecipherable.

Isa had asked herself the same question the night before. "There is only one answer I can come up with. She baked us all cookies. I couldn't feel anything at the time, but there was just so much power everywhere... I can only guess that she used some sort of Sorthileige."

"Couldn't it have been the other food?"

Isa shook her head. "According to the children, she spoke with every child, asking them their parents' occupations before giving them their treats." Now that she thought of it, why hadn't Sacha talked to Genny or Henri? Perhaps she had but did nothing to them because they were orphans. They had no parents to affect.

"But why all the different maladies?" Ever looked back at the children over her shoulder.

"She chose what she knew would hurt each family the most. The boy with sores is the son of a healer. Who would visit a healer who can't heal his own son? The girl without a voice is from a family of minstrels. The one with blisters comes from a family of bakers."

"But what about you? Did you tell her you were the queen?" Ever looked incredulous.

"I know better than that," Isa huffed. "I told her you and I protect the region." Isa sighed. "Still, any wife would have one overarching duty for such an important calling."

"Which would be?"

"Produce an heir to follow in our footsteps."

Ever's jaw tightened as he closed his eyes again. "When were you planning to tell me this?" he asked in a low, dangerous voice.

"I wanted to! Last night, when you came to me and the dream and pain had passed, but then you told me about the children and I didn't want to worry you even more!" She took one of his large, calloused hands in her own. "I didn't understand the connection until this morning. I am sorry, Ever. Truly!"

"One might think," he pulled his hand free, "that our ability to have children could actually be my concern as well, worry or no." He stalked toward the tent door and motioned to his soldiers. Isa followed more slowly, trying desperately to keep her tears at bay. It hurt to hear, but he was right. Her pain was his business, and by hiding it from him she had only muddled things further.

"Get the med packs," Ever was quietly telling his men when she caught up to him. "We're going to do what we can for these children before heading back up the mountain."

The men exchanged looks of confusion, but they knew better than to question him. Soon they were all attending to the children. Isa helped one of them set the little boy's broken arm, but her attention remained on Ever, who was furiously mixing a salve for the boils and blisters. All around her, Isa could sense the confusion and frustration of the parents and the others who had come to watch the king work his miracles. Why hadn't the mute girl's voice been restored by his fire, and why wasn't he using that fire on any of the others?

And sensing the state of Ever's heart was even worse. Though it was vague, as usual, she could still feel pangs of panic. Fear. Frustration. Self-doubt.

And sorrow. One wouldn't know it by looking at him, ferocious as he appeared, but inside, he was mourning, just as Isa had done the night before.

When they were all done, Ever and his men quickly gathered their supplies before reloading their horses, and they were just about ready to go when the skinny woman ran after them.

"Wait, Agnes!" A man named Emile ran after her, but she shook him off before jabbing her finger up at Ever.

"What now? Are we too lowly for your precious fire? Are you that much high and mightier than us peasants? You won't even have mercy on our children?"

Since the night before, Isa had felt like a piece of string being wound tighter and tighter. Now, that string snapped. Dismounting her horse, Isa strode back to the woman and stopped when their noses were less than a hand's breadth apart. "You would dare to speak to your king this way?" she hissed. "The king comes all the way from the Fortress to your home, and you attempt to shame him so?" She took a step forward. "If the Maker does not deem it the proper time for your daughter to be healed, do you think anything my husband does shall change that?" She grabbed the woman's wrist and gripped it tightly, despite the woman's protests.

Isa focused all of her energy on the truth that she had just spoken. As she continued to hold Agnes's wrist, the woman's pulling and thrashing stopped, and she fell to her knees in the mud.

"Forgive me," she sobbed. "My husband passed last year." She looked up at Isa through red, glassy eyes. "She's all I got left!"

Isa's anger dissipated at the woman's pleas. "We will pray for guidance and continue to search for answers," she said, letting go of the woman's wrist. "Perhaps the Maker has another way in mind." After helping the woman stand, Isa mounted her horse once again, and they set off to the Fortress.

As they went, though, Isa could still feel the tension they were leaving behind. Agnes's change of heart wasn't reflected in all of those who had witnessed Ever's failure. Or even many of them. Most of the crowd still consisted of confused, angry parents, grandparents, and friends. Isa got the feeling she would be using her gift more than ever before in the coming days, and she prayed she would be up to the task.

As soon as they were at the foot of the mountain, Ever turned to one of his men. "Hamon, show me the gash you received two days ago in training."

The red-haired man looked startled but did as Ever said, removing his glove to reveal a puckered scar above his fourth knuckle. Ever placed his hand above it. As the fire burned brightly for a brief moment, Isa wondered whether or not it would work. But to her relief, when Ever pulled his hand away, all signs of the man's scar had disappeared.

"Thank you, sire," Hamon said, bowing his head.

Ever looked up at his men. "I want the rest of you to return to the Fortress. Hamon, report to Garin what happened here today. I need to speak with my wife alone." He dismounted, then held his hands up for Isa to do the same.

Isa's stomach did a flip as she dismounted and turned to face him, and she suddenly felt like a little girl when her father would call her to his chair to admonish her for some wrong she had committed.

Rather than rebuking, however, Ever only took her hand in his and began to run his fingers over her knuckles, a nameless expression upon his face. Isa tried to read his heart, but it was too muddled.

"I am not angry," he finally said in a soft voice. "I only wish you had come to me sooner." He met her gaze, the fiery rings capturing her in their depths. "You of all people should know by now that we must do this *together*. You've never wanted me to leave you behind." He arched an eyebrow, inviting her to challenge him. But of course, she couldn't. "Now I have this request of my own. You cannot try to shoulder your burdens alone." He clasped her hand tightly in his own, and Isa reveled in its warmth and strength. "Are we agreed?"

Isa nodded, despite the tears that were running freely down her face. Ever gave her a sad smile and reached up to wipe them away. Was it possible for her to love him any more than she did now?

"Now, though I am afraid of the outcome, let me see what I can do for you." Gently, he laid his right hand over her belly while he held her arm with his left. "I will be using a much stronger fire than usual," he warned her. "This may hurt a bit." And with that, he pressed in.

At first, it was just a flicker of warmth, the way it felt when one sat too close to the hearth on a cold day. But the longer he pressed, the hotter the flames became, and it took everything in Isa not to leap away. *Please let this work!* she begged the Fortress, gritting her teeth and mashing her eyes closed as hard as they would go. She could vaguely feel Ever stroking her hair as he continued to work, but it was of little comfort. The pain was too severe. If it could heal her though, she could survive anything.

Finally, however, the fire was simply too hot, and Isa let out a cry of pain. Immediately, Ever stopped and grabbed her arms so she wouldn't fall. Isa hobbled over to a large, flat rock and lay down. Ever sat beside her, drawing her close until she was recovered enough to breathe and take stock of herself.

"Well?" he asked, hope rising up within him even though Isa could feel him trying to quell it.

"No," she whispered. "It's still there."

15

A BOY'S TOUCH

"Where is Miss Isa?" Henri asked the servant tending to the garden.

"The *queen*," the servant woman gently corrected him, "is with King Everard in the Tower of Annals."

Henri sighed. Exactly where they had been for the past three weeks. Did the king and queen ever do anything besides sit up in that tower?

If it had been up to him, he and Genny would have been spending the day differently as well, *in* kitchens, rather than outside of them. But Genny had insisted on coming outside to chase butterflies. One of these days, he swore to himself, he was going to stop letting his little sister always have her way. Butterflies were fine, but Cook's bread was delicious.

It wasn't Genny's fault that he was in a bad mood, Henri reminded himself as he munched on the tomato he'd snatched when the servant wasn't looking. It was King Ever's fault. Or perhaps it truly was his. He wasn't sure anymore.

During their second week at the Fortress, long after the other children had been returned to their parents, the king had taken to reading books at the table while they ate. Henri could tell that Miss Isa didn't approve of the king's habit much, judging by the little frowns she would send him and his books every few minutes. But she said little about it, often spending her time talking with the children instead. And Henri didn't at all mind missing out on the king's company. The king frightened him.

Though Henri had seen taller men, King Ever had arms and legs thicker than both of Henri's legs put together. The king's voice boomed, and his ability to fight would have put Henri's brawny father to shame. The king was generally in a rather short mood, and though he would make attempts to talk to the children now and then about little details such as the weather, Henri simply preferred to stay out of his way completely.

The night before, however, which had marked three weeks since he and Genny came to the Fortress, Henri made a grave mistake. As they sat down to supper, something that seemed a nightly tradition at the Fortress, Cook brought out a new frothy drink, one with foam and bubbles that nearly spilled over the sides of the cups.

"Madame Gigi told me you two might enjoy a new kind of treat," he had said, a twinkle in his narrow brown eyes. Henri had immediately taken a sip, and to his delight, had found it the sweetest thing he'd ever consumed. Genny, on the other hand, seemed to have plans other than actually drinking her treat. As soon as Miss Isa stepped away from the table, the little girl had giggled then blown a few pieces of foam onto her brother's plate. Without thinking, Henri had returned the favor with his own foam. Unfortunately, he blew much harder than he'd meant to, and to his horror, a large bit of the foam flopped down right on the ancient text the king was reading.

Henri's face had flushed with embarrassment as King Ever fixed his steely blue eyes upon him, and the look the king had given Henri had made him want to run upstairs and hide in his new room forever.

"This text is over four hundred years old." The king's voice reverberated in Henri's chest in its low, menacing tone. "I do not think blowing our drinks across the table is appropriate supper behavior."

Henri's horror had only grown when Genny piped up without hesitation, "But Miss Isa says readin' at the table is not *app-er-o-piate* supper behavior either!"

The king had stared at them for so long that Henri thought he might toss them outside right then and there. Finally, however, he only slammed the book shut and stomped out of the room, probably, Henri guessed, to head back up the tall tower, taking his supper with him.

Now, as he watched his sister chase the butterflies, Henri wondered again what he would do if the king and queen threw them out. He couldn't deny that he had quickly grown accustomed to a warm bed and full stomach. It was nice to see Genny happy, and no one, not even the king, had raised a hand against either of them since they'd arrived. Though he was far from trusting that the situation could last, for it seemed quite too good to be true, Henri wished to the Maker desperately that it might. Being rejected by parents who had never truly loved them had been bad enough. He didn't know if he could stand being rejected by someone as kind as the queen.

Henri had never known a woman like Miss Isa. He remembered little of his own mother, and whenever Helaine had turned to address him directly, it was usually to bark out an order or to make sure he remembered his place, often with the backside of her hand. Miss Isa, though he would never admit that he liked it, was full of hugs and kisses. She reprimanded them enough, but her words were never cruel. And she made Genny happy.

Henri stood and walked out to where his sister had collapsed on the ground, breathing hard after nearly an hour of running in circles and jumping up and down. Plopping down on the grass beside her, he asked, "Do you think Miss Isa looks more tired today?"

"No." Genny shook her head as she kept her eyes trained on the robin-egg blue sky above them. "Miss Isa always looks beautiful."

"I don't mean that she doesn't look beautiful," Henri scoffed. "I mean I think she looks tired. Her eyes are dark, and I think she seems... sad."

"No," Genny chirped again, still unperturbed.

"I don't know why I even bother asking you." He stood and brushed himself off before heading for the kitchens. Sometimes he wished Genny were just a few years older. Having a conversation with a four-year-old could be nearly impossible. If she was so determined not to talk sensibly, then she could lie there by herself. He was going to get some of Cook's sweet bread.

Just before he made it back to the vegetable plot, the door was blocked by Gigi, the older servant who fussed over the king as though he were Genny's age and not thirty-one, as Miss Isa said he was.

"There you are!" She smiled at him, though he thought her smile looked strained. "The queen is sorry she cannot have the midday meal with you today. She's very busy. But Master Garin has informed me that he would like to speak with you over the meal instead. He's sent for a picnic so you can all eat out on the Fortress's front lawns."

She said something else, but Henri didn't hear. All he could think about as he looked at the size of the basket Gigi carried was the loaf of bread his parents had given him before leaving them in the forest.

The king was sending them away. If it had been the queen who had suggested the idea herself, he might have thought otherwise. But the horrible memory of the foam-stained page from the night before was suddenly all he could think about.

They were being rejected again.

"I don't think so," Henri said in a small voice, shaking his head vehemently as he fell back a step. "I think I will just wait for Miss Isa."

"Nonsense." Gigi *tisked* as she reached for his hand.

Henri panicked, and before he knew what he was doing, a thin blue flame had not only engulfed his hand but hers as well. With a cry, Gigi fell back, clutching her hand to her chest. Henri couldn't move. He stood frozen in place as he watched her cradle the hand, already red and swollen.

Like a rabid wolf the king was suddenly there, although Henri had not the slightest idea as to where he had come from or how he had known what had happened, as there were no other servants about. The king gently took the older woman's hand and rubbed his own hand over it. He was asking her something, but Henri couldn't hear it for the sudden roar in his ears. Then the king grabbed Henri's arm so tightly it felt like it might break. Without pause, he dragged Henri all the way up to the children's room, where the king practically flung him onto the bed and slammed the door behind him.

Trembling, Henri hugged his knees to his chest as he rocked himself back and forth on his bed. He had never hurt anyone before with his trick. He'd only used it to provide light at night or for Genny's amusement. In fact, he hadn't even known that his fire *could* burn someone. He truly hadn't meant to hurt the old woman. His flame had been instinctive, as though it had a will of its own. Shame and fear took turns riding the tide of dread within him.

At best, he and Genny would merely be cast out of the Fortress. At worst... Henri shivered. He didn't even want to think about the worst that King Ever could to do him.

Miss Isa had spoken before about the power of the Fortress, how it heard her thoughts and created power within her. She had also said that the Fortress knew one's heart, even when others couldn't see it. *Well,* he thought feverishly, *if that's true, Fortress, I need you now!*

16

STORY ABOUT A BOY

*I*sa let herself fall into bed, allowing her weary limbs to relax one at a time in its feathery depths. How many times had she tried to hide away in her room like this, just to be thwarted by another knock at the door? It seemed there was always a needy servant or a desperate parent begging her to return to Soudain to see to a child whose condition hadn't changed in weeks. Not that she wished to shirk her duties, but rather, Isa simply longed to have an hour to herself to pause and breathe.

Just one hour.

As if on cue, Isa could hear her husband's heavy, quick footsteps fast approaching their door. She sighed up at the red canopy above their bed, counting down the seconds until he burst through the door with some new emergency, no doubt, that simply could not be remedied without her.

Sure enough, the door banged open. "Come here." His voice had an edge to it that Isa hadn't heard in a long time.

She sat up. "What is it?"

Ever's face was an alarming shade of red, and the anger within him was nearly palpable. "I need you to see what he's done."

"Who?"

"That boy of yours. Come with me."

Scrambling out of the bed, Isa was immediately alert, all memory of exhaustion gone as her heart pounded away. She considered asking him what he'd meant by *her boy* but decided against it. She had learned long ago that nothing good came of arguing with her husband when he was in a mood like this. Better to let him calm down and then discuss whatever had roused his ire. But, she wondered, how long would that take this time, for she had not seen him in this kind of temper for a long, long while.

While Ever hadn't exactly been taken with the children as Isa had been, he had tolerated their antics rather well, even venturing cautiously to speak with them now and then. To his credit, he'd tried, considering he'd never spent much time around children even when he was a child himself. But the way he walked now frightened Isa, and she hurried even faster as they headed downstairs and rounded the corner to the first sick room.

"Gigi, what happened?" Isa ran to the older woman's side and gently lifted the hand that the healer had just cleaned. Bright red puffs of skin covered her hand, wrapping around it the way another hand might. Though Isa was no healer, she knew a bad burn when she saw one.

"Your boy did that," Ever fumed.

"Please, Ever," Gigi stuttered, seeming close to tears. "It was an accident. I only frightened him, that was all!" From the way her voice trembled, though, and the paleness of her round face, it was obvious that Gigi had been shaken by the incident.

"I wanted you to see this before I healed it," Ever said, still fuming, "so you would know exactly what he is capable of!"

Isa didn't answer him. Instead, she gently lifted Gigi's burned hand and placed it in Ever's hands before squeezing Gigi's shoulder. She focused on what Gigi had told her, that the boy had meant no harm. As that truth flowed from Isa's hands into Gigi, Isa could feel the older woman relax. Her white curls ceased to shake, and color returned to her cheeks. Hopefully Ever could do his part now. Isa held her breath.

Just then, Isa noticed Garin standing in the corner of the room, a tight, intense look on his face.

"Where are the children now?" Isa asked as Ever set to healing.

"Locked in their room," Ever said. "Where I told them they would stay unless they wished for the direst of consequences to befall them."

Isa closed her eyes and said a quick prayer. It was very possible that Ever had just done more damage than good, but she would need to talk him into a calmer mood before she took any drastic measures. As she opened her eyes, Ever let go of Gigi's hand. Isa sighed with relief as Gigi moved her fingers. It seemed that at least for this ailment, Ever's powers were still effective.

Ever gave Garin a meaningful look. Garin nodded, and the two of them stepped out into the hall. As their footsteps faded, Gigi looked up into Isa's face, her eyes imploring.

"Please, Isa!" she said, her voice hitching again, "don't let him be too hard on the boy! I should have known better, given their... circumstances. I know Henri didn't mean anything by it. You should have seen the look on his face when he realized what he'd done!"

"I promise," Isa said, leaning over to place a kiss on Gigi's soft cheek. "We will get this all sorted out." As she spoke, an idea came to her, an answer to the prayer she had uttered only a moment before. She knew exactly what she needed to say. But first, she had to catch Ever.

Isa broke into a sprint, but as she ran, she wondered with annoyance at how quickly the exercise was tiring her. When was the last time she'd gotten more than four hours of sleep uninterrupted? Her tired mind couldn't recall. What she wouldn't give for a nap right now. Thankfully, she didn't have to run far before overtaking Ever and Garin, for they had been stopped by one of Ever's soldiers. Isa stopped, too, but waited just close enough that she could hear what the man was saying.

"... healing people in the southern woods. The parents who have brought their children to her claim they've shown no symptoms since."

"How many people know about this?" Ever asked.

"Enough. Bartholomew says there is a line every time she appears, and that she never heals every single one. Mostly the woods people are those who have been going to her thus far, but news is spreading fast."

Ever stood perfectly still for a long moment. Finally, he told the soldier in words nearly too quiet for Isa to hear, "We'll set out tomorrow before first light."

Isa wanted to groan.

"How many days should we prepare for, sire?"

"It's a three-day ride to the town." He paused. "We will travel without speed this time. I will need to save my strength for the meeting, should it go badly." He glanced up at Isa, then told the man that he would be down to discuss logistics with him soon enough but for him to relay the plans to Acelet in the meantime. Isa took that as her signal.

"Please." She approached her husband and took hold of his arm, keeping her voice low so the passing servants wouldn't hear. "Let me talk to the children."

"I think not."

"Ever," Isa said, "you are angry right now. I know how much Gigi means to you. But how much good will it do for you to frighten Henri more? That is how this mess began in the first place."

Ever glared at her for a long time, but to her relief, Isa could feel him beginning to soften. She hated using her gift on him but sometimes it was necessary when he refused to see sense. Thankfully, however, she did not have to use it this time, for he finally let his head droop to his chest as he let out a gusty breath.

"Take Garin. I don't want you alone with them until I know what the boy is capable of."

"Actually," Isa leaned in, "I was hoping you would both accompany me. I believe this is something you need to be a part of."

Ever hesitated, casting one last look of longing in the direction of the soldier he had just sent away, then nodded reluctantly. Isa sent him the most confident, peaceful smile she could muster, praying all the while for her plan to have success. For if it didn't, this could end very, very badly.

By the time Isa and Ever arrived at the children's door, Garin had unlocked it and was standing by the hearth with his arms folded. Genny seemed oblivious to the fact that her brother was curled into a little heap on his bed, or that there was a problem at all as she pulled at Garin's trousers and begged for him to tell her a story. The little girl's blue eyes lit up as she spotted Isa, but as soon as she spotted Ever, she wilted like a flower in the dead heat of summer. Ever must have noticed, too, for Isa felt a flash of guilt move through him as she wrapped the little girl up in her arms. Good. He hadn't needed to scare Genny too.

"Are you ready for bed?" Isa asked the little girl as she plopped her upon her bed and began to braid the child's hair. Genny gave her a big grin.

"But it's early! Cook only just brought us supper! Plus, we still need a story." Then she turned her little face to where Ever stood and drew her lips up into a pinched frown. "Except from him. I don't want a story from him."

"Well, I have a special story tonight for both of you." Isa tucked Genny in, then went over to Henri and began to unfold him from his little ball. "In fact, it is one of my very favorites because it's a *true* story." As soon as the children were both beneath their covers, she sat down beside Henri.

"Long ago, there was a boy, a prince, who had special powers from the Fortress."

"This Fortress?" Genny sat up, her eyes wide.

Isa laughed. "Yes, this Fortress. You see, the prince was very strong. Even as a boy he could best grown men with the sword, and with only his hands he could create a power so strong that it was like the lightning from the sky." As she spoke, Isa watched Henri. He still looked terrified, but the more she spoke, the less he hid his face beneath the blankets.

"When he was thirteen, the prince was in a royal procession with his parents. Many people came to see the prince, for news had traveled far and wide of the young prince's power *and*," she added, "his kind heart. And his heart was indeed kind. For when a girl fell into the street, he climbed off his horse and helped her stand."

"That was nice." Genny nodded matter-of-factly.

"Yes, it was nice," Isa said with a sad smile, flicking her gaze over to where Garin and Ever stood by the door. Garin's arms were still folded in front of him, but his eyes were closed now. Ever's face was slightly twisted in a way that made Isa's heart ache. But, she reminded herself, bones needed to be broken before they could be reset. Ever needed to hear this before he allowed his anger to carry him away.

"Unfortunately," she turned back to the children, "the prince also had a temper that often got him into trouble. And on that day, it did just that. You see, the girl didn't know she wasn't supposed to touch the prince, so when she ran up and grabbed his sleeve, hoping to thank him for his kindness, he lost his temper and accidentally hurt her with his power."

"Was it fire power?"

"Yes." Isa nodded, thankful Henri was finally talking again.

"What happened?" The boy studied his hands thoroughly as he spoke, still either unwilling or unable to look her in the eyes.

"He had to realize that the Maker still loved him, as did the Fortress and all of his friends who lived there with him. But that didn't mean there were no consequences. You see, his power hurt the girl badly, and it changed her life. She couldn't walk well, nor could she use her hand the way she once had. It took her many years to heal." Without looking at him, Isa could feel the shame burn through Ever as it always did when her old injury was brought up. Directing her next words to him, Isa lifted her gaze, wishing he would meet it.

"But the Fortress would not allow the prince to go on in sadness and loneliness."

"What happened?" Genny asked, somehow more out of the blankets than under them once again.

Isa smiled and tucked her back in. "The Fortress and the Maker brought the prince and the girl together so that neither of them could go on until she forgave him and he learned how to say he was sorry. In that forgiveness, they fell in love." Isa smiled to herself as the joy of that forgiveness filled her even now.

"Did they get married?" Genny asked.

"They did." Isa grinned as she leaned over to kiss Genny, then Henri. "They were soon married, and are *now* living happily." She stood to leave, but Henri's words brought her to a halt.

"I didn't mean to do it." Henri's voice was quiet. The way it cracked broke Isa's heart. "I never even asked for the fire. I just have it."

"None of us did." Isa sat back down and took Henri's hands. "But the Fortress has a purpose for everyone it gives strength to." She lifted his chin. "Including you. The hard part is waiting to see what our purposes are. Patience is a lesson we must learn." She looked up at Ever. "All of us."

Henri sighed and nodded before lying back down. "Fine. I'll think about it. But I'm not marrying Gigi!"

Isa laughed, and even Garin smiled, but Ever's face remained grim.

After Isa had snuffed out the candles and made sure the fire in the hearth had enough wood, for it was still chilly in the evenings despite the coming of spring, she, Ever, and Garin filed out quietly.

Before going his own way, Garin turned to Isa in the hall and gave her a wry smile. "Five hundred years I've spent in this place and yet you still manage to surprise me. If I ever need more humility, I shall be sure to come to you in the future."

"Does that mean they've won you over yet?" Isa asked.

"Perhaps," Garin said thoughtfully, "I am beginning to see that dealings with my own people are not as black and white as I remember them to be." Isa returned his grin, and Garin excused himself, leaving her alone with Ever.

"Come," she said, taking her husband's hand and leading him down the hall. "Let's get some air."

As they walked, she tried again to read him, to see into the depths of his soul. What was it about the children that bothered him so? But, as usual, she was shut out.

Isa had once asked Garin why it was sometimes so difficult for her to read Ever's heart. Others came more easily to her, but for some reason, Ever could close himself off like a bear in its den.

"You were privy only to the last few months of Ever and Nevina's rivalry," Garin had told her.

This mention of Ever's old enemy had surprised Isa. She'd been sure Garin would talk about Ever's father and all of his infamous lessons in denying his feelings.

"Nevina knew how to use Ever's feelings against him, and she did so until the day she died." Garin had given Isa a wry smile when she'd stared in surprise. "I know what you're thinking, and yes, King Rodrigue *did* have a great hand in teaching Ever to keep his emotions hidden, but much of that training is gone now. You, my dear, have worn it away. The shield Ever places over his heart at this time is one born of need. He placed it there to keep Nevina out."

"But she's long dead. How do I get past it?"

"I helped him build it for his own safety, but I'm really not sure how to break it now, to be honest. He was still building it even up until her death." Garin had shrugged. "I don't know how long it will be before he knows how to take it down, or if he'll ever even have the ability to do so himself."

Now Ever's defenses were up in full as he followed her out to the crystal balcony. No musicians were there, as the hour had grown late, but Isa pulled him to the center of the blue floor and began to lead him in a slow, simple dance. That her story to the children had touched him was sure, for his eyebrows were drawn into a thoughtful, somewhat pained frown, but to what extent she had really reached him was still a mystery.

"Ever, what's troubling you?"

In response, he drew her in for a kiss. It was gentle and sweet, but there was no passion in it tonight. Rather, his lips seemed to match the expression on his face, reserved and unsettled.

"What was that for?" she asked.

"For showing me the truth," he said slowly. "You were right. I reacted far too quickly with the children. My anger was out of place." He gave her another soft kiss on the cheek. "Now, you need to go to bed. You've been staying up entirely too much lately."

That was quick. Isa had hoped to talk more. Although, since he had mentioned it, bed did sound wonderful. "We all need reminders." Isa smiled up at him.

Ever gave her a tired smile of his own, then turned and began to walk away.

"Wait!" Isa called out.

He turned, raising his eyebrows in question, and Isa's blood suddenly raced, for she knew what she was about to say couldn't be taken back.

"It... It will take a while for the children to find their places here." She gave him the most hopeful smile she could muster. "They'll need time."

The blue flames that were always dancing around the pupils of Ever's eyes changed direction, and Isa knew immediately what he thought of her suggestion as his face settled into its most guarded mask. "Isa," he said softly, "I don't know if—"

"Your Majesty!" A young soldier, Eloy, burst through the door of the dining hall, stopping so fast he nearly fell over when he laid eyes on Isa. "My Queen!" He bowed, breathing hard. "I am sorry. I didn't know you were both here."

"What is it?" Ever stepped forward.

"We have found where the woman appears every day. She comes from..." He hesitated, looking at Ever and then Isa as though unsure whether or not they would believe him. "A tree. There is no door, no way to enter or exit, but she still comes from the inside of the tree every day. She melts through it, like a mist."

"Where?" Ever asked.

"Just outside the small forest village of Sansim where she does her daily healings. And not only that," Eloy still breathed heavily, the white of his dark eyes standing out in the low light of the moon, "the people are beginning to talk. Not just the forest villages either."

"What are they saying?" Ever asked, and Isa held her breath.

"Forgive me for uttering their words, Your Highnesses... but they are saying that you have failed them one time too many." Eloy's voice fell to a whisper. "They wish to make her queen."

17

TIES OF BLOOD

One day, Isa thought ruefully as she donned her bow and quiver, she would get a full night's sleep again. But this was not that night. For as soon as the mention of an uprising had fallen from the soldier's lips, Isa knew they were leaving. And though her exhaustion was great, she didn't dare mention it to Ever. Mentioning a weakness of any kind would only send him into a worried tizzy that would land her in bed. If she was lucky, he might let her out again in another decade.

So instead of complaining, she allowed the servant to help her mount her horse. She would sleep again, she told herself.

Eventually.

"Tell Henri that I will teach him to read his new book when we return," Isa said to Garin as the steward adjusted one of her saddlebags. "And please ask Gigi to tell Genny a story every night before she tucks them in."

"I think that by the time you return," Garin said with a sly smile, "Gigi will have spoiled them so rotten they care for nothing but sweets."

Isa had to smile at this, for she knew it was true. Despite Henri's incident, Isa knew that Gigi would spare no expense in making sure the children were cared for and happy.

"Let us go," Ever announced. The horde of servants that had come to help them prepare stood back as their king, queen, and five handpicked soldiers set out into the blackness of the early morning.

Isa tried unsuccessfully to quell the fluttering in her stomach as they began to make their way down the mountain road. If there was truly an uprising, there would most likely be blood shed at some point. And though no one could equal the strength or ability of her husband, Isa knew his reluctance to take up arms against any of his citizens. For all his hard exterior, Ever loved his people. And just as it had nearly killed him when the evil enchanter had tried to take the Fortress three years before, Isa worried that his compassion might lead to his injury now, or even worse.

She must not think of these things, Isa admonished herself. They had a three-day ride ahead of them. Ever did not wish to spend his strength on speed but rather wanted to save it in case there was a confrontation. Instead of worrying the entire time, Isa decided to focus on what she wanted to say to Ever about the children. What she *needed* to say to Ever about the children. They had been on the cusp of such a conversation before Eloy had interrupted them, and whether Isa wanted to or not, they would need to finish their discussion sometime. They might as well get it done sooner rather than later.

Her chance did not come that first night, however, for they rode straight through the rest of the night and then on through the following day, stopping only to rest their horses. Isa slept each time they paused, managing to get an hour of sleep here and there, but it was never enough. On the second evening when they finally did stop for the entire night, Isa fell asleep before supper was cooked. It was only on the third night that she finally got the chance to speak with Ever. The rest she had taken the night before had strengthened her some, and she felt as though she might burst if she did not speak to Ever soon.

Her prayers were answered when Ever took the first watch. Isa waited on her sleeping roll until she could hear the steady breathing of the three men who were not on duty, and Ever had walked far enough away that whispers wouldn't wake them. She wrapped her blanket around her shoulders and slipped out of the camp to stand beside him as he studied the moonlit landscape before them.

"I've never much liked these open valleys," he said softly without looking at her. "They make me feel vulnerable. I would much rather travel along those bluffs in the distance." He nodded at the tall shadows along the horizon. "But they're too far out of the way for where we are going."

Not sure what to say to that, Isa simply waited for her courage to catch up to the moment, her breaths coming too fast and making her feel almost dizzy. But this was her chance.

"Ever, I've been thinking," she began, suddenly unable to look at his face. "When this is all over," she gestured back at the camp, "with the children, I mean..." Despite her nearly incoherent words, she could sense him stiffen in the dark, and his heart began to seal itself up again.

"Before you fall in love with them," he said, his voice kind but firm, "have you considered the repercussions of such an action?"

"Giving two orphans a home?" Isa's voice was suddenly too loud and one of the men stirred. "Yes, I have considered that. I've concluded that taking them in permanently would mean we would have two fewer children in the streets!"

"Isa, I know you want a child. And I understand—"

"No, Everard! You do not understand!"

"Then please enlighten me!" He finally turned toward her.

"You want an heir! Someone who will follow the rules and take the kingdom and do exactly as he's told. But I want a child... children! Soft, warm children who make mistakes and make messes and say the wrong things at the wrong times. I want to hold a girl in my arms and whisper that all will be well when she cries, and to straighten her braids and have the tailor make her a dress that twirls when she spins! I want a son who is honest to the point of offending an odious supper guest because he is only saying what everyone else is thinking." Isa leaned forward. "I want us to be *needed*, Ever, and those children need someone to love and hold them, to undo all the hurt their parents inflicted upon them."

"I am sure they have family somewhere," Ever said, his voice growing stiffer. "Your parents have a wide range of influence in Soudain. Surely they would know someone who could take them."

"Henri has power. Genny might very well, too," Isa said. "Other homes wouldn't be prepared for such children. Genny told me that their stepmother didn't like Henri's fire. That might very well be why they were abandoned!"

"But you haven't considered the long-term effects!" The fire in Ever's eyes leapt wildly. "Suppose we do keep them! What happens if we die without an heir? Who do you think the people will crown?"

"Does it make a difference?" Isa's voice was as cold as Ever's. "You know that those children were sired by someone in the Fortier line, and we *both* know who that was!"

"Don't," Ever growled, but Isa ignored him.

"Those children are your blood! Your sister and brother! They deserve love from you before they deserve it from anyone else!"

"You think I don't know that?" Ever took a step closer, his voice dark. "You think I haven't considered that in all the weeks they've spent with us? Every time I look at that boy, I see myself! But they are also Fae, Isa." He stopped and took a deep breath. When he spoke again, his voice was resigned as he reached up to pinch the bridge of his nose. "I cannot afford to consider the fates of only a few. Once we are gone, Destin will lie in the hands of the crown prince. I can see that there is Fortier blood within them, but I do not know how strong the Fae blood runs either. I cannot be blind to what they are, whether I want to see it or not. I cannot be blind to the truth of their origins. You, of all people, should understand that."

He turned and began to walk away, but Isa followed him, ignoring the jabbing weight of his words.

"You are so blind that love could hit you on the nose and you'd never be the wiser!" She turned and stomped back to her sleeping roll as tears blurred her vision. Unfortunately, though, as soon as her head was quiet enough to think, she was struck with the truth of his claims that she had suppressed during their argument. What he had said about the children had verity. But her argument did as well. The children were Fortier *and* Fae, and though Isa could see the truth in their need, she could not see the future. If their natures were eventually to war within them, she could not confidently say which side would win.

For the first time since she had realized her power, the truths within Isa seemed to collide, and she could make no sense of them. Every time she shut her eyes, the world began to spin.

SOMETHING FAMILIAR

*T*he next morning, Ever's mouth was still set in a tight line, and Isa was feeling no less frustrated. But as much as she wished to continue their argument, doing so now would only be detrimental to their mission. They had come to gather knowledge about a possible enemy and nothing else. Ever then planned to return immediately and consult with Acelet and Garin before making any far-reaching decisions.

Thankfully, it was cool enough for everyone to wear their cloaks without seeming out of place. Before entering the village, Isa and Ever donned their hoods. People from the smaller outlying villages generally stayed put, rarely visiting Soudain or the Fortress. This gave Ever and Isa the advantage of more anonymity, but it was still best to take precautions. Being recognized would jeopardize their entire mission.

Before leaving the Fortress, Isa had asked Ever if he couldn't use his power to disguise their faces.

"I've heard there are some with the ability to make things appear as they are not, and I do not mean the way the Fae do it," he'd said, "but that particular gift is not in my range of skill."

So now, as they made their way to the little village of Sansim that bordered the woods, Isa did her best to push all thoughts of the argument out of her head and focus on blending in. That would be more difficult, however, as long as they were riding their horses. In most of the outlying villages, few individuals could afford to keep a horse. As their little party made its way through Sansim, Isa realized theirs were the only horses in sight. And it made her more than uncomfortable.

Ever, however, looked completely unruffled, as usual. The only sign Isa could find of his restlessness was in the way the blue flames in his eyes continued to jump and turn in short, agitated bursts.

The mysterious woman would not be healing until that afternoon, according to his men, but Ever had announced that morning that he wished to hide the horses before most of the people were milling about to see them. Without the royal crest on the soldiers' breastplates or Ever's ceremonial armor, they would be given only as much respect as their weapons could buy them. Isa had even removed her blue crystal ring for the event, something she had only done a handful of times since Ever had placed it on her finger.

The ride to the church seemed to take much longer than it should have for such a small town, but the streets were hardly straight, and they began to fill more quickly than Isa had expected. Rickety carts and stubborn mules moved at painfully slow paces, and many children seemed to prefer watching the goings-on from the middle of the street rather than the side. The roads here were naught but mud and the houses were hovels pieced together with sticks, mud, and straw.

The early risers who were out now in the pearlescent pink light carried axes, baskets, flax, and bundles of firewood. They watched the company of seven ride past with open resentment in their eyes. Isa shivered. By the time they finally reached the church, even Ever was flexing his jaw regularly, making his face seem even more angular and immovable than usual.

Degare, the eldest of their guards, dismounted and went to knock on the church door. As they waited for the holy man's answer, Isa studied the church itself. It seemed to be the only building in the town that was made of stone rather than mud and sticks, and the entire building could have fit within her own personal chambers at home. Three small square windows were carved into the church's right side. They did not have real glass panes, as most buildings in Soudain had, but instead were covered with thick animal skins stretched at an angle to keep the rain out.

Finally, the door was opened and the priest appeared. He must have been at least fifty years of age, probably more, his head completely devoid of hair. Bags hugged his eyes. His round face, however, wasn't unpleasant as he spoke to Degare. Isa couldn't hear what was being said, but Degare scratched his red beard thoughtfully as he considered whatever it was that the priest said. Eventually, he glanced up at Ever then Isa before turning back to the priest and nodding once.

"We'll go around the back," Degare said as he rejoined them, taking his horse's reins and leading them toward the left side of the church between the building and the edge of the wood. "He says it would have been best if we'd come sooner before anyone was awake, but he will do his best to keep the horses safe for us until nightfall."

As they rounded the corner, Isa felt very doubtful that the horses would be well hidden at all. A little covering stood upon four poles that stuck out of the ground, its roof made of the same straw thatch that covered most of the cottages around them. All she could do was thank the Maker that the church was at the edge of town. Perhaps there would not be so many people passing by who might see the seven great horses resting beneath the small shelter. If their horses were stolen, king and queen or not, it would be a very long walk to the next place they could purchase replacements.

The priest appeared at the church's back door and quickly motioned for them to follow him inside. Isa wondered at the urgency in his face, for Degare had been instructed not to mention their true identities to anyone. Did this priest guess at their purpose in being there? Or was he simply concerned for the group that was very obviously not from anywhere nearby?

They entered the church quickly in single file, as the door was too narrow for anything else. The small chamber they found themselves in was apparently not part of the church's main chamber, the one with the leather-covered windows. Instead, it was a windowless room with a small fireplace and just enough space for a few pieces of rough furniture. A small cot was pushed into a corner, and a little wooden chest beside it had clothing spilling out. Was this hovel where the man of the Maker lived?

"Your Highnesses!" The holy man quickly closed the door and turned around, the light from the flames dancing across his face. "It is not safe for you here!"

Isa didn't miss the rebuking look that Ever sent to Degare, but the priest only shook his head. "I've been to the capital. I know who you are. Now, pray tell, why are Your Highnesses here? I told your spies only last week that this region is full of traitorous whispers and schemes!"

"And for that, we are indebted to you," Isa said quickly, hoping to soothe the man's anxiety.

"We have come to see this woman for ourselves," Ever said, his face dark even in the light of the hearty fire. "She is dabbling in a magic blacker than I have seen before."

"Oh, she does more than dabble!" The priest squeezed through the group to lift a stack of parchments from a crooked little table in the corner. They were covered with ink scribbles, though Isa couldn't make out the words from where she stood. The holy man handed one to Ever, who squinted at the paper as he tried to read it.

"I have lived in this region since I was accepted to the church, and I have been making notes of the goings-on in these woods since I began." He looked at Isa, his round face scrunched into a troubled frown. "Dark arts are not so uncommon here, more common than even you would know, Your Highness, if I may say so." He nodded at Ever. "But in the last nine years, I have begun to see an inexplicable rise in the evil that sometimes pervades these woods. At first, the disturbances were only small, as if someone was testing himself, learning the tricks of wickedness and practicing them as one might practice smithing or sewing."

"Why was I not notified?" Ever frowned as he reached for another paper. "Father..."

"Oh, Lucien, Your Highness. And please forgive my boldness, but though it is a good deed done when you expel this or that bit of darkness as you always do, there are a dozen more for every one that is cast out. You would never have time to do anything else if you chased after every single one." The man looked at Isa desperately, as if hoping she would understand better than her husband. "But it stopped, you see, about five years ago. Then it began again last year."

He turned back to the table and pulled out a map that Isa guessed he had made himself. The drawings seemed to depict the region Sansim was in, encompassing the town as well as the southern woods to the east, direct south, and west of the church. The details were more intricate than any map of the southern forests Isa had ever seen at the Fortress.

"Last year, children began to disappear from our village, as well as the three or four nearest by," the priest said, pointing as he spoke. "Then they would be returned only a few days later. It frightened the parents at first, especially when the children returned speaking nonsense about mystical places and houses made of sweets. But when the children always returned no worse for wear, people eventually stopped worrying." The priest glanced up at Isa. "Again, my apologies, Your Majesty, but the people around here haven't much trust for the crown. I urged them to go to you, but they wanted to fend for themselves."

"That's why no children were reported missing from the southernmost villages," one of the guards murmured.

The priest nodded. "It happened often enough that the people began to talk of spirits in the forest who took the children to drink of their youth before sending them home again. Utter rubbish, of course." The holy man shook his head. "But that there was an evil at work, I had no doubt. Still, that was nothing compared to the sicknesses and injuries that began to shake the people a few months ago."

"Sicknesses?" Isa asked.

"Yes, my queen. People began to experience all sorts of strange maladies, but no matter how many healers saw them, they could not be healed. I, myself, went to pray for them often. Soon they began to despair, though, and brought in the dabblers of the Sorthileige to attempt their charms and incantations." The priest shuddered so hard his faded blue robe shook. "Of course, that in itself brewed a new pot of problems, but to say the least, nothing worked."

"Tell me," Ever said, his voice suddenly lifting the way it always did when he was excited. "No one died from these ailments, did they?"

There was a long pause. "No, Your Highness," the priest said slowly. "They are all still alive. They were even cured... all of them, about two months ago."

"What do you know of this woman?" Isa asked, suddenly fighting the urge to track down the woman then and there.

"Little," the priest said. "I went to see her for myself when she first appeared last week, and when she emerged from her tree, I knew immediately that darkness came from within her. I confronted her, but she mocked me in front of the people, and I was nearly driven out of the town."

Isa closed her eyes briefly and pressed her hand to her belly. The ache caused by the curse had left long ago. Still, her middle hurt from time to time, and her womanly cycle had never returned. Whatever force it was that had stolen her chance at natural motherhood could not be allowed to continue roaming like this. She wouldn't allow it. Though she had never killed another human with her own hands, nor had she any desire to do so, Isa felt a sudden fire flame within her. She would do whatever she must to remove this monster from the people.

The priest's sigh broke through her thoughts. "I know this village is not much to look at. Its people are rough, and they often lack in decorum." He lifted his shoulders in a helpless shrug. "But I love them. They are not all as you have seen. Many are simply trying to survive."

"We are indebted to you," Ever's voice rumbled as he finally looked up from the stack of papers that he had been reading. "You have done the Fortress and the kingdom a great service." The priest began to utter protests, but Ever held up a gloved hand. "When we are done with this debacle, I will return and you will accompany me to the Fortress. We will see what we can do to help your village and others like it."

"I would love nothing more, Your Highness." The priest's shrill voice quivered as he spoke. "But first, you must survive the day." He ran to the hearth and stooped at its edge, gathering ashes in his hands. "You are far too clean to look like you belong here." With that, he ran between each of his guests and began to smear the ashes upon their hair and faces. Isa didn't particularly relish the idea of being covered in ashes until they reached the Fortress again, but she didn't argue as he dirtied her face.

"Now," he brushed his hands off over the hearth and placed his fists on his hips, "after you finish watching her this afternoon, I would like you all to return here. It is the safest place you will find in this town." He gave a sardonic chuckle. "It is also the only place you will find to stay. Since word spread of the woman's healing, families have been flocking here from all over with their sick children. She emerges from her cursed tomb of a tree and heals at the third hour every day, but for one hour only. Then she returns and everyone waits until the next afternoon."

The way he ordered the royal party around made Isa smile. Few men or women were bold enough to tell the king and queen what to do. But Isa liked it. This man truly cared for their welfare and for the welfare of his little village. She would like to know him better if she ever got the time.

They spent the remainder of the morning and the early afternoon in the priest's cramped quarters. Isa found his stories and knowledge fascinating, and she discovered that he had been born in a part of Soudain not far from where her parents lived. Soon, however, the priest reluctantly told them that if they wished to get close enough to the woman to see her, they would need to leave and find a place in the crowd, despite it being only the first hour of the afternoon.

As they donned their hoods to leave, Isa was reminded of a comment Henri had made once about going to the church in his little village.

"Father." She turned back to the little man. "When we came to these woods and found the children in the Fae land, there were two without a home to return to. The boy, Henri, is nine years of age, and he once lived nearby, in the forest, I believe. He has mentioned several times that he used to come to the church and talk with the priest." She was suddenly praying that this man might be able to shed light on Henri and Genny's shadowy past. "He has a little sister named Genevieve."

A sad smile came to the priest's face. "Ah, yes. Young Henri and Genny."

Ever gave her a look of impatience as he ducked out the door, but Isa tarried just a moment longer. She needed to hear what this man had to say about her peculiar little charges.

"Henri is a special boy. He sees things differently from other children. He also has unusual... talents." The priest frowned slightly before giving her a more reassuring smile. "But I never found a child so desperate to belong. I am glad to know they have found a safe place where they can finally rest."

"Take these." Isa pressed two gold coins into his hand. "Buy glass panes for the church. No one should have to pray in the cold." She gripped his hand briefly, squeezing the coins so the man couldn't return them. Then, as she followed her husband and their men, she tried to steel herself for whatever revelations lay ahead.

As they found the crowd and moved toward the center, the guards began to separate, each one taking a particular position in the crowd where they would all have a different vantage point to watch and listen.

While Isa now partook in most of Ever's defense schemes and even made some of her own, military strategy was one area that held little appeal for her. So she simply allowed her husband to do as he wished, and she did as she was told. For this plan, she was to stand near Ever with her hood drawn, an arrow nocked and held low where the people pressing in around them wouldn't see it. Ever and the guards had more close-range weapons at hand, swords and knives ready and waiting. Isa prayed they wouldn't have to use them in a crowd so dense and so full of sick children. Families were already beginning to shove to the front.

Just as Isa was about to whisper to Ever that the number of people present had far surpassed her expectations, the crowd roared. Isa was tall, but even she had to stand on her toes and crane her neck to see what the cheers were about. She could only just make out a large tree near the edge of the clearing that was beginning to shimmer. Isa was reminded of her time in the strange world of the Fae and the way the surroundings constantly changed. And though she had somewhat expected it, Isa was still somewhat surprised when the woman that she had known as Sacha stepped forward and smiled sweetly at the people, holding out her arms and dropping a little curtsy.

"That's her," Isa whispered to Ever. "Sacha is the one who helped us escape."

Only now she wasn't wearing the simple purple gown that she'd worn in the Fae world. This dress was made of rich yellow tones and had much fuller skirts. Her ears, neck, wrists, and fingers dripped with jewels. She had also chopped off most of her hair so that it only reached the edge of her jaw. With her hair down and near her eyes, the woman suddenly looked very much like Genny. One glance at Ever and Isa knew he was thinking the same thing.

"Dear ones," Sacha clasped her hands in front of her and bowed her head once more, "I am honored to see that so many have come today. Since you are great in number and I can only heal for one hour, I will try to see each one of your loved ones as quickly as possible. Now." She held out her hand to a small girl in the front, one Isa immediately recognized as one of the children from Soudain. The one with the missing voice.

Green mist began to envelop the woman's hands. Gently, she tilted the girl's head back with one hand, and with the other she grasped at the girl's neck. The green continued to swirl until the woman let go of the girl's head.

"Now sing for them," she commanded. The little girl looked back at her parents, who nodded cautiously. Then she turned to the crowd and opened her mouth. Immediately, a lovely little melody danced on the air, inviting hushed tones of awe from the people and a feeling of icy dread from Isa.

"My lady!" a familiar voice called out. Isa quickly spotted the skinny, red-haired woman from Soudain, the one who had rebuked Ever in front of the tent. "Why is it," Agnes asked in her shrill voice, "that you can heal our children while the king cannot?"

"Ah yes," Sacha said, nodding her head. "I am asked that question often. But the time had not yet come to answer... until now."

Suddenly, Isa felt a fierce hatred emanating from Sacha. Before, she had been secretive and hidden, pushing Isa's abilities to their limits to read some sort of emotion in her. But now Sacha hid nothing in either her heart or her eyes.

"It was not time because my little brother was not present to hear what I have to say. But now he is here, so I can tell all of you." Sacha turned and looked directly at Ever. "Isn't that right, little brother?"

REMINDERS

*H*enri skidded to a stop when he saw the Fortress steward leaning intently over a book, a new candle upon his writing desk. Perhaps this was not the morning to visit the Fortress library after all. Despite his inability to read, Henri loved the books with their beautiful leather spines and their spidery words on each page. Miss Isa had told him that she'd added the room herself after she'd married, for she thought all Fortress inhabitants should have access to books. But looking at books was not worth another run-in with the steward.

Before Henri could fully retreat, however, Garin called his name. Henri looked up at the distant ceiling, just as he had often seen Miss Isa do. "I thought you liked me!" he whispered to the Fortress.

"Henri."

"Coming."

Slowly, Henri trudged back to the steward, staring at the ground as he waited to hear what new rule he had broken. Once he was standing before the steward, however, Garin was simply quiet. In fact, he was quiet for so long that Henri's curiosity finally got the best of him, and he sneaked a peek up at the older man.

The steward did not look young nor did he look old. Rather, his age seemed to change depending on whatever he was doing at that moment. There were deep lines at the corners of his eyes, and strands of silver glinted against the long, straight black hair that was tied neatly behind the man's neck with a leather thong. Henri had rarely seen the steward's thin face in anything but a scowl, particularly when the topic of conversation had to do with him and his sister. But today he was surprised to find only a thoughtful look on Garin's face as Garin tilted his head and rested his chin on his thumb and index fingers.

"You seem to have quite an attachment to these books." He glanced up at the three stories of shelves that vaulted up around them. "This is your third visit this week. Had you ever seen a book before coming to the Fortress?"

Henri swallowed hard before answering. "Yes, Master Garin."

"Where?"

Henri hesitated. Few people had ever known about his excursions to see the holy man in the Sansim, and he had tried hard to keep it that way. His father wouldn't have approved. "I would visit with our priest," he finally said, keeping his voice as low as he could make it. Perhaps Garin would become tired of hearing his quiet words and let him go.

But instead, the steward only leaned forward. "And what would you do while you were there?"

Henri shrugged. "Sometimes I swept the church floor. Sometimes he showed me the Holy Writ." Would the steward be angry that he had seen something so sacred? Would Father Lucien be punished?

"Why did you go to the church? Was it the one your parents attended?"

"My father and Helaine did not attend the church."

"Then how did you come to find it?"

Henri balked. This was a part of the story he did not wish the steward to know. Who knew if he would bring it up later to Miss Isa or King Ever? And yet, when the steward raised his eyebrows, Henri knew he had no choice. "There wasn't much food in the house. Genny kept crying because she was hungry, so I..." He paused, studying his foot. "I might have borrowed an apple from Father Lucien's storehouse."

"An apple?"

"And maybe some bread and cheese." Henri looked up at Garin, wishing desperately that the questions would end soon. "I meant to pay it back! But—"

But Garin held out his hands. "No need to go into all of that. I understand."

He did? Henri studied the steward's face again, searching for a sign of anger or disappointment. But to his surprise, there was none, only a slight frown. And for once, it wasn't directed at him, but rather, the floor.

"Surely your mother—"

"She was *not* my mother," Henri snapped. "My father only married Helaine because he didn't know what to do with Genny." He crossed his arms, suddenly not caring whether or not he was being impertinent. "Not that she ever took care of her."

"What do you remember of your real mother?" The steward's voice was surprisingly gentle.

Henri paused. What did he remember? "Not much," he finally admitted after a moment of thought. "She didn't hate my trick the way Helaine always did. Father said she was killed in a hunting accident nearby." He shrugged. "That's all I remember."

It was a long time before either of them spoke. Garin's eyes were distant, focused on someplace behind Henri, though Henri didn't know what. The silence was so long, in fact, that Henri began itching to move. He hated standing too still. It was temping to roll a bit of flame across his fingers, but he didn't dare do so in front of the steward.

Just when standing still was becoming nearly impossible, Garin's eyes softened as they refocused on the boy. "You remind me very much of a small boy I knew once." He placed a hand on Henri's shoulder, then knelt to look Henri in the eye. "I fear I must ask your forgiveness in misjudging you and your sister. I believe... I can only guess that you know little of the Fae?"

Henri shook his head, and Garin nodded.

"Let it suffice to say that our mutual relatives are not a people you should ever wish to meet. It is not your fault that their blood flows in your veins any more than it is my fault that I suffer the same fate. But the day will come, I fear, when you will be made to choose one side over the other."

"How do you know that?" Henri didn't like that idea in the slightest. How could he be forced to choose between things he didn't understand?

"I don't. It is only a feeling I have. But if one day you are told to choose either the side of King Everard and Queen Isabelle or the side of the Fae, remember the goodness the Maker has shown you in bringing you and Genny here. And if you understand nothing else, know that a strength lies in your blood that is of the Fortress, and thus, of the Maker. You may be young, Henri, but that strength is not dormant. It was given to you for a purpose."

With that, the steward began to stand and gather his belongings from the desk.

"Wait," Henri said. A question inside had been nagging him for weeks. He might as well ask it now while the steward was, for once, not angry with him. "When the king and Miss—Queen Isa return, what do you think they will do with us?" As soon as the question had left his lips, he immediately regretted asking. He didn't know if he could really handle a dismissal now, not when they'd come so far.

Surprisingly, however, a small smile lifted the steward's thin lips. "I do not know for sure, but the king and queen have very pressing matters to attend to currently, and will, it seems, for some time. I wouldn't go worrying about your place anytime soon. Now," he turned and began to walk toward the door, "would you and your sister like something to eat? I believe I smell blueberry tarts."

Never one to turn down food, Henri trailed after Garin, and for the first time, he didn't feel afraid.

AT WHAT COST

*Y*ears of practice kept Ever's face as unflinching as always on the outside. But inside, he felt as though he had just shattered into a million pieces. Though he had known deep in his heart that his father must have been unfaithful, Henri and Genny's ignorance about their own past had allowed him to at least pretend another explanation existed. But now, in front of hundreds of his subjects and even his own wife and guards, this woman was proof that Rodrigue had broken his word to the Fortress, to Queen Louise, and to his people. To his son.

Though Ever had always favored his father in appearance, looking at Sacha was too much like looking in a mirror. Her gray eyes, the shape of her neck, and the strong shoulders, though most definitely feminine, were all too familiar.

"So the tear between worlds," Isa called out, her voice much stronger than Ever's would have been at that moment, "was only a ruse."

"A test," the woman said, looking at Isa as though her presence was just a minor annoyance. "I was testing my brother to see if the great Fortress our father always spoke about was really with him. But when he failed to find the tear and you did instead, I realized that I had been right all along." She turned and raised her voice to the people, addressing them now instead of Isa or Ever. "Perhaps the Fortress has tired of these men that forever go on playing their games of war and self-righteousness!" Her low voice rang clear in the perfect silence of the crowd as everyone looked back and forth between their king and his sister. "And," she fixed her eyes back on Ever, "when you failed, Brother, I knew that it was the Maker declaring a new era. It's my turn now."

"You blaspheme the king!"

In one smooth motion, Degare had thrown back his cloak and drawn his sword. People stumbled over one another as they pushed out to give him space, trying to get away from the weapon.

"Degare," Ever called softly. Degare was one of his favorite guards and loyal to a fault. His temper, however, matched the color of his flaming beard, and if Ever wasn't careful, the man would take on the entire crowd to honor Ever's name.

Before Degare could take the hint, however, two dozen other members of the crowd raised their own hidden weapons, long skinny pikes with a bundle of thick green leaves tied together and hanging just behind the sharp pike heads. Hemlock, Ever realized, to poison the victim after breaking the flesh. By plunging the pike even deeper into the wound, the hemlock leaves would be dragged into the body behind the sharp head. They were crude weapons, but their damage could certainly be deadly. Ever guessed that there were more enemies hanging in mist form nearby.

Despite his men's skill in battle, Ever knew that there were far too many Fae for any sort of fair fight. Besides, the citizens that surrounded them would surely get in the way and be killed themselves.

"Admit it, Everard," the woman called out to him. "Four years ago, you brought a curse upon your great Fortress, and now, it seems, you have brought a blight upon these people as well. You are too much like our father."

"You think I did this?"

"I've been watching you, and the evidence is too great to ignore. Look around at the proof. Could you heal the Fortress four years ago? Answer me honestly."

"The Maker had to heal the Fortress. That was the point," Ever said, "to prove that I was not able to do so on my own..." Ever's words trailed off as he realized that he was digging himself into an even deeper hole. Arguing was not kingly, and by the sudden look of horror on Isa's face, Ever knew that true or not, his words had just spelled out his judgment in the eyes of the people.

"And if the Fortress is so intent on keeping your line upon the throne, why is it that your wife," she gestured to Isa, "has not yet conceived a child?"

Ever's mouth was suddenly bitter. Who was this woman to think she could insult his wife? To his surprise, however, even his anger was eclipsed by that which he felt coming from Isa. So great was her anger, it seemed, that he could feel her power for once instead of the other way around. And yet, Isa was not simply angry. He could feel her familiar power working on the woman's heart, trying hard to impress the truth of the Fortress's love upon her. But some hearts were stiffer and more hidden than others, and for all of Isa's glares and hard work, Ever's sister only smiled.

Whispers broke out around the crowd. But as the three continued to stare one another down, the whispers began to lose their whisper quality, and even without Isa's gift, Ever could feel the frustration rise within the air.

This had been a terrible plan.

Just as the first Fae soldier began to step forward, shimmering slightly as he went, and Ever drew his own sword in response, a blur of gray robes darted between them.

"Please!" Father Lucien held up his hands, gasping between words. "I know you are all confused, but please do not turn our home into a village of blood!" He turned in agitation from side to side in short, jerky movements. "Certainly there must be a more legal, civilized way to go about deciding this!"

To Ever's surprise, his sister spoke up, her voice suddenly gentle. "You are right, Lucien. There must be another way to bring these people what is rightfully theirs without fighting around their children." She turned to the Fae, her golden hair bouncing as she began to step backward in the direction of the tree from which she had first appeared. "We are done here today. I will heal again tomorrow."

The people began to groan, but she held her hands up. "There are children here. Do you wish violence upon them?"

Before Ever had time to hear their responses, the priest lurched at Isa and grabbed her hand, before fairly dragging her back toward the town with him. Immediately, Isa disappeared. She wouldn't be able to hold her invisibility for long, though. It was a skill she still struggled with. Ever used his power to project his own invisibility onto the holy man, something he had only tried once or twice before. The invisibility wasn't perfect, but it did the job of mostly hiding the priest as they raced toward the church.

As they rounded the back of the church building, Ever could hear footsteps in the distance behind them. Despite his sister's words of peace, the people hadn't listened, it seemed. They wouldn't have long to hide. Without a word, Father Lucien, Isa, Ever, and their men darted into the priest's hovel. There was no light inside this time, not even a fire. They did their best to crouch in the corners, but Ever knew it wouldn't do them much good if the door was broken in.

"We will have to fight," Olivier, their knife master, murmured.

"No." Isa's voice was quiet but commanding. "There are too many children."

"If we die," Degare pointed out, "then all of the children of Destin will be at risk from that witch!"

Ever felt a soft hand work its way into his. "I can do this, Ever." Her voice was quiet but resolved.

"It's too dangerous." He knew he wasn't fooling anyone, though. Even Ever knew this was a losing battle. Too many innocents would die if fighting ensued.

"This is my gift," she said in the same soothing voice. "Trust the Fortress. Pray for me, and let me talk to them."

Ever squeezed her hand so hard that it must have hurt. But she was using her gift on him even now, and as much as he abhorred it, Isa was right, as usual. She was their only chance of escaping without the shedding of blood.

"This will draw more strength from you than you have ever expended," he said in a voice that shook far too much. "You've been pushing yourself too hard."

He was interrupted by more shouts outside the door, but Isa simply squeezed his hand again, and in the dark, leaned forward to kiss him on the cheek.

"I love you."

With that, her hand was pulled from his, and he could hear her rise and walk to the door. Immediately, he made himself invisible and went to stand just beside her. She might be their only hope for peace, but he was not about to allow his wife to face the crowd alone.

Isa opened the door, the light of the fading sun touching her hair and making its copper strands shine almost blindingly. The crowd that stood just outside the door was mostly void of children, but there were still enough present to make a fight difficult.

Fortress, he prayed as he lifted his weapon, *give her strength.*

"Where is the king?" someone called out. Ever suddenly felt like a louse for hiding beside her. He nearly revealed himself, except for the slight flick of Isa's hand that reminded him to leave her be.

"Does it matter?" she asked evenly, her dark blue eyes searching each of the faces before her. "For you have seemed to forget that the throne was rightfully mine before it was King Everard's."

"And a fine job you've done then, as well," another man sneered, his bushy black hair streaked with mud and oil. Ever itched to teach the man a lesson for speaking so rudely to his wife, but another slight wave of Isa's hand kept him at bay.

"I understand your frustration," she said quietly, and the calm of her voice seemed to quiet the crowd somewhat. "You are worried for your little girl. Cyrille, was it? I remember her." Isa smiled in that gentle way of hers. "She has pretty green eyes." How did she recall these details? Ever could hardly remember what he had eaten for supper the night before.

"Yes," the man said in a more subdued tone, his eyes moving to his boots. "That's 'er."

Ever could feel Isa beginning to work the crowd. She had never tried to influence so many people at once. Even now, he could see the tiny bead of sweat that was forming on her temple. How much longer could she last?

Please, Fortress! he begged. *Just a bit more!*

"I can see in your face that you love your daughter, that you would do anything for her," Isa continued.

"That's what I'm doin' now!"

"Then would you want her to see you tear a person limb from limb, as you have been contemplating doing to me?"

The man froze, his eyes wide and full of terror.

But Isa didn't stop. "Would you be proud to tell her what kind of deed you had committed?"

For all of the mob's jeering and shouting just a few minutes before, the crowd had grown nearly silent and still in the quickly falling light of dusk. All the while, Isa maintained her calm and steady gaze. Only Ever could see her wrist as it trembled with the effort she must be expending. She couldn't have much strength left.

"No." The man finally swallowed and bowed his head. Without another word, he turned and began to walk away. Slowly, one by one, the rest of the crowd followed his example. Men and women dropped sticks, axes, and whatever makeshift weapons they had managed to grab on their way to the church. Finally, the last woman left, and Isa turned to them, a slight smile on her face.

"We will be safe tonight. But Ever?"

"Yes?"

"Catch me."

21

SHORT WORDS AND DIRE PLANS

*T*hough she never lost consciousness completely, Ever could feel Isa's utter exhaustion when her knees buckled and he caught her in his arms. He wanted nothing more than to let her sleep the night away in the church. Father Lucien advised leaving Sansim as quickly as possible, however, so Ever was forced to place her before him in his saddle so she wouldn't fall off her own horse. It would put a strain on his mount, but they would be at the Cobrien border by the next day. Surely she would be stronger by then.

The group was quiet that evening and then the next day as they rode. Ever was grateful for their silence. They had been by his side long enough to know his ways and when he did and did not wish to speak. Still, he could feel their curiosity and pity in the sidelong looks they cast him. But he didn't want pity. He wanted a solution.

"We're approaching a stream up ahead, sire," Leroy called from the group's point. "Do you wish to stop there and rest the horses?"

"That sounds wise. Is there shade?"

"Yes, sire. A grove of trees lies a little way to the north. We'll be mostly hidden."

They turned their horses off the rough road, and within minutes, Ever spotted the trees peeking up from a ravine. It would be the perfect place to examine Isa again, shielded from the heat of the late morning sun.

As they rode, Ever scolded himself once more for his negligence. Isa had not only worked tirelessly alongside him for the last month as they'd visited the sick children in Soudain, and searched every scroll and book in the Tower of Annals, but she had also continued to manage many of the Fortress's comings and goings that had nothing to do with their current problems. And as if she hadn't been busy enough, she'd spent every spare second with Henri and Genny. Last night had been the breaking point. Never had she tried to work so many minds at once, and now she was paying for it.

Ever wanted to kick himself.

When they had all moved down into the little ravine, Ever gently handed his wife down to Degare before jumping off the horse himself. Then, taking her back, he carried her to the edge of the stream and knelt so that he could fill his waterskin while holding her in his lap. As he poured a little stream of water into her mouth, Isa's eyes opened, and a deep sigh of relief escaped him. She hadn't looked so awake in hours.

"Why hello there." He put the waterskin down and propped her up a little higher, drinking in the alertness of her beautiful blue eyes like a man dying of thirst. "How are you feeling?"

"Better." She squinted and blinked a few times before pushing herself into a sitting position. Ever let her but kept his arm behind her back in case she collapsed again. "How long was I asleep? Where are we?"

"I don't know if you remember, but we left Sansim last night. You've been sleeping on and off since. We'll reach your brother at the border in just a few hours."

"Launce? Oh, right." She rubbed her eyes. "Why are we seeing him again?"

Ever spoke slowly, hoping his words wouldn't startle her into a true fainting spell. "I need to plan with him for the possibility that we'll need to relocate our troops. I sent a message the night that we left. I supposed you wouldn't mind?" Actually, he had worried very much that she would mind, particularly after her initial reaction to Launce's last little "revelation" at the party.

But Isa only gave him a tired smile. "I will be glad to see him." She looked around. "Do we have anything to eat?"

Ever leaned her against the bank then leapt up to dig a hunk of dried beef, bread, and a few pieces of fruit out of his pack. It was good to see her eat. She did so almost ravenously, as though she'd skipped two days of food rather than only two meals. Perhaps her strength would return sooner than he'd first thought.

"Can you walk?" he asked.

She smiled and nodded, and he helped her to her feet, keeping her hand tucked into his as they walked a bit away from the men. After riding through the night, their men deserved some sleep.

"Leroy, keep watch for a few minutes," Ever called over his shoulder. "I will take it when I'm done."

"You need sleep too," Isa said softly, but Ever only shook his head. Even if he had the time for it, his mind wouldn't allow him to rest now.

When they had walked around a little bend in the stream and were hidden from the sight of their men, Ever eased Isa down onto a large flat rock then sat beside her. "Isa," he started, "I must ask forgiveness for my poor judgment last night. I wasn't thinking clearly. If you hadn't been there to stop them..." Ever shuddered.

"You might be a gifted king," Isa said quietly, leaning her head on his shoulder, "but you are still human. Learning a secret of that magnitude would have shocked anyone."

"I have to wonder, though," Ever said slowly, staring into the stream as it bubbled up continuously around a boulder, "if perhaps she is right. I *was* the one who cursed the—"

"Everard!" Isa's voice and eyes were suddenly fierce as she grabbed his face with both hands and turned to face him. "You know that her words were lies, and I never want to hear you utter such blatant nonsense again! Do you understand me? Your father's infidelity says nothing about you, nor does it make you an unfit king." She loosened her grip, and her face relaxed slightly, but she didn't let go. "The Fortress loves you, and it has proven that time and again. I do not know why the Fortress has not allowed you to chase this evil from Destin's borders. But somehow we will. Together." The blue fire in her eyes blazed wildly, and the thin set of her lips told Ever that his wife was deadly serious. And as she held him there, he could feel her using her gift on him with all she had. All he could do was nod.

Before she began to tremble too hard with the effort, Ever gently removed her hands from his face and held them in his lap. "I believe you," he promised her. "No need to collapse on me again. Your brother might have my head if he finds you in such a state."

For an immeasurable time, they sat there together staring at the brook and its shallow sandy shores as she leaned heavily against his shoulder. For how long they sat, Ever didn't really know. "Leroy," he finally called out. "I'll take watch. You get some rest."

But there was no response. A nasty feeling settled in Ever's gut. Isa stared up at him, concern etched on her face. After another second of brittle silence, Ever grabbed Isa and pushed her back against the ravine then wedged himself beside her. When they were both flat against the bank, he prepared to peer out from behind the bend. Before he could, however, a change in the water caught his eye. Where the stream had run crystal clear moments before, a thick red now flowed down.

Glancing back at his wife, Ever swallowed hard. Usually he could count on Isa's sword just as well as he might Acelet's. Isa had spent many long hours training to ensure that. But the ghostlike color of her face worried him. She couldn't fight today. "Stay here," he mouthed at her, praying that for once, she would listen.

Finally, he leaned around the corner. Leroy was lying half in the water and half out, a long pike sticking out of his gut. To Ever's shock and relief, however, the other men were still only sleeping. It was as if there had been no fight, not even a scuffle. The only sign that Leroy had even tried to fight back was that he had drawn his weapon. Unfortunately, it looked as though he'd never had the chance to even use it.

A movement caught Ever's eye. Though the young man looked to be asleep,

606 | BRITTANY FICHTER

Eloy was gripping his sword so hard that his brown knuckles were turning white. But where was the enemy?

A cloud of something humid and warm flashed across Ever's face and yanked him forward. Ever found himself on the ground beside Eloy, his head dangling out over the stream and his sword hand pinned to the ground. In the blink of an eye, the mist had shifted from its cloud form into a man. And that man was trying very hard to push his head under the water.

With his other hand, Ever grabbed the Fae by the neck. With a yank, he had it off his chest and on the ground. Just as his sword should have bitten the creature's flesh, however, it was gone, the green mist rising instead. The mist darted up near his face, then brushed behind him. Ever tried to flip but was too late, and his sword was too slow to block the man's shove to his back. He fell forward, clipping the side of his face on a boulder.

Eloy leapt up with a cry, only to be knocked back down by another quick appearance of their attacker. Not wanting the boy to get himself killed, Ever tried to stand. But as he did, his vision doubled. Sensing a presence to his right, he rolled over to face his attacker head on, but it was impossible to tell which was the true opponent, for there were suddenly two identical Fae that raised pikes above him. Just as the pikes began to make their way down, a flash of silver knocked the pike out of the attacker's hands. As the world came back into focus, Ever realized that the only reason he hadn't been run through was the head of copper hair that had distracted his opponent.

Whether fueled by the Fortress or his anger, Ever didn't know, but immediately his vision was restored, and he leapt up in a rage, blue flame building dangerously in each of his fists. Just as the thin man raised his pike against Isa, he turned back to see Ever, and his slitted eyes went blank. Isa didn't hesitate, knocking the pike away, thin blue flame exploding from her hands. Then Ever's sword was in his heart.

Where their enemy should have slumped onto the sandy bank of the stream, however, he only dissolved into a heap of ash.

"Their lips!" Isa cried, drawing his attention back to his men. They rushed to the three guards lying limply on the ground. Eloy was able to sit, but his face looked unwell, too. Isa's eyes widened as she took in Leroy, but Ever was proud of her as she gritted her teeth and focused back on the men that still breathed.

"Hemlock poisoning," Ever said as he lifted Degare's head. "They've not been stabbed, but it's been rubbed all over them. Hold him in your lap for me. I will have to heal him, but it will hurt, and he'll thrash."

Isa nodded stiffly, and Ever was grateful that she didn't give voice to the fears that swirled inside of him. Would he be able to heal them? So many times, he'd failed... No. He couldn't afford to think that way now.

Please, he prayed to the Fortress, *let me help them!* The skin was already beginning to bubble around the man's mouth. If Ever didn't act soon, his throat might swell shut and the man would surely die. With Ever's heart in his stomach, he gently took hold of Degare's pale face, resting his fingers above the mouth and below the chin. After taking a deep breath, Ever exhaled. And then they waited.

The seconds turned to years, it seemed, before the man began to thrash just as Ever had predicted. But Isa held on tight, and to Ever's joy, Degare's eyes opened, and his flaming red skin began to recede.

"To Olivier!" Ever told her. By the time the noontime sun was directly overhead, all of their men had been healed.

All except for Leroy. It pained Ever that they could only do a short battlefield service in honor of his friend. Leroy had saved his life on more than one occasion in battle, and in the few times he'd been willing to share his opinion it had always been worth its weight in gold. Their small party watched solemnly as his friend's ashes were gathered and placed in a small bottle for the man's poor wife. *Let him know*, Ever asked the Maker, *that he shall be missed, and that I look forward to seeing him again when my night comes.*

"Why would only one Fae follow us?" Jori Blanc, the group's navigator, asked when they were back on their horses and a respectful distance from the ceremonial pyre. "Any why not kill us all?"

"It was a warning," Ever said as he glared at the road ahead of him. "She means to let us know that we are being watched."

"She can watch all she wants."

The ferocity in Isa's voice took Ever by surprise and he turned to look at her. With her copper hair swept back into a tight braid and her leather riding trousers sticking out from beneath her slitted skirt, his wife was a fierce sight to behold. But even more intimidating than her combat attire, or even the sword and bow she wore, were her eyes. Isa's eyes flamed in agitation as they fixed themselves upon Jori with dangerous care, like a panther ready to strike.

"Because if it is Destin that she desires, then she will have to pry it from my stiff, lifeless hands."

22

TAKING CARE

"What is she doing here?" Ever growled.

"They aren't aware of the gravity of the situation," Isa murmured, ever the peacemaker. Despite her gentle words, however, her stress was evident in the taut muscles of her face.

Ever grunted in response as they approached the border. White canvas tents were stretched out along the river that ran between the two kingdoms. Servants walked between them carrying food and other supplies.

"Does he think we're here for a festival?" Ever muttered, to which Isa shot him a frown. "It looks like a bloody carnival." The message he'd sent Launce had been short. *Meet me at the northern border near the crooked river. Bring men.* He hadn't expected Cobren's new prince to bring half of the royal court. Or his pregnant wife, for that matter. "Stay with her," Ever said to Isa. Guilt gnawed at him. "Keep within sight of my tent. I hate asking you to protect her, but—"

"Ever," she said gently, a tired smile on her pretty face, "I didn't spend all those hours on the practice floor getting bruised up for nothing."

Ever nodded, but it didn't make him feel any better. The Fae had killed one of his men and nearly him as well. Only between the two of them had the monster died. And yet, he didn't want Olivia to hear what he was about to tell her husband. A pregnant woman didn't need that kind of stress, and Isa was the best protection he could think to offer her. But that didn't mean he had to like it.

"Everard." Launce strode forward to greet him as they crossed the river over a thin stone bridge. Before they could grasp hands, however, Isa ran up and threw her arms around her brother. As he tried to hug her in return, she pulled back and gave him her fiercest glare and then punched him in the arm. Ever smothered a smile. Her punches hurt. He had seen to that.

"*That* is for not telling me you were expecting," Isa said. "Now where can I find her?"

"She's in that tent," Launce said, rubbing his arm. With an indignant flip of her hair, Isa turned and marched off.

"You really shouldn't have your wife here at all," Ever said as Launce turned back to him, still massaging his arm.

"She felt badly about making Isa uncomfortable last time we met. She wanted to apologize and make things right."

"Is there a place we can talk?"

"Yes. Behind me." Launce turned and led Ever into the smallest tent. "Out," he ordered the men that were gathered to talk inside.

As he watched the young man take control of the room, Ever had to admit that he had indeed grown since taking his place as prince of Cobren. When Ever had first met Launce, he'd been a skinny, angry young man with a hatred for much of the world. He'd hated Everard in particular. But his most redeeming quality had been his care for his sister. Before Ever had loved her, Launce had been there watching over Isa to the best of his limited abilities.

"I will put this as simply as I can," Ever said when the room was clear. "Before I was born, and then again after, my father opened an ancient barrier and had an affair with a woman of the Fae people."

"The Fae?" Launce's mouth fell open, but Ever held up his hand.

"Let me finish. There are two children back at the Fortress that Isa found among the missing that were lured into the Fae realm. They are, it would seem, my younger brother and sister, part Fae and part Fortier. My older sister, however..." Ever took a deep breath. No matter how many times he remembered the events from the day before, they still seemed surreal.

"My older sister has decided that it is her duty to claim the crown for herself using her own personal army of Fae to do so. On our way to meet with you, we were attacked by a Fae who killed one of my most trusted personal guards. That is why this is no place for your expecting wife."

Launce stared at him for a long moment before finally giving his head the slightest shake. "I... I'll send her home immediately." Then his eyes grew large, and he ran to the tent's opening and began to look around wildly. "Where is she?" he asked as if Ever had been keeping track.

Perhaps the young man had not grown up quite as much as Ever had first thought.

"Isa is with her," Ever said, wishing very much instead to let Launce wallow in his fear for a moment. It would be a good lesson to him, but Isa wouldn't approve of such a sentiment. "The reason I called you here was to make a plan."

"Did you know someone was after your throne?"

"Not for sure," Ever shook his head, "until she revealed it to me yesterday. But I had a hunch that someone was planning an invasion. The veil between the two worlds could never have torn by itself. When Isa discovered the Fae realm where the children were being taken, and my younger sister and brother showed up, I knew something was wrong." He paused and looked at one of the maps spread out on the table. It depicted the Fortress's mountain as well as the desert mountains and valleys directly to its north and the thick forests to its south.

"What do you want from me, Everard? Ask and it will be done."

"I do not yet know how to defeat the Fae."

Launce's eyes widened, but he said nothing.

"I will talk to Garin when we return. Hopefully he knows something."

"But why would Garin—?"

"A long story for another day. But if we are attacked before I can correctly train my men, I will need a place for the army to go until I've learned to fight the Fae properly. And when I do, I will call my men back with this." Ever took off his signet ring and placed it on the table. Launce picked it up and examined it.

"I may be the prince of Cobren now," Launce said in a soft voice, "but this wolf will always be in my heart." He handed the ring back to Ever. As Ever slipped it back onto his finger, the jewel-eyed wolf stared back at him with the same piercing look Rodrigue had given him often in his boyhood. At least the wolf had always been faithful.

"What I need is a place for my men to camp on your side of the border, just at the foot of the mountain. At a fast pace, it would take them only a day to make it up the back side of the mountain and to the Fortress."

"And what of the people?" Launce gave him a wary look, and Ever knew he was thinking of his parents and sister.

"Sacha is using the people to gain her the throne, manipulating them through a magic I do not understand nor am I familiar with. They are her path to the crown. She won't jeopardize their trust, for it is their good graces she is relying on." Ever shook his head. "They would be in more danger if I sent my men to find her. The war would be fought in the streets." He fingered the hilt of his sword idly. "I'll have to draw her out like poison."

"Consider it done," Launce said, still frowning down at the map. "I'll wait for them here with a number of our men as well. I assume you'll send a bird?"

"I will send whatever messenger is at hand," Ever said, his mouth suddenly feeling dry as he considered such a dire situation. "For if we are that far gone, I will consider it a blessing to find a drunkard in need of coin."

The two men stood there quietly. Would it really come to such things? Ever wondered. As if reading his thoughts, Launce gave him a weak smile and clapped him on the shoulder. "Let us pray we never find such a day, and that you will defeat her quickly." He glanced outside. "I assume you will be leaving soon?"

"We'll head out in the morning. Isa has been pushing her powers further than she should. She needs a good night's rest before we set out again."

"Let her go back with Olivia!"

The sudden fervor in Launce's voice took Ever by surprise.

"She can protect Olivia," Launce continued, "and they will both be safer with Olivia's father. Besides, if something should happen to me, someone should be there when..." his voice trailed off, and Ever's heart went out to the young man. He was willing to sacrifice his life for Ever's cause. Ever briefly imagined Isa bringing a child into the world without him, and it twisted his heart.

"As you said," Ever sighed, "we shall pray that nothing comes to fruition. Besides," his voice softened, "I need her. She has been gifted by the Maker in ways I will never even hope to understand."

"Surely you could spare her somehow."

"You know as well as I do that she would never go, even if I tried to force her."

Launce studied him for a moment. "Much has changed in the last three years." Then he looked down at his own golden ring, the one his father-in-law had given him on his wedding day, the promise of Cobren's crown. "Though I still don't agree with everything you do," Launce threw Ever a wry grin, "I must admit that I now better understand your decisions far more than I once did. And I thank you for being patient and trying to teach me. Just..." Launce hesitated, "you know I trust you, but as a younger brother..." He cast a look of longing outside again before looking Ever in the eye. "Please take care of my sister."

~

"Oh... Oh dear!" Olivia's face went so white that Isa nearly ran to fetch Ever, but Olivia just shook her head and lowered herself onto a large boulder. "I'm fine. I just need a moment to think." She looked out over the water, rubbing her belly as she did. Isa felt a stab of guilt over having to tell her sister-in-law about their newfound danger in such a disorganized fashion. If she hadn't, though, Olivia would have continued to insist that they take a long walk by the river. Isa didn't want her to take a walk at all, but at least Olivia had stopped now just at the edge of the camp. Isa kept her hand on the hilt of her sword, but all seemed peaceful for the moment. If only it could stay that way.

"How are you both doing?" Isa forced a smile and nodded pointedly at Olivia's burgeoning belly.

"Huh?" Olivia looked up. "Oh, thank you. The sickness has abated, it seems, but now I can never get enough to eat." She looked down at her belly and grinned. "The little thing is always hungry, and if I don't eat enough, likes to kick me in the ribs. My nurse says this is good, though, since it means the child is strong." She sighed and placed her hands behind her, leaning back and closing her eyes as the sunlight washed over them. "But sometimes, what I wouldn't give to be a tad less round." She laughed then, her warm brown eyes opening to meet Isa's. "There are days when I fear I will always be this large. And I still have a long way to go!"

"You look beautiful," Isa assured her. And truly, she was. Olivia's fine olive skin had always glowed as though she'd rubbed a sunbeam all over her skin. But now her eyes were alight with excitement whenever she talked of her baby, and though she had filled out quite a bit, it wasn't unbecoming. The loose yellow and orange wool dress that Olivia wore flowed over her soft curves, giving her the look of an ancient queen. Many of the old queens had once worn dresses like Olivia's, according to the paintings in the Tower of Annals. As much as Olivia might be tired of her new size, it made Isa happy, for it meant her niece or nephew would be healthy and strong.

"Isa."

Isa squirmed under Olivia's gaze. She'd thought she'd been concealing her feelings decently, but the concern in Olivia's warm eyes told her otherwise. "Are you well?"

"To be honest..." Isa hesitated. It was not considered queenly to share one's entire burden, for the weights of the monarchs were theirs alone to bear. Or so her etiquette instructor had told her. But Olivia was also a royal. And more importantly, she was Isa's sister now. "I know Ever is only being practical. He always is." Isa stared into the river as it flashed by, wishing she could toss her burdens into it and watch them be carried away. "We had an argument a few nights back about the children I told you about, Henri and Genny."

"Let me guess, you want to keep them."

"They're his blood!" Isa turned to face Olivia again. "Henri's already shown the Fortress's power. Who better to care for them than us? Besides," she pouted, "I want them."

"And you're sure they're his younger brother and sister?"

Isa shrugged. "They're not Ever's children. I know that for sure. But whenever I try to discuss their future with us, he's too worried about tainting the bloodline with Fae blood, particularly now that we've seen what his older sister has become."

"Does he say as much?"

"Some yes, and some no. But I can see it in his eyes. Our division is to the point where he has become wary every time I've spoken with him since we left the Fortress."

"Does she know about them?" Olivia shifted on the rock, frowning thoughtfully.

"I don't know. She saw them when they came to the Fae world with all of the other children. She even put me in their holding chamber. But she treated them no differently than the other children. Except..." She turned to Olivia, her heart suddenly racing. "All of the other children who were kidnapped were cursed with an injury or illness after they returned! I thought at first that Henri and Genny weren't cursed because they were orphans. But... she never even spoke with them! She *couldn't* have known they were orphans!" How had Isa not seen this?

"Isa," Olivia said in a grave voice, "I have no gifts as you do, nor am I familiar with the ways of your enemy, but it would seem to me that she knows exactly who those children are."

"I must tell Ever!" Isa took one stride forward, but Olivia managed to grab her wrist and pull her back.

"Before you go, I need you to hear two things," she said.

Isa stared down at Olivia's serious face, wondering what on earth she could mean.

"Rodrigue Fortier and my father were close enough that I have known Everard all of my life. I know he can be gruff and stubborn. Even as a young man, he was never good at having fun. His father didn't allow him to. But never in his life did he do anything out of spite. If he says he is concerned about taking these children in permanently, then he is genuinely worried. Your husband is a good man. Don't forget that."

Isa took a deep breath as she stared into her sister's sweet face, and a part of her couldn't help but soften. Olivia was right. That didn't mean that she agreed with Ever by any stretch. But as Olivia had pointed out, his intentions were always honorable. Isa couldn't deny him that. He was simply afraid.

If only Isa understood what moved through the minds of men to make them think as they did.

"What was the second thing you wished to say?" Isa asked softly, to which Olivia gave an ornery grin.

"I only wished to say that if you are intent on dashing off to talk to your husband this instant, I would be much obliged if you could first put me to rights and on my feet. For if I try to get off this rock by myself, I will end up in the water."

Isa laughed as she bent to help her sister stand. For all Launce's faults, he had chosen a wonderful wife.

23

THE WEIGHT OF SIN

"*A*celet's not going to like this," Isa said as they neared the Fortress gates.

"Let me handle him." Ever clucked to his tired horse.

Isa's smile grew mischievous. "Oh, I plan to. I have two children to visit with. The monotonous business is yours today."

Ever laughed, but inwardly, he allowed himself a deep sigh of relief. His conversation with Launce had only served to reawaken his worries about Isa's health. Launce was right to be concerned. They were traveling far too much and she was getting far too little sleep. Their run-in with the village mob had only made things worse. And though Isa was far healthier and fit than his own mother had ever been, Ever suddenly recalled the way Queen Louise's face had been pale and drawn in the final days before her death. He couldn't allow the same thing to happen to Isa. Visiting the children wouldn't allow any sort of real rest, but at least it meant she wouldn't be gallivanting about the Fortress grounds on official business.

The rest of the afternoon passed in a blur. As soon as Ever had given his horse to a groom, he changed clothes and immediately called General Acelet to his study. Isa's prediction about Acelet proved true. The general was not pleased with Ever's emergency defense plan, to say the least. But Ever wasn't in the mood to argue, and in the end, he won simply because he was the king. He didn't find such victories satisfying, as he much preferred to be in agreement with his general. But Ever had a more pressing conversation on his mind, one he'd been dreading since meeting his sister back in the forest. For there was only one person in the world who could shed light on such a situation. And Ever had been avoiding him as much as possible since the arrival of their two little guests.

True to his nature, however, Garin didn't even need to be summoned. As soon as Acelet walked out of the king's study and closed the door, Ever could hear the two men's muted voices outside. He caught something about "beyond trusting" and "not enough time" from Acelet, but as he responded to Acelet's agitation, Garin's voice was indecipherable in its usual maddening calm. Finally the door opened, and Ever could see Acelet shaking his head and stomping away as Garin glided in.

"He seems less than enthusiastic about your plan." Garin placed a tray of tea and biscuits on Ever's desk. "I must say, I understand his frustration." His eyes darkened a shade. "While I don't think your foe is yet ready to take the Fortress, I doubt we'll have the time to properly train the men before she is."

Ever ignored the tea and instead stood and went out to the northern balcony. "So I take it you've heard then, that she is my sister?"

"I had guessed as much."

Ever turned and gave his steward an icy stare, but Garin just shrugged.

"Word has been spreading that the Fae woman is a Fortier. I didn't want to jump to conclusions without talking to you, but I had my suspicions."

"You mean you suspected it even before I met her."

Garin looked at the ground. When he spoke, his voice was soft. "Don't be mistaken in thinking that I enjoy being right, Ever. This was one prediction that I was loathe to make." He looked back up at Ever. "Five hundred years is a long time to study man and his tendencies." Garin went back to the tray and poured himself a cup. "Nevertheless, the people are beginning to believe her now as the word spreads throughout the kingdom. Enough for a number of factions to have started forming."

"Factions?"

"Many in the streets are calling for her coronation. It's not a majority by any means, but the number is far greater than any rebellion I've seen."

In five hundred years this was the greatest? Ever swallowed hard. "But she created the sicknesses! I'm sure of it! Even Isa..." Ever's voice trailed off as he remembered that they weren't only blaming him for the sickness, but also his inability to wipe it out. Suddenly he needed to sit. "What do I do, Garin?" he groaned as he fell into one of the deep red leather chairs.

"Do you really want my advice?" Garin's words were annoyingly patient.

"What choice do I have?"

"How much time do you believe we have before she makes her move for the Fortress?"

Ever shook his head helplessly and shrugged. "I don't know. A week at least? Maybe two?"

"Then this is my advice." Garin placed a firm hand on Ever's arm and leaned over so that Ever had to meet his eyes. "Your people need you now more than ever. The best way to convince them that she is not their savior is by showing them that you still care. Heal them." Ever tried to protest, but Garin only held his hand up, then continued. "Heal the everyday maladies and illnesses as you usually do. Hear their needs. Attend the Seasons Ball. The guests will be arriving in a week. Don't worry about the army, for I will work with them myself. And Ever?"

Ever glared up at him, his head spinning with all of the reasons not to follow Garin's advice.

"Take care of Isa."

This last piece of advice took Ever off guard. His shoulders slumped, and he knew he couldn't argue with such logic.

A long silence ensued, interrupted only by the crackling of the fire. The biscuits smelled intoxicating, as Ever hadn't eaten for hours, but he couldn't bring himself to bridge the gap and get them from his desk.

"I was Fae on the night you were born, Ever." Garin's voice was almost too quiet to hear. "And I was Fae on the day I met your wife when she was a little girl. Has such a revelation altered everything I've done for you in the past?"

Of course it didn't. But, as Isa was fond of saying, truth often felt much like a surgeon's blade. Ever stared out at the Fortress's mountain through the balcony's open doors, still unable to look at the man who stood before him. Finally, Garin stood to go, and Ever's gaze didn't waver.

"You know where to find me," Garin called out, a raw undertone in his voice that Ever hadn't heard before. Just as the door clicked open, however, Ever turned.

"Wait."

Garin stopped and looked at him expectantly.

"How... How were the children?"

The ghost of a strange smile touched Garin's eyes. "You would be surprised at how much young Henri is like you."

"Actually, I wouldn't. Considering that he is none other than my brother." The anger that had been building within him warred with his morbid curiosity. Suddenly, the need to know burned so heavily in Ever's stomach that he stood and walked to Garin without hesitating as he had done for the last five weeks. The time for petulance was over.

"How did this happen?" he asked, choking as he spoke. "After all the lectures about duty and self-denial and selflessness, how could he treat my mother and me like this?" Rodrigue and Louise had never been close in the slightest, but it still irked Ever that his father could have been so unfaithful. "And the Fortiers always sire boys first," he bellowed on. "Why was she a girl?" It didn't matter, of course, but Ever was tired of mysteries and riddles.

"Walk with me," Garin said, holding the door open. Ever complied, and soon they were walking in the direction of the tower.

"As to why Sacha is a woman," Garin said, seemingly unfazed by Ever's childish temper tantrum, "that is easy. Whatever Fae woman birthed Sacha was not the crowned Fortress queen. Therefore, the Fortress traditions did not apply to her. As to your father, I've been thinking about that." He pulled out a key and unlocked the heavy door that led into the tower. After their run-in with the glass prince three years before, the door had been completely remade and now was three times heavier than before, thanks to its triple iron casings.

"Your father would take off on personal missions of sorts," Garin continued as he locked the door behind them. "I recall one such mission about two years before he was married to your mother. A bear touched by the Sorthileige was rumored to be running about the southern forest, and your father went to deal with it. He was gone an exceptionally long time, though, for the kind of errand it should have been, two weeks at least. When questioned upon his return by your grandfather, he simply said he had discovered more pockets of the dark power and had worked to rid the countryside of them. As this was in line with his character and dedication, we didn't think twice. After that he continued to claim that he was receiving messages from other individuals dealing with the darkness in the same vicinity, and he continued to return there, even after he was married and you were born."

"He was gone so much," Ever said as he began to thumb through a book, only to slam it shut in frustration. "I never questioned his intentions on such campaigns. His constant absence from Mother and from me was only duty, he said." And Ever had believed him, never considering that his father was absent because he might be finding familial fulfillment elsewhere. Ever had been an idiot.

"Your father loved you," Garin said in a gentle voice. "He was often at a loss as to how to show it, but for all of his pains, look at what you have become."

"An arrogant fool who knows how to shed blood better than he knows his own people," Ever said, the words tasting sour as he spoke them.

"A strong, vigilant leader," Garin corrected him, placing a hand on Ever's shoulder. This time Ever didn't shake it off. "Yes, you have sinned. But do not forget the first lesson you learned from the Fortress. Because it is one that many of your forefathers never learned. The Fortress loves you and uses you in spite of your shortcomings, even through them! Just look at the wife you were given, despite your doing everything in your power to push her away at first. You have been willing to learn and grow, and you have been forgiven. You are not the same man you were four years ago, Ever, nor will you be the same man you are now in another four years."

"Perhaps," Ever stared at the ground, "that is why I am not yet a father. The Fortress knows how I could still ruin the life of a child."

"Now whatever would make you say such a thing?" The shock in Garin's voice made Ever look up.

"My father, despite his best intentions, ruined so much in me. And look what he did or didn't do for this... sister of mine. He was with me often enough that he couldn't have given much time to her. Maybe the Fortress knows I'm enough like my father that I would do the same."

"Nonsense."

But Ever shook his head. "You said yourself that Henri is much like me. Such waywardness would devastate him. What if I do to him what my father did to me?" Ever could just imagine himself pushing the boy to his limits, forcing him into a role that allowed him no choices.

"What happens if no one loves him?" Garin asked, fixing two steely eyes upon Ever. "You maintained pieces of your natural self because I was here, and because of Gigi and the servants, and sometimes even your father. Because of the Fortress. Now, imagine yourself as a boy and ask yourself what ultimate rejection would have done to you."

Ever held Garin's gaze unhappily. He didn't want to even contemplate that outcome. It would have been disastrous for the entire kingdom.

"Because," Garin continued, folding his arms defiantly, "that is exactly what is happening to that boy right now. I can see it in his eyes. He's desperate to find a place for himself and his sister. And if he cannot find it through natural means, he will look in places that no child or adult should even consider."

Ever stood still for a long time. Part of him, the part that often sounded a lot like Isa, knew what he should do. The other part, which sounded more like his father, much to Ever's disgust, was very, very afraid.

"Isa has been asking," he began slowly, "about what we plan to do with the children." He took a deep breath. "What do you know of Blood Sealing?"

Garin frowned but didn't seem completely taken by surprise. "That is a serious matter indeed. I am not surprised Isa wishes to know, but how do *you* feel about such an undertaking?"

"They have no one." Ever shrugged. "The girl seems harmless enough right now, but the boy needs someone to teach him how to use his power correctly before he accidentally obliterates an entire village. And Genny has become Isa's shadow..." He looked at his feet, suddenly frightened of what he might see in his mentor's eyes. That the children were part Fae still concerned him, and he fully expected Garin to capitalize on such a glaring risk.

Instead, however, Garin simply said, "Follow me," and turned. Curious, Ever followed him to the northern side of the tower. Garin knelt beside an ancient chest that sat against the window wall, and then opened the lock with a large, rusty key Ever did not recognize. Ever wondered how he had never noticed this particular chest before. It was so old that the blue paint had all but peeled off completely. With a creak and a good deal of encouragement, the lid finally came up and Garin reached inside. Ever peeked over his shoulder to see a few dozen scrolls on yellowed, cracking paper inside. What on earth could those contain?

"Here it is." Garin's voice was muffled from inside the trunk as he rummaged around. Finally, he stood and pulled out a scroll that had been rolled and tied carefully with a ribbon. The ribbon was so thin that its crimson color was all but gone. Reverently, Garin took the scroll back out to the large wooden table and slowly unrolled it. It took Ever a moment to make out the faint markings on the page.

"This is in the old language!"

Garin nodded. "This oath is as old as the Fortress itself."

"Has it ever been used?" Ever leaned closer and squinted to make out some of the smaller words.

"No. There has never been a Fortier to go childless. Even when the first son was killed, there was always a younger brother or sister to take his place."

Until now, Ever thought unhappily.

"I will not try to persuade you one way or another," Garin said. "This decision is for you and Isa alone. But," he leaned forward, "should the two of you complete the covenant, the oath will be binding. The children will be your own flesh and blood in the eyes of the Fortress and the Maker. There is no going back."

"Thank you, Garin." Ever took the scroll and carefully rolled it up once again. Despite his love for his steward, he needed someplace where he could be alone. He needed to speak with the Fortress.

As Ever began the long walk down the stairs, he shook his head. It was all too confusing. *I need guidance!* He stopped and leaned against the wall. *I want to do what is right. But my fear is crippling me.* Ever sat on the step, placing his head in his hands. *Tell me what to do!*

"Your Majesty"

Ever's prayers were interrupted by a panicked shout that echoed up the tower, and with it, the prickling sensation that something was wrong. "What is it?" He stood as the breathless chambermaid paused just steps below him.

"A demon has come... in Master Henri and Miss Genny's rooms!" She doubled over as though she might faint. "Queen Isabelle is holding it off, but—"

Ever didn't hear the rest of the woman's words, for he was already halfway down the tower steps.

24

DECISIONS

*E*ver burst into the children's chambers. When he stopped he should have been between the hearth and the two large canopied beds, but instead, Ever found himself in a swamp. Stinking gas bubbles rose and popped at the surface of a rancid pond, and chirps, grunts, and all sorts of other sounds assaulted his ears. Only the sounds of the children's screams drew him forward.

Only then did Ever remember what Garin had said about the Fae creating illusions. Isa, too, had said the candy house was only an illusion for the children. Was this how the Fae had killed Leroy so easily, blinding him first? Ever inched forward. "Isa!"

"We're here!" Isa called back, much to his relief. The Fae must not have been strong enough to block their senses completely. "We're by the window!"

"I can't see you. You'll have to keep talking!" He needed to follow the sound of her voice through the mist that surrounded him. But as he was looking for Isa and the children, where was the Fae? Were there more than one? "What happened?"

"It was hiding under the bed when I arrived," Isa called back. Her voice was strong, but Ever could detect a tremble. "I was able to graze its arm with my sword, but nothing else."

"Where is it now?" Knowing the creature was there in the room with them somewhere, Ever felt like his skin was crawling. He still only felt the oppressive wet air of the swamp upon his skin and saw strange ripples in the stagnant water as he walked upon the moss-covered log that spanned the frightening, gray depths.

"I think it's in the hearth."

"Henri, Genny," Ever said, praying the children would listen, "grab onto Miss Isa's skirts. Isa, hold out your hand. I'm going to pull you back toward the door.

Then, Isa, I want you to find Garin, and keep the children with him until I kill this miscreant."

"Miscreant?" A thin voice warbled.

Ever froze, his left hand outstretched toward Isa. The voice had come from his right.

A hazy figure stepped out from behind one of the swamp trees, and two slitted green eyes glowed at him. "You are hasty to judge a creature you've never met, Your Majesty."

Ever's title was said like a curse word, and Ever gripped his sword more tightly as he stepped away from Isa and the children and toward the creature. "I *see* that you are in my home, uninvited. Hiding in the children's room is hardly a way to get in my good graces. Now that you have my attention, would you like to tell me why you're here?"

It didn't answer, though. In a second, the swamp was gone, and the room was blacker than any darkness Ever had experienced before.

"It's got me, Henri! It's got me!"

The little girl's shrieks awakened a new kind of anger in Ever. A ball of flame appeared upon his left fist. In the light of the blue flame, he could see Isa with her sword held out protectively before Henri, who clung to her skirts. But Genny was gone.

"Ever!" Isa shrieked, her eyes wide. Following her eyes, Ever turned to his right to see green mist materialize into the thin form once again. Its new form was more like a human than the reptilian creature that had appeared only moments before. But the slitted eyes were still too far apart, and its mouth was far too wide. And it was staring at his flame as though in a trance, even as it held Genny pinned to its side.

Henri let out a shout, then, and Ever kept his fire lit as he turned to see a second creature holding one of Henri's legs, trying to loosen the boy's grip on Isa's skirts. This creature was suddenly staring at his fire, though, too.

Isa met Ever's eyes and gave the slightest nod before yanking Henri back and pinning the creature to the ground with her sword. Ever whirled and threw all of his weight against the first Fae. It dropped Genny's arm as Ever slammed into it. The fire disappeared from his hand, but a few sparks fell into the hearth, and the tinder within it began to catch, giving light to the room. With a shout, Ever thrust his sword through where the Fae's chest should have been.

But before his blade could draw a single drop of blood, the creature dissipated into the green whorl of light drops, which swung around and wrapped themselves around Ever's throat. Invisible fingers began to materialize, crushing his airway.

"Isa!" Ever rasped. "Go!"

With the flame gone from Ever's hand, the creature that Isa had pinned looked back up at her and dissolved. Isa didn't wait for the Fae to materialize again. She darted past Ever and his foe and grabbed Genny by the arm, but just as she threw the door open, Henri let go of her hand and took a step back toward Ever. As Ever fought for air, he tried to motion to the boy to go and leave him be, but a determined look came into Henri's eyes.

"No," Ever tried to yell, but he was too late. Henri held up a hand, and immediately, a little blue flame appeared inside his palm. The Fae stopped squeezing Ever's throat. Instead of watching the little blaze as it had done with Ever's ball of flame, however, the Fae disappeared and then shimmered into being right in front of Henri. It reached out and grabbed his hand that held the flame, and with its other hand, it grabbed Henri's throat. But before it could squeeze, Ever threw himself upon the creature, blade down. And this time, his sword hit its mark.

A sharp cry rang out behind Ever. He turned to see the second Fae, horror in its eyes as it stared down at its dead brother. Ever sprang at the living Fae and grabbed it by its scrawny neck before it could escape. This time, he kept his flame burning as he pinned it to the ground. And no matter how it squirmed and fought him, it couldn't quite tear its focus from the flames that leapt from Ever's hand.

"Why are you here?" Ever growled as he pressed the Fae hard into the rug. But the Fae only spat on him. Ever lowered his hand until the flames began to singe the edge of the creature's human-like hair. It screamed, and Ever pushed down with even more force. "Why have you come?" he bellowed.

"It matters not," the Fae hissed as it glared up at the flame with its slitted eyes. Its form shimmered, but it managed to stay solid. "She is coming, and she will avenge us." It flicked a trembling finger at the dead Fae, which was now a pile of ash. "You think you have the right to—"

"I have the right to protect the children within my home. And I will rid that home of vermin like you and your brother." He squeezed the Fae's neck once more, bringing his flaming fist just inches from its face. "Now, when will she be here?"

"She already is." With those words, the creature tried to kick Ever in the stomach, but Ever was faster, plunging his sword into its heart.

The dark mist disappeared, allowing the light of day through the windows once again. As the light returned, Ever could see that the body at his feet was indeed human in shape, but only just. Lines that should have appeared around the eyes, mouth, palms, and fingers were nonexistent. The skin had no variations or spots of any kind but was one continuous color. Seconds later, it, too, dissolved into ash.

"These must have been young." Garin's voice came from behind Ever. "They weren't very good at imitating other forms yet."

Ever wiped the sweat from his eyes. "Thank you for keeping the door."

"I would have interfered, but you appeared to have it quite well under control."

Ever nodded. "Unfortunately, it seems you won't have time to work with the men after all." He finally tore his gaze from the pile of ash and met Garin's eyes. "She's here."

Garin's eyes began to fill with something that, if Ever hadn't known better, looked very akin to hate. "Shall I tell Acelet to take his leave then?"

Ever took a deep breath. "I'm only beginning to understand how to defeat them," he said softly. "The men wouldn't stand a chance right now."

As Garin nodded and headed off, Genny began to cry.

"Get her calmed down," Ever told Isa. "When they're better, give them to Gigi. I... I need to speak with you."

Isa looked at him curiously before picking the little girl up in one arm and taking Henri's shoulder in the other. As soon as she was gone, Ever looked down once more at the pile of ash beneath his feet and shuddered. He had a decision to make and much less time than he had expected to make it.

"Wait," he called out, catching them in the hall. They stopped as Ever knelt before Henri. "Do you like it here?" he asked, knowing that he must look like the biggest fool in the world to the child. After weeks of stomping around the Fortress and muttering about the children's antics, would Henri trust him enough to answer honestly?

Henri studied him for a long time, his blue eyes wary in his thin face.

The more Ever looked at the boy, the more he saw himself. From the golden hair to the angle of his chin, the boy was his spitting image. But Ever had spent so long trying to push him away that he suddenly wondered if he was too late.

"Why?" Henri finally asked.

"I fear..." Ever took a deep breath. Admitting his errors had never been one of his strengths. "I fear I have not been entirely fair to you. You are of the Fae and the Fortress because the Maker created you so, and I allowed my fears to blind me to that. For that, I am sorry. But now, I wish to know what you think of this place. If," Ever swallowed hard, "you could ever think of it as home."

"When I lived with my father and stepmother," Henri spoke slowly, "I never felt like I belonged. The cottage was there, and my family was there. I only cared about Genny, though. But here," he took a deep breath and looked at his feet. "I don't know how to say it..." He shook his messy golden hair, a look of frustration on his face. "Here I feel like there's someone watching out for me. For both of us. Like when those things came." He nodded at the bedroom. "Genny's been saying there was a monster beneath her bed for four days. But it didn't come out until—" He stopped and looked up in wonder. "Until you and Miss Isa were back to protect us."

Ever felt his heart stop. The Fortress had answered his prayers, even as he had uttered them on the tower steps less than an hour before.

"Meet me in the Tower," he said to Isa. "There is something urgent we must do."

25

SEALING WORDS

"Forgive me for taking so long," Isa said as she shut the tower's heavy door, her copper hair falling prettily out of place. When she turned, her eyes were wet with tears. "Genny was still upset, and it was nearly impossible to get them to go down the mountain without—" She stopped when she saw Ever and Garin standing at the heavy wooden table. Garin stood by the fire and Ever stood across from him. Between them on the table were laid two parchments. One was the ancient scroll that Garin had removed from the chest earlier that afternoon. The other was a new parchment, which had been written out by Garin himself upon Ever's request.

"What is this?" she asked breathlessly, looking back and forth between the parchments and the men standing before her. Finally, her gaze came to rest on Ever. Ever went to her, feeling suddenly as nervous as he had the moment he'd asked her to marry him. There were dark bags under her eyes, the same ones Ever wore constantly now, too. But in that moment, the flush of her cheeks and the slight parting of her lips was the most beautiful sight he'd ever seen. Gently he leaned down for a kiss, which she gladly gave him. Then he placed his forehead against hers.

"Garin has found the vow for Blood Sealing," he said in a voice that didn't sound at all like his own. Ever's voice was always confident, nearly always loud, and never betrayed any uncertainty. But now it wavered like an adolescent youth's.

"Blood Sealing?"

"You were right." Ever stepped back to search her midnight eyes. "Those children are creations of the Maker, just the same as you and I. They need love, and they need a home." He took her right hand and drew it up to his mouth, kissing each finger softly in turn. "I was stubborn and foolish—"

An amused snort sounded from behind him, but Ever ignored the steward and continued.

"As always, I wanted to protect the kingdom in my own way. But the Fortress has opened my eyes."

Isa's eyes grew wide. "Really?" she whispered.

"If you are willing, then we will complete the Blood Sealing now," Ever said. At this, a radiant smile began to form, but Ever held up his hand. "Before you make a decision, you need to know that should we ever have a child, he will be third in line for the throne. There will be no distinction between my siblings and our children, for they will be sealed as our own bone and blood. I have read the text, and there is no way out of the covenant once it is made." He drew her closer. "Are you prepared for that?" he whispered.

"Absolutely." She didn't even blink. When Ever gave her a wary look, her smile became fierce, and she clutched his hands tightly. "These children were given to us for a purpose, Ever! I don't know why or how, but I *know* these children need our love. And," she paused, reaching up to touch his face, "we need theirs, you as much as I. Only," she paused, looking down the mountain through the window wall, "do we have time? Sacha could be here any moment!"

"I have word that Sacha has been spotted hiding in the forest west of Soudain. We have at least two hours. But even if she comes sooner," he took her hands in his, "I believe the Fortress desires this, what we are doing now. It will provide us the time we need."

Isa responded with an even brighter smile.

"Then," Garin said, "let us begin." Clearing his throat, he began to read from the ancient scroll that he had translated earlier that afternoon. Though Ever didn't need the translation, Isa had not learned the old tongue, so it was for her that Garin read. Ever wanted her to know what they were doing through and through.

"The almighty Maker has seen it fit that man and woman should be joined in marriage, and they should beget children," Garin began in a low, clear voice. "At times, Darkness shall interrupt this sacred order, and such Darkness will work its contrivances, disease, illness, and evil to separate parent from child and child from parent. In the event that such harm should infiltrate man's native familial roles and interrupt such circles of devotion, the Maker has also seen it fit to bring new life to a man's empty home and new love to a desolate woman's arms."

A tear rolled down Isa's face, but when Garin paused, she quickly brushed it away and just shook her head. Garin continued.

"For the Maker finds it pleasing to confuse the schemes of evil, making it his desire and plan for evil's personal wiles to ultimately submit and serve the purposes of good. For this covenant such good will be borne by joining bone to bone, blood to blood, and flesh to flesh. Parents and children who were parted will become one, and there will be no difference between begetting and vowing."

What is vowed once will never be broken, for such a forged bond cannot be severed in the Maker's sight."

Garin looked up over his spectacles at Ever and then Isa. "If you are ready, my queen, you will take your vows first. Please present your ring."

Isa looked surprised but held out her left hand. The heavy blue crystal in her ring and its swirling silver filigree flashed in the light of the hearth's fire and bounced off the glass walls, which were now orange with the sunset's glow. Garin poured a little pool of silver wax upon the new parchment. Then he took Isa's hand and guided her ring into the wax, and as he held it there, he instructed her to repeat after him.

"Mortal bodies, precious ways..." he said.

"Mortal bodies, precious ways," she echoed.

"I will love you all my days. There in sorrow, there in joy, heartache e're will be destroyed."

As she followed Garin through the vows, Isa's voice became stronger and more resolute. Her chin lifted, and for the first time in a long time, she looked neither tired nor sad.

"Now it is your turn, Your Highness," Garin said, nodding to Ever. Again, he poured more wax, and guided Ever's signet ring to it, holding it there for the duration of the vow.

"Repeat after me. Holy vows and lonely kin, never will you be again. Fighting as with sword and bow, in my heart you'll stay and grow."

As Ever said the words, he wondered at how such beautiful words had never been used. Surely some king or queen had seen and pitied an orphaned child sometime in the last thousand years, even making it only a third or fourth born. And yet, here they were once again, doing what no king or queen had ever done before. But then, since they'd met and married, he and Isa had never been the sort to follow tradition's path.

"In the eyes of the Maker, the Fortress, and I, your witness," Garin said, letting go of Ever's hand, "you have completed the blood seal. The children are now yours."

Ever turned to look at his wife, then back at his steward. Such a short ceremony to reap such large consequences. He was a father now. And his wife, a mother. And yet, he didn't feel any differently. Was he supposed to?

"What now?" Isa asked. Before Garin could answer, a knock sounded at the door.

"Please forgive my intrusion," one of their personal guards called out, "but I could not delay. Sacha is approaching the Fortress, sire. She and her followers should be here within the hour."

"Thank you." Ever was already headed downstairs, clutching Isa's hand tightly when the guard caught them and spoke again.

"There is one more thing you should know, Your Highness. She is spreading the word as to what she is planning."

"And that would be?"

The guard paused and looked at the floor.

"She's telling the people, Your Highness, that the Fortress has abandoned you this night. She will be made queen. And you will die."

26

SACRIFICE

*I*sa couldn't help crying as they sent off the last of the servants. She would have cried even harder had they not sent the children down to Soudain already. The tears didn't absorb into her sleeves, though, as she was now in her battle dress. The leather leggings beneath her gown and the long leather sleeves that covered her arms and the tops of her hands were meant to keep water out. Well, that was fine then, Isa thought. If she was meant to let the tears dry on her face, then so be it. It only served to stoke the fire within her.

By the time Isa returned from dismissing the rest of the servants, Ever was already in the throne room. Isa marveled, in spite of her sorrow, at the warrior sitting in the throne beside hers. Ever wore his full battle armor as well. His large shoulders looked even more massive, as did his chest, beneath their steel coverings. Chain mail covered his sides and the lower part of his neck. Whether for ceremony or intimidation, she wasn't sure, Ever had donned his crown, a piece he rarely touched. But now, as it sat upon his brow, it only served to make him look even more fearsome with its blue gems glinting in the bright light of the thousands of candles that lit the throne room.

As she drew near, Ever stood and walked to her, holding Isa's own diadem. Thinner than his, with silver ivy upon the gold that matched her blue crystal ring, the queen's crown was the loveliest creation Isa had ever seen, and as such, she was rather hesitant to wear it except for ceremony. But now he gently placed it upon her head.

"This is so we remember who we are," he said softly, "no matter what she says."

Isa's throat tightened, and she had the sudden urge to kiss her husband as she never had before, a desperate, urgent kiss that would have done dangerous things to her concentration. Instead, however, she merely took his hand and held it as tightly as she could. His return grip was just as fierce.

"She's coming!" a guard called out from the hall. Isa closed her eyes. *I don't understand, Fortress. Why?*

Warm, familiar fingers placed themselves under her chin, and when she opened her eyes, Ever was inches from her face. "Together," he said.

Isa nodded, and then he led her up the steps of the dais. Once she was on her throne, he sat in his. The wait felt like eternity as the approaching party made a ruckus in their attempt to open the great doors of the Fortress's front hall. Wordlessly, four of their five remaining guards appeared beside them. The Fortress's holy man, and finally Garin, joined them last. As he often did during ceremonies, Garin stood just behind the two thrones where he could be quickly consulted should the need arise.

The air was heavy, as though someone had placed a giant boulder upon the earth itself, pressing everything down beneath it. Isa reached out and tested the hearts of her little group. Fear was the overwhelming emotion, but the guards bore it well. Garin was angry more than anything else and had a good deal of dread as well, something Isa could only guess would come from seeing one's people for the first time in five centuries. Ever's heart, as usual, was more hidden. Trying to read it was like trying to see the bottom of a pond while the water was being splashed about. His face was like granite. Once again, Isa wanted nothing more than to lean over and kiss it, melting away the man of stone into the gentle, kind husband she knew so well. But now was not the time. Now was the time to wait. And pray.

If only the Fortress would listen.

"Your Highness," the fifth guard called out, his voice dripping with sarcasm. "A woman is here demanding entrance. She claims to be the rightful queen."

"Let her in," Ever said in a voice so calm it surprised even Isa. And it was a good thing, too. Isa's response would have included words not fit for a lady, much less a queen. As they waited, she squeezed the silver-veined marble arms of her throne until her fingers hurt. At first, when she'd heard that Sacha was in Soudain, Isa had been filled with fear like their guards. But with each passing moment, the fear began to flee, and raw determination took its place. Ever's sister or not, this woman had much to answer for.

And Isa was determined to make her do just that.

Sacha did not carry herself like a queen as she stalked past the guard into the throne room. Her long, exaggerated strides reminded Isa instead of a dog's gait when it was warning others to keep off its territory.

People crowded in behind her, their dark rags and garments standing out vividly against the pristine white of the marble walls that surrounded them. Most of them were poor and many were dirty, no doubt from their long trek if they had followed Sacha all the way up from the south. Isa wondered how Sacha's gaudy golden dress had stayed so clean after traveling such a distance. Even on a horse, Isa's clothes had never stayed so spotless. The size of her puffed sleeves and the hundreds of jewels that bedecked the bodice of her gown were so numerous that Isa was sure they must be illusions as well. She was tempted to use her power to see, but then decided against it. She was likely to need all of her strength very soon. So instead, Isa sat up even straighter, pressing her spine up against the hard back of the throne. Jewels did not make a queen.

Sacha came to a stop just at the foot of the dais. A number of hooded figures, probably three dozen at least, came to surround her. Nasty hemlock leaves swayed gently from leather thongs tied beneath the pointed ends of their crudely hewn staffs. The citizens that accompanied the party filled in behind and around them, their whispers and tittles creating a low buzzing sound like many bees in a hive.

Isa closed her eyes briefly and tested the hearts before her. Fear. Anger. Hate. Uncertainty. There were hundreds of souls present, too many to count. And, to Isa's disappointment, there were at least a few dozen children in their midst as well. Would these people ever stop bringing their children to dangerous gatherings?

"Brother. I have come to stake my claim to the throne."

At the sound of Sacha's voice, the crowd went silent, looking back and forth between their monarchs and the usurper.

Isa chafed inside. Could no one remember *her* place in all of this? "Actually," she called out, lifting her chin and making certain her voice didn't wobble, "it is *me* that you should be addressing." Sacha gave her a strange look, at which Isa allowed herself a small, victorious smile. "The throne was mine first."

Sacha looked momentarily taken aback, and Isa allowed her half-grin to grow, reveling in the woman's temporary confusion. Sacha had hidden her feelings from Isa very well during that first meeting, but with each encounter since, Isa had become more convinced that the woman was loathe to do so. In fact, she seemed to struggle greatly with not giving wind to her whims now as her emotions wreaked havoc with her carefully laid plans. Even without her gift, Isa would have been able to tell such from the woman's stunned expression.

There were a few moments of silence before Sacha brought her face under control once more. "But you are a Fortier now, are you not?" she asked impatiently.

"I am."

"Well, I am, too." Sacha turned to the crowd and raised her voice. "Your late King Rodrigue was my father first before he sired Everard." She turned back to Isa and Ever. "And therefore, I challenge you for this throne."

"And how do you propose to do such a thing?"

Isa was amazed at Ever's calm as he spoke. For all the vague turmoil she could feel within him, his face was completely impassive, his voice unshaken. Meanwhile, Isa was boiling. "As my holy man and many of these citizens here can attest to," Ever swept his arm out over the throng of hundreds that had gathered before them, "we took the sacred vows. The Fortress has accepted us as its servants."

Sacha stared at them, and all at once, Isa could see what Garin had meant about the Fae changing so very quickly. The speed at which Sacha, who was only half Fae, changed her mood reminded Isa of the way a storm cloud might change its shape, tossed about and remolded continuously by the winds. Simply being near her was giving Isa a headache.

Just then, the woman's eyes focused on something behind Isa. "It can't be," she muttered.

"Oh," Garin said in a dry voice, stepping forward so he was standing between the two thrones, "but it is."

"How did the traitor live?" she bellowed, turning to some of her hooded cohorts. "It has been nearly five hundred years!" She looked back at Garin. "Stories are told of your treachery!"

"Then how do you know I am he?" Garin's voice was taunting now.

"I would know a Fae when I see one, particularly one who is the king's lapdog!"

Isa heard the holy man gasp, as did a fair number of the citizens in their midst. Isa and Ever hadn't made that bit of Garin's past known to the public, but it was too late to care now. Isa kept her eyes forward.

"It would seem the Maker still has a purpose for me then, wouldn't it?" Garin snapped. "Or I wouldn't be here."

Sacha stood silent for so long that Isa wondered if she might faint. Isa could sense her heart racing in frantic, stilted bursts. Finally, however, she merely tucked a single piece of straight golden hair behind her ear before shouting at someone behind her, "Get the child!"

Isa's mouth tasted sour as a little boy was brought forward. He looked to be around five years of age, just a bit older than Genny, and Isa vaguely remembered seeing him as one among the kidnapped. A surge of dismay hit her from the right, and Isa turned to see Ever staring at the child as well. Not a muscle moved in his stony face, but he paled infinitesimally.

"Before you make this challenge," Isa spoke, hoping to give Ever time to recover, "you should all know that this woman is the one who took your children and grandchildren in the first place. It was she that I met in the *otherland* beyond the veil. *She* was the one who stole your children and cursed them before returning them to you."

A murmur began to spread among the people, but Sacha turned to the crowd and raised her hands. "Deep claims, your queen makes!" She turned back to Isa, her eyes narrowing. "I would like to see you prove it."

Isa narrowed her own eyes in return. Oh, she would most definitely do that. *But...* she glanced up at the crowd. *If only the crowd weren't so very big.* Convincing the crowd in Sansim had taken nearly every ounce of strength she had. This crowd was more than ten times that size.

"I have a question," Ever's voice rumbled down to the people. Thankfully, he seemed to have recovered himself well, for there was no trace of hesitancy now as he spoke. "Have you not lived in peace and prosperity in these past few years?

What claims have you brought to me that I have not addressed? And considering that, what in this woman's history has proved to you that she should rule this kingdom? What does she know of stewardship, of keeping a treasury full or settling land disputes?" He stood slowly, and the people standing nearest him at the foot of the dais scrambled to step back. Relief nibbled at Isa as she felt the first wave of guilt work its way through the crowd. But just as people began to talk amongst themselves, a familiar mop of red hair appeared and began to push its way toward the front.

Agnes. How could one baker cause so much mischief?

"You have not healed our children, sire." The skinny woman spat out Ever's title. Then she looked at Isa. "And before you go saying such, Your Highness, I was patient! I was patient like you told me to be! I prayed without end that my daughter's hands would heal. And yet, this woman here was the one who healed her!"

With that, Agnes nodded to the two men who had brought the boy forward. Normally, Ever would not have allowed such flagrant disrespect to continue in a throne room hearing. But the only guards present were those who surrounded them, and losing any of them to wrestle away an unruly peasant would not only cost them bodies, but would show the crowd and Sacha that their numbers were indeed low. Better to let them think Ever was simply being unusually patient.

"Do you think then," Ever asked in the same calm voice, "it would be better to bring her on as a healer?" He looked back to Sacha, his eyes suddenly kind. "I would very much like to know the sister who was denied to me."

And, Isa could feel, he was being completely honest. One of the few areas in which Ever and Isa had never understood one another had been on the subject of siblings. As an only child, he'd never had the chance to enjoy the inexplicable bond that forms between brother and sister, older and younger. Isa had, of course, experienced such a bond with both Launce and little Megane. And as Ever continued to stare at Sacha with a sudden expression of longing, Isa was hit by the strength of his desire for a sister. In four years of marriage, Isa had never known that such a desire burned so strongly within him.

"You would make me another servant. How kind. No, I think you have been tested by this Fortress enough... and failed! And the people of this kingdom deserve new blood, not the line that has grievously injured them over and over and over again."

It took all of Isa's willpower to keep her eyes trained on Sacha's quick, angry movements. For beside her, she could feel the pain of transgressions remembered beginning to eat away at her husband. Again. Somehow, his sister had found the chink in his armor. If Ever doubted anything in the Fortress or Destin, it was himself.

Truly, Isa wondered as she scanned the crowd, how had so many come to join Sacha? What illusions had the Fae shown the people that they might believe what she was telling them about Ever? About her?

Ever turned to the holy man who stood trembling to his right. "What is there in the Holy Writ or the ancient texts that might suggest a legal path for what my sister demands?" He was stalling. Isa knew there was nothing in the texts that could justify ripping two monarchs from the throne who had sworn their lives to and been accepted by the Fortress. But it might buy them time. Though to what end, Isa wasn't sure. With so many children present, how could they fight?

Please, Fortress. Show us the way.

"There is no path to the throne," the holy man stuttered. "You have made a covenant with your lifeblood to serve it all of your days. The only way to fulfill such a promise is..."

Sacha smiled. Her smile should have looked like Ever's, as her face mirrored so many of the Fortier features. But rather, her smile was cold and hard. The people behind and around her began to hiss and boo, displeased with the holy man's answer, obviously missing what Sacha had not.

"See how little he cares for your children? I cannot heal this many without the power from this holy place. And though he cannot do it himself, he *still* denies you that healing!"

The shouts of outrage began to grow louder, and the crowd began to move like a creature being awakened from its slumber. Sucking in a deep breath, Isa pushed the truth out into the crowd, straining to cut through the lies they must have been fed. But every time she got one group calmed down, another began to rail against them even more loudly, and the effort quickly drained her. Yet she continued, straining until she shook with the effort. Until a warm hand gave her shoulder a gentle squeeze.

Isa opened her eyes and looked up to see Garin standing over her. A soft blue light shone from beneath his hand even though it was gloved, and Isa felt a rush of healing take her body.

"What can I do to appease you?" Ever stood. "For it seems your minds are made up no matter what the truth."

Taking the boy by the shoulders, whom Isa had nearly forgotten in the throng of angry people, Sacha led him up the dais until he stood before Ever. "Then show us the truth," she said, holding a hand up behind her. The people quieted but not as completely as the time before. "Heal this boy, and we will all know whom the Fortress wishes to sit upon its throne."

Ever stared at his sister for a long time. Then he placed his hand on the boy's head and closed his eyes.

A blue flame began to spiral above them, dancing in slow swirls as it radiated from his hand into the child. As it grew in intensity, the fire began to move up into the air before cascading back down around them like a fountain. The amount of power Ever summoned was immense, and caught Isa's breath in her throat. She had never seen him use so much power before. Never had he been so strong. When the boy opened his eyes, they glowed with the intensity of a full moon, large and luminous in his little face. Isa could hear exclamations as the people pressed forward to see. And yet, Ever's power continued to build until it swirled above their heads, nearly touching the ceiling in its reach.

Slowly the fire began to sink, slowly, slowly returning to Ever until the room no longer glowed blue, and the fire was gone.

"Well, son?" A man pushed forward, breaking away from the throng. "What do you see?"

The boy hesitated before answering, his eyes moving back and forth cautiously. Finally, he turned to face his father.

"Nothing, Father."

Isa's heart plunged. The boy was still blind. All that power and the boy was still blind.

Without a word, Sacha took the child's hand, and a blue light began to move down her arm and into his hand. But it wasn't the deep, pure blue of the Fortier power. Rather, it was tinted with green. Garin's grip on Isa's shoulder tightened ever so slightly as they watched the far less impressive display, Sacha's strange fire making a faint buzz as it moved through the boy. Finally, she let go, and the boy opened his eyes and turned toward the crowd once more.

"Papa!" he cried, looking directly at the man who had called to him moments before.

"Take them," Sacha ordered. "But I want *him* alive."

Isa's hand was on her sword in an instant, but Ever was faster. The two Fae that climbed the dais with their pikes in hand got their weapons sent clattering to the ground. Isa felt a movement to her left, turning just in time to block the strike from a third Fae.

Isa had spent countless hours with Ever in the training room and had even progressed enough to begin practicing swordplay with multiple enemies. She was growing proficient, he'd told her. But her best efforts had only included opponents of twos or threes, and they had been human. Now, as she and Ever fought back to back, Isa felt perspiration building quickly on her skin and running down her back and temples as she moved faster and faster to block the attacks of the spirit men. She could see now why Ever hadn't wanted his soldiers fighting an army of this. The creatures would lose their bodies in one location just to materialize in another. She heard her crown's clang as it fell to the floor. A quick glimpse told her that Ever had lost his as well.

Just as she began to lose her balance, a deafening roar filled the air. Fae screams mixed with the cries of the people as a great wall of black rose around them. As it shot up, the Fae disappeared along with Sacha and the mob. In an instant, the throne room with its towering rectangular windows and its glittering white walls disappeared, and there was only a single light from above, though Isa couldn't tell its source. Black surrounded them in every other direction. But it was not an oppressive black. Rather, it felt like the darkness of a gentle summer evening just before the stars began to appear. And it was quiet. Nothing stirred, save for the sounds of their own ragged breathing.

"Garin," Ever said, gasping for breath, "what is this place?"

Garin simply cupped their faces in his hands in the same way Isa's father had caressed her face as a little girl. Without a word, he pulled Isa toward him and softly placed a kiss on her forehead. And then Ever's.

"The Maker saw it fit for me to defend this sacred ground from the bloodied hands of my own son," he whispered. "But He gave me two new children in my boy's place. Now, my children, go!"

Garin placed his hands upon their shoulders and shoved them backward. As Isa felt herself hit the floor the black curtain disappeared, and they were once again on the throne room dais. The irate crowd still shouted, but this time, neither the people nor the Fae were looking at them. The people were looking at Garin as he walked toward them with the utmost calm.

Then Garin changed. As he removed his gloves and tossed them off to the side, his skin began to blaze so brightly that looking at his skin was like looking at sunlit snow. Silver wings unfolded from behind his shoulders. Once spread, the wings were wide enough that they spread all the way across the dais.

Even Sacha stood immobile, her mouth open as Isa felt the horror pulsate from her nearly as strongly as her hate.

With one final step to the edge of the dais, Garin turned once more, his eyes smoldering, a blue-white glow as they locked with Isa's. His silver wings began to shimmer like metal that was being put to the flame. "Go!" he ordered in a voice that shook the Fortress walls.

The Maker had indeed made him a being completely *other*.

Isa stumbled forward but turned when she realized that Ever was not at her side. Instead, he was still on the floor, lying exactly where Garin had pushed him. Crawling back, Isa took his arm and pulled him to his feet. She had to drag him all the way down the front lawn, down to the edge of the forest. Only when they were safely hidden within its sheltering trees did she allow herself a short sigh of relief.

But as they began the trek down the mountain, Isa still guiding Ever, a familiar voice gave a cry so loud that it escaped the Fortress's walls and echoed into the night. And Isa couldn't tell whether it was the cry of a warrior or a cry of pain.

G O

"So..." Isa's father shook his head as if to clear it of the horrible events Isa had just related, the lines in his face suddenly looking much deeper in the light of the single candle. "What do you need?"

Though Ever sat beside Isa in body, Ansel had eventually stopped directing any questions his way, as they could draw little from him except grunts.

"We'll need at least three horses and supplies for a week's journey," Isa said softly as she stroked Genny's golden hair. "The Fae can sense our power, so we won't be able to use our fire to speed the horses. It will take the full three days to get to the southern forest. I can only guess we'll spend a day or so there. Then it will take another two days to reach Launce."

"You can't go straight to Launce?" Deline pursed her lips tightly. "He could offer you shelter at least."

Shelter wasn't exactly what they were seeking. Rather, their rendezvous with her brother would be in preparation for war. But Isa didn't correct her mother, for doing so would have only brought on more worry. Instead, she continued to brush the little girl's golden locks with her fingers. Genny stirred in her sleep, but didn't awaken.

Henri slept, too, though his head was on a cushion Deline had provided rather than Isa's lap. Still, he was close enough that his knees were pushed up against her, something he wouldn't have allowed even a few weeks before. In the midst of all the dreadful goings-on, Isa took comfort in this little victory.

"And what of the children?" Ansel asked in a wary voice.

"Megane," Isa murmured, turning to her sister. "Take Genny for me?"

Megane nodded eagerly, taking Genny in her arms so quickly that Isa guessed she had wanted to do so all night. As soon as the little girl was resettled,

Isa motioned her father up out of the cellar. They took no light, leaving the single candle behind them with the others.

"Ever and I were going to... actually, we took the blood joining oath just before his sister arrived." Isa was glad she couldn't see his face through the dark. "They're ours now. They don't know it yet, but they will be coming with us."

Ansel paused for a moment. It must have been a strange night for him, Isa thought wryly. Not only was he sheltering his children on the run, but he was learning that he had suddenly become a grandfather as well.

"Wouldn't it be safer to leave them here?" Ansel finally asked, his voice trembling just slightly.

"No. We're not sure what she wants with them, but we're sure she has something planned. Unlike all of the other children, they were never cursed. And then she sent a Fae after them in the Fortress."

"Do you think she knows of their relation to her?"

"We believe so, but we would prefer not to find out."

"Huh," Ansel said. Isa nearly cringed as she waited for her father to warn her against the dangers of taking two children halfway across the kingdom while they were being pursued. But to her surprise, he only sighed. "And what of your steward?"

"He's in the Fortress's hands now. He ensured our escape when Sacha arrived."

One of the floorboards was lifted, interrupting whatever Ansel was about to say. Megane peeked through the crack, then emerged from the cellar.

"Where are you going at this hour?" Ansel asked with a frown.

"It's almost dawn," Megane said, nodding at the window. And to Isa's surprise, it was. The gray light was beginning to seep beneath their drawn curtains. "Mum says she wants me to get some salve and bandages for Isa and Ever on the off-chance they should need it. I'm also to ask Mr. Sager if we can borrow his spare horse."

"Be careful, Megs," Isa said. "I will not have you getting hurt over this."

Megane laughed, her blue eyes twinkling. "Are you in earnest? This is the first adventure I've gotten a part in. You and Launce have all the fun!" And before Isa could warn her anymore, she grabbed her basket and flounced into the street.

"That one is going to give me more gray hairs than you and your brother combined." Ansel shook his head as he frowned at the slamming door.

Isa wished she could argue, but Megane indeed possessed a flair for the dramatics. And it didn't help that she was still a few years too young to enjoy the court lives of her brother and sister. Granted, growing up as a merchant's daughter when one's brother was a prince and one's sister was a queen would be sure to rub anyone a little in the wrong direction. Hopefully, Isa thought, this taste of adventure would suffice for her until Megane was of age and a little more discerning.

As time passed, Isa prayed that her sister would keep her head. The errand that should have taken only twenty minutes turned into forty and then into an hour. Ever continued to brood in the basement, but the children eventually woke up and were kept quiet with cookies. Isa and Deline continued to exchange looks of worry as the sun grew higher and there was no Megane to be found.

Finally, just as Ansel was ready to grab his coat and go looking for his daughter, Megane came skipping in. "Mrs. Sager says they'll bring the horse over this afternoon. Mr. Sager has him out in the fields."

Instead of smiling at the girl's enthusiasm, Isa grabbed Megane by the arm and dragged her up to the attic. She didn't want her new children to hear the chewing-out she had planned for her sister. For judging by the look on Megane's face, she'd been up to no good. As soon as they were alone, Isa slammed the door shut and turned to glare at her sister. "What took you so long? We were so worried!"

"I was hurrying, I promise! But then Margot caught me just outside the Pottens's shop."

Isa groaned. Would that old busybody *ever* learn to mind her own business?

"She asked me where I was going in such a hurry, so I had to think up a story on the spot!"

"What did you tell her?" Isa almost didn't want to know.

Megane turned a light shade of pink and giggled. "I told her that Davin Crowley and I were going to be kissing on the old bridge, and that I was late so I had to hurry!"

Isa was horrified. "Megane, you are to be telling no such stories to people from now on! Do you understand me?"

"I had to think of *something* unless you wanted me to share your real whereabouts!" Megane smirked, then made a sour face. "Is that an order from my *queen?*"

"That's an order from your *sister*, and I have a good mind to tell Father what sort of mischief you've been up to!" She looked hard at her little sister. "You haven't been kissing Davin Crowley, have you?"

"No!" Megane's face had gone from pink to a near gray. "Oh, please don't tell Papa! I was only trying to help!"

"Yes, and you wanted your bit of fun while you were at it, didn't you? Now Mother and Father are going to have to listen to the whole town whisper of nothing but your upcoming nuptials, and possibly worse." Isa pursed her lips then sighed and drew her sister in for a hug. "Megane, what am I going to do with you? You are to tell no more such falsehoods, understand?"

Megane nodded miserably into Isa's chest. "I'm eleven now, Isa. You don't have to worry so much about me. I'm not a baby."

"And you sometimes think you're fifteen." She pulled back to study her little sister's face. "Part of growing up means doing what is responsible, rather than what sounds fun." Suddenly, something caught in Isa's throat, and it was difficult to speak around it without croaking. "Father and Mother are going to need you now more than ever. Launce and I can't be around to take care of them all the time, as much as we would like to."

"Isa." Tears began to run down the girl's face. "You will be coming back, won't you?" She wiped her face with her sleeve and tried to smile. "You promised you would take me to my first ball! You can't go breaking it on me now."

"I'll do my best, Megs."

"Wait now." Megane pulled back and gave a shaky laugh. "You'd better stop crying before your face gets all blotchy and ugly like it does when you cry."

Isa was about to smack her sister with her glove, but a flash caught her attention through the attic window that faced north. In one movement, Isa had shoved her sister down on the bed before running to the window. At first, there was nothing, only the rooftops of the city's northern quarter looking just as they should on any early summer day. But just as her fingers touched the open window, a swish of green fog appeared before her.

With a shriek, Isa jumped back then regretted it immediately. She had shown the Fae exactly what it was looking for. Who knew how many more were out there looking for them?

"Ever!" Isa grabbed Megane by the wrist and turned to drag her downstairs again, but the sound of breaking glass made her pause. A green wisp flew past them. Then a man with a vague, flat face and slitted green eyes materialized at the bottom of the attic steps.

28

SON

"You've been quiet," Ansel said, shooting Ever a sidelong glance.

Ever continued brushing the horse. It was disrespectful not to answer his father-in-law, and Garin would have given him a withering look for such behavior. But today, as with the night before, no words came. Ever simply had none left.

"I built this stable soon after we realized Isa would always struggle with walking," Ansel spoke again. If he was trying to make Ever feel better he wasn't doing a very good job. The last thing Ever wanted to think about was Isa's accident. But Ansel kept talking anyway. "Before that, we'd only ever needed one horse, so our old horse had made do with a lean-to that attached to the house. After her accident, though, I knew two horses wouldn't fit into the tiny space, and since I figured we would always have more than one horse after that, I thought I might as well build a decent stable."

Ansel stopped fiddling with the saddle he'd been mending and gave a distant smile. "You should have seen the look on her face when I brought her to the horse breeder. She immediately fell in love with this hulking midnight-black fellow, a giant of a horse. But when we asked the owner how much, we found that we couldn't afford him, and I realized very quickly that bringing her along had been a mistake. I'd raised her hopes only to break her heart again." He sighed. "I cannot tell you how ashamed I felt the next day when I brought home the most pathetic, half-starved beast you'd ever seen. An acquaintance had offered him for less than a third of what the black steed would have cost.

"I felt like a failure as I finally presented her with that sad excuse for a horse." Ansel went back to the saddle he'd been working on. "Isa was not a begging child. There was only one thing in the world she had ever truly asked of me, and it killed me that I couldn't get it for her."

"What happened?" There were few topics in the world that could generally entice Ever from his worries, and stories of Isa's childhood were one of them.

Ansel smiled as he placed the saddle on one of the horses. "It is funny how the Maker uses our failures. Isa was disappointed to be sure. But that pathetic creature was in such poor condition that it was only a matter of minutes before she was fawning all over the poor beast, brushing out the snarls in its mane, bringing it carrots, and doing everything in her power to restore it to health." He paused. "I think that's when she truly began to heal... when she had another creature that needed her. And the Maker knew she would never find that with such a fine horse as the first fellow she saw.

"You know," he said, placing a calloused hand on Ever's work, forcing him to stop. With resignation, Ever turned to look Ansel in the face. The wrinkles around his mouth and eyes had deepened considerably in the last few years, and the hair that had been peppered gray and black when Ever had first met him was now mostly gray. He stood a tad shorter than Ever remembered, and his midsection was a good bit rounder. But the intensity in Ansel's gaze held Ever to the spot. "I see the fear in your eyes," Ansel said, "when you look at those children."

"I don't see why I shouldn't." Ever snorted. "The first thing everyone mentions is how much I am like my father. And the older I get, the more I see it in myself. Now I'm taking children into my home, and I find I have no home to take them to." He looked at Ansel, suddenly desperate for the older man to understand, though he really wasn't sure why. "What if I slip?" He went back to filling the saddlebags. "What if I can't protect them? How could they even want me for their father after what happened last night?"

"Are you regretting your decision then?"

"Of course not. I just pray to the Maker that I don't fail them as my father failed me."

"Oh, you will fail them. There is no question about that," Ansel said. Ever gave him a skeptical look, but the older man just shook his head. "Every father fails his children. And he does it again and again. What I have found, if you wish to take my humble experience, is that asking forgiveness … and speaking *with* them instead of *at* them can strengthen our ties to our children far more than the best gifts ever could."

Ever chuckled without humor. "Now you sound like Garin."

"Good. At least one of us is—"

But before he could finish, Ever's skin prickled, and a scream sounded from the house. Ever dashed to the stable door. It was midday, and the sun nearly blinded him after being in the dark cool of the stable. After a second of squinting, he made out a broken window in the upper attic. Another scream sounded.

"Megane!" Ansel cried, but Ever was faster, his sword already drawn as he sprinted to the house. Before he could reach the back door, however, the house disappeared. Sand bit his eyes and tried to burrow into his skin, and the friendly noon sun became cruel and blisteringly hot. And there was nothing. Nothing for miles and miles except for dunes of loose sand and gales of wind blowing it around like walls of biting insects.

"What is this?" Ansel cried out.

"Don't believe what you see," Ever called back. "The Fae are here." But even as he spoke the words another shriek came from the direction that the house had been. It was Genny this time. Drawn by the scream, Ever began to push forward again, but just as he should have reached the house, a green whorl stood in his path. Ever stabbed at it, but the blade sliced through the cloud-like creature as though it weren't there at all. The green mist darted behind him, and Ever realized it was heading for his father-in-law who was still protesting, demanding to know where they were.

As the green mist began to whip around Ansel in circles, the older man stumbled and fell, fear filling his eyes as he beheld the ghostly creature. The green mist began to materialize into the shape of a woman, but before she could finish, her legs still invisible, she flipped her head and her strange green eyes widened as she looked at Ever.

What is she staring at? Ever looked down at his hand to see a ball of blue flame floating just above his palm. Then he remembered the Fae in the children's bedroom, as well as Garin's words.

Fae are sensitive to power of any kind. Even if it is one they can't use, they can still feel it.

"Cover your face!" Ever yelled to his father-in-law. "This might hurt!" As he spoke, Ever ran through the risks in his head. It was dangerous to gather too much power in a place as closely contained as the little city neighborhood. In his throne room, he had used the Fortress as his aid, and he had known exactly how well the great room could contain his strength. But here, with houses crowded beside one another and people still in the streets, there was always the chance his power would touch someone unintended.

Another scream sounded, but Ever couldn't tell whose it was. "Isa!" he shouted, hoping desperately that she could hear him. "I need to find the stable. I need to see!" He waited, holding just enough power to keep the Fae's attention. As he did, more Fae began to appear around him.

It wasn't fair of him to ask her to break their illusion. She hadn't been able to do it the day before, and there had been only two Fae in the children's room. But as the seconds ticked by, Ever knew he couldn't wait much longer. He began to inch his way to where the stable should have been. Each time he moved the Fae shimmered as though trying to awaken themselves from the spell he held them captive in, and he was forced to increase the fire just that much more. If he wasn't careful, the stable or house could go up in flames, and he wouldn't even be able to see it.

Just as he was about to give up that she'd heard him or that she was capable of breaking the vision, her familiar power pushed its way through, and the vision the Fae had cast cleared just enough for him to dart into the stable and leap upon one of the horses.

Much to his relief, the Fae gave chase. The faster he pushed, the more the vision faded, and Ever could once again make out Soudain's neat cobblestone streets. One glance back, however, told him that even more Fae had begun following him. Now that he was safely in the middle of the road and he could see, Ever increased the brightness of his fire, hoping it would draw Sacha's entire search party, however many that was.

But he hadn't expected the Fae to be quite so fast. Whether it was their desire to stay near his power or their rage at his escape, they began to gain on him. Ever pressed the horse harder, adding his strength to aid the beast's speed, all the while holding his left hand high to keep the Fae's attention. Once he was out of the city, he could lead them to a private place where he might take advantage of their obsession with his fire and pick them off one at a time. Then Isa and the children could make their escape.

But that, he realized as he glanced back again, was all contingent on getting the Fae out of the city's borders. Their green eyes glowed and their teeth gnashed as their horde continued to near Ever's horse. He would need more than just a flat piece of farmland to fight them in. He would need someplace with obstacles where they couldn't all descend on him at once. Twice now he had clashed with the Fae, and twice he had nearly been killed in the process. He would need to do more than simply get out of the town.

He would need a miracle.

29

DIVERSION

*P*lease, Ever begged the Fortress as he left the city, *I don't know what you wish me to do. But for their sakes, show me where to go even if it leads to my death!*

Just then, Ever remembered an underground cave five miles east of Soudain. The immediacy of the answer to his prayer was both relieving and a discomfort at the same time. Would this fight be his doom?

Ever nudged his horse off the main road and into a vineyard. He could barely see the raised lip of the cave over the edge of the vines. *Just a little longer,* he thought. But his arm shook with the effort of staying raised, and Ever gritted his teeth. *Just a little closer.* The cave would provide him some much-needed respite for his poor horse. And it would make the fight even.

Somehow he made it through the vineyard with his arm still up and then plummeted into the belly of the cave. His horse resisted, but Ever pushed him on into the dark, keeping to the walls of the cave as they skirted the pool of water that filled most of the cave. His blue fire threw strange shadows against the stone walls and the stalactites, which sparkled like knives hanging perilously from the ceiling. As he reached the back of the cave, Ever extinguished his fire, leapt from his horse, and rolled behind a pillar of rock. The horse pounded back through the entrance, leaving Ever alone to face the beings which he could now hear entering the cave.

His confidence in the plan wavered as he counted the green mists floating in. He had expected perhaps six or seven, including those that had first sought out Isa and the children, but not fourteen. Still, he was too deep into his plan to back out now.

The mists floated cautiously above the pool, pausing hesitantly beneath the glow worm colonies that hung between the stalactites like stars in the dark of night. Ever began to inch his way back toward the entrance of the cave along the outer wall. It was highly tempting to break into a sprint every time a green mist drifted near him. But Ever forced himself to breathe through his nose and take his time.

Finally, he reached the entrance of the cave. Mild regret filled him as he placed his hands against the largest white sandstone pillar and began to push. He had loved visiting this cave as a child. Cracking sounds filled the air as Ever continued to press against the sandstone, sending the whorls into blurs of green agitation. By the time they seemed to realize what was afoot, however, it was too late. Ever rolled out of the way as the pillar crumbled and the entrance collapsed with a deafening crash.

Except for the light blue glow of the worms on the ceiling, the cave went completely dark. The water of the pool lapped up against its edges, the only sound to follow the great crash, until, for the first time, one of the Fae spoke.

"What do you plan for us here, oh son of Cassiel?" a thick voice called out, taking Ever by surprise. How did the Fae know of the Fortress's first king? "You know there are many more of us back at the castle."

Ever didn't answer, but instead squinted through the darkness as he moved to his hands and knees again and began to crawl toward the center of the cave. A change in the lapping of the water and that one of them had spoken with human words told Ever that at least some of the Fae had transformed into their more solid bodies. *Good.*

Ever continued to crawl as his fingers touched the water's edge, regretting that he couldn't first take off his boots. Wet feet would be miserable, but cutting his foot on unseen rocks at the bottom of the pool would be even more miserable. He could heal himself, of course, but that would take time and power, neither of which he had any to waste.

Ever had nearly reached the pool's center when a green mist that had been hovering above him began to take its more human form. Suddenly a leg appeared right where there had been none before. And he had run right into it.

"He's here!" a female voice cried.

Ever jumped up and punched his announcer right in what he guessed to be the nose. It must not have seen him, he realized, for rather than driving his hand through a shapeless green mist, his knuckles made a satisfying crunch as the creature went down. Buoyed, Ever lifted both his hands into the air. A ball of blue fire blazed between them, and this time, Ever didn't hold back. Hotter and hotter, the flames grew between his palms until the ball began to lift of its own accord into the air. Sweating with the effort of keeping it raised, Ever left one hand in the air to guide the fireball and unsheathed his sword with the other.

Just as he'd hoped, the remaining whorls changed into their human forms. With their mouths agape, they walked toward the fire. Ever retreated slowly to give them more room. He would have only one chance at this.

In the dance of blood that he knew only too well, Ever began to meet his enemies. One by one, they were felled. Garin had been right. Their thirst for the power, their draw to it would be their undoing. And Ever would have felt much worse about exploiting such a weakness if it hadn't been for the fearful cries of his new children still ringing in his ears.

And Garin's cry.

It wasn't long before Ever had taken out ten of the fourteen Fae. But as he continued to fight, relying more on his senses than his eyes in the blackness of the cave, he began to struggle. He wouldn't be able to hold the flaming globe aloft much longer. As he decided that his power would hold for four more minutes, the sound of splintering rock above him broke his concentration. Just before the blue flame fizzled out, Ever had time to witness a great crack running through the ceiling. As the crack continued to grow, he could hear the thousands of stone icicles above him began their own chorus of snaps and cracks.

A sharp pain in his left shoulder made him cry out. Warm blood began to seep down his arm as his globe of flame fell out of the air and died in the water. Before he had time to resume the fight, however, he was thrown to the ground by a body, and he choked on the water as he went down. Hot hands pressed down on his chest, keeping his face beneath the surface.

Ever did his best to lift his throbbing left arm up out of the water, but the pain made it nearly impossible. With a garbled shout, he torqued his body until his hand was free enough to reach up into the air. It fizzled as the blue fire struggled to light on his wet fingers. Just before he should have passed out, however, the fire grew strong, then fizzled out again. The distraction was short, but just long enough for Ever to shove the Fae off his chest with his sword.

Leaping to his feet, Ever realized the three remaining Fae had returned to their mist bodies. He wrapped the blue fire around his hand once again, but this time, it didn't burn as brightly or as blue. He was tiring and wouldn't last much longer. Never in his dozens of previous battles had he faced opponents like this.

Unfortunately, the remaining Fae seemed to have more self-control than their brothers and sisters that lay at Ever's feet, for the fire did not bring them to their bodies as it had the others.

Instead, they began to circle around him. As they did, however, more cracking sounded from above. Ever looked up just in time to see the cave ceiling begin its collapse. Rocks started to rain down upon them, small at first, but then growing in size and weight. Glow worms fell into the pool with the rocks, taking even more of the light with them. Ever was forced to duck and cover his head. For unlike the mists, he could be crushed.

Another loud tearing sound echoed throughout the round cave, and again, Ever was underwater. A large boulder pinned his left knee to the ground. He couldn't breathe. Gurgled laughs sounded as the three whorls morphed into distorted bodies that walked toward him.

Ever had never been burned by his own fire before, but as the desperate idea entered his head he wondered if this trick might just be his last one. His mind was made up, though, when a foot delivered a kick to his ribs. Ever dropped his sword and stretched his hands out before him. *Once more,* he told the Fortress.

Hesitation did not hold him back this time as it often did. There was no wondering about whether his power would be too much for his surroundings. Ever dug down to his core and mined every bit of strength he had left.

Placing his hands beneath the water, he let all of his power go. The wave of flame left his fingertips with a hiss, and the water that surrounded him sizzled as it cut through the air. The three Fae screamed as the scalding water hit, so hot it turned into its own mist.

Then all was quiet.

30

THE HARD QUESTIONS

"I'm cold," Genny moaned.

"We only have two blankets, and you've got one of them," Henri reminded her, less patient with his sister's demands than usual. The hot, dusty three-day ride had made him grumpy, and the hard floor beneath him now only made it worse.

"How about you snuggle with me?" Miss Isa reached over and drew the little girl close before wrapping her cloak around them both.

"I still don't understand why I can't use my fire," Henri mumbled.

"The Fae can sense power the way you do. If you use your power, they have a better chance of finding us. We need to stay quiet and hidden until we rejoin King Ever."

"When is King Ever coming?" Genny asked as Miss Isa rearranged their blankets.

"Soon, I hope," Miss Isa said as she leaned back against the hard wooden bench, but Henri could see the strain in her smile this time. After the king had dashed away with the Fae trailing him, Miss Isa and the children had bolted with what little supplies had already been packed upon the two remaining horses. For who knew, Miss Isa had said, when more Fae would be sent? With tears and prayers, Miss Isa's family had sent them off, Miss Isa on one horse and Genny and Henri on the other.

The first day hadn't been so bad. On the contrary, Henri had felt like a warrior on a quest as they'd ridden through the countryside. But as they'd begun to draw closer to the southern forests, the pleasure had fled, and it was all Henri could do to keep from turning the horse around and racing right back to Miss Isa's family instead.

What he wouldn't give for a few more of Mrs. Marchand's cookies.

"I don't see why we have to stay here," Henri grumbled as he moved back up to the bench. Perhaps it would be more comfortable on the bench than the floor, though it hadn't been the last three times he'd tried. "Father Lucien is gone."

"Father Lucien must have been needed elsewhere," Miss Isa said. "But I know he would wish for us to rest within the church if he were here."

Henri frowned at the queen. The church had been locked up when they'd arrived, but she had shown no hesitancy in loosening one of the animal skins that covered the windows and climbing inside.

Breaking into the church wasn't exactly the kind of behavior Henri would have expected from the queen. He and Genny were the ones who were expected to break the rules, not her. It seemed wrong. But as the air had grown colder and dark had begun to fall, Henri had stopped objecting. Staying in the church seemed better than freezing out in the night.

They sat quietly for a long time as Genny's breathing became deep and even against Miss Isa's chest. They had no fire, as the church had no hearth, and it truly was beginning to grow chilly despite the fact that summer would soon be upon them. The dark of the night and the thin blanket Henri had wrapped around himself reminded him that he was tired as well, but he wasn't yet ready for sleep. They were too close to his old home, the cottage with the tree-smashed roof and nine years of memories that Henri would rather not possess. So instead, he decided to ask more questions.

"Why does that woman want us?"

Miss Isa looked at him, and even in the weak silvery light leaking in from the outside, Henri could see her look of surprise. They hadn't told him or his sister much about their enemy, but Henri had done enough eavesdropping to know that this mysterious woman was not a gentle spirit.

"I do not know," Miss Isa finally said. "I can only guess that she knows you are part Fae as well and thinks you should be within her ranks instead."

Huh. That was certainly not an outcome Henri desired. All his Fae blood ever seemed to do was get him in trouble. Living with people like him was the last thing he wanted. "If she's at the Fortress, then where are all of the soldiers? Shouldn't they have stopped her?"

"The king sent them to a secret place to wait until the time is right to retake the Fortress."

A brief silence lapsed before Henri decided to do something daring. It was the question he'd been dying to ask for weeks but hadn't had the courage. "Why have you kept us for so long?"

At this, Miss Isa frowned. And with each passing second of silence, Henri was sure she was searching for a way to tell him that they didn't want the children anymore, and that he and Genny would be sent off on their own as soon as possible. He and his sister had not been easy guests, he knew. They were too noisy and ate too much food. Genny was always whining for Miss Isa, and Henri seemed to be incapable of staying out of the king's way. So when Miss Isa finally answered him, he was taken completely by surprise.

"You need someone to love you." She paused before adding, "And we need someone to love us, too."

Henri gulped. Could she be saying what he hoped she was? There was only one way to find out.

"That boy from the story... Was he ever lonely?"

"Yes," Miss Isa murmured, sounding tired. "He had no brothers or sisters to play with, and most of the other children his age were afraid of what he could do."

"Does *he* want me?"

"Why do you ask?" Even in the muted light, Miss Isa looked weary as she held Genny and leaned back against the church bench, but Henri had to know. Because he was dangerously close to letting himself fall in love with a family who might not want to love him.

"I don't think he wants me," Henri continued. "I'm too much like him. And he doesn't like himself sometimes."

"He saved you, didn't he?"

Henri didn't answer. As though able to read his silence, Miss Isa pushed herself back up into a sitting position and reached out to take his hand. Henri tried to wiggle it free but the queen held firm.

"King Everard shows his love in a different way from many other people. He does things for others, keeping them safe and cared for. His father taught him to use a sword to show love instead of words. King Everard is learning to show his love in other ways now, but learning takes time." She smiled a bit. "Like the way you are learning to control your powers. Now," she yawned, "tomorrow will have its own troubles, but I think those troubles will be easier if we get some sleep tonight. Goodnight, Henri."

With a sigh, Henri obeyed. The queen's voice was sadder than he'd ever heard it. And though the king still made Henri nervous, Henri decided that he did indeed want the king to come back soon. For he could see how sad Miss Isa was without him. And the queen was too kind to be kept sad.

Henri was awakened some time later by the murmur of two voices. Stiffly, he rolled over to see a hulking form standing above the queen. Panic seized Henri as he tried to see her. Was she still breathing? Had the stranger hurt his sister?

"How is your knee?" Miss Isa's voice was quiet.

Relief made his limbs feel wobbly when he heard the king answer.

"It's a little sore, but it will be fine in a few days."

"You didn't *walk* here, did you?" She sounded alarmed.

"I had no choice. Your father's horse ran when I ducked into the cave. Hopefully, he went home. And don't worry, I healed it enough that I could run some."

There was a pause, and Henri guessed that the queen did not like that answer. Finally, she asked, "How long do you think until we reach them?"

The king groaned. "Four days at best. Maybe longer."

"Could you send Acelet a message, now that you know how to fight the Fae?"

Henri did his best to look like he was asleep. He didn't know why, but excitement tickled his chest when he realized they were talking about standing up to the enemy. He tried to peek at them from beneath his eyelids.

To his relief, the king had turned so that Henri could see what he was doing. He held up the ring he always wore, the one with the image of a wolf on the top. Its gold gleamed even in the low light.

"Launce knows not to accept any summons except this. I wasn't sure if my sister could create the illusion of me well enough to fool him, so he is not to follow a single word I say or send until he can hold this ring in his hand. Unfortunately," the king put the ring back on and ran his hand through his hair, "I couldn't find any birds when I arrived here."

"It was that way when we got here," Miss Isa said quietly.

Henri shivered at the memory. For as long as Henri could remember, Father Lucien had lived in the little windowless room behind the church. But when they had arrived that afternoon, Henri had nearly been sick at the sight of the blackened, torched hovel. The main room of the church had been left alone, but it didn't make him feel much better. Father Lucien, the one friend he'd had before the king and queen had come along, was gone, and the holy man hadn't left a clue behind as to where he went.

"How did you all fare?" the king asked.

"We did well enough. My father had at least packed us two blankets and enough food and water for a day. Yesterday we found a stream that had some apples nearby." She paused. "You would have been proud of Henri. A single Fae began to chase us after you left, but Henri was able to throw wads of his fire backward until it no longer followed us."

Henri nearly jumped when the king turned to look at him, the rings of fire burning into his eyes as though he'd known Henri was awake the entire time. Henri cringed, ready for the lecture. Instead, however, the king only stood and walked over to the bench where he lay. Laying a hand on Henri's arm, the king said quietly,

"You did well. I'm proud of you."

As the king then walked to the front of the church and lay on the bench closest to the door, Henri felt an immense wave of peace wash through him. For nearly a week, he had gone to sleep with the feeling of being chased. Even at the Fortress he'd slept poorly. But, for the first time in what felt like a long time, Henri let himself drift off to sleep. He felt safe.

31

HOLD THEM TIGHT

*I*sa studied the set of Ever's shoulders as his horse led the way into the woods. Because they had only two horses instead of three, Isa and Ever had redistributed their weight by placing Genny with Ever on his horse and Henri on Isa's. Now as he held Genny in front of him, he appeared confident enough, his back straight and shoulders high. There were even moments during their trek when Isa believed him. But whenever she tried to peer into his heart, to reach out and touch the man inside, there was too much turmoil. Confidence, yes. But pain, too. Duty. Abandonment. Longing.

"I don't like that tree." Genny's little voice interrupted Isa's musings.

"And why is that?" Despite his volatile mood, Ever sounded amused.

"It dropped me."

"You mean you fell out of it." Henri smirked.

Isa laughed, a strange sound in the midst of the skinny, crooked trees and the sickly yellow light that filtered through them. How she longed to be free of these oppressive woods. Heavy rains had kept them inside the church for the majority of the morning. Ever had gone out to inspect the tree from which Sacha had made her appearances, but nothing had been revealed. He had more faith, however, that they would find answers back at the cottage Sacha had lured the children to, which was still a day's ride away. That, he felt, was where the original tear between realms would be.

They found a place to spend the night just before the sun set. By then they had traveled deep enough into the woods that the light was weak, and Ever didn't want to be caught unawares in the dark without a fire. As soon as the horses had been watered, Ever made a little fire no larger than the size of his fist, though he used natural means so as not to attract any wandering Fae's attention. Then Henri showed him how to set a trap to catch a hare. Isa couldn't help giggling to herself as she watched that unfold, for Ever's annoyance at not knowing how to carry out the simple skill was expressed through his continually deepening scowl. Before long, however, two hares were caught, and everyone settled down to a hot supper.

"King Ever, I have a question."

Ever froze, his wide eyes meeting Isa's. Isa was just as surprised. Since arriving at the Fortress, Henri had done his best to avoid Ever, answering his questions in as few words as possible. And he had never spoken to Ever voluntarily.

"When you heal," Henri continued, "does your fire burn the people you touch?"

"No," Ever said slowly. "Why?"

"I have fire, but I can't heal people. I only burn them." Henri frowned and held out his hands. "My gift doesn't seem very useful."

"You might be surprised," Ever said, taking another piece of meat from their makeshift spit. "With the proper training, you could learn to use your fire in many ways."

"Do you have fire?" Genny asked Isa.

"A little, when I need it. My gift is different than King Ever's, but I can use the Fortress's fire for small things." Isa hated calling Ever by his title in front of the children. After all, he was their father now. But there hadn't yet been a time that felt right to tell the children about their adoption. It was not the kind of information one could spring on a child right before bed.

"I wish I had a gift." Genny pouted. "Henri can at least make fire. I can't do anything!"

"Now, Genny, your smile alone is full of magic." Isa tickled the little girl.

But Henri wasn't looking at them. He was still staring at Ever. "How do you make your fire heal?"

"Give me your hand," Ever said. Henri stared at him for a long moment before ever so slowly raising his right hand. Ever reached over and took it, placing it inside his own large hand. Henri looked nervous as Ever closed his hand over the boy's. "Do you feel that?" Blue fire engulfed both their hands.

Henri nodded.

"Good. That is my fire as it comes to me, raw and undisciplined as yours is."

"I can control it," Henri grumbled.

"Somewhat. But now feel the difference." The flame began to dance. Most humans wouldn't have been able to feel it, but Isa could, and even Genny's eyes grew rounder as Ever's fire changed its rhythmic pulsing. "It has taken me years of practice to achieve such, but I have trained my fire to do more than burn air. Instead, it can move through substances as well as people. I recently healed a man who struggled with fits of coughing."

"How?"

"Ever," Isa murmured, hating to break the moment, "the Fae might sense you."

Ever let go of the boy's hand and the fire disappeared. "I sent my fire into his blood. As it traveled his body, it purged him of the illness that resided within it. As fire takes away dross from gold, so can my fire do with sicknesses. It can also speed healing of skin and bones."

"That sounds impossible." Henri rubbed his hand.

"It is not my place to judge what is or is not impossible," Ever said, returning to his food. "Only to trust that the Fortress will do as the Maker wishes it to. I must be willing to serve as a vessel for those choices, whether that be in humility or victory."

Henri looked thoughtful but said no more. After supper, Isa wrapped each child in one of the blankets. Within a few minutes, Henri fell asleep, his head resting against one of Isa's legs. Genny, however, had other plans. Without a word, she marched up to Ever before turning and plopping herself in his lap. Ever looked at Isa with panic in his eyes, but Isa only smiled. So many times she'd imagined her husband cradling a child in his lap. And now he was, albeit involuntarily.

Still, as the little girl curled up in his arms, wonder filled Ever's eyes. Softly, so softly, he reached up and stroked her hair, and for the first time that day, Isa felt peace ripple through her husband like a little stone in a pond.

It seemed that Isa had no sooner closed her eyes than a distant explosion jolted her awake. Lightning filled the sky's holes in the forest canopy above them, lighting up the trees like daggers in the night. Isa turned to pull Henri to his feet, but Ever was already ahead of her and had both children off the ground. In no time, both the children were on the horses, and Ever and Isa were leading them on foot, though where they were going Isa had not the slightest idea. She thought she heard Ever saying something about ruining the horse's feet in a forest as this. But their progress on foot was slow at best, and the storm continued to build as it chased them deeper into the heart of the woods.

"Will we make it to the cottage?" Isa yelled over the wind.

"No!" Ever shouted back, squinting through the rain that was beginning to pelt them more steadily. "It's too far!"

"We can't stay out in this!"

As if to agree, a bolt of lightning struck a tree just behind them, and as it fell, Isa and Ever had to swerve dangerously, making their horses squeal in protest. Isa prayed the children would hold on.

"Wait!" Henri's call was so frantic that Isa slowed just a hair to look back at him. "I know where we are!" he shouted. "My old cottage is just that way!" Henri pointed south. "A tree fell on it, but we'll be out of the rain!"

Immediately, Ever turned and began to lead his charges south. As they ran, Isa prayed that the children's parents had not died in the cottage as Henri thought they had. *For the children's sakes,* she begged the Maker, *let someone have come and taken the bodies!*

But as they continued to push on, Isa made out what looked like a light up ahead of them, a faint yellow glow against the black of the forest. It was a lantern, she realized, which hung in the window of a fully functional little cottage. She thought about asking Henri if this was a different cottage, but a bolt of lightning struck so close that a tree not thirty feet away caught fire.

Moments later, they reached the cottage. Ever dragged both children off the horses and pushed them under the eaves with Isa, then he practically shoved the horses into the pathetic little lean-to that stood beside the house. "In!" he ordered, throwing the door open.

None too soon, either, for as soon as the door was closed, another tree even closer to the cottage burst into flames behind them.

"That was close," Isa murmured as she looked at her little band. They were all dripping and looked quite disheveled. They were also all staring in the same direction. Ever's face was drawn into a tight frown, and Genny's was one of timidity. Henri looked as though he might faint. When Isa turned to see what they were looking at, she found herself staring at two commoners, a man and a woman.

The man was stocky and short with a scraggly brown beard, and the woman was lean with a pinched face. They had been eating at the little wooden table just to the left of a glowing hearth, but now they both stood, looking as though they wanted to run.

Isa had thought at one point that her heart couldn't break any further. In the last few months, she had lost her home, her friends, Garin, her kingdom, and her hope of ever bearing a child. But she had been wrong. For the single word that Henri uttered caused her more pain than she could have known possible.

"Father."

A LUCKY THING

*T*he king looked down at Henri. "I thought you said your father was dead."

"But a tree fell on the roof..." Henri trailed off, looking back at his father. It was wrong, but he somehow felt more bothered by Claude's life than he had been by his death. Henri had seen the tree and the smashed roof. But as he looked around now, Henri realized that the house had been completely repaired. New glass windows were in place, unfamiliar stones strengthened the walls, and the roof was even higher than it had been before.

"Your Highnesses!" his father sputtered, finally seeming to awaken from his initial stupor before turning to his wife. "Don't jus' stand there gapin' like a fish, woman! Get 'em something to eat!"

Helaine blinked a few times before nodding blankly at Henri's father. But the look she sent Henri and Genny over her shoulder made Henri cringe. *That* look often came with an ear boxing.

"Forgive us for intruding," King Ever said in a tight voice. "I am King Everard Fortier, and this is my wife, Queen Isabelle. We were out in the forest when the storm hit. I appreciate your hospitality."

"Of ... of course, Your Majesties. I seen you before. In the town, I mean. Allow me to introduce m'self." Henri's father gulped. "My name is Claude Biscoup. This here is my wife, Helaine. And you, boy," he looked down at Henri, "go get some more firewood for our guests."

Henri swallowed the storm of feelings that raged inside him as he prepared to face the storm again, but a hand placed itself firmly on his shoulder, pinning him to the spot. Henri looked up to see the king glaring at Claude.

"He will do no such thing," the king's voice rumbled. "It is dangerous."

Henri could have hugged him.

"I want to go home," Genny whimpered, turning to Miss Isa and wrapping her arms around Miss Isa's legs. But the queen was distracted, too, staring furiously at Helaine much in the way King Ever was doing with Claude. A long, awkward silence stretched between the four adults.

"Thank ye for bringing our children back," the woodcutter finally mumbled, looking at his feet as he spoke. "We was looking for them for quite some time now."

"The boy says they became lost in the woods. Twice." The king's reply was icy. "They even found their way back once to find the cottage destroyed."

"Storm did that while we was out looking for the little buggers," Claude muttered.

"Of course." But the king's face was dark, and his mouth was in a tight line.

"I'm sure once you've eaten and warmed and the storm is over," Claude nodded at the window, "that you and Her Majesty will wish to be on your ways?"

Henri's chest suddenly tightened, and he silently begged the Fortress not to let the king push his father too far. Once the king and queen had gone, he and Genny would be all alone again. And who knew what kind of punishment Claude and Helaine would pour upon them for their subsequent humiliation?

Henri hadn't realized just how much he wanted to stay with the king and queen until he had seen his father and Helaine again. His stomach twisted into a knot. The king had moods, to be sure, but so did Claude. And at least the king's moods had a purpose. Claude's moods, and worse, Helaine's, could come at any time, often ending in purple and blue marks on his and Genny's skin. And for all of King Ever's stern words and expectant looks, never once had he struck either Henri or Genny in anger. Of course, this thought only made Henri shake harder.

"Actually," the king said, his grip tightening on Henri's shoulder, "we are in need of a place to pass the night. I am sure it will not be an imposition to stay here with you."

"As you wish, sire." Claude bowed his head and turned to throw another log into the fire.

"You two!" Helaine's grating voice snapped. "To bed with you. It is late, and you will be worthless in the morn if you get no sleep now."

Henri knew Helaine would make him regret it later, but he dared a glance up at the king, wishing suddenly with all of his heart that the king would carry them away again just as quickly as they'd come. Henri would never run in the Fortress halls again or spill the king's wine, and he would keep a tighter rein upon Genny. But King Ever only gave him one slow nod.

Surprisingly, Genny did as she was told, something Henri gave silent thanks for. But in spite of that miracle, wretched tears threatened to escape from his eyes as he slumped forward to obey his stepmother. It felt strange to lie upon the scratchy straw mat with Genny, now that he was used to sleeping in nightclothes and in the palace bed all his own. But the itchy straw pallet and lack of bedclothes were the least of Henri's worries.

Witch or no witch in the Fortress, Henri knew that under no circumstance could he live in this house again. Never again could he watch his stepmother lay a hand on his sister, nor could he endure his father's cruel words. After the king and queen left them, they would run to Soudain. He didn't know how, as they had no horse, nor did they have any food, but he would get them there somehow. Perhaps Miss Isa's parents would allow him to work in their store. They seemed nice enough. Anything was better than living unwanted and despised.

A lone tear rolled down his cheek.

"It's a lucky thing you're getting rid of these ones," Helaine was saying in a sour voice. "They're no innocents like other children their age."

"How did they come to wander in the forest alone?" Miss Isa asked, ignoring Helaine's comment. Henri wanted badly to see her face as she asked such a bold question, but he didn't dare. Helaine would double his punishment in the morning.

"They were out in a storm," Helaine said uneasily. "My husband had been cutting wood in the deeper parts of the forest. Some parts of the woods is more confusing than others. Anyhows, Claude here turned to find them when the storm got closer, and that's when he found they were gone. None too convenient, either. The lightning just got so close he had to come home. Nearly killed us it did." She paused. "The witch got them the next day when we went looking for them again."

The queen said something else, but Henri didn't hear what it was. Instead, his heart began to pound, and he began to shiver all over. Helaine was lying. Her story hadn't at all been how he and Genny had become lost. Such, though, he had expected from her.

But how did she know that Henri and Genny had been captured by the witch?

HALF-TRUTHS AND QUANDRIES

"*Y*ou're lying." Isa interrupted whatever gibberish the pale, stinking woman was spewing. Ever had been considering interjecting with some objection of his own, but Isa's quiet tone promised danger. Claude and Helaine stared back at her blankly.

"What happened? In truth." Isa leveled a dark look at them, Helaine in particular. Her voice was perfectly calm, like a lake of ice. But Ever knew that deep inside her heart must be breaking.

What Ever couldn't understand was how Henri and Genny had come under the care of this worthless man and his awful wife in the first place. Despite the fact that his world was falling apart back at the Fortress, Ever suddenly needed to know. It made sense, of course, that Rodrigue's mistress, the children's true mother, might not have wanted to raise the children in the Fae world. But if this couple disliked the children as much as they obviously did, then why had they kept the children for so many years before getting rid of them? Did they know where the mistress was? Did they know that the children had royal blood? Fortunately for Ever, he didn't have to ask many questions to get his answers. It seemed Isa would do all of that and more for him. She was still glaring at the silent couple across the rough wooden table.

"I would answer her," Ever warned them.

"I am not their mother!" Helaine blurted out.

"So the children have told us," Isa said.

"They belong to my first wife," the woodcutter added.

"Well," Isa asked after a moment of silence, "do you care to explain? Or shall I make you?" She raised an eyebrow, daring him to refuse.

"She was an odd little thing," Claude sighed. "Half starved 'n half mad when I found her in the gutter of a village not far from here. Kept mutterin' that the king was her father. I thought it was the hunger 'twas driving her mad, so I brought her back to the village church and asked her to marry me. Told her I'd feed her 'n give her a home." He paused. "Never thought the madness would stay after she was fed and rested," he then added with a grumble.

His first wife? Ever was reeling. Sacha was the children's *mother?*

"Her mouth was so dry she could barely say the vows—"

"You didn't have the decency to get her to her right mind before wedding her?" Ever interrupted in disgust. "You couldn't even wet her tongue?" His voice was louder than he'd meant it to be, and the man shrank back like a frightened rat. *Good.* When Ever glanced at Isa, however, he realized she didn't seem nearly as surprised by this sham of a marriage as he was. Only angry. How common was this kind of marriage, where one could carry the other away and the holy man would oversee the vows without question?

"I didn't want nobody to think I was bein' indecent with 'er." Claude swallowed loudly.

"Continue," Isa said.

"We... We gets home, and she has a fit. 'I can't find the veil,' she says over and over again. It was a few weeks with me before she stopped talking so much nonsense. Liked to take long walks in the woods, though. And never got terribly fond of me."

"Did she ever find anything on her walks?" Isa asked.

"Not for a long while. Another few months and she was too heavy with the boy to walk far anymore." The woodcutter frowned, scratching his wide chin for a moment. "I didn't know what she was until after the boy came, though." He glanced at Henri, who now snored quietly in the corner beside his sister. "I soon found that she an' him could do things... Came in one day to see them playing with fire!"

"What were they doing?" Ever leaned forward. He had an idea as to what Claude meant, but he wanted to hear more about Sacha's abilities. And Henri's.

The woodcutter held up a rough, meaty hand. "The boy was makin' some sort of fire with his fingers, rolling it and bouncing it upon them, and she was watchin'." Claude shivered. "When I saw th' look on her face as she watched our son, I figured for the first time that she was no ordinary woman. An' she was different after that. Like another creature. Somethin' had changed her. Somethin' like," he leaned forward and whispered, "the Sorthileige."

"What did you do after that?" Ever asked.

The woodcutter just shrugged. "What could I do? She was short-tempered and did as she pleased. Still went on walks every day. Left the boy with me most hours."

Would it kill him, Ever wondered, *to ever use his son's name?*

"Few years later we had Genevieve. As soon as she saw the child, she insisted on walking again, though she was dirty and still breathing hard from the birthing bed. Still didn't find nothin'. Began to get even more ill-tempered. It became that if I displeased her, something unpleasant would happen the next day. She all but stopped talking t'the boy. Would come back from her walks with books and such. I can't read, but they gave me shivers enough whenever I looked at 'em."

Ever was beginning to see why Henri had spent so many hours at the church instead of at home.

Claude sighed. "I knew that it wouldn't be long then from the look she got in her eyes whenever she looked at the children. Sure enough, soon as the girl was weaned, barely over a year, Sacha went for her usual morning walk. Never came back. After she left, I had the holy man come and bless the house." Claude's voice cracked as he stared hard at the table. "'Twas a house of darkness."

Ever glanced at Isa, but her face gave nothing away. "Is that why you remarried?" she asked.

Poor Isa. She must have been dying on the inside to hear how these children she loved so much had been cast off. And, Ever found, it angered him too.

Claude nodded hesitantly, the silver in his beard glinting slightly in the firelight as he mumbled something about not being able to care for two young ones on his own.

"And I tried!" Helaine squawked. "But soon it was obvious that boy had witch powers in him. He would set things on fire! The house, the woodpile, even—"

As she prattled on, Ever couldn't help but think that it was a wonder Henri hadn't caused any more accidents than he already had, especially with someone like her around to make him doubt and hate himself so much.

"You still," Isa snapped, "haven't explained how the children got lost in a place where they had lived all their lives. Why would they get lost here? And why now?"

Claude didn't answer. Instead he turned to his wife and slightly lifted a brow. Her gaze flitted back and forth between her husband and Isa before finally nodding and making a subtle noise with her throat.

"Before the children were lost, unlucky things started to happen. Accidents befell us. Common and uncommon sicknesses, fire... even more than the boy's usual upsets," Claude whispered. "I knew it was her, calling them. I could feel her near."

"So you *gave* them to her?" Ever stood so fast his chair flipped backward with a bang, but he didn't care. "You are their *father!*"

"What could I do against her?" Claude blanched, holding his hairy arms out before him. "With all due respect, Your Majesty, you have never been in my place, nor do y'know what you would've done, what with Her Majesty not being able—"

"I would never have traded them for mere peace and quiet! I can promise you that." Ever spoke through clenched teeth, leaning over the table so that his nose nearly touched the large man's face.

"Hold on," Isa said. "You say you heard her *calling* for the children?"

"More or less."

Isa stared at Claude. Her dark blue eyes flashed as Ever felt her reach out with her power and wrench the man's soul out from its hiding place. And she didn't do it gently, for which he was glad.

"Oh, just tell them!" Helaine crossed her arms and rolled her eyes.

Claude made a gagging sound as Ever felt Isa release him from her stronghold. "She came to us, and we made a deal."

Ever had a mouthful of words that he wanted to shout at the man, including a few words in particular that he rarely uttered. Before he could, though, Isa turned to him with fear in her eyes.

"She was the one who placed us together!"

"What?"

Isa shook her head impatiently. "When I hit my head and fell through the tear, Sacha was the one who placed me with the children! They weren't there by accident. And neither was I. She *wanted* me to fall in love with them! Ever!" Isa covered her mouth. "She's planned this from the very start!"

Ever stared back into her eyes as the words sank in. The whole thing had been a trap.

"Get the children."

Isa scrambled to do as he said, but Claude protested.

"You can't just take my children! You just brought 'em back!"

"You said yourself that you cannot protect them." Ever grabbed the stocky man by the arm, satisfied when he heard something snap. "I'm not about to leave them with someone who would use them again to purchase peace of mind." With that, he turned and stormed over to where Isa had awakened Henri and was trying to rouse Genny. Ever scooped the little girl up in his arms and strode toward the door. "We're going. Now."

34

THE RIGHT THING

"*E*ver," Isa called softly as he placed Henri in front of her and then lifted Genny up onto his horse with him. Henri stirred in her arms but quickly settled into another doze. Ever didn't answer her, so she called his name again and finally moved her horse in front of his to make him stop. When his eyes met hers, they were full of a kind of pain Isa had never seen before. And yet, she had to ask. "What are we doing?"

"We're going to meet your brother. You and the children will stay with him, and I will come back and look for the veil's tear."

"But, Ever, these aren't our children," she said, her voice breaking. "We can't simply leave them with him—"

"I know that." She prayed for the right words. "But I just need to be sure we're doing the right thing." Isa paused. "They're hers, too," she whispered.

"Well, what do you propose we do?" he demanded. "Leave them with the father who gave them up to his wife of darkness? Or should we leave them to the Fae when she sends another creature to chase them?"

A tear slipped down Isa's cheek in the dark. That hurt. "Of course not," she said. She wanted them so badly it hurt. Every moment she held Henri's sleeping form close it broke her heart just a little more. They had said the vows. For one fleeting moment, she had been a mother.

They sat silently, not looking at one another as the sounds of the forest echoed around them. Thank the Maker the storm had abated, although thunder would have been a welcomed alternative to the brittle quiet now. Finally, in the thin light of the moon Isa could see Ever rub his face with his hand, the stubble of his untrimmed beard making a scratching sound as he did. "We need to keep going."

Isa nodded and nudged her horse forward.

Hours slipped by as they passed through the forest. Isa could feel tingles run up and down her bones, some stronger than others, as they went. The darkness that seeped out of nooks and crannies beneath stones and in the shadows of the trees was cold and wet and made her shiver. Never had she felt the Sorthileige in so many places. How had they been so naive as to think the dark magic had been nearly banished from their land? But then again, they had been blind enough to miss the children's true connection to Sacha. It seemed so obvious now.

"Where are we?" Henri raised his head and rubbed his eyes.

"You won't be staying with them after all," Isa said into his hair, not answering his question.

"Is it because they lost us on purpose?"

How much did he know?

"Some of it, yes," Isa said cautiously, wishing she could see his face better, rather than sitting behind him.

"Why would my father do that?" Henri asked then, his voice suddenly angrier than Isa had ever heard it.

"Because some men are just bastards," Ever growled. Isa shot him a pointed look, but Ever just ignored it.

Another silence stretched until the fuzzy gray of morning began to break through the trees. Finally, Isa worked up enough courage to ask Henri a question she knew might hurt him. But it had to be asked.

"Henri, did you recognize the woman who tended to us in the Fae world? The one who brought me to you, and who gave you cookies?"

"No." To Isa's great relief, Henri shook his head. "Why? Are you going to give us to her?"

"We will be doing no such thing," Ever said in a stern voice. "It's still early. You need to go back to sleep."

To Isa's surprise, the boy only gave Ever a long look before nodding slightly and leaning back against her. In only a few minutes he was snoring lightly.

"I'm sorry," Ever said. When Isa looked over at him, his gray, fire-ringed eyes were burning into hers.

"For what?"

"For how I spoke with you earlier." He sighed. "It was just ... In the moment the bastard admitted to giving them up, I finally understood the pain you must have been feeling for so long. I ... I *wanted* them."

Isa's eyes must have been ridiculously wide as she listened, but she was too enthralled to care.

"I've always wanted an heir," he continued. "It was expected, just a part of life. But now... now I want children. *These* children. And it kills me that I cannot change the life they've had to live when I have been only a short distance away. And the things that monster did to my sister?" He shrugged helplessly. "Maybe I could have prevented all of this long ago. Or at least much of it."

Isa sighed as he spoke. Once again, her husband had managed to hide a world of pain from even her. And yet her heart soared as it dawned on her that she was no longer alone in such longing. That he felt it too.

"There's no use in such thinking," she finally whispered. "You had no way of knowing what your father had done."

Ever moved his horse closer so he could reach out and gently squeeze her arm. "You asked if we were doing the right thing in taking them from their old home. They might not be my siblings, but they are still my father's grandchildren, which makes them children of the Fortress. Let us content ourselves for now knowing that we are still protecting them. And that's what matters." He paused. "We will sort it all out when things are better and the danger is not so high."

In the early morning light, Isa wondered again at just how incredibly striking her husband was. The sharp angles of his face and the way the gray light reflected off his armor made him look fierce. But the vulnerable, gentle way he was looking into her eyes now made her want to melt. Suddenly, her tired muscles felt loose and relaxed, and Isa felt a serenity that she hadn't felt in a very, very long time. It was with a sudden intensity that she longed to draw him close and kiss him as she never had before, to hold his face in her hands and to run her hand through his short golden hair. Had she ever loved him so much? Had she ever needed him so much?

"How are you feeling?" he asked, the kindness still on his face as he searched hers.

"I might have been helping the children sleep, so a bit more tired than I would have been otherwise, but," she paused and smiled, "I don't think I have ever been better or happier in my life."

The look Ever gave her was a reward itself, for just then the sun rose and set his golden hair aflame, and his smile was like its own beam of light.

Oh, why did they have to be running for their life just at this moment? She would much rather have spent it with her lips on his, holding him tightly against her away from harm and sorrow. Just as she began to say as much, Henri startled awake, and then Genny. The brother and sister briefly looked at one another before Henri twisted around to look at Isa, his eyes troubled. Green mist floated through his irises as he gazed up at her.

"Someone's coming."

35

MOTHER

*I*sa tightened her grip on Henri as dozens of blank-faced men and women with pikes made a half circle about them. Sacha rode to the center of the semicircle and stood before Isa and Ever on her own horse. Isa wanted to scream in frustration. How had she found them? Then she remembered the two miserable creatures back in the cottage they had just left.

"You." Sacha turned to a nearby male. Wordlessly, he came and helped her down from her horse, where she stood and stretched for a moment before speaking. From the way she moved, Isa guessed Sacha was not used to riding horses for long distances. Isa hoped the witch's behind would bruise. She also wished bruises upon the two degenerates they had just left behind. Sacha must have been just on their trail the whole time.

"Henri."

Isa tensed as Sacha turned to her son.

The woman's voice was gentler than Isa had ever heard it. "Do you remember me?"

Henri leaned back into Isa as he studied the woman before him. "No." He paused. "Wait. You were the woman in the other world, the one who gave us cookies."

"Yes, that was me. But do you not remember me from before?"

Henri shook his head, and a brief flash of pain lit the woman's face before she smiled again.

"I'm your mum. Your *real* mum." When Henri didn't respond, she picked up a nearby stone and set it flat in her palm. With the snap of her fingers, she set the stone on fire and began to roll it along her fingers. "Do you remember," she whispered, "when we used to do this together?"

"That's Henri's trick!" Genny said, pointing.

But Henri stiffened beneath Isa's arm. "You look different from her."

She smiled wryly. "I look like the queen I am now, if that's what you mean." She eyed him up and down. "Just as you have come to look like the prince you truly are."

Isa closed her eyes briefly and tried to test the woman's heart. What was she up to, trying to contact the children she had abandoned? And why now? But unfortunately, it seemed that Sacha could be just as skilled at masking her feelings and intentions as her brother. What little Isa could taste was fear. But what was Sacha afraid of?

Sacha walked a few steps closer, and Isa clutched the boy more tightly to her until Henri turned and looked at Isa directly, his blue eyes full of questions.

"You knew she was my mother?"

"Your father only told us last night," Isa said, her throat tight.

Sacha's face was beginning to redden, and she had taken one more step toward them when Genny spoke up.

"King Ever, who's that?"

"My darling!" Sacha turned to the little girl as though just remembering that she had a daughter too.

Ever's eyes burned more brightly, and like Isa, he squeezed the little girl closer to his broad chest.

"You don't remember me," Sacha stretched her hand out, "but I'm your mummy!" Genny leaned back into Ever and frowned, but Sacha continued to stretch both arms out. "Give me my daughter," she said in a strained voice. "I have not held her since she was a babe."

"An injustice that is your fault entirely. If you think I am going to willingly hand over a child that you sent a violent Fae to fetch *after* you abandoned her twice, then you are sorely mistaken." Ever drew his sword with the arm not holding Genny. "Either of these children, for that matter."

In response, Isa drew her own sword, and the soldiers began to thin into green mists, staying just solid enough to hold their pikes. Sacha drew her sword as well.

In one swift move, Ever was off his horse and had wedged Genny in the little space between Isa and Henri. He slapped her horse on the rump. "Go!" he shouted. Just as her horse turned, however, it stopped and reared. Pain shot through Isa as she was slammed to the ground. Genny landed on her chest and Henri on her legs.

She wasn't allowed to recover her breath, though, for the Fae were upon them immediately. Green mists faded in and out as the Fae moved between forms like dozens of green snowflakes melting and then freezing once again. Isa leapt to her feet as well as she could, still holding Genny against her legs as Henri scrambled up to stand beside her.

Fortress, she cried out inside, *I will not pretend to know what you are about here, but please protect your children, just as you promised!*

Bringing her sword up, Isa could feel the Fortress's power move out of her like rain bursting forth from a storm cloud, heavy and dark. It was not the heart power that she usually felt, but rather the same fiery strength that Ever possessed. And today, it was hers.

Genny shrieked as the first Fae made its attack, thickening again and grabbing its pike from the ground as it moved toward them. But Isa met his attack easily. As more and more Fae, male and female, tried to touch Isa with the poisonous pikes, Isa could feel the power of the Fortress pulsing around and through her. The Fae gnashed the teeth in their blank, simple faces, but no matter how many seemed to pile in around them, only one at a time could step through the blue whirlwind of fire that surrounded her and the children. And Isa was more than ready, all thoughts of exhaustion gone as Genny pressed in at her legs and Henri at her side. The attacks continued to come, but each only further ignited Isa's raw determination to keep them safe.

Ever seemed to have received no such respite. The flash of his sword against his sister's was blinding, lightning striking repeatedly as they clashed. Isa peeked at them between her opponents' attacks and was dismayed to see that Sacha seemed to be just as skilled with the sword as Ever. Even her twists and turns were familiar as they battled over the rocky, pinecone-littered terrain. For the first time in her life, Isa wondered if Ever would defeat his opponent. His sister's power was palpable and her moves swift and deadly. His many times in battle should have given him the edge. But the rage Isa could feel radiating from Sacha's heart was vicious.

A shriek from Genny snapped Ever's head toward them and reminded Isa of her own fight. She had become lazy in her defenses. A female Fae had edged closer to them, despite the fire wind's blanket of safety. Isa quickly knocked the pike from the woman's hands, but the damage had been done. Ever's distraction had given Sacha the chance to spring at him and knock his sword out of his hand. Ever immediately grabbed Sacha's wrist, the one that held her sword. Back and forth the sword went, first closer to one face and then to the other. Ever cried out, though, when Sacha delivered a kick to his bad knee.

The Fae stopped attacking Isa, also watching their leader face off with Destin's king. The longer the siblings fought, however, for control of the sword, the more Ever began to lose his ground. The angle at which he gripped the sword was awkward, and Sacha had the higher ground.

"Stop!"

Everyone, even Sacha and Ever, turned to look at Henri. Before Isa could stop him, he broke away from her, darting through the dying fire wind and changing green mists, throwing himself between Ever and Sacha. "We're going with my mother. Genny and me."

Isa turned to resume her fight, for there was no way she and Ever would allow such a thing. But for the second time that day, she was tossed to the ground so hard her vision spun. A blurry figure pulled Genny from Isa's arms and carried her away. Not far off, Ever cried out. Then all went black.

36

NOT HERS

*T*wo whole days of travel passed before Henri could gather the courage to talk to his mother.

His mother. What a strange thing to say.

It seemed wrong to call her *Mother* when she was the one who had sentenced King Ever and Miss Isa to ride behind them as captives even after his sacrifice.

He had hoped that upon giving himself up and going with the new woman, the king and queen would be allowed to run to her brother as they had planned to do. Then they could return to the Fortress and save them all. He had never expected the Fae to strike Miss Isa upon the head, or worse, for another to stab the king. The pike head had gone so far into the king's shoulder that the two leaves tied to it had also been buried in the flesh. Now as they rode the king's face was deathly pale, and his body shuddered from time to time. He might have fallen off his horse if they hadn't tied him to it.

Perhaps, if Henri were brave enough, he might convince his mother to be kinder to them. Maybe, at the very least, she might let the king have some water.

Henri swallowed hard, clutching Genny tightly to his chest, before riding up beside his mother's horse. As he did, he was thankful again that Miss Isa had taught him to ride a horse so he didn't have to ride with one of the blank-faced Fae that surrounded them.

"How do you know him?" he asked.

"Hm, what?" His mother shook her head as though awakening from a daydream.

He repeated his question.

"Henri, that man is my younger brother, your uncle."

"Our uncle? Then why didn't we meet him before?"

"Oh, he was too busy guarding his riches and wealth and training his precious army." Her eyes glinted the way Genny's did when she was about to throw a fit. Henri would have to tread carefully.

"Is he why you left?" he asked.

She turned to look down at him, and her eyes softened. "In a way, I suppose."

"Because you wanted to see him?"

At this, her eyes bulged. "Why would I do that?" Henri looked down at the ground that passed beneath them, but his mother continued. "Why would I visit the man who lived only days away and let his nephew and niece nearly starve to death? That man is dangerous, cruel, and selfish, not at all the man he's tricked you into thinking he is. Never doubt for a moment that Everard Fortier is an instrument of evil." Her frown deepened. "Just as my father was." She stopped talking for a moment and studied Henri for the first time since she'd met them in the forest two days before. "Out of curiosity, why do you ask?"

Henri had to take a deep breath as he struggled to hold her gaze. What he wanted to say seemed very much like it would make her angry. That the things she and her people had done to the king and queen were cruel and nothing like what he could ever do to Genny, even if he were very angry with her. "I... I don't remember you much," he finally said in a low voice. Not a true answer to her question, but it seemed to appease her, for the intense glare once again softened on her face.

"What do you remember?"

"You taught me my trick." He held up his hand and briefly rolled a little ball of blue flame between his fingers.

She nodded. "What else?"

Henri looked back down at his sister's curly yellow hair. She hadn't said a word since the king and queen had been tied up. Not even their mother's best pleading and promises of treats had gotten her to speak. And, Henri realized with annoyance, she really didn't have any reason to. He might have vague memories of his mother's face, the way her chin had a handsome tilt to it, or how she rolled the fire around her fingers. But when it came to Genny, Henri had done it all. His mother had done nothing. He could feel the heat rise to his face, and before thinking better of it, he snapped.

"I remember teaching Genny to walk. And talk. And Stepmother made me learn to braid her hair so she wouldn't have to. And you didn't say anything when we were in that other world, even though you knew it was us!" He was suddenly shouting. "Miss Isa and King Ever talked to us and spent time with us. More than you ever did!"

His mother held her fingers up and snapped them, uttering something under her breath that Henri couldn't hear. His mouth immediately shut, though he wasn't done talking.

"Hold!" his mother called up to the front before moving her horse over to his until she was close enough to reach over and grab his chin roughly. Henri tried to jerk his face free, but she was too strong. As she leaned in, her short, golden hair swayed back and forth along her jawline. "I don't care what your uncle did with or for you before I was here. Everything I've done, including leaving, was for you and your sister. I wanted to give the world to you. *This* world! But I couldn't do that with your worthless father around, so I had to go! I even sent you with *her*," she jerked her chin back in Miss Isa's direction, "so you could live in the palace until I came. But from now on, you will respect and obey me, or you will be very sorry you didn't. Understand?"

Henri could feel Genny shrink into him, but something within him, a fire from deep down, would not allow him to look away. He nodded, but only because his chin was beginning to hurt.

As she let go and yelled for the group to continue, he felt the familiar flash of warmth move through him as he always did when he sensed someone about to use their power. His mother barked out orders and their horses began to pick up speed.

Something strong was stirring within his mother. She claimed that all she did was for him, but Henri sensed that whatever power she was harnessing was volatile and barely restrained. In fact, it didn't feel like it belonged to her at all.

Suddenly, Henri wanted nothing more than to hide in Miss Isa's arms once again. For that, he would happily trade having a mother.

THE OTHER ONE

"Take her to the dungeon and my children to their rooms," Sacha announced as they marched through the Fortress's grand entrance. "I want to speak with my brother." She turned and glared at her companions. "Alone."

Ever glanced at Isa, who gave him a weak smile and a nod as the Fae began to pull her toward the main dungeon. At least, it seemed, they didn't know about the outer dungeons. Not that either was highly desirable. His heart ached when the children also turned and looked at him, their eyes wide with fear. It killed him that he could do nothing. But the poison from the hemlock was thick in his blood by now. And even if he could fight, he couldn't best all of her men. They'd already proven that. Isa or one of the children might be hurt.

As he turned and began to follow his sister, he noticed that new banners already hung from the walls. A sickly mixture of green and yellow, it appeared, but his headache was painful enough that he couldn't really trust his eyes.

Ever's heart sank even deeper as they descended into one of the lowest levels of the Fortress. He didn't have to look up from the floor to realize they were headed toward the practice room. As they neared it, to his surprise, she fell back a step to walk beside him. When she did, he couldn't help but study her in the dim light of the torches hung on the walls. Seeing his father's familiar features in a female's face was strange. She wasn't what he would call beautiful, but handsome would have been a better word if his view of her hadn't been so skewed by her evil.

"So, little brother," Sacha said pleasantly, "I want to get to know you. Tell me about yourself."

"What is it you wish to know?"

"Did our father love you?"

Ever studied her for a moment longer, a bit surprised at the question. Her tone was friendly enough, but she was blinking too rapidly to be as calm as she appeared. "In his own way," Ever said slowly.

"How so?"

"He trained me."

"Ha," she scoffed. "He trained me too. What else?"

"Tell me where Garin is and I'll answer you."

"How about you tell me what I want to know, and I'll not kill him right at this moment."

Ever bowed his head in concession, but inside he was rejoicing. His mentor was still alive. For now, at least.

"Our father taught me to control my temper, a hot one that runs in the family, I'm afraid."

"Maybe," she said, not looking at him this time, "if you hear my side of the story, it will loosen your tongue a bit."

Ever was all for that. The long walk was beginning to strain him. It was far too much like the time he was cursed, for his breaths were beginning to come hard and fast, and sweat trickled down his temples and back.

"Rodrigue never lived with me and my mother in the Fae world. He couldn't, he said. It shifted too much. Nothing lasted, he would rant, and that was not his way. But he visited quite a bit, and always with gifts." Her gray eyes became distant. "He had the best presents. Toys, dolls, and as I got older, gowns, jewels, and weapons." The small smile that lit her face as she spoke looked strange in the flickering light of the torches.

"When I was six, he decided to train me. He would bring a new weapon every few months. A sword, a bow, a knife, and so on. I was good, he told me. I had a gift! Then about the time I was eight, he began to teach me how to use my special powers. Powers, he said, that came from a long line of strong warriors."

Her voice had become dreamy, but then she shook her head and lifted her chin slightly higher as she spoke. "I always begged him to take me with him whenever he left. Enough of his human blood was inside me for me to hate the Fae world. There is no continuity, and the older I got, the more I could see why he disliked being there. My mother cared little, for she had other men. Fae are not monogamous, you know."

Ever didn't know, nor did he really want to.

"But *I* was half human, and though my peers shared little care for their parents' affection one way or another, I did care. Still, he never let me go with him. He said his world was not the place for me, and mine not for him."

Finally, they reached the large wooden door that opened up into the great room of stone and walls covered in weapons.

"Choose," Sacha said once they were inside. Ever stared back at her until she rolled her eyes and gestured at the hanging weapons. "Choose one, or I shall choose one for you."

Ever trudged slowly over to the wall. The larger weapons were tempting. After the sword, he was quite comfortable with the short-handled mace or even one of the staffs. But his strength was waning quickly, and he needed something small and light that would allow him to fight without being hindered by its size.

"You're stalling," Sacha said.

Ever walked slowly to the wall and pulled down the claw blade, a knife no larger than his hand with a hilt and blade that curved up like a crescent moon.

"Interesting choice. Now it's my turn." Sacha went over to another wall across the room and pulled down one of the daggers. "This way we will be even, little brother."

"And what exactly are we fighting for?"

"I want to see how our father did with you."

"Didn't we just do that?"

"You were distracted by the others. This time if you are distracted, you have no one to blame but yourself." She backed up and began to walk a wide arc around him. He had no doubt his father had trained her as she melted into the stance of a great cat. It was his stance.

"He said nothing to me of you," Ever said quietly. "I swear."

"I'm sure he didn't." Her voice was bitter. "No king would want to admit his illegitimate child to his heir." She kept circling but regarded him with an unreadable expression. "I heard someone say one time that you grew up a lonely boy. But even *you* can't empathize with a half-human who grew up in the world of Fae."

Ever stood still as she circled him, trying to regain the energy he lost on the walk to the weapons room. "We reproduce," she continued, "but there are few family ties. There were once, I heard, but that hasn't been since ... well, since your precious steward betrayed us all. It was decided that loyalty to the people should be chosen over that of the family. Children are kept alive by their parents when they are young, but most simply fend for themselves within a few years of birth. Parents do little in the lives of their children now among my people. Keeping to the Fae people as a whole is more important."

"That makes little sense." Ever crouched but found his joints stiff.

"Does it?" She began to close the distance between them. "I don't know what your steward told you, but the young Fae that he killed to save the Fortier line? That was his son."

Ever stared at her, and Garin's last words came back to him from that awful night.

The Maker saw it fit for me to defend this sacred ground from the bloodied hands of my own son.

In one brilliant leap, Sacha crossed the distance between them. Ever ducked and rolled, but his shoulder screamed with pain, and the swift movement made him dizzy. Before he could orient himself, a thin line of blood rolled down his left arm, breaking, Ever was sure, the quick stitches Isa had been forced to give him the night before as they'd camped. Sacha hopped back a few feet.

"Too many died in the Fortress's final scourge because of your steward. After that day, the remainder of our people, thanks to the traitor, decided that families should not be tightly knit. Rather, children would learn from all. That way, there would be no particular ties to one individual or another. Along with families, monogamous bonds disappeared as well." She flipped her short blonde hair as she began to circle him once again. "It couldn't have been a difficult transition, I suppose. Our natures are transient enough."

"You don't sound convinced," Ever said as he pushed himself to his feet again, praying suddenly for some way, *any* way to reach her. The pain and loneliness on her face were clear. If only he could use that to show her what she could have if she joined him. Them. Everyone Ever held dear. A curious, childlike voice inside him wondered what it would truly be like to have a sister.

Sacha shrugged. "It's how the Fae are, and I have seen the efficiency of their methods now. But there was a long time before that when I didn't." She pranced forward again. This time, Ever was able to block her first strike. He leapt forward to grab her wrist and twist it. She grunted as he wrapped her arm around her back and stole the dagger. The fast movements were making his head spin, however, giving her the time to elbow him with enough force to bloody his nose and loose the dagger from his hands. In a second, it was hers once again.

"I always saw myself as lesser," she said, hopping back, "because I couldn't disappear completely as my peers could do. I longed for our father the way none of them had ever yearned for their parents. When he was around I could be proud, for he was able to show me what I was capable of. He even taught me how to use the power from *both* of my heritages. One day, I vowed, I would be like him."

"When did he stop coming?" Ever asked, trying to ignore the violent throbbing in his nose as he wiped the blood on his shoulder. A shudder passed through him, and for a second, his hand and wrist seized from the poison. He needed to keep her talking so he could catch his breath.

"As I grew older, he visited less and less, but when I was seventeen, he finally told me he wouldn't be returning again. He was needed elsewhere." She stopped moving for a moment, her face suddenly hard. "You wouldn't happen to know anything about that, would you?"

Ever didn't know how old his sister was, but a whisper in his head told him he knew exactly what period of time she was referring to. And from the cutting look in her gray eyes, a look his father had worn often, Ever knew he had just forfeited his chance of winning his sister over. Or rather, his father had.

"When he told me," she whispered, "I clung to him, begged and wept that he would take me with him. I couldn't stand living in that wretched world forever. But to no avail. The last time he touched me in my world was when he brushed me aside so he could return through his precious veil."

"I am sorry," Ever said, unable to think of any words more adequate. As harsh as Rodrigue had sometimes been with him, it now seemed incomparable to what his sister had lived with.

A small smile touched Sacha's thin lips. "He thought he'd sealed up the veil behind him, but I was able to use my powers to place a foothold as one does with a door to keep it from closing. I bided my time until I could hoard enough food for some sort of journey. Then, when I was eighteen, I slipped through the veil and set out in search of our father."

"How did you find him?"

"Sometimes people took me in. I looked and acted human enough not to raise too much suspicion. Other times I slept in the forest or on the road. I knew that I would probably find him near the beloved Fortress he'd told me so much about."

She stopped and held up her weapon, testing its edge on her finger. Ever didn't miss the hint. "It took me weeks, but eventually I did find him. When I did, he was making a speech at Soudain's edge, just at the foot of the mountain." She looked at Ever, tilting her head slightly and placing a finger on her cheek.

"You were there by his side. He had never told me I had a brother, but you looked so much like him that I knew immediately who you were. Still, I was so excited to see him, and I was so sure he had missed me, too, that I shouted out in the middle of his speech and ran to him as fast as I could."

"I wish I remembered." Ever shook his head, trying to clear the cobwebs inside that the hemlock was weaving in his mind.

Sacha gave him a sour smile then began to creep forward again. Ever tried to stand ready, but his strength was leaking like water from a cracked pitcher. His knee felt like it was shattered.

"It was probably no more than a nuisance to you. And you were young. I'm sure a more unacceptable sight could never be seen by a father, though. His unwanted daughter was running toward him with her hands burning blue and green, wearing a dirty dress some peasant woman had offered me along the way when my own gown had become too torn to continue properly.

"To this day," Sacha's voice was suddenly dead as she raised her knife, "I don't know what he did to me, but I could not use my power after that for a very long time. None of it, not even my Fae abilities. He personally dragged me to the edge of the crowd, and I'm sure would have gone farther, except that you ran up to him to ask him what he was doing."

Ever tried hard to recall that day, but he couldn't. How old would he have been? Had he truly seen his sister years before? Before he could remember, he was on the ground again. This time, the dagger traced his collarbone down one side and then up the other. Pain followed each slice. With a shout, he was able to shove his body over enough to knock her off his chest. As soon as she was off, he rolled backward until he could pull himself up to his knees. But no higher.

"He stopped to tell you to stay where you were." Her wry smile was gone, and in her eyes was only hatred. "I took that moment to run."

"Where did you go?" he rasped.

She lunged forward again, this time leading with her fists. He blocked her first flurry of punches, and even managed to hook his little knife around her neck, but he wasn't strong enough to hold her there. She shrugged out and danced away again. When would she tire of playing with him? *I can't hold out much longer,* he told the Fortress. In response, a tiny breeze fluttered around him, only strong enough to tickle the nape of his neck. Ever almost smiled. *If this is what you wish, then I will continue to wait,* he thought. His cuts screamed and his head throbbed and his vision was most definitely blurred, but the Fortress was there with him. For this reason, Ever would hang on.

"I wandered," Sacha said, "doing odd jobs here and there. I wasn't much use to most. Few people want a half-starved woman who knows how to use the sword. But eventually I learned how to feed slop to the pigs and corn to the chickens. Seven years of wandering will teach you that, you know. Then, after a particularly bad beating by my most recent employer, my *husband* found me in a gutter, filled me with wine, and dragged me down to some holy man not worth his cloth who married me to a stranger without as much as noting my sobriety."

Ah. This was why the Fortress had told him to wait. "You could have told me who you were," he said.

"You wouldn't have believed—"

"I would have felt your power, and so would Garin," he cut her off sharply. "Father might have denied you, but I never would." He leaned forward on one hand, begging the Fortress to let her *see*. If only Isa were here. "I always wanted a sister. I would have protected you! The Fortress would have protected you!"

She lowered her weapon and studied him with her too-bright gray eyes. For a moment, Ever saw the vulnerable, injured girl she must have been. Her eyes were wide, and despite the thin lines around them, she suddenly looked very young. And lonely. It was a look he had seen on Henri's face many times.

"You would have been sheltered," he whispered, stumbling to his feet, "just as your children were."

The open expression was suddenly gone, and her mouth twisted into a smirk. "And how well were they received by your steward? After all, he killed his own son."

"I still don't understand why you wouldn't come to me," Ever said again, ignoring the bait. "You could have at least tried."

"Let me put this clearly." She melted down into her cat-like stance again. "You were his spitting image, down to that quirked brow you hold now. I knew better than to place my hope in a man."

"I have changed," Ever said quietly. "I am not that man anymore."

"You're right. You aren't that man anymore." Sacha began to stalk forward, and Ever sensed she wouldn't be toying with him for much longer. Warily, he raised his own weapon one more time, trying to ignore the way his back and shoulders seized up.

"I might not have been in the Fortress courts," Sacha said, "but I have kept watch on you and your little wife since the beginning. She's changed you. Made you soft. If it hadn't been for her effect on you," Sacha crouched low, "I wouldn't have gained my foothold in your door. It took me five years, but I *did* find the veil's tear. And when I did, I returned to a people who had mocked me for too long. But unlike *your* people, we hold on to our legends. They do not become a thing of myth. There are few direct ties between kin, but as a people, we are strong! And when I told them that I had found the man whose ancestor banished us to our realm, they were thirsty for blood."

"Why are you telling me all of this?"

Instead of answering, she pounced. Ever's head hit the stone floor. His already queasy stomach nearly convulsed as she planted a knee in it. Her dagger was to his throat, and her face was so close he could feel the heat of her breath.

This was it then. *Take care of them,* he begged the Fortress. His fever was raging, and he began to shake violently, though from the head injury or the poison, he couldn't be sure. He'd been using his power to hold off the worst symptoms, but now there was little left to fight with.

"I told you so you would know," she said, "that I am not a complete monster. You see, I cannot blame you wholly for what our father did or did not do for us. I also, however, believe that I *am* the rightful heir since I came first." She moved the dagger down over his heart. When she spoke again, her voice was surprisingly soft. "I am going to give you this one chance to live and take my mercy. I'm sure by now your wife has informed you that her ability to grow her own child has been removed?"

Ever's anger that had subsided returned to him like a flood. With a roar, he shoved her off his chest and leapt to his feet, but she easily knocked the knife from his hand and had him at her dagger's point once again.

"Here's my offer. I remove the curse which I placed upon her if you swear to leave Destin and never return." Her voice grew nearly inaudible. "Find a quiet place and settle down. Have a family." She leaned back a bit and searched his eyes. "Be happy."

"And leave you with my people and the two children whom you sent two Fae after?" he growled.

"Oh, that. I wanted to know your strength. When the messengers didn't return, I knew more about you, and that you were willing to do what you thought was necessary to protect your hold on the kingdom."

"And had I failed," he ground his teeth through another round of shaking, "what would you have done if the Fae had killed your children?"

"They wouldn't have—"

"I know bloodlust in a creature's eyes when I see it!" he shouted.

"But you didn't let them hurt the children, did you?"

"So you sent your own people into my home to die? Life is quite cheap to you, isn't it?"

"And I would do it again!" she shouted back. Her hand shook as she held the dagger against him. Green mist rippled through her gray eyes. "If there was one thing I learned from Father, it is that I will do what I must for the better of my people."

"And so will I."

"So," she stepped back, "you would refuse your wife the one thing she desires, to save your own crown?"

For once, Ever had no answer. The pain in his chest was too tight. *Why,* he cried out to the Fortress, *are you allowing her to do this? How has she grown so powerful as to defeat even the power you have placed in me?* But there was no answer. Only that nagging sensation to be patient. So he said nothing.

"Then you may expect no other such offers from me," she said in a low voice. With that, she reeled back and smacked the butt of her dagger across his head. "Put him with the others. But I want them in separate cells."

Two Fae, a male and a female, came in and began to drag him toward the door by his arms. Ever thrashed, trying to break free, but it was no use. The hemlock's venom was sending his body into convulsions, and his efforts only brought him a severe bout of pain as he was dragged back to the hall.

"Oh," Sacha said, turning just before they led him out. "I will take this first, though." She lifted his left hand and slipped the signet ring from his finger.

38

RELEASE

*T*he poison had kept Ever's heart beating at an erratic pace for hours, sometimes slowing it dangerously and other times speeding it so fast he felt lightheaded. But he felt his heart come to a complete stop when his eyes adjusted to the dark enough to make out the limp body hanging in the stocks.

Before he could run to the body, however, one of the Fae delivered a sharp kick to his shoulder. Pain seared down his arm and even his chest and sides as he clutched at the bloodied hole the Fae's pike had left three days before. Through stinging tears, Ever raised his shaking head to look at the man in the stocks again. But before he could speak or reach out, both Fae guards picked him up and tossed him into an empty cell, sending yet another wave of pain through his body.

"Ever!" His wife's voice came from somewhere else in the dark room. There, in the faint light of the single candle, Isa knelt on the other side of Ever's bars in the cell adjacent to his. "You need to heal yourself now!" Her voice was strained. "The poison will kill you if you don't stop it."

"I don't have time for that," Ever panted as he rolled slowly to his knees. "Takes too long." He began to crawl toward the bars but was interrupted by a violent twitching in his right arm. The smell of mildew assaulted him, and odd lights briefly danced before his eyes. The poison was spreading, but all Ever could do was grind his teeth as he waited for his vision to return to normal and his arm to stop moving. He'd had brief sensations like this over the past four days, but this was by far the worst. With Garin on the other side of the bars, however, Ever hadn't the time to pay heed to his wound. As soon as he was able to sit up straight, he crawled over to the bars in stiff, awkward movements. "Garin?"

At first, Ever feared the man in the stocks wouldn't move at all, but finally, his head rolled to the side just enough for Ever to see that Garin was still there. Ever grabbed the bars in front of him and began to pull. Isa protested and scolded away about his health, but Ever didn't listen. The bars gave way a little, but much less than they should have. His strength was almost gone.

A sharp object was thrust through the bars, just inches from his face, and Ever looked up to see the Fae woman guard standing just outside his cell, her face taut. Ever grabbed the pike's end and was about to loose the rest of his strength into this evil, mystical creature, when he heard a soft voice to his left.

"Slow down," Isa said softly. "Let me handle this."

Ever wanted to retort that he didn't need her help in tearing this monster limb from limb, but as he opened his mouth, the Fae's face smoothed, losing what little emotion it had held before. Ever turned to see Isa closing her eyes, one hand on the bars and the other outstretched palm up to the Fae woman.

"We need time alone," Isa whispered. "We will not be escaping tonight." Normally, it would have bothered Ever to have his wife promise a guard they wouldn't try to escape, but this time he knew she was right. Garin wasn't moving anywhere in such a poor state, and Ever was not going to leave him again.

It took longer than usual for Isa to convince their captor to see the truth, so long that Ever thought it might not work. But finally, the Fae woman nodded once before returning her pike to its upright position. To Ever's surprise, she even took out a key and unlocked both his and Isa's cell doors. She shut the prison door behind her as she left.

Isa let out a sigh but didn't open her eyes. "Go on," she said. "Let him loose."

Ever nearly passed out in his attempt to lift Garin out of the stocks, and when he finally did, the older man's body dragged along like Genny's rag doll.

"Garin," he started, but he could say nothing else. Dried blood matted Garin's face and his long gray hair, and even in the dark his skin seemed nearly transparent. Ever delicately lifted the steward's head and shoulders into his lap, and Isa, seeming to have recovered herself, scrambled to sit on Garin's other side.

"There you are." Garin's eyes opened a slit, and though his breathing was labored, he gave Ever a ghost of a smile. "I wondered what was taking so long."

"Forgive me!" Ever pulled him closer and laid his head on the steward's shoulder. "I shouldn't have gone! I should have come back for you."

"You did exactly as I told you." Garin burst into a fit of coughing. The spell lasted so long that Isa also placed her hand under Garin's head, her face puckering with worry as she wiped the beads of sweat off his forehead with the end of her skirt.

"What did they do to you?" Ever whispered. But even as he asked, he knew what he needed to do. Closing his eyes, Ever gathered what little remained of his strength, taking the steward's hand in his own. The moment felt eerily familiar.

And like his father, the steward pulled his hand free. "No, Ever," the steward said.

But Ever wouldn't lose another this way. Not again. Determined, he firmly placed his hands over Garin's heart, and the blue light began to drip from his battered body into his friend, a light blue glow emanating from Garin's chest.

"Ever." Isa placed her hand on his. "This isn't going to work."

But Ever only shoved her hand off. Why wouldn't they just let him focus? Again, he pressed, and again, the blue light began to trickle out, but it was getting harder by the second, and Ever began to shake with the effort.

"Everard!" Isa took him by the arms and shook him hard, briefly reigniting the pain in his shoulder. "You need to stop! You're killing yourself!"

"What if I want to die?" he shouted back. The words were out before he had time to consider them. He didn't miss the look of pain on Isa's face. "I can't do it." He hung his head as tears began to drip from his eyes. "First she'll take Garin. Then she'll take you. I cannot keep watching this death." Sobs racked his body.

"No need to be so dramatic, Ever." Garin's voice was surprisingly mild, as though he were actually smiling. "We all die."

"Why, Garin?" He stared hard into his mentor's face, trying to memorize its features in the dim light. "Why would the Fortress allow this? Why must so much evil abound?" His words were hard and cold as he spoke them. There was no excuse for this, no reason that the evil should have its way so easily.

"That is simple. Because my duty is now fulfilled."

"It can't be. I still need you. I need you more than ever now, to tell me what to do!" Another spasm tried to take him, but Ever fought it with all his might. As he did, though, something inside warned him that his ability to ignore the poison's effects would soon be gone.

Garin reached up with a shaking hand and gently touched Ever's face. "You helped heal a heart that had been broken for centuries. I lost my son to the evil of my people, but the Maker has kept me here for so many years, waiting until I found another."

"But I'm not your son. And I brought the curse! I have pained you again and again with my folly. And yet you bore it with patience! I cannot have been the good son you deserved to have!"

"You may not be my son by blood, but you became my life. From the moment I looked into your eyes, I knew I would love you in a way I hadn't loved anyone in five hundred years." He chuckled softly, which sent him into another coughing spell. "There were moments, to be sure, when you tried my patience. For example, all those times salt magically appeared in my tea." He squeezed Ever's hand. "But you are a man now. And I couldn't be more proud."

"But—"

"That's what a father is, Ever. You watch your children fall, and you help them get back up. And you love them through it all." Garin turned to Isa, his breath becoming fainter each time he spoke. Still, he managed to reach up with a shaking hand and touch her cheek as well, wiping at the tears that were rolling silently down her face.

"Be patient with him, my dear. And never lose that heart of yours. I knew you were special the moment I saw you as a little girl, with your bouncing braids and bright eyes. In the last four years, you have far exceeded even my expectations. Now that I will be gone, it will be your duty to take care of Ever." His eyes twinkled even in the dim light. "Someone has to do it."

Isa wiped her tears on her sleeve and nodded, still crying as she leaned down to plant a kiss on the older man's forehead.

How dare she nod? Agreeing with Garin was admitting defeat.

"I need to know, though," she said in a shaky voice, "why couldn't Ever heal them?"

"Because they were never sick."

"What?"

Garin let out a raspy sigh. "I should have seen it before, but I've spent a long time away from my people. I happened to see one of the children more closely as they prepared to punish me for my crimes."

Ever burned with rage as he listened, but he let Garin continue uninterrupted.

"I realized that the children's symptoms, like so much else, were only illusions."

"But the pain!" Isa said. "They were in pain!"

"My people are skilled deceivers."

"Then why couldn't I see through it?" Isa sounded indignant.

Garin laughed again, his chuckle hardly more than a whisper. "You are strong, but there is still much of your power that you haven't even tapped." He broke into his worst coughing fit yet, and when he lowered his hand, Ever could see drops of blood on his palm.

"So it was all a ruse," Isa whispered. "Just like the house."

"Don't you see why we need you?" Ever leaned closer. "We cannot defeat her on our own!"

Garin let out another rattling sigh, the gleam no longer in his eye. "I have been working for over five centuries, Ever. I am tired, and the Maker has seen fit to finally bring me to my eternal rest."

Ever shook his head at this, tears beginning once again to fall, but in the dark, Garin smiled. "You will see me again when it is your time." He wheezed out a chuckle. "That, of course, gives you no right to try and see me sooner than you must. You have a family to care for now. Your wife needs you, the kingdom needs you ... and those children need you."

"They cannot be ours. Both of their parents live." Ever's voice came out more bitter than he'd expected.

"That does not mean they need you any less. You, of all people, know what woman you leave them to if you allow her to keep them. Now, promise me, Ever, that you will not give up." Garin suddenly jerked forward, grabbing Ever by the collar and pulling his face down. "Promise!"

But Ever could only shake his head. "I don't believe it," he whispered. "The

Fortress *will* restore you. It always does." It had to. Ever had never needed Garin so much in his life as he did now.

Yet Garin closed his eyes, a small smile on his lips. "Not this time, son. But," he squeezed Ever's hand once more, trembling as he did, "the Maker has left me enough life that I may finish this final task."

"No!" Ever cried out. He tried to pull his hand out of Garin's trembling grasp, but it was too late. Garin's hand seemed to be sewn to his. Blue whorls of light began to ebb out of the steward's body and into Ever's. The waves of light looked like water flowing out of a crystal pool. Ever could feel the power entering his body, and he begged the Fortress to make it stop. But the power continued to come until it slowed to a drip. Finally, it grew so thin that Ever didn't know whether it was still coming or not. He clung to Garin's body, praying until he broke into a cold sweat. *No,* he told the Fortress. *Not now. If you love me, you won't take him from me. If you truly love me, you'll leave him for just a while longer.*

How many hours passed, Ever didn't know, nor did he care. And finally there came a moment when Garin let out one breath and did not draw in another. For a brief moment, the room grew as bright as day in the flash of a blinding light. Azure fire glowed, lighting the edges of Garin's body, the protector of kings that Ever held in his lap. Fierce wings exploded upward, and in that short moment, Garin himself shone like a star in the night skies. Then the light went out, and the man Ever had cradled was gone.

39

REASONS

*A*s the Fae led him up to the Tower of Annals, Henri was suddenly very glad his sister hadn't been allowed to come. He had always been curious about this room, but the king had insisted that it was sacred and not a place for the children. Now as he entered, the large room with its circular wall of windows would have been a pleasant sight had it not been for the sickly warmth that wriggled through his arms and legs and into his chest.

His mother was bending over a large book on the sturdy rectangular table near the hearth that stood in the center of the room, her short blonde hair falling in front of her eyes. The sick chill, however, wasn't coming from her but from the black cauldron hanging over the fire.

"There you are." She looked up from her book and beckoned him forward. "Help me with this bundle before we stir it in." She held out a little bundle of twigs, herbs, and flowers all tied together, about as long as the palm of her hand.

"What is it?"

She tilted her head and studied him. "What do you know about your power?"

"I can still make fire in my hands."

She nodded, as though she had expected such. "You, as I do, have not one but two sources of power that flow through your blood. Did you know that your blue fire was given to you by the Fortress?"

"What do you mean?" He frowned.

"You have the blood of the Fortiers who get their power from this very place." She gestured around her at the tower they stood in. "And you also have the power of the Fae."

Henri shuddered. He had never questioned his ability to feel power, to sense it when it was nearby. It had always been a part of who he was, something he thought everyone felt until Father Lucien told him otherwise. But he wanted nothing to do with these green misted beings that floated about.

"You know," she said, eyeing him as she stirred the cauldron of sickly bubbling brown goo, "you shouldn't be ashamed of your Fae blood."

But Henri didn't answer, studying the herbs on the table instead. As he did, a sparkle caught his eye, and his heart fell as he recognized the king's ring on the table beside her knife. Now King Ever couldn't even send for help.

"Come here, son."

Henri took a step forward but stumbled backward when he felt the wave of raw force surge from the cauldron. "What is that?" he whispered.

"Your uncle is very strong, and so is his wife. In fact, she's much stronger than I would have ever expected, considering the pampered wench that your grandfather picked for *his* wife." Henri's mother sniffed. "I am strong, too. Even with my Fae power and Fortier fire, though, I'm not sure it will be enough to best both of them. So this," she gave the cauldron a stir, "will be our third source. I had to work long and hard to find the recipe. But," she added, looking thoughtfully at him once more, "it will be even more potent with another's assistance. Stand here. You're going to help me."

Henri hesitated, suddenly wanting very much to run and hide behind the many shelves of books that filled the room.

"Henri," she said, lowering her voice, her eyes pleading, "I'm not strong enough to do this on my own. I need your help."

And yet Henri couldn't move his feet. Whatever was in that cauldron, boiling, bubbling, and snapping as it was, smelled so sour it made him want to retch on the ground at her feet.

"Then let me put it this way." His mother's affectionate tone melted. "If you won't help, I suppose I will just have to fetch your sister to come up and do as I say instead."

Henri's feet suddenly had the ability to move once again. Trembling, he went to stand beside his mother as the roaring heat of the fire scalded his ears and eyes from being so close. With a cry, he jumped back once again.

"What is the matter now?"

He stared at her. How could she not feel that? His skin felt as though it might dissolve if he stood near the cauldron for more than a few seconds. "It's too strong." He shook his head.

"I told you, it will take an enormous amount of power to defeat my brother. That's why it is so important that you do exactly as I say. One wrong move and this entire castle could go up in flames."

Henri's breaths came in and out too fast, but he did as she told him, creating a fire in his palm and holding it out as she picked up the bundle of herbs once again. A pungent odor wafted from the bundle as she held it over his flame. It was not a friendly smell. Henri grimaced, but his mother acted as if she were used to such a scent.

Her calm disappeared, however, when sparks began to fly from the herbs.

His mother leapt back with a yelp, and Henri gaped at his hand. His flames had never done *that* before.

"What did you do?" she cried, holding up the charred bundle of twigs. After examining it closely she looked back at Henri. Henri wondered what she saw, for something in her face changed, though he couldn't exactly say what it was.

With the slightest shake of her head, she dropped the burned herbs on the table and began to cut more. "That is enough for today," she finally said. "You may go back to your room now."

Henri was out the door in a flash, gasping for fresh air as he fled down the winding stone steps. The air he sucked in as he descended was stuffy, but anything was better than the scent of that vile concoction his mother was brewing upstairs.

As Henri reached the bottom of the steps, though, he realized that his original escort had fled. Whether he, too, had gone up in a puff of green mist, or whether his mother knew Henri would never try to escape without Genny, Henri was free for a few precious moments. Before he knew exactly what he was doing, Henri found himself on the way to the dungeons.

He hadn't been to the dungeons before, but he'd once watched Garin accompany a drunk down with one of the guards. He had watched them for long enough to know that it was in the northern wing of the Fortress. Henri kept to the shadows when he could and darted from corner to corner where there were none. Though he'd come to love the Fortress in his short time there, the building now seemed eerie without its bustling servants and constant stream of visitors. Every so often a green mist would float by, or a blank-faced Fae with a pike would walk past, but to Henri's relief, there were very few to witness his four failed attempts at finding the dungeon door. Two storage rooms, one room with nothing in it, and one sick room later, Henri finally opened a door that reeked of dank soil and mildewy rock.

The room was so dark that Henri nearly tumbled down face first. He caught himself, however, on the second step and crouched there until his eyes adjusted to the dimness, for the room was lit only by one candle.

A nudge to his arm nearly sent him screaming until he saw that it was only a Fae guard poking him with the butt of his pike, a thin frown on his flat face.

"I'm just sitting here," Henri grumbled. After looking at him a moment longer, the Fae shrugged and dissolved before floating back outside the door. Henri peeked around the corner to see Miss Isa and King Ever kneeling on the ground, a limp body stretched out between them, its head resting on the king's lap. Henri squinted, trying to think of who it might be. Then he heard the steward's voice.

Henri couldn't hear what Garin said, but whatever it was, the king responded by choking out a sob that made Henri's heart hurt as the king cradled the older man in his arms. King Ever was brusque and often stern, but Henri had long ago stopped questioning his motives. Seeing the king's body shiver with tears and jerk back and forth at random was more frightening than his mother's concoction upstairs.

Suddenly, Henri understood why the king hadn't fought back after that initial meeting with his mother. It was the same reason Henri hadn't fought his mother in the tower. Henri had Genny, and the king had Miss Isa, Garin, and the rest of the kingdom. And his mother was using them all.

Henri wandered slowly back up to the main level. *Fortress,* he thought, *I don't know if you're listening to me. I know I'm not the king or anyone important like that. But ... I want to stop her. For my sister ... and for them.* Henri stopped where he was and looked up at the glistening white molded ceilings that vaulted above him. He strained to hear an answer the way he had seen the king and queen do on many occasions. But no words came. There was no sign that anyone or anything had heard him.

Annoyed, Henri kicked at a corner as he headed toward the kitchens. Well, if the Fortress wasn't going to help him, he would just have to find something to eat, as he and Genny hadn't eaten since noon. There was no soft, warm bread waiting for him as there always had been before, but after a bit of scrounging through the cabinets Henri found some dried salted pork and a few cold biscuits. With his arms loaded up he was about to start walking back to his room when a movement caught his attention. What was that?

Henri turned back and walked to the window. To his disappointment, he realized it was just a bird picking a berries out of the garden, blue ones, almost the color of the stones in the king's ring.

Henri nearly dropped his food.

After stuffing his pockets with as much meat and biscuits as he could carry, Henri dashed out of the kitchens and back to the stairs. Once he made sure no one was near, he skittered up the steps, taking them two at a time. Only when he reached the door to the annals did he realize he had no idea as to how he would explain his entrance to his mother. To his joy, however, the room was unlocked, and upon peeking inside, he found that his mother was nowhere in sight. The ring, however, was still on the table.

Henri sprinted over and snatched the ring up, only to hear voices coming from the other side of the room. His mother's and the flat, disinterested voice of one of the Fae. Henri raced back out of the room and down the stairs, not stopping until he reached the bottom, panting. His first thought had been to simply get the ring. But now what should he do with it? How was he supposed to get it to the soldiers at the bottom of the mountain that King Ever had spoken about?

The birds. King Ever had wanted to find Father Lucien's birds! Once again, Henri took off. As he tried to recall where the animals were kept, he begged the Fortress for the bird boy to still be there.

"You!" he shouted as soon as he was through the door of the bird coop. But there was no one there. Henri's heart sank as he found himself in the empty stall. He threw himself down on an empty cage and ran his hands through his hair.

"It's not fair, Fortress," he mumbled. "If you love them so much, why don't you save them?" His voice cracked, and Henri felt a lone, traitorous tear slide down his face. He was so tired. Suddenly, all he wanted to do was go back to his room and sleep for a hundred years.

Something nudged his elbow. Henri jumped up, but there was no one there, not even a Fae. Then again he felt a nudge, this time toward the door. Henri continued to find himself pushed along until he was standing before the cage closest to the door.

"I don't know what you want me to do," he grumbled, staring at the bird inside. "I think King Ever was going to use his power to make it go to the right place. I don't have his power."

Once again he felt the nudge at his hand. This time, however, a trickle of peace began to flow through him. "Fine," Henri sighed. "If this is what you want me to do." Henri opened the cage and gently pulled the bird out. It fluffed its warm feathers against his hand and tilted its head. "The bird boy told me you only fly home," Henri frowned at the bird, "but if the Fortress thinks you'll go to the right place, then I guess I'll send you."

Henri found one of the little packs hung on the wall, took it down, and tied it securely to the bird's back. It looked crooked, but it should stay on at least, he thought. The ring itself seemed nearly too heavy when he dropped it inside the pack, but once again, he felt the gentle push.

Shouting jarred Henri from his focus. Panic struck as he looked out the door to see his mother and a dozen green mists charging straight for him. "Go!" he shouted at the bird, tossing it in the air. Then he turned and began opening the other cages. He'd only succeeded in freeing three by the time his mother caught his arm and threw him to the ground. As he fell, more cages fell open and more birds were set free.

"Where is it?" she shouted. "Where is the ring?"

Henri didn't answer her. Instead, he scrunched his eyes up and tried to put his arms over his face as he curled up in the hay and dirt.

"Bring them down," his mother yelled. Henri's heart sank as he saw one of the Fae pull a bow from his back. As his mother began to drag him away, he could hear one soft thud after the other as the little bodies hit the ground.

"The Fae want you dead, just so you know," she said through gritted teeth as she dragged him back into the Fortress. "Because you are my son, and only because you are my son, I will give you this one last warning. But if you fail me again, your sister will take over your responsibilities!"

"But she's too little!" Henri protested, trying to keep up as his mother marched him toward his room. "She doesn't have the fire like I do!"

"Then if something happens to her, you can take comfort in knowing that it was your fault."

40

A SCORE TO SETTLE

"*E*ver?"

But Ever didn't answer her. Not so much as a muscle moved. Instead, he stayed curled up as though he still held Garin's empty body and it hadn't disappeared with the steward's soul.

She tried again. "You heard Garin. We need a plan. Sacha won't wait much longer."

Still nothing. Isa felt a flash of irritation. It wouldn't be long before another set of spasms took him, shaking his body until it seemed it would burst. If he were an average man without his great power, the poison surely would have killed him by now. "I need you to heal yourself," she said, making her voice as severe as she dared. "You will die if the poison stays inside you much longer. You need to fight it!"

But there was no response. Dismay threatened to make her panic as Isa prodded at his heart. Usually she could sense other emotions there, even if she wasn't wholly aware of his exact sentiments. This time, however, there was nothing. No anger, no rage, no fear, no sorrow. Not even longing. Sacha had done what no other creature had done before.

She had broken him.

Before Isa could think of anything to say, a convulsion shook Ever so hard that he slumped to the ground when it was done, his eyes closed.

"No!" Isa rolled him over and smashed her ear against his chest, listening, praying for the heartbeat. Seconds felt like hours, but finally, she heard it. The sound was faint and uneven. And yet ... Isa stopped listening and focused instead on what she felt. Beneath Ever's skin was the smallest of vibrations. Garin's gift, it seemed, was still present. *Don't let Garin's sacrifice be in vain,* Isa prayed.

After a long stretch of waiting, Isa was sure Garin's power was working. Ever's heart was slightly less erratic. It seemed that the miracle would simply take time. Well, that suited her just fine. Isa laid his head and shoulders gently on the ground and stood. Sacha had managed to break her husband's heart. But Sacha had not broken her.

She had a score to settle with Sacha.

Isa closed her eyes and leaned back against the bars of the prison cell. She was tired, but her exhaustion was incomparable to her determination. She would not lose Ever so senselessly, not after all they had survived together. Isa wouldn't let Sacha have him in either body or mind. So in her own mind, Isa traveled the length of the Fortress, searching the halls, the chambers, the king's study, the kitchen, even the gardens until she located Sacha's heart. It was in the tower.

A few minutes later, a new Fae appeared. Instead of merely replacing the Fae Isa had sent away earlier, however, he motioned for her to follow him. Isa laid a soft kiss on Ever's cheek before straightening and following the Fae, holding her head up high as she did. She might be a prisoner, but she was still the chosen daughter of the Fortress. This was her home, and she was queen.

"I thought that tugging sensation might be you." Sacha didn't even turn away from the fire as Isa followed the guard into the annals. "What do you want?"

Isa was surprised to see that the sun was fading once again over the mountain. Had they already been here a whole day?

"I must admit," Sacha continued, "I'm rather curious to know the woman who changed my brother so." Sacha had changed clothes since Isa had seen her last and was now wearing Isa's new red dress, the one Ever had liked so much. Did this woman have no end to the ways she could aggravate her? Isa shoved that thought aside and focused on what she had come to do.

"I am here to discuss the current state of affairs."

Sacha motioned to a chair near the fire, but Isa stayed put. "I know about the children," she continued, "and that they were never sick at all."

"There is something you should know that I did not tell my brother, for I feared it would only puff him up more than he already is." Sacha spoke as though Isa hadn't said anything at all, finally turning to face Isa, her gray eyes sweeping up and down the mess Isa must look. But Isa only stood her ground. She wouldn't be intimidated by such paltry judgments.

"I never wielded my fire as easily as Henri does, but," Sacha said, her eyes growing distant, "the first time I showed my father how I could make a flame, Rodrigue promised me that one day he would take me away from the Fae world and that I would be queen." She turned to stir whatever was inside the black cauldron upon the fire, though Isa could not see what. "I would be loved by all, he promised. And revered. I can only assume this was before Everard was born, for I was quite young. But," her face hardened, "he chose Everard."

"It matters not whom he chose to be king," Isa said, "for I was chosen to be queen of the Fortress before your brother was ever coronated. In fact, he only became king because he married me." How did *no one* remember this? She took a step closer to the woman, her arms crossed. "So if you're here to squabble over titles, it is *me* you should be dealing with."

"I want what is mine by right!" Sacha exploded, hurling a little glass bottle to the floor. It shattered, and Isa wondered what had been inside. "I deserve this! My children deserve this! We will be loved by the Fortress and its people forever!"

Isa wanted to spit every vile word that she knew at the woman, but something held her back. *Tell her*, it said, *what it means to be my daughter.*

Isa wanted to groan. *Now* the Fortress was telling her what to do? Yet she knew better than to ignore its instruction. That never ended well. Taking a deep breath, Isa sought to calm herself.

"If you truly wish to be a daughter of the Fortress, you must be willing to be molded and wrought into a creature of compassion and sacrifice."

Sacha rolled her eyes before turning back to the strange cauldron that hung over the hearth, but Isa continued.

"It is a hard, painful path, and your brother has been melted down and recast time and time again upon it. But if you want to know true love," Isa took a step closer, her heart pounding, "then surely it is a lesson you could learn. We all do in time."

Sacha didn't respond, only continued stirring whatever was in the pot. For the first time, Isa picked up a whiff of something sour, like rotten cabbages. She also felt a strange twinge ripple through her body as she stepped closer to the hearth. What was in the cauldron?

"You think your husband would be willing to allow me to stay by his side to learn such a lesson?" Sacha's voice was petulant, but Isa answered anyway.

"Ever has always wanted a sibling! I know he would open his arms with joy if you would only join us and give up this darkness." She eyed the pot. "You could live with us, and we could rule together! But you must be willing to withstand crippling blows for the sake of your duty to this place. For the Fortress shapes those it loves."

"You seem so confident of your place in this great castle." Sacha turned once again to glare at her, and Isa could feel the hatred in the woman's heart begin to coalesce. "Feather beds, full bellies every night ... This hardly feels like sacrifice and destitution to me! I *know* sacrifice and hardship!" Her words moved to a high pitch. "You cannot speak to me about hardship until you have been shunned by your people and your father abandons you, and then he casts you out and you are taken advantage of by a greedy man with even lesser means than he has compassion!"

"There are many kinds of suffering," Isa said quietly.

"You know what? You are right! And since you seem so intent on belittling mine, I shall prove to you how set I am in my ways, and that you shan't dissuade me." She jerked her head in the direction of the hearth. "Come here!"

Hesitantly, Isa did as she was bid. The Fortress had brought her here. It would not abandon her now. But that didn't stop her from trembling. The closer she drew to the cauldron itself, the more suffocating the air seemed to get. Isa's skin prickled as though unseen eyes watched her, and the heaviness in the air was suddenly so intense it was dizzying.

"Tomorrow morning," Sacha said, "you will stand before your kingdom. I've already summoned as many people from Soudain as will fit in your courtyard and down the mountain road. They will bear witness to the change of crown. I will finish this spell, and you will burn from the inside out. And after they watch you die, they will know who their queen is!"

"You do not have the power for something so dark." Isa fought to stay upright as she stood beside the bubbling mixture of evil. "I can feel your heart, and it is dark, but it is only so strong."

"Perhaps you are correct, and I do not have the power necessary. But my son does."

Immediately, Isa's vision adjusted and she could see more clearly. That this woman would dabble in the dark arts was bad enough. But to involve Henri? Isa clenched her fists, wishing with all her heart to knock the woman into oblivion. And then it occurred to her. A question that no one should have to ask a mother, but one that might allow Isa a peek into her heavily guarded heart.

"Do you love your children?"

"What?" Sacha had bent over a thick book on the large wooden table. In it were all sorts of drawings of circles and stars and herbs.

"Do you love your children?" Isa demanded more loudly this time. And as she did, she was suddenly caught up in a vision.

Generally, Isa could sense the temperature of the hearts of those around her, sensing both their version of truth and showing them the real truth at the same time. But this vision was much stronger than any she had ever experienced before. It wasn't just a feeling. Isa saw into the woman's very soul.

"You're afraid of them!" she gasped. She could feel Sacha grab a handful of her dress and shove her up against a wall, but the vision was still too strong to escape.

"I fear no one!"

"You're going to kill them!" Isa watched in horror as all the woman's plans and imaginings came to life before her eyes. Repeatedly and in different ways, she watched the children die.

As her sight returned to her, she realized that Sacha had placed her elbow across Isa's chest and shoulders, pinning her hard against the wall. Sacha clapped her other hand over Isa's mouth and leaned in close. Isa bit her fingers hard. Sacha leapt back with a shriek, cradling her hand.

"You hate them," Isa continued in a rush, "because they're too familiar for your comfort! You thought you wanted them until you came back and found them just as you were once, unwanted half-breeds. Henri especially! He frightens you with his power. It's growing quickly, and it leans far more to the Fortress side than the Fae!" Isa felt like she could sing for joy. It was a fierce joy.

Sacha dashed over to the cauldron. Lifting a large ladleful of the brown liquid up to her lips, she began to whisper into it. Immediately, a sharp burning, like holding a candle too close to the skin, began to eat its way through Isa's insides. Isa's knees hit the ground with a sharp crack, but it was nothing compared to the scorching inside.

Sacha said something, but Isa couldn't hear it over the pain. Two sets of hands grabbed Isa by the shoulders, but just after they lifted her, Isa felt someone take hold of her hair and yank it back.

"For all that talk of being the Fortress's chosen queen, the Fortress doesn't seem to care much about you now. Does it?" Sacha whispered. And with that, Isa was dragged all the way back to the dungeon.

41

THE CONDEMNED

The Fae guards tossed Isa down into the dungeon, worsening the pain that already racked her body. The fire still burned inside, so hot that Isa couldn't seem to find her voice to cry. Whether or not Ever was still on the ground Isa couldn't tell, nor did she have the strength to look. She could only draw her knees to her chest and silently beg the Maker to extinguish the fire inside her, to kill her if He must, but to just end the pain.

One arm was slipped beneath her knees and another behind her back. "I tried to go after you," Ever whispered hoarsely, "but I'm not strong enough—"

"Heal me!" she gasped into the darkness.

"What did she do?"

"Just do it!" she tried to scream, the fire clawing its way up her throat. "It's burning me!"

"I can't heal you if I don't know what she did!"

"Sorthileige, Ever!"

One hand was placed on her head and the other on her stomach. A weak blue glow began to move into her. But the longer she waited, the more scorched her insides felt. No relief trickled in like the cool stream Isa had expected. She moaned, and tears streamed down her face as he tried again and again. But he couldn't seem to manage a fire greater than anything Henri might have produced.

Ever finally shook his head. "It's too strong. It's the sick tent, all over again."

The fire inside her continued to burn, but his words cleared a hole in the cloud of smoke that filled her mind. Isa clenched her teeth and fought to slow her breathing. She focused on what little precious truth she knew.

Sacha was terrified. Though Isa couldn't see exactly what she feared, the woman's fear was nearly visceral. In her fear, Isa was sure that Sacha would use no less than all the powers she could summon. And though that meant she was using her Fortress fire as well as the Sorthileige, it also meant that she would be using her Fae powers, too.

And the Fae power was only a lie.

Slowly, ever so slowly, drops of release began to dribble through her. And though the pain was still there, Isa could finally breathe again. Wearily she let herself droop against her husband. For a long time they lay that way, Ever against the wall and Isa against Ever.

"I tried to go after you," he said again into her hair. "As soon as Garin's power began to clear my mind, I fought them, but I wasn't strong enough yet."

Isa didn't think she'd ever heard so much shame in his voice. "Shhh." Her throat was so parched that she broke into a coughing. "You did nothing wrong," she rasped when it was done. "I went on my own accord." She twitched as a tongue of flame licked her chest.

"This is my fault," he said into her hair. Isa wanted to ask how that was so, but talking was still hard. "Sacha offered to heal you," he continued. "She said that if I was willing to leave Destin and never return, she would lift the curse on you. We could go somewhere quiet and alone." His voice moved to a whisper. "She gave us the chance to be happy. And I threw that chance away."

Isa squeezed his hand. "I've seen enough of her heart," she croaked. "She would have chased us down eventually. There's," she paused to swallow, her mouth still unbelievably dry, "no way she would have allowed us to live. She's too frightened."

"I feel as though I've asked the Fortress a hundred times in the last hour, a thousand times in the last month, why it would let this happen." He began to rub his hand up and down her back, and though it didn't help quench the fire, the touch was at least soothing.

"All I can imagine is this." She pulled back to look up at him. Even in the weak light of the candle, the sheen of sweat on his face was easily visible, as was its unusual pallor. "We have asked the Fortress *why* in all of our darkest hours. When the curse was cast. When Nevina attacked. When Bronkendol nearly killed my brother." Isa drew a deep breath. The more she spoke, the less power the fire seemed to possess. "But we never question the Fortress when the good happens. Why were we brought together, despite our hatred for one another? Why did the Fortress use my kidnapping to show me my true strength? Why were Henri and Genny pushed into our lives? For every *why* there has been a gift ... one that neither of us deserved." She gave a shaky laugh. "I may have little strength left in me, but in my heart ... I feel peace."

Whether the burning was truly beginning to dull, or whether she was just beginning to go numb, Isa didn't know, but she was immensely grateful for whichever was bringing her relief. And with it, clarity of mind. "We need to fight this. She's going to execute us at dawn."

"And just how do you propose we do that?" His burning eyes locked onto hers. "I'm improving, but I'm not exactly battle fit. And please do not take offense, my love, but you are hardly looking well-rested and ready yourself."

"Ever, she's going to kill the children."

He stiffened beneath her. "She wouldn't dare." His voice was deadly. "They're her *children*."

"I think she always meant to be reunited with them, but Henri threatens her. He's far more powerful than she expected." She paused. "And I think you are right in that we cannot defeat her. But," she brushed a piece of hair from his eyes, "the Fortress can. And as for me, I've seen too much *not* to trust the Fortress. And I will not be taken quietly."

They were silent for a long time. Ever stroked her hair as Isa snuggled beneath his chin. Her stomach, chest, and even her arms and legs still hurt as though she'd left them uncovered in the summer sun for hours. But she was well enough to think and pray and hope.

Ever, as usual, was closed off. She could still feel the pain and shame flowing from him like a river cresting during a storm, but his exact emotions were hidden. *Please, Fortress,* she thought, yearning overtaking her as it never had before. *Let me know his heart. Before we die, break down his walls and let me know him!*

Then it hit her. For weeks, they had studied the ancient writings in the Tower of Annals. They had hunted for their enemy, and they had tried to take the kingdom back by force. In the same way, Isa had been trying to shove the truth in her husband's face whenever she thought he needed it. Then when it didn't work, she'd allowed frustration to take her every time he'd failed to see the light. Isa had been wielding the truth like a hammer to prove to everyone that she was right. And yet, the peace she felt now was anything but a weapon. Instead, it was gentle and quiet, a rain on a summer's day.

And it was the most potent peace she had ever felt in her life.

She moved in stilted, slow motions until she was kneeling before him. With shaking hands, she took hold of his shoulders. "Kiss me."

Ever leaned forward. The kiss he gave her wasn't nearly the passionate, exuberant, wild kiss she'd been wishing for back in the southern forest. But it was real. As his lips softly molded to her own, Isa breathed out the peace that was within her. For her peace was the truth. Whatever the Fortress had planned for them, it would be for the best. Perhaps they would be saved or perhaps they would join Garin in eternal bliss. If that happened, maybe Henri would one day become the great king the people deserved, despite his mother's intentions. Then when it was their time, Henri and Genny would join them in eternity as well. The pain for Isa and Ever would be only a moment in comparison to eternity. But for the short seconds they might suffer here, the Fortress would be with them through whatever fire they might walk. The Fortress had never failed them before. It would not fail them now.

As she poured the truth of her own heart into the kiss, Ever's own kiss grew eager and even desperate. Gripping her arms, he pulled her tightly against him. He trembled, but she could sense that his shaking wasn't from fear or even from the poison. His mouth was hungry, kissing her lips, her temples, her neck in turn. His fingers wove themselves into her hair, and Isa closed her eyes as she thanked the Fortress for bringing him back not just from death's door, but also from despair. Pain still lived in his heart as it did in hers. But his determination was quickly beginning to eclipse that pain.

And then, as if the heavens had exploded above her, Isa saw into Ever's soul. Resentment for his father, like the color of dried blood. White-hot mourning for the loss of his mentor. Sunbeam-yellow streaks of pride for his men and the kingdom he loved so much. A brilliant violet surprised her with its intensity, mourning the child they'd never had and the children they were losing now. The black of a bottomless pit for his sister and the pain she'd caused them. A wave of silver thanksgiving and devotion to the Maker and the Fortress. In that instant, though, his overwhelming flood of emotion was his desire for her.

Until that moment, Isa had never understood just how deeply her husband needed her. Memories of their early days were a deep hue of twilight blue, interwoven with more recent memories of emerald green the color of grass. But most of all, Ever's heart was red like spring's first rose. Isa sighed into his kiss, her pain suddenly overshadowed by her bliss. His heart was marvelous.

How long they lingered in that kiss, Isa couldn't say. Again and again, his hands explored her face and her neck before sliding down to the small of her back. In turn, she also memorized his features, the curve of his stubbled jaw, the straight lines of his neck, the way his arms felt as he wrapped them around her.

"I am greatly curious to see," she finally leaned back and let out a short breathless chuckle, "how we might find our way out of this predicament. I think I should like more nights like this, rather than letting this one be our last. The last time we were in prison, Garin had the plan."

"First of all," Ever nuzzled her jaw with his nose, "I think this getting thrown into prison is a terrible habit that we ought to break. It sets a bad example for our children."

Isa giggled. *Our children.* How her heart soared when he uttered those words.

"Second," Ever said, "whatever my sister has planned for us we will face with dignity and faith." He took her face between his hands, and with his thumbs he traced circles beneath her eyes. "Do you forgive me, Isa?"

"For what?"

"Despairing." He shook his head. "If I have learned anything, it is never to underestimate this Fortress." He softly turned her head to place a lingering kiss on her cheek. "Or you." Then his lips were on hers again, and he hugged her so tightly to him that Isa's ribs hurt. "I do not know what destiny is ours," he whispered in her ear. "So for now, in this moment we have been given, I will no longer ask why."

"What will you do then?" Isa's heart beat fast.

"I am going to give thanks and enjoy these beautiful moments with my wife." His voice was suddenly gravelly and breathless once again.

In spite of their dingy, dark surroundings and their pending executions, Isa's happiness became one she had never known before.

42

WHAT LITTLE STRENGTH

*I*sa woke with a start as the dungeon door banged open. It took her a few hard blinks in the light of the torch before she could clearly make out the Fae who seemed to be holding the door open for them. Her determination to fight was still there, of course, but Isa wouldn't have minded just a few more hours of sleep before they faced whatever nightmare Sacha had prepared for them.

When Isa tried to get up, though, Ever's arms stayed tightly wrapped around her, holding her to him. "I am afraid you shall have to tell us what exactly you want us to do," Ever said, shrugging helplessly. Isa glanced up to see his face full of innocence. He was taunting them. "That lovely hemlock did a lovely job of addling my mind, you know."

"Her majesty wants you," was the Fae's terse reply.

"Do you hear that, my dear?" Ever looked down at her, his smile polite and his eyes gleaming mischievously. "We have a queen calling for us!" He looked back up at the guards, still smiling pleasantly. "Send our regards, and please apologize for our absence. But as you can see, we are quite busy and cannot spare a second. Perhaps," he wiggled his eyebrows at Isa, "we should send a gift to make up for our absence. Do you suppose a stuffed pig would be to her liking?"

The Fae didn't respond, but Isa felt something in the creature's heart flutter. She wiggled out of her husband's arms and stepped through the open cell door. The Fae's eyes widened as she approached, but he stayed still.

"Isa?" Ever's voice was no longer mocking.

Isa placed her hand on the Fae's arm and looked into his green misty eyes. What she felt from his heart surprised her. "You were not meant for this world," she whispered.

The Fae didn't answer, only stared sadly back at her. His attitude was very different from that of the Fae Isa had encountered earlier.

"Why do you follow her?"

"Because ... we deserve more?" it said slowly.

Isa studied him, reaching deep within his heart. And while she couldn't put her finger on any one emotion, she could suddenly see why the Maker had created such a realm for them, one that was pliable and ready for shaping again and again. They were too changing, too fluid to live in a world with rules and hard structure. They were meant to wander. If they continued to reside in Destin, it would not only injure the Destinians. The Fae would die as well.

"You need to go home," she whispered.

The Fae only continued looking at her with his large frightened eyes, shivering slightly every few moments. Suddenly, he tilted his head as if listening. "Come."

When Ever joined her he no longer wore his obnoxious smirk. Instead, he allowed the Fae to bind his hands behind his back, slipping Isa a wry smile as he did. The plan they'd pieced together the night before wasn't as glamorous as anything Garin would have come up with, but it rested on the Fortress's faithfulness and on Isa's revelation about Ever's heart.

They were herded across the Fortress and up the tower steps. During their long walk, Isa was relieved to see that her husband's gait was once again strong and sure. Garin's gift seemed to have restored at least most of Ever's health. Now if only Isa, too, could survive whatever horrors Sacha had planned for them. Her whole body ached, and she felt as though she might drop into a deep sleep at any moment. If she was still able to stand by the time they climbed all the way up to the annals, Isa would count it as a miracle.

When they finally entered the tower, Sacha and her Fae waited out on the balcony in the fuzzy gray of early morning. The tower's balcony was wide enough to hold at least a dozen men between the window wall and the ledge, but crossing it felt to Isa like a lifetime of its own. She knew what awaited her. Her heart still caught in her throat, though, as she got close enough to the edge to see below.

Just as Sacha had promised, the Fortress's front lawn and the road down the mountain were filled with hundreds of people. Fathers, mothers, and children, old and young alike were there to witness their demise. From the crowd, however, there was none of the bravado or excitement she'd felt from the mob on the day the Fortress was taken. Instead, Isa sensed overwhelming fear rising like a storm cloud nearly full to bursting. These people didn't want Isa or Ever to die, she realized. They'd only come because they were summoned, like her. Were her parents there? She hoped not.

"You look well." Isa turned to see Sacha eyeing Ever suspiciously. "No matter, though." She waved her hand dismissively and walked to the balcony's edge.

"Destin!" Sacha's voice echoed down from the tower to the people below.

"My name is Sacha Fortier. I am the firstborn of the late King Rodrigue, and I have come to take my place." She began to list all the ways Ever had failed the Fortress and its people, but Isa didn't listen. Instead, she stared into the beautiful gray eyes of the man beside her. At any time now they would need to set their plan into motion, but oh, how she wanted to linger in the stormy depths of his gaze.

"So you don't think me heartless, I will offer my brother mercy one more time," Sacha said, turning back to Ever and Isa. "Do you renounce your claim to the throne and swear never to enter this kingdom again?"

Ever turned to look at his sister straight on. "I swore to serve this Fortress until death. Doing anything less would be dishonorable," his voice boomed. "So no. I will not surrender what I have sworn to protect."

"And you?" Sacha turned to Isa, her eyes hard. "Do you renounce your title?"

"I took the same oath as my husband. Honor will be for us both."

"Fools," Sacha muttered before turning back to the people. "Since they won't renounce their claims to the throne, even though the Maker has clearly delivered the Fortress into my hands, it is my duty to take it from them. By fire they have lived, and by fire they will die. Henri."

Only then did Isa realize Henri and Genny had been brought out onto the balcony as well. Henri whispered something in Genny's ear before letting go of her hand and trudging out to join his mother. Genny screamed as she fought to free herself from the Fae, but Henri only walked forward. Behind him, two of the Fae carried the boiling cauldron out, placing it between Sacha and Ever. Despite her resolve to stay calm, Isa fought the urge to lunge at Sacha. Whom had Sacha threatened to coerce the boy into such evil? Isa could guess only too well.

"Henri," Isa called out softly. "You don't need to do this. Trust the Fortress! She cannot touch you without its permission—"

Sacha's hand was sharp and fast, and it made Isa's face sting. Ever looked as though he might tear his sister to pieces, but Isa bumped into his arm and shook her head. They needed to wait for the right moment. She needed to get to Henri. If she couldn't convince Henri, they were all doomed.

Sacha walked back to the cauldron and held her hands out, then she looked expectantly at Henri.

"Henri, no," Isa whispered, but Henri raised his hands as well, refusing to look at Isa as he stared stubbornly into the cauldron's brown bubbles. Thin gloves of blue and green fire wrapped themselves around his hands, and he placed them on the side of the cauldron.

Sacha began the incantation, and as her voice rose the burning began again, this time in Isa's feet. The sensation reminded her of walking barefoot on Soudain's cobblestone streets after they'd been too long in the sun.

"Isa." Ever had leaned down, his eyes burning brightly. Knowing it might be her last, Isa craned her neck up and met him for a brief, beautiful goodbye. His lips were feverishly hot, and she knew he was feeling the Sorthileige's heat as well. Still, it was a strong kiss. One that made Isa smile. As they said goodbye, Isa felt the rope around her wrist burn off with his fire. They were ready.

In one instant, Isa was kissing her husband. In the next, he was gone. Ever jerked around and threw himself at the nearest Fae. It disintegrated, and he fell hard on the ground. In another second he was up, swinging the Fae's pike around in the air like a staff, his fire flaming from it at both ends.

Sacha's surprise showed on her face, and for a moment she forgot to chant. Isa took that moment to throw herself down at Henri's feet. She considered pushing his arms down, but the green and blue fire that encircled them convinced her that was a bad idea. Instead, she placed one hand on his face. "You don't have to do this," she whispered.

"Get away from him!" Sacha screeched, but Isa ignored her. If her hands hadn't been held out above the cauldron, Isa was sure Sacha would have killed her in that moment. As it was, the burning not only intensified in her feet but moved up to her ankles as well. Isa stifled a short cry. Sweat began to roll down her temples, and Isa clenched her muscles tightly to try and repel the burn as she forced herself to look back up at Henri.

"She said she would hurt Genny," Henri whimpered.

Sacha's incantations became a shout, sending another wave of pain over Isa.

"Do you remember all those times," she gasped, "when I told you we needed to trust the Fortress?"

"Yes."

"This is the most important time of all."

"Shut up!" Sacha screamed at her, but Isa kept talking. Whenever the woman became distracted, the burning that now had risen to her calves would lessen for just a moment. Behind her, Isa could hear the sound of fighting as Ever shielded her from the Fae. She needed to move quickly.

"Your mother needs you for this because she is not strong enough to unhand us on her own. If you stop helping her, she will not be able to continue." Isa sucked a quick breath in. The fire was now at her waist, and the world was beginning to tilt. Shaking her head to clear it, Isa continued. "Did you know that before we met your father and mother, King Ever and I decided to keep you as our own—"

Isa's words broke off in another bout of pain, but Henri's fire flickered.

Drawing in air was becoming more and more difficult. The burning was now up to her lungs, and Isa had to place a hand on the ground to remain upright where she knelt. *Please, Fortress,* she begged. *Just a little longer!*

"We love you, Henri," she gasped. "If... If we hadn't been attacked that night, you and Genny..." But she couldn't continue. The pain was too much. Clawing its way up her throat, her world exploded into one burning chasm of fire. The ground began to rise again, and Isa hit the balcony floor.

"No!" Henri cried out.

"Henri! Get back here!" Sacha shouted, but instead, Isa felt a small hand clutching her arm. Somehow, she pried her eyes open one last time.

"You were going to keep us?" Henri whimpered, his golden hair falling in his eyes as tears began to stream down his face. He still held one hand against the cauldron, but the other hand was holding her.

Isa smiled, reaching up to caress his face with a trembling hand. "We love you and Genny so much..." she sucked another breath in, "... that we vowed to go to the ends of the world for you. And this is me doing just that." Isa's body felt as though it should imitate the Fae and fall into a pile of ashes. But in slow agonizing movements, she pushed herself up on her knees and wrapped him in an embrace. As she held him tight, Isa gathered all the love in her heart and impressed it upon his.

Just as she'd opened Ever's heart the night before, now Isa wrapped the truth around Henri. There was no more hammering away at the walls he'd erected around himself. Instead, she wove the truth of their love in and out of his soul as one might weave a ribbon of silk. She showed him the way she felt when the children entered a room. She let him feel Ever's anger at their father's careless-ness. She sang to him of the tears of joy she'd cried as they'd sealed the blood vow.

Slowly, ever so slowly Isa felt Henri's heart begin to open. His fear began to melt away, and his breathing grew deeper. And Isa thanked the Maker as Sacha's screams sent waves of fire up her arms and face. He had answered her prayers. And though Sacha's fire was great, the fire of the Fortress within Isa was greater. Sacha might burn her body to nothingness, but Isa's soul could not be conquered.

Isa would have gone on hugging Henri forever, but eventually she could hold on no longer. Briefly she saw the blurry form of a boy reaching out for her as she let herself fall. As the fire ravaged her body from the inside, her strength melted like wax.

People shouted from all around her. Men's voices in particular began to drown out the others. She could feel Henri still battling with himself over whether to continue aiding his mother or to let go of the cauldron completely. He longed to let go, but there was just enough fear left to keep him from it.

"Henri," Isa whispered. She could vaguely make out the sound of weeping, and a small hand found its way into hers. Sacha was screaming something again but Isa didn't care. The pain was so great she was nearly numb. "The truth is that you are loved. You need no longer fear." As soon as the words had left her lips, Isa felt herself slip away.

Her life at the Fortress had not been long. But Isa's four years had been good. Oh, how good they had been! Her journey, which had begun with a broken body and broken heart, had brought her the purpose she had so long craved. Ever, once the hated prince who had ruined her life, had become the friend who valued her life above his own. And even if it was only for a brief time, the

Fortress had brought Isa children as well. Not a detail would she change in the life she had been given.

Take care of them, she silently asked the Fortress as she pushed the last of her strength into the boy's heart. *He's seen the truth. Now let him believe.*

43

INTO THE FLAMES

*E*ver wondered how much longer he would be able to hold up. The burning was more painful than the hemlock's poison had been, but at least it didn't send his body into convulsions. Still, both hurt more than Ever had once thought possible. Only by the Fortress's mercy was he still fighting.

At least he didn't have to think much about his fighting tactics. With each Fae it was the same.

Burn the fire brightly on the pike.

Wait for the Fae to come, like moths to a flame.

Wait for the Fae to materialize while drawing close to the flame.

But just as he would kill one Fae, another would come. Then he would have to mesmerize that one, too. How many had Isa said there were? Over two hundred? Still, Ever wondered, where were the others? He'd witnessed at least four dozen Fae with them when they'd first arrived at the balcony. Though his opponents here were still coming fast and steady, there weren't nearly as many as there should have been. And that made him uneasy.

Unfortunately, another bout of burning punched him in the gut, and Ever hit the ground. A swift crack to the head from his latest foe's pike sent his vision spinning as well. Ever swept his left arm back blindly and managed to knock the Fae over. She quickly rematerialized on her feet, this time with four more Fae at her side, but he couldn't seem to rise again. Without his fiery torch to distract them, the Fae crouched back ready to spring, with more joining them by the second. Ever did the first thing he could think of and threw a little ball of blue fire high above their heads, just as he had in the cave. The Fae stopped advancing to watch it as it rose. But where was his pike?

Panicked, Ever searched the ground for his weapon only to realize it had rolled away. Just as the Fae began to look back down from the sky, their eyes once again focusing on him, two of them gave a rasping sound and collapsed before turning into a pile of ash. Ever looked up to find the last person he had expected to see.

"Acelet!"

"Keep drawing them!" his general said, crouching low to meet another. "We'll pick them off!"

Ever didn't stop to ask how his general had known to come, but in his heart, he was in awe. The Fortress had answered his pleas. Somehow, the fire continued to build in his hands, though his body felt like it should collapse at any minute. And yet, he felt at least temporarily invigorated as his men flooded the balcony around him. As they tried their first attempts at fighting the airy creatures, Ever had an idea. *I can't do this without you*, he told the Fortress. *I'll need more fire than I've ever wielded before.* Then he balled his fists and raised them up to the sky.

In response, each of his soldier's weapons burned bright blue with his flame. Ever was so surprised that he nearly forgot to focus. It was an incredible sight, the glowing green eyes of the Fae meeting the blazing blue weapons of his men. As the men fought, different flames would go out here and there, and Ever had to rebuild each. Every ball of blue flame was harder to make than the last, as was the glow of each sword. If he could just hold on, though, his weariness wouldn't matter in a few minutes, for Acelet's men would have won the day and Ever would be free to face his sister. And with that in mind, Ever was able to push out the pain just enough to continue the fight.

A cry interrupted his focus on the balls of fire, however, and immediately, the burning lessened.

There was no celebration, though, when he turned and saw Henri staring in horror at the ground. Henri clutched at Isa's arm with the hand that wasn't touching the cauldron, tears slipping down his thin cheeks.

The world stopped. Ever stumbled then found his feet, only to fall again. Pushing, shoving, crawling, and running, he might as well have been wading through tar. The way her eyes were closed and the absence of color in her skin were too real. They looked too much like death. But Isa couldn't be dead. He wouldn't allow it.

Finally, Ever broke through the battle raging around them to collapse at Isa's side. He could hear his men's dismay as their fires went out, but he didn't care. Lifting her head up, Ever placed his ear on her chest. It wasn't moving up and down.

"Henri," Sacha screeched, "if you stop now, the Sorthileige will kill you!"

"That's not what Miss Isa said!" Henri took a step closer to where Ever cradled Isa. The boy touched the edge of the cauldron with only a few fingers.

"You will die!" Sacha's voice was hysterical.

"No!" Henri shouted. "You're lying!"

"Henri, I will kill you myself if you don't finish this!"

Rage took Ever as it hadn't before. This woman must die.

Before he could intervene, however, Henri turned to his mother. "No," he said, his young voice suddenly as calm as a pond.

"No, what?" Sacha's shoulders heaved as she threw even more green flame into the cauldron. The pain took Ever by surprise, and a cry slipped out against his will. "You worthless piece of—"

"I am not worthless! Miss Isa and King Ever were going to keep me and Genny because they loved us. And the Fortress loves us. So I don't need you." Henri looked from his mother to his hand. "And I don't need this."

An inhuman shriek tore itself from Sacha's lips as Henri let go of the cauldron. Genny screamed from another part of the balcony, but Ever couldn't see her.

"Get down!" he shouted, praying desperately that Genny was out of the way. Ever grabbed Henri and threw himself over the boy and his wife. As he did, the dark swell of Sorthileige that Ever had felt building inside the cauldron broke. Sacha was enveloped in one quick burst of green flame that burned brighter than the sun.

Then she was gone.

The remaining Fae that had battled around them collapsed into the familiar piles of ash, their pikes making clacking sounds as they hit the ground. In awe, the soldiers watched their enemies' remains float away on a sudden wind.

A cry of victory was raised from one soldier, and soon they were all shouting, as were the people on the ground below them. But not Ever.

Now that the burning was gone and Sacha was dead, he lifted Isa's lifeless body into his lap. "No," he whispered. *It can't be true, Fortress! She's not gone. She can't be!* Tears began to run down his face, and before he knew it, sobs racked his body more violently than the poison ever had. An emptiness filled him, one as black as ashes and even more suffocating. His world was devoid of light, of air. It was a thing of nothingness and death.

"Everard?" Launce called from somewhere behind him, but Ever ignored him.

This woman was his beacon. She was the voice of purity when the siren call of his own demons haunted him. No one else had been able to reach him when he had been in his darkest days. Not even Garin had touched his soul like she had. The memory of the night before floated before his eyes. It had only been hours ago that her arms had held him, her slender hands tracing the contours of his face as she whispered, "I love you," over and over again. He could have ... should have loved her more. Four years wasn't enough, not with all of the wrongs he still had to right. He still needed to tell her he loved her one more time.

If only Sacha had killed him too.

"Let's give your father a few minutes alone," Ever heard Launce say in a low voice. He felt Henri rise, as if being pulled.

"But she's not dead!"

Ever looked up to see the boy frowning at Isa. "Henri." He tried to speak through his tears, as he knew Isa would want him to do. "She's not breathing." It felt like death to say that.

"But there's power still inside her. I can feel it!" And before Launce could grab him again, Henri had shrugged out of Launce's grip and threw himself down beside Isa's body. "We just need to pull her out." He stretched his hand out over Isa's heart, then looked at Ever, his thin face falling a bit. "I still don't know how to control my fire like you do."

Ever stared at Henri in disbelief. Was the boy telling him he'd missed his wife's spark? Ever wanted to retort to the boy that this was foolishness, and that he was just holding on to a dangerous, damning hope. But just as he was about to say as much, Henri touched Isa's hand, and a green mist filled the boy's eyes.

Ever moved so quickly he nearly toppled. Shaking, he held his hand over her heart. At first he felt nothing. But reassured by Henri's eyes, he pressed harder.

Sure enough, after an immeasurable moment, the slightest ember still burned within her. "Take her hand!" Ever ordered the boy as he scrambled to lift her head up. "On my command, press your fire into the palm of her hand!"

"Genny!" Henri waved her over. "Come here!"

Ever wanted to point out that as the little girl didn't have the Fortress's fire yet, she would be of little help to them. But the way she tore herself from Eloy's grasp and threw herself down next to Isa kept him quiet. That was fine then, as long as she didn't get in the way.

"Now, on the count of three!" Ever closed his eyes and began to focus all his efforts on reigniting the spark inside her heart. "One, two—"

"Genny, what are you doing?" Henri cried.

Ever opened his eyes to see Genny leaning over Isa.

"Wake up, Mummy." With those soft words, Genny placed a little kiss right on Isa's lips.

Isa's eyelids fluttered.

EPILOGUE

Just Wait

"*Y*ou certainly act as though your tummy is feeling better," Isa said, smiling wryly as Genny bounced on her bed.

"My tummy has been better for a long time!"

"Then why did you tell Cook that you needed cake for supper because greens made you feel sick?" Isa quirked an eyebrow.

Genny sighed dramatically, falling back on her bed like a rag doll. "I was just making sure it was better. But as you can see, it is!"

Isa shook her head and proceeded to tuck her wiggly daughter into bed. *Her daughter*. The words felt so wonderful to even think.

"When is Daddy getting back?"

"You ask that every night." Henri frowned as he walked in. "And I thought you were still sick."

Isa stepped back and watched, amused, as Henri began to tuck his sister in again. Though he had a room of his own now, the boy never failed to see his sister to bed. Nine years without a true mother had created some habits in him that were proving difficult to break. But taking care of his sister? Isa was more than fine with that.

"Alright, you two. I think that should suffice. Genny, remember what Daddy said. He will be home as soon as he can. And Henri, how about I tuck you in now?" Henri nodded, so after a quick prayer and kiss for Genny, Isa walked with him to the next room over.

"How are *you* feeling tonight?" she asked him.

He shrugged. "Fine, I guess. My stomach hasn't hurt in a few days."

"Good. Let's keep it that way by getting some sleep." Isa waited as he climbed into bed. Just as she was about to blow out his candles, however, Henri sat back up.

"I have a question."

Curiosity sparked as Isa sat on the edge of the bed. "What would that be?"

Though Henri had seemed relieved and even a bit excited with his new title as Crown Prince of Destin, he was still finding it more difficult to open up than Genny. And that was to be expected, Isa knew, as he was much older than Genny and had seen far more rejection and danger than his sister had. Still, she yearned for him to talk to her as he seemed to want to do now.

"If you have ... if you and King—Father have a baby, will we still be..." He let the question die, but Isa drew him into a fierce hug.

"When your father and I swore to keep you, we meant that as long as we live and breathe, you will always be our first son, and Genny, our first daughter." She ruffled his hair. "Besides, I don't think there is much chance of that. It seems the Maker wanted me to have a boy and a girl, and I am overjoyed to have you both. I wouldn't change a thing about you if I could."

Henri nodded, seeming mollified. As Isa left his room, she wished to the Fortress that she could convince him of their commitment once and for all. But, she knew, it would take time. There were some truths that needed time rather than power. He would simply have to see that their love was faithful. And that was a gift she was more than willing to wait for.

Isa paused and rubbed her own sore stomach as the door of her chambers closed behind her. After Ever had left to chase down the remaining Fae, giving them the choice to either return to their world or die, the Fortress staff had returned. It had been a wonderful reunion until half of the Fortress occupants had fallen ill with some awful stomach sickness. Henri, Genny, and Isa had held off for a while, but three weeks before they had succumbed as well. It was strange, though, Isa thought as she began the weary walk to her bed. The sickness seemed to linger for a week or so in most, but she was taking far too long to recover. The healer was nearly beside himself with worry. She had taken quite a beating from Sacha and had been feeling ill since the curse had first fallen. Perhaps she would call for the healer again in the morning.

She paused before the full-length mirror, suddenly glad Ever wasn't there to see her. Not that he would have minded, but the bags beneath her eyes were nearly purple and her skin was still too white. And though she hadn't been able to keep much food down at all, her belly was still slightly swollen as well.

Isa frowned, stepping closer to the mirror, squinting in the evening light that shone through the balcony. She turned, pulling her gown tight to see better. Isa's gowns had been snug as of late, but that had been from the upset stomach. Hadn't it?

The nausea.

The constant exhaustion.

The stiff muscles.

Her small but undeniably round belly.

"Someone get Gigi!" Isa ran back to the door and shouted at the first servant she saw. "Get Gigi!"

Isa had never seen Gigi run so fast as she did when she burst into the room. When she took one look at Isa's face, however, and one glance at the way Isa clutched her belly, the old woman's face broke into a glorious smile.

"I don't understand!" Isa said as Gigi began to gently feel around her stomach.

"Oh, Isa," Gigi fussed as she stepped back and looked her up and down, "you're at least four months along!"

Isa stared back at her, her mouth falling open in shock. "But the curse! My cycles stopped when Sacha cursed me!"

For some reason, this made Gigi laugh. Isa frowned, trying to figure out what she had missed.

"Oh, me!" Gigi exclaimed between giggles. "You are not to blame, my dear, for you're the one with the muzzled mind of the expectant, but I've no excuse!" She grabbed Isa's hand. "Garin said the children's illnesses and injuries were deceptions, illusions, yes?"

Isa felt so foolish. Of course! The curse she had felt must have been an illusion as well!

"But why would the Fortress have allowed me to think I was cursed? I surely would have known much sooner than this!"

Gigi drew Isa in for a deep embrace, then patted Isa's tummy as she turned to leave the room, to boss the Fortress staff into preparing a nursery already, no doubt. "Would you have fought so desperately for Henri and Genny if you had?" And then she stepped out, leaving Isa to puzzle in wonderment at such a thought.

~

Ever sucked in a breath of air that smelled of roses, fresh grass, and his beloved mountain. Never had he guessed it would take three months to track down every Fae in the land.

"I was beginning to think you'd never find all the little buggers," Acelet called as he greeted Ever from the stables.

A sharp pain gripped Ever's heart as he remembered every time Garin had come to meet him in such a way. The three months had lessened the shock, but the hurt was still strong. And he wasn't sure if it would ever quite be gone. Not, at least, until he was in that blessed eternity as well.

"I didn't either," Ever admitted.

"It is done then?"

"Yes." Ever hopped off his horse and took a long swig of water from a nearby bucket. "Most of them were surprisingly ready to return. But the veil is finally sealed. I think we should hopefully have a moment to breathe before the next disaster befalls us."

"I certainly hope so," Acelet said, a sudden ornery gleam in his eye.

"Oh, and Acelet, please send for Eloy. I have a task for him before I go up and see everyone."

In just a few moments, the men Ever had brought with him had dispersed, and only Eloy stood before him in the stables.

"Walk with me." Ever clapped the young man on the shoulder as they slowly started for the Fortress. "So what did you think of guard duty?"

Eloy gave him a big grin. "It was an honor to keep your children safe..." he paused, "when I was able to keep up with them."

Ever snorted out a laugh. "Good then. Because I have a position I would like you to consider."

Eloy's eyes went wide, but he said nothing.

"I grew up under the watchful eye of my father," Ever said, his laughter quickly dying, "but I became a man under the guidance of Garin." His chest tightened as he said the steward's name. He drew in a deep breath. "If you are willing, I would be honored to have you continue on as the personal guardian for my children."

Eloy's mouth dropped open, and it was a moment before he could speak. When he did speak, he stuttered terribly. "Sure...surely ... y...y...you must have s...s...someone else more qualified than I, Your Majesty. I have only just begun—"

"You saved Genny's life when the cauldron exploded. In that, you have already proven your worth as a soldier. But if you must know more, the children trust you. And that is no small feat for Henri." Ever frowned. "He needs someone with a good heart who will help him see himself as he is, not who he fears himself to be." He turned a sharp eye on the young man beside him. "But I warn you, watching over them will age you, making you far older than your years."

Eloy's grin spread across his face once more. "You have been gone for some time, Your Majesty. How do you know that Henri is such a hooligan as you make him out to be?"

"Because I was a hooligan."

"Ah, I see." Eloy stopped and gave him a bow. "Then it would be an honor, Your Highness, to guard your most precious possessions." His face grew more serious as he looked back up at Ever. "I will keep them with my life." Then he looked slightly confused. "You do mean all of them, don't you?"

"Both of them, yes." What a strange thing to say.

"Oh, then ... of course, sire." Just as Acelet had left him with an ornery gleam in his eye, so did Eloy now. Ever shook his head as he continued to the Fortress alone. What had gotten into everyone?

As he drew closer to the Fortress's front steps, he could see the crowd waiting for him in the distance, and he couldn't help but marvel at how the Fortress had saved them one small miracle at a time.

To begin with, Henri's bird shouldn't have reached the army. He couldn't have known which one to send, nor did he know how to use his power to alter the animal's mind so that it might fly to the right destination. On top of that, Sacha's Fae had killed nearly every homing pigeon they owned. But somehow, Henri's bird had survived, and it had arrived at Launce's camp at just the right time. An hour later and none of them would have survived. It was a gift of the Maker, Father Lucien had told him.

They had found the holy man walking along the road between towns. Apparently, the priest had caught wind of the coming uprisings. He had taken the church's messenger birds and the church's holy writ to a larger town nearby, where he stayed with the priest there until he heard that all of the sick children had been healed. That, he'd told Ever, was when he realized Sacha had been defeated. As they traveled together after that, he and Ever had made plans to discuss Sansim's future once the kingdom was put to rights.

Ever was pulled from his reverie by the shrieks of a little girl. He barely had time to hold his arms out when Genny bounded into them. Ever laughed, hugging her close.

"I missed you too!" He put her on the ground. "Where are your brother and mother?"

"Henri's back there." Genny pointed behind her. "And Mummy—"

"Don't you say a word!" Henri darted up and clamped his hand over his sister's mouth. "She's in the tower." After he was done reprimanding his sister, Henri looked up at Ever and, to Ever's surprise, slipped him a small but genuine smile. Ever squeezed Henri's shoulder then set off for the tower. After a few steps alone, however, he turned. "Aren't you coming with me?"

"Yes!" Genny said, but Henri shook his head.

"I think Cook has some sweet bread for us to try." He looked at Genny. "Wouldn't you like some sweet bread?"

"No." Genny pouted. "I want to stay with Daddy."

"Oh, come on!" Henri took her by the arm and dragged her away. Ever watched them go, mystified, but finally shook his head and continued his walk to the tower. Perhaps now that he was home, he would eventually learn to somewhat understand those two.

He didn't see Isa at first when he entered the tower. Since the battle, new panes of glass had been fitted into the walls and balcony door, and the shelves, books, furniture, and rugs had been put to rights. All signs of the black magic were gone. It was a peaceful, sacred place once more.

Then he saw her. Standing out on the balcony, Isa wore a long flowing dress made of a lavender fabric that looked thin and cool, fitting for the late summer heat. He paused on the threshold and knocked on the glass of the open door. "May I have an audience with the queen?"

Then she turned, and all of Ever's teasing words fled him. "Is... Are you?" As though in a dream, he walked toward her. When he reached her, however, he stopped, unable to touch. For touching would make it real, and this could only be a dream.

Isa gave him the most beautiful, radiant smile he had ever seen. She reached down and took his hands in hers, then gently placed them on her belly. And though Ever had thought he couldn't be more amazed, he wanted to shout when he felt the slightest movement within her. Her baby.

His child.

Ever heard a shuffling sound behind him and smiled to himself. His *third* child.

"You can come out now." Isa smiled around him, and Genny and Henri crept out to stand beside Isa. Genny looked quite pleased with herself, but Henri seemed unsure.

"How?" Ever managed to whisper.

Isa shook her head and grinned again. "The Fortress does as it pleases." But that was as far as she got, for in a second, his lips were on hers. He wrapped his arms tightly about her, holding the world's most beautiful soul close, in awe again as her belly pressed against him.

"Ew." Genny made a gagging sound.

"Oh, you think it's disgusting when I kiss your mother?" Ever turned and raised his eyebrows. Before Genny could answer, though, he had fallen to his knees and pulled all of them into his arms. "Just wait until I kiss you all!"

Genny squealed and tried to wriggle free, while Henri groaned and tried to push himself away. Isa laughed, and Ever felt tears prick his eyes.

"Thank you!" He let his head fall back as the tears fell freely. "Thank you!"

All he had ever wanted was here in his arms. He had gone from a lonely, angry prince to a king, married to the most worthy woman in all the world. And in five months, they had gone from having no children to three.

"Will we be happy now?" Genny pulled back from his crushing hug to study him quizzically.

Ever laughed through his tears at her serious expression. "Yes."

"How do you know?"

"Because we have each other. And no matter what comes, the Fortress has us all."

Dear Reader,

I want to thank you for journeying with me through Before Beauty. *As a favor, if you enjoyed this book, please consider leaving a review on your online retailer or Goodreads.com.*

If you like free stories (including more about Isa and Ever) visit BrittanyFichterFiction.com. By joining my email list, you'll get free access to:

An exclusive secret chapter from Before Beauty

A short story about Everard's very first encounter with Isa
(It wasn't at the parade!)

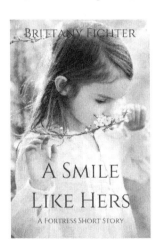

You'll also get sneak peeks at books before they're published, more secret chapters as they
come, chances at giveaways, and much more!

Sign me up!

∾

For the next book in *The Classical Kingdoms Collection*, read on...

ALSO BY BRITTANY FICHTER

The Becoming Beauty Trilogy:

1. Before Beauty: A Retelling of Beauty and the Beast

2. Blinding Beauty: A Retelling of The Princess and the Glass Hill

3. Beauty Beheld: A Retelling of Hansel and Gretel

The Becoming Beauty Trilogy Boxset: Before Beauty, Blinding Beauty, & Beauty Beheld

The Classical Kingdoms Collection

4. Girl in the Red Hood: A Retelling of Little Red Riding Hood

5. Silent Mermaid: A Retelling of the Little Mermaid

6. Cinders, Stars, and Glass Slippers: A Retelling of Cinderella

The Classical Kingdoms Collection Novellas

The Green-Eyed Prince

(Coming soon…)

A Curse of Gems

The Autumn Fairy Trilogy

The Autumn Fairy

(Coming soon…)

Autumn Fairy of Ages

The Last Autumn Fairy

Entwined Tales

A Goose Girl - K.M. Shea

And Unnatural Beanstalk - Brittany Fichter

A Bear's Bride - Shari L. Tapscott

A Beautiful Curse - Kenley Davidson

A Little Mermaid - Aya Ling

An Inconvenient Princess - Melanie Cellier

ABOUT THE AUTHOR

Brittany lives with her Prince Charming, their little fairy, and their tiny prince in a ~~sparkling~~ (decently clean) castle in whatever kingdom the Air Force has most recently placed them. When she's not writing, Brittany can be found enjoying her family (including their spoiled black Labrador), doing chores (she would rather be writing), going to church, belting Disney songs, exercising, or decorating cakes.

Facebook: Facebook.com/BFichterFiction
Subscribe: BrittanyFichterFiction.com
Email: BrittanyFichterFiction@gmail.com
Instagram: @BrittanyFichterFiction
Twitter: @BFichterFiction